ROAR

ROAR

American Master
The Oral Biography of Roger Orr

A NOVEL

compiled and edited by

BRUCE WAGNER

Arcade Publishing

Arcade Publishing books may be purchased in bulk at special discounts for sales promotion, corporate gifts, fund-raising, or educational purposes. Special editions can also be created to specifications. For details, contact the Special Sales Department, Arcade Publishing, 307 West 36th Street, 11th Floor, New York, NY 10018 or arcade@skyhorsepublishing.com.

Arcade Publishing® is a registered trademark of Skyhorse Publishing, Inc.®, a Delaware corporation.

Visit our website at www.arcadepub.com.

10 9 8 7 6 5 4 3 2 1

Library of Congress Cataloging-in-Publication Data is available on file.

Jacket design by Erin Seaward-Hiatt

Print ISBN: 978-1-956763-22-5
Ebook ISBN: 978-1-956763-26-3

Printed in the United States of America

for my publisher

ROAR: Roger Orr, American Master *is a work of fiction. Roger Orr is a chimera. My intent was to create a subterfuge—a dream—whose scaffolding is the traditional form of an oral history. I hope that by the end of the novel the scaffolding will fall away.*

CONTENTS

BOOK FOUR
Imaginary Prisons
1985–2000

BOOK FIVE
Bye Bye Blackbird
2000–2018

EDITOR'S NOTE

In the end, it was thought that an oral history—a kaleidoscope of voices, both famous and obscure—was best suited to convey the life of one of the most celebrated, complex, controversial artists of our time. For a more orthodox presentation of the life and works of Roger Orr, the handful of extant biographies and documentaries will serve the reader well.

No doubt there will be many more.

I met Roar in the early Seventies, in my twenties. For the next four and a half decades our lives intersected personally and sometimes professionally. I can't remember exactly when I proposed a biography; I must have been kidding (or drunk) because the idea of myself, a novelist, embarking on a nonfictional history of a human being was outlandish. Yet the ambitious prospect of it did make me swoon. Roar himself proposed I interview friends and family—and critics too—instead. That sealed it for me, for in my mind, I would simply take dictation; I could lazily have my cake and read it too. There was no deadline, no contract, no pressure. Still, I couldn't help but feel a sense of urgency because there were a thousand people I needed to contact—many of them, as Roar described, "with a foot in the grave. They may as well put the other one in their mouth."

I arrived at a hundred doorsteps armed with an elegantly handwritten letter: "I, Roger Orr, do hereby grant you sanction to speak with the gentle soul named Bruce Wagner. (Please insist he show identification.) Torah! Torah! Torah!" I wouldn't understand the "Torah" reference for years to come.

Some of those whom I interviewed passed away years before I met Roar; some died while I was literally en route to their homes; two expired mid-interview. In many instances, when I felt it important for the voices of the departed to speak from the grave, the medium of archival material has been employed. Through the years, when respondents rudely expired before publication, Roar enjoyed saying, "Another one bites the dustjacket."

I thank all of the living and dead who contributed to this book.

But my heart and my gratitude begin and end with Roger Orr. It's a cliché to say the worst clichés are true but here it is: we will never see the likes of him again.

No doubt he'd add, "You should thank God every day for that, bubbeluh."

Here are two friends, at the end of one life.
—headstone of Jan Morris and her wife

FIRST LOOK

VINCE GILLIGAN (*showrunner*) He was more than once-in-a-generation, he was that thousand-year storm.

GWYNETH PALTROW (*actress, entrepreneur*) You couldn't have invented him: a film and theater director of genius, an Academy Award-winning actor, a legendary stand-up, and celebrated songwriter, playwright, novelist, sculptor, and dermatologist.

A dermatologist! Most people don't know that.

JOHN LAHR (*writer*) In terms of multiplicity, one thinks of Chaplin, whom of course Roar knew. He knew everyone on earth. But Chaplin never wrote a novel, and if he did, one doubts it would be the masterwork of *The Jungle Book*. And Chaplin certainly wasn't a dermatologist.

CHARLIE CHAPLIN (*actor, filmmaker*)[1] We met in 1971. A puzzle piece, but the most adorably charming one I'd ever met. He laughed when I started calling him "the Enigma Variations"—after Elgar—but it was true.

STEVE ALLEN (*comedian, entertainer*) He used to say he was a riddle wrapped in an enigma. But he'd always add, "a *Nelson* riddle."

JASPER JOHNS (*artist*) Easy to know—yet hard. Erudite, with a virginal, rapacious intelligence. One of the rare souls one feels instantly comfortable with. At first blush, you had the sense of having known him forever. You knew nothing about him, of course, nor ever would.

---

1 *Chaplin: Conversations*, ed. Thomas Ward (Aperture Press, 1972), p. 218.

DENZEL WASHINGTON (*actor*) A white man raised in great privilege who learns in midlife that his biological mother was Black—and his biological father a violent racist. He'd say, "It don't get any better than that, Denz."

MERYL STREEP (*actress*) I have a photo on the piano of him with Sinatra, Streisand, and Muhammad Ali—but your eyes go only to Roar. The rest are just staring at him, wanting his love and attention. And laughing, you know, glamorous big-laughing, larger than life, like that famous photo of Gable, Cooper and Stewart at Romanoff's. I don't know where they were, what party or event, but everyone was in a tux, even Barbra. Roar's looking straight at the camera with that sly little trademark smile but you have the sense he's alone. That sadness . . . oh! I get tears.

DICK GREGORY (*comedian*)[2] We used to gig together. At the hungry i . . . and in Reno. This was a long time before Roar knew where he came from. Before Bird and all that jazz. The boy was white as a sheet of paper! We were friendly competitors—you know, always telling each other our shit wasn't funny. He'd hear me do my act on a *good* night and just shake his head. Click his tongue and look real, real sad. "Only connect," he'd say. "Only connect, Sandman." He called me Sandman 'cause he said my act put people to sleep! We fucked with each other like that. He called me Sandman so I started calling him Sad Man 'cause he had that thing in his eyes. The cat was wounded. You're born with that look. Can't be taught.

WOODY ALLEN (*actor, filmmaker*) He was the inspiration for *Zelig* but in reverse—he was Zelig in the center, not the fringe. Everyone else, regardless of their fame, was reduced to being Zelig just by standing next to him.

TREVOR NOAH (*comedian*) He and Dick Gregory were close but the one nearest to his heart was Richard Pryor. They were born in the same year, 1940. Pryor was raised in a bordello, a far cry from "Parnassus," the palace in Pacific Heights where Roar was brought up.

DICK GREGORY I was writing my memoirs and he said, "I got a title

---

2 Dick Gregory, *Nigger, Please! Monologues in Black and White* (Division Street, 1993).

for you, Sandman: *Black Out*." Damn good. But I was a little ambivalent. 'Cause I didn't want black to be out, I wanted it to be *in*. "White Out"? Ha! The main thing was, I needed to make the name of the book my own. A few months later, I told him, "Gonna call it *Nigger*." His face got all kinda deformed and I thought *Oh shit, the motherfucker hates it!* Which would have hurt, feel me? 'Cause I respected the fuck out of that man. I got all tense. Then he smiles—remember that smile he had? Big as the sun—and gives me a hug. "Sandman? That's genius. And that's why I'll never be you. I'll never have those big balls." He had *mad* balls, was born with 'em, but was generous to a fault. But it was important to me that he liked it—loved it— because I was still waking up at three a.m. and saying, "Do I really want to call my book that?" I was worried it was too forced-outrageous. Sensational, exhibitionistic, whatever. After he said the title was great, I *still* had doubts. Called him one morning for a little reassurance, and he said he'd kill me if I backed down.

That's the gift he gave everyone: the truth. The truth, and an unconditional generosity of heart and spirit. And he was always right, except when it came to himself.

But even when he was wrong about that, he was right.

MARVIN WORTH (*producer*) [Pryor] was his first choice for *Coloring Book*, Roar's version of the Sirk movie, *Imitation of Life*. He was always going back to that theme. The movie never got made and that's one of the regrets of my life. Did you know Pryor was arrested in Germany when he was in the Army? In the late Fifties. Richard was watching *Imitation of Life* and there was a white soldier in the audience, some piece of shit who thought it was funnier than a Road Runner cartoon. He shouted at the screen, you know, mocking the Susan Kohner character—the girl who was "passing"—and generally laughing his cracker ass off. Richard and a bunch of black soldiers beat the shit out of him. Pryor did time for that, two years in the stockade.

So much for joining the Army and seeing the world.

GOLDIE HAWN (*actress*) We had a house in Point Dume, not far from the place Roar had at the Cove. We threw a little dinner party for him. I was giving him a tour of the house. We were in the bedroom and he said something so insanely funny, I wouldn't dare try to tell you what it was. Then he did a dancer's pivot and vanished into the hall. A master of timing, a master of the exit. I laughed so hard I shat myself and blacked out.

ERIC IDLE (*author, comedian*) He was legendary for being able to do that. He'd drop a bomb and leave, then people would shit or piss themselves and fall unconscious. It's where we got the idea for the *Python* sketch, "The Funniest Joke In the World." The joke that literally kills.

MARIANNE WILLIAMSON (*author, activist*) I really do think he was a bodhisattva. Late in life, he got recognized as a *tulku*—a reincarnated master. So was Steven Seagal, because of the donations he made to a monastery. When I told Roar that, he said, "Why, of all the nirvana!"

EDDIE IZZARD (*actor, activist*) I don't know if it's apocryphal but he was in the UK because he was made a KBE, which is quite rare for an American. He spent time alone with the Queen and she roared with laughter—how aptly named he was! Servant scuttlebutt was that a neat rivulet of stool dribbled down her leg but I don't believe it.

Still, that was the effect he had "on cabbages and kings."

ELON MUSK (*inventor, entrepreneur*) People think it was my kids who were responsible for the Tesla fart app. Nope: it was courtesy of Mr. Roger Orr. He said he wanted to be the Dylan, the Kanye, the Sondheim of electric farts. True to his word, the man got *involved*. He didn't come up with "Short Shorts Ripper"—but "Gentle Roar" was all his.

AMY SCHUMER (*comedian*) He was the greatest stand-up, *ever*—Pryor himself said that. Chappelle's obsessed with those early performances. We all are. And that he did them when he was a *kid* was just . . . impossible. Patti Smith said he was the Rimbaud of comedy, but I thought she was talking about Stallone. . . . Those LPs he did had amazingly surreal moments— totally worthy of Perelman. I heard that Spike Milligan lifted some of the bits for *The Goon Show* but don't know if that's true . . . classic vaudeville and hyper-cerebral too. They're all on YouTube. I don't know a comic who hasn't studied them like the Dead Sea scrolls. Scroll down!

HOWIE MANDEL (*comedian*) He did one of those famous cold calls. I don't know how he got my number but hey, it's Roger Orr, he's got everyone's number. Right? I thought it was a prank because I talked about him all the time in interviews. He said he wanted to be a judge on *AGT* [*America's Got Talent*]. I burst out laughing and said, "Okay now, *seriously*—who is this?"

RUPAUL (*drag queen, television personality*) Growing up, he felt he was a girl trapped in a boy's body. We talked and talked about that. He came to embody so many things about this contradictory age. That's always the way it is with visionaries. They don't come along too often. God gives you a tiny allotment then says, "*Th-th-th-that's all, folks.*"

CAITLYN JENNER (*activist*) He said I was the bravest person he ever met. But without Roar I'd never have had the courage. So, he was being kind. The most fearless soul I'd ever met.

JAN MORRIS (*writer*) He wanted to do an opera about my life. I loved him but that was something I simply wasn't interested in. He wrote *Swan Song* instead. I was the oyster who made that pearl—it makes me smile. Naturally, it's entered the canon, like everything Roar did.

KATY PERRY (*singer*) He wrote an opera about a hermaphrodite, a word that's fallen into disrepute because it's considered . . . whatever. I have a lot of trans friends who love that word. But the opera was about him. He called it "my schoolboy *Madame Butterfly*."

STEVEN SONDHEIM (*composer, lyricist*) *Swan Song* was far better than Puccini. Much closer to Mozart than Puccini.

CAITLYN JENNER We talked about *everything*, including the Pronoun People. Roar'd say, "I don't mind being called 'they' but when I got implants, my tits thought they were being spoken about in third person. They said, 'How rude!'"

DR. TERRY DUBROW (*plastic surgeon, television personality*) I was at a party with Brooke Shields, and somehow Roar's name came up. I was such a fan. Well, of course she knew him and said, "He loves your show." I was, like, "Huh?" Roger Orr was a fan of *Botched*! I'd read his book in med school— *Orr's Textbook of Dermatology*. So I reached out to ask if he'd do a guest consult on *Botched* for a patient with vitiligo and rheumatoid arthritis. We do something like that now and then. I was instantly embarrassed—the note was fawning—and worried I'd get an angry call from Brooke, saying, "You *idiot*. Why did you *do* that? What were you thinking!"

Months later I got a response. A lovely thank-you, ending with "Sorry— no skin in that game anymore." It's framed and on my desk.

GWYNETH PALTROW He was a friend of Dad's. I was probably about seven years old when he came to the house for dinner. My mom loves scented candles, and they were burning all over the place whenever we had guests. He came back from the bathroom, sniffed the air and smiled. Mom said, "Vanilla rose." And he very *dramatically*, you know, very arch, stared into space, and mused. "No. It smells like . . . my vagina." This was a long time before he had the surgery! My parents fell on the floor. I'm so glad he lived long enough to see the Goop candle—my homage. He asked if he'd be paid a royalty— kind of half-joking?—and I said something stupid like, "Oh c'mon, Roar, you already *are* royalty."

He held the candle in his hands, smiled and said, "Gwynnie? Stop making scents."

KEITH RICHARDS (*musician*) His chemical intake was . . . Promethean. Drank like Dylan Thomas and drugged like Neal Cassady. Good songwriter too; *great* songwriter. Very Jacques Brel. Wrote a lotta crap for his movies— "soundtrack songs" I call 'em—but did some amazing ballads that were never recorded. Mystical love songs on par with Leonard Cohen, like "Heaven Can't Wait." That's one I wish I'd done.

FRANCIS BACON (*artist*)[3] He showed me some sculptures. He called them "doodies," sardonic doodles, throwaways. The call of doodie was how he referred to the moment inspiration came. I thought they were as good as anything Giacometti had done.

---

3 From *Francis Bacon, The Dishing Pope* by Lendrick Harris, pp. 181–185 (Black Arch, 2008).

TOM STOPPARD (*playwright*) A consummate alchemist. Paul Allen rented an entire cruise ship and had it completely redone for a weekend party he threw in Saint Petersburg. (Yes, a weekend party.) I was at a dinner table with Roar, Carrie Fisher, Terry Gilliam, James Watson, Martha Stewart, and Deepak Chopra. I don't remember a thing anyone said—except for Roar telling me he loved *Rosencrantz and Guildenstern*, and "You should really write something about Shakespeare in love."

He had a way of planting seeds.

FRANCIS BACON[4] He enjoyed dressing like a girl when we went out. He was beautiful. I was quite in love. This was a bit before he became "Roar," Renaissance Genius of the World. He was still Rodge, soaking up theater in London and whatever spilled anywhere near. He was rough in bed. I liked it cruel though that's not what he was about. But he could *play* cruel. A chameleon, with a cock fatter than Lucien [Freud]'s. With Rodge, you never knew exactly *who* you were fucking. Wasn't that the thrill.

VINCE GILLIGAN I met him during *The X-Files*. A party at Matt Groening's. Seductive and compulsively gregarious but that winning smile saw right through you. I was expecting him to be "on," you know, to be Roger Orr. "Entertain me." That sounds kind of sleazy but it was true—I was in awe. *Everyone* was. He told some very funny stories then did the laser eye thing. "So, Young Invincible Gilligan, what are you going to do next that isn't yours?" No affect at all—like asking if I had travel plans for the holidays. That's why it was so deadly. He added, "What's your next idea for the Man?" He wasn't talking about Chris [Carter]. . . . "The Man"—a very Sixties thing to say, but I got it. I was so shaken that I left the party.

I blasted the radio in the car and by the time I got home, *Breaking Bad* was mapped out in my head, from pilot to final episode.

STEVEN SPIELBERG (*director*) As if his other talents weren't enough—if you can politely call them "talents"—he made six films in the top twenty or thirty of the best ever made. I don't think that's even arguable. He was like

---

4 Ibid., loc. cit., op. cit., id. est., PRN, b.i.d. with food, p. 213.

Kubrick in terms of his effortless exploration of genres: comedy, noir, sexual tragedy, war. But Kubrick with a heart. Stanley was cold; Roar was hot.

QUENTIN TARANTINO (*director*) We met in 1990, before *Reservoir*. I was working at the video store. People came in wondering what to watch, and I pushed his movies on customers like dope. I was his dealer *and* his pimp! Then one day the man himself comes in and asks for all the John Fords. The studio would have screened them but he wanted laser discs. . . . I was a pretty big poster collector and gave him one of my own—the Tippi Hedren movie, *Roar*. He loved that. We became friends and I couldn't believe it. I showed him the rough cuts of all my films. His was the only opinion that mattered.

MERYL STREEP The day he died—well, the first thing I thought, the first thing anyone thought when you heard something like that was of course COVID. This was before the vaccine, when the other shoe kept dropping. Most people survived but I had friends, and friends of friends—mostly their parents—who didn't. People with comorbidities, which Roar certainly had. All the heart stuff, all the abuse he'd done to his body. You white-knuckled it whenever there was a surge, and there was *always* a surge. He was just about eighty and of course vulnerable. I was in complete denial about that because he was one of those people you think will never die. The life force was so damn strong, he was like some *kid*. My head started racing and I went to was it suicide? Because as much as he was surrounded by light—blinding light!—there was *so* much darkness. He tried it once before, the suicide thing, maybe more than once . . . but I hated the possibility—taking his own life—so I started thinking, *Was he sick? Was it cancer and no one knew?* Some of that was selfish because if I knew, I would have gone to see him one last time. I thought, who can I call to find out what happened? I was frantic. There were a *lot* of people I could call, starting with Laughlin, Leslie, and Ali Berk. We hadn't spoken since our last film together. . . . I was going to give him the Twain Prize but he canceled, so something was up. Did I talk to him right after that? After he canceled? I must have. I would have *had* to. Why can't I remember? I'd given him so many awards! The Special Award from the Academy . . . he'd already gotten the Presidential Medal of Honor, the Kennedy Center Honors, the National Book Award, the Grammy Lifetime Achievement. My God, he was an EGOT! He called *that* one the "EGO." Roar hated awards but loved them too. That's him in a nutshell.

I remember what he said when he took the stage for something or other—oh, he loved "taking the stage." No matter how depressed he was, it breathed life into him. Loved walking into a party and knowing all heads were just *ratcheting* toward him. You could hear people's neck bones! I remember one time before he left the stage clutching whatever glass and gold hardware they'd given him, he told the audience, "See you next year in the memorial montage."

Big laugh, but not too far off.

AMANDA GORMAN (*poet*) I knew the twins from school. Ava and Emma, Roar's godkids. My mom's a teacher. She has eclectic taste but loves watching old films. One time I was about fourteen and heard her *crazy*-laugh. I walked into the room and she was watching Tyler Perry in her favorite Roar flick, *Hallelujah Boogie*. I mean, Tyler wasn't even twenty years old . . . I wasn't a big fan of Madea, but I've changed my tune now. Oh, I was haughty when I was younger! But I knew enough to be impressed because by then Tyler Perry was a huge star and directed movies and built his own studio. Not easy for a Black man, not easy for *anyone*, not then and not now. But *Boogie* was before all that, *way* before. I started watching and got sucked in 'cause Tyler was *funny*. I tried not to laugh. Turned my little nose up and said, "Well, he did a good job directing." That's all I'd give her! I thought he was *born* directing, you know, came out of the box that way. She said, "*Tyler* didn't direct this! He was a *baby*. Roger Orr did—'Roar!'" I knew Roar through the twins but for some reason it didn't really register. A day later I heard her laughing again and walked in—but it wasn't laughter, she was just bawling her eyes out watching Denzel in *Grace War*. Three minutes later, I'm crying just like Mama. And, of course, Roar directed *that*. I remember thinking, How do you go from *Hallelujah* to *Grace War*? How do you even do that? How does a person hold so many different things in their hands? That was my aspiration. He's what got me thinking that way. There are no limits. The only limits are those we put on ourselves.

KANYE WEST (*musician, entrepreneur*) I ran into him at the Mercer. I never called him Roar, never called him Roger. Just "Mr. Rogers." He called me Constantinople but with a K-A-N. Whenever I saw him. I'd say, "Mr.

Rogers! Is it a beautiful day in the neighborhood?" "Kanstaninople? It's a *shit* day." I'd sing back, "Would you be mine? Could you be mine?" He always sang back, "Yes, I'll be Jim Nabors." [*laughs*] He knew I was interested in fashion but hadn't found a way in. That day outside the hotel, he said, "The secret's right under your nose." Then he got into the back of the limo, rolled down the window, and winked.

"The *sneak*ers right under your nose," and the car pulled away.

I went to my room at the hotel and sketched out the first Yeezys.

TYLER PERRY (*actor, director, producer*) I called him once for advice. There's no better consigliere than Roger Orr. I was developing *Diary of A Mad Black Woman* with one of the studios. Hell, this is almost twenty years after Roar gave me my first job—in *Hallelujah Boogie*. I said I was in a bit of a tussle about directing *Diary* myself; they were giving me push-back. And there were some other things like script notes that I was beginning to compromise on. I downplayed it and told him I'd power through. You know, that I was strong but would win in the end. How all in all, they'd been pretty good allies—that kind of bullshit. Roar said, "*In the end*, I think it's good to have a nice little house on the plantation." That night, I decided I was going to raise the budget money myself—and build a movie studio of my own. . . . There's that story about Steve Jobs wanting to poach the president of Pepsi. Jobs said to the guy, "Do you want to sell ●ugar water for the rest of your life? Or do you want to come with me and change the world?"

For me, Roar was my Steve Jobs. And with all he'd been through? He was Job too. Steve *Job*.

SCOTT DISICK (*reality show personality*) He was a big fan of pop culture, believe it or not. We first met in Vegas when I was having a tough time. I sobered up long enough to have a drink with him. He'd say, "You need to beam yourself up, Scottie." I thought he was making a Jim Beam joke but he was talking about rehab. I knew who he was and couldn't believe he was even *interested*. He said, "Are you going to be a toy poodle on that ladies' show forever? [*Keeping Up With the Kardashians*] Is that the major plan? Are you going to jump into bed with one amazing, anorexic eighteen-year-old after another? Forever?"

That night, I decided that was *exactly* what I wanted to do. Forever.

LAUGHLIN ORR (*sister*) He was just a baby when our family took him in. I was already seven years old. When I asked where he came from, my mother said, "He's a gift from God." I didn't believe her. Now I do.

STEVEN SPIELBERG He was the one who planted the seed for *E.T.* All of his films are about aliens—"the other." Especially *Gift from God*. You know, the little boy who thinks he's an alien and goes searching for his father. Every Roger Orr movie is a false flag metaphor for that.

MEGHAN MARKLE (*activist*) The other day, Archie was watching *Gift from God*—just glued to the set, totally focused. Harry told me his mum loved it too and I couldn't believe it! I said, "Archie, are you watching Grammy's favorite movie? Is that what you're doing? Watching Grammy's favorite?" He didn't turn to look at me at all.

MICHELLE OBAMA (*author*) Roar saw *all* sides of a story. That's what made him a great director, a great storyteller. He was developing something for Barack and me when he died. An adaptation of a book of Toni Morrison's for Netflix.

He had such compassion. Apparently, his biological father was a very charming man. They met in prison. He was in jail for murder. He raped Roar's mother and killed a bunch of Black folk—white people too. But Roar got along with everyone, even unapologetic racists. Folks would ask, "How can you even *speak* to Nazi sympathizers?" He'd smile and say, "Easy. I get that from Dad; he had the gift of gab." Always funny but with a dark, dark edge.

WOODY HARRELSON (*actor*) We bonded over our fathers being in prison together. That's a true story. Only for a few days—a prison in Georgia.

Roar would do both their voices and it was Lenny Bruce meets Richard Pryor. Chappelle and I were at the Paradise Cove house and he did twenty minutes. The routine was like one of those comets you'll never see again in your lifetime. Dave went insane. Out of his mind. Dave laughs a *lot* but I never saw him go that hard.

DOLLY PARTON (*singer-songwriter*) We met at the Grammys in 1972. He'd written "Try A Little Tenderness" ten years before—when he was twenty-one! And written songs for his films, and some for singer-friends, "as a lark." That's how he put it. If you want to call "Storming Heaven" and "Catapult" *larks*. Lord, I'd give my left tittie for a lark like them. Give *both* titties—well, almost. [*laughs*] We became fast friends. I was working on "I Will Always Love You" and sang it for him in his brownstone in New York. He kinda knew it was my goodbye song to Porter [Wagoner]. I was having trouble with a lyric, which is rare, 'cause most the time it just flows. He grabbed a scrap of paper and scribbled something. "We both know I'm not what you need." And it was so . . . right. He was shaking. I was too. He had tears in his eyes. I realized that for him, my song was about everyone he'd ever loved and lost. He thought he was a freak—all geniuses think that, and it's true. God's freaks. That's a heavy weight to carry 'cause you're always leaving folks behind. Turning your head to say "I'll always love you" but by the time you get the words out, they're gone.

I wanted to give him a record credit for giving me that lyric, no big thing. "A special thanks to Mr. Orr" in the liner notes. He wouldn't hear of it.

ELON MUSK He was an angel investor in Zip2, in '95—that's when we met, through a professor of mine at Stanford. Roger had a breakdown a few years later—not the first!—and did a lot of ketamine. Said the ketamine saved him. . . .

We were in Maui, talking about our fathers and mothers. He had two sets of parents; it's hard enough having one. By then, even though it'd been a long time since he found out about Bird, he still hadn't processed his shame. He hid that pretty well from the world. Not the shame that she was Black—no no no!—but the shame of how he reacted to finding out that he was adopted. When Roger discovered he wasn't who he thought he was, he literally lost his mind. Do you remember? They had to hospitalize him. As sophisticated as he was—knowing spiritually and intellectually that identity is merely a construct—it was a horror to him that he couldn't accept his fate. A fate with grandeur, with magnificence. Instead of embracing the weirdness of it, the *religiousness* of it, he went into the fetal position, and that he responded in such a way filled him with self-contempt. People who don't know him got it all wrong. They still say, "It was racial shame." Roger hated that sort of gossip—that he was ashamed of Bird, ashamed to have a Black mother. Hated it. Which couldn't have been farther from the truth. Yet what should have been a joyous revelation, a liberating one, sunk him into a profound existential despair. See, the major thing about Roger Orr, the major trait was that he was always in control of the narrative. Complete control. That's why he was such a great director; he did narrative for breakfast. In one of his journals he said the sudden appearance of his new origin story was "the bull in the china shop of bourgeois complacency." He never forgave himself for the primal timidities—his phrase—that he considered to be a fatal flaw of character. Roger was a radical artist but when he found out where he came from, he woke up worse than an emperor with no clothes. He was an emperor running naked through the streets in a nightmare, chased by a mob of alternate selves. It was a wound that never closed.

AMANDA GORMAN Toni Morrison's my total hero. And there they are on YouTube when she won the Nobel in Stockholm! She insisted Roar be onstage when they gave her the award. No one had ever done that, and I don't think the Swedes were happy, but what could they do? Of all the people on this blue-green Earth that Toni could have chosen . . . I know they were collaborating on a musical of *Othello*. He'd already written some of the songs. And was working on a film adaptation of her last book, *God Help the Child*, that the Obamas were going to produce. He was working on it till the end, they *both* were, and died within a few months of each other.

That's how I'd like to go. With my poetry boots on.

ELON MUSK When we had our baby [X Æ A-XII], he called and said, "You should have just gone with 'Roko'—so much easier to pronounce." Then he whispered, "Every child needs to kill his parents for the greater good."[5]

AMANDA GORMAN I never got the chance to meet Ms. Morrison. I wrote to her after I became the national youth poet laureate—she wrote back! That was *crazy*. She was incredibly supportive when I started my nonprofit, One

---

5 "Roko's Basilisk" is an AI thought experiment postulating that robots could justify the killing of human beings if those deaths resulted in a greater human good. The theorem remains a favorite of Musk and Grimes, the mother of his child.—*ed.*

Pen One Page. But I did get to go to her memorial. So many heroes were there to eulogize her: Angela Davis, Edwidge Danticat, Ta-Nehisi Coates. Oprah . . . but Toni's instructions saved Roar for last. He was very, very sick. It took him *hours* to get onstage, and he had a lot of help too.

He began with a spot-on Vivien Leigh: "After all, tomorrow is another day!" Folks tittered and gasped. He took a long, theatrical pause. Then his voice broke and he said, "No!" That voice *boomed.* "No! I *lied.* Tomorrow has been *canceled. Today* has been canceled. There are hereby no *tomorrows* or *todays.* They have been *suspended* until further notice. Only *yesterday* has currency, because that's where Toni is. Today and tomorrow are foreclosed, bankrupt, without value. There will never be another today or tomorrow •ithout Toni in it. And that is unacceptable."

You'd think an earthquake hit, the way that cathedral shook. Like God was crying too. God's a big Roger Orr fan, oh I'm sure of that.

ELON MUSK We were big fans of *Tucker.* The Coppola film. I told him I was going to buy an electric car company, and we tossed around names. He closed his eyes and said, *"Electra Glide in Blue"*—another movie we both liked—and we shortened it to Electra, of which I grew quite attached. Tesla came very close to being Electra. It was the corollary to his little Roko joke: Electra wanted to kill her mother, Clytemnestra.

LAUGHLIN ORR He used to tell me he'd be the first to go, but I never believed it because he'd been saying that from the moment he could talk. When I argued the point, he'd make the concession that "We're the Either/Orr Kids. It'll either be you or me. It's a race to the ether."

BOOK ONE
Birth of a Nation
1940–1955

CHAPTER ONE

Tennessee's Partner

> And I say to myself
> What a wonderful whirl
> (*"For Louis," Bird Rabineau*)

BIRD RABINEAU (*singer, Roar's mother*)[6] Far as I've traveled from Leipers Fork, that's where I am when I wake up. Isn't that funny? That's where I am when my head hits the pillow too. Don't matter if I'm in L.A. or Paris or Stockholm—I could be in Botswana, zoomin' after a lioness as she chases down some poor squealin' warthog—or that time in Monaco watching fireworks from the yacht club, you couldn't even *be* there unless the Prince himself invited you—or riding a German stallion in Mallorca like the one time I did . . . but in the mornin' or late at night, I'm always right back in Leipers Fork without shoes, runnin' around the neighborhood at night with Callico. A black sky of stars just whirling above you fast enough to make you dizzy at the mystery of God's world. Runnin' 'round and dreamin' of the mysteries I've now seen, not even *able* to dream what I've seen. That little girl had no idea, oh, but she had ideas of her own that are still mysterious even to me. They say you can't go home again but that's bull 'cause you never left. Ain't it all funny?

CALLICO PRIDE (*Bird's childhood friend, age 97*) Bird was perfect. Just a perfect, beautiful soul. They named her Mika. Albert, her daddy, wanted a

---

6 *Bird of Prayer: A Bird Rabineau Convocation*, edited by Cilia Wheathouse, Introduction by James Baldwin, pp. 216–223 (Simon & Schuster, 1980).

boy and was gonna call him Michael, after the archangel. That's in the Book of Daniel. Albert was a preacher, you know. Mika means "gift from God," my great-granddaughter told me that just two days ago. It's a mineral too, all shiny, you can see right through it. And that was Bird all right. I used to call her Kiki but after she put her lips on mine—just that once—I called her "Milky" in my head. I never told my kids that, never told a soul. I should be old enough not to care but still do, just a little bit, but I hope she kiss me again when I see her. Oh, the Milky Way had *nuthin'* on my Milky. I went straight to the stars with that kiss. Now I don't know where *she* went, but I know I went further. Mind you, she's the only girl or lady I allowed such a thing to ever happen. Everything *about* that child was milky. You could look right through that skin, see a big heart in there beatin' like a drum. Had little webs between her toes, between the pinkie and the one beside it, and Bird didn't like folks to see that. You couldn't hardly anyway, even if you looked (and you were lookin' everywhere else). That's why she didn't run barefoot like the rest of us. When she didn't have shoes—that's how poor we were—she ran around in socks. [*laughs*] Freckles? They was *everywhere*, like stars you see through a telescope. And that birthmark . . . a pink butterfly on her forehead, where the third eye is supposed to be. She was light enough you could see the pink. They call that an angel kiss, did you know that? Yes, they do.

BUCK SNOWCRAFT (*historian*) Elbert Williams was lynched in Brownsville. That was the summer of 1940. You know, the Klan was founded in Tennessee in 1866, in Pulaski, about an hour's ride from Leipers Fork where Roger Orr's mother lived.

Elbert was the son of sharecroppers, and his grandfather was a slave. He was active in the NAACP, and it didn't help that he wanted to invest in a local hardware store; his entrepreneurial streak was the straw that broke their backs. The sheriff jailed and interrogated him, then he was released in the dead of night. A crowd of good ol' boys was waiting to see him safely home. A few days later, they pulled the body out of Cinnamon River. Of course, the perpetrators were never brought to justice. One of the mob wasn't local—no one knows what "Wriggle" Petry was doing up in Brownsville in the first place. Probably just on a Havoc Tour. After the deed was done he traveled east, on his way home to Macon. Stopped in Leipers Fork long enough to rape Mika Rabineau.

CALLICO PRIDE They didn't start calling her Bird till she was sixteen. Lillian gave her that name—Lil Hardin, Louis Armstrong's wife. Mika didn't like it at first cause she thought they were making fun of her webbed feet! She told me that years later 'cause I didn't see her for a long time after she ran away. Billie Holiday said *she* gave her the name but nope, it was Lillian. They all took a lot of guff from white folk, the black entertainers, even after they got famous. Drunks and all-around troublemakers. What do they call 'em, hecklers. Doesn't seem like the right word for what they do. It was dangerous being up onstage—wasn't no joke. Charlie Parker once said if they were ever on the same bill, best be careful. Mr. Parker told her, "Easy to kill two Birds when they're stoned." He was a funny man. But I don't think they never did play together.

BUCK SNOWCRAFT Leipers Fork is close to Franklin, where a lot of Confederates were killed. You can still talk to locals who say it wasn't about slavery. You know, "Those damn yankees wanted our land and our cotton and ambushed our boys. Mowed seven thousand of them down." There was some truth to that.

ROSIE LEVIN (*biographer*)[7] Colson "Wriggle" Petry was twenty-four years old and two hundred pounds; Bird Rabineau was fourteen, a skinny little thing. She's lucky she didn't die. For years, she said, "If luck had been with me, I *would* have died that night." Eventually, she did come to think of it as luck. "It brought me closer to the Lord."

BUCK SNOWCRAFT Of course, no one went to the police. That'd have been suicide. And nothing would have been done, anyway. Worse than nothing because they'd have killed whoever reported it.

BIRD RABINEAU[8] My friend and I used to flit all over the neighborhood like little sparrows. All we wanted to do was hear the radio. We were too poor to have one; fleas on stray dogs had more earthly goods. We'd fly around till we heard Judy Garland or Billie on the radio—Mama had to tell me what

---

7 *The Sparrow's Eye: The Rise and Rise of Bird Rabineau* by Keg Sweeney (Norton, 1999).
8 Ibid., pp. 16–21.

Billie meant by "Strange Fruit." I must've sung "Over the Rainbow" till I was on the other side of the rainbow myself. That night after Callico went home, I took a little shortcut, stumbled right into a campfire. I knew right then I was going to die. My eyes saw what they saw and I felt it on my skin and in my bones. There were two others but the big one told 'em he was having me for himself. "Not sharing slave cunt tonight, boys." That's just what he said. I looked in the sky the whole time, wanting God to reach down, reach down and smite him and snatch me up. But He didn't. It was just that poor little girl and those stars, the ones He made, winking at her like they was in on the plan. That's when I broke with the Almighty and didn't find my way back for many years. Big fat Mr. Campfire had a radio and put it close by, like a boy might, for romance. I heard the others laughin' and spittin' and doin' whatever kinda shit they do when somethin' like that goes down. A tune was playing. Tommy Dorsey—I didn't know it then but that's what it was. "You're the tear that comes after June time's laughter, you see so many dreams that don't come true, dreams we fashioned when summertime was new." The man was so heavy on me I passed out. That was a mercy. Don't even know how I got home. Don't know why he didn't just kill me—guess that God's plan too. Parts of me managed to die but not all of me. I prayed and prayed for the parts that didn't to join the parts that did, but I couldn't get out from under Mr. Campfire. I prayed to go right through him if I could and just levitate to the stars. I've spent a lot of my life chasing those dead parts! Chasing after that poor dead little girl to wrap my arms around her and give comfort. Then I changed my mind, you know, I didn't want to join her, I wanted to rescue her, take her away with me because those stars didn't deserve her, ooh I was so mad at those motherfuckin' stars! I couldn't sing "Indian Summer" for a long, long while, couldn't even listen to it. I knew I had to. *You're the ghost of a romance in June goin astray.* . . . When I finally did sing it, I think that was my ticket back to the Lord Jesus. And I forgave that campfire Wriggleman for what he'd done. The needle and the heroin were tellin' me I forgave him, that's what the Devil does. But noddin' out ain't forgivin'. So often what we *wish* to believe isn't so—we want to believe we've healed but we haven't. That speaks to our selfishness and arrogance. The Lord says to His children, "You've come so far but there are miles to go before you sleep." Mr. Robert Frost said that! I met him in 1972 and couldn't believe he wrote that! I was sure it was from the Bible. I was embarrassed, but Mr. Frost was so kind. . . . The Lord says exactly that, you have miles to go, do not rest on false laurels, for such is vanity. That's His way of keeping our eyes on the prize. Of keeping us right. I do believe you have to *feel* you've forgiven your enemies—"for they know not what they do"—even if you haven't in your heart of hearts. Belief is the first step. Don't matter if your forgiveness isn't true, if it isn't righteous, it *shall* be righteous and true when we meet the Lord. He will lift up His arms and His embrace will make it true and wash everything away. We shall be washed clean in the arms of the Lord. That's God's will and His way.

Heroin helped me get to forgiveness. When I tell folks that, it's controversial. God made heroin too. But pickin' it up? Well, I still don't know if that's God's way or the Devil's.

CALLICO PRIDE Her skin was light as Etta James. She and Etta didn't meet till the Sixties. Bird was about twelve years older but called Etta "Little Daughter." Etta had a white daddy too, a pool player called Minnesota Fats. Jackie Gleason made a movie about him. I *loved* Jackie Gleason. "Bang! Zoom! To the moon, Alice!"

ROSIE LEVIN Roger Orr was born at the Hermitage Hotel in Nashville. That's where they brought Bird when she was six months pregnant. They wanted her someplace they could keep an eye on her and make sure she was eating well. Interesting factoid: toward the end of his life, Minnesota Fats had a suite at the Hermitage. They set up a pool table for him in the mezzanine and he'd regale the guests. That pool table's still there.

CALLICO PRIDE Etta always wanted to sing like Bird and came pretty close. Bird had that *voice* from before I can remember. From another world. From . . . [*points heavenward*] there. Even when she was humming, it sounded like an opera. She used to sing "Summertime." Billie put that out in 1936 when we were ten years old. We didn't have no radio, you know, just skulked around till we heard it in the white folks' houses. We hid in the bushes—all Bird needed was one listen to make it her own. Like that song knew she was in the bushes and waited all its life for her. [*sings*] "One of these mornings, you're going to rise up singin' . . . then you'll spread your wings and take the sky." Lord, gives me chills to remember! That's just what Bird did. She took the sky. Even after that Klan motherfucker did his rape. (He was the first but weren't the last.) She took the sky and limped home. But that sky was *hers*. She's a constellation now. And you better believe it.

GWYNETH PALTROW [Spielberg] always wanted to make a movie of her life. A few months after Roar found out Bird Rabineau was his mother—the early Eighties, right?—Roar told Steven about it at a party. That he was her son. And no one knew, this was before it got leaked in the tabloids. Roar just blurted it out, like, very kind of cavalier. Probably he was loaded! Steven thought he was joking. Who wouldn't have, right? Steven was already a huge fan of Bird—"Soar Eyes" was on the soundtrack of *Sugarland Express*—and couldn't believe that Bird Rabineau was Roar's *mom*. No one could; my father told me that Roar himself couldn't, not for the longest time. I think that's why he was cavalier because he was still in shock about it. Roar used the word "preposterous" a lot when it came to his life—oh my God, I just remembered he named his production company "Preposterousaurus"! But it was such a weird, amazingly beautiful story: a cosmic *Ripley's Believe It or Not*. Right? That just made Steven want to make his movie *more*. He was going to call it "Bird of Pray," which they later used as the title of a book of collected interviews, but fate had other plans. This was 1983 and he was already pretty far along with *The Color Purple*. Years later, the project came back to him again— it was always coming back! He couldn't let go. He wound up doing *Amistad* instead. Roar told me, "It's like Steven's Preakness of black oppression. Ma keeps losing by a nose. Or should I say noose."

CALLICO PRIDE Bird's daddy was a drunk. A preacher too but in name only. He had charisma to him but they didn't let him preach no more 'cause Albert was just too scandalous. Drank turpentine when there was nothin' else available and finally got the wet brain. He was handsy, always tellin' me how curvy I was. Bird and I got our periods early, when we were eleven. He was like a bloodhound on the trail. She was a prude, the boys were fingering all the girls—but not Kiki. That's why it was even worse when the "Wriggle" pulled that devil shit. Everyone thought it was Albert who done her like that. Even my mama thought so. Bird's mama, Leticia, wasn't slow but her mind didn't walk at a normal pace, either. To this day I don't know what that woman thought about *anything*. She did what Albert told her to and she suffered.

Knocked a tooth out of her once. After that campfire business, Bird swore me not to tell what happened so I kept my mouth shut. I was the only one that knew. When she started to show, my mama was sure it was Preacher. All I'd say was, "Naw, it ain't him." She'd say, "Well if it weren't that sonofabitch, who was it?" She knew I was hidin' somethin' and slapped me silly. We finally had to tell the truth 'cause word got out there was a gang of men—rough black boys with crushes on Bird—who were gonna do Preacher Albert serious harm. They was gonna hang him and blame it on the Klan.

LETICIA RABINEAU (*Bird's mother*)[9] She changed after those white boys had their fun. Yes she did. Got more reserved. I couldn't put my finger on it but one day I knew what it was: she stopped singing. That's it, that's what it was. The funny thing is all the birds stopped singing too. You'd have to walk a distance till you heard 'em again. Like there was some kind of dome dropped down over the whole house like a glass cake cover that you couldn't see. Sometimes I wondered if it was a dream but that's how I remember it. Like the birds were protesting against their Maker for having allowed such a terrible thing.

CALLICO PRIDE Bird tried to kill the baby by drinking some of her daddy's hooch, but all she got was bad sick. She was too scared to put a hanger up there like some of the girls did. We knew one who died like that. Then some white people came and had a talk with Albert. Said they was church folk who'd find a nice home for the baby and pay him for his trouble. They took Kiki away, and Albert got drunk and boasted to anyone who'd listen that he got $500 cash money. Now that was more money than any of us ever looked at. The whole neighborhood lined up to come in and watch him fan those bills. 'Course someone stole most of it and Albert started sleeping with a little pistol under his pillow, which didn't make Leticia too comfortable. A rusty old thing, prob'ly would have blown up in his face if he pulled the trigger. Twenty years later, Bird told me the church folk put her in a big hotel with fancy food, all she could eat. Chocolate sundaes, every day! Had the time of her life being waited on hand and foot, but *I* know she was scared. She delivered at the hotel and they took it away. Why

---

9 Ibid., pp. 83–84.

was everything always being taken away from my Bird? Even the second baby, that beautiful little girl . . . The day she came back to Leipers Fork—they didn't even let her rest, just threw her right out of that hotel—she was dead in the eyes. Albert bought a truck with the money left over and drank himself to death. Oh, happy day. That truck never did run. She was sixteen when she left home for good. I cried so hard I couldn't see straight for two weeks. I went blind. You know that Etta song? "I'd Rather Go Blind"? [*sings*] "I would rather go blind then see you walk away from me, child."

I could have wrote that for my baby Bird.

BILLIE HOLIDAY (*singer*)[10] I was twenty-seven when we met. She was so shy, she couldn't even look at me. That voice! I gave her the name—Bird—cause you could almost see the feathers. But she wasn't a sparrow, no she wasn't. She was a hawk.

ROSIE LEVIN Bird's maternal grandfather, Porter, was thirty years older than his wife, June, who was born in 1891. They married in 1909. A year later, Bird's mother, Leticia, was born. Porter Cant was one of about a dozen African Americans elected to the Tennessee House of Representatives. This was after Reconstruction, but it didn't take too long for the Blacks to get banned from the House. Porter was tarred and feathered. Broken. He died of alcoholic poisoning just like Albert Rabineau. Cant had a congenital condition—webbed feet, something Bird inherited. And her grandmother had a birthmark on her forehead, what they used to call a "stork's bite," a patch of blood vessels that marked her specialness.

Little anomalies were in the DNA and one of them presented itself in Roar's polymastia: a "supernumerary" nipple. When Bird gave birth at the Hermitage Hotel, the adoption people saw that third breast and just about lost their minds. They were certain the not-insignificant balance still owed them would go up in smoke; the buyers would reject a circus freak out of hand. To their great relief, Bunny Orr didn't care. I've often wondered why it was such a concern. They sort of had their priorities scrambled, because they'd neglected to tell anyone the baby's mother was Black.

---

10 Interview with Billie Holiday, *DownBeat*, November 1954.

LAUGHLIN ORR In some ways, I thought our mother was closer to Roger than she was to her biological kids. I don't think [Jonny] felt that way . . . probably just me being insecure. But the drama of it, the mystery, the *impossibility* of it—a payoff to some sketchy group in Tennessee providing babies to barren high-society women!—all those things appealed to Mom deep down. Her father was a Texas wildcatter. A tough, tough Jew. Jews had their run-ins with the Klan too. Grandpa Langdon used to tell her stories of violence and derring-do that I think fueled a lot of choices in Mom's life. . . . We didn't really keep a Jewish household, but the one thing she always did was light yahrzeit candles when "important" Jewish people died. That's how I learned Douglas Fairbanks was a Jew—she lit a candle for him and was quite upset! A few months later, she lit one for Grandpa Langdon. I was seven years old when he died putting out a fire on a rig. I actually remember him—his smell. He smelled like a tree, like one of those big old live oaks they have down in Texas. Mom had a hundred of those planted at La Piedra. When I visit, I still feel him there. An ancient oak, with its smells and battle-scarred bark.

CHAPTER TWO

Golden Slumbers

GRACE SLICK (*rock singer*) Laughlin was the rich girl on the scene. Man, she had the right name—that amazing, deep-throated laugh. We met in San Francisco, probably 1966. The quintessential rich hippie: smart, patchouli-sexy, flaxen-hair wild. Gave the Diggers money, kept Morning Star [commune] afloat, helped Stewart [Brand] start the *Whole Earth Catalog*. Laugh was like the chick you met in a hot tub at Esalen at four in the morning and you find out a week later that her family *owns* Esalen. Ha! She didn't—own Esalen—but she could have. That was the vibe. She was only six years older but living a life *way* over my head. This gal who poured money into the Free Clinic and the Panthers was also part of the family that built the Presidio and funded the San Francisco Opera with the Gettys. I mean, the girl was balling Robinson fucking Jeffers! She knew all the Beats—fuck, Allen Ginsberg was *physically attracted* to her. And women were invisible to Allen! She might have slept with his crazy husband and definitely slept with Neal [Cassady] and Jack in the Fifties. Supposedly, Allen said she was the one who got away.

He wrote a poem about her, "Laughing Golden Gate Heavy Menses Sutra." It's got that great line, "blackgold spore of vortexarkana"—a nod to her grandfather, Langdon Desmoines, who was from Bowie County.

DICK GREGORY Laughlin and I were about the same age. I met her in Chicago—can't remember why she was in town but the lady *traveled*. She introduced me to Roar. She always called him Baby Brother. She said, "Listen to this Baby Brother shit!" and played the 45. When I heard the "comedy stylings" of this kid—they used to call it that, comedy stylings—the 45s were already this underground thing and it blew my mind. At the time, no one knew Roar was fourteen years old. Fuckin' unreal.

Laughlin wound up doing a lot for the Panthers. Fred [Hampton] loved her; they all did. I won't say she was involved with the Weathermen but I *can* say she helped Eldridge out when they were hiding Tim Leary in Africa. I can say it because she's already written about it.[11] Laughlin paid for the defense of Bobby Seale, most of it anyway. She didn't want that known and I respected that. . . . Oh, she had a good time on the red carpet—loved the glittery show-biz bullshit, just like Baby Brother—but when it mattered, when it was life and death, she ran silent and deep. She didn't like to leave fingerprints. Which was smart because Laughlin didn't want to attract attention to certain things she was doing; the publicity *would* not have helped. Her mother Bunny was a straight-up classy lady but there were lines that couldn't be crossed. I don't care how rich or "eccentric" you were, you could only get away with so much.

Bunny Orr knew that and so did her daughter.

GRACE SLICK Laugh was a huge figure in the Urban League—at thirty years old. She had that weird, old-money Zen thing in the way she carried herself. It's in the bones. She changes the room when she floats in. Her grand-father was this oilman from her mom's side, incredibly handsome, very Daniel Day-Lewis *There Will Be Blood*. And Laugh's father, Mug Orr—a.k.a. "the Commodore"—was a tobacco king. I love saying "tobacco king." [*laughs*] Charming, seductive, treacherous. And fuckin *funny*. The marriage of two dynasties, two patriarchies, so I think the women were rebellious and always needing to prove themselves. Mug's family wasn't wild about him marrying a Jew; Laugh told me that. Her mom was a trip. You could totally see where Laugh got her shit. Bunny was probably sixty when we met, and gorgeous. Maye Musk-gorgeous. The weird karmic thing is that I used to wait on her when I worked at Magnin's in the early Sixties. She'd sweep in and buy her Chanels and Balenciagas in every color.

He loved his sister. They were very, very close. Everything changed when Roar found out he was adopted. He held that against them—totally irrational because it wasn't like Laugh and Jonny were conspirators, they didn't know a

---

11 In *The Last Laughlin: A Memoir* by Laughlin Orr (Blue Rider, 2006).—*ed.*

fucking thing. But Roar needed a punching bag. Laugh *especially* paid for the sins of her parents, the sins of omission.

HOPE "HOOP" RADCLIFFE (*socialite*) Laughlin and I were born the same year but were never really friends. I traveled so much and went to school in Europe—Le Rosey. We were neighbors but didn't click. But Mother [Sunny Ambrose Radcliffe] and Bunny were thick as thieves. Mother was the only one who knew the backstory and I heard a lot about it when I was much older. It's complicated.

After Bunny had Laughlin, she and the Commodore—they nicknamed him after a friend of the family, Commodore Cornelius Vanderbilt—after she had Laughlin, they kept trying for another baby but nothing worked. Bunny wanted a passel of kids and was heartbroken. Every specialist in the world examined her case: in Denmark and Germany and even that famous place in Montenegro—they went everywhere and anywhere but it was no-go. Then, in an act of defiance that was pure Bunny Orr, she got pregnant! And sent every one of those doctors a note on her bespoke Itoya stationery. You had to keep opening and opening these beautiful envelopes, very matryoshka, until about ten minutes later you got to the very last one. And there it was, a card that said, in that beautiful tiny handwriting of hers, "Go fuck yourself." Mother showed it to me: you needed to get close to the page and squint in order to read it. And of course, the *worst* thing happened—she miscarried at five months. Mother said Bunny was so . . . embarrassed. She cursed herself for sending out those notes. You know, the curse of hubris. That's when she decided to adopt. Mother said she didn't see it as a compromise, because she was determined to have that baby like it came out of her body. Which maybe it did! In the end. Who's to say? She was witchy that way. Sometimes I thought Roger was more hers than Laughlin or Jonny ever were. There was a special bond between them. Laughlin said the same thing once. . . .

A year after Roar "arrived," Bunny had Seraphim. And Jonny, five years later. The so-called experts were wrong after all. But she never sent out any fuck-yous. She was done tempting the Fates.

JONNY "STAGE DOOR" ORR (*adopted brother*) After Mom died— when I found the diaries—there was a card in one of the pages, like a bookmark, a placeholder. She'd written on it something from Scriptures: "Whoever brings up an orphan in his home is regarded as though the child had been born to him."

I wondered about it but didn't realize the true import until I started reading.

HOPE "HOOP" RADCLIFFE When my brother Trevor had his terrible injuries from the war, Bunny Orr was the only one outside the family who visited him at the hospital. It brings tears to my eyes even now. No one else had the stomach, no one else had the heart. I know I didn't. I just couldn't. It was too hard . . . It saved Mother in a way—to have a compatriot, someone in the trenches, because that was a real war too, the war of trying to save our brave, darling boy. No matter how I feel about Laughlin, she's connected to the woman who eased Mother's burden, eased *all* our burdens.

And Roger was a big part of that. It's why he became a doctor for the brief period he did. Roar made a *difference*. What he did was saintly. It was the real thing.

LAUGHLIN ORR[12] These people in Nashville were well-known in blue-blood circles. It was like the Underground Railroad. Not really, but . . . They serviced the infertile crème de la crème in California and New York. There was an attorney called Peter Gramm, he was actually *from* Nashville. A shady character—at least I always thought so—but a very important man in San Francisco. On all the boards. I wonder how *that* happened. Dad used to joke that Peter Gramm knew where all the bodies were buried, because Gramm buried them himself. It was perfect because Tennessee was far enough away to soothe the nerves of the high-toned ladies who didn't want people knowing their business. These women would "go to Europe" for six or eight months and come back with a baby. They'd leave around the time they would have started to show. What happened with Mom was she miscarried in her fifth month and went straight from the hospital to La Piedra, our ranch in Sonoma. She couldn't bear to go home with a flat stomach and tell the world over and over that her little boy died inside her. Yes, it was a little boy . . . *Sooooo*, she hatched a plan, forgive the pun, and Daddy spoke to Mr. Gramm. The mystery

12 *Golden Slumbers: A Family Album*, Laughlin Orr (Haight Street, 1991), pp. 153–154.

is, those people in Nashville would have *known* the mother was black! Regardless of the lightness of the birth mom's skin, they definitely would *not* have overlooked—lying about something like that would have jeopardized their lucrative ongoing business with Mr. Gramm. It was utterly bizarre . . . Could Mr. Gramm have known? Could he have known all along? It baffles me. Because he was such a careful, ruthless man. Maybe he only found out when the baby was born. Then made the executive decision to come clean to Mom and Dad. My mother was many things, but she was *not* a racist. Neither was the Commodore. Mr. Gramm knew this all too well and not just from their activism in the Urban League—they'd given millions. Maybe Gramm cynically thought it was the one thing that would save him from his snafu or blunder, his what have you. There was no way Mom or Dad would say, "No negro babies for us!" My parents had a perverse sense of humor. Dad probably loved the idea of everyone thinking Mom took a black lover. Ha!

HOPE "HOOP" RADCLIFFE Did Laughlin say that? I never read her book. She means well but isn't famous for giving credit where credit's due. She probably doesn't remember that *I'm* the one who told her all of that because my mother said it was exactly what happened. Peter Gramm did not know. He found out when the baby brokers called, in a panic. The first thing they told him about was the third nipple—the second was, "Oh by the way, the mother is Negro." Well, it was what Mug used to call a real clusterfuck. He had very colorful language. And Bunny *did* have a failure of nerve, even though she knew in her gut she would keep that Tennessee child—the prod-uct of a violent rape no less which made her heart cry out. But she did waver. She told Mug, "What if it's black as the dark side of the moon and the world thinks you're a cuckold?" He got all ruddy like he did whenever he imme-diately had the answer to a Big Question. "Fuck em!" he said. My mother said that she didn't think there was a moment in Bunny's life when she loved that man more. Bunny cried in the Commodore's arms and said, "*Thank you thank you thank you*," a ten-minute seizure of thank-yous. That's what mar-riage should be like in its ideal but never is, is it? Two heads with one magnifi-cent heart. Like Fredric March and Myrna Loy in *The Best Years of Our Lives.*

JONNY "STAGE DOOR" ORR My sister's embroidered her theo-ries through the years about Mom and Dad not giving a flying fuck about adopting a black baby. A liberal's wet dream. That idiot "Dope" Radcliffe climbs into the telephone-game echo chamber with her bullshit gossip. She's a pig, a totally useless human being. Most of the conversations with Mom that Laughlin wrote about in her book were invented from whole cloth, as they said in ancient times. *Seeds* of truth were there, in the characteristics, the "humanistic philanthropy" of Mom and Dad. Their capacious spirit and all. But the mythology kept growing. Laughlin crocheted away until the narrative ended with our parents knowing all along that Bird was raped by a Klansman—knowing fucking *everything*, like the rich white gods they were—when the truth is they were scared shitless. In the what-have-we-got-ourselves-into sense.

Did you know Roar spoke to Peter Gramm before Gramm died? Gramm was the Ray Donovan of his time. He had an office in the Embarcadero with Diebenkorns and John Registers on the wall—in between snow globes, tchotchkes from Sausalito, and hideous sports memorabilia. Framed photos all around: Bill Kunstler, Bill Graham, Billy Graham—Peter paid his Bills! They paid *him* too, God only knows for what.

Roar told me the *real* story, which he never shared with our sister because he knew she'd Play-Doh it. Can't help herself, God love her.

VIOLA DAVIS (*actress*) People were always telling me I looked like Bird when she was young. . . . Steven [Spielberg] spoke to me about the project. He wanted Melissa Mathison to write it. Melissa wrote a little movie called *E.T.*—ever heard of it? [*smiles*] She and Harrison [Ford] were a couple, they were married. Anyway, I wanted Roar's benediction and went to see him. To that beautiful house he had at the beach. And he was conflicted. He didn't come right out and say it but that was my impression. He loved and respected Steven. Roar wanted the story to be told but at the same time needed to protect *both* moms, Bird *and* Bunny. I had the feeling the whole idea made him uncomfortable and that he wished he'd never entered into an agreement with Amblin. He was uncomfortable because it was obvious the story was his to tell, but he just couldn't. Just didn't want to go there.

When I left that day, I knew the movie would never be made.

JONNY "STAGE DOOR" ORR Roar told me that the woman in Nashville who made the "arrangements" got very, very ill. The baby-pimper. Pimp Baby was dying! That's what Gramm told my brother in the meeting they had before ol' Pete croaked. Helen Carver was her name. Gramm called her outfit "the Stork Club," yuck yuck. He said that Carver became deathly ill a few weeks after making the deal but didn't want to jeopardize the business arrangement. So she had her larcenous niece take over. The fee my dad was paying was something like ten grand, a totally crazy amount for that time. But hey, you were buying a kid! And I'm sure Gramm was getting something off the top, no doubt. It was supposed to be five thousand for the surrogate and five for the Stork Club, half of that payable when the surrogate was found, and half, ahem, on delivery. Apparently, the thieving niece was the one who found Bird. She gave her parents $250 and embezzled the rest. Psycho-niece *hated* Auntie Helen and didn't give a shit about the consequences, didn't care if it brought the whole house of cards down. 'Cause Auntie Helen would *never* have gone for a black baby—no fucking way. The niece knew Helen would never make it out of the hospital anyway and was only sticking around long enough to collect the five grand that was due. With which she was going to *abscond*. Gramm insisted they take a picture of the baby, something the niece wasn't expecting. Not a problem, though, because Roger looked, crawled and gurgled like he was white. The niece must have been some kind of dope fiend not to have conscripted white parents in the first place. If it came out black, no doubt she'd have found a white baby to pose for the color Kodachrome. But that pesky third tit! Psycho-niece thought it would queer the deal. You know what Roar used to say? "Welles had *The Third Man*, I had the third nipple." Ha! So the niece calls Gramm in a panic with the information. He wasn't thrilled but such are the vagaries of the game. Gramm tells Mug and Bunny, and they're all right with it. Then some errant Stork Clubber betrays the niece and gets in touch with Gramm bearing important "additional" information that'll cost him another grand. He tries getting in touch with Carver but oops, she's dead. Calls the Stork snitch back. Now, Gramm could be a very scary guy, he was old when he and Roar met up but still a brawler. My brother said behind those cataracts the man still had that dead-eyed killer look. So Gramm calls and says he *might* give them $250 if what they had to say was meaningful. God knows what else he said but he put the fear in the whistleblower. That's when they confessed that Bird was black and about the rape and all. Gramm was so angry he wanted to kill those people! He drives up to La Piedra. No choice but to bite the bullet, fall on his sword, whatever. Mom had already been there three months, hiding out after the miscarriage. . . .

VIOLA DAVIS He didn't want his parents to be crucified. You know, buying a child, a *Black* child, wrenching it from its mother. Which of course wasn't the whole truth; the whole truth is always far more complicated. But— what's that word?—the "optics" weren't good. The optics were terrible. And remember, Roar had experience, up close and personal, with the firebombing of public opinion. The mob's rush to judgment. Time and again the tabloids hanged him in the public square. By the time Steven wanted to make the film, Roar's skin was thick, but when the arrows went in he still bled. He didn't have any confidence in human beings' ability to parse, to look at nuance. In a way, he sort of adopted Bunny's own shame at having lied to him about his origins. The Big Lie kinda seeped into his DNA over time. But *his* shame was rooted in a refusal to accept that his idea of what he was—so-called "reality"—had been shattered.

Now, *that's* a true existential crisis, my friend. The phrase is thrown around a lot. It's misused. Not in this case.

JONNY "STAGE DOOR" ORR They were drunk when he finally told them. Gramm thought the third nipple bulletin could wait a beat! So, he comes right out with *Your kid's black*. Mom and Dad were taken aback—Roar called it "taken a-black"!—then started to laugh. I mean, they just wouldn't stop. Gramm couldn't understand the *revelry*. He thought they didn't believe him and kept trying to set them straight. The more he explained, the harder they laughed. Finally, it became clear to him that they didn't give a damn. "They relished it"—that's what he told my brother. As it turned out, Laughlin didn't entirely have it wrong. Gramm showed them photographs of Roar in his crib, the ones taken by psycho-niece. And they fell in love. Doris Duke told Mom it was meant to be. Doris was one of the few people Mom trusted. Doris said, "If you don't want him, he's mine." Anyway, I think by then Mom'd had enough. She missed her friends in the city. She was a very social person and the quarantine was taking its toll. She was more than a social butterfly; she was a fucking *lepidopterarium*. [*pause*] I know that word because my girlfriend Chickweed's a butterfly freak. Hope you're impressed.

CICELY TYSON (*actress*) It was the most significant, most *spiritual* thing that happened to him in this strange, marvelous, God-given life. To finally learn where he came from. And that mother! Well—he had the mother of all mothers, so it was like winning the lottery. The fear of death that dogged him since he was little just shriveled up and died. That's what my grandson likes to call a bonus burger. "It's better than a nothingburger, Gray-Gray." He still calls me Gray Gray like when he was little.

What's tragic is, so many ignorant people thought he was ashamed of being Black. He was thrilled! But shattered at the same time—if that makes any sense. *Shattered from birth.* Sometimes being shattered like that becomes the source of one's greatest strength.

LAUGHLIN ORR[13] One thing we wondered was: How did Mom live with that buried truth? Roger said it was like Kafka by way of Ralph Ellison, you know, "The boy wakes up to find himself an enormous Negro cockroach." We laughed about Bunny checking the bed every morning to see if Black Roger hatched! But he stayed white as can be.

The real mystery is why she kept it a secret at all. The Commodore wouldn't have cared, but when it came to Mom's wishes he toed the line. "Bunny Orr" was so ashamed that she couldn't face her friends after the miscarriage—not her friend-friends, her society friends. The worst thing for a fearless woman is to admit you're afraid of being pitied; that's complete surrender, complete defeat. (And what made it worse, what made it sheer torture, is that her embarrassment would be interpreted as racist.) She hated people who cared about the opinion of others. She drilled that into me since I was little: never, *ever* care what anyone thinks. When she lost that baby, she found herself locked in a cage and couldn't find the key because she threw it away herself. There comes a time—in many families—when a big secret calcifies. It doesn't just get swept under the rug but buries itself under the floorboard like something out of Edgar Allen Poe. In those dark nights of the soul, she told herself, "This is my karma for being so prideful in my life. So severe in my judgment of people's lack of generosity. This is the millstone I will carry to my grave."

How does the saying go?

"Mom plans, God laughs."

Ha.

---

13 Ibid., pp. 400–401.

PETER GRAMM (*attorney*)[14] I've been asked many times to write a book. I'll leave that sort of enterprise to Bill [Kunstler], Lee [F. Lee Bailey] and Herb [Caen]. I can barely scribble my name.

LAUGHLIN ORR I was on summer break in Sonoma. Up at the ranch. Mom only wore muumuus and tented paisley blouses. I hadn't seen her in a few months, because Daddy said she'd been sick. She looked thinner but I didn't notice too much. I was six years old. Looking back, I *must* have asked, "When's the baby coming?"—I was excited about having a new little brother or sister. Which would *not* have been well-received. I do remember she wouldn't let me fall asleep on her tummy the way I liked when she was still in the city. In her first trimester. I'd try to hear the heartbeat. Then one day, Daddy said she was sick and needed to stay at La Piedra till she got better. I finally went to see her. We didn't play the tummy-heartbeat game anymore. I tried but she pushed me away. I remember crying and she apologized and said, "Mama's still not feeling well." I probably stayed less than a week. It's kind of a blur.

I went back to the city, back to school, and the next time I saw her she was on her big blue chair in the bedroom of Parnassus, the big house in Pacific Heights.

Daddy said, "Come meet your baby brother."

---

14 "Mr. Fix-It," *San Francisco Chronicle*, Sunday profile, Pat Dugan, 1988.

CHAPTER THREE

Seraphita/Seraphitus

ROGER ORR
(*letter to Steven Spielberg*)

You asked about my childhood. I was a sponge—a little alien dropped down to memorialize the natives. Which, as it turned out, was literally true. A marvelous episode of that old show *The Outer Limits* struck a chord. I was probably twenty-two or twenty-three when I saw it, and it hit pay dirt. David McCallum played a rough Welsh miner who becomes a guinea pig for a professor who's conducting evolutionary experiments. The miner's unremarkable brain goes forward thousands of years—in just a few days, he can speak hundreds of languages and play classical piano like Sviatoslav Richter—he absorbs and conquers the world of man then moves on to the universe. He's telepathic as well. It's called "The Sixth Finger" because he grows one, a crude, TV-cinematic way of showing his advancement. (Made an even bigger impression on me because of my third breast. It's all a numbers game, Steve, as you well know; more is better.) His head becomes huge. Egg-shaped. . . . I was a bit of a prodigy, a little Napoleon. My fantasies were about absorbing the world of the arts then moving to the cosmos "and beyond," as Arthur C. Clarke so eloquently put it. But prodigies never end well—I was quite aware of that even at a tender age. And it didn't end well for the poor miner. He was gorgeous, McCallum, when he was young . . .

* * * * * * * * * *

I had my birth mother's beauty. When we finally met face-to-face, in the Eighties, Bird showed me pictures of her when she was sixteen, and it took my breath away. We looked exactly alike. . . . I was a bit of an androgyne. The Balzac story "Seraphita" made a deep impression. I must have heard about it from Henry Miller. Seraphita was a great, spiritual epicene. Some saw the creature as a woman; others saw it as a man, "Seraphitus." That was my aspiration, what I wanted to attain: the corporeal and the transcendent. To be what everyone *wanted* to see, what they wanted to touch and be touched by. Pasolini's *Teorema*. . . . I loved wearing wigs and dressing up in Bunny's haute couture. Boys flirt with that, but I knew it was something more. More is better!

But I never had the kind of beauty Bird had when she was young; few do. That "hurt," ineffable beauty. Oh, I was definitely effable! Thin as a rail, with horsey equipage. Too much information, Steven? All the boys and girls wanted me; all the big people too. And I wanted *them*. For a long, long time, it was paradise.

Now here I am: after the fall. Paradigm lost.

* * * * * * * * * *

AMANDA GORMAN It's *crazy* how that baby looked. Like a Rubens—a Rubens baby. He gave Mama a faded old picture from his San Francisco days and she took me down to the Met and pointed out a Rubens that looked just like him. She told Roar about it and he said [*laughs*], "I'm certain the Commodore would have preferred a Reuben sandwich."

LAUGHLIN ORR The most beautiful baby I'd ever seen. Not that I'd seen too many. I was seven years old, and none made that kind of impression before or since. Which I suppose was normal, because *this* one was my precious baby brother. I can still remember: He looked up at me, a deep look that went on for the longest time. All babies are like that I guess—busy downloading. Then he looked away without so much as a fare-thee-well. "Been there, done that." On to the next download.

JULIANNE MOORE (*actress*) That's what Roar was—"The Great Observer." Before I did *Hannibal*, I watched *The Silence of the Lambs* a bunch of times. Clarice says, "You see a lot, don't you, Doctor? Why don't you turn that high-powered perception on yourself and tell us what you see? Or maybe you're afraid to." [*laughs*] It always made me think of Roar!

Of course, he *did* turn that power of perception on himself. And told us what he saw. Told the world.

MERYL STREEP He hated the name "Roger." Maybe that's too strong but he wasn't fond. His family got away with calling him that but look out if you tried to do the same. I asked Laughlin if she knew how Bunny picked it. She said her mother always loved the name Aurora but Mug thought it was too ethereal. He said, "Save ethereal for the next one." (They did, naming "the next one" Seraphim.) Anyway, it was moot when the little boy from Nashville came. The Commodore got the idea to call him Roger after his dad's middle name. Bunny was *not* thrilled. But when he pointed out that *Roger* plus *Orr* could be *Roar*—which was close enough to Aurora—and that the boy was an August baby, a Leo/lion baby—she softened.

That's a lot of calisthenics, huh. The Name Game.

JULIANNE MOORE When he did mushrooms, he said he became *everyone*. Every mother, every father, every child—every orphan. He became everyone who ever lived and died on the battlefield, every pregnant woman who lost a child, every fetus who died in the womb or got thrown in a dumpster. He became all the people who were tortured and all the people who died peacefully at home, surrounded by family. He was a supreme . . . empath. I think that's why he was able to be so many things: a songwriter, novelist, actor, painter. A comedian. Doctor! That's why he was such a great director, because he had this amazing access to inhabit consciousness, to climb into the awareness of others, and their physicality as well. Behind it all was this great, organizing intelligence; behind the omniscience was a very engaged yet disinterested computer. Without the motherboard, he'd have been lost or gone mad. He did go mad a few times in his life but always made his way back to the motherboard. He was able to reboot. A gift not all artists have. Oh Bruce—did you hear the Word Police are trying to ban "motherboard" from the dictionaries? Isn't that the dumbest, silliest thing? What a scary place the world's become.

RICHIE "SNOOP" RASKIN (*detective*) You know about Pete [Gramm] getting an anonymous call from the gang that couldn't shit straight, right? I don't know who you've talked to but you know about it, right? Some scumbag from the Stork Club, which should have been called the Schmuck Club, tried to muscle Pete with an amateur-hour grift to make him pay for the privilege of finding out that Roar's mother was black. As you can imagine, Pete wasn't too happy about the *fukakta*ness of the whole enterprise. He was a cautious, meticulous man and you better believe loose ends were on his mind from day one. He starts thinking, "What else do these dunderheads know?" Now, understand: *No one* knew where any of the babies he got ahold of were heading, not even Helen Carver. The way it worked was he'd send his people to pick them up, precisely to avoid this kind of nonsense—Mug answering the phone three years later to some blackmailing ding-dong on the other end. But Pete didn't like the way any of it smelled. Plus, he was extremely pissed off. He had very important, very *rich* clients—if something went south, if something went public, these people would not hesitate to burn him. As tough as he was, he was vulnerable; his clients were too big to fail. If you were going to muscle somebody, it better be anyone in the world but Pete Gramm. He knew some rough people in Nashville. Of one thing I'm certain: that person who called? They aren't breathing anymore. The whole group vanished. Draw your own conclusions.

SUZE BERKOWITZ (*former wife*) My father was in advertising, and one of his biggest accounts was OTG, the Orr Tobacco Group. Dad came up with print ads that were really popular during the war—handsome models smiling from the newspapers and magazines, thanking the enlisted for their service. The ads were clever because it wasn't obvious they were sponsored by OTG. But *subliminally* you'd notice the models always had a pack of King's in their pocket, which was OTG's biggest brand. So, you can thank the enlisted—but thank Daddy for those brilliant ads!

Mug inherited OTG when his father died. OTG's only real rival was the American Tobacco Company, owned by Jim Duke. Doris Duke's dad. He died back in the Twenties, and I don't know who inherited it; I don't think it was Doris but coulda been. Did you know Doris and Bunny were great friends? Anyway, my parents took me to parties at the house in Pacific Heights. "Parnassus." My God, those grand parties at that grand house . . .

which Bunny and Mug actually bought from Doris Duke! Small world, huh. The richer you are, the smaller it gets. The Orrs literally had Rafael's fresco, "Parnassus," hanging in a ballroom they built specifically for its display. Probably bought it from Doris.

Mom and Dad always wanted to get a babysitter—they didn't want me cramping their style—but Bunny insisted they bring me along to entertain Young Roar. Young Roar needed to be entertained at all costs! Roger called me "Wifey" right from the beginning. He must've got that from the radio— Henny Youngman or *The Milton Berle Show*, we listened to those all the time. At just seven or eight years old, "Wifey" stuck. He still called me that after we got divorced, but with a wink. No one but Scatter knew it'd been going on since the beginning of time.

JONNY "STAGE DOOR" ORR Dad gave me that nickname "Stage Door." He loved puns. My brother did too. Runs in the family. Or maybe just walks in it. I was *going* to say Roar inherited that from the Commodore, but—oops, wrong dad! Though I suppose you *do* get traits from someone who isn't blood but it's more like you pick them up. You know, imitate. It's true though, they both loved wordplay. After he won the Palme D'Or at Cannes for *Grace War*, Roar started writing me notes addressed to "Stage D'Orr." Called it the "Palmed D'Orr," all that . . . It's funny you're doing this now because he said he never wanted a standard biography, he wanted an "Orral History"—*yuck-ety yuck*—all that punning got exhausting.

The Commodore started calling me Stage Door when I was a wee boy 'cause I was always waiting by the door for Roar to come home from school. Dad would say, "Stage Door Jonny waits breathlessly in the wings." I idolized my big brother. The truth is that I was named after an uncle—my *father's* big brother, who *he* idolized. Jonny jumped off a building after the crash of '29. Nice, huh? I guess Stage Door's better than *Jump* or *Splatter*. I mean, if you had to choose.

LAUGHLIN ORR By then we'd moved from Russian Hill to the house in Pacific Heights, Doris Duke's old place next to the Gettys. It was two homes put together. Auntie Doris was a childhood pal of Mom's. Doris and the Commodore's dads were the sultans of tobacco but that was purely coinci-dental; Mom and Mug didn't meet until she was a debutante. She spent a lot of time at Shangri La, Doris's place in Hawaii. She'd fly there on Doris's private plane—a Boeing 737. I don't think either one of 'em wanted to grow old but hey, join the club.

Parnassus was the ultimate petri dish for Roar. The people who came through there! Sheesh. I didn't appreciate it till later, when I was writing my first book and went through all their photo albums. There was Mayor Lapham, who visited all the time—my parents were big supporters. There was Harry Bridges; oh, that man made me laugh. Know who he is? Was? Head of the Longshore Union. I was at Brentano's and stumbled across a biography about him. It was a thousand pages. Every celebrity on Earth danced through that ballroom. Babe Ruth. Tony Curtis. Roz Russell and Louis Armstrong . . . Chaplin! *Jiminy Christmas.* And Jiminy was probably there too. Dad told me that Albert Einstein was supposed to come but his plane got delayed; he didn't give a tinker's curse who was there but was quite upset about *that* one. I saw Fred and Ginger dancing together! Boy oh boy. Florine *Stettheimer* . . . In the Sixties, I threw fundraisers for the Free Clinic. In the early Seventies I had benefits for Delancey Street, which had just been started by John Maher and Mimi Silbert. John was a junkie who was originally part of Synanon, down in L.A. He had a theory that you needed to relocate addicts from the hood, away from their dope connections. To get sober, addicts needed to *move on up,* into wealthy neighborhoods. So he and Mimi bought defunct embassies in Pacific Heights that were just around the corner from where we lived and filled them with pimps and ex-cons. They named the buildings "Russia" and "Estonia." . . . I remember we had a gala, Moscone and Harvey Milk were there, the night before they were killed. Daddy didn't like the junkies moving in. He'd say, "There goes the neighborhood," but Mom couldn't contain her glee. You know, *épater les bourgeois* and all that.

SCATTER HOLBROOK (*friend*) As a boy, he was especially interested in the behavior of adults. A miniature anthropologist. He particularly studied artists. His waking hours were spent as a voyeur; come nighttime, he sifted through the day or night's gathered material, curating and prioritizing. *What does this person have that makes them special? That makes them unique? And how can I use it?* That famous poem about two roads diverging in a yellow wood—Frost, by the way, was his mother [Bird Rabineau]'s favorite—with Roar, it was a hundred roads, a thousand roads diverging. He took so many of them. Went all the way down and all the way back again, woods into woods, fields into fields, roads into *other* roads, when most of us are lucky to take just one. I'd rather just take the one but that's me. He wasn't like most mortals that way. The roads diverge and the one who speaks for Frost is "sorry I could not travel both." Roar's motto was "diverge and conquer" and he took them all. That house he grew up in *was* called Parnassus, right? The sacred mount, home of the Muses. Genius never takes one road. And when it does, it's Every Road. But Every Road equals no road at all—as Roar might put it.

SUZE BERKOWITZ He was viciously bullied at school. He wouldn't take his shirt off for sports or to swim. The school knew about his "condition"— the extra nipple—and exempted him from certain activities. But kids being kids, they lasered in on his defect and were terribly cruel. They'd make disgusting sucking sounds with their lips when they saw him. He got beaten up but never retaliated. "I turned the other breast," he used to say. There was a boy, a real sadist whose mission was to make Roar suffer. The boy didn't come to school for a few days. When he finally did, he saw Roar and went pale, then ran like hell. Rumor spread about something having happened between them, something unspeakable. The sucking sounds stopped. They were all afraid of him now.

LAUGHLIN ORR Mom wanted to yank Roger out of there and home-school him—and it was one of the few times my parents came to blows. The Commodore said, "He's got to fight back, Bernice, because that's the fucking world!" Bernice was her birth name, and the rare times my father used it, holy shit, you knew he meant business. She talked to some plastic surgeons about removing the nip, but Dad was opposed to that too. And I'm glad because Roar kinda loved it. I was surprised Mom had such a thing about it, but understood; she hated seeing him suffer. It wasn't the breast but the bullying that was traumatic for her. As much of a disrupter as my brother was, he was like all children—all adults!—part of him only wanted to be liked and accepted. To be loved. In that way, he got the ultimate revenge because he was loved by millions.

SCATTER HOLBROOK It was all rather savage and mysterious, like something out of Stephen King. Years later I asked him what went down and he got that cagey smile. *I* think he raped that boy. . . . the Commodore had a "hotspot" in his library at Parnassus—a cattle prod. He got it from Langdon Desmoine, Bunny's dad. Desmoine had a ranch in Texas, in Palo Duro Canyon. Mug loved that thing! My theory is, Roger waylaid him. Lured him somewhere, promising to give him money if he'd stop the bullying. Then *wham*, hit him with the hotspot and did some other stuff.

SUZE BERKOWITZ I heard that story from Scatter but never asked Roar myself. I wouldn't put it past him; he had a kind of gangster courage. Bravado. I do remember something about that prod. It was kept in the library and one time we came in and the Commodore nodded toward it and said, "You don't need *that* again, do you?" With a wink. If something did happen, I'm pretty sure Mug knew all about it and was proud. It might even have been his idea in the first place. But I don't know about the "other stuff" Scatter talked about.

JOHN LAHR[15] One of the first things he wrote was a screenplay. He was nine years old. His father, the tobacco king Mug Orr, took him to see *The Third Man*, and Roar loved it. He promptly wrote a murder mystery about his birth anomaly called *The Third Teat*. That's how he spelled it—he told me "teat" was much funnier than "tit." He searched for years to find that lost script. "It would have made my name," he says ruefully, looking like Buster Keaton having yet another bad day. "I coulda been a contender."

SUZE BERKOWITZ He invented all sorts of games. He was very imaginative that way. Parnassus had a screening room and we watched a ton of movies. It was an amazing education. *Top Hat, Gold Diggers of 1933, Show Boat* . . . I loved *The Wizard of Oz*, but Roger wasn't that keen. He said the Wizard was made too much of a fool, which was "libelous." I didn't know what the word meant . . . We played all those other games too, doctor-patient games. Fooled around like most kids. Displayed our private parts. We fooled around with Scatter—a ménage-a-trois des enfants! *Les Enfants du Paradis* was more accurate, because life on the hill *was* paradise. Oh yes, we saw the Carné film too, when we were ten years old. Can you imagine? As Laughlin would say: *Sheesh.*

---

15 "The Hero with a Thousand Faces," Lillian Ross, the *New Yorker,* 1991.

CALLIOPE LEVY-LEVY (*therapist*) I think his life began, his true life, when his sister Seraphim died. Snakes shed their skin before giving birth, and that's when Roger Orr, the artist, was born. A life of perpetual shedding, a life of trying on new skin, began. Though the metaphor of the salmon is probably more apt. In breeding season, the males grow teeth then return to where they were born. Again and again, Roger went back to the "scene of the crime" for artistic sustenance: the death of his sister Seraphim. He died and was reborn a thousand times, growing new teeth, new faces, new films, books and works of art, in failed attempts to bring her back to life. I called him "the hero with a thousand faces" and he liked that; a writer wound up using that as the title of a magazine profile and even gave me attribution.

SUZE BERKOWITZ Seraphim came a year after Roger did. It was a great shock to Mrs. Orr because the doctors said she'd never be able to conceive. . . . Sera and Roger were inseparable. He was her total protector. He sang to her when she got fussy, and she went right to sleep. No one else could do that. These . . . beautiful lullabies. One of them made its way to that record he did in the Nineties, *Roger Orr Sings Himself to Sleep*. It's called "Safe Unsound." I sang that to Ali when she was a baby—and can remember him singing it to Sera.

When she died [*at nine years old*], he went dark.

CALLIOPE LEVY-LEVY Please do not leave out that he gave me permission to speak after his death! You must or I'll take you to court.

SUZE BERKOWITZ Elvis had a twin who died in the womb, and they say it haunted him forever. But to me, this was so much worse because Roar had her for nine years! Loving her, holding her, being her. He used to say he'd been given the dull, earthly name—Roger—and she, the celestial one. Like it was predestined. That was something he told himself, to deal with the pain. That her time here was *meant* to be short. That she belonged—was needed—elsewhere.

STEVEN SODERBERGH (*director*) Everything he did was about saving his sister—the "twin soul" who died when he was nine. He told me they had a secret language that was "close to Glaswegian dialect."

I don't even think he was kidding.

LAUGHLIN ORR He told Steven about that? God, I haven't thought about that in a long time. There was no way to decode it; it was like a talking Enigma machine. I thought it was gibberish for the longest time. One day I hid in a closet and listened. I must have been there for half an hour. I'm telling you, Bruce, it was too real to be made up. The give-and-take, the pauses, the outbursts of laughter, the serious moments—all the hallmarks of human conversation. Could it have been just an extended, brilliant improvisation? I mean, for their own surreal amusement? Maybe. Anything's possible. But I was convinced.

SUZE BERKOWITZ They wore each other's clothes. But I don't think they ever fooled around. I don't think it ever got sexual—though I wouldn't have been surprised because it was a completely incestuous relationship. Maybe "symbiotic" is more appropriate; when one inhaled, the other exhaled. They had the same skin. The same body.

DOLLY PARTON My husband loved him. And Carl doesn't just love anybody. . . . Do you know why Roar became a doctor? It wasn't just that friend that he wanted to save—the one who got hurt in the war. A few years after we met, Roar told me if he'd been a doctor he could have saved "my angel Seraphim." I told him, "Darling, angels don't need saving. We do." He said, "You're right. I guess angels just wing it."

JOHN LAHR[16] There's an untitled short story he wrote when quite young—it's now at the Roger Orr Archives of the Prescott Scott Library in Oklahoma—about a boy who time-travels to save his sister, struck dead by lightning. Seraphim died of Batten disease, but the metaphor was spot-on; her death hit him like a lightning bolt. The result of Batten disease is juvenile dementia, and for years Roger worried it would happen to *him*. Over time, it became a phobia. As a boy, he expressed those morbid concerns to his adoptive parents and the event of his sister's death would have been a good time for them to tell him the truth—that he had nothing to fear because he and Seraphim didn't share the same DNA. Obviously, the conversation would have been more than that but the door would have opened.

They chose to keep it shut.

---

16 Ibid.

In his early forties, when Roar learned about his parentage, it stung two-fold—not just their deception but the needless, untold suffering he endured for decades, a suffering that would have been alleviated by the truth . . . and yet, the terror of early-onset dementia remained at the core of his breakdowns, even after realizing there was no basis for it.

JULIANNE MOORE I saw him at the Globes when I won for *Still Alice*. He just . . . descended on me with that *vulpine* smile. Isn't that the word? Like a wolf. It always blinded because of the vast intellect behind it. Always threw me for a loop. I said something autopilot-stupid, which isn't like me. Something like, "Didja like it?" I don't think I'll ever say anything that dumb again in my life, I couldn't even *try* to outdo that one. He had a blank look and was trying to connect the dots—you know, as if what I'd asked had been in some weird language he was struggling to translate. Finally, he said, "Oh *no*, I won't see *that*, I'll never see *that*." Smiling away and kinda crazy-looking. I cringed because *of course* he wouldn't see a movie about a gal getting dementia in her fifties. That was one of his primal fears! Which I knew but had totally forgotten.

DOLLY PARTON We had some things in common that brought us closer. I'm from the Smoky Mountains, and Roar was born in Nashville. Daddy was a sharecropper on a little tobacco farm and Roar's adopted daddy was the Tobacco King! Oh, we laughed about that.

The biggest bond was losing our baby sisters. Rhoda Lee passed when I was eight and Roar was ten when he lost Seraphim. Mama put "Angel" on Rhoda's stone. So there you are: Angel and Seraphim. . . . One day he asked how I coped. I said, "Well, I made up my mind to cry later and I ain't cried yet. I'll do it when I see her." He liked that—liked it so much he wrote a song ["Cry Later"] that won the Oscar! He thanked me in his speech. After, at the Governor's Ball, I said, "Speeches are one thing—royalties another!" I was just havin' fun. Anyway, he returned the favor when he helped me out on "I Will Always Love You." He didn't get a royalty either, so we were even-steven. [*laughs*]

LAUGHLIN ORR When Seraphim died, our father was the strong one. "The Commodore" was aptly named: he kept that ship from breaking up on the rocks. I'm an Alanon so I was one of his sailors, making sure Bunny and Roger didn't drown. (Jonny was two years old and oblivious.) Mom retreated to the ranch like she used to; I was older and took solace in friends, fucking, and dope. But there was nowhere for Roger to go. Looking back, he was clinically depressed. But there was this steely resolve, like an Olympian athlete preparing himself to break every world record in her memory. All the Palaces of Story that were to come, all the wonders and music and magic tricks to come, were dedicated to her. She *was* those palaces—and the only way to survive was for him to become Seraphim. To eat the wafer. And boy, did he. It was an overeater's communion.

SCATTER HOLBROOK We both tried on Sera's clothes—before and after she died—but it was more of a giggle. *Before* she died, it was a giggle. After, it became more of a séance on a wet afternoon . . . The literal mother lode was when he discovered Bunny's couture closets. We were twelvish, a few years after his sister died. He put on Bunny's Balenciaga gown and we laid on the bed. Bunny and Mug were up at the ranch or in Europe, wherever. He said that his heart was pounding so hard, he almost passed out. My heart pounded too. The varieties of religious nonbinary experience.

JONNY "STAGE DOOR" ORR I was just a rug rat when Seraphim died. I barely remember her but Roger sure kept her alive, for me and everyone else. She was Dorian Grey. That was my brother's gift. He was always talking about her, dressing like her, being her—this constant communion. Someone said Dickens's characters were more real than real people. She kind of became realer—to me—than when she was walking the earth.

SCATTER HOLBROOK Sometime after she died—six months?—the Orrs took us to Europe on holiday. My parents gave their consent because it was the kind of education they never could have afforded. Traveling the world was a way of healing for the Orrs—maybe their way of running. The two can be the same thing. We wound up at Cannes; it was only the third or fourth film festival ever. This was '50 or '51. Bunny and Mug knew all kinds of Hollywood people. So many had come to Parnassus, which was kind of a rite of passage. You'd really made it when you attended a gala at the Orrs'. Not too many of that crowd knew Seraphim died, at least that was my impression. Or if they did, you wouldn't have known it. Generally, Tinseltowners are narcissists, and that was attractive to Mug and Bunny because it gave them respite from the grief parade back home. Death really did take a holiday. In Cannes, they weren't the hosts. They were free to mingle without having to dodge all those contorted, pitying faces coming toward them, mouthing condolences.

The festival really spiked Roar's punch. It was a dream he never woke up from. One of the seminal events in his life. So many things came together there: he saw *All About Eve* and even met Preston Sturges—*Eve* and *The Sin of Harold Diddlebock* were both in competition. Roar insisted on seeing *everything* and his folks, God bless 'em, coddled the hell out of him. *Miss Julie* was his first taste of Strindberg. And Buñuel! He was mesmerized by *Los Olvidados*, not one of Buñuel's bellyachers, but Roar knew genius when he saw it. Buñuel became his lodestar, the one to beat, right up until Roar died. (In the Seventies, he made pilgrimages to Mexico and became a friend of the family.)

His love affair with art and glamour began in Cannes, at the Eden Roc. That's when he became an official fame whore.

SUZE BERKOWITZ I almost went on that trip but got scarlet fever instead. It was awful! I was so heartbroken I prayed I'd just die. When he came home, Roar was very sweet, very dear, said they had an absolutely miserable time, which I knew from Scatter was a bald-faced lie.

He still called me Wifey but started calling me Scarlet too. Whenever I got bossy, he'd say, "Frankly, *Scarlet*, I don't give a damn!"

SCATTER HOLBROOK After Cannes we went to Panarea, off the coast of Sicily. It's part of a chain of volcanic islands no one but the superrich knew about. Onassis and the Gettys were there and the painter Francis Bacon, who Roar had an affair with in his twenties. Both claim not to remember meeting one another—which I never believed because they're among the most memorable people you'll ever meet in your life. Francis must have been around forty—we were ten or eleven—but nothing happened. Not that I know of. Roar *may* have had a dalliance with a fisherman's son but nothing as advanced as a genius British painter four times his age!

LAUGHLIN ORR That trip! It was insane. I sorta got adopted by Visconti and Zeffirelli. Liz Taylor was there for *A Place In the Sun*. She was nineteen, a year older than me. We fucked each other like men and I nicknamed her pussy "National Velvet." Roger did a portrait of us. Still have it somewhere. He did portraits of everyone and they were just extraordinary. Painting was his way of storyboarding—my brother already had images in his head but couldn't get his hands on a movie camera till we got back to the States. So, he painted and wrote little plays that he and Scatter and a few of the fishermen kids put on after supper. Oh, they were a big hit. But I had other interests.

SUZE BERKOWITZ He brought back a sketch he did, to prove I'd been on his mind. I did a double-take: it looked just like Seraphim. I had the same blue eyes and dark hair that Sera did, everyone always commented on that. . . . We had a secret wedding ceremony. That's so touching to me now. In a way, I think he was marrying his sister. *In sickness and in death.* Scatter pretended to be the minister: "I now pronounce you man and wifey." Roar kind of scowled at him for that. We did a lot of fooling around but never went all the way. This was the early Fifties! But I wouldn't exactly call us repressed.

I was always Wifey but if I called him Hubby, he got mad. For him, Wifey was a joke name—it wasn't a joke for me!—but when I said Hubby, he lost his sense of humor. Scowl, scowl, scowl.

TOM LUDDY (*film archivist*) He was barely in puberty when he saw the Buñuels. Buñuel hadn't made too many films, maybe half a dozen. Mug Orr got hold of all the prints. Parnassus had a screening room; of course it did. For Roger, the essentials were *Un Chien Andalou* and *L'Age d'Or*—particularly *L'Age d'Or*. He couldn't believe what his eyes were seeing. The scales fell away . . . At the ripe old age of twelve, he was seized by the horror that he'd created *nothing.* Time had passed him by! Because he did have an awareness: he knew he was a prodigy and instinctively sensed there was nothing worse than a wunderkind without an art form. For him that was hell. . . . He was *obsessed* with the giants who began as baby polymaths: Mozart, Rimbaud, Pascal. Even went through a Sor Juana phase . . . Roger was haunted by the "ex-prodigies" who died alone in cheap rooms, broken and forgotten. He'd see someone mumbling to themselves on the street and say, "Oops, there goes another rubber tree plant." What he meant was they could have had the keys to the Kingdom but dried up and died instead. He was absolutely haunted by that happening to him.

SCATTER HOLBROOK We started making movies when he got home. We learned all we could about cameras and lenses and lighting, that sort of thing. He wanted to be Buñuel so naturally he wrote "L'Age d'Orr"—starring Suze Berkowitz as "Wifey." In another, he played the girl and Suze played the boy. He was trying to shock but finally settled in and did things in a lighter vein. He had both those things in him: to shock but entertain, to be popular. To be accepted. He always said he had a sentimental streak and that's definitely true. He wrote songs and soundtracks for all the Roger Orr Productions. He was finding his voice and I remember him doing a rip-off of Chaplin's "Smile." He couldn't believe Chaplin wrote that song. That was another revelation: you could step outside of what people thought you were, and well, do anything. You could do any and everything and make timeless things of beauty.

LAUGHLIN ORR We could hear him in his room singing stuff he'd written. Mom stood by the closed door, stunned. I think she cried—the song was so melancholy, so bluesy, so beyond his years. Which makes sense, considering who his real mother was.

BEVERLY D'ANGELO (*actress*) The strange thing is, Bunny was a huge fan of Bird Rabineau but didn't have a clue that Bird was his biological mom— she died without ever knowing. Bird got famous in the early Fifties and you could hear her songs on the radio starting in '53. Doris Duke was totally plugged into the Black music scene and turned Bunny onto her. I loved her and used to sing her shit when I was in a band with Ronnie Hawkins, in Toronto. I asked Roar if he was even aware of Bird or if he knew that his mom was into her. He said yeah, he knew she was one of Bunny's favorites, but he himself didn't spark to Bird's songs until his early twenties, when he was going to med school in Chicago. But he didn't *have* to love Bird and her music, right? I mean, she was in his blood. She was inside him. The sun can't see itself rise or set. Don't you think?

CHAPTER FOUR

On the Road

SUZE BERKOWITZ We were rehearsing a scene he'd written. We must have been, what, thirteen? Roger loved movies where men cross-dressed. You know, *Kind Hearts and Coronets*. Early Chaplin. The Three Stooges did tons of stuff in drag! He was obsessed with the Stooges. And Abbott and Costello . . . We raided Bunny's closet and he put on a little number. He always called them "little numbers." It was jokey at first, you know, nervous-making burlesque. Because I think we must have known where this might be heading. He looked gorgeous. Much hotter than I did. He put on a wig—Bunny had a hundred wigs and he knew his way around them!—and pretty soon it was obvious that both of us were turned on. We were *shaking*. That was a revelation. It was like we'd come home: taboo meets natural inclination. Then he got this look and said that he thought he was going to come. Right when he said it, *I* started to come. Serious fabric queens! That's still one of the most erotic things that's ever happened to me. There was a lot of wardrobe cleaning after that.

BEVERLY D'ANGELO Have you seen pictures of him when he was young? The most beautiful boy ever. *Death In Venice* beautiful. An American Tadzio, with brains. With brains, heart, and soul.

JONNY "STAGE DOOR" ORR I know he started going into town and leading a phantom life. Our parents were progressive, if that's the word you want to use. Mom was a Summerhill freak—gave all kinds of money to A. S. Neill. Gave money to R. D. Laing too. It's funny how both those guys were from Scotland. . . . The house rule was "let well enough alone." I don't know about the well enough part. They pretty much turned a blind eye.

Laughlin was his guide to the underworld.

SUZE BERKOWITZ Laughlin was half-hippie, half-Beat—and all bad. He was her prize pupil. Roger graduated with honors, surpassing the teacher. The student became the master for sure. And I was hurt because I was excluded from that life. Not that I could have been a part of it; my parents kept a pretty close watch. Maybe she was jealous of my relationship with Roger. I don't know. Mostly, I was scared for him.

BEVERLY D'ANGELO He told me he got crabs so often, he gave them names. That he wanted a "crab act," like Chaplin with his fleas in *Limelight*. He started using aliases; his last name was too recognizable. He was Buster Crabs for a while—hee-hee—Buster Crabbe played Buck Rogers so *of course* he started calling himself Fuck Roger. Because that's *exactly* what he wanted: to be fucked "by anything with a pulse." That was an exciting discovery for him. He said, "I finally came into my own, and my own came into me." He told me Allen [Ginsberg] gave him the clap twice, "which made sense. Both of us were suckers for applause."

MELISSE ANNE PAXTON (*writer*) There's a lot of previously unpublished material in Brett Shaughnessy's meticulously researched book.[17] It's not enough to say "that was a different time"—the Beats were prolific pedophiles. The worst was Lawrence Ferlinghetti, whose nickname was the "Nappy Whisperer." On the occasion of his 102nd birthday, a City Lights groupie gifted him her three-day-old son for a celebratory liaison.

DAVE CHAPPELLE (*comedian*) He made that record in a little studio his sister set up. Laughlin got it out to ten thousand people, you know, tastemakers and shit. She was his Colonel Parker! His Berry Gordy too. Shit, his *Suge Knight*. She had that kind of clout and access to funds. Roar's parents didn't know what the fuck was happening. It had a different name[18] but came to be known on the street as "Cult 45" because it was a 45—a 45 RPM. Before long, it became known he was fourteen years old, which made no sense at *all*. How could a mutherfuckin' fourteen-year-old come up with the shit he did? Dylan was a year younger than Roar when he listened to it in Minnesota. In

---

17 *The Beats and Ephebophilia*, Brett Shaughnessy, pp. 17–21 (Columbia University Press, 1991).
18 "Either/Orr: 14 going on (a) 45" (Parnassus Records, 1954).

Hibbing.[19] It was always an underground thing. I mean, until they released a fancy version once he got famous. It was a bootleg thing. Laughlin pulled that off. They spliced in applause—Roar's idea!—and that was genius. The shit was so far ahead of its time it was crazy. It sounded like he was performing *live*, you know, they put in ambient sounds too, glasses clinking, nightclub shit. It's like the early rappers. Because they were saying "I can't sing, they'll never let me sing—but I can do *this*." He knew he was never going to be performing, you know, too scared, too young, whatever. But he could make *that* and no one was going to take it away from him. You know, like Brian Wilson said, he could make it "in my room." You have to remember that Roar's generation came from radio. . . . And it was *sophisticated*. Talkin' about *coming* and all this shit, I was like, *huh*? I couldn't even understand a lot of it. But the rhythm, you know, and the *content* predated Lenny Bruce, predated Nichols and May. The motherfucker was like Elon Musk! I don't even know what I was doing in my room when I was fourteen but it wasn't *that*. I take it back. I do know what I was doing. I know exactly. But I wasn't writing monologues about it.

* * * * * * * * *

ROGER ORR

from "Either/Orr: 14 going on (a) 45"—1954

Did you hear what they added to the Pledge of Allegiance? It's official: "under God." They added "under God." *I pledge allegiance to the Flag of the United States of America, and to the Republic for which it stands, one Nation under God.* Under God . . . isn't that the missionary position? [*scattered laughter*] What do you say when you're "under God"? What do you say when God's *inside* you? With that Ten-Inch Commandments cock? Do you say, "Ow! Ouch! *Ow*"? Do you say, "My Creator! You're hurting me! [*raucous* laughter] You gaveth— now taketh the fuck away!" Do you say, "Wrong hole, Father!" Or,

---

19 "It gave me some kind of hope. I was already writing songs but 'Either/Orr' had a humor I thought my 'serious' songs lacked and would make them more powerful. When I found out he was my age, I was jealous." Bob Dylan, *Chronicles, Volume 1* (Simon & Schuster, 2004).

"Be gentle [*laughter*] Be *gentile* with me . . ." And when you come, instead of shouting "God!", do you shout, "Humankind!" *Oh the humanity! I'm coming!* Do you smoke cigarettes after? [*a guffaw*] Maybe God lights up a whole forest [*laughter, applause*]. Maybe God drops a bomb on Hiroshima [*gasps, laughter*] . . . Do you think God's insecure? What if on the way to the bathroom, God turns and says, "Uh . . . did you come?" [*some gasps, laughter*] What happens if you say, "Actually, no. *No,* God, I didn't. Sorry!" [*laughter, applause*] God says, "Is there something I could do different next time?" And you say, "Won't *be* a next time, God. 'Cause you can't fuck for shit."

* * * * * * * * *

CHRIS ROCK (*comedian, actor*) I was fourteen when someone gave me a tape—all scratchy because it'd really been *listened* to. They'd recorded it off the original 45, many generations removed. I was the same age as Orr when he made it, so it gave me hope. You know, "I can do that." Well, no I *couldn't*, but I sure as hell could try. And you learn pretty quick that it can't be done, not without your ten thousand hours. You get humble damn quick. That's what was freakish about Orr. I had the chance to thank him later on. My mom was a minister, and, God bless her, she chaperoned me around to comedy clubs on open mic nights when I was fifteen. And when I finished high school and went to New York, that cassette never left my pocket. Every time I got booed off a stage it gave me energy. I'd rub that tape like it was a genie bottle. *Fuck y'all,* you know, *I'm gonna be a legend.* Jerry [Seinfeld] still has an autograph of Carl Reiner that he got when he was nine years old. I still have that tape—it's signed now!

I need to goldplate the motherfucker and put it behind glass.

DAVID STEINBERG (*comedian*) Because people were listening to the 45, word got out about this young comic. And I mean fucking *young*. Laughlin knew the owner of the hungry i, a newish club in North Beach. Used to be in a basement at Columbus and Kearney but moved to Jackson Street. I played there in the late Sixties and it was pretty much just folk singers. They did a few live albums there, the Kingston Trio and whatnot, but kind of overnight it became a magnet for stand-ups. Mort Sahl was one of the first. Lenny, Cavett, Woody . . . It must've been '55 or '56 when Roar went onstage. Laughlin kind of pushed him because open mics weren't a thing yet. He was a nervous wreck—Enrico [Banducci] told me that himself. Roar did some of the stuff from his record. "Under God" and a few others. And a guy in the audience is going insane. Very drunk but laughing in all the right places. Most of the crowd didn't know what to think of this skinny, androgynous kid but the out-of-control superfan wanted to buy Roar a drink after his set. Enrico made sure it was a Shirley Temple. Turns out to be Jack Kerouac.

MELISSE ANNE PAXTON This was 1955, right before Halloween. Kerouac hadn't published a thing, except for *The Town and the City*, but that didn't really count. He'd famously written six or eight books including *On the Road*, but no one would publish him. He was a legend in his own mind, and the minds of his friends: the man who would be King of the Beats. In that moment, though, the Beats weren't yet born.

A few days after Roar and Jack met, Ginsberg planned to do a reading in a shithole over on Fillmore called Gallery Six. He was going to read a poem no one'd heard before. A poem called *Howl*.

BILL MORGAN (*Beat historian*)[20] Over time, Laughlin became the Mama Bear of the Beats, doling out cash because it was always sorely needed. This was her first contact with Jack. At her baby brother's urging she gave the perennially broke writer $500. As a way of thanks, Jack invited the wealthy scions to a poetry reading of "a collection of angels" (to be held at a car garage-cum-event space) but Laughlin was otherwise engaged.

Roger went alone and was transformed.

They were all there: Ferlinghetti, Rexroth, Lamantia, Whalen, Gary Snyder, Michael McClure—and Neal Cassady, who was drunker than Jack. (If that were possible.) Gregory Corso was MIA, but a week later Jack took him to see "this gone jazz kid" do his thing at the hungry i. Corso later became a kind of mentor to Roger, involving the brilliant but callow youth in some minor criminal enterprises, one of which ended in tragedy. The fifteen-year-old heir got something from the attention of the Beats that he couldn't acquire from his father, Mugs [*sic*] "The Commodore" Orr. Mugs wasn't equipped to appreciate or understand his adopted son's genius.

---

20 *The Typewriter Is Holy*, Bill Morgan, p. 212 (Free Press, 2010).

GORE VIDAL (*novelist*) It was common knowledge that the Commodore was gay. He covered the waterfront—or was it the Fisherman's Wharf? He was quaintly known in certain circles not as the Commodore but the Commode, which was the favored place of assignation in various Haight homo porn palaces. After a few arrests, each expunged from the record by his bagman Peter Gramm, "Mug" was playfully extended to Mugshot... Gramm always got him out of jams with friends in low places, much like he did when Mugsy's son got into big trouble in not-so-little Oakland.

SAM KASHNER (*author, Beat memoirist*) Mug was definitely threatened by the libertinism of the Beats—more jealous I think than frightened—but his antipathies took the form of rage. An impotent rage. Because in terms of respect and attention, how could he win? And he *did* want Roar's respect. What Ginsberg and the rest had going for them was alien to Mug: the whole spiritual thing. Peripatetic Bisexual Buddhist Poets on Peyote! Whee! Whoopee! Holy, holy, holy! Their anarchic, pagan, prescient, zeitgeisty energy opened Roar's eyes, his coming of age. He's written that the image he carried in his head from that time with the Beats only came later, courtesy of Mr. Kubrick: Malcolm McDowell's eyes held open with metal clamps, forcing him to *see*. But instead of the pedestrian, high-toned horrors of the world, *Mug's* world, the dead-end, pickled Parnassus world, Roger in Wonderland was force-fed a Boschian garden of earthly delights, a garden ruled not by flowers of evil but flowers of transcendence.

Suddenly, all of Roar's dalliances—his cross-dressing, his *bad thoughts*, his myriad transgressions—for which he held a surprisingly strong measure of guilt—became insignificant, puny, laudable. He could talk about it all and be celebrated! He could act out and be celebrated! Whoopeeeee! Wheeeeee!

Off to the races.

BEVERLY D'ANGELO He made a few more 45s before the "Roger Orr: Basement Tapes" era came to a close. Before it did, Albert Grossman got in touch with Laughlin. Al had opened a club in Chicago—in a basement!—called the Gate of Horn. Though maybe it was just Gate of Horn, without the "the." This was years before Al collected Dylan and his other illustrious clients. Joplin, blah. Al wanted to book Roar at his club and even take him on a tour, but it was complicated because he was a minor. The Commodore wouldn't hear of it, but Bunny got all excited; she had an artistic streak and lived vicariously through her son. Most biographies say Mug "won the day" but Roger said if he'd wanted to go on the road, the Commodore would have caved. He said he was just, you know—been there, done that, it was fun while it lasted. *Bye bye mein Lieber Herr, it was a fine affair . . .* But he made a *perfect thing.* Those recordings are masterworks. They could have been written by someone in their forties, at the top of their game. Fucking uncanny. I always think of him like that French poet who stopped writing poetry at seventeen and became a gunrunner! And they keep getting rediscovered. You saw the Apatow documentary on Netflix, right? Roger said he stopped recording 'cause he got "distracted," which was the understatement of all time. Because not long after he met the Beats, that horrible thing happened with the girl in Oakland and he wound up spending months in a psych ward. Baby snakes are the most dangerous because they haven't learned to control their venom; everything they bite gets the full load. Roar was out to kill with each bite.

And one day, the inevitable happened: he bit himself.

ANN CHARTERS (*writer*)[21] I was at the [Gallery Six] reading. He was fifteen and I was nineteen. He was perfect. Beautiful. I remember him like a blurry morph of James Dean and Dominique Sanda. And *so* brilliant. He sang the most beautiful songs to me and one day I finally asked who wrote them. "I did," he said.

I didn't believe him.

SAM KASHNER I was pretty much the very first student—for a while, the *only* one—at the [Jack Kerouac] School of Disembodied Poetics.[22] I was Ginsberg's amanuensis. Allen conscripted all of them to guest-teach or just be guests: Burroughs and his son; Gregory [Corso]; Whalen; Ann—everybody. Ann and I ended up at a coffee shop and she told me about Roar and her "unrequited infatuation" for the boy genius. I was a little jealous because I had unrequited feelings toward Ann myself.

---

21 Ann Charters, *Beats and Company: Portrait of a Literary Generation*, pp. 117–118 (Doubleday, Garden City, 1986).

22 Naropa University, Boulder, Colorado.

ANN CHARTERS Nothing happened between us, not that it couldn't have. Not that I didn't want it to. He was young but it wasn't like he was a babe in the woods . . . and that was a different time. He was more wolf than babe! Between the two of us, he was much more experienced—and I was five years older. Something in me just didn't want to go there; I'm grateful I never crossed that line. Plus he slept with *anything* . . . so that wasn't much of an incentive. You always want to feel special.

The Beats liked to call themselves angels, but here was a *real* angel in their midst. I was protective. I knew what was going on, that Allen seduced him—though it was probably the other way around—and he'd fooled around with Jack. They introduced him to Benzedrine. They used it for writing but it's a big sex drug. I didn't like that they did that. The only one on my side was Nunz [Gregory Corso]. Nunz was always shouting at Allen, "You're going to destroy that little baby!"

As it turned out, Nunz was the one who took Roger down.

* * * * * * * * *

from The Dharma Bums[23]

"Wellllp," said Japhy,[24] "it may be that the boy's a bodhisattva, but a man doesn't always make a mandala."

He talked in riddles, pulling you up short like an old brakeman of God when you strayed into flowery vain enthusiasms.

We stared a while at the Kid [Roger Orr], who watched the goings-on with akoodle eyes, mandalas in themselves. He had a bead on Rheinhold Cacoethes and another bead on the doomed, swollen fruit of Rosie Buchanan.[25]

"He's the real thing," I said. "There's a lot of clay there. A real fledgling Looney Tunes Zen master and doesn't even know it. You can see the golem *and* the saint."

"Lotta clay, huh," he said, winking a sagely Nobodaddy wink.

---

23 *The Dharma Bums*, Jack Kerouac, pp. 54–55 (Penguin Classics, 1991).
24 Kerouac's literary pseudonym for Gary Snyder.—*ed.*
25 "Rheinhold Cacoethes" was a pseudonym for the poet Kenneth Rexroth. "Rosie Buchanan" was the fictionalized name of Natalie Jackson, a lover of Neal Cassady.—*ed.*

"Welllllp . . . you know what Avalokiteshvara said. 'What doesn't *kiln* you makes you stronger!'"

He let loose with a great, mad Shakyamuni guffaw then chugged a half gallon of California burgundy like an ox at a mountain stream.

* * * * * * * * * *

BOSLEY CANTICLE-JONES (*critic*) Corso was a junkie and small-time thief. Handsome, charming, volatile. A dead-end kid from Little Italy. Went to prison for stealing a toaster. Everything he did was on a small scale, including his art. He had a huge inferiority complex that dogged him to the end of days. He never felt he had his due, which he didn't, and for good reason. He eschewed fame, always put on a firework show about his contempt for those who chased it, but that was just a defense mechanism against the avalanche of resentment he had toward Kerouac, Burroughs, and Allen for leaving him in the dust of their careers—careers that seemed to grow more legendary by the hour. And then came Roger Orr. He must have been ferociously jealous. Subconsciously, I think he wanted to murder that boy, as sure as Lucien Carr murdered David Kammerer. *Kill your darlings* . . . Kerouac was the only one Corso really respected and loved. Corso was always pontificating about artists. He'd say absurd, lofty things, like his theory of artists being broken into three categories: talent, genius, and the "divine." Kerouac was divine. It begged the question; which category did Corso consider himself belonging to? In my humble opinion, he was holding on to "talent" by his fingernails and knew it. So, he threw in his cards and settled into the tiresome role of poète maudit. The cantankerous, sacred thug, the disrupter, the holy heckler. He found his calling in being a caricature, a buffoon, a cartoon figure. He had his groupies—lost souls and scavengers content to lick the gravel at the bottom of the Beat Mount Rushmore of Burroughs, Ginsberg and Kerouac. That's where Corso could be found.

Some are born to fame; others have footnotes thrust upon them. In the end, Corso was a footnote.

SUZE BERKOWITZ Nunzio [Gregory Corso] was staying at Parnassus—more like hanging out. You know, seeing what he could see. What he could get out of it. He liked rich people because they were afraid of him but at the same time sort of mesmerized. There was always a banquet, and he knew if a dog stayed under the table—though Nunzio stood on the table and danced!—he knew food and money eventually made their way to the floor. Roger introduced us. I thought Nunzio was sweet and funny and a little dangerous. *Handsome . . .* He probably did stay over a few nights though I doubt Bunny and Mug were aware. Though actually Bunny might have been. . . . That house was just so big and he snuck girls in. I caught one leaving once. She looked like a stripper but was probably just a junkie.

I was jealous of Nunzio, because I wasn't allowed to go into the city on Roger's plastic fantastic dark-side explorations. I guess I looked at him as the ringleader. I was just really happy when I got the chance to meet *any* of those people; like pages of a novel coming to life. My tiny broken heart took it as a sign of hope that one day I too might be invited on the gypsy caravan—good luck with that. All I cared about was spending time with Roger, and I was mad at anyone else who had the privilege. I got so angry I told him not to call me Wifey! I had little to offer in comparison to those . . . *grown men.* Those big, grown, hairy poet-men, those footloose manchildren! How could I compete? A genius, I was not. . . .

Nunzio sort of seduced Bunny, not literally, but he could have. She was always sponsoring artists, very de Medici, and there was a lot of flirting going on. It probably would've been good for her! [*laughs*] Laughlin was wary but let it happen. You know, what-will-be-will-be. She was twenty-two, an *old*, dissolute twenty-two. A few years younger than Nunzio but just as streetwise in her way. She had a fondness for him too, I don't know if anything ever happened between them—*probably*—but when he asked for money she never gave him a penny. There was no way she was going to fall for his bullshit but she *was* amused by the strange bedfellows of it all. God knows, Parnassus saw its share. But when things started disappearing, Laughlin got pissed. Servants noticed: the odd curio went missing. Then silverware. Then a Tiffany lamp. It was Nunzio of course; he needed to buy his dope and was always cash poor. The Commodore finally had enough. Nunzio *was* charming but there was always the threat of a ruckus. One time I heard him shout at Roger, "Your daddy's a stone fag, baby!" That may have been the truth but it certainly wasn't something you said in the house of your host, *particularly* not to the host's adolescent son. I guess I'm a prude. Mug found out—that Nunzio called him names—and was livid.

He was a fearless man. He took Gregory by the shoulders, marched him out the door, and threw him down the steps. Nunzio didn't make a peep! That's typical of certain types of rabble-rousers, isn't it? All bark, no bite.

JONNY "STAGE DOOR" ORR Roger wasn't too happy about Corso getting 86'd. He ran away and Dad sicced Peter Gramm's hounds on him. As it turned out, Corso put him up to scoring some dope. Roger wasn't using a needle but was snorting the stuff and acquired a taste for speedballs. He loved the romanticism of it. Allen became *huge* after the "Howl" reading and being crowned Beat Mascot turned my brother's head. Anyway, Roger wound up somewhere in the Riddles, looking for Corso's connection. The Riddles is a *very* rough part of Oakland. Violent and desolate. He probably didn't know he was in trouble until the cab flew off like a bat out of hell and left him there.

RICHIE "SNOOP" RASKIN There were all these lookouts, and one of them directs the kid to a warehouse. Roger's starting to sweat. He keeps saying "*Gregory Corso* sent me, *Gregory Corso* sent me"—like the fucker's name was the magic safe word. More like an unsafe word. Remember, Roger was this beautiful boy, this beautiful boy-girl. In about ten seconds he's lying on a dirty mattress. Tied up, no clothes. They're gonna do all kinds of things to him. He looks to the right and some nigger's stripping down and getting ready to fuck his ass. Looks to the left and it's white girl gang-rape city. And she's fighting like hell. She gets loose from the ties, scratches the face of her attacker. He yelps, stands up and *bam bam* shoots her. She lets out a blood-curdling scream and everyone splits. Roger gets himself free, crawls over to help, and she dies in his arms.

JASPER CAVENDISH (*historian*) The girl who was killed was a member of the Hopkins family. Mark Hopkins was one of the "Big Four" that founded the Central Pacific Railroad.

HERB CAEN One of the ironies is that her father owned the warehouse in the Riddles where she was murdered. She was a troubled girl, like so many children that come from great wealth. Her parents were acquaintances of the Orrs, not friends. I'm sure they'd been to parties at Parnassus.

When the police chief learned the identity of the boy found at the scene, he made a single phone call, resulting in Roger Orr's presence being "disappeared." Mug and Bunny had funded Mayor Robinson's reelection campaign and he owed them. Peter Gramm did his part in keeping it out of the news, which took some doing because it was a big story, a national story—the lurid death of a society family's wayward daughter. Reporters were digging deep. I know personally that Gramm paid off ambulance and hospital workers who'd acquired the habit of supplementing their salaries by selling information to the tabloids.

BOSLEY CANTICLE-JONES Rumor had it that the Commodore wanted Corso dead and Gramm, of all people, talked him out of it. Mug wanted to hunt down *le Poète Maudit*, shoot him up with dope, and have him tumble from a roof like Natalie Jackson.[26]

LAUGHLIN ORR They put Roger in a private hospital in San Rafael under an assumed name. He was in terrible shape, and I felt one hundred percent responsible. It was my come-to-Jesus moment . . . I had PTSD for years over what could have happened to him in Oakland. And I thanked that poor girl—if she hadn't fought like she did, I think they'd have killed my brother. She was the sacrificial lamb that allowed him to live.

Of course, the *weirdest* part was her name: Seraphim. Her name was Seraphim! None of us could believe it. The only person that wasn't rattled about it was Roger. The symbolist in him thought his beloved little sister rose from the grave to warn him what was coming if he continued down the path he was on. I couldn't argue with him on that one.

For a while, he wanted to convert to Catholicism. He was all about Sor Juana, Dorothy Day, Saint John, Saint Hildegard . . . but Mug just wanted to ship him off to Switzerland—to Le Rosey, where Sunny Radcliffe's daughter went. Mom begged him to put Roger on "probation," and he finally agreed. When he came home from San Rafael he was a model prisoner. He was a different person. He made amends to Mom and Dad and to the ghost of his sister—the ghosts of *both* Seraphims.

He stayed clean and sober for a while.

---

26 A month after the Gallery Six reading, Jackson, who was part of the Beat coterie, slit her wrists and fell from a roof to her death while being pursued by the police.—*ed.*

* * * * * * * * * *

ALLEN GINSBERG
(from a letter to Laughlin Orr, "xmas 1955"[27])

. . . rereading Diamond Sutra and meditating on ineffable wonder-wall of suchness, phenomena, and essence. One Undifferentiated Purity. The contamination of mind (born mind, not unborn, which is pure) is One with the heavy heavenness of this dumb luminous dream called Life. (Lifedeath.) Gregory is a coward, yes, a scoundrel, a knave, a foolsaint perilously close to sharing Holy Visions with the pilgrims if he could only stop his nonsense (which is holy too). He's just a stone's throw away—that's why he calls himself a "pebble without a cause." It's ugly what he goaded the Golden Boy naïf to do. But we're all that: no separations, separateness being the ONE&only corruption. Separateness = downfall of enlightenment. This is no bullshit. But OH you and Bodhi-Buck Roger have been in my thoughts and fractious fractured heart. I hear he's back home safe and pray he didn't/doesn't suffer too much. Remember: Howl came from my own snakepit time (seven months) and was given/dedicated to great foolsaint Carl Solomon; no doubt one day your brother will write a Golden Boy Saga & with a Mahayana yelp shout his own holy dedications _____

THANK YOU for the dana (which sent me back to reread Dana Charity chapter of the Diamond Suitra [sic]) that you sent to Bill [Burroughs], who was touched by your thoughtfulness, and bestows regards. $250 goes a long way in Tangier. Have been in letter exchange with the other Laughlin[28]—he wants to make chapbook of Roger's 45s cut-up routines, if any interest on your end. City Lights also desirous tho may be too soon for all involved.

Don't be too hard on your luminous Self.

---

27 Jack Kerouac and Allen Ginsberg: The Letters, Bill Morgan and David Stanford, pp. 118–120 (Penguin, 2010).
28 James Laughlin, publisher of New Directions.

* * * * * * * * * *

LAUGHLIN ORR There was a producer named Bob Thiele. He founded a record label when he was seventeen. Signed Lester Young, Coleman Hawkins, Mingus. Put out most of Coltrane's most important work . . . Bob was a real prodigy—like Roger—but was twenty years older when *On The Road* came out. He called [Kerouac] and they did a recording in New York, Jack reading poetry while accompanied by Zoot Sims and Al Cohn. "Blues and Haikus." You can hear Bob on the track, whooping it up from the mixing board. Jack told him about my brother, "a great, beat Max Jacob angel." He felt terrible about the girl getting killed. And Gregory's part in it. Jack knew her name was Seraphim, same as our sister; he had a sibling who died at the same age Seraphim did—his brother Gerard. He was working on a book about him.[29] Allen told me Jack had great suffering about Gerard and suffered too over Roger holding Seraphim when she died.

Anyway, Jack played "Cult 45" for Bob, who was blown away and immediately wanted to sign him. But Roger had zero interest in his old life. He was off on his medical savior thing and couldn't be bothered.

* * * * * * * * * *

from **Interview** *magazine*[30]

JIM JARMUSCH: What did you think of the movie Gus Van Sant made about that time in your life?[31]
ROAR: I love Gus. And loved Leonardo's performance. Who wouldn't want to be played by Leo? I do think he was better a few years later, in *Gilbert Grape*. That's pretty hard to beat. [River Phoenix] would have been closer to how I looked; River was more *ectomorph*. But that's a quibble. I really don't have any complaints. Jim [Caviezel] was a revelation [as Neal Cassady] but Neal wasn't all

---

29 *Visions of Gerard* would not be released until 1963.—*ed.*
30 "The King Who Would Be Everyman," December 2011.
31 *Golden Gates*, Killer Films/Warner Bros. (1991).

that much a part of my story. A little bit of window dressing, hard for a filmmaker to resist, because Neal's de rigueur. He's such an entertaining figure, and if you're presenting even a swatch of Beat tapestry, well, you need to weave him in. It's great fun and the audience loves it. Sean Penn was marvelous as Gregory but . . . too on the nose for my taste. I wish they'd found a young Robert Blake, because Blake had Nunzio's energy—that's what we called him, from his middle name. Blake had that improvisational, hurt-wildcat spirit. It was hard to watch Seraphim—the warehouse scene. Very, very hard. The actress who played her later came to a tragic end.[32] . . . It's pretentious to complain. You know, Jim, it's impossible to watch something like that with any objectivity. Everyone's life has a mythic aspect. You just have to look closely, which isn't an easy thing to do. But watching a coming-of-age film about oneself is tricky! By the time you do, old age has arrived with bells and whistles. More like sirens and wheezes. And you can't help imagine the movies—the travesties—that are coming down the pike after you're gone. As if any of it matters!

JIM JARMUSCH: Have you been in touch with Corso? Have you seen him?

ROAR: Twice. The first time was at Jack's funeral in Lowell. In 1969. It was wonderful to see him, to see *them*—even Ann [Charters], who I had a tremendous crush on, one that remained to my great sorrow unrequited. Jack laid in the box in a bow tie and loud shirt. I did a lot of crying then, a gentle rain falling down from all the years. By then I'd had some fame and Allen was especially gracious about that. "Our son turned out well," he said. Gregory was conflicted and broke my balls. But only a little. He never acknowledged what happened but said everything with his eyes and all was forgiven. It was very emotional. Unfortunately, the second time I saw him was in Rome. I was doing a film there and got a call from a documentary filmmaker. There was going to be a ceremony for Nunzio and would I come to the cemetery? I couldn't just then but went after the shoot. The old bad boy's buried with Keats and Shelley—but fifty yards away.

---

32 Jane Sookh died in a car crash as she drove cross-country with her fiancé after the film wrapped. *Golden Gates* was her debut.—*ed.*

Always a bridesmaid, never a bride. That's Gregory. For some reason, it made me think of that wonderful lyric, "And I'm sure it wouldn't interest anybody outside of a small circle of friends." Because no one ever really *was* much interested in Nunzio, outside of those remarkable men and a handful of second-rate academics. He was his own worst enemy.

"Burn, burn, burn, like fabulous yellow roman candles." I hate that quote of Jack's [*from* On the Road] because they plastered it on greeting cards and T-shirts. But Nunzio never burned. He stewed and simmered. [*laughs*]

JIM JARMUSCH: After the Oakland incident, you were in San Rafael, detoxing—

ROAR: A polite way of saying I had a complete nervous breakdown. I was decompensating, as the men in white coats used to say.

JIM JARMUSCH:—for three months. Then what happened?

ROAR: I went home. Parnassus was my Magic Mountain. Went home and did a lot of reading, a lot of thinking. I might've written some songs too, not very good ones, I'm sure. Mostly laid fallow. Broken. Got very . . . *sentimental.* Read things that calmed my mind. All the wonderful Sherlock Holmes stories. Kipling's glorious *Kim.* And Bret Harte, who meant the world to me. I don't know how I discovered him. I'd just sob and sob over "Tennessee's Partner." A slow-witted "partner" loves his overseer, Tennessee, a sadistic criminal who gets hanged for his crimes. The story ends with the partner on his way home to meet his hanged friend, imagining he's still alive. A ghostly, maudlin reunion like the one at the end of *The Man Who Would Be King.* There's Kipling again. I'm crazy about ghostly, maudlin reunions, Jim.

So: see you in my dreams.

BOOK TWO

Snakeskin

1955–1970

CHAPTER FIVE

Razzmatazz

RIVER PHOENIX (*actor*) I got a call from Roar around the time I wrapped *Running On Empty* in '88. You know, he wanted me to do *Golden Gates* and I was incredibly flattered, but there were scheduling issues and I couldn't make it work. Leo was amazing though . . . When they finished—maybe they were even still shooting!—he invited me to his place in Paradise Cove for lunch. He'd written a "little sequel" about being in the hospital after that girl was murdered. He was kind of funny about it. He called it "my *Cuckoo's Nest*, for kids." I asked if Gus was going to direct it and he said no, it was something Roar was going to direct. I thought, *Whoa*. The script was called *Seraphim* and began where *Golden Gates* left off. I sat in a tiny shed overlooking the ocean and read straight through. Now and then I'd hear him far away in the house, on the phone laughing. That famous laugh coming in waves, like the water. The script was—I cried my eyes out at the end. To be in a movie directed by Roger Orr is the pinnacle. Every actor's dream. But to play him as well? I just hope we get the chance to make it before I'm too old. I told him, "I'm already too old!"[33]

JOHN LAHR Roger was distraught when River died. He was inordinately fond of that boy. Absolutely infatuated. And they'd had such a marvelous time working together on *Gift From God*. That was River's last film and many—myself included—believe his best performance. *Seraphim* was to be their next collaboration. By the time they got their financing and schedules

---

33 From *Premiere* magazine, September 1990 interview with Anne Thompson. (Phoenix died October 31, 1993, when *Seraphim* was in preproduction—*ed.*)

together, River would have been twenty-three, playing a fifteen- or sixteen-year-old kid, but I think he'd have been wonderful. . . .

He raged a lot about that senseless death—a towering rage against God. He was just livid, literally shaking his fists at the heavens. It was almost stage-craft. After that, Roar was convinced the project was doomed, and railed at his own vanity—the hubris of believing anyone could possibly care about his exhumation of that very personal time. (Of course they would have, 'cause he'd have made a marvelous work of art.) Twenty years later I ran into him at Claridge's and asked if the project might ever see the light of day. "No, no," he said, with a smile. "It's deep-sixed, Johnny. Ain't no River deep enough."

JONNY "STAGE" ORR I was ten or eleven when he returned from the hospital in San Rafael. He was spun. Gained a bunch of weight from all the Thorazine and shitty food. He was pretty clear-eyed, though, so I think he must have been weaned off the drugs by the time he returned to Parnassus.

I remember hugging the daylights out of him. Just would not let go. I'd logged a lot of hours by the stage door waiting for him to come home. He was friendly enough. Brotherly. Cordial might be the word. Not cold, not standoffish but you could tell he was . . . somewhere else. He grew up, I guess, from the whole experience. You know, crossed the threshold.

I said something stupid, like "How was it?" Like he'd been away at summer camp.

GWYNETH PALTROW My dad said that after Roar left the hospital, he entered his "Catholic saint period." Jewish mothers want their boys to be saints too—or doctors. Same difference, right? And he *did* become a doctor—though not from Bunny's influence. With Bunny, it wasn't "My son the doctor!" so much as it was "My son the artist!" Loved that about her.

MARLENE BOCK (*critic, biographer*) In that post-sanatorium time, he read Huysmans's *L'Oblat*, a very weird novel about liturgy, Catholicism, suffering. He was *possessed* by Hildegard of Bingen. At sixteen! Hildegard also composed songs and music, which wouldn't have been lost on him. He conflated fame with sainthood and dreamt of becoming a saint himself—but became a doctor instead. There were many doctor-writers he admired: Céline, Chekhov, William Carlos Williams, Arthur Conan Doyle. . . . He got his MD in record time but never practiced, not in the conventional sense. He did manage to invent a new way of healing burn victims. It may not have been sainthood but came damn close.[34]

SUZE BERKOWITZ The Orr School of Medicine at the University of Chicago was kind of waiting for him—like the monolith in *2001*. [*dramatically hums* Also sprach Zarathustra] If you want to be a doctor, nothing beats a medical school with your name on it.

As Mama used to say: "Couldn't hurt!"

REV. THOMAS B. REVEILLE (*friend*) I was a young seminarian at Saint Patrick's. The rector believed in what he called "local missionary work." His biggest thrill was shoving us out of the nest. None of us had any life experience. I, for one, had this absurdly romantic idea that I'd be shutting myself away and reading medieval manuscripts by candlelight . . . He had us ministering at the hospitals, ministering on Skid Row. It was quite the education. I was absolutely terrified, but that experience became the bedrock of my spiritual practice. I ministered to Sunny Ambrose Radcliffe's son Trevor; that was an awful thing. She was one of the city's great socialites and a close friend of Bunny Orr. Everyone knew "Bunny and Sunny." Well, Sunny's boy was one of the first casualties in Vietnam. It happened on Christmas 1955. He was a sergeant looking for pilots who'd gone MIA. I don't think he crashed in a plane or anything like that; I think something blew up in the mess hall or a tent caught fire. When they finally brought him to the hospital in San Francisco, I spent hours at Trevor's bedside. He was a brilliant, gentle boy. He told me he'd always chafed against the wealth and frivolity of his parents. That's why he entered the military. If you want to get spiritual, I suggest a visit to the burn ward. It either breaks you or brings you closer to God. The Monsignor always said one has to be broken to get close to God. Needless to say, Trevor didn't have many visitors. The average person couldn't withstand prolonged exposure to that kind of suffering. And there was no young lady in his life.

Bunny Orr became a mainstay at the hospital. She visited three times a week. I remember Trevor saying that she was the only one who didn't pity

---

34 *The Boy Who Cried Later: A Biography of Roger Orr*, Marlene Bock, pp. 117–132 (Pantheon, 1996).

him. She *never* referred to his burns and he was so grateful. All he wanted was to be treated like everyone else.

SUZE BERKOWITZ Trevor was seven or eight years older, but Roger remembered him from parties at Parnassus. So, there was a connection. He knew what happened to him in Vietnam—everyone did—and that Bunny often visited. He begged his mother to bring him along and one day she did. A turning point in Roger's life.

REV. THOMAS B. REVEILLE The ladies in her social circle were appalled. "How could you bring your child?"—he *wasn't* a child, he was sixteen and had already seen things no adult has a right to see—"How can you bring him to a place like that to see a *creature* like that?" Hypocrites, all. Not that Bunny Orr ever gave a damn what anyone thought. You know, we spend so much time shielding our children from the suffering of the world, rightfully so, but when they come of age they need to start using their eyes and hearts. Roger was an early bird to the worm of trauma and sorrow; the circumstances of his birth certainly attest to that. He and Trevor got along like a house on fire, if you'll pardon the phrase.

SCATTER HOLBROOK He was determined to save Trevor Radcliffe, who was constantly in and out of hospitals for infection. Roger became obsessed.

REV. THOMAS B. REVEILLE I first met Bunny and Mug at the funeral of the murdered girl—Seraphim Hopkins. Her parents were prominent Catholics. This was six months or so before Bunny and I reconnected during one of her visits to see Trevor at St. Francis Hospital. I certainly didn't learn the details of Roger's "misadventure" until much later; that he was with Miss Hopkins on the night she got killed. I can't fault the Orrs for covering it up. Their son was blameless. I'm still uncertain whether Seraphim's parents knew that Roger gave comfort to their daughter as she lay dying.

The Orrs struck me as exceptional people. Bunny was Jewish and Mug fairly agnostic but they both indulged Roger's mania for Catholicism. Perhaps fervor is the better word. I had a bit of that myself at his age.

SUZE BERKOWITZ When he was back from San Rafael we didn't see each other for a few months. We talked a few times on the phone, barely. Finally, at dinner one night, my folks said Bunny and Mug thought it'd be a good thing for me to visit. A normalizing thing. I was so nervous! We had to fall in love all over again.

SCATTER HOLBROOK Roger was wobbly for a while. He didn't talk too much about his stint in the loony bin—and I didn't ask. He basically finished a college education in two years. For his homeschooling, tenured professors made the pilgrimage to Parnassus. Some got $100,000 or more, but his degrees weren't bought, he earned them. He was hell-bent on becoming a physician; he was incentivized and nothing's scarier than Roger Orr incentivized! Did you know he had an altar in his closet? He was heavily into Catholicism—the rituals appealed to his theatrical aesthetic. He'd had a sly, early introduction to that through his hero Luis Buñuel, who couldn't get enough of the Church's perversions. But Roar wasn't satirical about it, he was serious. That altar had saints, dead flowers, rosaries . . . and little buddhas too, a hangover from his exposure to the Beats' infatuations. He called the whole thing his first midlife crisis, a crisis of faith and identity that prefigured what was to come.

True prodigies have their midlife crises early.

JULIANNE MOORE His Abelard and Héloïse phase! Oh, he went deep. Abelard and Héloïse fired on all cylinders: forbidden love, castration, monasteries, and lesbian convents!

It gave him the idea to marry his childhood sweetheart.

Of *course* it did.

SUZE BERKOWITZ Roger was in Chicago, doin' his Doogie Howser thing. He was just turning seventeen. I went out there a few times on Mug's private plane—oh my God, *that* was exciting. I'd come for a week but hardly saw him. He'd give me envelopes of hundred-dollar bills to go shopping at Marshall Field. He was up before dawn to do rounds, just insanely focused on his studies. He'd come home and say, "I have an idea for Trevor," "I'm totally going to fix Trevor."

I remember exactly where I was when he proposed. I was interning at Berkowitz & Squibb, on Telegraph. My father's main office was in New York, but he loved the West Coast. Because OTG was such an important client—and he and Mug had apparently become BFFs—Dad set up shop in San Francisco. I was futzing around with ad campaigns for I. Magnin. I could futz because I was the boss's daughter. The best part was being mentored by Margaret Larsen, the gal who invented those iconic Parisian Bakery baguette paper bags that everyone used to carry around. (Don't they still?) But I digress.

Roar strode in, dropped to his knees and said, "Will I marry you?"

I thought he was stoned. I said, "What are you *talking* about?"

He said, "Wifey, that's the best proposal a narcissist can make." He handed me a little box with an emerald the size of the Fairmont. It belonged to Bunny's mom. Margaret rushed in and I cried in her arms.

We were nineteen.

DICK GREGORY Oh, that wedding was a *scene*. Chicago, '59—a fuckin' fairy tale. Sam and Barbara Cooke were there. They just got married too. Sam's father was a preacher and Roar wanted him to officiate, but he turned him down. I wondered how that marriage was gonna work. Suze was all right, she was cool. A good lady. But Roar? A stone wild child. Too much brain, too much dick, too much money. Too much everything.

I was working for the post office during the day and doing gigs at night in the black clubs. I opened a little place[35] but that didn't work out so well. Laughlin sent me a check for five grand, 'cause that ship was *sinking*. I called to thank her and she said, "By the way, Baby Brother's in Chicago going to medical school." I said, "Say what?" The Orrs were full of surprises. I think she wanted me to check up on him and give her a report. He came and saw me perform. He was with some stringy-hair tranny. [*laughs*] I tried getting him onstage but he wasn't havin' it. The next year, I did the gig at the Playboy Club and my life changed forever. One time he said, "What's it *like*, Sandman?" All bug-eyed and crazy. I said, "What's what like?" "What's it like to be *famous*?" I think deep down, he thought there were only two kinds of people: the famous and the unknown. Not the rich and the poor or the ugly and the beautiful or the happy and the unhappy. He seriously called it the brass ring. I called it the *ass* ring and said, "You can have it. Just slip it on like a turtleneck—you won't even know it's a noose." He said, "I've always been

---

35 The Apex Club.—*ed.*

an ass man. Not only will I wear it, Sandman, I'll melt it down, sit on it, and fuck it."

Nobody made me laugh like Roar.

ANN CHARTERS I was kind of surprised to be invited to the wedding. I was representing for the Beats. When they read their vows, I cried. Sam[36] and I got married the year before but I guess I still had feelings for Roger!

REV. THOMAS B. REVEILLE He sent me a plane ticket. He wanted me to preside. I was thrilled and asked if I'd be traveling with his parents. He laughed and said they didn't know; he wasn't going to tell them until after. Well, I just couldn't. I couldn't do that to the Orrs. It would have been a betrayal to Mug and Bunny—not on a grand scale but it didn't feel right. I should have told him the truth but instead called the next day to say a parishioner had died and I had to be at the funeral. Roger said marriages and funerals were the same and I should come to *his* because he "died first"! When I demurred, he started singing, "I'm getting buried in the morning! Reverend, come kiss me, show how you'll miss me!" But he was gracious, because he understood the bind I was in.

SCATTER HOLBROOK True to form, instead of "Here Comes the Bride," the *Marche Funèbre* came through the speakers as Suze walked down the aisle. Ken Kesey's wife gave her away . . . by the way, Suze's folks didn't know about the wedding *either*, and she wasn't too happy about that. But Roger insisted: top secret.

STEWART BRAND (*writer, editor*) Ken and Faye were there. (Laughlin was the one who introduced me to Ken.) I wasn't invited—but *almost* crashed it. Ken encouraged me to. I have no memory why it didn't happen because it was just the sort of mischief we were up to in those days. It certainly would have been memorable. . . . But Laughlin wasn't invited either! And the Kesey's weren't even close friends. Go figure.

---

36 Samuel Charters, a record producer and historian. Shortly after the wedding, Charters released Orr's "Try a Little Tenderness" (LaVern Baker, Charter/Wildcat, 1961). It sold over a million copies.—*ed.*

Ken was a prodigy himself—God, he wrote *Cuckoo's Nest* at nineteen or twenty. He was just a few years younger than Roger. We both met Roger when he was eighteen and back from Chicago for a few weeks, I guess for the holidays. We were in Chinatown at Sam Wo's, the old Beat hangout. Me, Ken, Laughlin, and Roar. I think Paul—Krassner—might have been there too. We'd all heard the 45s, the "legendary" 45s, and thought they were *beyond*. Roger held court with these amazing stories about being in a psych ward for ;uvies, you know, acting out all the parts. It was sublime. At the time, Ken was working at the veterans' hospital in Menlo Park, about an hour's drive from where Roger was locked up in San Rafael. He was already deep into writing *Cuckoo's Nest* and when Roar did his lobotomized toddlers-on-Thorazine act, Ken's eyes *bugged*. When he got home, Ken announced to his wife that he was going to rip the book up and start over—"I'm gonna set it in a children's nuthouse!" Faye thought about it for ten seconds, blinked, and said, "No, you are fucking not."

FAYE KESEY (*friend*) I had no idea why he sent those plane tickets, because Ken had only met him the once. He was in the middle of *Cuckoo's Nest* and having one of those moments where he was really struggling with the book, so a break was welcome. Not even Allen [Ginsberg] was invited! Or Laughlin. . . . She was *very* pissed off and made her displeasure vehemently known, but Roger swore us to secrecy. What could we do? The whole guest list struck me as kind of random. . . . then Suze, who of course I'd never laid *eyes* on, asked me to give her away!

Ken dropped acid for the wedding. Did you know that he and Allen were volunteers in Project MKUltra at Stanford? They took *lots* of drugs, courtesy of the CIA: LSD, mushrooms, mescaline. But he was very well-behaved for the ceremonies—not so much the after-party!—and quite touched to be there. I was too.

LAUGHLIN ORR I didn't know about the marriage and that hurt. All those people there, that he didn't really know. . . . But I *got* it. I was kind of a mother figure and maybe he still had a resentment about the Corso-Seraphim Hopkins debacle. That he somehow held me responsible. I don't know. I got used to taking it on the chin. That became a tradition with us. Thank God my jaw wasn't glass. It was iron, like my mother's.

FAYE KESEY After the *I do*s, Suze took me aside and whispered, "You're the reason all this happened." I wondered what on earth she meant. She said, "You and Ken were sweeties in junior high—just like we were—and got married at nineteen. Roger took that as a sign. He said, 'It takes two to tango,' he said. 'But four to cuckoo.'"[37]

ROSIE LEVIN The strange thing is that at the time of their wedding, Bird Rabineau was gigging at the Black Orchid, right before it went bankrupt. Everyone played the Orchid: Sarah Vaughan, Ella, Johnny Mathis . . . and Chet Baker, with whom Bird had a long, destructive affair. Her big song was on the charts—"Come to Me" hung around in the thirties, always trailing "Beyond the Sea." Still, to be on the Billboard charts was a very big deal for a singer like Bird, who wasn't considered mainstream. "Come to Me" was upbeat and more accessible than her usual stuff, and popularized her for about a minute. Chet was jealous and gave her grief.

When Roar saw a notice in the paper, he said, "Oh shit, the *Bird* . . . Mom's favorite!" He had this lightbulb moment to get her to sing at the ceremony, which ultimately he never pursued because he thought somehow it'd have made the news. Which I doubt—it was a very clandestine affair—but he didn't want Bunny finding out like that. He knew how angry she'd be when she learned of the elopement, how heartbroken. Bunny Orr always talked about wanting big weddings for her kids. Jonny was the only one who delivered, but that wasn't until much later. She was of that generation—a great, classic, society wedding at Parnassus was important. You can't always get what you want; she never lived to see her grandchildren, either. But Roar didn't want to add insult to injury. A rare moment of tact! It'd have been an astonishing thing, though, for his birth mother to sing at his wedding, with both of them completely oblivious.

If you put that in a movie, the critics would call it preposterous. Crude, contrived. The type of thing that could ruin a film.

ANN CHARTERS Aretha Franklin's dad was a semi-famous preacher and

---

37 From a phone conversation with Resnick Whittle, 2012. By then, Faye had married the writer Larry McMurtry [in 2011], a friend of Kesey's from the Stanford University Creative Writing Center.—*ed.*

self-promoter who enjoyed calling himself "the million-dollar voice." When Sam Cooke's dad turned Roar down for the nuptials, he asked Reverend Franklin—but the man was a little dismissive. Said he wanted a fee, some crazy number like five grand. Not that Roger didn't have it, but it left a bad taste.

JOHN CUSACK (*actor*) My father and his friend Philip Berrigan were at the wedding. I think Philip was visiting from New Orleans; he taught high school there. He was close to a young chaplain in San Francisco, Thom Reveille, and Thom couldn't come, so Philip took his place with Roar's blessing. He'd only been ordained a few years before and probably wasn't thrilled to read the vows Roar had written—some were profane—but he was a good sport. He wasn't priggish and saw the giddy spirit behind it.

DR. EUNICE LAVAR (*friend*) There were perks about sharing a dorm room with the future Dr. Orr. Not that he was there all that much. He had all kinds of plates spinning. There was the apartment on the Gold Coast, where Suze stayed when she visited, and that suite at the Drake. If those walls could talk, no doubt they'd ask for penicillin. But sometimes when he was too exhausted to move, he'd flop at the dorm. I was absolutely in love with him—platonically. He might have made a move or two when he was stoned but that wasn't my thing. We had a great time together.

He went home to San Francisco with some frequency. Mostly, to see a friend of the family, a soldier burned in Vietnam. That war wasn't really on the national radar yet. We're talking fourth- and fifth-degree. It kept Roger awake at night. He told me that's why he was in med school: to find a way to end that boy's suffering. It was a race he wouldn't win.

DR. TERRY DUBROW He was very much into [studying] Domagk and his treatment of burns—this was Germany, 1935—and Wilson's experiments with tannic acid. The effectiveness of neutralized tannic acid with soluble sulfonamide, which causes pain to immediately go away. Sort of like the oil of cloves that Olivier used on Dustin Hoffman in *Marathon Man*. [*poorly imitates Olivier*] "Is it safe?" [*laughs*] Wilson's work led to sulfanilamide and paved the way for Charles Fox and silver sulfadiazine—I can't believe I remember all this shit. What Orr did was change the antimicrobial game by reducing sepsis. He pioneered silver-based therapy for burn victims.

There's an apocryphal story about him listening to Bing Crosby sing "Silver Bells" then having an LSD-induced epiphany about sulfadiazines. It's probably horse pucky but I always wanted to ask him about that. The truth is, he was a brilliant, intuitive clinician, and it's *crazy* to think what he may have accomplished in medicine if he hadn't done the hundred other things he did in the arts. For selfish reasons, I'm glad he branched out. If he'd stayed in the doctor lane, there's a boatload of songs and movies that wouldn't exist. They were great seduction tools—which means a *shitload* of my all-time great performances in bed would never have happened!

DR. EUNICE LAVAR That friend who burned in the war wound up killing himself. I remember being startled when Roger told me that because he didn't have much emotion about it. Like he'd already moved on. He compartmentalized pretty well, maybe *too* well. I think part of him thought, "I did my best but was too late." Which was actually a healthy response. As much as he was a fantasist, he was a pragmatist as well.

ANN CHARTERS I kept my feelings in check but totally lost it when he sang that song to Suze at the wedding. He'd only written it the night before. He sang a cappella, and I'd never heard that *voice* before. My God, it was beautiful. I looked over at Sam, and he was crying too. Before Roger was even finished, my husband whispered, "That's gonna be number one. And I'm going to produce it." Two months later he did, with his old friend LaVern Baker on vocals. Sam wanted Erma Franklin to do it but after his experience with her dad wanting all that money to officiate the wedding, Roger nixed it. Sam also suggested that he sing it *himself* but Roger didn't want to. He hated his voice! Besides, he liked the idea of changing it up and having a woman sing the lyrics. Roger hadn't given it a title, and Sam said, "What about 'Tenderness'?" Roger smiled, touched his arm and said, "'Try a Little Tenderness.'"

SUZE BERKOWITZ LaVern altered a word by mistake. It was supposed to be "shabby" but she said "shaggy"—"shaggy dress." We laughed about that. He said, "What does *shaggy* even mean?" But it stuck. Every cover of that song had "shaggy." And there were about a thousand covers.

LANGLEN CUTTERBEE (*musical theorist, historian*) The genius of "Try a Little Tenderness" is that it's in the medieval Dorian mode, from the Greek—the theorist Ptolemy. It uses the white notes, D to D.

In other words, the diatonic scale—a heptatonic, made of five whole steps and two semitones in each octave. That's what gives the song its transcendent insistence, its ascension. Its populist emotionalism.

ANN CHARTERS It reminded me of Allen doing *Howl* that night at Gallery Six. You *knew* you were listening to something timeless, something that would change the world in its own big or little way. That song of Roar's was the tsunami that began his public life.

SUZE BERKOWITZ He wrote "Tenderness" the night before we married. We were both a little prickly. Nervous, I guess. And I was still nursing a grudge about my parents not being there. He was in another room, and I heard dribs and drabs but didn't give a shit. We'd just had some stupid argument and I was pissed. I *do* remember saying, "Don't be so rough"—probably phrased less delicately!—and he got sweet after that. Kissed his fingers then touched the hem of a nightgown I was wearing. My comfort nightgown. I'd worn it to death. Of course, that made it into the song, "wearing that same old shabby dress." If Bird *had* sung at the wedding, I think Sam would have definitely used her for the recording instead of LaVern. That's a lot of *what ifs* but wouldn't that have been beautiful and outrageous?

DR. EUNICE LAVAR It was the first and last time I was anyone's best man. I was honored but didn't kid myself: I was the only one he trusted with "medication." I carried a little black doctor's bag in those days, filled with goodies. We all used barbiturates to sleep, Benzedrine to stay awake, and Percodan to take the edge off marathon hospital shifts.

Marriage rhymed with triage.

STEPHEN SONDHEIM The *real* marriage vows were exchanged when he made that appearance on Jack Paar's show and sang "Try a Little Tenderness"—because Fame was his true bride. The quiet, cerebral courtship ended on the Paar show; he'd won her at last. He quit med school, a thought he'd been mulling from the moment Sunny Radcliffe's boy blew his head off with a pistol that one of his soldier buddies smuggled into the hospital.

Long before "Tenderness," gee, even before those preternaturally brilliant 45s, Roar was nostalgic for something he hadn't yet tasted: *razzmatazz*. Look at his lineage: showbiz razzmatazz was in his blood via Bird Rabineau. (Along with lots of other pathogens and pharmaceuticals!) When I told one of my godsons about my little theory, he said, "Sounds like a bad case of FOMOR." Fear of Missing Out on the Razzmatazz. [*laughs*] Well, don't we all have it. His agonies were redoubled by the fact that he *was* razzmatazz, the definition of it in its rarest, highest form: a consummate showman with authentic, transgressive, multitudinous gifts. No one in history succeeded in so many disciplines nor I doubt ever will.

After the Paar show, he rode tall in the rhinestone saddle. Then quite suddenly the Commodore died and Bunny was hospitalized with depression. All of his caregiver-savior stuff came to the fore. Because it was important to her, and because he really did love her, he put a lid on the razzmatazz and picked up a residency in San Francisco. See, she very Jewishly *implied* that his quitting medical school was the thing that broke her; and he just couldn't deal with the untoward consequences of dropping out. I always called him "Roar of the Greasepaint"—well, the greasepaint kept roaring but now there was nothing to apply it to. The actor's face was gone. In the middle of an ovation, he left the stage and embraced the loneliness of the long-distance dermatologist. It was a very dark time. The sexing and drugging were out of control, and Suze left him, again and again.

She's the true saint of this story, not his sister Seraphim.

SUZE BERKOWITZ He made a short film. I played Bunny—as Gloria Swanson, addled from shock treatment—and he played William Holden, "a fashionable, washed-up cross-dressing skin doctor," floating in the pool. It was cruel, but you couldn't help laughing. He called it *Sunset Boulevardier.*

STEPHEN SONDHEIM An old desire got reignited—his ticket out. He didn't want to be Louis Pasteur *or* the thinking man's Irving Berlin. He barely wanted to fuck. He got the movie bug again, big-time.

Like the old joke goes, what he really wanted to do was direct.

CHAPTER SIX

Fire Sale

SAM WASSON (*critic, essayist, film historian*) 1962 and '63 was what Roger called his "*anuses* horribiles"—the first of many! But it was also a rebirth—the first of many! The death of Bunny and Mug gave him wings to rise from the ashes.

STEVEN SODERBERGH He went through a time when he was obsessed with getting to the bottom of his father's suicide. I think Gregory Corso was the first to plant the seed that Mug was gay. And of course, when Roar came of age, he had ideas of his own. . . .

I got a call from him out of the blue—he was famous for cold-calling artists that were in love with him and his work. He'd just seen *Kafka* and wanted to know if I'd be interested in directing a film that would explore the time when he met Kerouac, all that. He was one of the most forward-thinking artists I've ever known but had a compulsion to look backward as well. He may have been stoned. He said he loved my movie, and loved *Kafka* since he was a boy. He segued into [Kafka's] *Letter to My Father.* He was, just, so emotional, and I was touched. He had a theory that his father killed himself because he was being blackmailed by a gay lover. More of a fantasy than a theory. When I asked about the details, he said, "We'll need to make those up." For whatever reason, he wanted revenge on Mug. And from everything I knew—and know—the Commodore wasn't the tyrant Kafka's father was! I mean, not even close. But who knows? I think the root of that anger was that he never got over his parents' betrayal; not telling him he'd been adopted. Maybe toward the end of his life he overcame it . . . He talked about Marvin Gaye, who'd covered one of Roar's songs—and was murdered by his father.

71

He kept returning to the Dad/Murder theme. He said, "Did you know Marvin's old man was a cross-dresser?" When I told him I *did* know that, he said, "Eureka! I've found my director!"

SUZE BERKOWITZ That last year in Chicago was a nightmare. I'd essentially moved there by then and was seeing a shrink because Roger was taking me down with him. Wifey was *not* doing well. He'd pretty much lost his mind and the only reason they allowed him to continue his "studies," such as they were, was because the Orrs kept putting out fires with that handy money fire hose. He lost his raison d'etre too when Trevor died but that wasn't the half of it. It was more of an *excuse*. He was using a new drug called fentanyl. And cocaine, lots and lotsa cocaine. The way it worked was, the day the interns got their MDs, the drug companies mailed them these, like, *vats* of pharmaceutical coke! A way of saying, *This is going to be a long, fruitful relationship!* Like a fucking welcome wagon. I don't know if that's still going on—probably—but it was batshit crazy. He'd do fentanyl to sleep then get coked up in the morning, plus whatever speed he scored during his night prowls. The meth was *nasty*; his skin smelled like metal. He OD'd a bunch of times but fortunately his roommate, who was our great friend and all-around boon companion [Dr. Eunice Lavar], revived him. I don't know why I didn't just fly the fuck home. I didn't want to stay alone in that big apartment anymore so he put me up at the Drake—Bird's favorite hotel, by the way. It was so awful. He'd say he was coming home for dinner—"home"! ha!—but wouldn't show up until dawn. Then twenty minutes later, he'd leave for rounds. I refused to sleep with him. I finally squeezed it out of poor Eunice that Roger was treating himself for syphilis! When my daddy got sick, I moved back to San Francisco; I wanted to care for him but needed to get away because I was becoming a cokehead myself and starting to get into some real mental trouble. I was crazy as he was. Maybe crazier.

When I got back to the city, I started throwing up. I was pregnant.

ANN CHARTERS LaVern Baker's "Try a Little Tenderness" became a big hit. There was a *really* good story behind the guy who wrote it—people were naturally curious—like, who was that masked man? This wealthy scion . . . this comedy record child prodigy . . . this *effing dermatologist* . . . Sam's PR machine, such as it was, went into overdrive. The media picked it up and Roar became clickbait before clickbait was even a gleam in Mark Zuckerberg's grandfather's eye.

Jack Paar was intrigued and asked him on his show.

And POW, he was a star.

HUGH DOWNS (*announcer, The Jack Paar Show*) Roger walked out and the audience immediately loved him. He was handsome and charming and had a kind of modesty about him that was very appealing. Whether or not it was an act didn't matter. Jack walked Roger through the whole history: the rich family, the underground 45s, the friend who was burned in the war. They spent a lot of time talking about Trevor Radcliffe and Roger deciding to become a doctor, in order to save him. The audience was riveted. People were crying. By the time they got to the part about marrying his childhood sweetheart, a star was born.

There was something so American about the story. Except it wasn't rags to riches, it was riches to riches.

CALEB GANNOWAY (*producer, The Jack Paar Show*) We were taping in California for a few weeks. José [Melis] had the biggest band we'd ever assembled because Judy Garland and Bob Goulet had been on the day before. Jack held over the orchestra, which cost a boatload of money. I wasn't too happy. Jack had a plan: he was going to ask Roger to sing "Try a Little Tenderness." You know, spontaneously. Which was a gamble, 'cause we didn't know if Roar would just say no—or freeze during the performance if he said yes. 'Cause remember, he'd never sung for a crowd of strangers, never been on television, never done anything *professional* . . . and, oh—did I mention Roger had already refused our initial suggestion that he sing the song? Sorry, I skipped over that. He didn't want to do it so we told him Goulet would. A complete lie. The plan was for Jack to tell him during a commercial break that Bob suddenly canceled and left us in the lurch.

Red Skelton stayed on the couch when Roar came out. Jack introduced his young guest, an unknown—more a novelty than anything else. He skimmed through Roar's CV, you know, the cult records he made when he was fourteen, the society parents, medical school. . . . Red was a little snide in that crude, shticky "everyman" way people used to love. He interrupted Jack and said, "The kid can do everything—but can he help my mother-in-law with her problem? She's a human whoopie cushion!" But "the kid" was a natural. I could relax! Even Red shut up because Roar had that kind of charisma. Jack asked how the song came about and Roar told the story about writing it the night before the wedding when he and Suze had an argument and he treated her unkindly. The famous story about the "shaggy" nightgown, you know, that it was supposed to be "shabby" . . .

People still say otherwise but I tell you here and now that Roger had no idea Jack was going to ask him to sing. (Jack forgot to tell him that Goulet bailed!) Obviously, he hadn't rehearsed. Go on YouTube and you'll see. The minute Jack said, "We just happen to have a full orchestra here," well—the rest is mystery, as Roger once said.

SAM CHARTERS (*producer, author*) His voice wasn't perfect. But it's bluesy—you hear Bird in it. What we call "black and white." A mix. You project onto it whatever you'd like to hear. That's why it's so friendly. Soulful and familiar. In many ways, the Paar version supplanted LaVern's single. I really do think of that moment as the birth of the Sixties singer-songwriter.

SUZE BERKOWITZ He was so happy we were having a baby. He took a break—the school let him—they had to!—and came home. After the Paar show, I was shocked he went back to Chicago anyway. He got sober. He really tried. He put on weight and looked so handsome. [*cries*] Oh! I don't know why I suddenly got so—sorry, Bruce! [*composes herself*] But it was . . . it was hard, because now there was this *other* thing: all the record labels wanted to sign him. He was kind of being pulled in all directions.

BEVERLY D'ANGELO He turned everything down. He made a promise to Bunny that he'd finish his residency. It's laughable now: Roger Orr setting up practice and burning off society dames' moles. Apart from all the hub-bub around his music—he told me he'd been offered a gig at the Sands—some acting opportunities came his way. Little-ish parts in *The Music Man* movie and *Whatever Happened to Baby Jane*[38] The only offer he seriously

---

38 When Ryan Murphy heard that story, he asked Orr to co-star in *Feud* (2017). Orr was flattered but would only agree to a small, uncredited role as an unscrupulous dermatologist-cum-plastic surgeon.—*ed.*

considered was the lead part in Herk Harvey's *Carnival of Souls*.[39] He just loved horror.

JONNY "STAGE DOOR" ORR I was fifteen when I saw him on Paar. It was like an earthquake. Every singer's manager, every *singer* wanted Roar to write for them. Patsy Cline covered "Try a Little Tenderness" and wanted to duet with him. But he was always a contrarian. Becoming a practicing dermatologist right in the middle of all that was the *epitome* of contrarianism. It was performance art! I know, I know, he was doing it for Mom. But part of that motivation was sheer perversity. I knew my brother.

SAM WASSON It was a huge news story when the Commodore blew his brains out. Peter Gramm was all over it. He put out the official narrative—"medical issues"—that Mug had been diagnosed with an inoperable brain tumor and didn't want to burden his family. Head shots were somewhat in the air because Hemingway did the same thing the year before. It all fit because everyone knew Mug was terrified of being an invalid; he had a real phobia because he'd watched his father die that way. Gramm took that as his cue and concocted the glioblastoma story. But "brain tumor" never made it into the coroner's report. Do I believe the fringe historians who say he was shot by his gay lover in the Tenderloin? That Gramm transported the body to Parnassus, where the suicide was staged? As Tommy Lee Jones said in *No Country for Old Men*, "Probably not."

LAUGHLIN ORR If my father had a so-called secret life, I never saw the evidence. It's tough to hide something like that—though it could be done. The Commodore was wily. He was born in 1908. We were flower children so being gay was kind of a shrug. But I guess it doesn't matter what generation you're born in; the closet's where many choose to live and I say more power to 'em. I was a big fan of Don't Ask, Don't Tell. Still am.[40]

SUZE BERKOWITZ The funeral was at La Piedra. Around twenty or so

---

39 Harvey wound up playing the role of the Ghoulish Stranger in *Carnival of Souls* himself.—*ed.*

40 *The Last Laughlin: A Memoir*, Laughlin Orr, p. 218 (Blue Rider, 2006).

people because Bunny wasn't in shape for more than that. The strange thing is that I can't remember too many of Mug's relatives being there. Laughlin flew back from Europe and was stoned out of her gourd. Roger brought a new "friend" called Boodles. I was miserable.

I was nine months pregnant.

REV. THOMAS B. REVEILLE I presided—and couldn't help remembering what Roger said about weddings and funerals being the same. Doris [Duke] was there to prop Bunny up. Roger brought along a very well-mannered, very presentable drag queen. Suze was heavily pregnant and pretended to turn a blind eye like everyone else.

SCATTER HOLBROOK His real name was Wilhelm Domino but he called himself Boodles—after the gin—and was one of the most beautiful girls I'd ever seen. In my mind now he looks just like Edie Sedgwick at the peak of her smudgy-eyed beauty. Roger was gorgeous too. They made this ethereal, aesthetically perfect couple—I called them "mourning doves"—and Suze got relegated to the role of top-heavy chaperone. I don't know how she got through it. She mostly sat with her dad, who didn't have to long to live himself. Mug's death was a terrible blow to him.

JONNY "STAGE DOOR" ORR Mom ended up having shock treatments at home. They wanted to do it in the hospital but she insisted, so teams of doctors and nurses would arrive with their boxes and apparatuses. When she came to, she didn't know who any of us were. As the effects wore off, she'd look at Roger and ask what he was doing there. "Why aren't you in Chicago?" Or worse: "The Commodore's dinner's getting cold!" It was a bad Tennessee Williams. And because he was her son *and* a doctor now, Roger was compelled to sit with her. It was like a Chinese finger trap.

BEVERLY D'ANGELO He told me that one time when Bunny was post-ECT, she asked the nurse to bring in Seraphim—then turned to Roger very casually and said, "Darling? What method was it that you used to kill her?"

Oh no no no. *Not* fun for him.

SCATTER HOLBROOK The Paar show made him a celebrity. The story was in all the magazines—remember those? Little glossy paper things you'd buy on a newsstand or read on a plane? We'd be walking down the street and people would shout his name from cars. His father had just died, his mother was a zombie—and there he was back at the hospital, with nurses asking for autographs. He enjoyed that. At the same time, he was humiliated because he felt like Cinderella. Looked like her too! Just a little.

LAUGHLIN ORR We weren't close at the time. I was in Europe going nuts without the benefit of electroshock. After the funeral I went straight back to London to catch the crazy-train. All aboard! All aboard!

HOPE "HOOP" RADCLIFFE Bunny got it in her head that the funeral was the perfect time to tell Roar he was adopted. I am serious. *Oh my God.* All those years of pent-up guilt—and Mug's death broke the dam. Bunny wanted to flood the whole village! She paced her bedroom like a madwoman, raving, kneading her hands. Mother sequestered her upstairs long as she could, trying to talk her down. When it was obvious nothing was working, she went "gangster"—Mother could be truly scary on the rare occasions she needed to be. "If you do *that*," she told Bunny, "on this of all days—if you choose to be an opaque, narcissistic, selfish *cunt*, I'll throw you in that grave too!"

Well, there wasn't a peep out of her after that. It was the splash of cold water on the face that she needed. Mother acted it all out for me when we got home. I could tell she was proud—and so was I. It seemed cruel but it was absolutely what was necessary: theater!

QUINCY JONES (*musician, arranger, producer*) Bunny never learned that Bird Rabineau was Roger's mother. Ahmet [Ertegun] told me she knew, but he was talking out of his ass. If Peter Gramm told her, as some people like to think . . . that's *bullshit*. And guess what: Gramm himself didn't know! And if he did, why the fuck would he tell *her*? Who would have benefited? From everything I know about Gramm, she could have asked with her last breath and it wouldn't have meant crap to the man. You couldn't have sucked it out of him with a pair of million-dollar lips. He got in a *little* bit of trouble when Roar found out—in the early Nineties, man! By then, Gramm didn't have anything to lose. He was a relic, a footnote with a dick and two feet in the grave. Motherfucker looked deader than Clive Davis! And being the perfect escape artist he was, Gramm went and dropped dead, avoiding any legal entanglements. Naw, Gramm didn't know. He found *out*, then told Roar. And that was half-a-century after the fact.

JONNY "STAGE DOOR" ORR Shock treatment helped because the woman could not stop crying. That was hard to watch. As Mom recovered, she began to conflate her grief over Mug with the lie about Roger's adoption. Her shrink told me all this after I found the diaries. She said my mother had this theory that if she finally told him, if she did the brave thing and told Roger the truth, it'd be like lancing a boil—a benefit to both of them. Which was probably true! She was a fairly candid person, arguably too candid, she prided herself on being completely transparent, so God knows what the poison of repressing all that did to her through the years. Dad was never bothered by deception; they were made of different stuff. Ain't nobody made of the stuff my father was. When he died, she lost her anchor. Just bobbing and bobbing out there, unmoored. In her diary, Mom said she was going to ask Gramm "once and for all." I'm assuming she was going to find out who the mother was. I have a theory about why she wanted to know. We all have theories . . . anyway, she knew Roger would be righteously pissed about being left in the dark, you know, the victim of a family conspiracy. We all were victims, in a way. I think she got a little grandiose and hatched a plan for a reunion. I think she wanted to reunite my brother with his biological mom. See, there was a ton of reasons for my brother to be angry. The big example was that from the moment Seraphim died, he thought he was doomed to have the same genetic fate—the Batten disease thing. You know, that he'd go senile. Going senile was a phobia of his, much worse than the Commodore's fears of being helpless or paralyzed. That was just *one* reason for being pissed off. My theory is, Mom's bright idea was to find the biological mother—to take the bullshit by the horns and martyr herself. Her way of atoning. In other words, when she made the announcement that he was adopted, she could soften it with pomp and circumstance: "Through great effort and expense, through great love . . . I have found her." Her fantasy.

Like most fantasies, it never happened.

RICHIE "SNOOP" RASKIN Want me to be honest? She never knew. Quincy's right on. And he wouldn't have told her anyway; Q was right about that too. Gramm was a cutthroat streetfighter with no morality whatsoever. He and the Commodore were kindred spirits in that regard. The suicide? Well, it eventually came out that half of Mug's family offed themselves— *another* secret Bunny closely guarded. But let's face it: Mug had his aberrations, and Gramm would have been privy to them. One hundred percent. But that's another story . . .

As I said before, Gramm was a thorough man. When that nonsense happened with the Stork Club, he left no stone unturned. Found out Bird was the mother—she was Mika then, so, Quincy was only half-right—found out *where* she was, and tracked her for a long, long time. Then let it go long before she became famous . . . but he knew where she was and kept tabs on whatever unsavory characters she got involved with. He didn't think she knew what happened to her baby, but he didn't want any surprises. By that, I mean blackmail. If Mug had asked him if he knew who or where Roger's mother was, Gramm might have said so. *Might* have. Because he respected Mug and knew he wouldn't have done anything stupid with that information, like gone and told his wife. She'd have gone to Herb Caen for chrissake! But Mug didn't give a shit who or where Roger's mother was; out of sight, out of mind. Another thing you need to remember is that if word got out, Gramm was vulnerable, because the whole friggin operation was illegal. Legit babies need paperwork. His network of clients would *not* be happy with the publicity. Reputations—lives—would be ruined. These were people who could crush Gramm. I wouldn't say he feared them, but they were the only folks he couldn't fuck around with; they could buy him, sell him, put him on the shelf, and forget about him. Not to mention he most likely had buried a few bodies along the way, literally, after being threatened and double-crossed by various amateur hour babypimper a-holes. Gramm didn't want a light to be shined on *that*. So there is just no way Bunny Orr would have learned anything more than what she already knew. You can take that to the bank and fuck it, as Baretta used to say. Gramm loved that show, by the way. Robert Blake became a client. I'll leave it at that.

HOPE "HOOP" RADCLIFFE It must have been a tremendous shock when she learned that Roger's birth mother was the famous Bird Rabineau. It probably dredged up all those feelings of guilt and shame. . . . My mother said Bunny wouldn't have been so affected if she found out they'd bought him from common trash. But from a woman she loved listening to on the *radio*? That made everything too real; it stopped being a fairy tale. I honestly don't think she would have taken her own life if she hadn't been depressed to begin with. But when she found out it was Bird—that was a bridge too far.

HERB CAEN The night nurse found Bunny with a plastic bag wrapped around her head. That wasn't until morning. Apparently, she'd been hoarding sleeping pills and swallowed two bottles. They could have filed a suit against the agency, because the RN was holed up in a Parnassus guest room with her boyfriend all night. But Laughlin and Roger were against that. Their feeling was, "We've had enough."

JENNIFER JONES (*actress*) They were both so young! Mug was fifty-four and Bunny was fifty-two. No one could believe it. Those two people were supposed to outlive *everyone*—like Philip and the Queen. They were supposed to die at La Piedra, holding hands. Centenarians! Isn't that the word?

NENA VON SCHLEBRÜGGE (*ex-wife of Timothy Leary*) Roar was hit hard by the surreal randomness, the transitoriness of our lives. He was always on a spiritual path, but the premature death of his parents is what galvanized the trip to India. He was a child of his time, yes, but Roar never dabbled. He had many lives, and each one of them went deep.

SUZE BERKOWITZ He didn't have to be a doctor anymore. It was like the cage door suddenly opened, and he froze like the songbird in that parable. Or like the monkey and the jar—you know, where the monkey's hand is stuck because he can't let go of a fistful of peanuts. Whatever.

SCATTER HOLBROOK It took a while to sort things out. There definitely was a will, but it needed "finessing." Enter Peter Gramm, who Mug had made the executor—without, I may add, Bunny's knowledge. God knows how much Gramm profited from *that* arrangement.

BILL GRAHAM (*promoter*) Millions were left to favorite charities and political causes. But the kids were all right. They were definitely all right. There was enough to go around, and then some.

JONNY "STAGE DOOR" ORR I bought land in Oregon with my inheritance and checked out. Turned on, tuned in, dropped out. Got heavy into Eastern religion and started a commune. And we're still here. Harvest Sun. We're a working farm. The most beautiful place you'll ever see.

SUZE BERKOWITZ We lived at Parnassus and I home-birthed there. Boodles lived there too but it didn't matter. Our daughter looked *so* much like Roger, like a Raphael baby in 3D. We were so happy for a while. What's that line from *Long Day's Journey [Into Night]*? Wait—I just googled it: "I fell in love with James Tyrone and was so happy for a time."

LAUGHLIN ORR Jonny was "the sane one." He was anointed the family archivist. He loaded boxes of Mom's personal papers and trucked them up to Oregon. He was supposed to be doing this careful cataloging but never touched them. They were up there at Harvest Sun gathering mold and dust. About a hundred diaries that Mom kept from when she was a girl.

SCATTER HOLBROOK Roar used some of the inheritance—a small amount, considering what he'd been left—to make a film. My credit was "Director's Executive Assistant." It was about the most fun I'd ever had.

SUZE BERKOWITZ Parnassus had a screening room, and we watched a lot of film noir. *They Drive By Night* was a favorite—Bogart and George Raft and Ida Lupino—and Roger made up a jokey title: *They Sleep By Night*. We thought it was hilarious, which it is. So, a goof became the world's first actual zombie flick. George Romero always said in interviews that *They Sleep By Night* was the inspiration for *Night of the Living Dead*. There was a lot of sly humor in all those movies George did but nothing compared to Roger's black-hearted wit. The *Blair Witch* guys were obsessed. And all the zombie movie tropes came from *Sleep*, especially the one they do all the time—my daughter just saw it on *The Walking Dead*—where the mom's holding her wounded daughter in her arms as the girl zombifies, forcing Mom to kill her own child. There was a lot of Jacques Tourneur in *They Sleep*—Roger loved *Night of the Demon*—and there was what he called "residue" of *The Tingler* and *Invasion of the Body Snatchers*, even *Night of the Hunter*. Sturges too . . . an alternate title for *Sleep* was *Undeadfully Yours*.

CALEB SCOTT DONAHUE (*cinematographer*) We shot it in fifteen days. I've done fifty movies since, won two Oscars, worked with every director on my bucket list. But I never, *ever* had as much fun as I did on *Sleep.* You spend a career chasing that first high.

No one knew what they were doing—except Roar. He knew more about shooting film than I did, which at the time wasn't saying a whole lot. But *way* more. He was like Altman; Bob cut his teeth making industrial films and came up with a lot of innovations for sound, for camera. Roar had a photographic imagery bank and learned everything from those marathon screenings his family used to have, starting from when he was nine or ten years old. Of course the best thing was that we didn't have a studio breathing down our necks because the man had written his own ticket. None of us slept more than two hours a night, except for the "twins," who had a guardian. We thought it was going to be tough finding parents who'd approve of their kids being in a low-budget horror film, but Sissy and Beverly's moms had both seen Roar on the Paar show and that really helped. They were enamored.

SISSY SPACEK (*actress*) Terry [Terrence Malick] was such a fan of *They Sleep By Night.* We talked about it when I did *Badlands.* He was a few years younger than Roar and really idolized him. He wanted to know what it was like to work with him and I thought that was so great that even someone like Terry, a genius, was reduced to being a wide-eyed fanboy.

That's what so wonderful about the movies.

JOAN HOSCH (*producer*) I don't think *They Sleep By Night* ever would have happened if Roar didn't fund it himself. We were having a terrible time. For months we only had one actor, Luana Anders, who was wonderful. A Susan Anspach type whose career never went anywhere, which I always thought was such a shame. A mystery to me, but that's how it is. Roar wanted Diana Sands for the lead because he loved her work in *A Raisin In the Sun.* Ruby Dee was in *Raisin,* and Roger knew Ruby from his sister, so reached out to Diana through Ruby. Diana said she wanted to do it but was committed to another film, *An Affair of the Skin,* which the critics just *hated.* Maybe Diana just didn't want to do *They Sleep* enough. Roar sensed that and I remember him being hurt.

MELLIE KOCH (*casting director*) He was adamant about having a Black lead. His heart sunk when Diana dropped out, and that's when he rewrote the character as male. I think he regretted it but that was Roar; he shook things up when he couldn't get his way. He'd paraphrase that Buddhist saying to, "Second thought, best thought." We found Duane [Jones], who of course George Romero later cast in *Night of the Living Dead*. Duane was an accomplished actor, academic, activist, and scholar. He'd studied at the Sorbonne and been in the Peace Corps in Niger. Good God, he headed up the literature department at Antioch! He was amazing, and as much as Roar wanted that character to be female, he was thrilled for the rest of his life that he had a hand in Duane's wonderful career.

BEVERLY D'ANGELO Sissy [Spacek] and I played the twins. I was twelve, and Sissy was a few years older—we didn't look alike, but it worked. Kubrick later told me that the twins in *The Shining* were drawn from us. When I told Roar that, he thought it was hilarious. But he was fuckin' proud.

SUSAN SONTAG (*essayist, activist*) I was teaching at Columbia when I saw *They Sleep By Night* at the Cinema Village. It had the misfortune of being released on the day Kennedy was shot. It was barely reviewed, dismissed with that typical bullying, American fervor.

The Europeans had a different view.

* * * * * * * * * *

THEY SLEEP BY NIGHT (1963)
by Luc Acoste Venier
Cahiers du Cinéma

With a droll, precocious nod to Raoul Walsh's 1940 noir *They Drive By Night*, Roger Orr's first film shows astonishing finesse, depth, and promise. The director, already famous in America for composing the international hit song, "Try a Little Tenderness," does a bit of costume changing early on: one discerns *Touch of Evil*, *Beat the Devil*, and a straight flush of Buñuel. In the end, Orr plays his own hand—beating not just the devil, but the house. Like the legendary corpse flower,

They Sleep By Night reveals itself in fetid bloom—slyly, comically, terrifying, seductively—as the first of a new genre: *horreur verité*.

* * * * * * * * * *

KENNETH TYNAN[41] Saw an outrageous—and outrageously good—film at the Savoy by a young American tyro with such natural gifts that one imagines he directed his own birth. Danielle loved it, and when we returned to her flat, I caned her bottom until it was bright scarlet. Afterward, we smoked and I inspected the marks. She said, "Better red than undead" and we laughed.

SAM WASSON If you listen hard, you can hear Bird Rabineau's "Come to Me" on the radio when the kids approach the farmhouse. I didn't pick up on that until years later when I saw *They Sleep* at Lincoln Center. Whoa! Just, *whoa.*

CALEB SCOTT DONAHUE To say that its release date was bad timing is an understatement. When JFK was shot, Roar said, "We needed *that* like a hole in the head." The other films that came out on 11/22/63 were a Jacques Demy, and *Fun in Acapulco* with Elvis and Ursula Andress. Roar always said that *Acapulco* was the *real* zombie flick. More perfect than anything we could have dreamt up.

JORDAN PEELE (*director, actor*) I watched that movie a hundred times before I wrote *Get Out*—that, and *Hallelujah Boogie*. He was crazy prescient, because, remember, when he wrote *Sleep*, he didn't know he was Black. And so much of that film was about race.

JONNY "STAGE DOOR" ORR He tried to minimize the failure of *They Sleep by Night*, but it definitely had an effect. He started calling himself Zapruder. But on darker days, he referred to its release as "the third suicide"—the one after Mom and Dad's.

---

41 *The Diaries of Kenneth Tynan*, edited by John Lahr, pp. 310–312 (Bloomsbury, 2001).

SCATTER HOLBROOK By the time *Sleep* tanked, he wasn't in the best shape. The deaths of his de facto parents did a number on him, and Roger escaped into making the movie. But with the "nonevent" of its release, the walls came tumbling down. He was very, very depressed. Sad, angry, the whole chihuahua. Not even the newborn gave him pleasure. Something was brewing; that famous *I'm-not-here* look was in his eyes. He told me he was thinking of going to London. He invited Suze, but there was no way she'd come, not with the baby, and he knew that.

He took Boodles. Of course he did.

WILHELM "BOODLES" DOMINO (*lover*) Sometimes Suze watched, sometimes she joined us. I'm talking about in bed. She was so in love with that baby, there wasn't time for resenting me—or Roger. Anyway, come on. Suze knew who she married. Part of why it worked as long as it did was she knew when to step forward and when to step back. When we went to London, she stepped back.

LAUGHLIN ORR The one bright light was Aurelia, their new baby. He sang her to sleep. It broke my heart. [*sings*] "This little light of mine, I'm gonna let it shine." He knew that the more he shined, the more Aurelia would. But at the end of '63, the bulb was burned out.

RAM DASS (*teacher, philanthropist*) He was a perpetual motion machine, but the core of him was static, impervious. The core was timeless. That's what India showed him. The magic trick—the trick of all tricks—is to outwit one's *unmagical* destiny. It takes a while to figure out how to do that, and he didn't know any better; he tried to outrun it. That never works. If you don't live in your core, unmagical destiny catches up, no matter how fast or how clever we are. Genius don't count!

It's the old Maugham story—the appointment in Samarra awaits.

SCATTER HOLBROOK He hadn't been to Europe since all of us trooped to Cannes in '51. He went straight to Czechoslovakia—probably because "Try a Little Tenderness" was a big hit in Prague. As it turned out, Miloš Forman was a huge fan of *Cult 45*—those early comedy records found their way across the pond. Roger had a little part in Cassavetes's *Too Late Blues*, and Miloš loved that movie. He and Boodles stayed long enough for Roger to star in *Candle, Book, Bell*, Miloš's first film.

He got a big award at one of the festivals[42] but was back in the States by then, burying Aurelia.

LAUGHLIN ORR He was wandering around Morocco, getting laid by street urchins. Ostensibly looking for Paul Bowles, who the Beats revered; as it turned out, Paul's wife, Jane, was the one he found and they grew very close. Scatter—poor Scatter!—was the one who impossibly reached him there. Oh, it was terrible, terrible. Terrible! Scatter said that when he told Roger the baby had died, there were all these weird noises on the line, this piercing feedback, before he realized it was *Roger*, canting, chirping, whimpering, screaming. Completely inhuman sounds that went on forever because he couldn't hang up—how could he? He held the phone away from his ears so his brain and heart wouldn't explode. It took forty-eight hours for my brother to fly home. My big fear was he'd never make it—that was a recurring fear— you know, like a scene out of *The Sheltering Sky*. When he finally showed up he looked like one of the zombies in *They Sleep by Night*. No amount of drugs could kill the pain.

SUZE BERKOWITZ She died in her crib in the middle of the night. The nanny was fast asleep beside her and the body was cold in the morning. Cold, cold, cold . . . still so hard to talk about. We never tried again [to have a child]. He called it "the curse of Seraphim" but Sera would never put a curse on anyone. It was more about Roger being cursed, or thinking he was. On some irrational level, replacing Seraphim with Aurelia was a betrayal. It made no sense. It was primitive.

I heard him late at night, talking on the phone in the library. I listened through the door but couldn't make sense of what he was saying. Then I realized where I'd heard the rhythm of those untranslated incantations: the secret language he shared with Sera. He wasn't on the phone at all. He was spirit-talking—communing—for solace.

WILHELM "BOODLES" DOMINO I should have come home with him

---

42 Locarno International Film Festival, 1964.

from Tangier but went to England instead. I just couldn't deal. He said he didn't care, that it was better for me to stay, but I don't think he ever forgave me for that. To make it worse, Francis [Bacon] and I became lovers; at that point, nothing had happened between them. Roar was really looking forward to seducing him when we got to London. . . . but after Roar got the news about his daughter, I sent Francis a note with a nude Polaroid. It was very explicit. I wrote "The Screaming Pope" at the bottom but crossed out the "Sc."

GORE VIDAL Ah, Boodles. I have a plaster cast of his cock. Ram Dass has one too. I visited Ram de Ass in Maui when he moved there in the Oughts, after his transient ischemic attack; invalidism paradoxically made his horns grow fonder. "Diff'rent strokes," as the groundbreaking sitcom reminds us. Ram de Ass had an altar in the living room, with incense, flowers, and guru statuettes—lined up like Oscars—and there it was: the notorious Boodlescock. Right between Obama and Jesus.

LAUGHLIN ORR Boodles was aptly named. Not only was he a drunk, but Webster's defines "boodles" as "a collection of persons"—which he was, because he had about seventeen personalities. Apparently, it's also a synonym for "bribe money." To be fair, he wasn't blackmailing my brother but was definitely living off him. And probably stealing from him too, now and then.

REV. THOMAS B. REVEILLE Aurelia was cremated. I don't know what happened to her ashes. In the end, perforce, Roger took the very spiritual view that she hadn't lived nor died. He didn't mean Aurelia hadn't lived in the sense that she had such a short life. Not in the sense of the temporal . . . but something else closer to the philosophies of the East. People have many different ways of coping with tragedy.

I never saw any of them again—no, that isn't true! I ran into Roger on the street. Why do I always forget? I didn't realize until that moment how much I'd missed his presence in my life. I *did* tell him what joy his songs and films had brought me, and the world. He said, "I do my part to balance out the senseless horror God brings like an espresso in the morning—and the hot chocolate He tucks us in with at night." Roger smiled and said, "Do you still believe in Him?" I think he really was hoping I'd say "No." I remembered what Noel Coward once said when asked the same thing. "Let's just say we have a working relationship." He threw back his head and laughed, kissed my cheeks, and got into his limousine.

BEVERLY D'ANGELO The only way he could survive was to make a *plan*—a consistent response to tragedy in Roar's life. To pick himself up, dust himself off and start all over again. "Time for the snake to eat its tail." That's what he always said.

And got down to business.

CHAPTER SEVEN

Pilgrim's Progress

KENNETH TYNAN The plan had been for them to leave Morocco and go straight to Francis Bacon's atelier. But that got derailed by the death of Aurelia, so Boodles went on alone. Boodles violently impaled the artist on the threshold; a tour of the studio could wait.

JULIE CHRISTIE (*actress*) In his own way, Boodles was as gorgeous as Roar. I'd just done *Billy Liar*; my social circle was expanding somewhat. I was at a party when the two walked in and everyone's mouths fell open. Boodles had pert little breasts—he took hormones—that Roar rather worshipped. I worshipped them as well! And he admired Boodles's *commitment*, you know, secretly coveted the courage it took for him to alter his body. But Roar wouldn't put anything into motion himself until the Nineties.

You see, Boodles was comfortable in whatever body he chose. Roar never made that sort of peace, which I think was a shame.

MARK STEVENS (*biographer*) In the early Sixties, Bacon was already ensconced at 7 Reece Mews, a former servants' quarters in South Kensington above a pair of seventeenth-century stables. Boodles made himself at home, lying around the place like a concubine. George Dyer, Bacon's lover, was not happy about it. Dyer was a thief from the East End. The phrase rough trade comes to mind, but of course it was more shambolic and complicated than that, as everything in Bacon's life was.

Roger and George got along quite well. I'm certain there was a dalliance there; Roger's payback for Bacon's rogueries with Boodles.

CLARE BARLOW (*writer*)[43] That trip, Orr met everyone who was anyone. Any given afternoon on Carnaby Street, he'd be introduced to Hockney *and* the Kray twins. It was like that.

Bacon's antipathies toward Hockney were well-known. He said, "Even the Krays say David's paintings are like quims filled with pastel shite."

STEPHEN FRY (*author, actor*) Bacon had met the whole family in the spring of '51, in Panarea. He got along quite well with Bunny and the Commodore but was *very* taken with Roar. Oh, nothing prurient—Roar was eleven years old, though I doubt that would have stopped him. I know from various sources that the introduction remained innocent. But he was fond of the precocious boy, admiring the little sketches he did and the plays Roar put on with the fishermen's sons. Bunny collected him over the years, because she loved having that personal connection, you know, having met him on that remote, lava-strewn island. Over time, she bought a little Pope painting and a grotesque rotund nude and hung them willy-nilly in the kitchen—the kitchen!—right beside a Cornell box and a Dalí she commissioned of herself.

JOHN RICHARDSON (*art critic*) Roger loved Bacon's work. Its raw, passionate, monomaniacal obsession with obsolescence and death. The corruption of the flesh and the trappings of domestic desuetude—the poetry of inexorable, ordinary isolation, the pulchritude of soiled mattresses and sweat-soaked hair . . .

The family took that trip to the island as a voyage of healing after Seraphim died, forever associating Francis, in the shamanic sense, not only with death but with healing.

DUSTY SPRINGFIELD (*singer*) In London, not too many people knew who Roar was, which I think was a tremendous relief to him. Otis Redding's "Try a Little Tenderness" wouldn't come out till '67, and while the LaVern Baker record finally made the Top of the Pops it hadn't been the hit in the UK that it was in America. And one had to be a real aficionado to have seen *They Sleep by Night*!

---

43 From *Queer British Art: 1867–1967*, Clare Barlow, p. 211 (Tate, 2017).

DUNCAN ROBINSON (*art critic*) In that first week, Roar met Frank Bowling, a friend of Bacon's. Bowling was born in Guyana and came to London when he was nineteen. They were both outsiders.

Like everyone else, Bowling was struck by Roar's great, magnetic beauty—and taken aback by his mysteriously deep pockets.

FRANK BOWLING (*painter*) Roger spent the dollars like he was printing them. I thought he was in bed with the Krays—that he was some sort of money launderer. Then Boodles told me Roger wrote "Try a Little Tenderness." Which made no sense at all! A cognitive dissonance. I said to Francis, "He made all that money from one little song?" Francis said no, he had *family* money.

I thought he meant the mafia!

VALENTINE DOBRÉE (*artist, novelist*) They clicked. There weren't many black painters of renown in the UK and Roger respected the quiet war Frank had to wage. And he loved that Frank married one of his instructors—and was punished for it.[44]

Frank had a son, about a year old, and Roar was so wonderful with that baby. All babies were stand-ins for the one he lost.

SEAMUS HEANEY (*poet*) Frank Bowling came to England wanting to be a poet, not a painter. One night at Wheeler's, everyone was stoned and Roger scribbled something on a napkin. Frank loved it so much that he made it into his famous painting, "Slipknot":

> Slipnot
> *who not—*
> *whatnot—*
> *when not—*
> *where not—*
> *why not—*
> *forget me*

---

44 In 1960, Bowling married an assistant to the principal at the Royal College of Art. As staff relations with students were forbidden, he was suspended, returning in 1962 when his wife left her position. He graduated with a silver medal; David Hockney got the gold.—*ed.*

FRANK BOWLING We'd go for Jewish salt beef at Bloom's, in Whitechapel. He didn't talk much about his sexuality. Mostly we rapped about painting. His eyes kind of popped open when I said I didn't care about being a Black painter—I just wanted to be a painter. It wasn't until he found out that his mother was Black that we reconnected. He'd been taking a lot of shit for not being political enough and asked me, "How do you do it?" Because I was strenuously apolitical. I told him, "That isn't who I am. You just be *you*." He smiled and said, "Tell me who that is, Frankie, and I'll try it."

FRANCIS BACON Roger was rather accomplished. No formal training but the daimon was strong. The second bathroom [in Reece Mews] was quite large and he took it over—made extraordinary things there. He got hold of some photographs John Deakin had taken on the burn ward of Shotley Bridge [Hospital]. Roger sculpted little clay maquettes of the burned men. Some, he made paintings of; others, he let stand alone.

I brought them to Geoff Hunter at Marlborough [Gallery] and he wanted to show them. Roger wouldn't allow it. I admired him for that.

GEOFF HUNTER (*art dealer*) Finally he agreed to exhibit his work under the name "Iwana Kant." I didn't find out until years later that Iwana Kant was the name of Victim #1 in his first movie, the zombie flick. I'm surprised some film geek never connected the dots; probably because it says "Ivanka" in the credits. But at the time, he told me it stood for *I want a cunt*. Prescient, that! He refused to give interviews and that's when they really started to sell.

With the help of Frank Bowling, he constructed a fake biography of Iwana. She was born in Mauritius. Frank and Paula Rego[45]—and Francis, of course—were the only ones who knew about the charade.

ROSIE LEVIN Say what you will—you can analyze all day how he came up with it—but "Cant" was Bird Rabineau's grandfather's name: Porter Cant,

---

45 Dame Maria Paula Figueiroa Rego, a painter, was born in Lisbon. She belonged to the so-called London Group, which included David Hockney.—*ed.*

who got railroaded out of the Tennessee House of Representatives. No way he could've known at the time.

How 'bout that?

GWYNETH PALTROW It's a beautiful name, "Iwana." It means "God is gracious." Right? I've heard the whole *cunt* thing but I think that's just "fanciful apocrypha," as Stephen [Fry] says. Dad said Roar told him the name was taken from the root of *cantare*—the Latin for "to sing." Which makes much more sense. I like that much better.

Roar loved to take a beautiful truth and graffiti it.

LARRY HARVEY (*cofounder of the Burning Man festival*) I'm a huge fan of everything that man does. I was thirteen years old when I saw him on Jack Paar. I was knocked out when he sang "Try a Little Tenderness"—and unexpectedly moved when he told the story of trying to save the friend who was badly burned. A few years later, I had a dream that Roar and his soldier friend were walking in the desert. When I woke up, I knew I was going to start a festival, and knew its name: Burning Man.

No one knew the Iwana Kant connection back then. When he died, I managed to buy one of the "burn ward" sculptures he did while living at Francis Bacon's studio. I had to mortgage the house.

Not too many people know that we invited him to perform at Baker Beach for our first festival, in '86. He declined. He sent a telegram—I have it right in front of me. "Sadly unable to attend because of current engagements—my ears are burning at both ends; they will not last the night. Sending prayers that your Burning, man, will give a lovely light to friends, foes and VIP ticket holders."

LARRY GAGOSIAN (*art dealer*) If he did nothing else, his legacy as a sculptor and painter would assure his place in "the lives of the artists."

Ed [Ruscha] loved him and did a series of wordplay paintings with the overall title "Google Trans" from epigrams provided by Roar:

YOUR WORD

AGAINST

MINE

THERE ARE NO WORDS

NO WORD IN ENGLISH FOR _____

THESE WORDS
WERE MADE
FOR TALKING

WHAT'S THE RIGHT WORD?

WORDS WITHOUT END, MEN

HE BEAT WORDS INTO TALK SHOWS

JONESING FOR WORDSMITHS

IF THE WORD FITS, SWEAR IT

WHAT—ME WORDY?

We just sold the entire suite to Jennifer Pritzker. Jennifer's amazing. She's trans, a Republican, and a retired lieutenant colonel in the Army. Her foundation honors vets and military personnel. The proceeds are going to the Transgender Law Center—Roar told Ed that was his wish.

SCATTER HOLBROOK He was tormented—the "tormented by" list was long. Close to the top was leaving Suze behind. For his own sanity, he really didn't have a choice. But the coldness of it, the cruelty, the *wreckage* of leaving his wife after the death of Aurelia was an exquisite agony. Hey, it wasn't a picnic for Suze, but that's for her to tell.

He'd been in London about four months when he finally called. Called *me*, not Suze. The first thing he said was, "You're taking care of her, right? You're with her now?" Which was totally psychic—and literally true because it was the middle of the night and Suze and was sleeping next to me. I stammered, "Yes."

"Good," he said. And he meant it. "*Good.* I love you. Now go back to sleep."

SUZE BERKOWITZ I don't think I would have survived without Scatter. I never felt so alone in my life. It was incestuous but it worked. Sometimes you can only heal with someone of the same tribe.

SCATTER HOLBROOK We didn't so much fall in love as rappelled to it. The love had always been there. The physical aspect was pretty spiritual, without getting into it too much . . . riven with tears, as the poets used to say—I love that word, "riven." But it wasn't enough. She was sinking and I just couldn't go there. She was Mariana Trench-deep. I finally realized that *Parnassus* was the stone tied around her neck; Parnassus was killing her, and dragging me along for kicks. At three in the morning, she'd hear Aurelia crying and stumble from bed in a sleep-run. I'd chase her down and shake her awake.

I finally said, "We have to get out."

A week later, we set up house in Maui. She was back from the dead. When we made love, she laughed instead of cried. She slept straight through the night and when I brought her coffee, I sang, "Good mornin', Starshine. The Earth says 'Hello.'" We left the stones of that haunted house at the bottom of the ocean.

JULIANNE MOORE Suze was *such* a strong woman. Todd [Haynes] wanted to do a movie about her for the longest time. Suze said, "Yeah! He could call it *Unsafe*." Ha!

LINDA LIPNACK KUEHL (*biographer*) Roar and Bird had that near-miss in Chicago, around the time he got married—an aborted plan to have her sing at his wedding.

So, it's interesting how they later crossed paths in London.[46]

GWYNETH PALTROW The London encounter with Bird always reminded me of the story about Steve Jobs and his biological dad. (I met Steve in 2000 because I knew his sister, the amazing novelist Mona Simpson.) Their father owned a restaurant in Sacramento where Steve always had lunch. At the time, neither of them knew they were related. Ultimately, they did find out, but

---

46 From taped archives, circa 1976.

never came together—out of pride, anger, whatever. I guess you could say Roar's story had a happier ending. [*laughs*] I guess not really! I mean, with his mother, *yes*—with his father, absolutely not! Oh my God, no!

JOHN LAHR Bird was in the midst of a tempestuous relationship with Chet Baker. To put it mildly. Heroin was "the other woman"—for both. He was in London doing a film, playing himself, "Chet Baker," in *Stolen Hours*, a remake of *Dark Victory*.[47] And having an affair with the star, Diane Baker. Bird was intensely possessive; it didn't help matters much when Chet joked about marrying Diane because "she wouldn't need to change her last name." One night, the couple found themselves at the Bowlings' for one of their infamous parties in Clapham. I think Julie Christie might have tagged along. And by the way, that's where Roar first met Peacock [Kenneth Tynan], who'd written that wonderful review of *They Sleep by Night*. Well, young Peacock was shocked and enthralled to see *l'enfant terrible Américain* in the flesh. The conversation drunkenly got around to their mutual predilections, which included flagellation, spankable bumholes, all that.

Suddenly, Chet and Bird swept in, freezing the room for a minute with the shock of their beauty—a dead silence fell, as Peacock later wrote in one of his diaries, "like a narcotic snow, blanketing everything but Eros." Chet started his time-tested, flirty, shy-gangster tortured-soul routine with Paddy [Bowling's wife]; his MO with the ladies. When Bird broke away in disgust, Roar made a beeline. He was hell-bent on seduction and immediately presented his bona fides: that he wrote "Tenderness"—he *never* told anyone that!—and how she "almost" sang at his wedding. Bird cooly said *Oh, really?* but was captivated. She must have known who he was but coyly pretended otherwise. Anyway, she was charmed. And it was tough to get that woman's attention! He was funny, smart, and beautiful, like her, in a different way . . . there was chemistry on so many levels. Sorry if that sounds rather artless to note.

---

47 Orr would direct a remake of *Dark Victory* in 1982, "during my Douglas Sirk period," with Debra Winger reprising the Bette Davis role. In the original, Davis sang "Oh, Give Me Time for Tenderness"; in her memoir *Undiscovered* (2008), Winger wrote that she pranked Orr by singing "Try a Little Tenderness" instead. The outtake footage was destroyed in the Universal Studios fire of 2008.—*ed.*

She began to dance with him rather suggestively, as a retaliation against Chet's lothario act with Mrs. Bowling—*and* Diane Baker.

DAVID HOCKNEY (*artist*) Chet saw what was going on and pried them apart. As fem as Rodge could look, *he weren't no poof*, so it was probably a good thing for Mr. Baker that Boodles stepped between the two men. (After seeing Rodge handle himself on the street when he was accosted, even the Kray twins said, "You're one of us, laddie.") Rodge started to laugh and Boods yanked him into another room where they collapsed on the floor. They shouted at each other like madmen: "Chet Baker!" "Bird Rabineau!" "Chet Baker!" "Bird Rabineau!"—they were *huge* fans—the lunatic callout game went on and on and on. I joined them mid-howl. I was just a few years older than Rodge but wasn't a jazzman; didn't know who either was—Chet *or* Bird—but played along.

Proper names soon devolved into barks, jeers, and a general filth of epithets and sobriquets. We sank into absolute paroxysms.

ELAINE DUNDY (*novelist, widow of Kenneth Tynan*) Thank God they left straightaway. Some of us worried Chet would return with a pistol. The Krays were supposedly his "sponsors"—maybe he'd come back with the twins. Who knew? I watched that front door for hours!

ALAN CUMMING (*actor*) Roar told that story many times over the years—before *and* after he found out Bird was his mum. You know, "the ménage-a-trois that wasn't." [*laughs*] He never fantasized about his mum sexually—or so he said—but *had* fantasized about Chet. So many of us did . . . the probability that he likely would have slept with Mum if not for the "altercation," well, he thought that delicious.

He told Rex Harrison about it and Rex said, "Let's *do* make a movie. I'll play Chet. Call the thing *Oedipus Rex Harrison*."

Roar loved him forever for that.

BIRD RABINEAU[48] When we finally met [in 1983], we laughed about that

---

48 *Bird of Pray: First and Final Interviews*, Introduction by James Baldwin, p. 78 (Simon & Schuster, 1988).

night in Clapham. *He* laughed but I chuckled because there was pain there for me. There was shame. It wasn't a sexual thing between us like how he scandalously tells it; my son and I clicked because of the heroin. Roar always leaves that out. That's something you know right away when you meet another user. Another parishioner in the Church of Smack. So, there was great shame because I knew the suffering that heroin had caused him in his life. There was great shame when I found out he was my son, shame for a long, long time that the apple didn't fall too far from the tree. Hell, it stayed right *there*, didn't roll away at all! Roar always leaves it out, 'cause he's protecting me. He didn't want to perpetuate that aspect of who his mother was. But I never liked sweeping the truth under the rug. I *was* in an abusive relationship and feeling vindictive, so some of that other stuff he says is true. I *did* use my boy to get a rise out of Henry[49]—not one of my finer moments.

Praise Jesus! The Lord nearly saw to it that I sang at his wedding—then set him down right in front of me in the United Kingdom and will make certain we are together *forever*, in the united kingdom come! The Lord made us dance together and it took me a while to see it wasn't a devil's dance but a Ghost Dance. That Native American thing? A return of the dead—He returned my son to me.

Praise God. Praise God. Praise God.

MARK STEVENS They went to the movies all the time. [Bacon] was something of a film scholar. He was enthralled by Eisenstein, *The Cabinet of Dr. Caligari, Metropolis*—and as big a fan of Buñuel as Orr. When it came to the Spanish maestro, Orr knighted the painter with his highest compliment: "Frannie *understands*."

TERRY SOUTHERN (*novelist, screenwriter*) I was told that *Dr. Strangelove* had an *outsized* effect on Roar—but '64 *swung* and he saw 'em all: *Pink Panther* and *Zulu* and the *7 Faces of Dr. Lao* and *Two Thousand Maniacs!*— *Muscle Beach Party, The Best Man, Black Like Me* and *Viva Las Vegas* . . . *The Pawnbroker, Night of the Iguana, Topkapi* and *Lillith, Goldfinger* and *Fail-Safe, The Naked Kiss* and *Zorba the Greek*. He was prepping for a monstro blockbusterama packed with king-thesps! He learned from experience that you

---

49 She called Chet Baker by his middle name.—*ed.*

needed to open as big as a Kennedy head wound! He loved *Sleep* but the showman in him, the Cecil B. *DeOrr*, didn't want another nouvelle vague rim job. *Jules and Rim!*

JOHN LAHR They heard Buñuel was at Shepperton, shooting interiors for *Diary Of A Chambermaid*—a ridiculous lie, most likely trumped up by Roar himself. He absolutely reveled in pranks, treasure hunts, that sort of thing. A rumor that Keith Moon went along on the night I'm about to speak of proved not to be true.

So, there they were: Boodles, Francis, George Dyer, and Roar—in a schoolgirl's uniform!—creeping around Claridge's like cat burglars. Which by the way George actually *was*. Roar insisted there'd been a fresh sighting of El Maestro. It was straight out of *A Hard Day's Night*, a film they'd seen that very afternoon. Sheer Buñuelmania!

ROGER ORR[50] I don't remember much about that particular outing but have no doubt it happened. Enough people have told me so!

Years later, I visited Allen Ginsberg when he was dying. In New York. I'm not sure how or why it came up but Allen said he heard that story over the years and happened to be staying at Claridge's that night. Some fancy sponsor put him up (Allen was very good at finding fancy sponsors) and when he looked out the window, he saw Francis and I crawling along like rooftop Buster Keatons. He knew Francis because they'd met in Tangier in the late Fifties, when Allen and Bill [Burroughs] were trying to get *Naked Lunch* in some kind of order. Francis could be prickly but Allen said everyone got along famously. The funny thing is, Frannie never mentioned them to me, not one word. Which would have been *strange* because he was a tremendous gossip and knew I was pals with Allen and Jack when I was young.

Now that I'm telling you this, I'm wondering if it wasn't an end-stage hallucination. Morphine's quite the mother's little helper.

WILHELM "BOODLES" DOMINO We got an entire suite at Claridge's— must have been five hundred quid—Roger called it a *"quid* pro *oh!"* George

---

50 Interview with Samantha Dunn, *Orange County Register* (2006), "Roger, Over and Out."

passed out while Rodge and I went at it in bed. Francis was very drunk and unable to join. Miss Otis regrets, I suppose . . .

ROGER ORR[51] . . . I watched our bodies, out of body, for hours and entered a chimeric space; down, down, down the rabbitfuck wormhole. "To whom do lions cast their gentle looks? Not to the beast that would usurp their den. The smallest worm will turn being trodden on, and doves will peck in safeguard of their brood." In my schoolgirl's skirt, Boodle didn't skirt the tissue, his worm turned within, the turn of the screwed, and *my* worm turned not in revenge or perversion but in love, pure Love. . . . All this presaged India and the reawakening of demonic work ethic culminating in *Romantic Comedy*, my thousand-armed Kali that slew Raktabīja box office vanities. That night at Claridge's was my Blakean vision, my dong of innocence: Ginsberg heard the voice of Master William but I heard the *vice* and was transformed by cosmic carnival knowledge. Underneath, then on top, Angel Boodle lorded over me with its perfect tits, elysian smells, cuntcave backside, sins and sinews, and we became One. (*How the West and East Were One.*) I knew *then* that one day I would transform, and had the great sense I was not yet what I already was: both woman and man. In that semenal [*sic*] moment, I tasted the Infinite. Joseph-coated by Angel Boodles in a jackedrabbithole jacket of gender-spirit hues.

The night I got sober.

KENNETH TYNAN Then suddenly, he was gone. Roger Orr had left the London studio, the building, the world. Without trace, tail, or trail. Francis was distraught. Boodles thought it funny—he knew that's what Roar *did*. When he had an epiphany, you could count on him to vaporize.

SCATTER HOLBROOK Suze and I were well-settled in Maui when he called, obviously manic. We bought a house on the beach with her father's inheritance—in Suze's name—but there wasn't much left after that. I was freelancing. Videotaping weddings and local events . . . Roger offered to help, and I told Suze absolutely not. There was no way I was going to agree to that.

Anyway, he called to say he was working on a script, "just steps away from

---

51 From *Long Day's Journal into Night* by Roger Orr, pp. 210–211 (Harcourt Brace, 1996).

where dear Keats breathed his last." A bit of a lofty thing to say for someone hell-bent on writing a film "that's going to make more money than *My Fair Lady*."[52]

SUZE BERKOWITZ He invited us to Italy but there was just no way. Plus, you never knew which Roar you were getting when you showed up. Besides, I was pregnant. We didn't tell him; we didn't tell anyone. I was too superstitious. To put it mildly.

QUENTIN TARANTINO *Gift from God* was kind of amazing on so many levels. First of all, Bird Rabineau was named "Mika," which means "God's gift," but of course at that point he didn't *know* she was his mother. And it's very *E.T.*—Spielberg talks a lot about it being an inspiration. But the version Roar wrote in Rome was *way* different than the script he pounded out in '68 after getting back from India. He showed it to me. Without India, it'd have been terrible. Maybe not *terrible*, but well—no! Shit! It would have been terrible!

* * * * * * * * *

from *ROARSHACH: ORR ON ORR BY SPIELBERG*[53]

SPIELBERG: What happened with the "Roman" draft of *Gift*? Quentin told me you showed it to him and I got jealous.
ORR: We were smoking dope, and I dragged it out and Quentin just . . . swallowed it whole. I watched his face and it reminded me of Herzog listening to the tape of that guy being killed by the bear.[54] You know, Werner says to the girlfriend, "You must never listen to this." I say to you: Steven, you must never read that!
SPIELBERG: What would you say was the main problem?
ORR: It was saccharine and very television. When I left

---

52 Released in 1964, *My Fair Lady* brought in $72 million at the box office—nearly $2 billion in 2022 dollars, adjusting for inflation.—*ed.*
53 Lighthouse, *American Masters*, Vol. 13 (2012).
54 In *Grizzly Man* (2005).—*ed.*

London—precipitously—my intentions were pure. But the method of delivery somehow became corrupted. I've always been fascinated with that kind of infection; the cancer of ambition. Genius gets away with it, *sometimes*, and when it doesn't, well, better a rare lymphoma than a garden variety basal cell carcinoma. I'm a dermatologist so I can say that. Welles is an example . . . The "problem" with the initial draft of *Gift* was simple. I lost my mind—in the worst Hollywood sense—and wanted to give the people what they wanted. Oh, that's the great tragedy of any artist. That's the beginning of the end.

* * * * * * * * * *

ANA DUVERNAY (*filmmaker*) He soldiered on, but the *Gift from God* script got worse and worse. Then one day he ran into a hollow-eyed man on the street, in Trastevere. A beggar wearing a spic-and-span dhoti.

Roar took him for an espresso, and his life changed forever.

STEVE SHAINBERG (*director*) I'm not sure "the American" ever existed but it makes a wonderful story. Roar was all about Story. Story was king.

DAN LEVY (*actor*) What is *wrong* with people? The American is *so* real, *one hundred percent*. They met on the Spanish Steps—don't you love it? "Roger and the Mystic." Can it *get* more romantic? I always call him Roger—not that I'm *always* talking about him, I only talk about him *most* of the time!—and when people ask why I call him *Roger* instead of *Roar*, I smile the way you'd smile at a stranger's child and say, "His close friends call him Roger." My sad little joke because I never got the chance to meet him. Which *kills* me, breaks my *heart*. It was even worse when I heard he was a fan of *Schitt's Creek*. We all *died* because Dad's even more obsessed with Roger than I am. If that's possible. Which it isn't. But Dad calls him Roar. So gauche.

Back to "the American": Roger described him in *Long Day's Journal*—*Volume 3*, if you must know—as a blue-eyed, Rasta-haired blonde with "an electric smile, as if still plugged into the Source." I *memorized* the whole passage! "The American's smile was incense and star musk." Star musk! I'm fainting. And the American *knew* things; he was definitely what they call an *adept*. He told Roger, "Your mother is not your mother." And that was in the first five minutes!

I *so* want to meet a hot mystic American on the Spanish Steps! I want to meet *anything* star musky. I don't even know what that *is* but I *want* it!

CHRISTOPHER ISHERWOOD (*novelist, diarist*) I do know that he saw "the American" every day for two weeks—a kind of *dokusan*. I'm old and the more appropriate word escapes me. The governing topic was Advaita, a philosophy Roger was inherently comfortable with . . . an old slipper, so to speak. "The American" was returning to India, which he'd apparently fled with his nondualistic tail between his legs; he committed the grave sin of having doubted his teacher. A similar thing happened to [Carlos] Castaneda. My God, it happened to *me*—it's quite common with students and seekers. When don Juan's teachings got "too much," Castaneda would retreat to L.A. from the Sonoran Desert, to lick his wounds and regroup.

Anyway, the fellow said he was returning to Varanasi and suggested Roger come along.

KENNETH BRANAGH (*actor, director*) Don't forget that *Kim* was one of Roar's great favorites—and Maugham's *The Razor's Edge*. In both, the protagonists meet itinerant gurus who profoundly change their lives. He'd always been a lover of spiritual adventure stories, "sorcerer's apprentice" stuff. What *really* happened? On a more prosaic level, Roar had the rude awakening that his script was abominable. He was too proud to admit it because his *exeunt* from Reece Mews had been so bloody dramatic. He was a *bit* of a drama queen. But with those awful drafts of *Gift from God*, Roar kept finding himself with egg on his face. I guess he thought, if it's going to be egg, it may as well be Kodi Guddu Gasagasala Kura![55]

KAY LARSON (*American Buddhism historian*) It's generally thought the American was a fictional character based on Bhagavan Das—Kermit Michael Riggs—a seeker from Laguna Beach who became famous after Ram Dass wrote about him in *Be Here Now*. Riggs introduced Ram Dass to his teacher, Neem Karoli Baba, who became Ram Dass's guru as well. The question is:

---

55 Indian recipe for boiled eggs.—*ed.*

did Roger and Bhagavan Das actually meet? Highly plausible. From the way Roger tells it, he and "the American" crossed paths in Rome in '64; we do know that before Bhagavan Das went to India for his first time, he did a lot of traveling around Europe. He felt especially comfortable in Rome. And yet, in Roger Orr's version, the regretful American had evicted himself from the Garden, so to speak, and longed to reunite with his guru—something that I know never happened with Riggs. So, I think "the American" was an amalgam, one more piece of fragrant, colorful cloth in a gifted storyteller's patchwork quilt.

SAM KASHNER Allen [Ginsberg] told me that Roar reached out around the time he would have been working on that doomed script in Rome. In '64? He said he was about to go to India and asked for a few tips—he knew Allen and Peter [Orlovsky] were there in '62.

Allen loved that "Old Angel Boy" (his name for Roar) was staying in the same room Keats died—though maybe it was Shelley's. I should know this. . . . No, it couldn't have been, because I'm pretty sure Shelley died in a boat. I *do* remember reading about Shelley's body being cremated but his heart wouldn't burn because it was too . . . calcified? His heart was calcified from TB. *Keats* died of that too—TB was like the uber-COVID of its day.

So, he asked Allen to hook him up. Allen said, "Go see Trungpa,[56] in Dalhousie!" I don't think Roar ever did though. I mean, go see Trungpa.

CHELSEA HANDLER (*comedian***)** What was he looking for? I don't know. Same thing anyone who went to India in the Sixties was, I guess . . . but compared to now? To fucking *now*? I'd go back in a heartbeat. Wanna know how people get spiritual *now*? They get ass implants and upload photos of their shit on #ratemypoo. And when the implants go south and look like stinky, black, moldy cheese, they want to show you pictures of *that*, from their hospital room. That's what fucking nirvana is *now*. You get spiritual by apologizing on IG for being *born*. That was a different time, a *better* time—especially because Roger Orr was in it.

---

56 Chögyam Trungpa Rinpoche later became Ginsberg's teacher in America.—*ed.*

PATTI SMITH (*singer, poet*) The guy he met in Italy was absolutely a real person, and *not* Bhagavan Das! There's a passage in *Be Here Now* where Ram Dass talks about Roar and "the American" passing through.

* * * * * * * * *

RAM DASS
from BE HERE NOW[57]

Bhagavan brought me into the small, white room—it was very clean and fragrant—and introduced me to Maharaji [Neem Karoli Baba]. The love that emanated from him gave me the jolt of my life. He asked us to sit and began to speak in Hindi, which I half-understood. He kept saying a word that I'd never heard before: *Roo-jair*. Which isn't too far from the Hindi "water" or "sap." Bhagavan was smiling away, as if in on a private joke. Seeing my confusion, one of the sadhus began to translate.

Apparently, I had instantly reminded Maharaji of a "very special boy," *Roo-jair*, who had visited a few years before. "Very rich boy, like you. But younger! More handsome! Richer! Richer!" They all laughed and Maharaji laughed the loudest. I pretended not to be jealous of Roo-jair, and suddenly got weirdly paranoid. My fragile ego only wanted to hear "You are the One, the one and only!" When I asked Maharaji if he was Roo-jair's teacher, he shook his head. "No need! Roo-jair already *has* teacher. *Roo-jair's* teacher: *suffering*. Suffering always best teacher!" The sadhu said that Roo-jair was brought to Nainital by one of Maharaji's other "favorites"—another Westerner, like Bhagavan Das. Now it was Bhagavan's turn to be the butt of the Maharaji's jokes. "But Ro-jair's 'American' more young! More handsome! More enlightened!"

Unlike me, Bhagavan seemed delighted by the ribbing.

* * * * * * * * *

---

57 *Be Here Now* by Ram Dass, pp. 113–118 (Lama Foundation, San Cristobal, New Mexico, 1971).

SCATTER HOLBROOK Suze wanted to get hitched. The whole City Hall thing never appealed to me—I was more like Roger's brother Jonny when it came to that—but Suze had a traditional side, and I was more than happy to oblige. I was crazy about her. Still am. When she proposed, I said, "Babe? The first argument we have, I promise I'll write you a song about whatever you're wearing. But it's gonna be the shittiest song ever written."

It wasn't an urgent thing but obviously they were still married and I needed to talk to Roger about getting a divorce. So, it was disconcerting on a *lot* of levels when he went missing. I even got in touch with Francis, who said Roger vanished into thin air. He didn't know where Boodles was, either, but was adamant the two weren't together and had gone their separate ways. Laughlin was distraught. Everyone was fairly certain something awful happened and we prepared ourselves for the worst. Eight nail-biting months later, I got the call. I didn't know who it was at first. The connection was good but he didn't sound at *all* like himself. I remember thinking, *Is this an imposter?* You know, a scam. I had brain static.

He was in a hospital in Bombay. I could have gone to see him but didn't want to leave Suze. Roger was away when Aurelia died—I wasn't about to dabble with *that* scenario again.

SUZE BERKOWITZ I finally grabbed the phone from Scatter. Roger said, "Hi, Wifey," and I just broke down. I said something like, "Where the fuck were you, asshole? We thought you were dead!"—the usual sweet nothings one grew accustomed to whispering in that impossible man's ear. He was sweet and remorseful, then of course I asked what had happened and if he was okay. He said he got sick with "traveler's diorama" and was on the mend. But I could hear the weakness in his voice and it scared me. I don't know why but I blurted out that I just had a baby.

He laughed then cried, and I did too.

SCATTER HOLBROOK He said, "You ought to marry that girl, Scat. We'll make it happen." Typical of him—to read our minds. I was just so damn happy. The only thing I cared about was that he was alive.

SUZE BERKOWITZ When I asked what he'd been doing over there all that time, he said, "I've been with my teachers." I said, "Did you find a coupla gurus?"

I was trying to keep it light. He said, "Oh yes, right here at the hospital. I didn't have to go a mountain cave to find Mother . . . Father . . . Seraphim . . . Aurelia . . . *you*. . . . " It was cryptic and unsettling, so *Roger*, and beautiful too. Part of me totally understood. But I was still afraid—that I'd never see him again.

How could I live without seeing him again?

DR. EUNICE LAVAR [Neem Karoli Baba] was one of the big guns. One of the important ones. He was Ram Dass' guru—and that piece of shit opportunist Larry Brilliant glommed onto him too. Even Steve Jobs went looking for Baba in '75, only to learn he had died the year before. . . .

A week after meeting Baba, Roger did a very Roger-like thing: he split! Later, he told me if he was going to wash anyone's tootsies, "it'll be the feet of a mountain." He was quite enamored of Sri Ramana Maharshi— the guru's guru—because after a near-death experience, Ramana found the ultimate teacher: the holy mountain of Lord Shiva. So, Roar left all the fools on the hill and commenced, as Granny said on *The Beverly Hillbillies*, to wander—an age-old tradition among sadhus. The hajj to nowhere, the circular trek to the gateless gate, the city-less city . . . He got dysentery and spent months being cared for by a family who believed him to be a holy man, which he *was*, by definition, because all kinds of things happen when you lose a third of your body weight and start hanging around the portal twixt this world and the next. You get strange. And he was strange to begin with.

Roger had a lifelong fear of inheriting Batten disease. His baby sister died of it, you know. Even if they'd been related by blood, the fear was irrational because he was long past the general due date of a Batten efflorescence. For kicks, we'd do blood tests in Chicago and they'd of course be negative. I'd say, "So—still think you'll get it?" He'd say, "Buddy boy? I'm Batten a thousand." If you haven't heard, med school's a laboratory of neurotic fears, which didn't help. Interns self-diagnose with fatal diseases three times a day. I was certain I had Creutzfeldt-Jakob . . . Now, Batten is typically an infantile or juvenile syndrome but does occur in adults—under CLN4 disease, or Kufs Type B— though that's very, very rare. Like, lightning strike-rare. It progresses slowly, often ending in dementia, which is the thing that terrified Roger most. When he got sick in India, his head meter broke and the needle spun; he thought fate had finally caught up. Roger had the revelation his guru wasn't a mountain at all, but a hereditary degenerative neurological disorder. Thank God he met Dr. Gupta Ganesh, a holy fucking mountain of a physician.

No one but Shiva could have arranged that.

CHRISTOPHER ISHERWOOD "Sri Ganesha" was the name Maugham used for the great guru Ramana Maharshi in *The Razor's Edge*. Dr. Gupta Ganesh's grandparents knew Ramana and for a time lived at his ashram in Tamil Nadu. Of course, Ganesh is the God known as "the remover of obstacles." In Roger's case, the doctor couldn't have been more aptly named.

DR. EUNICE LAVAR Gupta went to the Orr School of Medicine in Chicago—what are the odds of that? A perfect example of your karma and tax dollars at work. He graduated about ten years before Roger and I did, then returned home to practice in Bombay. They call it Mumbai now; what a bore. I heard that Gupta met Mug and Bunny when they flew in for some gala. But that's unverified.

DR. GUPTA GANESH (*epidemiologist*) It wasn't typical—though certainly not unusual—for the ward to see the occasional American hippie with dysentery, malnutrition, what have you. Or suffering from the effect of a drug or drugs ingested during their sojourn. The surname did get my attention. When he confirmed he was indeed one of *those* Orrs, I was of course intrigued. When I asked after his family—I'd never met his parents but there was a large, looming "welcome" photo of them in the lobby of the dormitory building—Roger said, "She's dead." He smiled and said, "Everyone's dead."

During my exam he was alert and present, but at the same time "elsewhere." Colors were very bright, he said, a phenomenon that sometimes prompted him to cover his eyes with his hands. The colors would quickly change, as in a kaleidoscope. He also saw himself as very tiny, as if just a few inches tall; other times he considered himself so enormous he had to bend his head to avoid being crushed by the ceiling. He added that time itself had become plastic. Wrinkled surfaces smoothed and smooth surfaces wrinkled . . . we call these sorts of descriptions and forms *metamorphopsia*. I wondered if he'd smuggled in a psychotropic, which wouldn't have been unheard of. When I brought it up, he smiled the familiar "ward" smile of all the youthful pilgrims who'd crashed against the hard wall of samadhi.

The prognosis wasn't stellar.

ROBERT THURMAN (*author, translator*) I got letters from the hospital in Mumbai. Very learned. Rough-hewn, auto-didactic, brilliant.

JOANNE LAMONT-DUPRÉ (*producer*) I received a few weird telegrams. I kept them. Here's one: "Dear Joanne"—spelled d-e-e-r—"I'm in the dark bollyWOOD doing PREVIEWS of ALICE IN WUNDERKIND. With her NOW. The WHITE RABBIS are eating the LOX OFFICE receipts!!!"

Triple exclamation points.

Yes. Well. I have a whole shoebox of them.

DR. GUPTA GANESH He knew that his mind was going and was rather calm about it. "Apparently," he said, "that's the whole point."

Tests revealed that during his travels, he contracted something called coxsackievirus B1. In his case, it caused "peduncular hallucinosis"—and something called AIWS, otherwise known as Alice in Wonderland syndrome. Those distortions of perception come from lesions in the cerebral peduncles, more typically occurring in adults with migraine and epilepsy. Sometimes it happens to a healthy individual, in the *bardo* of hypnagogia; the transition to sleep.

SCATTER HOLBROOK "Alice in Wonderland syndrome"—you couldn't make that shit up. Maybe Roger could, but he didn't have to.

DR. GUPTA GANESH A truckload of steroids, antivirals, and antibiotics did the trick—though once the doors of perception open, you never get them all the way closed, do you? Artists by nature have easier access to such things; Roger always had one foot here, one foot *there*. We stayed in touch until his death. The visions persisted, he said, though "without the flood." More like lovely canals he could watch from the balcony.

ROGER ORR[58] I experienced a panoply of visions—a panopticon—I was

---

58 Ibid., p. 85.

a guard in a vast, circular, Escherian prison. I saw *everything*, like that famous instruction given by Krishna in the *Bhagavad Gita*: that this life is a dream, a play, and one must act out one's part. Down the rabbit hole I went—with all the Lilliputian players,[59] including myself, already dead, and nothing to do but fulfill my destiny. Except in *this* vision, the dead were prisoners. There was Mother Bunny and Father Mug—I'm sure Bird and "Wriggle" Petry were in there too, because how could they not have been?—Seraphim and Aurelia and Suze and Scatter, the whole lot of them reified, magnificent zombies like in *They Sleep*, warriors all, not on the battlefield but clinging to the bars of their cells. Which I suppose is the same thing.

GAVIN DE BECKER (*author, risk management specialist*) I provided him with a protective detail in the Eighties and Nineties. He had some death threats when he learned who his mother and father were; white supremacists were targeting him and fanatics on the left as well, who weren't happy with what they interpreted as Roar's "historical polemics against Blacks." So, I knew him first as a client. I was already a huge fan of his films, his music, his writings . . . and knew a little bit about his transformation in India. I'd been planning on going there to see Ramesh Balsekar in Mumbai for my fiftieth birthday. Ramesh was an Advaita master and student of Nisargadatta Maharaj, who wrote the great *I Am That*. When I mentioned that Ramesh gave *satsang* in a neighborhood near Breach Candy, Roar's eyes lit up—that was where he recovered from the great sickness that befell him: in Breach Candy Hospital. He wanted to come but his schedule wouldn't allow.

ROGER ORR[60] I assumed that Dr. Goo (my name for the illustrious Dr. Gupta Ganesh) had set a record player by the hospital bed—but the music was in my head. I raised and lowered the volume with a single thought-command . . . songs of Schubert, Mahler's *Kindertotenlieder*, *The Isle of the Dead*, "Bali Hai" (transposed by Scriabin!), "Our Day Will Come," Doris Day singing a quite acceptable version of "Folsom Prison Blues"—and Coltrane's "My Favorite Things." I *accessed* Trane's new one, "A Love Supreme"—a brassily

---

59 In AIWS, a phenomenon called micropsia.—*ed.*
60 From *Either/Orr: The Rest of Roger Orr*, p. 83 (Juvenal, 2021).

cosmic, sinuous revelation that healed, nurtured, sustained. It wasn't lost on me (nothing was lost, everything was lost) that John and I were on Impulse.[61] *All pulse and impulses* were connected, all Everything. The dam of separateness broke, and the dawns did too. Furiously, I scribbled something on a scrap of the *Hindustani Times*: words and music to "Break of Dawn."[62] I thanked God/s for the privilege.

But Trane was my North Star—the miraculous Dr. Goo tracked down "Om" at a record store on Jubilee Street. When hallucinations came, the deep breathing-out of it saved me: *OMMMMMM*. I hadn't vibrated like that since Allen [Ginsberg] showed me how to chant when I was a kiddle. But AG was long gone: there was only Trane the prophet, Trane the cosmo-demonic, cosmo-symphonic, cosmo-shamanic Other: "I make all things clean. *I am OM*." I sang it ten thousand times and eventually replaced *OM* with *home*. I was willing myself home.

That's when I knew I would live.

GAVIN DE BECKER I told him a story that he said—his phrase—was a "diamond perfect encapsulation" of his own experience in India.

I went to see a Vedic astrologer in Los Angeles. His name was Chakrapani and he'd done the charts of Castaneda, George Harrison, many others. I told him I was thinking of going to India, and he suggested that if I ever made it to Bodh Gaya I should sleep under the Bodhi tree, where Buddha became enlightened. He smiled when he said it; I wasn't sure he was serious or if such a thing were even possible but the idea stayed in my head.

A few years later, I had the opportunity to go to Varanasi. It may be the oldest city on Earth; it's definitely one of the most sacred. I had the idea to leave my wallet and phone at the hotel and go wandering. All I brought with me was water. I spent hours sitting against a wall, meditating. No one bothered me, no one asked for money. I was feeling quite empty—and full of myself—when I decided, "You're ready to visit Bodh Gaya."

I got a late start. I hired a driver and we pulled up to a huge temple complex. It was closing time and the guard wouldn't let me in. I waved down a

---

61 Bob Thiele's label, Impulse, also released "Try a Little Tenderness."
62 "Break of Dawn," the theme from *Romantic Comedy*, won the Academy Award for Best Song.—*ed.*

well-dressed man who looked like he was charge and I made a large donation on the spot. He told the guard I could stay.

I walked toward some kind of distant commotion and there it was, like a dream: monks circumnavigating the Bodhi tree. I couldn't believe my good fortune. I went back to the car and grabbed a pillow and mosquito repellant from the trunk along with a large, thin piece of fabric to use as a blanket. I told the driver to come back at dawn then went back inside and laid down beneath the tree. The man I gave the donation to was gone. The sullen guard stared me down. Suddenly, klieg lights went on and the air filled with bugs. It was like being inside a snow globe when you shake it. I tried to meditate but was strangled by the hubris of sitting under the Bodhi tree. I began to compose my tellings and retellings of this amazing experience, to make a list of those with whom I'd share my "gift," then edited and reedited the list. At least I had some awareness and was able to watch the ludicrous calisthenics of Mind . . . occasionally, I opened my eyes and saw the monks walking silently around the temple. They never stopped. One woman took ten mindful paces toward the tree, then ten away from it—for hours. Next, my busy head became focused on impressing the monks with the stillness of my meditation. I resolved that my sitting meditation should appear more impressive than their walking one. From the looks of them—some aged, some stooped—they'd been doing this for twenty or thirty years . . . but I'd show *them.* Only later did I realize that the monks, dressed in white, were all women. I was the single man, the single being who wore black, the single one who didn't belong. It wasn't just mosquitoes that objected to my being there: locusts got under my legs and *pushed.* Pushed hard!

I watched a monk round the building and approach the tree. She scanned the ground, sometimes bending to study something—a dead locust?—then kept walking. I saw her pick up a leaf that had fallen. *Leaves from the Bodhi Tree.* I hadn't thought of that, how cool it would be to take away a leaf from the tree where the Buddha had been enlightened! Now I'd have so much more to talk about with friends—and strangers!—*women*—the story *and* a leaf. (Or two. Or three . . .) I was reminded of all the movies I'd seen where someone wakes up from a dream clutching a talisman brought back from another world. I became fully alert and on the lookout. When the first one floated down, another monk materialized and scooped it up. I thought, "Hey! That one's in *my* territory—that belongs to *me.*" Seeing how silly I was, I made my peace that the monk and I were One Being; that *her* having a leaf from the Bodhi Tree was the same as having it *myself*. I was growing more spiritual by the minute. The story was getting better.

A day earlier, I had a cough and scratchy throat and now I was shivering on the ground, balled up like a dog. Maybe walking would help—yes! I'd impress everyone by shifting gears—being fluid enough to do *different meditations*—walking around the temple like the others. I wasn't sure which left me in more discomfort: being stiff and freezing and feverish as I sauntered through clouds of insects or being paralyzed on the cold, wet ground. Near dawn, an aggressive guard ran toward me.

"You go now. Temple opening, you go now!"

I tried to convey that I'd paid someone for the privilege but that order was given hours ago by a man who meant nothing to him. I staggered through the darkness and out the back gate. Dogs were everywhere, growling and advancing on each other, fighting over territory—over leaves!—in the empty marketplace. The square came alive with morning prayers, soon replaced by the language of commerce, noisy enough that even the dogs couldn't be heard. I returned to the temple grounds, where a morning meditation ceremony was underway. I felt warm again and marveled at the beauty of the scene. I walked around the Bodhi tree again—my old friend. I resolved to get a leaf, but the grounds had been swept clean. As I was about to go, I spotted a large, perfect specimen—with no competing monk within sight. With great stealth, I slipped it in my jacket pocket. I had to pass through a gift shop to get to where my driver would be waiting.

There, in small baskets on the counter were items for sale: leaves from the Bodhi Tree, a dollar each.

As we neared the hotel, I reached into my jacket for the leaf, but it was gone. In the excitement of looking around to make sure that no one saw me claim it, I'd missed the pocket. There was only emptiness.

SCATTER HOLBROOK On New Year's Day [1965], we got a telegram saying he was coming back to the States. The house sitter in Maui read it to us— it was serendipity because we were in San Francisco for the holidays, visiting Suze's mom, who hadn't met the baby. The telegram was from Bombay; it was obvious he was already traveling so we didn't bother to respond. Suze thought it'd be a nice surprise to show up at the airport.

We went at the appointed time and it was an absolute madhouse. All those pesky holiday travelers. We brought the baby—a mistake!—but couldn't wait for him to meet her. She cried like crazy. The flight from India had a connection in Montreal, so by the time he landed he would have been in the air for close to two days. Customs took forever. We waited for an hour after customs seemed to have cleared and at a certain point looked at each other with the telepathic thought: *He's not coming! Of course, he isn't. What the hell were we thinking?* As we walked toward the exit, Suze turned back for a last look—and let out a great yelp. He was very thin, *very* handsome (as usual), with this magnificent light in his eyes.

Oh, we knew we were going to hear some stories.

SUZE BERKOWITZ He picked up the baby and held her to the sky. She stopped crying for the first time since we got there! There was *so* much joy. . . . He asked what she was called, and for a moment I thought he'd forgotten.

I realized that we never told him.

"Alice? Meet Godfather Roar!"

Well, his jaw dropped to the floor when he heard the name. He said that was John Coltrane's mother's name—and Coltrane's wife's too. He told us all the Alice in Wonderland syndrome stuff on the way home.

"In India, *Alice* showed me her world," he said, then looked into our baby's eyes. "I'm going to spend the rest of my life showing you mine."

CHAPTER EIGHT

Romantic Comedy

ROMANTIC COMEDY (1968)
by Andrew Sarris
The *Village Voice*[63]

I'll come right out and say it: not since Lubitsch's *The Marriage Circle*, Cukor's *Holiday*, or Sturges's *The Lady Eve* has a filmmaker delivered a nuanced, breakneck comedy of such dark-hued finesse, light-fingered genius and seizure-inducing, heart-strung hilarity. In *Romantic Comedy*, perhaps the first meta-look at the genre, Roger Orr has thrown in death, betrayal and the profanely sacred—everything that in the hands of another director would surely feel like the *kitsch* sink. A roller-coaster ride of heart and soul, a throw of the dice to the wind, it's got style to burn, and burn it does: it hits below the belt but in a good way. For ninety minutes, you forget where you are and *who* you are, remembering only that thing of which you're an honored, grateful player: the indefatigably poignant Human Comedy, antic, romantic, and otherwise. Putting aside the brilliantly spotty, heretical, ill-timed existential horror-noir *They Sleep by Night*—released on the day of the Kennedy assassination—it's the most impressive directorial debut of a young filmmaker since Truffaut's *The 400 Blows*.

* * * * * * * * * *

---

63 *Village Voice*, May 12, 1966, vol. 22, no. 32.

ROGER ORR (*accepting Oscar for Best Song, 40th Academy Awards, April 10, 1968*)[64] It feels obscenely frivolous to be honored for a song tonight—to be honored for anything—but I think I speak for everyone who was asked to come onstage and accept their little gold statuette: tonight, all honors belong to Dr. Martin Luther King. [*sustained applause*] The great Spencer Tracy [*he falters; applause*] privileged us this past year with two performances,[65] each written in that indelible, invisible ink Spence used so effortlessly—the ink of Everyman who is angry and hurt and just, Everyman who is tender and forgiving then angry and hurt and forgiving all over again—the mystical *American* ink he dipped into to write his characters and to write the character of a nation. [*looks skyward while clutching Oscar*] This one's for you, old man.

. . .

SCATTER HOLBROOK He was weak. He was still under medical care—a colleague of Dr. Ganesh's, in Los Angeles. He wasn't having visions anymore—none that he spoke of. His doctor thought Hawaii would be good for him, so he came to Maui and stayed a few months. It was good for us too. He swam in the ocean in the morning then worked on his script for the rest of the day. At night, he'd hang with the baby while Suze cooked a big dinner. We heard him singing to Alice. I think "Break of Dawn," which he wrote in India, and snatches of "Passages." I remember because he sang them over and over. He was workshopping songs with Alice!

SAM WASSON He jettisoned *Gift from God.* That was one of his strengths. He could "kill his darlings"—or put them in comas. He tucked the script away and didn't make that movie for twenty-five years.

SUZE BERKOWITZ When I asked what the script was about, he'd say,

---

64 Turning down the Academy's invitation to sing "Break of Dawn," Orr finally agreed to accompany Charles Aznavour on piano.—*ed.*

65 While Tracy's performance in *Romantic Comedy* was considered by many to be the capstone of his career, he was instead (posthumously) nominated for Best Actor in *Guess Who's Coming to Dinner.*—*ed.*

"Life. Just life." I'd be a little snarky. "Oh! How specific! *Thank you.*" He'd grumble and say, "It's a romantic comedy, Suze. Happy now?" He'd have that smirky little smile because he knew there was no way I'd believe that. He was *not* a romantic comedy kind of guy. And after what he'd just been through, the whole touch-and-go thing in India, it sounded so absurd . . . but it *was* a romantic comedy. I think he gave it that title just to spite me!

Ooh, such a devil.

GRACE SLICK He was in Maui and Laugh was trying to get him to come home—for her, that was always San Francisco. He said he couldn't, he was busy working on a script, yadda yadda. I don't know if he was commuting from the island to see doctors in L.A. . . . . They spent hours on the phone though. Why did she never fly out there? I have no fucking idea. Hawaii was never her thing. Anyway, I was staying with her in the Haight. *Everyone* came through that crazy Victorian house—it had twenty rooms and a cupola. Each room, even the outside, was painted in different colors. Stokely [Carmichael] stayed for weeks; they were having a mad affair. Shit got more urgent when Malcolm was killed . . . all of that was Laugh's *real* priority. She tried conscripting her brother for marches in Atlanta or wherever. He had zero interest.

STANLEY MOUSE (*artist*) He quoted Indian scripture. He'd tell his sister, "We're already dead"—nothing can be changed, you know, because everything's already happened. She thought it was all loony tune bullshit. I love her to death but Laughlin doesn't have a spiritual bone in her fabulous R. Crumb body. Allen [Ginsberg] used to tease her mercilessly about that. But she cut Roar slack because he'd been so sick and Suze kept telling her how worried she was about his brain being broken. . . . Believe it or not, Suze could be a tad square herself. That's why I liked to call her Suzy Creamcheese, 'cause Suzy Creamcheese she was not. Hell, in the Sixties, you met thousands of folks who rapped the way Roar did. And that was before breakfast.

JONNY "STAGE DOOR" ORR When I moved to Oregon after Mom died, I stayed with Kesey's folks at the family farm in Pleasant Hill. When Ken got busted in La Honda for possession and fled to Mex, I knocked around up there in my van for a few years, but around the time Roger got back from India I bought a place of my own just north of Coos Bay. A hundred and twenty acres—horses, chickens, hogs, hippies, the whole nine yurts. He'd call from Maui, and we had good talks. I'd share my own "explorations," how I'd been studying the stars. I was heavy into Aleister Crowley's tarot cards and learned how to do readings. Acupuncture too. And learning about herbs and shit for our garden. . . . He was genuinely interested, which meant a lot because I was still in thrall to my brother. Always seeking his approval. I'd have gone to Maui to see him but developed a convenient case of agoraphobia, which became chronic. I joke about it but it was actually kind of crippling.

He did invite me to the Academy Awards for the *Romantic Comedy* wingding. I felt that was important and bit the bullet. Smoked a bunch of weed and drove down with my old lady. I hadn't seen my brother in five or six years and bawled my head off. Went full Stage Door Jonny.

CAMERON CROWE (director) [In the spring of '65] he moved into the penthouse suite at the Pierre and typewriter-boogied on *Romantic Comedy*. Threw away everything he'd done in Maui—he needed New York City energy to get it right. But that same energy delayed things a bit. All his life, he bragged it never took him more than ten days to write a script; *Romantic Comedy* took six months. He finished on Thanksgiving Day.

SAM WASSON He went to the movies three times a day because basically he hadn't seen a film since London. 1965 was an amazing year: *Repulsion*, *Pierrot le Fou* and *Alphaville*, *Zhivago* and *Sound of Music*, *Help!*, *Loves of a Blonde*—his old friend Miloš—and Father Buñuel's *Simon of the Desert*. Roar was obsessed with *Simon of the Desert*, especially that freaky jet plane transition. When I interviewed him for the *Times* [2008], he said he saw *Red Beard* that year too and got so depressed by its majestic perfection that he took to his bed for a week. He was literally sickened and decided never to make a film again. Never write another song. . . .

Then there was *Darling* and *What's New Pussycat?*—*Pussycat* was why he cast Peter O'Toole in *Romantic Comedy*[66]—*Mickey One*, *Dr. Goldfoot and the Bikini Machine*, *The Hallelujah Trail*—

He was ravenous.

---

66 O'Toole was replaced by Tom Courtenay two weeks before shooting.—*ed.*

BADGE KEENER (*casting agent*) We had Julie Christie and Peter [O'Toole]—and for about a minute, Roar even wanted Nic[67] to shoot it. He begged Carlo Ponti to produce but Ponti was otherwise engaged. I think Carlo'd just been kidnapped again! When Peter dropped out, we got Tom [Courtenay], another *Zhivago* alumnus. Roger's little joke was, "Can we call this 'A David Lean Production'?"

ANJELICA HUSTON I was fifteen when I did *Romantic Comedy*. I had a teacher on set and sometimes Spenny [Spencer Tracy] "audited" a class. He would just sit very quietly and watch. It didn't make me self-conscious. . . . It was obvious he was sick, that he was suffering. Even at that age, I was mindful. After the lesson, we'd chat. He wanted to know about me—what I was interested in, if I had a fella. He talked to me like I was an adult. I remember him saying, "Always be true to yourself." When you're young, you really haven't heard that—it's not a cliché. And coming from him, it sank in. He spoke of my father and how much he admired him and told me something I never knew. He said he was visiting Kate [Hepburn] in Murchison Falls during *The African Queen* and that he was standing beside Dad when he got the telegram announcing I'd been born.

After *Romantic Comedy*, we became pen pals. Every few months I'd get a note from him on studio stationery and I'd write back. When Mother died, Spenny was the one I wanted to call.

I was seventeen, and he was the one I wanted to call.

But I never did.

TOM COURTENAY (*actor*) Julie and I had just worked with John Schlesinger on *Billy Liar,* and of course with David [Lean] on *Zhivago.* The verdict was still out on Mr. Orr's directing skills. We weren't convinced!

He was just so bloody young.

JULIE CHRISTIE *Tom* was the one who was skeptical of Roar's abilities; he was a great snob in those days. I was a bit more forgiving and could see something in our young director from the get-out.

---

67 Nicholas Ray, the original cinematographer on *Dr. Zhivago*, was fired early in the filming.—*ed.*

Did Tom tell you the moment he fell in love?

We were outside my dressing room prattling about Shakespeare when Roar interrupted. Tom was *not* at all pleased by this intrusion; when it became apparent Roar had nothing to say, that he was simply making an attempt to fraternize, Tom ignored him and continued on. Ever so slightly— or ever so largely!—rude. I grew concerned there might be a showdown. One of those *High Noon* things. Or perhaps I should call it *High Tea*. Because you see Tom was starting to be a real shit. He let it be known—in front of cast and crew, with a roll of the eye—that in certain instances, Roar may or may not precisely have known what he was doing as a director. So, there we were prattling about old Will in front of our trailers and there comes Roar, crashing the party. Well, an actor loves an audience, as you may know, and while Tom "ignored" him, he puffed up and continued having a go, very *actor-y*, about how for him the most difficult role was Malvolio. Now, Tom and I were absolutely certain he was a card-carrying heterosexual but Roar *immediately* announced he'd been lovers with the painter Francis Bacon, whom Tom was absolutely gaga over. The implication was that he and Bacon were still an item. Tom's face! He absolutely blushed and transformed. We both sort of giggled and gasped then Roger looked Tom in the eye and did his own bespoke Malvolio speech: "Some are born great, some achieve greatness, and some have greatness *thrust into them*."

Well.

Tom doubled over and the ice was broken. He was putty in Roar's hands after that—and came to believe him to be the finest director he'd ever worked with.

MARK HARRIS (*biographer*)[68] Spence died a few months after wrapping *Romantic Comedy*. He and Kate were living together in George Cukor's guesthouse, and she became his caregiver. Roar was in L.A. to see one of his doctors and dropped by for a visit. Moments after he left, she found Spence crumpled on the floor. The press release said he died alone.

LAUGHLIN ORR That death hit my brother *very* hard. Spencer Tracy was a father figure—gruff like Mug but with the soul of an artist. A fantasy dad.

---

68 From *Pictures at a Revolution: Five Movies and the Birth of the New Hollywood,* Mark Harris, pp. 338–339 (Penguin, 1972).

JOHN LAHR Sinatra and Jimmy Stewart were pallbearers, along with Cukor and John Ford. Ford was shaky and looked like he was going to collapse—he was getting over a flu—when Roar jumped up from his folding chair and rushed over. All the great men stood stock still, like palace guards, as he took Ford's place. Like the denouement of some showbiz opera. Or *West Side Story*.

Before they marched on, Roar caught Lou's[69] eye and she nodded, grateful. He was quite moved by that.

BEVERLY D'ANGELO He told me that his relationship with Spencer became sexual. Briefly. I'll read from a letter that Roar wrote: "We tried to speak the mother tongue, though father tongue is more appropriate—that's the language both of us seemed to dream in. But it was all pro forma and we had *proformance* anxiety: me from drugs, Spence from old age. Still, we were glad to give it the old college try. If every dad and son did the same, no doubt there'd be peace on Earth."

GORE VIDAL They were *all* queer. Ford—aka "The John"—was Cowgirl Caligula; that ol' cow loved a poke. Sinatra—"Saint Francis of a Sissy"— enjoyed his fellatio and was thereby anointed permanent guest of *boneur* at Cukor's famous stag parties. "I opened for Frank" and "Frank opened for me" became the wink-wink in-joke. Lionel Barrymore, Glenn Ford (who'd been dubbed "Used Ford") and "Grandma" Walter Brennan were usually in attendance. Thelma Ritter, Spring Byington and Margaret Hamilton too—the original "Strap Pack" whence the Rat Pack took its name. The Strap Pack was the next incarnation of the Sewing Circle: Garbo, Dietrich, Edith Wharton, and the greatest libertine of them all, Salka Viertel. The head of the snake was usually Cukor's legendary houseboy-pimp Mattelin; and a young Brit alternately dubbed the Eatin' Mess and the Eton Miss formed an ass-to-mouth conga line invariably ending in Ol' Blue Eyes' pink-eyed Wonder of the World. The private gala continued through the early Nineties. By then, they called Sinatra the Wheelchairman of the Board—"Cruise Tom," Jon Favreau, Vincent Gallo, and Matthew McConaughey labored over Frank's in-for-a-penny in-for-a-pound appendage; a now rather wonderless wonder,

---

69 Louise Tracy, Spencer's widow. Katharine Hepburn did not attend.—*ed.*

heroically fluffed and fussed over by revolving greased backdoor of mailroom boys known as the William Morrissettes.

DAVID UNGER (*talent manager*) When my father signed on for [Miloš Forman's] *Philip Phaethon*, Roger's first big acting role, they became great friends. Dad produced *The Magic Christian* and *Don't Look Now*, two movies Roger loved. I was an agent for a long time and whenever I ran into him, he told me an agent joke. It became our little tradition. I remember this one: an agent and his lawyer are at a party. The agent sees an actress and says, "I'm gonna fuck her." His lawyer says, "Out of what?" [*laughs*] Though maybe that's more of a lawyer joke.

JONNY "STAGE DOOR" ORR My brother said he had one of his Alice in Wonderland "visions" during Tracy's funeral—that he was a pallbearer for his own body. But he wasn't two inches tall and he wasn't twenty feet tall, either, like he usually was in the hallucinations. He was regular. And I didn't like that because it was just . . . too real. Didn't like it at all.

CALLIOPE LEVY-LEVY It's my belief there was a merging with Spence—who also happened to be a patient of mine—because Spence was tortured by the death of a daughter as well. Katydid was born blind and died in her crib like Roger's baby. Spence blamed the sins of womanizing for her death and spent a lifetime running. Now, Roger and Suze's situation didn't resemble the Tracy marriage in any way, though Roger did relate intensely to the part of him that compulsively ran from any sort of discomfort. He'd been broken by those two deaths—Aurelia's, and the "original sin" of Seraphim's passing—and loathed that he never really faced either of them head-on. He couldn't stop running. That was his nature and you can't fight nature.

Well, you can, but you'll lose.

SAM WASSON He joked about naming his entire body of work after the Kurosawa film—*Ran*.

DAVID STEINBERG He always talked about writing a memoir. Which none of us thought he'd ever do because his movies were his memoirs. His films and his journals . . . but Laughlin said he'd been talking about it from his *teens*. And he was so angry at James Jones for "stealing my title"—Jim wrote that book, *Some Came Running*. Which *he* stole from the Gospel of Mark. Roar was livid. For him, titles were a very big deal. When he got stoned, he just wept at the beauty of *Some Came Running*.

But as much as he loved the notion of running toward redemption, he loved running away from it even more.

DICK GREGORY He moved to New York and made the scene. There was a *lot* of scene to be made! I thought he was being frivolous—he was always jumping on a plane to go somewhere, you know, to *flee*—and underestimated him as usual. Guess I had a little chip on my shoulder. Maybe a big chip because his apparent indifference about what was going on in Alabama— what was going on all over the *country*—righteously pissed me off. He wouldn't do the marches, wouldn't speak out or speak up. . . .

But still waters run deep. All the time he was getting his ultra-white "romantic comedy" together, he had this *other* script cookin' about being Black in America: his adaptation of Sammy Davis Jr.'s *Yes I Can*. Talk about transgressive. It was transgressive as a motherfucker.

SAM WASSON Roar was working on a hundred projects while he in preproduction on *Romantic Comedy*. He felt superhuman and probably was. One night at the Pierre, he turned on *The Tonight Show* and there was Sammy, flogging his new book. Roar had a lightning bolt epiphany: "I'll do *Yes I Can*, with an all-white cast! And never mention race!"—it was pure Roar, completely subversive, surreal, perverse . . . all the things we've come to know, love, and expect. Sammy had a great sense of humor. He was well aware of who Roar was and respected him; Otis Redding's amazing version of "Tenderness" was already out, and the song was having an insane resurgence of popularity. Sammy started singing it in his Vegas act, and it almost outshone "Mr. Bojangles." So, Roar pitched his idea to Sammy at Birdland—an all-white *Yes I Can*!—but Sammy didn't get it!

No one did.

HARVEY FIERSTEIN (*actor, playwright*) When Sammy turned him down, it was a call to arms and Roar began to strategize. No way was he going to let it go. Around that time, Roar began a torrid affair with [Warhol superstar] Candy Darling—a key player in the seduction that eventually led to Sammy assigning Roger the rights to his book. Candy became Sammy's Molly Bloom: "He could feel my breasts all perfume yes and his heart was going like mad and yes I said yes I will *Yes I Can!*"

GEORGE PLIMPTON (*journalist, editor*) Candy out-Boodled Boodles; Roar became sexually addicted. He called her Breach Candy, after the district in Mumbai where he'd been hospitalized during the whole Alice in Wonderland syndrome business. I don't think she ever asked *why* he called her that; or what he meant by shouting, "Once more into the Breach!" during lovemaking. He used to go along when she got her hormone injections at Dr. Reveille's.[70] *That* was a big turn-on.

Afterward, they'd shoot speed with Edie over at Andrea Feldman's.

BETTE MIDLER (*singer, actress*) I didn't meet Andy Warhol until the Seventies. He said that Roar kind of pimped Candy to Sammy, that it was all part of the hustle—Roar would've done anything to get the rights to *Yes I Can*. Andy said that Candy Darling couldn't *believe* she was meeting Sammy Davis Jr. because she'd been obsessed with Kim Novak [Davis's former lover] since she was a kid on Long Island.

Sammy called her Candy Man but she didn't like that at *all* so he changed it to Candy Girl. She hated that even more! Andy said Roar called her Candygram because wherever they were, Candy's connection would show up with cocaine.

DICK CAVETT (*talk show host*) Roar was super-possessive but didn't seem to mind Candy and Sam fooling around because it was all a means to an end. . . . Taylor Mead said that one night Candy dressed up as Kim Novak in *Vertigo* and sucked Sammy off backstage before he went on in *Golden Boy*. Now *that's* something you wouldn't be able to unsee.

PAT HACKETT (*writer*) Boodles left New York a few months after Candy and Roger met. He went on and on about what an unjealous person he

---

70 No relation to Rev. Thomas B. Reveille.—*ed.*

was—those *types* are always most psycho-possessive!—but the truth was, Boodles just couldn't take it. He couldn't handle Roger's transfer of affections. It was the end of him.

BOB COLACELLO (*journalist*) Boodles relocated to California. He and Edie [Sedgwick] became roommates in a nuthouse in Santa Barbara. I don't know if someone arranged that or if it was serendipity . . . someone should write a play about that. After he was discharged, Boodles moved in with Edie and her husband. They were both in mourning; Edie was mourning the loss of Andy and Bob [Dylan], and Boodles was mourning the loss of Roger Orr.

They slept in the same bed. Not sure what her husband felt about that. On Thanksgiving Day, he walked in and found them. He said their arms were wrapped around each other and their skin looked like white Carrara marble.

DR. EUNICE LAVAR I reached out to him around that time. It was random—just one of our occasional catch-ups. At the time, I knew nothing about Boodles. We talked about this and that. Nothing memorable. But at the end of the call, Roger mentioned that a close friend had just died. Very unemotional, very matter of fact. I had déjà vu because he used the same kind of flattened affect when he spoke about the death of the young man that inspired him to become a doctor. The fellow burned in the war.

PAT HACKETT He *never* talked about Boodles's death. And neither did anyone else, at least not when he was around. Boodles was great fun, you know, she was a kick, but Edie was who everyone wanted to talk about. We talked around *that*, too, whenever we were with Roar—you know, just memories and stories, making sure not to bring up "the end," because of the two of them being found together. Roar had a force field around him when it came to Boodles, you know, a neon sign above his head that flashed *Warning! Do Not Approach!* Like a silent alarm. I think it helped that when Boodles died, Roar was still in the throes of sexual conflagration with Candy. The affair burned itself out six months later but did the trick.

Whatever gets you through the night, okay?

CHARLES CHAMPLIN (*film reviewer*) Roger didn't have the rights to *Yes I Can* yet but was looking for a producer. He spoke to his friend Miloš Forman and he suggested Carlo Ponti. This was before Miloš and Ponti had a falling-out.[71] Roger was a huge fan of [Godard's] *Contempt*, which Ponti produced, and loved the idea.

VITO RUSSO (*film historian*)[72] Did he need Carlo Ponti? Not really, because Orr decided to pay for the picture himself. But Ponti had produced the films of Godard, De Sica, and Antonioni (*Dr. Zhivago*, too)—and Orr wanted to be a rung on that ladder. He knew that *Yes I Can* would catch all kinds of shit, especially in America. As a counterbalance, he needed the critical acclaim—and the glamour of its festivals—that European firepower would provide. Lineage became essential.

JEAN PIGOZZI (*art collector, photographer*) Carlo was a very big collector. He had a slew of Bacon triptychs and *also* collected Iwana Kant, a relatively unknown sculptor at the time. Now, Bacon was possibly the only person other than Roger's art dealer who knew that Iwana Kant was Roar's *nom de brosse*—and certainly *Carlo* didn't know. Larry [Gagosian] told me all this himself. Carlo had a few of the "burned man" sculptures Iwana Kant made: the so-called Shotley Suite. Kanye West and Rick Owens own most of them now. And a few crypto pimps and YouTubers.

BOB COLACELLO We did an *Interview* piece with Francis Bacon and the "reclusive" female artist Iwana Kant. Rereading it, it's quite amusing. We were hoodwinked.

GEORGE PLIMPTON After Boodles died, Roar avoided the Factory. Candy was still around but Roar stayed away. Andy was hurt and upset by that. I think he was in love with Roar. Andy wanted him to fill the void when

---

71 Unhappy with Forman's *The Fireman's Ball* (1967), Ponti reneged on his $150,000 investment, putting the Czech director in legal jeopardy until Orr provided funding. The film was nominated for Best Foreign Picture one year after *Romantic Comedy* had its critical and popular triumph.—*ed.*

72 From *The Celluloid Closet: Homosexuality in the Movies*, Vito Russo, pp. 217–228 (Harper & Row, 1987)

he and Edie "broke up." Edie was twenty-three; Roger was pushing thirty. . . . He was obsessed by Roar for the same reasons he was obsessed by Edie—his evanescent, almost eerie beauty—and of course the pedigree of great social standing and storied family wealth. You can add genius to sweeten the pot. Andy certainly knew about the Orrs of San Francisco. Bunny was as rich as Dominique de Menil; her father Langdon L. Desmoine was great friends of the de Menils, and the Commodore had nearly as much money as she did.

PETE HAMILL (*author, journalist*) Sinatra had great success with his cover of "Tenderness" but Frank wanted something original. When he came to New York, he summoned Roar to Jilly's. They had a few drinks and Frank said, "Got another song for me, wonderboy?" Sammy had started doing "Tenderness" in his act and it was becoming kind of a signature. The Chairman wasn't too happy about it. He said to Roar, "I told Ol' One Eye"— that's what he called Sam—"to cease and desist or he'll be Ol' No Eyes." It wasn't like Sam was doing "That's Life" but Frank could be like that. He didn't want anyone playing on his turf. Point being, all that talk about Sam gave Roar a goose to chase the *Yes I Can* rights again. He'd slacked off because of the general *mishugas* of Boodles dying—the breakup with Candy—not to mention that he was about to go into production on *Romantic Comedy*.

DAVID STEINBERG (*comedian, director*) Roger took me to Birdland all the time. They named the club after Charlie Parker but Parker had nothing to do with it. He only played there a few times, but the other Bird—Rabineau— did showcases before it went bankrupt. This was *way* before he found out she was Mom. It's weird we never saw her there because we were both fans. The artist he never missed was John Coltrane.

GORE VIDAL "Birdland—the Jizz Corner of the World." More like the *Ah, men!* corner. George Shearing was the house whore. Wasn't a bottom, though; they said George had perfect pitch.

BEVERLY D'ANGELO All the Hollywood stars went to Birdland. Gary Cooper, Judy Holliday . . . Kerouac hung out in the early days before he was "Kerouac." Just, everyone. One night, Roar looks over and there's Sammy Davis. The timing's perfect because he'd just seen him on Johnny Carson, which was probably why Sammy was still in New York. Plus, he didn't want to approach Sammy through an agent or manager or whatever. So, Roar introduces himself; weirdly, they'd never met. And Sammy's totally knocked out to meet the writer of "Tenderness." Roar decides not even to mention wanting to make a movie of *Yes I Can*. Right place, wrong time. They're all having too much fun, why spoil the party. You need to remember that back then Roar had only made one movie—an arthouse zombie flick *no one* saw or even heard of.

But you want to hear the funniest thing? On the night he met Sammy, Roar was with Robert Thurman, who'd just been ordained by the Dalai Lama as the first American Buddhist monk in his tradition. He's crazy brilliant, speaks a thousand languages, translates from the Sanskrit. He's Uma's dad and used to be married to one of the de Menils. Had an accident in 1961 and lost an eye. When Bob shook Sammy's hand, he said something like, "Alas! The cyclopes meet!" Sammy spit his drink out and did one of his classic pre-Nixon bent-over convulsions. Roar said he wanted to do a movie about Bob and Sam—not a biopic but a *myopic.*

SAM WASSON Beverly said that? Well, she should know. I thought he told Sammy about his idea for *Yes I Can* right away. . . . I *do* know that Roar had a recurring fantasy of throwing a dinner party where none of the guests were told who else had been invited. And it'd be Sammy, Robert Thurman, Peter Falk, Sandy Duncan, and Alice Walker—all of whom had one eye. I didn't know that Alice Walker had one eye, Bruce! Did you? He riffed that it'd make an amazing movie, like *Dead of Night*: each guest would recount the story of how they lost an eye. He wanted to call it "Doctor My Eye," after the Jackson Browne song. He loved that song!

TONY KUSHNER (*playwright*) Sammy *loved* Roger. How could you not? And it didn't hurt that they were both sex freaks and went on to have all kinds of scenes together: with men, with women . . . with women who wanted to be men and men who wanted to be women—

It was all part of Roger's long game: the seduction of Sammy D.

DAVE CHAPPELLE Sammy thought Roger was—what do the *English* call it? "Taking the piss"—when he said he wanted to do a black-and-white film adaptation of *Yes I Can*. No niggers in it at *all*. Oh shit.

JOHN LAHR Suffice to say, it wasn't the film version anyone expected. It was a complete subversion that almost destroyed his career. But it has quite weathered the test of time, hasn't it?

* * * * * * * * *

YES I CAN (1970)
by Pauline Kael
The New Yorker[73]

Oh yes he did.

The nuclear audacity of Roger Orr's revisionist historical tone poem cum musical is matched only by its funky, flamboyant artistry. Shot by James Wong Howe in glorious, in-your-face black-and-white—a satirical game of stylized checkers recalling the great cinematographer's work on *Sweet Smell of Success*—this adaptation of Sammy Davis Jr.'s memoir *Yes I Can* is exorbitantly elegant and unexpectedly moving. It shocks and offends, all while teaching a lesson about race in America sans pedagogy. (Orr has said that an alternate title would have been *Grace War*.) The cumulative revelations of *Yes I Can* make you lose your bearings.

Called an avant-garde minstrel show by its detractors, *Yes I Can* is actually a courageous act of tender terrorism—one that's garnered unprecedented opprobrium and death threats for the director—and made Sammy Davis Jr. a "whiteface collaborator"/enemy of all colors of the rainbow. One wonders if such critics have dared to see the film. And if they have, one wonders if they're capable of *really seeing*: for beneath the "whitecaps" (the name Orr gives to the police) are the macabre, racial shipwrecks that still haunt the Division Street called America.

Orr has made those watery schooners and battleships spectral, beautiful, and somehow uproarious.

Of one thing you can be certain: *Yes I Can* is *not* a sequel to the director's breakout three-hankie feel-good hit of last year, *Romantic Comedy*.

---

73 *Village Voice*, May 12, 1966, vol. 22, no. 32.

* * * * * * * * * *

JORDAN PEELE That movie was some kind of wicked wizardry. What he tapped into was Sammy's own ambivalence about being Black—and let's not even talk about Roar being a Black man *himself* and not yet knowing it. So, Roar was ambivalent too, on a completely unconscious level. You know what Leslie Bricusse once told me about Sammy? He said that his major conflict was "Am I Black? Or am I white?" That's what got Sammy spun: that Roar homed in on that.

He made his Faustian deal and when the movie came out, Sammy was all, *Oh God, what have I done?*

SAM WASSON He was going to divide *Yes I Can* into three parts: Johnny Whitaker as the boy Sammy; David Cassidy as the teen; Roy Scheider as the grown-up. For Sammy, it all suddenly got too real and he said *absolutely not.* They hadn't signed the contract yet and Roar realized he'd made a tactical error by oversharing. That's when he went into overdrive. He said the film would be very *European,* which appealed to Sammy—that it'd be a *political statement* about the erasure of Blacks by whites. That got Sammy's attention. But what really changed his mind were the aces up Roar's sleeve: John Coltrane agreed to do the soundtrack (which he probably *hadn't* agreed to at the time)—and the $3 million check Roar would give Sammy for the rights.

Do you know what three million was back then? $30 million in today's money. A completely insane amount.

BOB THIELE (*record producer*) Coltrane needed the money. Trane *always* needed the money. But he got what Roar was doing, you know, the madness of it. The absurdist, apocalyptic goof of it. And they bonded over India—both had been to a lot of the same places. Trane had that deeply spiritual side.

MICHAEL ERIC DYSON (*author, professor of sociology*) Some saw Roar's adaptation of *Yes I Can* as brilliant social commentary; others, straight-up racist pornography. Whatever it was, it was a hand grenade.

SPIKE LEE (*filmmaker*) It felt like genocide to me. Still does. And the shit got worse in the rearview, when Roar found out his biological father was a white supremacist. A Klansman! The shit got complicated. Begrudgingly, there's art to it. *Great* art. I almost hate to say it. Man, [*Yes I Can*] haunted me a long-ass time. Two hundred percent.

DAVE CHAPPELLE I mean, why not? If I was white, why not make a movie about middle-class, Norman Rockwell, Fifties America—*without the whites.* Tom Hanks, a nigger! Scarlett Johansson, a nigger! I'm gonna do it! I'm gonna direct that shit!

Better yet, remake *Yes I Can*—with white actors, *again*. That's what I'll do. I'm always looking for fresh ways to get fuckin' canceled.

QUINCY JONES He reached out when Coltrane bailed. I was going to do *Romantic Comedy* but it didn't happen. Roar liked what I did with *In Cold Blood* and *Bob & Carol*. And we had lots in common—you know, I've got white ancestry. One of George Washington's sisters is kin, that's for real. And a stranger thing is that I'd produced one of Bird's albums, *Flygirl*, long before anyone knew their connection. My mother had some issues like Bird did, but Bird wasn't schizophrenic. . . .

Yes I Can was misunderstood. I think it's gotten its due now. Folks still go after it—but hell, they banned *Lysistrata*. They rioted over *The Rite of Spring*. You ain't nobody till they want to kill you over what you create. And they almost did. They almost killed him.

ADELE (*singer*) It's *outrageous*. Fucking *genius*. Fuckin' *love* that movie.

MO'NIQUE (*comedian, actress*) I heard Lee Daniels wants to remake it— with an all-Black cast. I hope he *does*. You always hear about stuff like that now; avant-garde theater productions going all-Black for an old play with all-white characters. In *this* case, do that with something that should have been all-black to begin with! World's gone crazy. Time to uncrazy this shit.

QUINCY JONES When the fur began to fly with *Yes I Can*, I probably could have stepped up a bit more. I have some regrets. People thought I distanced myself because I was ashamed to be involved. Or that I didn't like the outcome.

But I was proud of the work I did. Proud of the film. I just didn't step into all that glare. I like to say I never had time for that bullshit but maybe I could have made a little time. I understood what Roar was doing from the beginning and knew there'd be heat. But I tend to walk away from the noise and let the work speak for itself. Maybe I walked too far, and that's on me. I talked to Frank about it. He said, "Q, you don't need to be a mouthpiece, that's not your thing." You know, "Sam's a big boy in a little boy's body, he'll be all right. Let the storm blow and zip it." I listened to him and I'm glad I kept my mouth shut.

After that, he didn't call me Q for a while. He called me Q. T.

COLSON WHITEHEAD (*novelist*) Roar went to see Sam when he closed *Golden Boy* on Broadway, a week before shooting started on *Romantic Comedy*. Roar loved the dissonance of doing something "popular" like *Romantic Comedy*—then following it with something *out there*. But he was still cultivating Sam, still trying to seal the deal for the rights to *Yes I Can*. Sam had yet to sign on the dotted line.

They were already pretty tight from hanging at Birdland and running in the streets, gold-paved that they were. Roger introduced Sam to Anatole Broyard and "the three musketeers" got close. *All* of 'em were serious pussy hounds. I don't know who was more physically beautiful, Anatole or Roger. The mind-boggling farce is that Anatole was a book critic for the *Times*, who was notoriously hiding his Blackness[74]; and Roar was a Black man who didn't *know* he was Black.

Someone should do *that* movie.

BLISS BROYARD (*daughter of Anatole*) Roar heard all the rumors about Dad being Black but that was something they never discussed. After my father died, Roar gave me some insight. My father's reasons were personal and complicated—but Roar said that if he'd revealed himself, he would forever be known at "the Black writer," "the Black critic." Which Dad would have hated. No one spoke of Joyce Carol Oates as "the white novelist" or Lewis Mumford as "the white critic." Philip Roth *hated* being called a Jewish novelist. Dad just wanted to be known as Anatole Broyard, critic. Anatole Broyard, memoirist.

"Anatole Broyard: writer."

---

74 Broyard was a mixed-race Creole who passed as white in New York.—*ed.*

SAM WASSON Without telling Sammy, *Yes I Can* went into preproduction in the summer, a day after they wrapped *Romantic Comedy*. That was a huge gamble, because if Sammy said no, everything would be kaput. The weekend before principal photography, he flew to Vegas to get him to sign. The weekend before! Sammy knew he was coming and by then I think someone told him what Roar was up to. Apparently, Sammy wasn't pissed. He may have been *incredulous* but was also sort of in awe of the chutzpah of it!

He was recording "The Sounds of '66" at the Sands with Buddy Rich. It started at three a.m. so that all the Strip headliners would be able to come after their shows. Tony Bennett, Frank and Dean, the Lennon Sisters—even Howard Hughes was there. Sammy sang his signatures, ending the show with a jazzed-up version of "What Kind of Fool Am I." For the single encore, he got *very* quiet and the spotlight hit him. He was sitting on a stool and went into that inense *confessional* mode. Staring down at the stage with a kind of religious humility. The Church of Showbiz, writ large.

"As some of you may know, I wrote a book called *Yes I Can* that was very important to me," he said. "I'm going to sing a song for you that was written by a genius-cat who's here tonight. It's all about being gentle. About being kind. The world would be a beautiful place if we followed the message of this song. And I have a message of my own for Genius-cat . . ." He looks up for the first time and the spotlight hits *Roar*. And Sammy says, "Genius-cat? *Yes You Will.*" Sammy makes a little pantomime of signing his signature on a contract in the air. Then he does the best "Try a Little Tenderness" anyone would ever hear. Roar was home-free.

But only Sammy knew what the feral genius-cat had in mind.

ROY SCHEIDER (*actor*) My first film was *The Curse of the Living Corpse*, a zombie rip-off of *They Sleep by Night*. We shot that in black and white too. I went to his production office in Chelsea for the audition. I was scared shitless. Roar had kind words about my performance in *Curse* and I couldn't believe he saw it. I thought he was bullshitting.

Yes I Can was half a musical. Certain gifts an actor may or may not have were required. I wasn't a singer or dancer but I was a boxer. A welterweight who'd fought professionally. Roar already knew that and said he liked the way I moved in the ring. Years later, Fosse told me I almost didn't get *All That Jazz* because of *Yes I Can*. You know, "You already did that." But I guess he saw something in me that Roar did—an energy that fit their vision of what they wanted or needed.

Bob was a big fan of *Yes I Can*. It influenced not only *Jazz*, but *Lenny*.

CEDRIC ROMAINE (*trainer*) Roy used to take Roger up to Tommy Boy's, a gym we had in Harlem. Taught him to box. Showed him the ropes. Roar was a natural and held his own in the ring. Gave as well as he got. The first time I saw him spar, I thought, "This ain't his first rodeo. No way."

MO OSTIN (*record executive*) I have no idea when Roar slept. But apparently, he did. He said that "Piece of My Heart" came to him in a dream and that all he had to do was jot it down when he woke up.

SUSAN SONTAG Roger was a fan of *Visits to St. Elizabeth's*, the song that Ned Rorem did from the poem Elizabeth Bishop wrote about visiting Ezra Pound when he was in the psych hospital. Roger had the idea to do a hallucinatory opera, conflating the time he spent as an adolescent in lockdown and the time he spent in Breach Candy Hospital. The results were something of a disaster. He and Ned had a falling-out when Roger changed his mind midstream and announced he wanted to do *Candide* instead—which he later staged to universal acclaim, with a female protagonist.[75]

NED ROREM (*composer*)[76] It's become impossible. We swim in the morning, as if to shake off the antagonisms of the day before. Some days he looks like Lautréamont, and others, like a very young Harry Truman. He talks endlessly of becoming a woman, off-putting to me, because I want him to be a *boy*, which of course he is—Essence of Perfect Boy. He's more Ravel than Rimbaud: *Pavane pour une infante défunte*.

GORE VIDAL He collaborated with Rorem—*Roarem?*—but that didn't work out so well. Perhaps certain extracurricular activities—*extracaligula?*—got in the way. Ned was a very busy boy. Rumor had it he'd bang Harry Truman in the Oval Office then take the train to Nassau Point and do Einstein

---

75 Retitled *Candida*. Orr hired his old friend David Hockney to do the stage sets.—*ed.*

76 *The Later Diaries of Ned Rorem, 1961–1972*, pp. 358–361 (Feuilleton Calypso).

for lunch. The senescent became Ned's subspecialty; it was all very continental. *Incontinental?*

BOB THEILE He was writing, writing, writing, all the time. It was a meditation for him, a way of calming down. He'd do highbrow, lowbrow, and everything in-between . . . jazz, country, soul, R&B—just astonishingly fertile. Sometimes he'd collaborate because there was such an overflow. He cowrote the Tammy/Marvin song with Harvey [Fuqua], Johnny [Bristol] and Vernon [Bullock][77] but "build my world around you" was his lyric. For a while, every R&B song had that motherfucking callback, everyone was building a world around anything that flew, fucked, or shit. He was the first to pair rivers and mountains in a song—and you know where *that* went. . . and the first to say "You found somebody new" in a country western song. Go ahead and google "Roger Orr, Uneasy Street." It's right there in Wikipedia. He *rarely* gets credit for being the first lyricist to write about going back to Tennessee. A lot of country singers wrote songs about *being* in Tennessee, *missing* Tennessee, *loving* Tennessee—but no one until Roger Orr ever wrote about *going back*. After he did, people couldn't get enough of going back: to California, Colorado, El Paso, Alabama, wherever.

KEHINDE ASÉBÁYỌ̀ (*essayist, musicologist, cultural critic*) Orr sang the track of "Piece of My Heart" himself, and Bob Thiele sent the demo to Erma Franklin, Aretha's sister. Years before, Thiele wanted Erma to record "Try a Little Tenderness" but that didn't happen because of Orr's antipathy toward her father, C. L. This time, though, bygones were bygones; Erma was available and Orr gave the green light.

Erma laid down "Piece of My Heart" on Thanksgiving Day. That was the only time the studio had a slot because Simon and Garfunkel were in the middle of recording *Sounds of Silence*.

BOB COLACELLO Some say he wrote "Piece of My Heart" about Boodles.

HOPE "HOOP" RADCLIFFE That song was about Seraphim—definitely. So sad.

---

77 "If I Could Build My Whole World Around You" (1967).

SUZE BERKOWITZ It was his way of saying goodbye to Aurelia.

MARIANNE WILLIAMSON (*activist, spiritualist*) "Piece of My Heart" is about God, the Buddha, whatever. About all the things that unknown, unseen forces do—they tear us apart before showing us Love is the answer. Lennon said it best in "Mind Games." *Love is the answer. And you know that for sure.*

ALI BERK (née Alice Berkowitz-Holbrook, *daughter of Suze and Scatter*) Oh, that song's about my mom! That's what Daddy always said. Uncle Roary wrote it when their divorce became final, so she could remarry.

It's such a sad song though!

LAUGHLIN ORR Do I think "Piece of My Heart" was about Suze? No. Nope. *No.* I'm pretty sure it was about *himself*—his shadow side. That song's about the part Roar could never reconcile with. He was this . . . amazing *racehorse*, with a rider who kept whipping and would never let him sleep. A visionary, disruptive rider. But you need to merge with your shadow, you gotta make friends with it. Marianne [Williamson] tells me that all the time. It sounds New Age-y but it's fucking true. Phil Stutz calls it Part X. He's my shrink. Stutz calls it the death cookie.

He always says, "You gotta eat the death cookie."

BLISS BROYARD When he found out Roger was doing an all-white version of *Yes I Can*, my father severed the relationship. It was too close to home. Dad told my mother never to tell his own *kids* he was Black, and, in my father's eyes, Roger's film was a weird satire of the very personal choice he had made. He felt used. Exploited. He was especially sensitive after the whole Chandler Brossard deal.[78]

Betrayal got him crazy.

REV. JESSE JACKSON (*minister, social activist*) When the movie came out, I went by myself to see it. I thought it was a travesty. A white director—we

---

78 A character in Brossard's *Who Walk in Darkness* is a Black man passing for white—generally considered to be a thinly veiled portrait of Anatole Broyard. Until then, Brossard and Broyard had been close friends.

didn't know differently at the time—a white director literally whitewashed the Black experience. I couldn't see beyond that. I was looking at it through one lens. And did a terrible thing: judged Sammy in my heart. I said, "You are a co-conspirator." I canceled my brother. Just . . . shunned him for a few years. And that is a terrible thing. That is a small, petty thing. You cannot shun your brother. You cannot turn your back on him. I could not see the art in it, not at that time. I could not see the message through the filter of my rage. We get blind in all kinds of ways. And it wouldn't have mattered if there was *no art to it at all.* You do not turn your back on your brother.

DICK GREGORY Sammy was destroyed. Then just when folks were beginning to forget and forgive, he goes and hugs Tricky Dick! He became the most vilified Negro in history. Was that fair? Hell no. But what is? You tell me what's fair. I'll sit here and listen.

SHIRLEY MACLAINE (*actress, writer*) The worst part was the white supremacists. They sent letters to all the Black actors, activists, and entertainers: "Y'all should do what Brother Sammy said in his wonderful movie: y'all should disappear!" Sam had all these formal invitations to speak at Klan rallies as the "honorary white guest." They were delivered to his *home.*

AUDRE LORDE (*poet, essayist*)[79] It didn't matter that the movie was a masterpiece. And Roar hated that it was politicized. Because it *wasn't* political, not to him. You could say he was a naïf . . . or that he was criminally out of touch—or you could just refer everyone who got uptight to the Lillian Hellman quote: "I will not cut my conscience to this year's fashion." *Art does not cut its conscience, ever.* He looked at *Yes I Can* as pure Buñuelian satire. (By the way, the proudest moment of his life was when Agnès Varda told him *Yes I Can* inspired Buñuel to make *The Discreet Charm of the Bourgeoisie* a few years later.) Roar could have taken a lot of pressure off if he'd gone on Cavett for the dog and pony, you know, stumped about his film being an antiracist polemic . . . Roar had become friends with Christine Jorgenson after she famously walked off the Cavett show—and friends with Cavett too because he was touched by Dick's apologia to Christine. So Cavett would have been a

79 From *Sister Outsider: Essays and Speeches,* 1991, pp. 228–229 (Crossing Press, 1984).

sympathetic ear and given him carte blanche. But he chose not to. He didn't want any part of that nonsense. It always backfired. He used to say, "A funny thing happened on the way to the public forum . . ."

He did have some private meetings with the Panthers. He acquitted himself eloquently, and they said, "Well, if you feel that way, if you're so passionate about it, come march with us." He wouldn't! He said that he was an artist and his Art spoke for itself. Art *is* activism—when it's done right. He really did believe that all human endeavors are fleeting. Even the most righteous social movements are fleeting.

LAUGHLIN ORR Roar knew what would happen. How could he not? That's the trouble with genius: people get trampled underfoot.

I ran into Sammy at a march somewhere. He was going to a lot of those, you know, trying to make amends to the Movement. Sammy took me aside and said, "Rosa Parks got escorted off the bus. Your brother threw me under it." But he said it with a wink and a smile because Sammy knew he played his part. He *also* knew—regardless of the fireworks and the bullshit—that Roar made an amazing, beautiful film.

Sammy was a lot of things, but he wasn't stupid.

DICK GREGORY Hey, Sam took the money. He'd already converted to Judaism in '61, which was a big part of the film. So you had this one-eyed black *Jew*, taking money like a Jew—to erase Black history! Man, it was nothing but a lose-lose situation that just kept *on* losin'.

And no one seemed to care that Sam gave a million of it to the NAACP— no one gave a *shit* about that little detail. Ain't that a bitch?

RENATA ADLER (*author, film critic*) When *Yes I Can* came out in 1970, it won the Palme D'Or but was otherwise censured and vilified. It's now of course considered to be one of the most politically powerful, most poetic films of the Black experience ever made. The bookend was another masterwork, *The Jungle Book* [2008]—a novel, not a film.

QUENTIN TARANTINO *Romantic Comedy* was released in the summer of that year and he finished shooting *Yes I Can* right before Thanksgiving. He told me that Truman Capote's Black and White Ball was his wrap party.

GORDON PARKS (*cinematographer*) He privately called *Romantic Comedy* his "experimental film" because it was mainstream-traditional. Now, I don't think that's at all true, but it's how he put it. There's no question that his pride and joy was *Yes I Can*, which he playfully described as "a pitch-black, white bread two-reeler in black and white."

What could have been more perfect than ending the year with a Black and White Ball?

BOB COLACELLO Truman wouldn't allow plus-ones. Andy came without an entourage and it was *hell* for him. Husbands and wives were forced to show up without spouses. Roar switched table cards with a willing George Plimpton because he wanted to sit with Mia and Frank. (George preferred the Buckleys' company.) Mia was nineteen, and Roar was, what—twenty-eight? He was utterly entranced. Mia didn't know a single soul, with masks or without. But Frank got bored—"Frank Got Bored" sounds like one of those Tom Wolfe profiles, doesn't it?—and the Sinatras left early.

KEHINDE ASÉBÁYỌ̀ Roar wore a dress to the Black and White Ball. Oscar de la Renta. Everyone had masks on sticks—designed by Adolfo—but Roar didn't want to be holding something in front of that beautiful face all night. He had this glow-in-the-dark rectangle covering his eyes, very *Day the Earth Stood Still*, something you'd see on a chic Cubist/Constructivist robot. Have you seen pictures of it? Do you know what I'm talking about? The dissonance of that tech-looking thing atop a classic gown was genius. De la Renta was there and couldn't get over it. Because the thing didn't draw attention away from the gown, it drew attention *toward* it.

In everything you read about that night, there were really only two people to look at in that ballroom: Roger Orr and Penelope Tree. You ping-ponged between the two.

PAT HACKETT Even Cecil [Beaton] didn't recognize him at first—it'd been a long time since anyone saw Roar in a dress! Apparently, that used to be his thing but when he started getting famous, he got shy about it. It took a masked ball to free him; the Factory certainly hadn't.

The lady was dying to come out!

JAMES JONES (*novelist*) I think Cecil said to Tru, "You *must* invite the boy." Roger was a little disdainful of Capote because of that infamous remark he'd made about Kerouac—"that's not writing, that's typing." Roger was quite loyal that way—he certainly defended me enough through the years—and was of the mind that Jack was at least as important as Whitman. On that night, he had a few drinks and said as much to Truman. Truman kept his cool. He looked up at Roar—*way* up—and said, "Well, I'm sure you're right, and I apologize. I should have said *stenographer*." Truman kissed his hand and thank God Roger laughed.

KATHARINE GRAHAM (**newspaper publisher**) Herb Caen was with the Sinatra group. Herb was an old friend of the Orrs and Roger knew him since he was a child, from parties at Parnassus. They did some catching up because they hadn't seen each other since Bunny's funeral.

Bennett Cerf told me that he saw them sitting at an empty table and Roger was staring down. Herb had an arm on his shoulder—like a father. They must have been having a moment.

DICK CAVETT He swanned about and networked. Picked Virgil Thomson's brain. Charmed the *pantalones* off Jerry Robbins and Harold Prince, softening them up for a musical he had in mind. And it took a lot to get those boys soft.

BENNETT CERF (*publisher*) Mailer was very, very drunk. In that ratty raincoat he always wore over a tux . . . When Norman got lit, he did the tiresome routine of inviting people "outside." It was ugly and dumb. He'd start talking in that bizarre street accent—the most absurd bully who ever lived. If someone brought their pet parakeet and it looked at him the wrong way, that noisome clown would've said, "Step outside, Polly!" Lillian [Hellman] was there and he asked *her* outside. There's no doubt in my mind who would have won. Lillian, hands down.

NORMAN PODHORETZ (*editor*) [Mailer] cornered Tallulah Bankhead, who wasn't well, and said, "Step outside, you leprous old cunt." Roger overheard it and spoke up; Mailer's retort was rather misogynistic. Remember, he believed that Roger was a girl, not that it would have stopped him from asking "her" to step outside after he was finished with Ms. Bankhead. In light-ning speed, Roger shoved him in a vestibule off the kitchen and gut-punched him. Roar knew how to handle himself; Mailer didn't.

Mailer gasped for air as Roger seized the moment, pulling Norman's pants down straight to his shoes. Roger hiked up his skirt, lowered his *own* panties then shoved his cock into the novelist's mouth, jerking him off with a free hand . . .

BETSY BLOOMINGDALE (*socialite*) The next thing you knew, Norman was out on the street dazed and half-naked, hailing a cab. His wife chased after him. Oh, that was a sight. Everyone thought he was smashed but the truth is he was absolutely destroyed.

SCATTER HOLBROOK When I heard that story, I immediately thought of how Roger handled the bully, back in our school days. Borrowing Mug's hotshot and all. And the rumor he'd raped the boy . . .

GORE VIDAL I was an enormous acolyte of Mr. Orr after that! What one *didn't* hear was something Lee [Radziwill] said she got from the mouth of a kitchen worker: Norman had a raging hard-on, no doubt an autonomous reaction to being pantsed and *manipulated*, with the added frisson of finding strange meat in the mouth. The epiphany both exalted and ruined him: in one fell swoop, he was a bigger faggot than his idol, "Poppers" Hemingway.

The only difference was that Poppers liked to suck on cold, hard steel—when nothing else was available.

. . .

DAVID STEINBERG It was Christmas 1970, when it happened. And when it did, it suddenly seemed so inevitable—why did none of us see it coming? Roger and I were taking one of our long walks through the city. We ended up on Wall Street, admiring the World Trade Center. They'd just topped off the tallest building on Earth.

I still associate his being shot with the World Trade Center.

Its absence calls back that time, to this day.

BOOK THREE
Grace War
1970–1985

CHAPTER NINE

The Horror

LAUGHLIN ORR I was in Mississippi with Stokely. He'd been married during the last few years of our affair[80] and it was, um, complicated. The phone rang, and it was Ruby Dee. I met Ruby and Ossie [Davis] on the Freedom Rides, and we became quite close. She knew Roger and they hit it off. She understood what he was doing with *Yes I Can*; no one was going to tell Ruby what to think. So, I picked up the phone and it's Ruby. All she said was, "They got him, baby." I said, "Got who?" "They killed your baby brother." Everything went black—then the world just exploded. I was falling, falling, falling. Stokely was in the room and was cold about it. He was *not* a fan of my brother. I saw the look on his face. It wasn't a smirk but was definitely, you know, like, "That's payback." In that moment, my love for Stokely died.

BOB COLACELLO They took him to Mother Cabrini, the same hospital they brought Andy when he was shot. The whole Factory came down— Paul [Morrissey], Candy, even Billy Name—everyone but Andy. Andy just couldn't. The déjà vu was too strong.

JONNY "STAGE DOOR" ORR It sounds like a shitty thing to say but part of me was relieved the shooter wasn't a black—he was classic nerdy whiteboy American sociopath who hated *They Sleep by Night* and wrote a manifesto supporting zombie rights! I remember praying; that was a first time because I definitely considered myself to be an agnostic. I even called Father Thom [Reveille], who talked me down from the ledge.

---

80 Carmichael married the South African singer Miriam Makeba in 1968.—*ed.*

145

LAUGHLIN ORR My gut reaction was, "It's political." Because after *They Sleep*, there were *so* many threats. Roger shrugged them off, but a few times the FBI got involved. This was during a long season of assassination. Malcolm and Martin, Fred Hampton . . . *George Lincoln Rockwell*—remember him? The fucking Nazi? Taking people out was the new normal. The new American pie—or maybe just the old one, served up again à la mode. I got real paranoid, which wasn't my natural tendency. Carried a *pistola* in my purse for a while.

ALICE COLTRANE (*musician, spiritualist*) Sammy flipped out when he heard. Because he loved Roar, he really did, but couldn't shake his hurt from everything that went down when that movie came out, the movie of his book. Couldn't stop the blame game. Sammy was in a quandary because he wanted to reach out to Roar in the hospital, but couldn't. He was paralyzed. I said, "You love that man and you know it. And he loves you too. It would help him to hear you say it." He'd start to dial—right in front of me!—then hang up. I'd say, "Ain't nuthin' stoppin' you but you."

JESSE JACKSON I was with Sammy and Altovise in Palm Springs when it came on the news. An array of emotions ran through Sam like an electrical current.

I knew what he must have been thinking: "I'm next."

LARRY FLYNT (*publisher*) When I was shot ten years later, Roar called the ICU.[81] He used the term from old gangster movies—"ventilated." You know, "Welcome to the ventilation club!" Made me laugh, which was a bit painful at the time. He always called me Hairy, never Larry. Someone held the phone to my ear and a voice says, "Hairy? Blue Balls Orr has a message for you and here it is: bein' ventilated ain't for sissies. But if you *live*—which sadly he's told you will—it's 100% guaranteed to grow hair on that sad, shaved puss of yours."

---

81 Flynt was gunned down by a white supremacist outside a Georgia courthouse on March 6, 1978. Flynt later said that his assailant, Joseph Paul Franklin, was an enlistee in Project MKUltra, of which Ken Kesey and Allen Ginsberg were volunteers. Franklin and Orr's biological father, "Wriggle" Jones, became prison pen pals.—*ed.*

The call meant a lot because not too many people have gone through it. As Groucho said, you don't want to join that club.

DAVID STEINBERG Whenever we passed a particular bench in Washington Square, the pigeons tried to shit on us. We always joked about it. The last thing Roar said before they put him in the ambulance was, "That was some pigeon, Dave."

DR. EUNICE LAVAR The bullet perforated a lung and broke his clavicle. It got infected and they put a drain in. The irony was that when they closed him up, the third nipple got swallowed by the skinfold.

Poof, it was gone.

JONNY "STAGE DOOR" ORR I was just glad Mom and Dad weren't alive to go through that. Mom, anyway. She was tough but not *that* tough.

DAVID STEINBERG When I saw him after surgery, he was groggy but . . . *alive*. [*emotional*] He was alive. I burst into tears because I was so damned happy. His brow furrowed and he said, "Is it in custody?" Like a stage whisper. I didn't know what he was talking about. "The *pigeon*," he said, kinda testy. "Did they collar the pigeon?" I said no, they hadn't yet made an arrest. All was fucking well with the world.

HOWIE MANDEL The kid who shot him has the distinction in shooter trivia as the first in a long line of American assholes who carried a copy of *The Catcher In the Rye* during hits on celebrities. A fad was born! Trending! Trending!

I still carry a copy with me on the subway. When someone gets too close, I hold it up and say, "Stop or I'll read!"

SCATTER HOLBROOK The press went to town, as is their shitty wont. The pot got stirred—all that imminent race war hogwash surrounding the *Yes I Can* movie. But when they arrested the little white punk, all the "controversy" evaporated overnight. Perversely, Roar getting shot was the best thing that could have happened, because it lanced the boil. A lot of sympathy was garnered and there were even some favorable critical reassessments of the film. He called me in Maui—I stayed home with the baby when Suze flew to New York to see him—and said, "Taking a bullet was good for the Jews."

His pet phrase.

SUZE BERKOWITZ Laughlin and I couldn't believe he was alive. But that's all we knew. Alive, but what *kind* of alive? They wouldn't give us any information. Until you get to the hospital and see him with your own eyes, your head's going crazy. You're already at the funeral, you're *arranging* the funeral . . . then, in two seconds, the world has color again. You see him hooked up to all kinds of machines—horrible!—but he's fucking *smiling*. I cannot tell you what that felt like. For the first time, you breathe, your whole body and soul just breathes. . . .

When they came in to do some tests, Laughlin and I went down to the cafeteria. We lost it in the elevator. Hugged and hugged and cried and cried.

BEVERLY D'ANGELO I was singing in Toronto[82] and we used to cover some of his songs. "Tenderness" . . . "Go Lightly" . . . once in a while "Piece of My Heart." I hadn't seen him since *They Sleep by Night* but still thought about that whole experience. To be that young and suddenly sort of starring in a movie—I played one of the twins—is a *very* big deal for a twelve-year-old girl. Sissy and I had huge crushes on him. When *Romantic Comedy* and *Yes I Can* came out (loved them both), I thought fuck it and sent a funny mash note. Well, *I* thought it was funny. Probably sent it to William Morris but never heard back. Don't know if he even got it. I'd just turned nineteen and should have sent a nude—that might have got someone's attention. The Morris mailroom boys, anyway. But the *genius* of those two films, and the *impossibility* they were directed by the same man! When I heard Janis sing "Piece of My Heart" and found out that Roar wrote it, I couldn't *believe*. Literally. I was like, *What?* Like, *No.*

I wasn't the only one who thought: This is God. (Or the next best thing.)

About a week after he was shot, I bought a nurse's uniform and snuck into the hospital. By the time I got to his room, I was a nervous wreck. When I peeked in—I hoped he'd be sleeping—he was looking straight at me.

---

82 In Ronnie Hawkins's band, The Hawks.—*ed.*

He shouted, "Aubrey!"—my character's name in *They Sleep by Night*—"I thought you'd never come."

ANDY WARHOL (*artist*)[83] Cabbed ($6) to the Pierre Hotel, where Roger Orr has three big suites. Marisa [Berenson] begged to come because she's obsessed. Sunny Radcliffe, an old friend of Roger's mother, was just leaving and said she wants me to do her portrait. I told Roger I wish I could have painted his mom. I remember meeting Bunny at Ferus, a few months before she died.[84] She'd have looked so good [for "Society Ladies"] hanging between Dominique [de Menil] and Lynn [Wyatt]. Bob said he heard that Dominique hated the painting I did of her but that turned out to be just another lie spread by Gerard [Malanga]. Roger was really surprised when I told him I lived in a shack on Orr Street in Pittsburgh when I was a boy.

Roger is so handsome and still in so much pain. They keep him stoned and he looks like a floating Chagall angel. He talked a *lot*—about stained glass windows and wanting to open a fag bar called The Stained Ass and how he'd put in a lesbian bar next store called The Stained Lass. Then he changed the names to "Stained Lass Widows" and "Stained Ass Widowers." He's so funny and smart but it doesn't come across as trying too hard. He talked about the movies he's going to make next year. One of them is about Albert Pinkham Ryder—he's going to play Ryder himself—and a horror film starring Barbara Streisand! But she turned him down because she didn't want to play her mother. She said, "I'm going to turn into her anyway so what's the rush?"

He showed us his scars, and Marisa almost fainted, not from the scars but his beautiful body. He wanted to see mine, but I said he should just look at the Avedon picture instead.[85] I told him that when I was in the hospital, I was watching the news and there was a bulletin about Robert Kennedy being shot. It confused me because I thought I died and somehow they were rerunning President Kennedy's assassination on TV. That made him laugh, but I

83 *The Andy Warhol Diaries* by Andy Warhol, edited by Pat Hackett, pp. 313–318 (Twelve Tree, 2014).

84 Warhol had his West Coast debut at the Ferus Gallery on July 9, 1962. Bunny Orr died on Christmas Day of that year.—*ed.*

85 Richard Avedon famously photographed Warhol's gunshot wounds.—*ed.*

felt bad because laughing is the worst thing you can do after you're shot. It hurts so much.

Candy Darling was hiding from me in one of the suites and there was a big black nurse from the Bahamas named Jimmy who kept coming in to tell him it was time for physical therapy. Candy finally came out and they did coke in front of Jimmy, and he rolled his eyes and left.

I made a faux pas and asked if he'd heard from Boodles. He said no, because "he" was living in L.A. with Edie—Roger used "he" instead of "she" after they broke up—and made it sound like Boodles was in the Amazon or somewhere in Africa with Peter Beard. Like being in L.A. meant Boodles wouldn't have heard the world news about Roger being shot and if even he did, there wouldn't be an easy way to call. We talked about the trial[86] and how it's become a big fad for killers and wannabes to carry around *A Catcher In the Rye*. Roger said it could have been worse, he could have been carrying *Black Like Me* or the S.C.U.M. Manifesto. When I told him Valerie Solanis [sic] was still after me, he shrugged.[87] We wondered if Sirhan Sirhan had been carrying a copy of the Salinger book.

I said he should be on the cover of *Interview* and he said yes, but only if Avedon took pictures of his scars too. "I want to be an Andy Warhol Superscar." So that was funny. Then he started talking about the *Interview* piece we did with Francis Bacon and Iwana Kant. He kept asking me what I "really" thought of Iwana's work, just went on and on about Iwana Kant and how great she was like he was her publicist. There was a knock on the door and a beautiful girl named Beverly came in. Candy sort of cowered and left. Jimmy insisted it was time they take their daily P.T. walk down the halls of the Pierre. I didn't want to run into Candy downstairs so I talked to Beverly for a few minutes. She's really beautiful and is going to be a big star. She whispered that Candy was supplying Roger with drugs. Like that was a news flash. Roger shrugged and changed the subject. He said Beverly visited him in the hospital in a nurse's uniform. I told him about Vera Cruise, who did the same

---

86 Orr's assailant, Mason Rigby Carpenter, was ruled insane by the Supreme Court of the State of New York and remanded to Bellevue, where he hanged himself.—*ed.*

87 Warhol had been shot by Solanas in 1968. After her release from the New York Prison for Women, she was rearrested and subsequently institutionalized for stalking Warhol. —*ed.*

thing when *I* was shot. Vera was a car thief and always wore a leather jacket over a nurse's outfit. Now Roger wants to meet her.

Marisa didn't say two words the whole visit, she said she was too star-struck. She cried in the cab ($8) and said, "I'm such an idiot."

SUZE BERKOWITZ Bev's an old soul. She'd just turned twenty and had a Lauren Bacall vibe. Husky-voiced, sexy, gorgeous. She could outdrink, out-fuck, and outthink anyone at the table.

We didn't meet that time in New York; I was only there for a few days, because I needed to get back to Maui. I missed Alice *so* much—Scatter too!—but I *really* missed Alice. Once I knew Roger was gonna be okay I went back. Beverly and I got to know each other over the phone because she spent so much time with him during his recovery and gave me updates.

When we finally met, she looked exactly like I pictured her.

JOHN LAHR The speed of his recovery was remarkable. By spring, he was in Maui, starting his script for *Hollow*.

He brought Beverly D'Angelo with him.

BEVERLY D'ANGELO Maui was when it first got sexual—there wasn't *time* in New York because I was trying to get him away from all the enablers, the superstar dope fiends. I hadn't met Suzie yet but we started colluding on the phone about an escape plan. She's the big sister I never had.

I never had a little sister, either.

SUZE BERKOWITZ Maui was a homecoming. Scatter and I represented that—home—and Alice was the gravy. Alice was the embodiment of Seraphim and Aurelia, all the little girls he'd lost. But she didn't have an aura of tragedy around her. He knew she would live. He even said that to me once: "This one will live."

ALI BERK I was seven or eight years old when Sammy Davis Jr. came for lunch. I don't remember much but I do remember him singing "Candy Man" to me. In my memory, it was Sammy singing his signature song—but after he died, I noodled around on the internet and saw that he didn't record "Candy Man" until a few years *after* the Maui visit. So, I guess I conflated it with something else. Maybe "Bojangles"? The funny thing is that he hated "Candy Man." His signature song and he hated it!

Isn't that so perfect?

RENATA MINT (biographer) After the film version of Yes I Can, Sammy was persona non grata—not just to Blacks but liberal Hollywood. He stopped performing, which he needn't have, because Vegas certainly never blackballed him. If you were making money for the casinos, which Sammy was, they stood by you. In some ways, he was even more of a draw. The trouble is, he was getting heckled. There were always drunks in the audience who thought it a good idea to shout "Traitor!" Plus, you had the white supremacist contingent coming to the Vegas shows to voice their "support." It was intolerable. He decided he'd had enough and locked himself up in the house in Palm Springs.

A few years later, an opportunity came up for him to act in a movie. He told Frank and Elvis about it—the two people he felt closest to—and they went to "the fortress" to see him. Both said, You need to do this. It was a huge studio production [Tora! Tora! Tora!] and the part they offered was smallish but great. He'd play the father of an African American cook that won the Navy Cross for heroism during the attack on Pearl Harbor. A true story by the way. It was a natural fit because Sammy was drafted into the Army at eighteen and had a tough go because of the rampant racism. He was a wonderful actor, and this wasn't From Here to Eternity, mind you. But it was a way of getting back in the business.

And a way to get out of his head, at least for a little while.

ROGER ORR[88] Around noon, Suze woke me up and said there was a guest arriving. I was perplexed but she had that look in her eye. "Roger, you have to come—now."

I wrapped myself in a robe and stumbled through the house to the lawn. Servants stood in absurd, rigid attention—apparently, Suze hired some locals and dressed them in uniform. You could tell they didn't want to disappoint; they wore the flop sweat of amateur greeters.

---

88 From Long Day's Journal, Vol. 2, pp. 313–315 (Harcourt Brace, 2002).

I became even more perplexed (Suze wasn't what I'd call a pranker) and wondered if I should have at least gotten dressed.

A helicopter materialized in the distance. Scatter appeared on the porch with a goofy grin, holding Alice in his arms. It was obvious he was in on it. As the chopper got closer, I'm thinking: the Aga Khan? . . . General MacArthur? . . . Barry White (big fan of "Tenderness")? . . . Spiro Agnew?

Then out he steps: Sammy.

He was shooting a dumb WW2 flick in Oahu and had a few days off.

For the remainder of the visit—to honor the poignant grandiosity of his arrival—I dubbed him "Tinker Bell, the uncommon fairy."

I didn't realize until then how much I missed him—and loved him.

Before he left, we made a pact to never again abandon the broken-down warship of fools and friends. The *worship* of fools and friends.

BEVERLY D'ANGELO I never met a Black man who ate pussy like Sam.

SCATTER HOLBROOK I'm pretty sure Roger encouraged the affair with Beverly. I know it was brief. They were free spirits. Suze always said Bev was freer than Roger and Sammy put together.

ALI BERK Uncle Roary was really good at playing. He was like a big kid himself. We did little movie scenes together and it wasn't until I was older that I realized he'd been auditioning me for the part of Iris in *Hollow*. I think Mom must have known. Dad, not so much.

You know, in terms of him being shot, I just . . . wasn't really aware of what happened. I knew he'd been in the hospital in New York but they pretty much shielded me from that. I wouldn't have been able to process it. How could I? Why would someone want to shoot Uncle Roary? It would have made me sad and scared. I was shielded from a *lot*. I didn't even know that Mom and Uncle Roary used to be a couple until I was fifteen!

SAM WASSON After that idiot almost killed him, Roar redoubled his productivity, if that were even possible. Because his output was crazily prodigious. *Some* of the urgency could be credited to his fixation that someone would come along and finish the job. For years, he lived under that sword. Every time it happened—John Lennon's murder sent him into hiding—the fear was exacerbated. He had this geographic view of his oeuvres and envisioned his violent, random, premature expungement as tantamount to the erasure of an entire continent of still-gestating, uncreated work.

George Steiner's *My Unwritten Books* had a huge impact on him. He said that he wanted to write something similar and call it *Undone*. He had to, he said, because "what if the one regret I have at the end of my life is never having written about the movies, songs and books that I never made?" An Escherian dilemma. And when he told me that, he was already an old man . . . As a teenager, he made copious lists of all the films he planned to direct: the John Ford Western; the "Billy Wilder film noir"; the *Apu* trilogy—which, in compressed form, became *Gift from God*, his adaptation of a tale from *Arabian Nights*; the Buñuelian comedy. As he got older, the list stayed remarkably the same but was revisited after the shooting. By then [1970], Kubrick had done *Spartacus, Paths of Glory, Lolita, Strangelove, 2001,* and had begun shooting *Clockwork Orange.* Roar coveted that sort of range even though he already possessed it. Added to all those films, those templates, were the "subversions," which he wouldn't get a chance to make until the Nineties. . . .

One of his heartaches was that he wanted to do [Thomas] Bernhard's *The Loser*; it was his *Elective Affinities*.[89] When that didn't happen, he wanted to adapt Bernhard's *My Prizes*, which he saw as a kind of bookend to the Forman film he acted in.[90] But the famously difficult Bernhard refused to grant the rights.

He'd already decided to do a space opera next, an adaptation of Philip K. Dick's "I Hope I Shall Arrive Soon"—sort of Terrence Malick meets Tarkovsky—how's that for mainstream?—when *Hollow* [1972] got into his head and wouldn't decamp. Roar really did want to make his mark in horror again. *They Sleep by Night* didn't count because no one saw it. And he succeeded: *Hollow* launched a thousand freak-children horror films. The idea came from a dream, and the dream became the famous trailer—Roar dreamed in movie trailers! A three-year-old boy goes into his parents' room while Dad's away, wakes his mother up, and says, "Mama? Do you want to know what fear is?" That was the whole trailer! Which was kind of a big deal

---

89 After years of struggle, Francis Ford Coppola failed to adapt Goethe's novel *Elective Affinities* to film.—*ed.*

90 *Philip Phaethon* (1975).

because it was the first of its kind, you know, a fifteen-second trailer. That was back when they were at least two or three minutes long. The studio thought it was a terrible idea and begged him not to do it. Their brilliant logic was that it wasn't enough time to give the audience "traction." But when the trailer was shown before another Warner Brothers film, *Deliverance*, the audience went completely insane. A few weeks later, another one dropped that was five seconds longer. The camera widens a wee bit—and *something's in bed with Mom*. A lumbering shadow, moving from behind, *clearly* sexual. The kid says, "Let it, Mama. You let it! You let it! You let it!" The hairs on your neck stood up. People lined up outside the Village [Theater] for a mile.

An old Warner's projectionist told me Friedkin watched *Hollow* about twenty times, making notes on legal pads. *The Exorcist* came out the next year but that whole lines-down-the-block horrormania phenomena started with Roar. His fingerprints are all over Friedkin's film—Blatty even sent Roar a thank you note. It's on display at the Margaret Herrick Library.

DAVID UNGER He was having trouble financing *Hollow*, which was stupid because *Romantic Comedy* made so much money. The genius Hollywood strategy was: Do another *Romantic Comedy*! Do something just like it—*again!* Horror was considered niche; it wasn't what the people wanted that particular year, month, whatever. Noel Marshall was his agent for a while and Roger said, "If you put the financing together, you can produce." Noel was getting tired of agenting anyway.

Noel was married to Tippi Hedren. Years later, he wrote and directed a movie about big cats in Africa—actually cast *himself* opposite Tippi. A lion bit him and he got gangrene! The thing took five years to shoot and tons of people on the crew were seriously injured.

Can you guess the name of the movie?

That's right: it's called *Roar*.

CHRIS SILBERMANN (*agent*) After *Hollow*, Noel Marshall became the executive producer of *The Exorcist* because he represented [William Peter] Blatty and was instrumental in financing its development. Friedkin wasn't happy; he didn't want his film to be considered *Hollow's* stepchild.

QUENTIN TARANTINO He came to the house for a table read of *Pulp*

Fiction—a table for two. We did all the parts, and it was a gas. We were amazingly stoned.

After, he got real quiet then said, "What about Travolta for Vincent?" John had become *invisible*. I mean, in the ten years before *Pulp*, what had he done? *Look Who's Talking, Look Who's Talking Too, Look Who's Talking Now*. . . . I didn't have to think twice. It was done. The best mindfuck *ever*. We called John at home—somehow we got his number. He was in Florida so it was, like, four in the morning. Neither of us knew him and we were sure he'd hang up. At first, he said, "You guys got the wrong number." But he was sweet as could be. We still joke about it. He calls it "the 'wrong number' that changed my life."

Roar loved resurrecting forgotten stars. He cast Miriam Hopkins in *Hollow* at the end of her life, right? She was a favorite of Lubitsch and Mamoulian and won Best Actress for *Becky Sharp* in 1935. She did *four films* with William Wyler. The last role she had before *Hollow* was in a 1970 slasher/*Sunset Boulevard* flick called *Savage Intruder* that was released under the title *Hollywood Horror House* . . . one of the Three Stooges played the driver of a Hollywood tour bus! John Garfield's son was in it—and a silent star named Minta Durfee who was married to Fatty Arbuckle. We just showed it at the New Beverly.

BEVERLY D'ANGELO Whenever I see Quentin, he tells me I look different. I always say, "It's the New Beverly."

MELLIE KOCH I saw Meryl Streep and Sigourney Weaver in a wonderful play—God, this must have been 1968, because they were barely out of their teens. The Yale Drama School was a dysfunctional, crazy cauldron of upstart talent; all the upstart casting directors went trolling for talent. We called it the Yale Trauma School. The play was written by two student grads, Chris Durang and Albert Innaurato. Wow, huh. Meryl played an eighty-year-old in a wheelchair and I was just knocked on my ass. Roger and I talked all the time so of course I told him about her right away and he stored it in that vast mental archive of his.

When it came time to find the mom in *Hollow*, he was very interested in Joanna Frank.[91] He'd seen her in an *Outer Limits* where she played a queen

---

91 The older sister of television producer Steven Bochco.—*ed.*

bee—literally. He loved *The Outer Limits* because it was so friggin' weird. Some of the episodes were sort of freakish hybrids of Cassavetes films, with sexy, hyper-contemporary couples encountering cheesy, B-movie aliens. Robert Towne wrote one.[92] The aliens were always having some kind of existential crisis. The one with Joanna Frank was called "ZZZZZZZ."

Roar screened the episode for me. It was about an entomologist, an expert on bees. Joanna appears in the professor's garden one day, on the ground, unconscious—this absolutely gorgeous, sensual girl in a slinky dress. You can see her bosoms! Suddenly, she wakes up with a smile. See, all the bees got together and decided that if they took human form, their short lives would be extended; for them, seventy or eighty years seemed like immortality. Her mission was to sleep with the professor. Of course, he'd die in the act—in a nice script touch, the professor's wife was unable to conceive—but would have millions of children with the queen, as his legacy. Queen Bee Joanna hires on as his seductive, haughty assistant. She's goes to the garden in the middle of the night to lick pollen off the flowers . . . Joanna was wonderful: quirky, assured, luminous. A *star*. To this day, it's a puzzle to me why she never became an immortal herself because even from that dumb little show you could see she had it all. For some reason she wasn't available, I can't remember why. That she missed her chance to be in *Hollow* is one of those tragic acts of fate that befalls so many forgotten actors.

Roar said, "What about the gal from Yale?"

I didn't know who he was talking about. For some reason—that day, anyway—Meryl just wasn't on my mind!

MERYL STREEP *Hollow* was such fun. Rod [Taylor] told me these amazing stories about Liz Taylor and Montgomery Clift, and about being on the set of *The Birds*—he said the birds were all stoned and they hung raw meat on the cameras so they'd attack. *Why* they were stoned, he didn't say! Miriam Hopkins was such an extraordinary woman. And famous for her legendary parties—she told me that one night the guests were Stravinsky, Thomas Mann, Coco Chanel, and J. Robert Oppenheimer. I was *fainting*. Roar said she reminded him of his mother because of the incredible parties at Parnassus when he was a boy. He was so kind to Miriam, you could cry.

---

92 *The Chameleon* (1964), starring Robert Duvall.—*ed.*

BEVERLY D'ANGELO I didn't have a big part in *Hollow*, but it was a good one. I used to regale Meryl with stories of my life on the road with Ronnie Hawkins. She was kind of prudish, so it was fun blowing her mind.

I told her about a girlfriend who was broke. She got a random phone call from some guy who offered her $2,000 to go to a hotel room and fuck him in the ass with a strap-on. So she meets him at a Chinese restaurant in Brooklyn and they go to his ratty little car. He pulls out a wad of traveler's checks but they're dirty—almost like a prop he uses—and my girlfriend vibes he's been down this road before. She starts to panic. They're by the freeway and she says she really has to pee. When she gets out, she bolts. Turns out this guy gets arrested a few months later—there's even a book written about him—he'd make phony phone calls and lure chicks to hotels then drug and rape them.

Meryl looked like she'd been stabbed.

"You *know* this girl?" she said.

"She's still my closest friend."

Which she was and still is.

Meryl was struck dumb. I love her but she's a Yale girl, right?

MELLIE KOCH For a while, we tried getting Elvis—ha! But I think that was Roger's folly. Because he really wanted the husband to be older and loved the idea of Cassavetes, who was nearly twice Meryl's age. John couldn't do it because he was about to shoot *Minnie and Moskowitz*. That's when Roger focused on Rod Taylor, who was about the same age as John. He adored Rod. He told me he *still* loved watching *The Time Machine*; somehow it was the magic potion that calmed his nerves. Roger said he was a sucker for any film with characters that were dedicated, compulsive bachelors who had huge libraries with roaring fires and old, big-chested housekeepers that cooked, cleaned, and worried over them. No mommy issues *there*, huh. He called them "smoking jacket" movies because the hero changed costumes at night and sat by the fire to work things out: Sherlock, of course, who obsessed him, and James Mason in *Journey to the Center of the Earth*. *The Time Machine* was at the top of the smoking jacket list for obvious reasons. Roger wanted to reverse the deaths of Seraphim and Aurelia, he wanted to *save* people. What handier way could there be than to travel back in time?

There was so much he wanted to undo.

Much like all of us, I suppose.

ALI BERK Those three months were like a dream. I still think of everyone—the cast and crew—as my extended family. I never stopped working after that. Everything that happened in my career came from *Hollow*.

ROD TAYLOR (*actor*) We laughed our arses off—part of that was a legitimate reaction to how absolutely terrifying the script was. Well, you know he's brilliant, Roar, he's absolutely brilliant. A songwriter, a wonderful director—a bloody good painter too and I know something about that. I was a professional illustrator before I was an actor. He did sketches of everyone that were just marvelous. They skirted the line between caricature and classical portraiture, but with a mysterious twist. Unique. Magnificent, really. An astonishing man all-around.

AI WEIWEI (*artist*) The shoot was in Atherton—one of those *E.T./Poltergeist* Spielberg suburbs, but pre-Spielberg. I was fifteen when I saw it; how was it possible that an underground print made its way to Shihezi? I devoured the history of the making of that film and recently read something online on the first AD's blog. He said that everyone was nervous because of the proximity to San Francisco. All of Roar's drug connections were there. But he was very well behaved. The AD said that within a short while, he knew they had a serious hit on their hands. "Though maybe Roar knew all along."

* * * * * * * * * *

ALL-TIME HORROR FILM BOX OFFICE GROSSES

Rank	Film	Worldwide gross	Year
1	*It*	$700,381,759	2017
2	*The Sixth Sense*	$672,806,292	1999
3	*War of the Worlds*	$603,873,119	2005
4	*I Am Legend*	$585,349,010	2007
5	*Kong: Skull Island*	$566,652,812	2017
6	*King Kong*	$562,363,449	2005
7	*World War Z*	$540,007,876	2013
8	*The Meg*	$530,243,742	2018

(Continued on next page)

9	*Godzilla*	$529,076,069	2014
10	*Hollow*	$503,048,471	1972
11	*It Chapter Two*	$473,093,228	2019
12	*Jaws*	$470,653,000	1975
13	*Godzilla vs. Kong*	$465,763,133	2021
14	*The Exorcist*	$441,306,145	1973
15	*The Mummy Returns*	$433,013,274	2001

* * * * * * * * * *

LAUGHLIN ORR We trooped over to the Village, in Westwood. That's where they used to have all the big movie premieres. Jonny even came down from Coos Bay. He was trying to get over his agoraphobia and hadn't seen our brother since the Academy Awards. Since *Romantic Comedy*.

Roger was *very* stoned. It was fucking scary. I had two burly guys walk him around the hotel suite until he sobered up enough to get in the limo. What happened is, earlier that day, Boodles died. They found him and Edie [Sedgwick] in bed together. Both bodies. I forget who called with the horrible news—it might have been Paul [Morrissey]. The phone wouldn't stop ringing after that so we unplugged it from the wall. Roger shut himself up in his room and just . . . caterwauled. Then he got *angry*, saying all kinds of crazy things, like Boodles did it *deliberately*, you know, killed himself on the night of his premiere. *How could he, how dare he*, all that. The hectoring and the tears. But mostly, the tears. What's funny is, I thought Boodles died a while back, during Roger's Factory phase. Isn't that strange? Almost as if I'd read it somewhere—and even read about my brother's muted reaction, which was nothing like the hysteria he exhibited on the night of the premiere.

JOHN LAHR Roar sat in the front row of the theater, always his favorite place. An hour or so into the film, a character named "Boodles" suffers a spooky, grisly death. Roar meant it as a mischievously playful homage, a little dig that he thought—misguidedly or not—Boodles might get a kick out of. Well, you can imagine everyone's horror when the forgotten-about scene came on. . . .

It all reminded me a little too much of the storied death of Francis Bacon's former paramour, George Dyer. On the night of Bacon's opening at the

Grand Palais, Dyer overdosed in the bathroom of his suite at the Hôtel des Saints-Pères. Many of the paintings in the exhibition were of Dyer—and as Bacon mingled with the crowd, he felt his dead lover's eyes following him around the room.

BEVERLY D'ANGELO Oh, that was hard. Boodles wasn't the Big One— like Aurelia or Seraphim—but was definitely up there. And not just because Roar had never had a physical attraction like that before. The depression and panic that followed turned out to be rooted in something else.

We wouldn't know *what* until later the next year.

NOEL MARSHALL (*producer*) Miriam Hopkins was quite sick and couldn't come to the premiere. She died a few weeks later. Roar was always trying to resurrect mothers. Years later, he did the same with Susan Kohner, the Weitz brothers' mom—Chris and Paul—in *Act of Kindness*. That one had a much happier ending. Susan won an Oscar.

GWYNETH PALTROW When Miriam Hopkins passed away, Roar said it was déjà vu, because Spencer died not long after they wrapped *Romantic Comedy*. He read into it, which was kind of a reach because these people were old and not in great health, so it wasn't unexpected. But it was his nature to take these things—death—as signs and omens. He had such a fear of being frail, of being mortal. That's why he worked so much; to *not* work was another way of creating a space for mental and physical weakness. In it would creep... . He was always on the lookout for signs of deterioration. Signs and wonders! Like, if he occasionally had trouble remembering some piece of trivia—oh my God, hello! Happens to me ten times a day—and this was when Roar was in his *thirties*—he'd turn to Dad and say, "My mind's going, isn't it?" My father'd say, "Mine already went." Ha! But Dad learned not to even joke about it.

SUZE BERKOWITZ He'd say, "I'm cognitively failing." I mean, apropos of nothing—just out of the blue, like he was thinking out loud. His two favorite things to say were "I'm cognitively failing" and "It's good for the Jews." I'd say of course you're not and he'd smile to show that he wasn't serious. But he was. It always went back to Sera. One of the hallmarks of Batten disease is incipient dementia—which she never even had!

BEVERLY D'ANGELO Social faux pas rattled him, even after learning Seraphim wasn't his biological sister—which swept "hereditary" off the table.

He met Salman Rushdie a few years after the fatwa ended, I think at a party at Carrie Fisher's, and asked Salman if he'd ever been to India. He thought Salman was born in England but it was still an idiotic thing—certainly one *I'm* capable of—to ask the writer of *Midnight's Children* if he'd ever been to India. Without condescension, Salman said, "I was born in Bombay." Roar was mortified and went to bed for three days. Two of those three were spent on the phone with specialists. But his *dick* was failing, not his mind.

Or should I say his mind was failing his dick.

Still, he thought the end was near. And it nearly was.

CHAPTER TEN

Silver Hill Linings

STEPHEN FRY (*actor, writer*)[93] The only real secret I ever knew Roger to have was that he felt he'd been born in the wrong body. Which, my God, is such a cliché now. He suffered because it was his nature to be an utterly transparent being, and was painfully, exuberantly forthright about everything in his life—everything but that. We're such perplexing, haunted creatures, aren't we? The irony is that he thrilled at taking to the streets in ladies' dress, *loved* being a bottom, he'd lay on his tummy and thrust that pert little behind in the air; or upon his back, legs spread wider than legs had a right, playing the raptured, ruptured demimondaine. And *never* hid his unabashed envy, his intense infatuation with and attraction toward those brave enough to alter themselves by hormones or surgery. For Roger such alterations were inexplicably—at least, for a long, long while—a bridge too far. He hated himself for not having that courage, an *artistic* courage, because ultimately that's how he saw it. The best of him thought of himself as others did—fearless. The worst took undying notice of his cowardice, the dirty little secret that was slowly driving him mad. He saw the pot of gold at the end of the rainbow but kept getting derailed, like "a perverse Dorothy on the Yellow-Bellied Brick Shithouse Road."[94]

I'd like to say that secret-keeping was in his DNA and he was carrying on the tradition—Bunny's record-setting big whopper being that she managed to hide his adoption until Roar was middle-aged. Though *she* turned out not

---

93 Diary, *London Review of Books*, vol. 41, October 1991.
94 The phrase is from *Either/Orr: The Rest of Roger Orr*, edited by Simon Callow (Pegasus Press, 2016)—*ed.*

to be his mother, so DNA doesn't apply. But nurture has a way of seeping into nature.

Mother Nurture's a motherfucker.

KENNETH TYNAN He first met Jan Morris in London, at the Travelers' Club. She was in her forties and still "James Morris." She'd yet to begin hormone treatments—swallowing thousands of pills made from the piss of pregnant mares. Roger liked to say they got along like a "bathhouse on fire" but it wasn't true; *Roger* was the one who liked his rump saunas and frottage cottages, certainly not James.

VITA SACKVILLE-WEST (*writer*) Roger told James that he was keen on making a film about Hemingway, who died a few years before. James was an inveterate admirer of Papa's books and their talks led of course to Africa. James had written a book about the Dark Continent,[95] spent a fair amount of time with the Xhosa people and so forth. He told Roger that a Xhosa medicine man—woman?—told James that one day he would be a woman. Well, a shaman once told me the same thing and it was quite a shock, being that I already *was* a woman and so remain.

Perhaps I missed some nuance there.

EDNA O'BRIEN (*novelist*) Was it the Travelers'? I thought they met through Peter Beard, on safari. In fact, I'm sure of it.

JONATHAN PRYCE (*actor*) He kept his friendship with [Jan Morris] rather secret, which I found strange. He cultivated an air of embarrassment around them being close. As it turned out, he was shamed by his own lack of courage—which Jan had in spades. He had a serious case of what the Americans fondly call low self-esteem.

CHRISTOPHER HITCHENS (*essayist, critic*) I'm sure you know that before he became Jan, James was in the Queen's Royal Lancers. He notoriously joined Sir Edmund Hillary on the Everest expedition and scooped all the newspapers about the ascent. He wasn't the only military man who had a

---

95 *South African Winter* by Jan Morris (Faber & Faber, 1958).

genitalian change of heart: April Ashley *neé* George Jamieson was a Merchant Navy boy who got discharged after a suicide attempt. As it happened, George had his surgery done by the same doctor as James, in Morocco.[96]

Jim often spoke of seeing the dead—that was the Welsh in him. He regaled his fellow Lancers with eerie, comical tales of ghosts in the streets. The yarns he spun were cannily reminiscent of Lafcadio Hearn, rather like *Kwaidan* meets Wodehouse. As you listened, skepticism melted away under a bright light of charm and erudition; one came away a believer in spectral things—or, if one had the proclivity, *more* a believer. I used to josh him about his atheism. He'd say, "Dear boy, I am not an atheist. I'm fagnostic."

LADY ANTONIA FRASER (*author, biographer*) James and his wife Elizabeth had five children. He was a very open person—under the right circumstances—and doubtlessly would not have withheld personal details from someone like Roger, who was a bit of a walking wound. Roar was a tenderheart, a brilliant artist, and it would have been like looking into a mirror. And Jan—James—sorry, it gets confusing but we're talking about the time before the surgery—James would have been touched and charmed, though not seduced, because he hadn't a homosexual bone in his body. And I'm certain he would have shared about his daughter, Virginia, whom he and Elizabeth lost at two weeks old; a detail that would have irrevocably bonded them. It was the grand theme of Roger's life and his heart synchronized with the veterans of such a terrible experience.

PHILIP PULLMAN (*novelist*) He said that Jan was one of the "most sober" people he'd ever met—and the wisest. Naturally, those of us who knew her were well aware of that divine quiddity: her quiet, indisputable authority and the bouquet of grace with which it was always delivered. She was a friend's friend, and empathic *consigliere.* Roar was enthralled by the Welsh—the icing on the cake—and their melodious, mystic, chthonically spelled language. Jan always said she only spoke a "pidgin" version of the Cymraeg but Roger tried to learn as much of it as he could. The first word he claimed as his own was *hwyl,* meaning, the passion, energy and magic that animates the world.

---

96 Dr. Georges Burou, a pioneer of sex reassignment surgery.—*ed.*

Something like the Chinese *ch'i* but with a cabalistic, soulful bent. I may not have that quite right.

In short: he loved the weirdness of the Welsh.

MICHAEL PALIN (*actor, writer*) He used to say, "Jan lives in *Llanystumdwy*." He'd give all the Welsh words this heightened, elongated, feverishly bizarre emphasis. "Shall we motor to *Llanystumdwy*?" Or "Jan just named her little boy *Twm*. Shall we go see Tiny *Twm* in the wee fair village of *Llanystumdwy*? Or shall we wait till he's gone to university at *Prifysgol Aberystwyth*?"

BARRY HUMPHRIES (*author, comedian*) He sent Jan letters from India while in hospital . . . wait—did he send those from India? Or the psych ward in Boston? I suppose it's all the same. If you've had shock treatment in one, you've had shock treatment in 'em all!

JAN MORRIS[97] I was born in 1926, the same birth year of Mika "Bird" Rabineau—technically, I was old enough to be his mother. And I did feel that for years I had the privilege of being Roger's father *and* mother, though just as often he was both those things to me. He sent the most glorious, cocksure, numinous, educative billets-doux while he lay ill in Bombay. He was in hospital for some time and the letters signed off with "Your ward," "On-ward!" "Stay Mum," "Mum's the ward"—he delighted in wordplay. (I laughed at the irony of that city being renamed: *Mum*bai.) His notes—delicious love letters to the Divine—were like cracked stained glass in a Gaudí cathedral, a catalogue raisonné of the carnal and the ineffable. One of the horrors of my life was when they were destroyed in a flood at Trefan Morys; after his death, they were being sorted for publication and boxes of them littered the ground. Someone from the British Museum came round to have a look. He said the ink had been written in such a light hand and the paper so thin, they were completely unsalvageable—this was a man who was able to restore manuscripts from the Cotton Library fire! I had to become quite Buddhist about it, something, in retrospect, that Roger greatly helped with. I did one of his "boneyard meditations": the ink that wrote my own life—he loved to say, "We do not write, we are being written"—soon will

---

97 *Allegorizings* by Jan Morris, pp. 218–221 (Liveright, 2021).

unsalvageably vanish . . . You see, one spends one's life *desiring*, wanting to preserve and protect, as the motto of the wonderful police department in Los Angeles has it; we spend our lives in an illusory, hectic chase and never look back to see the hot pursuit of relentless forces bent upon our extirpation.

We kept no secrets. Before the surgery, it was a bit of an emotional roller coaster—especially tough when the National Health, due to bureaucratic nonsense, informed that I must divorce Elizabeth. Which of course I had no wish to. Roger was wonderfully supportive because he dreamed one day of having the surgery himself. We'd get on the phone like teenagers and chat up a storm whenever I found myself in a doubtful phase. He'd say, "Lancer?"— he adored calling me that—"We shall do it *together*. We shall *de-lance* yet still be queens!"

I thought of him the other day during a silly Q&A. The *very* young journalist was tiptoeing around the usual topic when I dredged up something "my old friend Roger Orr" once told me. I think it's quite brilliant. He said that if one's lucky enough, one can experience both genders in a single lifetime. And then, after achieving such a duality, *one must aspire to be neither*. Roger schooled me in the Vimalakīrtinirdeśa, a marvelous book that tells the story of a goddess that swaps sexes with Śariputra—without his consent, I might add!—to prove there is no such thing as male and female.

APRIL ASHLEY, MBE *(model, actress)* Everyone said [Jan Morris] was so warm and so wonderful but she never showed me that side. She was right cunty. I think it boiled down to envy, pure and simple. Because I'm the one who blazed the trail, didn't I? And she was never easy on the eyes, and right knew it. It's important to be easy on the eyes, ain' it?

LILLY WACHOWSKI *(filmmaker)* Toward the end of Roar's life, we spent time together. We were in Malta—with Elon [Musk] and Bono—and Pink and her husband, who'd been traveling with Pinchas Zukerman and the gifted Canadian psycholinguist Steven Pinker—when Roar asked me about *Cloud Atlas*.[98] I can't remember *what* he asked but he said he liked the film very much . . . just conversation in front of the fire. When I mentioned Tom

---

98 The 2012 sci-fi film written and directed by the Wachowskis and Tom Tykwer.—*ed.*

Tykwer, his eyes twinkled. "Do you know how the Welsh spell Tom? *T-w-m*." Then he said, "That isn't actually true—but T-w-m *does* happen to be the correct spelling of the name of Jan Morris's son." I was blown away that he knew Jan Morris, and knew her well, because she was my great hero and someone I'd always wanted to meet. He said, "Easily arranged"—and we finally did meet a few years after Roar passed. Oh—and this is a footnote to the story I'm about to tell—I just remembered Roar whispering to Elon that Jan was obsessed with him! With *Elon*. Elon didn't know who she was. I thought Roar was kidding about her having a crush on Elon but he swore it was true, which made me love Jan even more.

Then Roar got melancholy. We all did—not uncommon when you sit in front of a fire on a cold, dark night with a billion stars wheeling above. There's always that moment, that lull when cosmic sadness descends. It's all fun and games until cosmic sadness descends! You're laughing and flirting, having a grand old time, then the fire and its dancing cinders have their way and shut you up as you stare into the furnace of the Universe, humbled by your sheer insignificance. During "the lull," he told a story about Jan that was so moving and intimate, so *confessional,* that the flames of the fire were a perfect witness.

She had her surgery in '72—at last—a few months before *Hollow* premiered. He said they spoke all the time, sometimes twice a day, but when she was in Morocco for the operation Jan was incommunicado. He didn't hear from her until she got back to the UK. She told him it all went very, very well—her surgeon was a genius French doctor who everyone called "the wizard"—years later, he drowned—I need to make a movie about him! She said she needed a few more procedures but could do all that in London. Jan was in high spirits. He was thrilled that she'd done it in Casablanca and insisted they call themselves Rick and Ilsa. Jan said, "No, no, let's *both* be Ilsa." I love this woman. What Roar said next was one of the bravest things I'd ever heard: that the success of her surgery was a terrific blow "because to my own horror and dishonor I prayed it wouldn't go well." He was afraid to go through with it himself, you see, and said that a botched job on his dear friend would have let him off the hook. I don't think I could have admitted such a thing to *anyone*—not even my shrink!— and instantly admired him for it. I remember the way the flames looked, dancing on his face as he unburdened himself, and wondered if we were the first he'd told. He went on to say that Jan must have sensed his perverse disappointment—but if she did, never let on. "She wouldn't have. Because she was fluent in the language of Shame, and the last thing she'd do was bring me more of that. She was sanguine, so *English*—Saint Jan." Roar said that she knew he was afraid—and wanted to be the same cheerleader *he* had been all those years. He said, "Jan would have been the perfect sponsor—this virgin *Mary's* Virgil"—yet couldn't bring himself to go through with the surgery. "I worried that the newly knighted Dame, the least judgmental person on Earth, thought I was a big pussy; or worse, decided I didn't need one. Jan had one carved, and now fully understood: *mine* was installed at birth. Not a pink badge of courage, but a red one of rageful self-loathing and cowardice."

The old friends didn't speak for a long time after. And something she said cursed him: that without the surgery, she would have killed herself. Because she couldn't see a way of continuing life in the physical form of a man.

When Roar was done, Elon asked if he'd ever thought of suicide. Roar said that he had. And that he'd dreamed of writing a little fable about a man who takes his own life because he's an incurable coward—the irony being the act itself becomes the ultimate refutation. Because he really believed that suicide was "heroic." Or could be . . .

All that suicide talk was worrisome but I thought: *As long as he's still thinking of writing something, he'll be all right.* I hoped it was true.

CAITLYN JENNER I read Jan's book[99] until the pages fell out. I was only twenty-five and had secrets of my own. . . . I can't even imagine what that was like, the courage it took in those early days. The passage describing the hospital in Morocco—the intake, surgery, post-op—is like a movie. A horror movie! You shudder at what might have gone wrong. What struck me is her utter commitment, her *stillness*.

The complete fearlessness.

I think I've been courageous in my life, but nothing on the scale of Jan Morris.

BEVERLY D'ANGELO He was floundering with all these projects—"Grace War," his old script "Gift from God," and the Philip K. Dick adaptation—but

---

99 *Conundrum* by Jan Morris (Leviticus Press, 1974).

nothing was coming together. I worried about the drugs. He came home one night with a bloody nose—he got beat up outside a bar—and that's when I called his sister. "We need to do something or Roger's gonna die." I wasn't being dramatic; I could see it.

I *saw* his death.

Laughlin was in the Dominican with Oscar de la Renta and flew up for the intervention. McLean said they could take him tomorrow but he resisted. He didn't want to go to Massachusetts. He said, why not New York? He lobbied for Payne Whitney. "If it was good enough for Marilyn, it's good enough for me." Laughlin said, "Apparently, it *wasn't* good enough for Marilyn. Because she fucking overdosed." Laugh could be funny like that and kinda brutal. The original Miss Tough Love. But we didn't really want him hanging around in New York, not even under lock and key. Too many "lower companions."

I'd done some research and stupidly said *The Bell Jar* was based on Sylvia Plath's experience at McLean in the Fifties and that it was "harder to get into than Payne Whitney." *Oy.*

LAUGHLIN ORR[100] He was *such* a snob. But his interest in McLean perked when Cecil Beaton told him the grounds were designed by Frederick Law Olmsted—and that Ralph Waldo Emerson's brothers had been hospitalized there. What finally won him over was Howard Nemerov[101] telling him, "Bob Lowell used it like you use the Pierre." Howard said that a poem Lowell wrote during one of his stays was still taped to the wall of the nurses' station.[102] When Sondheim said that Lowell and Ezra Pound became pen pals while patients in respective nuthouses, Roger said, "That'd make a marvelous one-act."

The deal was sealed!

BEVERLY D'ANGELO When we checked him in everything went to hell in a handbasket, as my mother used to say. We thought we'd made a terrible mistake. I jumped on the phone to Payne Whitney but the not-so-funny farm's five-star vacancy was already filled by a two-time Pulitzer winner.

Roar promptly "decompensated"—that's what the shrinks called it.

---

100 *Golden Slumbers: A Family Album* by Laughlin Orr, pp. 217–225 (Haight Street, 1996)
101 The brother of photographer Diane Arbus.—*ed.*
102 The poem referred to is "Waking in the Blue" (1959)—*ed.*

Became totally, insanely manic. It's one thing when he's monologizing in his suite at the Pierre, you know, the "angel delirium"—Allen Ginsberg's phrase—that came over him in the throes of creating. There's a certain glamour, and everyone gets high from being around it. You're thinking, "This is what genius looks like!" So, *observe* and let it fucking flower. It's selfish, I suppose, and there's an excitement. But seeing him *cathect* in an institutional setting—no Louis XV furniture! no room service!—with everyone around him either raving or zombified with that thousand-yard Thorazine stare . . . is somehow less attractive. Plus, he'd managed to paint all kinds of tattoos on his body, like the hobo in *The Illustrated Man*.

Overnight, he lost his charm.

DIANE MIDDLEBROOK (*biographer*) Anne [Sexton] was admitted for depression just a few days before Roger. She'd been infatuated by McLean for a multiplicity of reasons—her teacher, Robert Lowell, did many stints there, as had Sylvia [Plath], whom she envied—and her dream was to finally "matriculate."

She even arranged to teach a poetry class on the ward but that was years before she was hospitalized.

JOANIE SMALL (*former McLean patient*) I dropped out of Radcliffe because of "difficulties." I was a poet, in thrall to Lowell and his handmaidens, and was accepted to McLean in 1969. Oh, happy day! Every serious poet yearned to be thus confined; I felt like the bride of John Berryman. I walked its hallowed halls as if in a dream, hungering for the laurel crown of my first rendezvous with ECT [electroconvulsive therapy].

One day [Margaret Ball] asked if I'd be interested in attending a poetry workshop. About five of us gathered in the hospital library. Ten minutes later, this breathtakingly stunning woman appeared and introduced herself as Anne. Well, of course I knew it was Professor Sexton, though part of me refused to believe it. Anne said the class would be held each Tuesday—why had I ever bothered with Radcliffe?—and because *If It's Tuesday, This Must Be Belgium* had just came out, the workshop would be known as "If It's Tuesday, This Must Be Bedlam." Some of the attendees were on suicide watch and had chaperones guarding against sudden moves. I thought, *Work hard enough and you'll be given a chaperone too.*

I relapsed in '73 and returned to McLean for post-graduate work. It was so strange running into Anne at Belknap Hall. I assumed she was teaching the workshop again but she'd had a breakdown and was admitted to the coed unit. She looked awful: that "awful rowing toward God" had begun.

Roger spent four days detoxing and was in worse shape than Anne. I didn't have a clue who he was. But Anne completely changed the moment she saw him; a case of coup de foudre. She started looking after herself. She did up her hair and put on watercolor mascara. Roger told her, "I'm drawn to you like a moth to a celebrity." I heard him say they should synch their periods. Anne said, "Sorry, that bloody ship has sailed." You've never seen two more glamorous people in your life! When they walked the corridors arm-in-arm, even the nurses were agog. Anne wore big dark glasses like a movie star but it wasn't a pose. She'd become photosensitive, a side effect of Thorazine.

DIANE MIDDLEBROOK She hadn't seen any of Roar's films. She *did* know some of his music—through her daughter Linda.

One afternoon, *They Sleep by Night* came on in the TV room. No one knew Roger directed it and he never let on, not even to Anne, who became completely engrossed. I'm told she said, "This may be the best fucking movie I've ever seen."

BEVERLY D'ANGELO He didn't want me there. Visiting. I was a little hurt. Then someone—Laughlin?—told me he was *seeing* someone, and it all made sense. "Seeing someone" in the snake pit! The ultimate Meet Cute, right? That was so Roger. I didn't know that it was Anne fucking *Sexton* but that made perfect sense too. Ha. Anyway, I *got* it. And honestly? I was happy for him. God knows *I* wasn't being faithful. Not that we ever had an agreement. The only thing I wanted was for him to come out the other end, sane and sober. Healthy and happy, or an approximation thereof.

It's weird but I was thinking the other day: the age gap between Anne's daughter Linda and Roger was the same as the age gap between Roger and Anne. And I was around Linda's age at the time . . . I don't even know why I thought of that or why I'm mentioning it now. It's *not* weird, it's irrelevant. Delete.

LINDA SEXTON (novelist, memoirist)[103] I never visited her at McLean;

---

103 *Searching for Mercy Street, My Journey Back to My Mother, Anne Sexton* by Linda Sexton, pp. 381–348 (University of Irvine, 1994).

we were pretty much estranged by then. But for whatever reason, I decided to call and she sounded happy to hear from me. We'd only been on the phone a few minutes when she said, "I have a new boyfriend."

"Oh? Doctor or patient?"

In an arch-conspiratorial tone, she said, "*Patient.*"

It broke the ice because we really didn't have much to say.

"Let me guess. Would he be . . . the Boston Strangler?"

"What makes you think it's a 'he.'"

"Fair enough. Would *she* be the Boston Strangler?"

My mother started to sing:

"'Some enchanted evening, you may meet a *strangler*. . . you may see a strangler across a crowded room . . .'"

When she stopped, she said, "Your future stepfather is Roger Orr."

BO WOJCIK (psychiatric orderly) Everyone called him "Roar"—but not Ms. Sexton. She thought it was a silly name. She liked calling him "MGM" or "Mr. MGM" instead—after the lion at the beginning of movies. You know, because it roared. Personally, I'm not a big fan. I liked the Carl Reiner he was in though. He's a good actor. But as a director I don't care for him.

DIANE MIDDLEBROOK Anne was forty-five and worried that her looks were going. She was lonely. And concerned that her recent divorce was a tragic mistake. She even "computer dated" but didn't have much luck. It was a big boost to her ego that this famous, handsome, charismatic younger man was so interested.

His interest *was* genuine. For a time.

JOANIE SMALL I kind of stalked them. I was the official scribe—I wrote down everything they said and did. They stopped paying attention to me, like reality stars who forget about the camera.

One day, he said, "I just turned thirty-three. The age of Christ, crucified."

Anne said, "That must have hurt."

"Only when I scream. Or cry like a bitch."

"You better tell your dad. He's the one with the long white beard and the cheap sandals."

"Naw. That's a pussy move."

"Speaking of which, I thought you were gonna nail me. Y'mean, I'm supposed to do the nailing now?"

"Yup. And don't be cross."

It was goofy and cheesy but sometimes became this amazing, brilliant stream-of-consciousness. The other day I saw a movie on TCM with Myrna Loy and Clark Gable and it reminded me of them *exactly*.

SAM WASSON I love that they had a "scribe." It's too good! And I think the movie that girl was talking about is *Test Pilot*—one of Roar's favorites, by the way. Howard Hawks wrote it but didn't direct.

BEVERLY D'ANGELO He and Anne fucked a lot. Roar said all the nurses seemed to know what was going on. He told me, "We were a handful—there was *no way* to separate us. The one time they tried, the poor bastards paid dearly. In the end, the shrinks shrugged and said, 'It's good for the Jews.'"

JOHN LAHR He was in awe of Sexton's poetry. He always wanted to be a great poet but felt it was the one thing he could never properly become because he "didn't have the goods." Which wasn't at all true—look no further than his song lyrics or the epic, superlative prose-poem of *The Jungle Book*. He meant that his talents were too diverse, too spread across different genres. To be a great poet, Roar believed one had to do be a "Jill-of-one-trade"—poetry alone.

In one of the *Journals*, he wrote, "I could never write a 'Warning to Children' or 'Cuchulain Comforted'—so why bother?"[104]

SCATTER HOLBROOK He said they used to play truth or dare. He told Anne that he used a cattle prod to rape a boy who'd bullied him about his extra nipple. (Something I always suspected but until then never confirmed.) Roger didn't have many secrets but that was certainly one of them. He told her about dressing up in Bunny's clothes, not a big secret in itself but the admission led to his sharing that he was a "lesbian" who wanted to have transsexual surgery one day. At that time, Jan Morris was the *only* person who

---

104 Poems by Robert Graves and W. B. Yeats, respectively. Many of Orr's lyrics are written in terza rima, the verse form created by Dante for the *Commedia*. Edward Hirsch has written that tercets suggest the feeling one is "always traveling forward while looking back."—*ed.*

knew. I think that speaks volumes about Anne—the high regard Roger had for her, not just as a poet but a human being. He trusted her.

JOANIE SMALL They wouldn't let me hang around when they played the Truth or Dare game, so I don't know what they told each other. I *think* he may have finally admitted he directed the zombie film.

DIANE MIDDLEBROOK Anne told him about her mother's talismanic fur coat—that she'd put it on and masturbate while breast-feeding Linda. How, when Linda was seven years old, she wore it as she laid atop her daughter and rubbed them both to orgasm.

Roger wrote in his diary that after her confession, she suddenly winced—as if realizing she'd said too much—and backpedaled, ascribing her actions to a "fugue state." But he'd been terribly aroused by Anne's disclosure. Not by the incest. By the fur.

JOANIE SMALL When they finished the game, I sat with them for dinner. Anne was saying how she and Sylvia Plath were students of Robert Lowell and after the class he was teaching the two of them would have martini lunches in a fancy hotel. They'd sit at the bar planning their suicides the way polyamorous cultists plan a wedding. They called Death "the groom at the top"—even though it was a marriage in Hell. She was so upset that Sylvia was the first to go.[105]

---

105 Sylvia Plath died in a kitchen gas oven suicide in 1963. In 1969, Assia Weevil, the lover of Plath's widower Ted Hughes, killed herself and the four-year-old daughter she shared with Hughes, also by kitchen gas oven. Anne Sexton committed suicide in 1974 by climbing into the kitchen-adjacent one-hundred-square foot oven of a brass foundry in Cambridge. In 2006, Janet Barclay, the biographer of Plath, Sexton, and Weevil, herded her seven children into a makeshift outdoor kitchen and shot each in the head before accidentally toppling over the oven that crushed and killed her. In 2009, during a tour of Auschwitz-Birkenau, Nicholas Hughes, Plath's and Hughes's son, had just been shown the camp's kitchen when he slipped away and hanged himself inside one of the notorious Topf & Söhne three-muffle ovens installed by the SS, where a thousand people a day met their end, many of them aspiring poets. In 2012, at a Renaissance Faire in Hampstead Heath, Peter de Montessant, noted memoirist of Nicholas, Plath, Sexton, Weevil and Hughes, took his life in 2012 by lowering himself, his wife, mother-in-law, two sets of twins, and the family borzoi into what appeared to be the oven of an open-air kitchen in Hampstead Heath but was in actuality a wastewater vat.—*ed.*

* * * * * * * * * *

ANNE SEXTON

(*from* Live or Die, *1966, Houghton Mifflin*)

Whoop dee-do,
the oven's clean,
of you and me and toddler shouts.
Cooked too long,
it all burned up—
the swastikas and brussels sprouts.

* * * * * * * * * *

BARRY HUMPHRIES (*actor, satirist*) They had a sham wedding before being discharged. The bride wore a T-shirt Roar designed, with GO FUGUE YOURSELF painted across the chest. He told me the marriage was real as any performed at City Hall—and that he still considers Anne "the door behind Wife Number Three." Whatever that means! But it's brilliantly funny, don't you think? *The door behind Wife Number Three.*

GWYNETH PALTROW My dad said that after they "divorced," Anne wrote a poem about him called "MGM." It had the line "in like a liar, out like a lamb." It's in her amazing, posthumous "Lollipops & Cuntblood [1979]." Goop's publishing it in the fall on our new imprint. Exciting!

JIMMY FALLON (*talk show host*) He told the story of the McLean wedding at a little dinner party I had for Jeff Bezos, Paul McCartney, Bob Dylan, Michele Obama, Karl Schwab, and Anthony Fauci. I said to Roar, "Buddy, that's so amazing!" I wish Anne was still alive because she'd be a great guest on the show. I'd give her a hug and say, "It's gonna be all right, buddy! Everyone loves you and you're amazing."

BEVERLY D'ANGELO The lithium didn't work for Roar but shock therapy sure did. Wham: turned off the mania switch. For the first time in—I don't know, a year?—he was himself again. Within putting range, anyway.

BO WOJCIK When I took him back to his room he would still be pretty out of it. He'd smile and say, "ECT is good for the Jews." Every time.

STEPHEN SONDHEIM He returned to New York in an artistic fury. A good fury, not the kind that presages a collapse. It was a marvel to behold.

He did that terrible play about Plath and Sexton—"Unselected Poems"—with Teri Garr as Sylvia and Amy Irving as Anne.[106] Off-off Broadway, with Hal Prince directing. I was in the middle of previewing "A Little Night Music," which Hal was *also* directing. I was incensed that he was spreading himself so thin but Hal was Hal; his amount of energy nearly matched Roar's. He was doing the Philip Barry, "Holiday," and the Dürrenmatt[107] at the same time. He phoned in "Unselected Poems"—though Hal phoning it in was equivalent to any normal director being involved up to ass and eyeballs. I was folded in half with fatigue and went to see "Unselected Poems" because Hal begged me. And after all, Roger was a friend. . . .

It was a complete, unmitigated disaster, a lazy fiasco filled with bad poetry and worse sex. Roger tried to rip off *O! Calcutta!*—which was having its ten-thousandth performance just a few miles away—the revue style, the blackouts, the sketches. But "Unselected" was just a shit bastardization of what I think could have been a lovely, moving play. Absolutely none of it worked. What was he thinking? What was *Hal* thinking? The answer is, neither were thinking at all . . . I simply didn't know what to say, where to *begin*. Hal said Roger wrote it in three days—it showed—from notes taken during his stay at McLean. Sexton gassed herself in a garage a few days before opening night, which gave new meaning to advance word of mouth. Boy oh boy. The whole critical world came after him; time to bring the whiz kid down a few notches. Kenny [Tynan] was kind enough not to write about it but the *Times* ripped him thirteen new assholes. Mailer reviewed it for the *Voice*. You know, Norman was said to have had a famous vendetta because of the apocryphal thing that happened at the Capote wingding, the what's-it-was, the infamous Black and White Ball. When I asked Roar to tell me the *truth*, he was always evasive. Mailer titled the review "Career Moves" and ended his

---

106 Orr's play became the inspiration for *Three-Martini Afternoons at the Ritz: The Rebellion of Sylvia Plath & Anne Sexton* by Gail Crowther (Simon & Schuster, 2021)—*ed.*

107 "The Visit"—*ed.*

titanic evisceration with a callback: "Those witchy, twitchy lady poets knew a thing or two about good career moves" and Roar should follow suit. "You've made your garage, now lie in it." Boy oh boy. When Roger shut it down, the audiences were actually growing—there were crowds outside the theater, like something out of the *The Producers*. It was quickly becoming one of those legendary, must-see horror *hoots*. Sad, sad, sad. Such an ugly betrayal of poor, dead Anne's confidences . . . and actionable, I'm sure.

Her daughter could have sued but had better sense.

Footnote: when Truman died, Vidal got a lot of press with his snappy eulogy: "Good career move." Stole the line from Norman's review! Gore really *scored* with that one, you know, the "tossed off" remark made its immortal way into all those bitchy *le dernier mot juste* anthologies—he got more play than Oscar Wilde. A *very* good career move for Gore!

ANTHONY BOURDAIN (*chef, author*) Vidal was pithy but cruel. Suicide causes such horrific collateral damage—imagine how your loved ones suffer! Particularly the kids . . .

What type of monstrous person would do that?

GORE VIDAL Sexton and Plath? I never understood the allure of those tell-all, fatherfucking "Take my life—please!" bughouse Rockettes. *Mademoiselle* Sylvia looked like a callow moo-cow and L'il Oven Annie—or do I mean Garage Sale Annie—became hard and patrician, every bit the caricature of a vituperative, opiated old queen. I knew them well but *Ted* [Hughes] was the pretty one. Such a decorous hole: like a little briar in the Cotswolds.

GILBERT GOTTFRIED (*comedian*) Roger licked his wounds over the Plath/Sexton debacle—he should have called that play "The Aristocrats"!— by working on two scripts: the Hemingway [*Gigi*], which took another thirty years to make; and one of his masterworks, *Grace War*. Around then, he was offered a major role in a film that his old friend Miloš Forman was shooting in London in the spring of 1975 [*Philip Phaethon*]. Forman should have called it "The Aristocrats"!

AUDREY RANK-SHAWCROSS (*critic*) *Philip Phaethon* is about a reclusive novelist, a perennial short-lister for the Nobel who gives a famous, aging biographer access to a trove of personal documents so that he can write the story of his life. On the eve of publication, the novelist changes his mind and revokes all permissions. The court rules in the novelist's favor and the books are pulped, erasing ten years of the archivist's meticulous, illuminating work. The jilted biographer seeks revenge.

Phaethon was like a cross between one of those magnificent Henry James stories about writers—and *The Blue Angel*.

PETER SHAFFER (*playwright*) *Philip Phaethon* was a kind of reverse *Amadeus* if that makes sense—though more a preamble to Forman's *Valmont* [1989]. A down-on-his-luck American book critic wagers a wealthy biographer that he can lure the narcissistic novelist who spurned him into showing up to accept a fake literary award. Roger plays the catty, amoral critic, an idea he particularly savored after the drubbing he got for *Unselected Poetry*. Besides, he had such great fun doing *Candle, Book, Bell* [1964] with Miloš.

London was just the tonic he needed. He reconnected with old friends— Tynan, Frank Bowling—but most importantly, Francis [Bacon], who was smack in the middle of creating the *Black Triptychs*, those towering, cathartic paintings of George Dyer. Dyer had committed suicide only a few years before; when Roar shared the news about Boodles, he was quite shocked. One would have thought he'd have already known—the pairing of Boodles with Edie Sedgwick had made their deaths somewhat of an international affair. But Francis was insular and typically had no idea what was going on in the world.

He remembered Boodles—and the famous Claridge's expedition—with great fondness. They bonded over whatever guilt they still harbored toward their phantom lovers and made a duet of atonements-by-proxy.

NED ROREM Roar said that he [and Bacon] gave each other "grief hand jobs." "Grief hand jobs don't give you the *la petite mort*," he said. "They give you *la petite vie*."

ANTHONY B. UNGER (*executive producer*) Ralph Richardson was extraordinary as the megalomaniacal novelist. Roar was known as a songwriter and film director but certainly not as an actor; he was an unknown commodity in that regard. After Sir Ralph signed on, Miloš thought it safe to propose Roar for the part of the critic. The financiers wouldn't allow it. They were adamant.

But when Gielgud agreed to play the biographer, the money people shrugged and finally said okay. It was good for the Jews! Good Lord, that sounded a bit anti-Semitic, didn't it? For the record, that's not my quote at all! It's Roar's. I'm Jewish, by the way.

PENELOPE HOUSTON (*critic,* Sight & Sound) Harold Pinter did the screenplay and had a rather public squabble with Miloš over the very last scene in the film. The script of *Phaethon* was great but Miloš thought the ending fell flat. In Miloš's opinion, it was too cool. Too . . . Pinteresque.

When they couldn't agree, Harold walked away. So now they didn't have a proper ending, and this was just days before they wrapped. Roar wound up writing it, uncredited—arguably the most tragically poetic, most *operatic* scene in all of cinema.

ANTHONY B. UNGER Funded by the scorned biographer, the critic invents the "Janus Literary Foundation" as part of an astonishingly intricate, believable ruse. The novelist is offered an enormous sum to accept the very first Janus Award. Of course, he's cynical, you know, he's above all that and laughs in "the Foundation"'s face. They chip, chip, chip away . . . and it doesn't *hurt* that the lovely Helen Mirren—a "Janus" operative and sometime lover of the critic played by Roar—is sent to the novelist's bolthole in Sussex to grease the wheels. But the man won't be swayed. An ace in the hole allows this megalomaniac to stand his ground; oddsmakers have tipped him to win that year's Nobel. When he loses to a writer whom he abhors, he accepts the Janus Award out of spite—*and* because its purse is larger than its Swedish counterpart!

The plot's far better than any of those long cons Mamet came up with for his little trifles—and as good as any of Poe's gloriously labyrinthine contraptions. Sondheim left a screening just enraptured; he was always a puzzle freak and a brilliant player of that game. When we passed muster with Stephen, I knew we had something.

MICHAEL CAINE (*actor*) It was a tremendous influence on *Sleuth.* Just tremendous . . . the behind-the-scenes story of *Philip Phaethon* makes for intriguing movie lore. I love reading about that sort of thing—bit of a bus-man's holiday. And here's some *television* lore for you: did you know the Monty Python boys were such fans of the movie when it came out that Terry Gilliam brilliantly changed the opening credit to *Monty Phaethon*?

You see, Pinter's script ends with the novelist—Sir Ralph—showing up in a Rolls sent by Ms. Mirren and "the Janus Foundation." Helen's told him the plan: his arrival shall be at the very *end* of the ceremonies so that he can make the grandest of grand entrances. He shall be ushered into the auditorium to a standing ovation—the hundreds of black-tie guests will already have been cued to bring their attention to the front of the theater to welcome the esteemed first winner of the Janus Prize. He's met on the sidewalk by photographers and an escort—his tormentors have thought of everything!—and after having his picture taken, triumphantly steps into what we know will be a ruinously empty auditorium. But in the Pinter script, the camera remains outside. End credits were meant to begin as the chauffeur leans on the Roller having a smoke. You never *see* his crack-up upon realizing he's been had. Now, I do sympathize with Harold—sometimes there's far greater power in withholding—though I believe his version would play best in a novel, where imagination is king. Or in the theater, where you could hear the novelist screaming offstage. It's quite different with film. Roger told Miloš the finale should be closer to *Nightmare Alley*, when Tyrone Power goes daft. "The people want to see him bite off those chicken heads!" You must *always* give the people what they want. That's a hard rule in show business.

I spoke to Roger at a dinner party and asked him all about it—I couldn't get enough. I remember he said something quite interesting, quite marvel-ous really. He said it was important to show the *annihilation* of the carefully crafted Self—its absolute collapse when the coronation is unceremoniously, brutally canceled. What struck me is that he said we should all be lucky enough to endure "a palace coup" such as the novelist experienced. "Because on the other side—*if we make it through*, Michael—there are absolute won-ders." He would know, wouldn't he?

Anyway, he wrote some new pages and Miloš went bananas for them.

HELEN MIRREN (*actress*) That last bit in the film brought Ralph some-where else. It's like he left the Earth. . . . Nabokov wrote that wonderful essay and called his performance "four-dimensional Shakespearean."[108] The condensed, *sustained* performance—losing his mind as the catacombs of vanity caved in and entombed is unwatchably grotesque, unwatchably wondrous. I've seen it a thousand times and can't imagine how he did it.

BEVERLY D'ANGELO I was on set, standing behind the director's chair.

I never saw anything like it and never will.

Cosmic performance art.

That's the only way I can describe it.

To see Ralph Richardson *collapse* then *recover* then *collapse*—to see that *face* morphing from charming, heartbreaking innocence into the darkest of darknesses by way of these adorable, frightening tics and elegantly unpredictable *universe* of eccentricities—raging *forward* then pulling *back* like some moonlit black tide . . . *fast*-motion, *slow*-motion, *fast*-motion, *slow*-motion—a Turner nighttime seascape. And the Shostakovich piano concerto bleeding in, on playback, and then the fucking *Supremes*—Miloš was so *musical*—I wouldn't have done *Hair* if I hadn't met him through Roar—Miloš had the idea to do playback during that scene—there wasn't any dialogue, so blasting music didn't matter. Only he and Ralph knew about it—the playback—except of course for the sound people and the cameraman. I've been on psilocybin trips where the shaman or guide or whatever plays music as you're coming out, it roughs up your heart, you *become* Heart.

And that's just what it was like for me as I stood there trying not to sob, hearing that music, watching Sir Ralph.

The devilish angel-magician Sir Ralph.

When Miloš said cut, there was dead silence. No one moved. Finally, Ralph cleared his throat and said, "Yes, well."

The whole crew unraveled then broke into soundstage-shaking applause. *One take.*

SIMON CALLOW (*actor*) If you blink, you may find me in *Philip Phaethon*. It's the very first thing I did on film . . .

---

108 The phrase is from "Philip Phaethon's Phantom Phaeton" by Vladimir Nabokov, *London Review of Books* 18, 1973.

One weekend, I tagged along with Roar, Miloš, Francis [Bacon], Sir Ralph, and Kenny [Tynan]—how's that for a posse?—we all went to Glyndebourne for *The Marriage of Figaro*. That was Peter Hall. Peter was obsessed with conscripting Richardson for the National. He considered him a god. We all did.

KENNETH TYNAN Richardson was enamored of Roger—I never saw him laugh so violently. And Roar? Completely captivated by "the magus." He was always looking for father figures and Sir Ralph shot to the top of the Daddy List.

ORSON WELLES (*actor, director*)[109] Miloš was quite angry; he'd asked me to play the lead in *Phaethon* but I didn't like Pinter, just loathed him— the man, not the writer—and wouldn't do it on principle. You see, I knew Antonia [Fraser] and she'd told me everything about their affair.[110] I was her therapist and confessor; some of *Punter's* bedroom hijinks were grimy and miserable. But it wasn't all that. I just hated the way he looked—like some cut-rate Michael Caine—hated his *smell*. So, when Miloš asked, I said, No no *no*. He got Ralph Richardson, who did all right with it.

Months later, I happened to be in London doing a voiceover for *Ten Little Indians* and went down to Glyndebourne to see Kiri Te Kanawa play the Countess in *Figaro*. I saw her do the part a few years before in Santa Fe and fell madly in love. In Glyndebourne, not without great sadness, I learned that the countess was happily married and impervious to suave innuendo. Oliver Reed was my wingman and we were *very* drunk. At some point, Ollie said something to Roar, who gave him a stare—one of those looks I've learned in my wisdom to steer clear of. But Ollie got his blood up and I intervened because Roger was known to be handy with his fists. He'd killed a boy, a bully, when he was young, and gotten away with it. I know this for a fact because I knew Peter Gramm, who told me everything about *everyone*. But I'll say no more—less will be revealed! Roar was a hell of a boxer too, very gifted. A scary customer. And that glorious business of getting Mailer to suck his cock

---

109 From *My Lunches With Orson: Conversations Between Henry Jaglom and Orson Welles* (Peter Biskind, editor), pp. 217–219 (Metropolitan Books/Henry Holt, 2013).

110 Pinter was married to Vivien Merchant when he began an affair with the historian Antonia Fraser in 1970, whom he married in 1975.—*ed.*

. . . which I know for a fact as well because I was friendly with a waiter who witnessed the deed. The man hid behind pots and pans and took *notes*; he'd been hired by Truman for the Ball and couldn't wait to tell *all* when I came into La Côte Basque for lunch the next day.

I like Roar, always have, he was really quite good [in *Philip Phaethon*] but is so much better when he sticks to composing a ditty. My *God* was that picture overrated. In the end, *Phaethon's* just pretentious S&B: Shit & Bathos. Miloš always had a fatally sentimental streak.

But they did well with it, didn't they?

BURT BACHARACH (*songwriter*) Roger told me that the night after seeing *The Marriage of Figaro* he went back to his hotel and wrote two songs: "Second Look" and "The Air That I Breathe." The Hollies had a big hit with "The Air That I Breathe," which is kind of a hybrid—typical Roger, you know, bringing a sly, Everyman mysticism to a pop fluff anthem—but nowhere near as interesting or complex, nowhere near as *Sondheimian* as "Second Look."

ROGER ORR[111] "The Air That I Breathe" was my decrepit homage to the Beach Boys' "God Only Knows," which no one can touch. I was a bit ashamed of even having tried.

HELEN MIRREN After *Phaethon*, I did *Hamlet* with Quentin Crisp, straight-away—and Roger went off to LA to do a Carl Reiner picture. The pop culture ponies did well at the races and he was a betting man. They brought in the money and that was important to him.

LAUGHLIN ORR Miloš did *Cuckoo's Nest* after *Phaethon* and my brother arranged a dinner with Kesey in San Francisco. We trooped over to the Haight—maybe Zam Zam? Probably Zam Zam. I brought Grace [Slick] and when Roger told her he was directing *Grace War* next, she said, "You better hire me or I'll fucking sue you for using my name without permission." She'd never acted before, but everyone was stoned and thought it was a really good idea. Like, *the best idea in the history of the world.* Roger drew a contract on a napkin that we all signed and witnessed. Stewart Brand

---

111 From *Either/Orr: The Rest of Roger Orr*, edited by Simon Callow (Pegasus Press, 2016).

showed up, then Stanley Mouse, then the poet John Wieners . . . then—
surprise!—*Ginzy* [Allen Ginsberg]. I kind of brokered that, because they
hadn't seen each other in years, since all the bullshit trouble Gregory
[Corso] started. I was like come on, guys, it's enough already. They started
bawling because they loved and missed each other so much. Total Old
Home Week.

I kept looking at the door, thinking the ghost of Jack might walk in.

PETER BART (*producer, journalist*) *Who Loves Ya, Maybe* was an absolutely forgettable Carl Reiner date movie starring Roar, Richard Benjamin,
Teri Garr, and Walter Matthau that made four hundred million dollars. After
the heady arthouse Sturm und Drang of *Philip Phaethon,* the well-oiled
Hollywood hitmaking machine was just what the doctor ordered.

He and Teri might have had a little thing.

TERI GARR (*actress*) Roger and I laughed about the whole *Unselected
Poetry* debacle. Oh, boy. Oh God! (I did *Oh God!* with Carl right after *Who
Loves Ya, Maybe*—ha!) Time had passed, so we could laugh. I mean, laugh
kinda. More of a teehee. Definitely not a guffaw.

We had some strange shit in common. A movie I was in with Elvis, *Fun
in Acapulco,* was released on the same day as the first movie Roger ever
directed—*They Sleep by Night*—the day JFK was shot. And then I played
Sylvia Plath in *Unselected Poetry* . . . holy moly. So when we were shooting
Who Loves Ya, Maybe we started calling each other Kiss of Death. You know,
we'd see each other in front of our trailers and say, "Mornin', Kiss of Death!"
When we wrapped the day, it'd be, "G'night, Kiss of Death!" Foul weather
friends for life. But fair weather too.

He was a huge help with my book.[112] I was doing press for it and he went
with me for the Letterman show [in 2007]. Picked me up in a limo with tons
of roses in the backseat. . . . That was *another* thing we shared in common
because we both had this very kind of special relationship with Dave. Roger
had of course been on the show not too long before, when he told the world
about his surgery. And I'd been on a thousand times but was terrified because

---

112 *Speedbumps: Flooring It Through Hollywood* (Plume, 2006) chronicles Garr's career and
    health struggles after being diagnosed with multiple sclerosis.—*ed.*

now it was *my* turn to come out—after being diagnosed with MS. I'd been out of the public eye, as they say, because it was just too hard, physically, emotionally, bla. I thought, What's the audience going to think when they see me? My right arm atrophied and I had trouble walking—*Are they gonna gasp?* Hey, I'm vain. Happens to the best of us. I freaked out and was going to cancel. But Roger propped me up, and Dave was wonderful; he walked me to the couch like the gentleman he is, and it was fine. I was *shaky* but it was fine. I knew everything was going to be all right when I looked over and saw Roger beaming with love from the wings like a dad—I mean mom!—because he was wearing a floral midi.

I loved him *soooo much.* Think about him every day.

MELLIE KOCH Financing suddenly came together for *Grace War,* and we pretty much started preproduction while he was still shooting the Carl Reiner movie. *Grace* had locations in Marfa, Iowa, and Alabama—Roar was incredibly excited. He'd say, "This is the one." He said that about every movie.

BEVERLY D'ANGELO [*Philip Phaethon*] was in competition in Berlin [1976] but we didn't go. The money kept falling through on *Grace War,* and Roger was too focused and depressed to travel. It was getting impossible. A very difficult time for him.

Grace didn't shoot until the long, hot summer of '78.

PETER BART It was a great year at the Berlinale. *How, How, How Can You Keep Saying That* [Lina Wertmüller] was pegged to win; bookmakers had *The Man Who Fell to Earth* [Nicolas Roeg] losing by a nose. But the Special Jury went to Altman [for *Buffalo Bill and the Indians, or Sitting Bull's History Lesson*] and *Philip Phaethon* won the Golden Bear. The biggest surprise was Roger winning the Silver for Best Actor—a vindication of sorts because the Americans and even the Globes put him in the Best Supporting slot. *Phaethon* was totally shut out of BAFTA and Miloš wasn't happy about that at all. But *Cuckoo's* swept a few years later.

JULIANNE MOORE The critics went bonkers. They *loved* him in *Phaethon.* It was one of those trials by fire because the whole world's gunning for you. Overnight, Roar added Actor—with a capital A—to his amazing technicolor dream coat. Miloš seemed to be the only one who knew that was *exactly* what would happen. He'd been saying it from day one, but everyone thought it was just a confidence-builder—and that he was going a little bit overboard!

LAUGHLIN ORR I suddenly had a problem—like, literally the mother of all fucking problems. Jonny called. The first thing he said was, "You need to come to Coos Bay." Which was a weird opener, especially because he didn't sound like himself. I mean, at *all*. I said, "What happened?" He just kept repeating, "You need to come." I said, "Jonny, are you okay?" Long pause. "No, I am *not*, Laughlin. I am *not*." He *never* used my name like that. He said he'd finally gone through the boxes—the ones he trucked up from Parnassus—and read Mom's diaries.

JONNY "STAGE DOOR" ORR None of us were particularly close around that time. There was a big sis-boom-bah when my brother was shot—everyone rallied together—but once he was out of the woods we kind of drifted back to our original positions. Like families do. Everybody's got their own lives, doing their own thing. My old lady and I were pretty involved in the commune. Harvest Sun was a working farm, and we started a bookstore too. My OCD hermit shit was starting to chill and I was getting comfortable in my own skin.

The diaries were sitting in the attic above the bookstore, stacked in metal boxes—kind of like a final resting place. They'd been in storage in San Mateo and I brought 'em up when I got the farm. To be honest, I forgot they were even there. I was busy. And it wasn't my life's work, you know, to read Mom's diaries. That's more something a daughter would want to do, not a son. But Laughlin didn't seem to be interested.

This was in the fall of '75.

Twelve years since she died.

I remember it was raining.

I closed the store, smoked a joint, and went up to the attic.

It felt like I was sleepwalking—like I was being controlled by some outside force. I watched my legs climb the staircase, *bop bop bop*. I totally wasn't in my body. . . . I *was* stoned—but this was something else. I watched my arms reach out and lift the lid off the top box. Saw myself staring at a notebook resting on top, marked "1940." . . . I didn't even say anything to Chickweed about it—my old lady—not at first.

I knew I had to tell Laughlin but definitely didn't want to do that over the phone. My sister was involved in so much political crap; I was pretty sure the FBI would be listening. She was in her early forties and still crazy as fuck. She almost got in trouble with the Patty Hearst deal because she knew all the folks in the SLA—she met Cinque at UC Berkeley and used to ball him when he was in Soledad. I don't even want to know the details of how *that* was arranged. But she was always hiring Kunstler to get her out of some kind of bogus bullshit, and that's why I didn't want to say too much on the phone.

LAUGHLIN ORR It took me, I don't know, about a month to get to Harvest Sun after Jonny called. I was in the middle of a bad breakup and couldn't get it together. I've gotten a lot better but at the time, you know, "It's Laughlin's world, everyone else just lives in it." I was terrible.

That commune was so fucking beautiful—I couldn't believe I'd never visited. Never had the curiosity to check it out. How self-involved is that? I was just so proud of my baby brother because he created this beautiful life for himself. And maybe a little jealous because it felt like Heaven on Earth. Looked like it too.

So, we go to the bookstore—everything reeks of incense—love my hippie bro!—and he points to the dark, rickety stairs. "Up there," he says. I go up like I'm a hundred percent in a horror movie. The attic's even darker than the stairs but there's a desktop lamp spotlighting a journal. *It's shining on an open page.* Crazy cinematic. Staged by the famous impresario Jonny Stage Door.

I settle in and start to read. Mom's writing about a miscarriage, and I got confused about the time line—but then she wrote that I'd come up to La Piedra to visit, and I suddenly remembered her in a muumuu, how she wouldn't let me play the game where I touched her stomach . . . *because there was no baby there.* I wasn't even in denial, I was just massively anxious and bewildered. Then the entries got fucking weirder. She wrote that Peter Gramm "found a baby" in Nashville, and it had a little deformity. *An extra nipple.* I thought, "Oh, that's interesting"—Mom came right out and *said it* but I just couldn't process. For some reason I started reading out loud—maybe to help my brain slow down—then closed my eyes and sunk deep until the words scuba'd up like a Magic-8 Ball: *Roger was adopted.* More words sur-faced: *Roger's birth mother was Black.*

I sat there in the crow's nest like some scholar discovering a tale from *A Thousand and One Nights.* Like a scene from one of my brother's movies.

BEVERLY D'ANGELO It's easy to think, "Of course they should have told Roar—*tout fucking suite.*" But it was complicated.

Jonny and Laughlin were like a small country that stumbles across an undetonated roadside bomb—then realize it's a nuke. Who you gonna call? And they were super protective of Roar: *First, do no harm.* He'd only been out of the hospital a few years and was still "McLean and sober." Going to AA, working a program . . . and about to do a big new film, *Grace War*—strangely enough, about an interracial love affair. Which *wasn't* so strange because Roar was a warlock, a witch, he was both, he surfed the collective uncon-scious. Jonny would have followed Laughlin's lead but she was paralyzed. She was the one designated to give Roar the news but didn't want to be the mes-senger; we know what happens to messengers. She thought, "Tell him or not, he's going to hate me either way." And that's exactly what happened.

LAUGHLIN ORR I had three abortions before I was thirty. Followed by three miscarriages—the last, only a year before I read Mom's diary. The doc-tors finally said I'd never be able to "conceive." Hate that word. The same thing that happened to Mom, but in my case, I was done. I did MDMA a few months later to work through a lot of shit. It was heavy. I felt Bunny's pain—how prideful she was, how ashamed. How vulnerable. I just wanted to *hold* her. I saw myself as a little girl, my arms wrapped around that terrified, bereft woman, the one who couldn't *conceive*, draped in that . . . tragic muumuu—the muumuu of mourning!

SUZE BERKOWITZ Roger was so angry they didn't tell him right away, mostly at his sister but I understood what happened. He *should* have been pissed at Bunny and the Commodore—instead, he put his rage on Laughlin and made her part of the conspiracy. Which couldn't have been further from the truth. She was an innocent. So unfair. To me, it would have been like blaming Seraphim for what happened.

GRACE SLICK Laugh knew how important *Grace War* was and didn't want to take an action that would derail it. So, she decided to wait until the movie was done before telling him. But there wound up being so many delays . . . We talked about it. I was one of the few people who knew, one of the few she could trust. Her plan was to have a sit-down sometime around his forti-eth, which wasn't too far off. He'd finish the film, have a birthday bash, then learn the truth that had been hidden from him for all the usual dark, incom-prehensible, fucked-up family reasons. Until then, ignorance was bliss—so, what was the rush? That's what Laugh told herself, even though it gnawed a pretty big hole in her tummy. It was easier for Jonny. He was much more insular, more of a compartmentalizer. The dirty work would be left to his sister anyway. He was Baby Brother: "Not my job!" Jonny literally told me that he didn't think it mattered if Roger *ever* knew!

Maybe if Laugh did tell him earlier, we wouldn't have had *Grace War*, which would have been a tragedy. I am *so* Team Laughlin.

BEVERLY D'ANGELO We were in New York. *Grace War* was locked and loaded, with a summer release—four months away. He'd just had a birthday when Laughlin brought him the diary—was he thirty-eight? Thirty-nine? I don't think he was *forty*, because I think I would have remembered that . . . no—he was thirty-nine, because I'd just done *Hair*. And that was 1979.

The three of us were in the room. That huge suite in the Pierre. Laughlin gave me a heads-up the day before, so I knew what was coming. Better to lower the boom on one head instead of two. Right? He read the perti-nent passages and looks up with a smile, nonplussed. Said something like, "This is Bunny's diary?" A non sequitur. He didn't have too much emotion. Obviously, he was in shock but I think Laughlin and I were relieved the first round seemed to be going okay. We knew there'd be a delayed reaction, but if this was an indicator . . .

He even got excited about making a plan to go to the West Coast to see Peter Gramm for more details. All in all, he took it well.

"A little *too* well"—that's what Laughlin said to me when we left.

The day before he was supposed to leave for San Francisco, a maid found him. He took a bunch of Nembutal and had a bag over his head—exactly what Bunny did when she finished herself off. If the housekeeper hadn't walked in, end of story. Laughlin put him in Payne Whitney and he was there for a month. It was awful, because I had to leave for Oklahoma to do *Coal Miner's Daughter.* Thank God I had Sissy to cry to, because she knew how close I was to Roger.[113] She was the only one I told that I was pregnant. . . . It was all so fucked.

Laughlin had so much guilt. She said she should have burned the fucking diaries and carried the secret to her grave. She was in agony. But you know what? There was no way he *wouldn't* have lost his mind—which was the best thing that could have happened. He *had* to lose it.

That's what he always wanted.

HARVEY FIERSTEIN The broken sword gets forged into something unbreakable. The spiritual side of him knew that. Like Narsil in *Lord of the Rings*—forged by dwarves, broken, then put back together again by elves! What's that old showbiz saying? "Dying is easy, comedy is hard."

Dying is easy.

Rebirth is the motherfucker.

---

113 Spacek and D'Angelo played twins in 1963's *They Sleep By Night.*—*ed.*

CHAPTER ELEVEN

Grace War

JAMES L. BROOKS (*producer*) There we were in Marfa. And this was before Marfa was *Marfa*. Oh, Donald Judd was already there. Was he ever not? There's something addictive about the place, for sure. You couldn't wait to go to sleep, just so you could wake up there. What's that drug in the *Dune* books? The one the worms are always digging for? Marfa was like *that*. You walked around in a kind of sunlit, euphoric delirium. You felt more alive than you did anywhere else. It was like Shangri-La. You never wanted to leave.

Roar called it Marfan Syndrome.

BEVERLY D'ANGELO Denzel [Washington] had a serious case of Marfan Syndrome. He couldn't believe such a place existed. His dad was a minister and his mom was born in Georgia—Denzel's character in the film was being extradited to Alabama but Roger changed it to Georgia when he found that out. Denz had only done summer stock and a tiny TV movie when he got cast—this was a few years before *St. Elsewhere*. Marfa just opened him up. The funny thing is, he told me he'd always had a big fantasy about living in Texas and going to school in Lubbock.

Who'd a thunk.

We took over this little motel called the Tangleweed. The Tangleweed! I'm just remembering . . . *such* a magical time. Denzel had to learn how to ride, which took him about three minutes—you've never seen anything more gorgeous on a horse. You'd pass his room and the door was wide open, the Stones blasting out. You'd peek in and he'd turn to look at you with that mischievous virgin smile, his face split open like a lysergic cantaloupe. He'd grab me and we'd sing, "*Wild horses . . . couldn't drag me away.*" True, that.

MELLIE KOCH Bev played a single mom, a junkie trying to get clean. She wasn't yet thirty, but in the script, her kid's half her age. She's trying to break away from her pimp but he wants her daughter in exchange, so they run away to Texas. Bev starts working at a diner and in walks Denzel. She's never seen a cowboy, let alone a Black one. They had a *lot* of chemistry.

Jim Brooks called them the Chemistry Kids.

ALI BERK People thought Beverly and I looked alike, so playing her daughter totally worked . . . Uncle Roary used to joke that I *was* their daughter! Oh my God, I would blush!

Mom and Dad came to visit once, just for a few days. I don't think they liked movie sets very much. I had a guardian, you know, to help with schoolwork, but everything was a lot more lax than it is today. I got close to Donald Judd's kids, Flavin and Rainer—I kind of became the big sister. They lived in this amazing place, rows and rows of barracks, with huge marble stones and cubes of crushed cars inside. The experience of doing *Willow* was amazing but *Grace* was a "coming-of-age." I even made out with one of the stuntmen. That's the first time I've ever told anyone that! I'm going to write about it all one day.[114]

GRACE SLICK I was "Crystal"—the salty, world-weary Mama Bear waitress at the diner Beverly worked at. I was just happy to be there. Happy to be anywhere, as they say in AA. But especially happy to be in Marfa. I'd just been fired from Starship for some hijinks at a concert in Germany. Told the audience they were fucking Nazis—some such standard, heinously offensive rock and roll shit—and Paul [Kantner] busted me for TUI: Talking Under the Influence. Haha. You know, I still have that napkin contract Roger and I signed at Zam Zam. Have it *somewhere.*

Roar ran these AA meetings at the Tangleweed Motel and I'd sit in. He knew I wasn't sober—that didn't happen till the Nineties—but was really gracious. In AA, you don't preach or judge, you lead by example. Actually, I was pretty well-behaved because I took the gig seriously—and because China[115]

---

114 She would, in *Travels with My Uncle: A Remembrance* by Ali Berk, pp. 137–145 (Pantheon, 2019)—*ed.*

115 China Wing Kantner, the daughter she shared with Jefferson Starship guitarist Paul Kantner.—*ed.*

was there. She was the same age as Don Judd's kids and they all had a blast. Thank God I didn't bring the Quaaludes.

Best decision I ever made.

RAINER JUDD (*actress*) I saw [Roger Orr] in SoHo in 1993, at the opening of the Spring Street house we grew up in. We wanted the public to be able to see it, but it was weird that it was now a museum. My father died ten months later and Roar sent the most beautiful note . . . We'd run into each other through the years in funny, unexpected places—once in Prague and once at my dad's place in Switzerland.[116] I was shocked to see Roar magically appear—I hadn't seen him since the *Grace War* shoot. He was unsteady on his feet. And softer, much softer—I think he'd begun taking hormones. He still had that smile, an alien, benevolent smile, welcoming you into the secret organization he called "the Club of Alien Hearts." Roger gave me a pendant with the letters CAH intertwined. I still wear it on special occasions.

ROGER ORR[117] Why do all these man crushes of mine crudely summon the Commodore? It's just too obvious and absurd, too comical. . . . I think of Don J. the way Jack wet-dreamed Neil [Cassady]. "I think of Don Judd, I even think of Old Don Judd the father we never found, I think of Don Judd." . . . I think of his *art*—but how perfect can a stool or simple wooden table be? They're out there, spread over America—the perfect stool, perfect bench, perfect table—the primitive-modern, the modern-primitive—and Don *knows* they're perfect. And knows they cannot be his . . . because they're . . . *out there*. I abhor this strangely magnetic impulse to swallow perfection, then present it in a perfect little alcove—a gathering of ten thousand stools and chairs and table and benches—to capture them as you would so much bark in a petrified forest—I abhor it because all of those impulses reside in me. The impossible dream: to reach the unreachable wooden stool, to dream the impossible perfect metal shelf, as the song goes. And yet, the fetishization of *les objets banals*, the more mundane the better, is a noble pursuit. Perhaps *the* most noble. God knows I've spent a lifetime doing the same. For me, it's not so much the fetish

---

116 In 1991, Judd restored Eichholteren, a family inn on the shores of Lake Lucerne that had
fallen into disrepair.—*ed.*

117 From *Long Day's Journal Into Night*, *Vol. 3*, pp. 515–523 (Harcourt Brace, 2008).

that allures but the fetishists: for they are the fanatical acolytes of a phantom world, they are the sad soldiers and tidy ghosts. That's what Don J. is—a great general, a *generalist*, not a private. Don Coyote, tilting at objects: I was reading one of the rules that Chuck Jones concocted for Wile E. Coyote and the Road Runner. "The Coyote could stop anytime—if he were not a fanatic." Mr. Jones goes on to quote Santayana, of all people! "A fanatic is someone who redoubles his efforts when he has forgotten his aim." (Note to self: need to meet Mr. Jones.) . . . poor Don, with his shelves and barracks of endless fabricated steel, the boxes and tables and benches meant to *last*, for Eternity! The comic, cosmic OCD of it. And I've heard he insists on writing up legal contracts to ensure his installations will never go away. Autistically designing Infinity . . .

He showed me his Land Rover, with its perfect bespoke metal appendages designed by Don J.—in a century, books or their equivalents (for books will be extinct) will record that DJ, at one time, owned every home, car, bird, and insect in Marfa *and surrounding areas*: owned/designed the very dirt mounds and dogs; designed the breath that came from the mouths of all living things (designed the unseeable breath of dead things too)—acquired endless *ownership* of the abstract and (literal) concrete, a monstrous assertion of Self camouflaged by superior aesthetics, relentless Beckettian erasures and repetition—the delusion being that by sheer scale and force of will, he might erase *himself*—all of it belied and bellied up by an obsession with legacy & permanence. "ME!" is the antiseptic anti-Ganesh on display in all the hangars and bullshit barracks . . . yet I adore him for trying. Perversely, DJ's world— the thing his Christina yearns toward—with its Brobdingnagian ceilings and barracks made holy by their quixotically strange, heroic American moribundity—like great churches of nostalgia for the Unknowable, already perfect in their striving—those barracks and vault-ceiling hangars only bested by the celestial vaults of Marfan sky—is a world I *understand*, a world I covet and aspire to—I, the hypocrite—a world I can taste and smell and love, a world that gets me *hard*. (Wonder if DJ feels the same.)

It's a dirty job, but Don has to do it.

There but for Don, go I . . .

I did make him smile though. He was railing about the idiots who call him a minimalist and I said, "You're not a minimalist, you're an empiricist." He liked that so much, he got quiet. You've never seen a more handsome object when it shuts up.

When DJ sleeps, he dreams of his thousands of acres metastasizing into carpets of wooden tables and stools—toadstools!—perfect calibrated bookshelves and boxes and drawers made of steel and ice, a divine cascade, until the world's hills, plains and valleys are rid of people, a world that is the loveliest, pluperfect place to *look-see*—a museum created by gods who can finally forget they ever made a human creature.

In short, Donald Judd is my ideal husband.

BEVERLY D'ANGELO A lot of the crew was local. There were tons of wives and lovers and babies running around and even our DP was pregnant, so maybe Roar got triggered. There were the Judd kids . . . and Daria Halprin visited with Ruthanne, the angel-faced little girl she had with Dennis [Hopper]. Dennis was shooting *Apocalypse* while we were doing *Grace*, but they'd already divorced. Daria's amazing, she was in *Zabriskie Point*, she's a dancer and a healer. I think she started a commune in Marin with her mom—Stage Door probably knows her! That's just what Marfa felt like: a commune. Location shoots can be like that.

Procreation was in the air. . .

One day, we're sitting around the firepit at the Tangleweed, and Roar asks if I want to have kids. Completely out of the blue—that was something we *never* talked about. I mean, ever. The vibe was: off-limits. Plus, he told Laughlin that when Aurelia died, something shifted—having a child got swept off the table forever. So I was stunned he brought it up but went with the flow. I was like, "Gee, I dunno. Haven't really thought about it." Which of course I had. Then he says, "Want to? With me?" I almost burst into tears but stayed cool.

I said, "I'd love that."

And threw out my birth control pills.

SUZE BERKOWITZ He sent love letters from Marfa and that made me a little . . . I don't know, uncomfortable. They were *surreptitiously* about us getting back together one day but not really. I mean, I didn't take them seriously. He was always a flirt. When he visited us in Maui, he'd sing "Maybe I'm Amazed"—though never when Scatter was around! That was my favorite song. But there wasn't anything . . . sexual. The attraction was long gone. From my side, anyway. And I'm pretty sure from his too.

I didn't want Scatter to find the letters but couldn't bring myself to burn them, either. I wasn't in love with Roger anymore, it wasn't that; he was family. Scatter wouldn't have cared. He'd probably have laughed. But *part* of me—the part that fell in love with Roger when I was literally just a kid, the part that honored the sacredness of what we had and the baby we'd lost—*that* part had trouble throwing them out. The Wifey part. The writing was so beautiful. *Duh.* I knew he didn't mean what he was saying, not really. He was just reveling in his words and his love: for me, for language, for the world.

And of course I was right because some of what he wrote to me turned up in that song—"Matadors."

BEVERLY D'ANGELO He asked me to mail something to Suze, along with a bunch of other stuff to his agents and whatnot—we did Marfan mail runs every few days, like they do in the communes.

On the way to the little post office, I opened the letter—why did I do that? No idea. It wasn't *like* me. Whatever.

It was a love letter to Suze, and I got hurt. I assumed she was writing him back but found out later that it was a one-sided affair.

I did wind up sending it though.

Then took some deep breaths and tried to let it go.

* * * * * * * * *

Letter to Suze Berkowitz from Roger Orr

stigmatador!
how gorgeous your note, tho Scattered: elegantly turning down my advances on this Marfan epistolary dawn: so goes the impeccable turn-down service in the Infinity Hotel. to watch your fearless walk on golden bough: i never saw that branch of you. (couldn't see the forest for the Thee.) i admit I can be thick: you've always been my thicket out.

now
this gored old bullshitfighter
bows.

as for your wings, don't flutter a word, butterfly (and by the way, did you know
Grace Slick's maiden name is Wing?)____

i'll butter your fly.

maybe i'm a maze, at the way you pull me out of time . . .
maybe i'm a maze at the way i____

cellmates in that prison, we never showed our tiers
we were always planning the Great Escape.

and look
hey look
now they've got us in a holding cell
(finally have our own holding company)
those *fuckers*
we're rated ex
you'd think by now
those wardens would know
they'll never be able to break
two
true
blue
lifers

* * * * * * * * *

SCATTER HOLBROOK I *did* see that letter. She didn't show it to me until
after *Grace War* came out and "Matadors" won Best Song. I said, let's hold on
to that. If we sell it, that's Alice's college fund right there.

JAMES BROOKS The Marfa shoot went very well, but Georgia was another
story. If I ever write about it, I'll call that chapter "Roar and Peace."

. . .

CASS ROUARK (*biographer*)[118] Billie Holiday took her name from the silent film star Billie Dove ... Roar gave a lot of money to the Motion Picture and Television Hospital in Woodland Hills and in the last year of her life, Dove lived there. Roar used to visit. He loved seeing the old actors—people like Bud Abbott, Mary Astor, Buddy Rogers, and Loretta Young. Everyone "dressed" for lunch, and it was poignant. The waiters wore tuxedos and kept linen on the tables, very *The Shining*. When Roar mentioned to Billie Dove that Billie Holiday named herself after her, she said, "Isn't that lovely?" He could tell she didn't know who he was talking about. She was probably ninety-five and had dementia. Roar loved telling stories about the motion picture home because they reinforced that "all is illusion." The mantra he picked up in India.

Usually that led to an anecdote about his old road dawg, Francis Bacon. Bacon had a friend, a gifted painter whom he eclipsed. (Who *didn't* he eclipse?) It was beyond schadenfreude; Bacon took enormous pleasure rubbing the poor man's nose in it. The embittered friend became obsessed and blamed Bacon for destroying his career. The macabre thing was, he had a point—Roar said that Bacon was perverse and had actively done damage to many artists' reputations, for sport. At the end of his life, the friend was impoverished and critically forgotten. As he lay dying, the doctor said, "What can I do to make you more comfortable?" The friend said, "Tell me Francis Bacon is dead!" The doctor said, in complete earnest, "Who's Francis Bacon?"

Maybe Roar *wasn't* the one who told me that; maybe I read it in Francis's biography. Or maybe the *Times Literary Supplement*. Or maybe Wikipedia. Or Twitter. Maybe I've plagiarized it! Regardless, the point is, *All is illusion*. That was always Roar's cosmic punchline.

SAM WASSON Billie Dove is the only woman who ever turned down a marriage proposal from Howard Hughes. Hughes himself said she was "the one who got away." And she was a pilot too! She *did* star in a film he produced called *Cock of the Air*. That's the title, I fucking kid you not.

---

118 "Grace Roars," Cass Rouark, *Harper's* magazine, November 2003.

ROSIE LEVIN[119] When Bird left Leipers Fork, she was possessed with finding her idol Billie Holiday. Billie was touring with Artie Shaw and when Bird learned they were gigging in Oklahoma, she was bound and determined to find them. She was a heat-seeking missile.

And there was a lot of heat.

Artie had just divorced Lana Turner. On their own, he and Billie were sexually insatiable—together, they were nuclear. Q [Quincy Jones] used to say, "Motels didn't even have to burn the mattresses when they checked out, 'cause Artie and Lady took care of that for them. There wasn't anything left."

ETTA JAMES (singer) Bird was fifteen. She was fearless. Oklahoma City was ten hours from Nashville by car. That little bitty girl hitchhiked. She doesn't talk about it much but I know she paid a price. I *know* she was raped more than once before she got to Deep Deuce, the club Billie was singing at. That was the night Billie named her. She called her "Bird" even before she heard her sing.

"You got a broken wing, honey—maybe two of 'em—but when they heal, you'll fly higher than the rest."

Lady Day became a mother to her. Kept the men away too. For a while.

SAM CHARTERS Bird kind of auditioned for Billie. She started with "Strange Fruit" but it sounded too much like Billie so she cut her off and said, "Don't do *me*. Do *Bird*. Live up to your name!"

Bird took a deep breath and sang "The Glory of Love," real slow. No one could believe it. Billie had tears in her eyes.[120]

BOB THIELE Artie worried about them harboring a runaway but there was no way Billie was gonna give that child up. By then, Bird told her everything that had happened to her and Billie could relate; she'd been raped all kinds of times, starting at nine years old. Billie cleaned up [from heroin] for a time. She kept drinking but stayed away from dope because she abhorred the thought of Bird seeing her nod off with a harpoon in her arm.

---

119 *The Sparrow's Eye: The Rise And Rise Of Bird Rabineau* by Rosie Levin, pp. 91–93 (Norton, 1993).

120 *The Country Blues* by Sam Charters, pp. 283–287 (Da Capo Press, 1975).

BILLIE HOLIDAY (*singer*) She was like a puppy dog and stayed close. Watched the shows from the wings. I tried not to curse around that little girl. But one night some cracker called me a nigger when I was onstage. I told the man that if he wasn't the motherfuckin' faggot that he looked like, he could come right up and suck my motherfuckin' hot-pink nigger clit. He said all kinds of things back and Artie and the boys had to wrestle me offstage 'cause I was gonna jump into the crowd and beat that piece of shit to death with the mic stand. Would have, too.[121]

BIRD RABINEAU There was always some kind of drama going on. I remember a peckerwood called her the n-word and they stopped the show. But he got his, in the parking lot. Oh yes he did. And it wasn't just the band members. A coupla white boys got a piece of him.[122]

QUINCY JONES When Lady got back to New York, she introduced Bird as her niece. No one asked questions, and that was the end of it.

PETER BOGDONAVICH (*director*) It wasn't a secret that Billie had a big affair with Orson during *Citizen Kane*. The publishers made her take that out of *Lady Sings the Blues*. Orson told me he was furious about the omission. They met through Duke Ellington in 1940, when Orson was ginning up to do *It's All True*. Duke was going to do the music for "The Story of Jazz," with Louis Armstrong playing himself. Billie signed on and Orson met Bird too, because Bird never left her side. When Billie came to L.A. to see him, it was Bird's first time in Hollywood.

Anywhere Bird went outside the South was for the first time.

JOHN SZWED (*writer*)[123] Bird started heroin when she was sixteen. Rumor is that the actor Fred MacMurray "turned her out." He was married and twice her age, already a leading man who'd done a bunch of Westerns. But still a few years from the fame that *Double Indemnity* brought him.

---

121 *Lady Sings the Blues* by Billie Holiday and William Dufty, pp. 236–238 (Price Waterhouse, 1956).
122 *The Sparrow's Eye: The Rise and Rise of Bird Rabineau* by Keg Sweeney (Norton, 1993).
123 *Billie Holiday: The Musician and the Myth* by John Szwed, pp. 418–421 (Rapunzel, 2015).

PETER BART The studio hid MacMurray's drug problem for years.

KENNETH ANGER (*filmmaker, author*) Fred MacMurray began as a singer and musician. He played clarinet in the "Chi" Fanter Orchestra and did revues on Broadway too. This was the early 1930s. He loved going to Harlem to play with Kick Eddy, Snook Weeve, "Saint" Ezra Stint—all those old great jazz players. That's where he got a taste for skag. He used to humblebrag to Barbara Stanwyck and Gloria Grahame about being a "gentleman junkie."

JOHN WATERS (*filmmaker, artist*) Fred's double life . . . talk about double indemnity! Squeaky-clean Dad Next Door was a hophead whoremonger. *Son of Flubber*? *The Absent-Minded Professor*? Maybe absent-mindedly putting a *needle* in his arm . . . No one but the Boomers remember him, anyway—and most of the Boomers are senile ex-junkies!

SUZE BERKOWITZ When Roger told me that business about Fred MacMurray being a hype, I thought he was joking. But who knows what's true? Roar is the perfect example of that. All his life, he thought he was from a rich Jewish family in Pacific Heights. As it turns out, his mom's Black, his dad's some KKK serial killer—and he was born in Tennessee!

So who am I to have *opinions* about Fred fucking MacMurray?

We get used to *anything*, we adjust to alternate realities. Roger's right, "It's all illusion," but most of us pick just *one*. One illusion to a customer seems to be all our poor little hearts and heads can handle. You know, "That's my story and I'm stickin' to it." There's something sad about that, don't you think? Like being a grown-up who still believes in Santa.

HOPE "HOOP" RADCLIFFE Fred had a huge ranch up in Sonoma, cheek by jowl with La Piedra. Bunny and the Commodore used to drop by. Fred came to a couple of hoedowns at Parnassus after he married June [Haver]. The ranch is still there—Gallo bought it. They make wine under the MacMurray label.

MARTIN TORGOFF (*writer*)[124] . . . they stayed at the Dunbar Hotel, but

---

124 *Bop Apocalypse: Jazz, Race, the Beats, and Drugs* by Martin Torgoff, pp. 410–423 (Skyhorse, 2007).

Billie spent weekends in Pasadena with Orson. Bird had her own room. During the week [while *Citizen Kane* was shooting], Lady went back to Central Avenue and got loaded. Just tore it up. The musicians at the Turban Room and Club Alabam would entice her onstage. You had a lot of whites from Beverly Hills slumming down there, and Fred MacMurray was the novelty draw that gave them that extra layer of comfort. (Billie used to call them "whitefish out of water.") He played alto sax and played pretty well. The musicians liked him, because he knew all the East Coast boys—and always brought bags of black tar and China white. Fred brought Christmas to Central Avenue.

He took a shine to Bird, but Billie looked the other way. Lady had a full plate; she'd been on Anslinger's shit list since the Thirties and was being watched.[125]

ORSON WELLES[126] Oh, [MacMurray] was a *very* bad boy! We knew each other from Wisconsin, when we were kids, did you know? Freddy *loved* to "burn coal"—the darker and younger the better. "Orson," he'd say. "Don't call me 'Freddy.' Call me Kurtz! Because I'll never leave the jungle."

BOB THIELE They spent five years together before Bird finally broke away from her mentor and started doing gigs on her own. She learned so much from Lady Day, vocally, but her voice was distinctive—closer to Bessie Smith, and Billie knew it. Bessie was Lady's biggest influence. She used to joke that Bird was Bessie's child. Some jealousy there, no doubt.

BIRD RABINEAU[127] She was overbearing. Like a mother to me, God rest her soul. But I was a colt in a barn fire. All those teenage hormones and all that dope didn't help. I know Lady felt some guilt, too, 'cause the truth is, she turned me on to heroin. So when I left, she might have actually felt some *relief*—you know, not to see my face and what she'd wrought. It was more

---

125 Harry Anslinger was the commissioner of the Federal Bureau of Narcotics.—*ed.*

126 *My Lunches With Orson: Conversations Between Henry Jaglom and Orson Welles* (Peter Biskind, editor), pp. 114–117 (Metropolitan Books/Henry Holt, 2013).

127 *The Sparrow's Eye: The Rise and Rise of Bird Rabineau* by Keg Sweeney, p. 616 (Norton, 1993).

about that than her bein' jealous of my voice. Ain't *nobody's* voice she was jealous of 'cept maybe God Himself.

And that was a maybe.

QUINCY JONES Bird worked the Chitlin Circuit. Did some recordings on Ace Records . . . some work with Bob Thiele too, for Bluesway Records. Bob put out Errol Garner, Lester Young, and Bird, all in one year. But she was like a phantom. She wouldn't play in the big clubs. She was using, and got paranoid the feds would bust her; she got that from Billie. So, she was hard to find because she mostly played in speakeasys. You'd only know where she was gonna pop up by word of mouth. Ella [Fitzgerald] used to make pilgrimages. Oh God, all kinds of folks did the same.

That's how she met Chet [Baker]. He heard about her—this old-young genius chick—and came down to Louisiana or wherever to see her. He was a few years older, but what a lot of people don't know is she was the one who turned him on to H. They usually assume it was the other way around. That's what held her back. The drugs and arrests, the paranoia . . . she and Chet found common ground.

By the mid-fifties her mental illness was pretty flagrant. She'd be hospitalized somewhere in the sticks, and no one knew where she was. What that gal must have endured in those hospitals! Lord. She went to Hell and back. I don't know how she managed, but she always got a round-trip ticket.

BOB THIELE Gus Dunnock saved her. Gussy was an anomaly back then— a Black attorney, and gay. One of the kindest, gentlest souls I've ever met, but you better not cross him. I saw him pound the bejesus out of three muggers. They must have rued the day they took him for a mark. He became Bird's protector. The father *and* mother she never had.

BERT WHYATT (*historian*)[128] Gus Dunnock befriended her when she gigged at the Black Orchid in Chicago. She and Chet had a baby by then, a little girl. But Chet was "the worst father in all God's creation"—that's a direct quote from one of Chet's twenty other kids. Baker could get physical and

---

128 *Chicago Jazz: the Second Line* by Derek Coller and Bert Whyatt, pp. 218–221 (Hardinge Simpole, 1979).

when Gus saw him lay hands on Bird, he swooped in and knocked him out cold. Chet couldn't play the trumpet for three months.

She moved into Gus's penthouse apartment on the Gold Coast and loved it there. It was a safe haven for her and the baby—the décor reminded her of the Heritage, where Bird stayed when she was pregnant with Roger Orr. That hotel room in Nashville was the first place she could start to dream of another life for herself.

ROSIE LEVIN Between entanglements [with Baker], Bird had a long-term thing with Etta James. She was much older than Etta; in many ways, their relationship mirrored Lady's and Bird's from back in the day. When Bird later found out that Billie and Etta were having a clandestine affair, she felt betrayed. Billie *knew* Bird would find out. Lady had no boundaries but it was clear she wanted to lash out at her protégé.

There was a lot of crazy incestuous stuff going on. Bird was friends with Sam Cooke, and *that* family was a demented soap opera.[129]

BOB THIELE I stayed in touch with Bird, and Gussy became a friend. I'd go over for dinner whenever I was in town. One day he called to say that Bird was writing songs again and I was happy to hear it. But he worried it would lead to performing—she'd taken a long sabbatical to look after herself and the baby—worried like a father about the drugs in the clubs and the "wrong element." I was of two minds. Because Bird was thriving and her daughter [Neva Baker] was thriving. But the part that needed nourishing—the songbird who belonged to the world—was dying. I finally said, "Gus, you can't keep her caged forever."

A few months after we spoke, Gus brought her into the studio to record "Come To Me." He sat in the booth and cried because it was so beautiful. I cried too! Mostly, he cried because he knew it was time to say goodbye. He

---

129 Bobby Womack, Sam Cooke's protégé, married Cooke's widow Barbara, just months after his death. Cooke's daughter Linda married Womack's brother Cecil. While married to Barbara, Womack began an affair with his stepdaughter Linda. When Barbara found out, she shot and wounded Womack, and they divorced. But instead of marrying Womack, Linda married his brother Cecil. There have long been rumors that Fred MacMurray was involved romantically and sexually with Barbara, Sam, Bobby, Cecil, Linda, and various grandchildren—and that MacMurray also bedded sundry attorneys and executors of Cooke's estate.—*ed.*

was smiling like crazy but the tears were falling down his face like a downpour on a sunny day.

I heard him whisper, "God's way."

QUINCY JONES Over the next few years, Bird recorded "Pray Tell," "Dream Coat," "Astonish Me," and "There Can Be No Mountains"—an amazing series of songs that established her voice and created her legacy.

ROSIE LEVIN She hooked up with Chet again, and they gigged together. They did that gorgeous duet, "Ever Apart." . . .

She was staying clean, as best she could. She was doing that for Neva, who remained at home with "Grandpa Gus"—thank God she knew better than to take Neva on the road. And Bird still kept her room at Gussy's, though she was there less and less. "Come To Me" was a big hit. Sarah Vaughan asked her to share the stage—unusual for Sarah but it made good business sense. Bird was becoming a big draw and Sarah benefited. This was right around the time Roger and Suze got married.

Doris Duke was a jazz aficionado and introduced Bunny Orr to Bird's first recordings; Bunny became a serious fan. Of course, we now know the supreme irony of Roger's adoptive mother being the one who gave him the idea that Bird should sing at his wedding.

SARAH VAUGHAN (*singer*) It was 1959, and we were just having a ball. I was about to ask Bird to tour with me when one of the girls came rushing up to say Billie Holiday died. The look on Bird's face! I watched that girl fall apart right in front of me. Like death in slow motion.

She started using again *that night*. Could not take the pain. It was . . . complicated. They had their set-tos over the years—the rift over Etta and whatnot. But oh how they'd loved each other. In so many ways, Lady Day was the mother she never had. And whatever else Bird was to Billie, she would *always* be her daughter.

Artie Shaw understood that. He asked her to come to New York and sing at the memorial. She did "Strange Fruit" and "Come To Me," and time stood still. It was like she opened a door—and Billie walked in, and sat awhile. Everyone looked at each other with twitchy noses; the smell of gardenias filled that room. It was like being at a seance. Three folks fainted.

CALLICO PRIDE I remember seeing Neva there with Gus. They were on one of the front benches. It was a solemn occasion, but Gus was so proud. It touched me mightily because I knew what he'd done for Bird. For both of 'em. He'd been a father to both. Neva the little sparrow! She looked beautiful, and just like her mom. Bird showed them the town before they went back home. Coney Island, the Empire State Building, the lights of Broadway— the whole kitchen kaboodle. I'd a gone but my stomach had a little disagreement with something I put into it.

* * * * * * * * * *

Gold Coast penthouse fire: 2 dead, including daughter
of singer, 3 others in critical condition including
Chicago firefighter
by Scott McCauley

Two people perished after a Gold Coast apartment fire Wednesday. Six others, including a Chicago firefighter, were taken to hospitals in critical condition. Names of the injured have not been released.

Fire officials reported that Neva Rabineau, 5, and Gus Polk Dunnock, 63, an attorney, died in the early-morning fire. Both Dunnock and Rabineau, the daughter of singer Mika "Bird" Rabineau, were dead at the scene from smoke inhalation. Neighbors said that Dunnock and his godchild had just returned from New York where they attended a memorial service for Billie Holiday at St. Paul the Apostle Roman Catholic Church. The service drew thousands and was attended by such luminaries as Benny Goodman, Frank Sinatra, Nina Simone, Tallulah Bankhead, Martin Luther King, and Fred MacMurray.

About 4:10 a.m. a resident on the tenth floor of a building in the 1400 block of North Jasmine Drive reported a fire in a same-floor apartment, according to multiple Fire Department sources. A neighbor said that the woman in the room where the fire is suspected to have started was a heavy smoker. "She drank too and was always falling asleep with a cigarette in her hand. This happened once before but it was during the day and we put it out before it did any real damage." Fire Commissioner Lance Canberry said the fire was quickly upgraded to an extra-alarm, "because of a mayday, firefighter down."

"We ask that everyone pray for all the people injured in this fire," said Canberry.

Rabineau, the mother of the deceased and a close friend of Holiday, is reportedly still in New York.

* * * * * * * * * *

GERTRUDE SAUNDERS (*singer*)[130] The death of her daughter was the end for her. She never even processed Gus being gone, because Neva's death was just too big. Too big. I know what that's like.

ETTA JAMES Bird had just turned thirty-three and never went back to Chicago. Ever. She'd already lost one baby [Roger Orr] and now she'd lost another. She felt cursed, which she *was*. Aren't we all? Even Jesus couldn't help her; she wasn't ready to let Him.

Not for a long, long time.

CALLICO PRIDE The coroner asked if she wanted Neva to be cremated. Because the body was intact—the smoke's what killed her. But Bird said, "Ain't gonna burn my baby twice."

She put little Neva in the same place as Billie. She wanted her to be with family, and Billie was the only family she knew. She loved that poem by Mr. Robert Frost and put it on the stone.

EDMUND K. CARTER (*cemetery groundskeeper*) She only came once that I remember. But I wasn't there every single day. She sat and talked to her

---

130 Saunders was the longtime lover of Bessie Smith and Alberta Hunter. Smith and Saunders acquired a child through Helen Carver, ringleader of the infamous "Stork Club" used by Peter Gramm to provide babies for Bay Area socialites. In 1943, Saunders, Smith, and the four-year-old girl they adopted were traveling from Nashville back to Chattanooga when the car swerved off the road. Smith and her daughter were killed instantly; Saunders suffered minor injuries and died in 1991.—*ed.*

poor little daughter, but I couldn't make out the words. I don't like to get too close to people when they visit loved ones. I try to be respectful.

She sat and talked then began to sing real soft.

* * * * * * * * * *

Gravestone at Old St. Raymonds Cemetery in the Bronx

NEVA BAKER-RABINEAU

1954–1959

"Miles to go before I sleep"

* * * * * * * * * *

BENEDICT ROWTHER-PRYCE (*historian*)[131] She spent the next fifteen years out of the country and didn't release a record in all that time. In comparison, Nina Simone's troubles begin to look like Xanadu. Bird Rabineau blew through every jail and hospital in Europe. She had "benefactors"—a lobster quadrille, with mock turtles thrown in—the usual merry-go-round of tosspots, tattered royals, and aging Mr. Ripley's, most of whom were inherited from Alberta Hunter and Josephine Baker. That she *lived* is a testament to a Herculean will.

She was a survivor nonpareil.

HOWARD W. KOCH (*producer*) "Lady Sings the Blues" had been nominated, and Diana Ross was going to sing it at the Oscars. But a few weeks before the Academy Awards [1973], she had emergency surgery to remove a cyst on her vocal chords, so there was just no way. That's when Berry Gordy tracked Bird down in Paris, in some Pigalle shithole. I don't know if it was a brothel or an opium den. Probably both.

BEVERLY D'ANGELO Everyone thought it'd be impossible, but Berry pulled it off. He sent a doctor and nurse to Paris and flew everyone back

---

131 *Unsung: Bird Rabineau in Paris* by Benedict Rowther-Pryce, pp. 218–219 (Knightsbridge, 2003).

to New York on the Concorde. Q told me it was the Concorde's maiden flight. . . .

They put her up for ten days at the Plaza, under guard—IV penicillin took care of the infections in her lungs and whatever else was going on between her legs. A psychopharmacologist handled the rest. Berry hired a cook and a nutritionist, and she gained fifteen pounds. Two days before the show, he checked her into the Beverly Hills Hotel and she was good to go. I always thought it'd have been amazing if Roar was at the Academy Awards that year, but he was at McLean that night, presenting Anne Sexton with his own statuette for Best Nuthouse Blow Job.

RALPH GLEASON (*music critic*) When she walked out onto the stage of the Dorothy Chandler, the audience gasped. She was only forty-seven and looked like a ghost. But she was luminous; *numinous.* That mysterious metamorphosis—the mouth-to-mouth, heart-to-heart resurrection of a moribund entertainer by an audience—had begun. She smiled at the crowd; everyone stopped breathing. It was the audience's turn to be revived. "They tied Billie's hands to the hospital bed when she was dying, God bless them. . . . But that womanchild still had her own, yes she did. God bless Lady Day." She beamed at the sky then looked across the sea of famous faces. "God Bless us all."

I think I can rightfully say she outshone Billie that night, not that it's a competition. The house came down so hard, half of us thought it was the Big One.

ALICIA KEYS (*singer*) I watch that on YouTube *all the time.* And it *kills* me, *all the time.* [*softly sings*] "Mama may have, Papa may have . . . but God bless the child that's got his own. That's got his own."

I've cried so many tears over that damn video.

SUZANNE DE PASSE (*producer*) All the winners and presenters who took the stage after her were still stunned, and each said something extemporaneous about the miracle they'd just seen: Francis Coppola, Liv Ullmann . . . and Cicely [Tyson], of course, who was especially eloquent. Bird even got a shout-out from Sacheen Littlefeather!

ROBERTA FLACK (*singer*) That performance began one of the great comebacks of all time. But she was very, very sick. Quincy did a lot to raise money for Bird's medical care. That was really the beginning of the idea of musical artists taking care of their own.

REV. THOMAS B. REVEILLE She started recording again—and found God. He leaves it to all of us to find our way back. Often, the more you struggle, the greater His rewards. They say all God's children get free lunch but that's a lie. The food tastes much better—and is more nutritious—when you pay for it. Bird Rabineau paid dearly. She bought herself a whole banquet.

SAM CHARTERS Bird said she wrote "Soar Eyes" in an hour. Spielberg used it in *Sugarland Express* [1974], and it just took off. But the apex of that comeback—even greater than her performance at the Academy Awards—was Carnegie Hall in '78.

* * * * * * * * *

NAT HENTOFF
(*The New Yorker*, June 11, 1978)

The art and suffering of Bird Rabineau are legend, but only her Art—glorious, restorative, transcendent—was manifest Saturday night at Carnegie Hall. It is a *religious*, otherworldly Art, born of the phrasing and intonation earthbound suffering makes: the sound of a warrior angel's wings beating swords into plowshares as it lifts up our dented hearts. We become angels too. There was humor as well—and sorrow—and sentimentality—and ineffable tragedy. Like Dante, she led us from the depths until by concert's end we stood on our feet and blinked our eyes, clipping off tears at the realization she was singing her encores in Paradise. It was not hope she was abandoning, but despair.

We can never see the likes of her again.

. . .

ROGER ORR[132] When we wrapped in Marfa and went to Georgia for the last month of the [*Grace War*] shoot, I had a memorable dream.

I was in Grand Central Station with my mother—she looked like Bunny, anyway, though not quite. She wore a nun's habit. I saw something on the ground; a perfect, miniature movie camera. I picked it up and held it in the palm of my hand. I told "Mother" that I was going to keep it.

"The hell you are!" she shouted. "*Go turn that in.*"

I stammered that I hadn't been serious about keeping the camera but the mother-composite saw through the lie. She pointed to a man behind a counter who was like a priest in a Buñuel film. I have no explanation for the embarrassingly unimaginative iconography, other than having gone through a Catholic phase in my troubled teens.

I walked toward him, tiny camera in hand.

"I just found this! Maybe the person it belongs to will claim it."

He took it from me and smiled.

"Did you feel shame for wanting to take it?"

He looked more and more like Fernando Rey.

Without a moment's hesitation, I said, "I don't need to *take* shame—I was *given* it at birth."

As he recoiled, I felt a surge of power. I woke up with an amazing feeling of self-confidence. I knew I had uttered an *essential truth*.

DENZEL WASHINGTON (*actor*)[133] *Grace War* is about a Black man who's falsely accused of terrible crimes and jailed for life. Booker makes a promise to himself to become the very thing the court accused him of being: a monster. And he does. Becomes the most violent inmate in that prison's history, becomes a legend. But he pays a price. And he can see it, he can feel it. He pays the price of enslavement—to anger, to hatred, to the system itself. Because the system has different roles that it needs people to play. The Warden; the Snitch; the Good Guard; the Bad Guard; the Model Prisoner; the Monster. Years later, he reads a book on Buddhism, and a light

---

132 *False Posthumous: The Rest of Roger Orr*, pp. 17–23 (Cavalcade, 2022). —ed.

133 From *Hollywood Black: The Stars, the Films, the Filmmakers* by Donald Bogle, introduction by John Singleton (Cambridge, 1998).

goes on. He begins his training to be a monk. And slowly, very slowly, the bars of his cell melt away. He's free.

Roar called the world a "prison planet." He said we get so accustomed to the steel bars that we don't see them. We think we're free but don't know what the word means. Like in the Kristofferson song—"Freedom's just another word for nothing left to lose." Except what it *should* be is "just another word for nothing *left.*" Maybe that's the same thing; I ain't gonna argue with Kris. It takes a lot of work to understand "free," to understand what it truly means. Roar said the same thing about the word "love" too. We don't know what it means to love, truly love, with no questions asked. Most of us never know what it is to love.

Words were important to him—maybe the most important thing of all. Words set you free. Words show you how to love. He thought it was obscene to throw them around without knowing what they meant. But he knew words could trap you, too. Knew that better than anyone else.

JAMES L. BROOKS A lot of monks dropped by the set. Not Hollywood monks, *monk* monks. Bob Thurman was the consultant on all things Buddhist. In the script, Booker—Denzel's character—is visited by an old *roshi*, the teacher of one of the men he's wrongly accused of killing. A young, wandering monk who was stabbed in a city park.

The roshi visits him throughout the years and eventually Booker takes the formal Buddhist vows.

JEANIE REY HALLIBURTON (*script supervisor*) The monks started a class for the inmates and it was a sensation. I was surprised the warden let them do that. There were killers in that class but you'd never know it; they looked and acted just like us. Made you think twice. I'd go home and look in the mirror and see "the killer within." But I was glad to be able to *go* home. Glad to be able to leave.

WARREN OATES (*actor*) All kinds of folks visited. Richard Gere and Philip Glass—they were friends of Bob Thurman's. I didn't know until later that Bob was the first American monk to be ordained by the Dalai Lama himself. And that's no shit. . . . The air got pretty thin. Dylan came down with Sam Shepard and Allen Ginsberg, and Allen knew Roar pretty well. Dylan was a big fan of *Yes I Can*, that wild movie he made where white people played Blacks. Dylan was kind of in awe of Roar. When *Chronicles* came out—Dylan's book—there was a whole section in there about Roar's music. The sneaky sophistication and crazy diversity of his songs. Dylan called it "not human." Patti Smith tagged along; she was startin' to be a pretty big deal. "Because the Night" had just come out and was all over the radio. I was starting to feel like shit on a shoe. (*laughs*) No, it was cool. Everyone was good people and I knew pretty much all of 'em anyway, one way or another. Sam's [Peckinpah] sets tended to be a lot like that. You never knew who was going to show up.

By the time we shot *Grace*, Thurman shucked his robes 'cause he didn't want to be *celibate* no more. He wanted to marry Nena [von Schlebrügge]! Hey, I'd have married her too. She was a groovy lady. But the most interesting visitor to *me* was one of Thurman's teachers, Geshe Gassho. That guy was a big kahuna in the Buddhist world but he was regular. Zero pretenses. All the legit enlightened guys are like that—I mean, the few I've met. Sometimes it'd get on your nerves because he had these monks around him, kinda like groupies, you know, laughin' too hard at his dumb jokes. And those jokes were *dumb*. Schoolboy jokes. He'd see me and say, "Sowing wild *Oates* today?" Hardy har har. I used to tell Geshe his comedy act was shit and not to quit his day job. He loved that.

Roar wanted him to be in the film—to play the roshi—but Geshe wouldn't do it. He just laughed, great big bellyachers. Geshe didn't want to play that game. Not even a little. When Geshe turned him down, Roar just shrugged, turned to me and said, "As Bill Goldman once remarked, 'Everybody knows everything.'" I still don't know what the fuck he meant.

PATTI SMITH Roar would sneak up and whisper, "I want to look like you, talk like you, fuck like you"—and I'd say the same thing right back. Because it was true! I remember funny little things about that time in Georgia . . . like when I was talkin' to Richard [Gere] and he used the word "reductive." I don't know the context—or why it stayed with me—but that might have been the first time he ever used it in a casual conversation. He was kind of trying the word out and it had a weird impact. *Richard Gere saying reductive.* Almost fifty years later, I was talkin' to Lena Dunham and she used the word "performative."

Somehow those two things got linked in my brain.

I don't know why I'm tellin' you that. . . .

Back to Roar: he was just so—incomprehensibly *comprehensive*. He "strode worlds." There was something psychedelic about his appetites. He was kinda like a dervish. A Sufi . . . he wrote a ballad with the most beautiful bridge I ever heard. He played it for me in his trailer, and I was knocked out. I told him I wanted to send it to some friends I knew in England, some kids in a band who were fans of mine. Why would I even have suggested that? I don't know, but I did. Which was stupid and presumptuous of me because he hadn't put it out there, the song wasn't out there in the world. *It belonged to him.* And why would he even have said yes, go ahead and send it to the kids? I don't know, but he did. Maybe I'd put him in some kind of corner and he was just being gracious. He was a very gracious man.

I almost put it on *Dream of Life*. I can't remember why that didn't happen. But I did sing it at his memorial.

ROLAND ORZABAL (*musician*) I was a fanboy of Patti's and sent her a mixtape and a mash note, from Somerset. Never heard back of course. Was rather embarrassed about it. Then one day a little package arrives with "P. SMITH" and a box number on the return address. I thought one of my mates was taking the piss. What's freakish is that I'd been writing a song and having trouble with the bridge. And there it came, a tape from Patti Smith, *singin'* it. "And I find it kind of funny/I find it kind of sad/The dreams in which I'm dying are the best I've ever had."[134]

Bloody fucking genius. We didn't know it was Roger Orr until much later. We thought it was Patti. And the truly *mad* thing is, the boys and I were going to originally call the band *They Sleep by Night* because that movie was *everything*. It played for a year at the cinema, at midnight. We must have seen it ten months straight. We had a little more time on our hands back then.

BEVERLY D'ANGELO Those monks were horny. I flashed 'em just to fuck with 'em. I had to be careful that the prisoners didn't see, because most of the extras were played by real convicts, and I didn't want to be cruel. Didn't want to cause a riot—a pussy riot. I really had to restrain myself because there's

---

134 "Mad World," Tears For Fears, Roland Orzabal and Roger Orr © BMG Rights Management (1982).

something so *hot* about a guy with MOM tattooed on his forehead, especially when you find out he's in there for decapitating Mom.

JAMES L. BROOKS We got there one morning, and the whole penitentiary was in lockdown. There'd been a murder during the night. *That* was scary. Thank God it didn't happen while we were shooting. But we had to find another location. We shut down for a week and finally found something in Bibb County, an old jail we spent three days dressing up.

JEANIE REY HALLIBURTON Roar was excited about the homicide at the penitentiary. I mean, *really* excited. He had a violent streak but hadn't killed anyone . . . not that I know of! Whenever he said he wanted to *experience* that, experience what it would be like to commit murder—he talked about it more than once—I could never tell how serious he was. He'd known his share of killers or so he said. I do know that one of his AA sponsors was a straight-up gangster that could do the *New York Times* crossword in six minutes. A guy cut him off in traffic one day then flipped him the finger. The gangster chased him down and forced him to pull over. He held a gun to the guy's head and said, "If you don't shit your pants in the next thirty seconds, I'll blow your head off." Nice! Roar knew some vets who were in that supersecret Phoenix Program during the Vietnam War. They'd go into villages and kill every man, woman, and child. He was entranced by what it took to do such a thing.

But he always spoke about those people with great . . . affection. On the set once—we were still in Marfa—the DP was talking about Richard Lester's film *The Knack*. The title referred to the knack of seducing women but Roar said, "You wanna know what the real knack is?" He quoted a passage of his favorite book, *Red Cavalry*, I think it's Russian, something about a timid man begging God to teach him "the simple knack of killing a man." I do think Roar believed that killing was an art, equivalent to that of a great filmmaker or novelist or songwriter. It's romantic—and juvenile—but part of him thought if you haven't killed anyone, well, shut your mouth.

NED ROREM During *Grace War*, he'd write songs in his trailer during lunch or between camera rehearsals. He sent them to New York to have them transcribed. [Some] absolutely breathtaking choral music—mesmeric sea shanties in the style of Percy Grainger's *Shallow Brown*. Roar had a little Hammond installed at his hotel and became quite proficient . . . Years later, he spent days on end playing the magnificent pipe organ residing at his friend Howard Shore's home in Tuxedo Park. The house originally belonged to an industrialist, one of the survivors of the *Titanic*. The poor man saved his son when the ship went down and when the boy died in a car wreck a few years later, built a music room in his memory. He put in a Welte Philharmonic Autograph Pipe Organ in 1915, which Howard meticulously restored—the first of its kind to have a pneumatic system with paper music rolls.

But Roger still wrote his signature bread-and-butter "earworm" pop songs, with that catchy mix of Orrian high and low. One of them, "The Death of Love," was based on Schubert's *Impromptu* in E flat-major (Op 90, No. 2). He could never get too far away from the longhairs. Had 'em by the shorthairs!

ALI BERK I was so sad when we wrapped *Grace*! I had a big affair with one of the gaffers. I never told anyone that. You know, underage and all.

CAM SARGEANT (*editor*) *Grace War* took a long time to cut because he was in love with every frame.

LANGLEN CUTTERBEE He was going to use his own songs [for *Grace War*] but all that changed when he saw Karen Dalton perform at a hole-in-the-wall on 10th Street. She and Dylan sang together at Café Wha? in the early Sixties—and it's funny because Dylan once said Karen had a voice like Bird. Which seriously pissed Karen off! I guess no one likes being compared to anyone, not most artists anyway.

By the time he met Sweet Mother K. D., she was in decline—Karen was one of those doomed souls they call "hope-to-die" dope fiends—but it sure paid off. They actually recorded "Wolf Tickets" in the bathroom of his suite at the Pierre. She had her kids and dogs with her. You can hear her doing a lot of shushing on the soundtrack album. Roar decided to leave it in.

LAUGHLIN ORR I sat on Mom's diary like a mother hen from Hell, praying the eggs wouldn't hatch—or break—before their time. I obsessively stayed in touch with Beverly, getting updates on when that fucking movie would be done. You know, "Hey, Bev, how's it going? *Is it fucking over yet?*" It felt like they were editing *for years*. I hadn't told her what was going on—I didn't want to burden Bev with keeping the secret—and she kept wondering why I was so frigging anxious for *Grace War* to be locked . . . I'd wake up in the middle of the night with the sheets soaked, sit bolt upright in bed, and shout "Fuck!" to the ceiling. I kept wanting to throw caution to the wind and just *tell* him, but couldn't. I didn't know how he'd react. I knew how good that movie was gonna be—and also knew that my brother was perfectly capable of getting the I Can't Believe I Was Adopted Blues—the *Why The Fuck Didn't Those Motherfuckers Tell Me Blues*—and just. . . blowing shit *up*. He loved doing that, ever since he was a kid he blew shit up just to watch it blow. He'd blow up *his* life, *your* life, your *dog* and your *cat's* life, on a dime. I had these dark fantasies of him nonchalantly lighting a match to the negatives of *Grace*, just destroying the *world*, then taking to the hills of Bumfuck, India, where none of us would ever see or hear from him again.

It was a horrible, horrible time for me.

BEVERLY D'ANGELO I was pregnant but wouldn't find that out until I was shooting *Coal Miner's*. It was Roger's, of course.

BRUCE WAGNER Roger got in touch. He was in New York, I was in L.A. I don't know how he tracked me down [because] he definitely didn't go through my agent. He wanted to talk about one of my novels. Apparently, Michael Imperioli—of all people—handed him a copy of *The Empty Chair*.[135] I got one of Roger's infamous cold calls, and he said some very kind things about my book.

A character in *The Empty Chair*, "the American," goes to India and becomes a guru, a kind of Vedantic cult leader. Ultimately, he vanishes and becomes a sadhu—a wandering monk. Roger said the narrative reminded him of his own "Indian sojourn," and how he'd "met" my fictional American's counterpart on the streets of Rome in 1964. He talked for hours and I was mesmerized. Stories within stories, like the *Arabian Nights*—in fact, some of what he told me *was* from the *Arabian Nights*. He recounted one of Scheherazade's stories, "The Hunchback's Tale," which of course later became *Gift from God*. He was so easy to talk to, but it was wonderful just to listen.

---

135 *The Empty Chair* by Bruce Wagner (Counterpoint Press, 1991).

He told me about meeting a young American in Italy, "while I was in the middle of a decorous nervous breakdown"—whom he eventually accompanied to India. I have to say, the parallels *were* striking. As an example, one of the main characters in *The Empty Chair* is a rich hippie named Queenie, who *intensely* reminded him of his sister. Queenie's boyfriend, Kura, is a gangster with a spiritual bent ("a bit like Corso," he said); Queenie's just seventeen when Kura takes her to India, intent on finding a guru. The one he encounters isn't at all what he bargained for: in my book, the guru's called "the American." Roger and *his* American went to see Neem Karoli Baba. He said he got very sick toward the end of that trip, recovering in a Mumbai hospital just like my Kura did. The similarities went on and on. We must have been on the phone for three hours. Then, almost as an aside, Roger said he thought *The Empty Chair* would make a lovely, "panoramic" film—I *think* that's the word he used—and might I be interested in writing the script? Interested was an understatement. I'd have *paid* to work with Roger Orr. "As it happens," I said, "I'll be in New York in two days." I was lying, of course. We made a plan to meet at his hotel.

I was on my way to the airport when the news broke on the radio.

LAUGHLIN ORR I wanted to be sober when I told him but when I got to the Pierre, I went straight to the bar and did shots. I'd finally told Bev what was going on, but just a few hours before. She *had* to know; two paddles are better than one when you're up Shit's Creek. I'll never forget the look she gave me when she opened the door. A "We'll get through this" look, which neither of us believed.

And there he was, beaming at me from the couch.

He was so happy—*Grace War* was in the can.

BEVERLY D'ANGELO She had some of Bunny's diaries in a Lord & Taylor bag—which was very Laughlin. He knew something was up because of her demeanor: weirdly resolute, weirdly shaken. It was obvious that Laughlin wasn't herself, which I thought poetically appropriate, in light of what was about to be revealed: that he wasn't *himself*—at least not the "himself" he thought he was. Roar about to learn he was someone *else*'s self . . . I can't remember if Laughlin came right out and said "You were adopted" before or after handing him the evidence. It's kind of a blur.

He started to read and eventually came to the offending passages, the same ones Jonny and Laughlin read in the attic. . . .

A shock wave went through him. Have you ever seen people when they come on to mushrooms? It was kinda like *that.*

He thought Laughlin was kidding; then he thought Bunny was kidding; then he prayed that someone, *anyone,* was kidding.

LAUGHLIN ORR His eyes watered up but the tears never spilled. Bev handed him a tissue . . . I remember his smile. Half-astonished, half-enlightened. A cosmic smile. What do they call it—beatific.

BEVERLY D'ANGELO He stood up—which made us nervous—and walked over to one of the suite's bloated Louis XV commodes. Opened a drawer. That made us nervous too. Pulled out a little black book. That's exactly what it was: *a little black book.* I'd literally never seen one before, I'd only heard the phrase. Walked back to the couch and plunked himself down. Flips through a few pages then gets a number. Picks up the phone and dials. Almost immediately, he says, "Is this Mr. Gramm?" *That* was a surprise. Peter Gramm was part of family folklore—I'd heard about him for years but was shocked that he was still alive. Roar said [*imitates*], "Well, Mr. Gramm, this is Roger Orr. Bunny and Mug's son." Did I just sound like Jimmy Stewart? [*laughs uproariously*] That's *exactly* how I remember Roar sounding! Like fucking Jimmy Stewart! But the part where he said "Bunny and Mug's son" just killed me. . . . Then he says [*deliberately exaggerating the "Jimmy Stewart"*], "I'm here with Laughlin and she just told me about the adoption. That's right . . . that's right. Right. Yes. Uh huh. Uh huh. And I'd like to come see you in San Francisco, Mr. Gramm. I'd like that very much. How's your schedule this week?"

Gramm was almost eighty years old and still showing up to the office. His body was failing, but his head was clear. Of course he agreed to see him, and Roar's assistant booked a flight.

LAUGHLIN ORR I kept waiting for the other shoe to drop—for him to ask when I knew all this. He starts reading the diary again then asks Beverly if *she* knew. Bev says no—a very white lie, by the way, because I'd basically only just told her. Then my brother asks me if *Jonny* knows. I couldn't help myself.

I said, "No." Then, the shoe dropped. He asked when I found out. Not really in an interrogatory way. You know, nothing aggressive. More like he was distracting himself. I said, "Not too long ago." A bit of a soft-shoe but he rolled with it. I hemmed and hawed about the bottom line being that I didn't want to lay it on him while he was still editing. I'm so caring and helpful! (*sardonic*) Best big sister *ever*. You know, all for a good cause. . . . But I guess I did kinda made it sound like I just learned all of it a few days ago.

My bad.

BEVERLY D'ANGELO He wanted to be alone that night. I kept saying, "Ya sure?" Laughlin couldn't ask him that, it was better coming from me. But at the same time, I didn't want to nag. And I understood him needing to be alone so he could process. Plus, there was *zero* indication that he was fucked up. It was the opposite. He was pretty chill. But he had a lot to unpack, and the general feeling was, he doesn't need us watching.

Were we being naive? I don't know. What *should* we have done, had nurses waiting outside with a straitjacket? I think what happened is we got lulled because the worst part was over, or so we thought. Because at least now Roar knew. I thought maybe there was a group kumbaya moment coming. Wishful fucking thinking.

But something in him *did* look like this amazing weight had lifted off. We were relieved. We were human. Was that selfish?

Maybe—probably.

* * * * * * * * *

Roger Orr Hospitalized After Suicide Attempt
VARIETY
by Variety Staff

Roger Orr is in stable condition after being transported to the same New York City hospital where he was treated in 1971 after being shot on the streets of Manhattan. The actor/director/songwriter was allegedly found in his room at the Pierre Hotel by a housekeeper. Several empty prescription bottles were on the floor along with plastic baggies in what sources are calling an apparent suicide attempt.

The Academy Award–winner's latest directorial nod, *Grace War*, is due from Paramount in the summer. . . .

* * * * * * * * *

BEVERLY D'ANGELO His dream finally came true—he got into Payne Whitney. I'm kidding. After a few days, they moved him from the ICU at Mother Cabrini, over to Payne, where they put him in a regular room. He was very, very depressed. I was visiting before I went off to do *Coal Miner's Daughter*. I was having morning sickness but didn't put any of it together. I didn't even *think* of getting a pregnancy test.

So, I'm sitting there holding his hand while he's in bed. Watching cartoons without sound and shoveling Fritos down my throat. This sweet-faced young man appears at the door with beautiful flowers. He had an expressive, poignantly comical face—like a silent movie star's. Roar kind of stiffened when he saw him. We didn't know if it was a fan or a delivery boy. And the kid was startled; his little eyebrows went up. Clearly, he had the wrong room.

It was Nathan Lane, before he got famous.

Roar didn't see him again for another year, a few weeks after he found out that Bird was his mother—and Nathan was her caregiver. But the day he showed up with the flowers, she'd just been admitted for "psych eval" and was a few rooms down. I still get walloped by the strangeness of this world, Bruce.

CHAPTER TWELVE

Arrival

LAUGHLIN ORR He graduated from Payne Whitney, summa cum laude. Or *summa Lance Loude*, as Roger liked to put it.

J. HOBERMAN (*film critic*) Cal [Robert Lowell] used to say he was married to McLean but Payne was "the other woman." Marilyn [Monroe], of course, sashayed through its halls—you know, anyone who was anybody. Candy Darling showed up for quarterly shock treatments, which she called "chic treatment." When Gloria Swanson and Tennessee came to visit Candy, the RNs thought Tennessee was her dad. He wound up there too, more than once. He'd say, "Let's just say I'm a Payne freak, baby."

Lou Reed even wrote a song about the place.[136]

JOHN LAHR Stephen [Sondheim] went to see him toward the end of his stay. With great seriousness, Roar announced that he wanted to do a sequel to *Company*, by way of a French-door farce performed in the rooms and hallways of Payne Whitney. He proposed that in *Bad Company*, the character "Robert"—from the Sondheim original—would be played by "the *real* Robert," Robert Lowell. And "Ladies Who Munch" would be sung by a troupe of schizoid lesbians. The ghosts of Payne Whitney suicides would crowd the stage for the finale, belting out "Being Alive." Sondheim said he laughed so hard they almost committed him.

BEVERLY D'ANGELO I miscarried in Nashville, where Roger was

---

136 "Kill Your Sons" (1974).

born—how's that for full-circle irony? We were filming at the Opry, and I bled into the toilet. No one knew. I shot my scene two hours later. I'd just gotten back to my trailer when the phone rang—it was him. He must have had a psychic moment. He asked if everything was okay and I blurted out "I lost the baby." That's something I would *never* have done—I might not have told him at all if he hadn't called at that exact moment. Because he had too much on his plate. . . . Plus, I didn't want to be part two of the dead baby narrative. Aurelia was a tough act to follow. I'm not sure I even cried. I was out of body; the baby was *definitely* out of body. Roger, over and out. So, I said I lost it, and he said "When?" "Uhm, sort of just . . . now." He never asked, "What baby?" It was like he already knew I was pregnant, knew all along, and knew it was ours. But he was okay, he was all right—even though I didn't believe it in that moment. It was déjà vu, because he'd been so calm and collected the afternoon Laughlin told him about Bunny and Mug lying to him all those years. So, calm and collected wasn't cutting it for me and I was spooked. I could just see him reaching for the Nembutals and a plastic bag, but he really *was* okay. About losing the baby. He was super sweet and wanted me to come home as soon as I could. And I think . . . equanimity came with finally knowing the truth about his origins. The mother of all origin stories! Equanimity was the gift . . . He had his little crack-up, but when the smoke cleared, Roar was able to step outside the details of this life and revel in the absurdity of it. Revel in pure Story. Before the scales fell from his eyes, he only pretended life was "story"—his life, our lives—because it hurt too much otherwise; and felt like a coward because he knew that *stories shouldn't hurt*—they're just stories. But when he found out he was switched at birth, it proved his mantra: "All is illusion." A peace came over him. He was right at the beginning of his own mother/child healing, his "mother and child reunion."

The truth really does set you free.

I envied him. Because I'd never have a reunion with the child I lost.

GEORGE PLIMPTON Why did he try to kill himself? He's been rather eloquent about that. He wanted to kill what he calls "the harlequin"—the marionette, dancing on the strings of a great lie. He wrote that marvelous essay about it for the *New Yorker*, "Harlequin Romance." Lovely title.

CALLIOPE LEVY-LEVY It was as if all the mirrors cracked; he ran straight through the looking glass and got badly cut up. The rage erupted like a volcano and there was no chance to process it. He felt that his entire history had been erased by the Orrs—his so-called saviors—who in reality were hijackers and colonists. For a while, he saw only conspiracy. And malevolent intent.

ROGER ORR[137] I became a hanging judge, an immoral moralist—a lunatic accountant who saw nothing but cooked books. I tore my hair out; I tore out the hair of others. At last, I realized the numbers added up. There was no one to blame because fraud wasn't possible. The outrageous arrogance of believing one's destiny *could* or *should* be different than what it is. . . . I was walking in the woods when self-pity left me as surely as a fever breaking. I'd taken shelter during one of those gorgeously haywire, pie-in-the-face summer storms—a do-si-do of torrential rain and blinding sun—and emerged from the thicket, cleansed.

My new life began with the apprehension that early and late Frost were the same: all things were golden, and all gold can stay.

LAUGHLIN ORR I had to convince him that Jonny and I weren't coconspirators—you know, part of the cover-up. There'd just have been no reason for Mom and Dad to involve us in that, *apart* from the fact they knew we wouldn't be able to keep such a secret from him. He finally conceded the point. But the worst was when Jonny told him he'd been the first to read the diary entry and that both of us sat on the information for more than a year. (Thanks, Jonny!) The idea that we—that *I* was protecting him—and his film—was repugnant because Roar said that Bunny and the Commodore had "protected" him out of existence. It was a drag to bear the brunt of that. . . .

The sins of the adoptive father, and the mother too.

DAVID STEINBERG Naturally, he wondered "Who is she? *Where* is she?" He knew he'd go looking for his birth mother but it didn't occur to him while he was in Payne. (That's Payne with a "y.") It was too soon.

His new best friend was the mirror. He stared into it for hours, searching for what he sardonically called "Negroid characteristics." He loved Joseph Conrad and began referring to himself as "the N-word of the Narcissus"—of

---

137 *Roarshock* by Roger Orr, pp. 210–215 (Liveright, 2003).

course he did. And by the way, he *hated* that word; I'm talking about the six-letter one. He *never* used it until he learned he was biracial. He'd race into the dining room where all the patients were eating and shout, "Are there any N-words here tonight?" Which didn't go over well, for those without knowledge of Lenny Bruce.[138] He used *nigger* too—forgive me for saying it but I want to be clear—*along* with "N-word" [*Steinberg uses air quotes*], the latter tending to be employed exclusively for comic effect. But he was ridiculously promiscuous with the six-letter one. Like a rapper before his time.[139]

There was a paucity of information but we knew his biological father was a Klansman and that Roar's mom was *probably* light-skinned. Though maybe not . . . but that was the "guessology." The one who came to mind was Susan Kohner in *Imitation of Life*. He'd say, *Oh shit! I'm Roger Kohner!* He was starting to mellow but got into periodic uproars over Mug and Bunny's "treachery." "What would they have done if they lifted the blankie of the little basket Peter Gramm brought them—and I was black as a Br'er Rabbit's Tar-Baby? I'll tell you what. They'd have left me at the door of the NAACP."

JONNY "STAGE DOOR" ORR One time on the phone—after he left Payne Whitney—the issue came up of how or when to tell the world about the whole adoption thing. What do you do, put out a press release? Because he led a very public life. I started to think maybe you don't tell the world at *all*. Who the fuck's business is it? When I expressed that thought, he got righteously pissed. [*imitates*] "I will *not* be a closet nigger like Anatole fucking Broyard!" I didn't even know who he was talking about. But I got it. He was tired of all the lies and the bullshit. He was over it. And he was right.

It got scary because for a minute he was going to give his money away—I mean, every dollar. He called it his "reparations phase." Thank God for Dick Gregory. Laughlin couldn't tell Roger what to do with his money; if my sister said *don't do that*, he'd have set the whole inheritance on fire in front of her,

---

138 One of Bruce's famous routines began with that line albeit with the six-letter version of the racial epithet. The comedian said that he wanted to strip the word of its power, "until nigger didn't mean anything anymore. Then you could never make some six-year-old black kid cry because somebody called him a nigger at school."—*ed.*

139 Orr's friend Richard Pryor ultimately chastised him; after a trip to Kenya, Pryor vowed never to use the word "nigger" again. Orr made no such promise.—*ed.*

for spite. So, she called Dick, who did a little intervention. He sat my brother down and said, "Giving away money is an *art*. You ain't been a nigger two *minutes* and you already actin' like you been one all your life!"

BEVERLY D'ANGELO We knew it would be the biggest news story of the year. But he was determined to find his mother—dead or alive—before going public. Making headlines with a splashy, premature announcement would have offended his sense of narrative. Roar thought in terms of three acts and for now we only had act 2.

Only a few people outside the family knew. Like Stephen [Sondheim] and Sammy ... *maybe* there were a few more. There was no one he told that couldn't be trusted a thousand percent.

ALTOVISE DAVIS (*wife of Sammy Davis Jr.*) When Sammy went to see him in L.A., Roar was drunk. That surprised me because we'd been hearing he was sober. The big joke during that visit was Roar getting a nasty look on his face and asking Sammy, "Did you fuck my mother?" You know, like that children's book *Are You My Mother?* I guess he was saying it because of Sammy's taste for white women in the past. But the joke—if you can call it that—was really just about Roger the little boy wondering who his daddy was. He made a joke of it instead and rode it into the dirt.

One time, Roger said, "It's okay if you fucked Mom, brother—it was good for the Jews."

SUE MENGERS (*talent agent*) *Grace War* opened in the summer to astonishing reviews and popular acclaim. There was this *huge* outpouring of affection for what Roar had been through—the suicide attempt, the hospitalization, the ongoing struggles with addiction—and he was so touched. He was a rock star on the red carpet. Give the public what it wants—a horror story and a resurrection—and they'll love ya every time. As far as the studio went, they could barely hide their hard-ons. The distributors said that his crack-up added $20 million to the receipts. The rumors of him being uninsurable died on the Hollywood and vine.

ELSA GRAMM (*Peter Gramm's daughter*) My father was in his office familiarizing himself with some *very* old files—he was expecting Roger to show up the next day—when Laughlin called to say that he tried to kill himself and was in the ICU. She told him to sit tight, you know, "we have some time now." But Dad being Dad, maybe knowing or sensing that *he* didn't have much time, began to dig. By 1980, the file was pretty much deep-sixed. He picked up where he left off and got some people on it.

For years, he kept tabs on Roger Orr's biological mother. The reason was simple: he often arranged adoptions for people of great wealth and didn't want a donor coming back to bite anyone in the ass—you know, to come out of the woodwork and say, "That baby is rightfully mine and you're going to pay for my silence." Those adoption mills were horrible but they did serve a purpose and I don't judge my father for what he did. But he was a businessman, with clients to protect.

It sounds awful, but what would have happened to Roger if he'd stayed in Leipers Fork? Think about it. There's two sides to that story.

RICHIE "SNOOP" RASKIN When I told Pete [Gramm] that Orr's birth mother was Bird Rabineau, he said, "So?"

Never heard of her.

Music wasn't his thing.

JEAN STEIN (*writer*) In Bird's life, three men rescued her. Gus Dunnock was the first; and Roger Orr, the son her parents sold in 1940, was the last. But in-between was a young, gay stand-up comedian named Nathan Lane.

GEORGE PLIMPTON Nate [Nathan Lane] was in his twenties when he met Bird. A jazz hound and a musical theater freak. His name was Joseph but he changed it to Nathan—a tip of the hat to Nathan Detroit from *Guys and Dolls*. While developing a not-so-great stand-up act, he waited on tables at Delatorre's. Needless to say, he was having a tough time. But he always managed to go see Bird and Etta James perform—they were having a worse time than *he* was. I don't think those two ever did a show together; there was still bad blood over Etta's affair with Lady Day. . . . Etta had been arrested at Minton's, while onstage. And the Vanguard wouldn't hire either one of them. When Bird got 86'd from the Blue Note, she started gigging at some of the punk venues. Club 82—the famous drag club near the Bowery—CBGBs, whoever would have her. Patti Smith loved her and had to shout at the audience to shut up.

It was heartbreaking to see this towering genius of American jazz, American blues, reduced to that.

One night Bird was playing to a trainwreck crowd at Sapphire's, in Chinatown. Little Nathan's in the audience watching like a moonstruck calf as she sang "Come To Me" for the ten-thousandth time. And she *recognizes* him—finally! the superfan!—and gives him a squinty, *Hey don't I know you from somewhere?* look—he's been at every show she's ever done in New York right?—and starts talking to him from the stage. Suddenly, he's in the act. She says, "You *Bird*-doggin' me, baby? You better be careful now, 'cause you know what the early Bird like to eat." Nathan shoots back, "Then, the worm is safe. Because you've never been early in your life!" She just *howled.* And the audience loved it. Nathan's very smart, acerbic, and it was the comedy relief needed between stoned suicide ballads. She asked him backstage and gets to know him, she's genuinely curious about this sweet and funny young man. He'd walk her home and pay for groceries—he was broke himself but somehow found a way. And saw that she got *paid,* because a lot of those club owners were taking advantage of her. Pretty soon she'd call him up if she got into a fracas—with man, animal, police—or got scared of things that went bump in the night. Nate was pretty fearless and got into the face of more than one drug dealer. Nearly got killed once. But he always managed to scrape together bail and made sure she took her doctor-prescribed meds. Cooked for her too.

Sometimes she passed out in his apartment, which wasn't a picnic, because his place was the size of a closet. The toilet was in the kitchen.

EDMUND DANZIGER (*writer*)[140] Lane began to open for her. That sounds a little grand; Bird's performances were becoming scarce, and the crowds were too. Sometimes she was so loaded that they couldn't get her out of the dressing room. But he had the chance to do his stand-up and it wasn't half-bad. More important, he got comfortable performing and went on to great success—Tonys, Emmys, Golden Globes.

BEVERLY D'ANGELO He finally reached out to Peter Gramm. A lot had happened since Roar made that original plan to see him in San Francisco; he

---

was pretty grounded. *Grace War* had done well and things were settling. It was time to begin his search.

He apologized for not showing up at the meeting they'd set. "Mr. Gramm," he said. "I feel terrible about standing you up. So terrible that it makes me just want to . . . *kill myself.*"

I'm not sure Gramm got the joke.

ELSA GRAMM When Dad called Laughlin to say he'd found Roger's mother, she screamed, "Tell him yourself!" and slammed down the phone. He didn't even get the chance to tell her it was Bird Rabineau.

I'm not sure why Dad called Laughlin—instead of Roger—with the news. Probably because he'd slowed down quite a bit and didn't want the hassle of dealing with a headcase. But the Orrs had been such an important part of his life that it really was a duty and he was beholden to see it through.

Anyhow, he called him in L.A.—Malibu?—and said, "Your birth mother's name is Bird Rabineau and she's currently living in New York City. If you'd like an address, I can give you one." Dad was a *just the facts, ma'am* kind of guy. He told me that Roger didn't speak for the longest time; he thought the line went dead but he could hear Roger breathing. After a minute or so, he said, "Thank you, Mr. Gramm"—it was always Mr. Gramm, never Peter—"I have just two questions. Are we talking about the singer? Or someone coincidentally with the same name?" A silly question but probably not so silly at the time.

By then, my father was thoroughly informed about Bird and her career. He said, "We are talking about the singer. The jazz singer."

"And does anyone other than you and I know about this?"

Dad said no, no one else knew, which technically was a lie because Snoop Raskin was the one who tracked Bird down. But Snoop didn't count. There was a third question.

"Does my sister know?"

"She does not. She has not been informed."

When Dad said no, you knew he meant it.

He thanked my father for his time—and that was that.

HERB CAEN The day after they spoke, Peter Gramm had a stroke. He died a month later. Soon, the world would know everything about the secret contract he made in 1940 between a dodgy Nashville baby broker and the grande dame of a fabulously wealthy Bay Area dynasty. Peter always had a bit of Houdini in him—he got out before the house of cards fell and buried him alive. Even so, the scandal became his legacy. Do one of those Ask Jeeves[141] computer searches, type in his name and see . . . you'll get the picture.

SCATTER HOLBROOK He didn't tell any of us. Roger was determined to keep it under his hat until he made contact with Bird. This time *he'd* be the one calling Laughlin with a shocker!

LAUGHLIN ORR He lashed out at me for years. For no reason, really. Someone said they were talking to him about me and said, "Your sister . . ." and he shot back, "She's *not* my fucking sister!" Just mean and awful and so uncalled for. I got to the point where I stopped being so compassionate.

CINDY SHERMAN (*artist*) He came back from L.A.—he cut his trip short—and walked around with those bottomless, smiling brown eyes that were brimming with tears. When I saw him, I always thought of photographs in *National Geographic* of ecstatic pilgrims on a *yatra*. Or the aborigines who follow song lines . . . because that really *was* what Roger was doing. Tracking dream pathways. He found his mother. No one knew that he looked like an emaciated saint because *he'd found his mother*. His friends were hypervigilant because of that big breakdown; he'd only been out of the hospital a few months, and we couldn't help looking for red flags. Playing amateur shrink, trying to spot the signs of mania, whatever. We'd huddle over lunch and say, "Do you think he stopped his meds?"

We all turned into moms and nurses.

CAROL KANE (*actress*) Roar hired some detectives. He wanted to know Bird's daily and nightly routines. Where she walked, where she went for lunch or breakfast, who she knew . . . Instead of telling them she was his mom—he was super paranoid about anyone knowing—he said he was thinking of doing a biopic about her and was in the "information gathering" phase. I don't know if they thought that was weird but they probably already

---

141 Caen was interviewed for this book in 1997, months before his own death.—*ed.*

knew Hollywood folks were weird. And they were getting paid. A *lot*. And why would they care? Can you imagine the things they'd been paid to do? The people they'd been paid to follow? He was just too terrified to approach Bird himself, which would have been a lot easier!

Anyway, he learned from the detectives that Taylor Mead was a pal of hers. Roar knew Taylor from the Warhol days—they were acquaintances, not friends—and called him up. He used the biopic "cover" with Taylor too and of course Taylor *immediately* wanted to introduce them but Roar said he "wasn't ready." Taylor thought that was charming, you know, that Roar was shy about meeting her. He said, "The person you *have* to talk to is Nathan Lane!" Nathan had been out of town dealing with his own mother—she was pretty crazy herself—that's why he wasn't on the detectives' radar. Taylor, Nathan, and I lived a half block from each other on Ludlow Street.

SUSAN SONTAG[142] Saw Roger Orr on street with Bird Rabineau. Brief talk of *Yes I Can* and *Le Mépris* . . . and Perelman broken by grief over brother-in-law Nathanael West's death. Mutual love of "Monkey Business" + Walter Benjamin (*Arcade*)/Queneau + Oulipo/Barthes (*Sarrasine*), Saussure, Julia [Kristeva] . . . Lacan, Henry Winkler/Beckett *Happy Days* opera + Pound's (canto), recited aloud in unison: 街上的脏玫瑰. Mutual love of Pepto-Bismol, its campy All-American effectiveness.

NATHAN LANE (*actor*) I received a phone call—*several* phone calls, but the line kept going dead. I thought: *pervert.* The phone rang again and when I picked up I yelled something like, "Are you *masturbating*, asshole?" Not that I didn't find it a little . . . *exciting.* A very *timid* voice says, "Is this Mr. Lane?" I thought, *Oh no! It's a casting director!* I said, "Yes, I'm so sorry! Who's this?" "This is Roger Orr." I say, "Who?" He introduces himself again—of course I knew the name!—and I'm thinking, *Pervert!* I said, "Do you mean Roger Orr . . . as in *Roar*?" He said yes. I said something like "Well, I don't understand," and then he mentions Taylor Mead, how he's a friend of Taylor, and Taylor told him all about me and Bird. For a minute, I thought I was being pranked because Taylor knew what a hero Roar was to me. I was completely in denial.

142 From *Journals and Their Metaphors, 1985–1996* by Susan Sontag, pp. 415–423 (Picador, 2003).

So, "Roger Orr" says he's going to—no, that he's *thinking* of making a film about Bird. Well of course I knew *all* of his films but really just worshipped him as a songwriter, first and foremost. As this singular genius. I loved all the pop stuff but was a cognoscenti of the obscure—the weird organ music and the song cycles he did with Ned Rorem. *The Rake's Progress*! There used to be a little place in the Village called the Vinyl Solution—not to be confused with the eponymous record store on Portobello Road that appeared six or seven years later, those people even admitted to ripping off the name—and The Vinyl Solution was big on *Orriana*, I mean they had *everything*. All his 45s too, the ones he did when he was a kid. "Cult 45." I'd committed the monologues to memory but couldn't afford them. I have all of them now. . . .

I knew about his recent "troubles"—the whole world did. You know, "Roger Orr: The Payne Whitney Years." But he came out of that pretty well, didn't he . . . *Grace War*, which I admired but wasn't my *thing*, was a succès d'estime—it was much more than that really. Sorry—why am I being such a cunt? Anyway, he asked if the three of us could meet and I thought he meant me, him, and *Taylor*. But of course, he meant Bird.

My head was just spinning.

BEVERLY D'ANGELO When I got back from shooting *Coal Miner*, things were different between us. We made love but I had a sense the physical aspect of the romance was over. Not because of the miscarriage—I don't think that played a big part. It was more about the nuclear bomb of finding Bird.

Not much from his old life survived that.

I remember we were in bed and I heard this . . . voice. It was so loud, I was surprised Roar didn't hear. The voice said, "You're just going to be friends." You know, I always envied people who heard voices—the genius artists, the visionaries. There was a kid like that from middle school, in Ohio. I had such a crush. It was like having a crush on a saint. I wanted to hear voices too!

But when I finally did, it was something a girlfriend would say. Instead of some amazing prophecy or revelation, it was, "He's over you."

NATHAN LANE The three of us met for dinner at the Knickerbocker. Do you know the Knickerbocker? In Greenwich Village? I used to go there with Chris Noth and Alec [Baldwin], in kinder, gentler times. Roar ordered for everyone—which was weird—he *over*-ordered!—though not much eating went on. Drinking, yes. Before we got there, I was pretty sure he was going to recognize me from the hospital. I was telling you, Bruce, about the time I brought flowers to the wrong room and suddenly found myself staring at Roger Orr and Beverly D'Angelo. . . .

As far as Bird and I knew, dinner was so they could get acquainted—it was all about that cockamamie "biopic." There was an awkwardness, not just from Roar, which was understandable, but from Bird as well. And I didn't know the reason for that until a *long* time later: they *had* met before, in England, at a party at Kenneth Tynan's. Nothing sexual happened, but as Roar tells the story there *was* an undertow. An innuendo. A soupçon. That night at the Knickerbocker, neither mentioned it. I think Bird wouldn't have brought it up because she was embarrassed by how she looked, how she looked *now*. She was still beautiful—one of the great beauties of the world—though a stormy life had washed out some roads and broken a few guardrails. She could be quite vain. She must have thought, What does he want from me? . . . You know, one more man who wanted to use and abuse her. She'd been fucked over by so many men, her guard rails were up.

He had *other* things on his mind than remembering the schmuck who showed up with the flowers! But I was nervous and made it about me. Because I was in such awe of the man, I took it personally. Oh no! I'm unmemorable! At the beginning of our little guess-who-came-to-dinner dinner, there were some brutally uncomfortable silences. To break the ice—some icebreaker!—I leapt into the fray and said, "Remember that time at Payne Whitney . . ."—*awkward!*—"do you remember that time someone walked into your room by mistake, holding flowers? That was *me*! Bird had just been admitted and . . . *blah*."

Roar was seriously nonplussed, like he couldn't fathom what I was saying. He smiled and said, "Isn't that something?" Some bromide or other . . . to make things *worse*, Bird hated sharing about her periodic psych ward vacays. Add *that* to faux pas hell. She looked at me with great *annoyance* and said, "Oh, that was nuthin' serious. Just my hemagoblins acting up." She was always talking about her "hemagoblins." Her euphemism for psychiatric emergencies.

I'd just done *Present Laughter* and was starting to get busy in my career. How 'bout that? The downside was that I couldn't look after Bird as much as I'd have liked, so his timing—the prodigal son's return—was perfect. It wasn't official but the baton was being passed. We had a few more meals together before they started going out on their own. He *still* kept up the ruse of the biopic. She was flattered but perplexed. She definitely knew some of his songs—which she loved—she sometimes sang "Tenderness" as part of her act—but hadn't seen any of his films. Bird wasn't a movie person and had no idea about her son's importance as a director. So, she had trouble putting together why a songwriter would want to make a movie of her life.

In retrospect, that may have been a little cruel. To lead her on. Because she was starting to get excited about the prospect. But who knew? Maybe in Roar's head he thought he *was* going to make that biopic after all. The truth is, he was stalling because he was scared shitless. How do you tell a woman you've barely met that she's your mother?

With each day, it got harder.

CINDY SHERMAN When I finally met her, they had the same eyes. A soft, almost fragrant woundedness. Dark pools of tragedy, with these glinty, blinding flecks of redemption. I saw madness in them too.

BIRD RABINEAU[143] Our Lord is mischievous! But his heart is the World, His compassion boundless. He knows He needs to show us that heart—His heart—slowly, because if we see it all at once, we shall go blind. He teaches us the virtues of patience. There are some whom He does not bless for that is also His way: to bless by not blessing, not on this Earthly plane. But others, like my son and me, He blesses with a tornado of diamonds and roses! Hosea 8:7 says we reap the whirlwind, a tempest that demolishes all the rickety buildings and warehouses, but the churches—*His* churches—remain. All those years my son and me hid in our shelters till we got blown to the sky like a couple of Kansas Dorothys, holding on to each other tight as the foundations trembled and the uprooted trees and blown-off rooftops swirled around us: the lean-tos of Leipers Fork and the mansions of the City by the Bay . . . you could even see the roof of the Hermitage Hotel where they took him from me, blasting off like a rocket.

---

143 *Bird of Pray: First and Final Interviews*, Introduction by James Baldwin, pp. 223–230 (Simon & Schuster, 1988).

BEVERLY D'ANGELO When he was discharged from Payne Whitney, he wanted to move back to the same suite at the Pierre—the one the housekeeper found him in. The hotel was a bit *concerned*, but he persuaded them. He gave the manager a bunch of money. Some fancy people were in the suite and didn't want to leave . The hotel comped them new rooms, which Roger paid for.

When I finished shooting *Coal Miner's Daughter*, we talked on the phone from Tennessee. I told him I was thinking of going home to Ohio. He knew how fucked up I was about losing the baby. That's when he asked me to stay with him at the Pierre. He said, "Come, I'll take care of you."

It's funny how the brain works. I'm watching *The Philadelphia Story* on TV when I hear the key in the door and they walk in. I *know* who she is—it's Bird Rabineau!—and of course am aware they've been hanging out. That whole thing about the "documentary" he was going to make . . . but, as far as I knew, he hadn't told her anything. That he was her son. So, I see her standing there with him and it does not compute. Then . . . I rise to my feet and burst into tears. The ugly cry of all ugly cries. She comes over and holds me, mothers me. I get chills now. What a privilege. If it's the last thing I flash on as I lay dying—such a fucking privilege to be there, to witness that. To be held in the arms of that myth, that mother, the lost mother of the great love of my life.

"I once was lost, but now am found, was blind but now I see."

STEPHEN SONDHEIM I met them for drinks at the Pierre after he told her, right before the proverbial shit hit the tabloid fan. Bird was by the window, sipping a martini. She wore a simple, elegant dress he'd bought for her at Bergdorf's. Holding that glass in her delicate hand . . . those long arms scarred by track marks, abscesses from yesteryear—maybe yestermonth. But she was clean now; she'd been cleansed. She looked out at the floating garden of the world, soaking in Central Park. Staring, staring, staring over the trees at the pond and skating rink, a wild grin on her face. Then, without turning to us, she said, "Praise God" and started to softly sing. I couldn't make any of it out. It sounded like a hymn, yet so contemporary. Ageless, I suppose I mean. We just watched, Roger and I. He reached out for my hand and we sat beside one another, watching.

The image of Bird looking out that window of the world stayed in my head and I used it for "Finishing the Hat": "Mapping out a sky/What you feel like, planning a sky/What you feel when voices that come/Through the window..."

LAUGHLIN ORR I found out from the newspapers like everyone else did. [*pause*] That hurt. But I understood. It was such a precious, strange, *primal* thing that he needed to control. He needed to control who he'd let in—and when. I think it was his way of getting even with me for having withheld what I knew. But at least we were even now. And could start to rebuild what we had.

The irony, of course, is that he had no control whatsoever. The whole noisy, awful world found out, without his consent.

PETER K[144] AA meetings often end with, "What you hear here, when you leave here, let it stay here." Sadly, human nature being what it is—and the rooms being filled with character-flawed alcoholics such as myself—some jackass secretly taped Roger's share then leaked it to the press for money. I have no doubt the person who's responsible died drunk.

Roger was raw, emotional, vulnerable. Who wouldn't have been? He felt safe in AA. Which was a little naive, but I sympathized. He'd been sitting on that information, and it was cathartic to tell a bunch of drunks about what happened. He left out the names but that wasn't enough to stop folks from finding out the dramatis personae.

I've said a lot of intimate things in AA, terrible, shameful things, and for the most part, people are very respectful about the sacredness of the rooms. But some things I *never* talk about at meetings. Some things, I only share with my sponsor. I don't think Roger had a sponsor—a rookie mistake. A sponsor would have guided him to *pause* when agitated. That a little withholding can be "right-sized" and healthy. We call it "restraint of tongue and pen."

BEVERLY D'ANGELO He wanted to shout it from the rooftops: "I am the son of Bird Rabineau!" He didn't care about the consequences. He should have, but was tired of all the lies and secrets.

You know: "The buck stops here."

---

144 A friend of Orr's from the twelve-step program. K. added, "I always follow the AA tenet to remain anonymous at the level of press, radio, and film."—*ed.*

ROGER ORR[145] I have a goddaughter named Alice. I asked her once what it meant to dream. She said, "That's when you wake up." A few months ago, I dreamt that I was adopted. I dreamt that I found my mother. I dreamt she was living four miles from where I slept at night. I dreamt that I found her and told her I was her son.

I dreamt that we woke up.

HAMISH BOWLES (*fashion writer*) The tape was sold to the *New York Post*. All they needed to hear was "four miles from where I slept at night." They followed him for a week and tracked his clandestine, hide in plain sight meetings with Bird. There was also a rumor they tapped his phone.

* * * * * *

New York Post headline, November 1980

"ROAR"
TO
"BIRD":
HI, MOM!
Roger Orr finds out he was hatch-snatched;
Mother is down-and-out jazz singer

* * * * * *

CINDY ADAMS (*gossip columnist*) I was so angry. I was having a "disagreement" with the *Post* editor at that time—he's long gone!—and the cloak-and-dagger operation was deliberately kept from me. I knew Roger; he would have talked to me. I was furious.

---

145 The complete audio of Roger Orr's AA share is available in aeternum on many Internet sites; even so, I struggled over publishing this brief excerpt. I polled many twelve-step program members, who were equally divided. Some feared that even a short quote might encourage those who are prone to violating the safety of the rooms; others said the information was already out there and assured me that "AA will be just fine." In the end, I decided it was an important contribution to this history.—*ed.*

BETSY BLOOMINGDALE (*socialite*) That story was bigger than the Lindbergh kidnapping, but with a much happier ending. I thank God every day Bunny wasn't alive for all the *mishugas*, as she'd say. She'd only have been seventy years old, rest her soul—she would have been painted the villain and gone through terrible suffering.

JIMMY BRESLIN (journalist) I was at the *Daily News* when we got scooped. They had more coverage than the Son of Sam. Something touched a nerve. At first, no one believed it—not anyone I knew. Everyone thought it was some kind of Hollywood publicity stunt. And nothing was real until it was in the *New York Times*. And then, of course, it was. Five pages of it. The Gray Lady kept it alive for weeks.

DICK GREGORY The Blacks that turned against him after *Yes I Can*. . . . Motherfuckers just turned *harder*. They called him "Roger Whorr"—a white whore. Ain't that a bitch? Then they said, "You ain't white. You ain't black. You just *wack*." I told 'em, "You know what? The man's more nigger than y'all ever be." [*laughs*]

JONNY "STAGE DOOR" ORR A week after the news broke about Bird being Roger's mother—early December, 1980—John Lennon was shot. That pushed them out of the headlines. It's shitty but I still associate Lennon's murder with a sense of relief. Not to say Roger and Bird stopped being news, no way. But the heat got turned way down.

HENRY LOUIS GATES JR. (literary critic) All the high-, low-, and mid-dlebrow rags did their tag-team thing . . . the *Enquirer* made out like Bird was Bigfoot—the Black Ness Monster! Both were on the cover of the *Rolling Stone*, which at least made sense because of their musical careers. Robert Frank took that picture. Folks couldn't get enough; running those stories was like printing money. And there were some marvelous things as well. Jimmy Baldwin did a wonderful essay in the the *Atlantic Monthly*. I cried when I read that. And Joan Didion, in the *New Yorker*—one of those novella-length profiles like they used to do. She called it "Awake and Sing," after the Odets play.

ED BRADLEY (*journalist*) A year after he and Bird did *60 Minutes*, the

French gave him the Commandeur de la Légion d'Honneur. He took his mom along for that. She was pretty well-known in France, which was probably why they gave it to him. Roger's own merits stood him well, but she was the icing on the prize so to speak.

LENA HORNE (*singer, actress*) The public went wild. There was enormous curiosity and suddenly she was back on the charts—her whole catalog was part of the national conversation. She became kind of a hero, a figurehead, not only because of her preeminence as a singer. Her association with Billie Holiday and so many others added to the gravitas ... And just as prominent was the fact that she was a disenfranchised young Black girl—raped by a Klansman, no less—forced to give up her baby. A baby sold to the highest bidder, like a slave child. There was a lot of finger-pointing at the adoptive parents and some of that was unfair, but you know what they say about the fairness of life: *ain't* none. She was in demand to perform, but Roger wouldn't allow it, not at first. I give him great credit for that. There was just no way he was going to allow her to be thrown to the lions. She needed to get her health back and her head too. He was the only one she'd listen to. "I do what my son tells me; and I do what my Lord tells me, too." She'd wink and say, "Just not in that order."

CICELY TYSON (*actress*) He wanted to get Bird out of the media storm, which was impossible because there was nowhere to hide. But you could mitigate it. He bought her a house in L.A. because there were good hospitals and the climate was right. Bird was always saying she was tired of being cold. "I've been cold my whole effin' life."

I lived right around the corner in Bel Air and we got close. I was riding high. I'd done *Roots* and was getting ready to play Marva Collins, but was still an East Harlem girl. And in so many ways, Bird never left Leipers Fork. We connected on that level.

CALEB FEMI (*poet*) Critics did their revisionist number on *Grace War* and *Yes I Can*. He had it coming from both ends: the praise and the damnation. That's when you know you're doing it right! One of the magazines put a picture of him on the cover with the headline, "Blackface Like Me." At the same time, there were beautiful essays, thoughtful, poetic ones, like Baldwin's in the *Atlantic Monthly*—"Notes of Native Sons and Mothers."

I was very young when I discovered him—his novel *The Jungle Book* was my first encounter—and he saved my life as surely as the music of Headie and K-Trap, as sure as the poetry of T. S. Eliot and the *Odyssey*. To this day, many still claim that he knew his true parentage all along, that he was *complicit*. They cling to the notion of him being a racial P. T. Barnum, "the Greatest Show and Tell on Earth," all that nonsense. How else to explain his films, music, and writings—I'm speaking mostly of the *Journals* now—as being consistently, linguistically, *sublingually*—durably and subdurally—focused on the difficulties of being Black in a white world, white in a Black world? The answer is that genius doesn't explain. It never explains. Genius just *is*.

Genius *knows*.

TA-NEHISI COATES (*writer*) He called that interview with *Playboy* his Emancipation Proclamation. Said he wasn't going to be a slave to reality *no more*—not that he ever was. It's like that moment in *Quixote* where the characters learn they've been written about in an "alternate" *Quixote*. Fitzgerald had that remark about the test of a first-rate intelligence being the ability to hold two opposing ideas in their head and still function. Try two opposing *worlds*. Try ten—try a *hundred*. That's what Roger Orr was capable of doing. Holding a hundred parallel worlds in his head and overthrowing the petty "one-world" Weltanschauung.

He was living proof of that and a lesson to us all.

ROSIE LEVIN Bird got a kick out of calling herself a Beverly Hillbilly, but the house he bought was actually in Bel Air. Apart from Cicely [Tyson], their neighbors were Judd Marmor—a famous psychiatrist—Henry Fonda, and Brian Wilson. And of course, Spielberg.

Cicely Tyson called herself Elly Mae, but Bird didn't want to be Granny. She wanted to be Mr. Drysdale! "I'm the banker, baby, and don't you forget it." She loved that Aretha never let go of her little purse when she did shows. People thought she carried a pistol in there, but Bird said that's where she kept the money. She made the promoters pay her in cash and when the purse got too small, that's where she put the *check*.

STEVEN SPIELBERG I'd just done *E.T.* and *Poltergeist* and was prepping *Indiana Jones*. Roar and I used to go for little jaunts around the neighborhood.

He was only five or six years older than me, but it was like taking a walk with Capra and John Ford, with Ernie Kovacs and Lenny Bruce thrown in. *And* *Lenny Bernstein!* I was an enormous admirer of Roar's work, just huge. The scope of it, the *breadth* of it exhilarated and panicked me at the same time. He had access to something none of us do. An access to the comedic, the tragic, and the holy. I wasn't competitive because there was no way to compete.

I was starting to executive produce films [e.g., *Continental Divide*] for others to direct. I made it clear I'd be thrilled to take on that role. Not that he needed my help because he was very much in demand—maybe even more so since the revelation of his biracialism, a movie in itself that I hoped to make one day. I just wanted to be involved in anything the man was up to.

He took me up on that with *Arrival.*

SAM WASSON One of the things he spoke to Spielberg about was his idea of "subversions." He wanted to do a movie like *The Best Years Of Our Lives* or *Little Shop On The Corner* or *It Happened One Night*—a classic, perfect, quintessentially *American* film—with a ten-minute ending that, in essence, *destroyed* what came before it. He called it "blowing up the cathedral." Spielberg gave his full attention to everything Roar said, but it's no surprise that he never warmed to the "subversions"—and signed on for *Arrival* instead.

DR. ARNOLD KLEIN (*dermatologist*) Roger brought his mother in; she had a melanoma above her breast. He'd already diagnosed it. He was five years younger, but I had a well-worn copy of *Orr's Textbook of Dermatology* on the shelf above my desk. It's still the gold standard. I assumed that David [Geffen] had referred him because he was always sending clients my way. David and I first met at a Cedars fundraiser. He told me it was *essential* to have an office in Beverly Hills but of course I couldn't afford the rent. He loaned me the money and in six months, I'd paid him back. Years later, Roger said he found my name in the yellow pages, the white pages, whatever they used to call it. I remember he said, "Arnie? Always let your fingers do the shtupping."

Because I was a doctor, he felt safe. He *shouldn't* have, because I love to gossip! I'm kidding. Everything between us was confidential. He talked about being gay—being *more* than gay, being *everything*. He called himself "liminal." He was fascinated with bodies, fascinated by trans surgery; I helped steer him to the right people when he started getting serious about it. We traveled the world together, from mud huts in Burundi to fabulous Bavarian castles in the air . . . with Ted Turner and Jane [Fonda], with Kissinger and his "boyfriend" Tituss Burgess, with Liz and King Fahd, with Bishop Tutu and his "wife" Jim Parsons . . .

He *loved* my then-assistant Debbie Rowe. When Michael and Debbie got married in Sydney, Carrie Fisher and Bird were ring bearers—and Roger, best man.

CANDACE HOWARD-SHULTZ (*television producer*) The *60 Minutes* interview—Roger and his mom's official "coming-out"—wasn't the carefully orchestrated, meticulously planned event people thought it was. Not by a long shot.

Bird loved the show and had a huge crush on Ed Bradley. She was watching one night when we did a segment about Patrick Lichfield, the famous photographer and cousin of the queen. He shot nudes of models—*and* the wedding of Charles and Diana. The way Roger tells it, Bird said, "We oughta go on that show. You're looking at the future Mrs. Bird Bradley." She held up her finger and said, "Ed Bradley gonna put a ring on it!"

Anyway, we got a call the next day from Ted Ashley, Roger's agent.

TED ASHLEY (*talent agent*) They couldn't believe that Bird and Roger wanted to do *60 Minutes*. There was just silence over the phone.

Easiest call I ever made, and I've made a few.

SHANA ALEXANDER (*journalist*) Roar always wanted to make Bird happy. That was his mission. And the showman part of him knew it was time for a public debut. The mother and son reunion had been big, loud news for months but Roar instinctively knew the cycle of that sort of thing. Once the swelling goes down, it enters the realm of myth.

60 Minutes was the first, necessary step of that evolution.

GENE SHALIT (*journalist, television historian*) They devoted the entire show to them, something they'd never done before. The first segment was about Roar: his birth into San Francisco's storied, fabulously wealthy Orr family; the early, underground comedy tapes and hushed-up controversy of the warehouse murder and subsequent hospitalization; becoming a doctor;

marriage to his childhood sweetheart, and a brilliant, improbable song-writing career. There was a lot to cover! The early movies, the death of his parents, the attempted assassination in New York, his foray into acting—the whole enchilada. The second segment was all about Bird: her abusive preacher father and childhood rape by a Klansman; leaving home in search of Billie Holiday; and how she managed to make great art amid her struggles with addiction and mental illness. The last part of the show was the "money shot"—mother and son sitting down together.

ABE LASTFOGEL (*agent, president of William Morris*) They sang a soft duet, a cappella—"Try a Little Tenderness"—so understated, so unexpected. It wasn't planned. Of course, the next day the Morris office was inundated with requests to book them. They could have done a stadium tour. I'm being serious.

AMANDA GORMAN Toward the end of the interview—it's on YouTube, you've probably seen it—Ed Bradley asks Bird, "What was it like when he said, 'You're my mother—I'm your son'?" She smiles and seems to transform before our very eyes into what Buddhists call the Great Mother. Then, with this . . . otherworldly *vitality* she hadn't yet shown—she'd been so shy, almost withdrawn—maybe because of her crush on Ed!—she says, "What was it like, Mr. Bradley? For this Bird?" And went straight into that magnificent poem from memory . . . crystalline, vivid, perfectly spoken:[146]

> I know what the caged bird feels, alas!
> When the sun is bright on the upland slopes;
> When the wind stirs soft through the springing grass,
> And the river flows like a stream of glass;
> When the first bird sings and the first bud opes,
> And the faint perfume from its chalice steals—
> I know what the caged bird feels!
>
> I know why the caged bird beats his wing
> Till its blood is red on the cruel bars;
> For he must fly back to his perch and cling

---

146 "Sympathy" by Paul Laurence Dunbar (1899) is what follows.—*ed.*

When he fain would be on the bough a-swing;
 And a pain still throbs in the old, old scars
And they pulse again with a keener sting—
I know why he beats his wing!
I know why the caged bird sings, ah me,
 When his wing is bruised and his bosom sore,—
When he beats his bars and he would be free;
It is not a carol of joy or glee,
 But a prayer that he sends from his heart's deep core,
But a plea, that upward to Heaven he flings—
I know why the caged bird sings!

She put her hand on her son's hand after saying that last line and said, "Thank you, Jesus, for the gift of sons and hearts . . . and cages."

CANDACE HOWARD-SHULTZ After she read that poem, it wasn't just Ed who was crying. It was the entire crew. You can still hear the great sob of a cameraman. (We left that on tape.) "Fly Away Home" had the biggest audience in *60 Minutes'* history. The Clintons came on ten years later, after Monica Lewinsky, and got 37 million viewers. Roger and Bird had forty-two—*without* the Super Bowl lead-in.

SCATTER HOLBROOK It worked. *60 Minutes* lanced a boil. Roger said, "For one time only, the best laid plans of moms and men did not go awry."

DICK GREGORY After they did their "This Is Your Life" act with Ed Bradley, Roger asked me to reach out to a group of people. Could've done that himself but asked *me*. Now, some of the folks he wanted to sit with had problems with *Yes I Can*; some just had problems, period. Problems with Roar being *rich*. Problems with him being a motherfuckin' genius. Problems with him looking so *fly*. And if the niggers didn't *have* problems, they were gonna *make* some. A lot of 'em felt Roar hadn't done enough for his *people*— I hate that "Your people, my people" shit—it's *our* people, it's *we the people*. Roar hadn't done a motherfuckin' thing for "his" people 'cause he didn't motherfuckin' *have* any, God bless him. That ain't who he was. Nigger didn't have a people-having bone in his body! 'Cause he didn't consider himself a color. Didn't even consider himself motherfuckin' human! [*laughs*] And that's the truth. I *still* don't know what he was . . . but with the revelation of his so-called Blackness, things changed for him. Shit got stood on its head. He went to the garden and started yanking out the white roots. Put a hair shirt on and decided, "I need to make amends and reparations." I said, "To who, motherfucker? And for what?" Quincy told him not to do that. A whole crew of us did. But he was hardheaded.

He met with Sidney [Poitier] and Harry [Belafonte] and Jimmy [James Baldwin]—none of whom had a problem with him *ever*. They *loved* his shit. The movies, the music . . . loved *everything*. Motherfuckers wanted to *be* him. When he started his groveling act, you know, saying how *sorry* he was— they'd all come over to the Pierre—they were, like, Say *what*, nigger? [*laughs*] You know, "We just came for dinner, we don't wanna hear this bullshit. Pass the caviar." [*laughs uproariously*] I said to Roger, "Baby, you are preaching to the wrong Black choir!" It took a while for him to defrost. He met with Henry Louis Gates Jr, a young professor at Yale. A very smart young brother, tip-top smart . . . helped organize that famous *symposium* with Muhammad Ali and Calypso Gene [Louis Farrakhan]. Roger "repented" for *Yes I Can* like it was the devil's work.

He was in shock, that's all. I told him he had PTNSD—Post-Traumatic Negro Stress Disorder. He lost his footing for a while, plain and simple. 'Cause he'd been white all his life and now that he was *Black*, he wanted to be accepted by his new family. Wanted to be brought into the fold. And if *groveling* was what it took . . . we do funny shit when we're in shock. The White man ain't the only one who likes a slave. And it was the opposite of what should have happened; all those people who thought he hadn't done enough "for the cause" should have dropped to the ground and kissed his feet, 'cause he was the motherfuckin' *Black Picasso*, that's right, he brought all of us up a notch on the world stage. In my mind, Roger Orr did more than anyone with the exception of Martin Luther King to change the idea of who and what Black people are, what they can become, what they deserve, what they can do, the *genius* of Black people—did more than anyone by just *being Roger Orr*. He was like a walking freedom march.

The showbiz pimp in him thought it'd be a good idea to bring Bird along for the meet with Ali and the Charmer [Farrakhan]. You know, a little fire-power . . . and he was right, 'cause Farrakhan's appreciation of Bird *would not stop*. He couldn't take his eyes off her. Mom was Roar's backstage pass, his get-out-of-White-Negro-jail-free card. Laughlin brokered a tête-à-tête with Huey Newton and Bobby Seale—her ex, Stokely Carmichael, was there but refused to come out of the kitchen. Ain't that a bitch? If you can't take the heat, stay in the kitchen, nigger! [*laughs*] And Bobby was a nickel-and-dime, envious motherfucker. Roger reached out to his old running partner Anatole Broyard but Broyard wouldn't see him, either. As pretty as Anatole was, he hated looking into a mirror, and that's what Roger was. A mirror.

Huey and Bobby gave absolution as he kneeled before them. All those press conferences of my boy weeping were a degrading spectacle. I had to look away. To me, it was a minstrel show.

TOM WOLFE (*author*) Roar got radicalized, which wasn't him at all. For about a minute, he wanted to go full-tilt boogie Islam and jettison his "slave name," but Bird talked him out of that. He later told me he'd been suffering from Black-and-White-Man's Burden Syndrome. That was *recoil*—not just from the Blacks who said "You'll never be one of us" but from the racists who had no problem shouting the n-word when they saw him on the street. He *did* become a Panther for a while. The Panthers never accepted him but were very good at self-promotion. In truth, Roger and his big sis were a bit of an embarrassment; deep pockets were the only thing they brought to the Party. So to speak.

The "syndrome" finally ran its course, and he got back to the busy, complicated, operatic business of being Roger Orr.

BILLY CRYSTAL (*comedian, actor*) Richard [Pryor] had his famous trip to Kenya in 1979, and Roger wanted to make the pilgrimage too. He became obsessed. He wanted to get away from all the noise and politics of America; Mother Africa wasn't interested in what he did or didn't do for Black people—she loved him unconditionally. Richard was very encouraging. He *almost* went along. Roger and Bird wound up taking their dermatologist [Arnie Klein] instead.

DAVID BRENNER (*comedian*) The late-night comedians had their fun. All those Oreo jokes. *Yecch.* Johnny Carson's monologue had Roar starring in a new miniseries with Levar Burton called "Dyed Roots." Redd Foxx did the

Morning Show and said he'd known Bird Rabineau for years, which was true. "Nice lady. My Mama's a 'bird' too—a *vulture*. But I ain't need to go to Africa to look for her. She right on the porch." Even Cavett jumped on the band-wagon in his own smarmy, inimitable way. He used to be a writer on the Paar show, and when Jayne Mansfield was a guest, he wrote Jack's famous intro-duction: "Ladies and Gentlemen, here they are, Jayne Mansfield." Cavett reprised the line when Roar came on his show. "Ladies and Gentlemen, here they are, Roger Orr." Which wasn't too far off. Roger seemed to appreciate it. The first thing he said when he sat down was, "I am large and contain mul-titudes." Cavett shot back, "I am small and can't contain my pleasure that you're here tonight."

Dick was in good form that night.

C. RILEY SNORTON (*author*)[147] During all the race hoopla, Orr's primary issue took a backseat. For the world to learn you're Black is one thing; for the world to learn that you identify as a woman trapped in a man's body was something else. They weren't handing out medals for it back then. Everyone at the circus of public opinion loves a flamethrower, but bearded ladies are definitely an acquired taste. He'd been to Africa but gender dysphoria was the *true* Dark Continent—the undiscovered country from which no traveler returns.

CICELY TYSON After being reunited with her son, the proof was absolute: God is good. Bird was *feelin'* it. She'd dance around saying she won the Lord's lottery, that He'd put the winning ticket in her hand. She got physically better each day. Was clean and sober. Spent the whole day at Elizabeth Arden and was lookin' *good*. She started singing again! She was just delirious with God's love.

LLOYD GARVER (*television producer*) Roar told me that his only purpose was to make his mother happy. That's how they ended up on *Family Ties*— Bird loved our show. I think someone at Morris got in touch. . . . Abe! Abe Lastfogel called me himself. He said Roger wanted to surprise his mother on

---

147 *Black On Both Sides: A Racial History of Trans Identity*, pp. 318–325 (Harvard University Press, 2007).

her birthday. I asked him if Roger wanted to be on the show too but he said no, "He wants it to be his mom's day." The writers' room was on fire. Bird was a real ham. We had to tell her to stop acting like Moms Mabley. We kept saying, "Just be you."

When we wrapped, they wheeled in a big cake that Roger ordered from Hansen's, on Beverly Drive—five tiers, with "Happy Bird-day" on it. The cast and crew brought LPs for her to sign, and she was absolutely gracious.

TRACY KRAMER (*talent manager*) Abe [Lastfogel] lived at the Beverly Wilshire. Every morning, a chauffeur picked him up at the hotel and drove him about fifty feet to the Morris Agency—then drove him back at five p.m. Abe's workday consisted of watching thirty-five-millimeter prints of World War II movies in the Morris screening room. Roar loved that. He couldn't get enough of Abe Lastfogel. When Streisand wanted to sign with Abe, she was told he was "emeritus" and went with Sue Mengers instead.

DONALD E. PALUMBO (*author*)[148] He was determined that his next film have nothing to do with race. Much of Orr's oeuvre can be described as an iteration of the Hero's Journey; now, in midlife, he was halfway through his own epic voyage. The Philip K. Dick short story "I Hope I Shall Arrive Soon" was a funhouse mirror of such a quest, with a protagonist—the fractured hallucination of a Hero—that appealed immensely to Orr's sense of deified failure. In Dick's brilliantly skewed narrative, you *can* go home again; the trouble is, you can't *stop*, and the journey home becomes a tortured, ad infinitum loop.

He was having trouble with financing, but all of that went away when Orr used his ace in the hole: Spielberg fulfilled a promise he made some years before and would exec produce.

JAMES DICKEY (*novelist*) Phil published "I Hope I Shall Arrive Soon" in *Playboy*.[149] That short story became Roar's bible during his stay in Payne Whitney. He said it kept him from going mad—which is interesting, because

---

148 From *The Monomyth in American Science Fiction Films: 28 Visions of the Hero's Journey* by Donald E. Palumbo, pp. 111–115 (Harcourt Brace, 1983).

149 The magazine ran the story in 1980, with the non-PKD-approved title "Frozen Journey."—*ed.*

it's a very claustrophobic tale of a man who is going mad. Rather terrifying. Roar read it aloud to anyone who came to visit—and I mean, read the *whole thing*. It took about an hour. I went through two of those performances and both times he cried at the ending. The last few lines are memorable . . . [*retrieves pages*]

Here:

"'We should have framed it,' he said. 'We didn't have sense enough to take care of it. Now it's torn. And the artist is dead.'"

JOHN JOSEPH ADAMS (*producer*)[150] The Wachowskis had been heavily influenced by Roger Orr's *Arrival* by the time they did *The Matrix*. Philip K. Dick's story "I Hope I Shall Arrive Soon" is about a distant time when life expectancy is two-hundred-plus years. Victor Kemmings is on his way to a vacation planet with a group of tourists. Everyone's asleep in cryonic tanks because the voyage takes a decade. But something goes wrong, as it tends to in the genre; Victor wakes up and can't move. The computer—PKD's "Hal," I guess you could say—informs Kemmings that he's going to be conscious for ten years, essentially buried alive with only his thoughts for company. He can't be taken out of cryonic suspension because there's no air or food onboard. The computer begins the emergency protocol of downloading Victor's personal memories of the last 150 years, starting with the time he had a girlfriend in Berkeley in the 1960s. When those memories become too traumatic, the computer brings him back further, into his childhood. That goes south too. The computer decides its only recourse is to simulate Victor's arrival to the tourist planet, which it does—thousands and thousands and thousands of times: *Victor Kemmings never stops arriving.*

The computer arranges for the woman he lived with in Berkeley to be there in person when the spaceship actually *does* arrive, believing her presence will be the only thing that saves him from terminal insanity.

It doesn't end well.

PHILIP GLASS (*composer*) I think the Dick story appealed to him because of the twin themes of paralysis and the porous nature of reality. Remember, he didn't find out who he really was and where he came from until his

---

150 From *Geek's Guide to the Galaxy* podcast, episode 17, 2011.

mid-forties. So, at the time he made *Arrival*, the news that Bunny and Mug weren't his parents—that Seraphim wasn't his sister—was fresh enough that he still harbored a phobia he had all his life about inheriting Seraphim's disease, with its genetic promise of early dementia. In many ways, Roar was so immensely prolific because he was in a race against time. And there's something else—the question of "Where *is* 'home'?" He would always be arriving in Nashville, he would always be arriving at Parnassus, in Pacific Heights . . . the discovery of multiple selves effectively obliterated any chance of traditional, definitive arrival. But more than anything, *Arrival* is a movie about the simulacrum of dreaming. Like PKD, Roger was possessed by the question, *What is real?*

Buddhism finally gave him the answer: nothing.

STEWART BRAND Not long after his release from Payne Whitney, Roger made a voyage of his own to California to meet PKD, who was teaching in Fullerton. They had friends in common. Kesey knew Phil and so did Burroughs; both Roar and Phil knew John Lilly, who invented the isolation tank. Lilly was addicted to ketamine; I was there when he died and his stomach's ten thousand pincushion injection scars leaked green fluid that smelled like fungus and ambrosia . . . but somehow Phil and Roger had never met. Oh, here's another thing: Tim Leary introduced them—independently—to the Shulgins.[151]

PKD's twin sister died when they were six weeks old. That ticked the loss boxes for Roar: losing Aurelia, losing Seraphim, "dying" as an infant when he got yanked from his birth mom. Both were bipolar dope fiends and sex freaks; and Phil tried to kill himself once, too. They called themselves "brothers from another Other." When Roger shared his plan to transition surgically, Phil was bewitched. He told Roar to keep a diary about that and Roar said, "I'm going to call it 'Transmigration.'" PKD shouted, "You can't!" because he was working on a book—it turned out to be his last—called *The Transmigration of Timothy Archer.*

---

151 Alexander Shulgin and his wife Nina were Berkeley chemists who wrote a pioneering, legendarily comprehensive two-volume catalog of psychoactive drugs, *PiHKAL* (vol. 1) and *TiHKAL* (vol. 2)—abbreviations of *Phenethylamines* and *Tryptamines I Have Known and Loved.—ed.*

Phil graciously provided another title, the one Roar wound up using: *Transfixed.* I like it much better.

JONNY "STAGE DOOR" ORR He visited Phil for three days and as far as I know, they didn't sleep. I'd have liked to have been a fly on *that* wall. Though maybe not! When Roger was about to leave, Phil said, "Didn't you say there was something you wanted to ask me?" Roger said, "Oh shit. *Yes.* I want to make a movie of 'I Hope I Shall Arrive Soon.'" Phil instantly agreed and they scrawled out a contract on the back cover of *Ubik*, which both of them signed.[152]

ROBERT HEINLEIN (*novelist*) When Roar visited him in Fullerton, *Blade Runner* was still a year or more away from production. That film has a long, complicated history that I won't get into here. Phil *hated* Hollywood, especially its approach to his work. He'd call me up and rant. He was very, very cynical about the mechanism, the whole enterprise. But when he met Roar, he was just so impressed. Roar was unlike anyone he'd ever encountered, in Hollywood or beyond. That's why he didn't hesitate when Roar asked for his blessing to adapt "I Hope I Shall Arrive Soon."

Phil showed him the journal he kept, detailing the religious "visions" he'd had in '74[153]—something Phil hadn't shown *me*, and we were extremely close. And Roar shared the "Catholic" visions that overtook him in adolescence. They were a marriage made in Heaven and in Hell. Cue William Blake.

DAVID UNGER When Philip died in '82, my father said it was a horrible blow to Roger, that he cried like a baby. Dad said he wanted to abandon *Arrival.* You know, "I can never do this film." That was his first impulse—he was just so distraught. Then, over time, it became, "I *have* to do this film—for PKD."

He got the idea of sending the story to Pinter because he suddenly lost faith in his ability to properly adapt the book, which needed to be expanded

---

152 Mark Cuban bought the paperback *Ubik* "contract" for $460,000 at a Sotheby's auction in 2016.—*ed.*
153 The thousand-page diary was posthumously published as *The Exegesis of Philip K. Dick* (Houghton Mifflin Harcourt, 2011)—*ed.*

quite a bit. Pinter hadn't written a script since *The French Lieutenant's Woman*, and the idea of a "space movie" piqued his interest. He read the short story and loved it; it was that easy. Remarkably, they'd never met because Pinter was gone by the time Roger started filming *Philip Phaethon* and for some reason their paths hadn't crossed since. Initially, Roger thought Pinter would turn him down because of the grudge he may have held about *Philip Phaethon*—that whole business about Roar rewriting the ending—but Sir Harold's beef was with Miloš, not Roger. In fact, privately, Pinter was said to have been enormously pleased with the result of Roar's contribution.

SIMON CALLOW Harold shortened the title to *Arrival*—he liked the symmetry because *Betrayal* was just a few years before. The titles became bookends in a sense . . . *Arrival* is about regret and botched homecomings; I still think it's the most emotional film Roar ever made. Though "botched" is probably the wrong word. What I think it's trying to say—part of what it's saying—is the tragedy of humankind adrift, imagining it can't find its way home.

Of course, the real tragedy is failing to see that home is everywhere and nowhere. So, we can never be adrift, can we. Rather Buddhist, isn't it? I'm not a Buddhist myself—but I play one onstage. And sometimes in interviews!

SAM KASHNER Orr loved that in *Journey to Ixtlan*, don Juan tells Castaneda, "Genaro left his passion in Ixtlan: his home, his people, all the things he cared for. And now he wanders around in his feelings; and sometimes, as he says, he almost reaches Ixtlan. All of us have that in common. For Genaro, it is Ixtlan; for you, it will be Los Angeles."[154] Or Nashville . . .

DENIS VILLENEUVE (*director*) When I was young, I dreamed of making a movie like *The Day the Earth Stood Still* or *Forbidden Planet* or *The Incredible Shrinking Man*. I was obsessed with the [John Varley] story *Air Raid* and thought, with the preternatural confidence of youth, "This will be my first film." I was fourteen. For some reason, I didn't see [Tarkovsky's] *Solaris* until I was seventeen . . . then a week later, *Arrival* came out and changed the way I'd been thinking about cinema. It completely rewired my brain.

---

154 From *Journey to Ixtlan: The Lessons of Don Juan* by Carlos Castañeda , p. 373 (Simon & Schuster, 1991).

When I made my own *Arrival* [2016], I got in touch. We knew each other en passant—he'd been president of the jury at Cannes in 1998 when my film *Un 32 août sur terre* was in Un Certain Regard. I asked for his blessing to name my film after the one he made that forever changed my life, as an homage. He said the honor would be his.

He could not have been more chivalrous.

MELLIE KOCH He wanted Harrison—but *that* wasn't going to work because Harrison had a now-famously shitty experience with Ridley on *Blade Runner*. Which of course we weren't aware of at the time. And as much as Harrison respected Roar, he definitely wasn't in the mood to extend the PKD franchise. Roar wanted to reach back in time and snatch Burt Lancaster from *The Swimmer*. He kept saying he wanted someone with that kind of "burned-out, acrobatic grace."

We cast Martine first—the girlfriend of "Victor Kemmings." Debra Winger was our first choice, and she agreed right away. Written by Harold Pinter and directed by Roger Orr was all she needed to know. It came down to Nick [Nolte] and Jeff [Bridges] for the role of Victor. Roar thought Nick was a bit hard and Jeff a bit soft—it was Goldilocks time—but either of them would work because he felt that Debra would magically even them out. Roar needed to see the chemistry, so each of them read with her, which was unusual because at that level agents don't want their clients auditioning. Nick and Jeff were lovely about it; every actor in Hollywood wanted to work with Roar. Actors' catnip.

Then, out of the blue, I get a call from Malcolm McDowell. Malc's an old friend, Lord, we go back to the Seventies when I cast him in *Figures in a Landscape*. He happened to be in L.A. doing a rather silly rock 'n' roll movie[155] and wanted to have lunch. A catch-up lunch, nothing to do with business . . . now, Malc's performance in *O Lucky Man!* was high on Roar's All-Time Greatest. And it was the perfect moment because Malcolm was a tad past his shelf-life date—oh, that's a *terrible* expression, forgive me, Malc!—those bright, wounded eyes, that *face*, always so time-worn and expressive, always so tragically, boyishly handsome, were now even more so. Well, sparks just flew between him and Deb, and that was that. And as wonderful as Debra was, Malcolm swept the awards. She got the Golden

---

155 *Get Crazy* (1983).

Globe, but Malc got the ones that mattered: the National Society of Film Critics, the New York Film Critics Circle, the Silver Bear, the BAFTA, the César, the Cahiers du Cinéma.

Orgiastic is the actor's head who wears the crowns that matter!

BEVERLY D'ANGELO I really wanted to play Martine. I told Roger I'd come in to read, and he said, "No, no, that's demeaning. I know what you can do." He kind of strung me along. Then I ran into Meryl and she said Debra Winger was already cast. I was like, *huh?*

He associated me with . . . I was in the pre-Bird group, and he wanted post-Bird people. It was simple as that.

DAVID UNGER *Arrival* won the Golden Bear—I can't remember why it was at Berlin, not Cannes—and all the BAFTA awards but was completely shut out of the Oscars. After seven nominations! The film lost money for the studio but its reputation grew exponentially. It's much more than a cult film now. It's on par with *2001*. It's *2001*, with heart.

SUZE BERKOWITZ Ali had a little part in *Arrival*, so Scatter and I came to L.A. for the wrap party. Of course, the *real* reason was to meet Bird; we still hadn't met Roger's mom! Can you believe it? I loved her on sight. And couldn't stop bawling . . . It was more than a little surreal because suddenly you had two narratives—I kept seeing Bunny and Mug but didn't quite know what to do with *Bird*. My brain was short-circuiting, you know, making bogus memories of Bird in a gown, sweeping down the stairs for a Parnassus gala, and creating alternate histories of Roger and I getting married in Tennessee while Bird sang us "Tenderness" . . . I was trying to integrate. Scatter said his brain was doing the same thing too. It was all very *Arrival*.

There'd been so much written about Roger and Bird, the "origin story," what have you—I read it all!—but there was stuff I didn't know. Stuff *he* knew, but no one else did. At least, that's what I thought. I had the feeling there was a big piece missing. Something that was being glossed over. . .

We used to talk on the phone late at night after Scatter went to sleep. A couple of night owls. I'd be in Maui and Roger would be wherever he was in the world—I'd pick up the phone and he'd say, "Put on the hair dryer." That was our code for Gossip Time: you know, two yentas trashing the world while they're under those old-timey hair dryer hoods. *Nothing* was off-limits. So, a few weeks after the wrap party, we're hair-drying away—who's fucking who, who's dropping dead, the usual. And suddenly I say, "Did you ever ask Bird about the rape?" He got real quiet then said no, he hadn't. I thought, well, *that's* strange . . . that he didn't want to go there. Part of me understood: "Hey, Mom, tell me about the rape!" But it wasn't like him not to ask, to not get the details. Maybe a daughter would have been more curious. Maybe if a son finds out something like that, he reacts in a kind of . . . [*sings the phrase*] "Baby, I don't want to know." That's from "Silver Springs"—Fleetwood Mac. *Love* me that song.

But that's what was missing—for *me*.

And I felt it was important.

BEVERLY D'ANGELO It was definitely on his mind before Suze brought it up. I mean, to find his father. Because adopted kids zero in on that shit like lasers. *I found Mom, time to find Dad.* Bird knew that; she must have. But how do you find a cold case rapist from, like, fifty years ago? Or almost fifty. I think Roar was hoping it was a lost cause and that he'd never be able to find the sonofabitch. He was preparing to just let it go and sit with his gratitude for what *is*, not what was.

When he finally asked about that night, Bird was a little blasé. A little laid-back, which was kind of her way. Probably a defense mechanism too. She kept saying the guy "wiggled in there" and Roger got in a rage. "Goddammit, he didn't wiggle in *anywhere*! The piece of shit *raped* you." She laughed and said, "That's his *name*, baby." Roger said, "What are you talking about?" Bird said, "Wriggle—that's his name. His boys called him Wriggleman."

That was something not even Peter Gramm knew.

RICHIE "SNOOP" RASKIN That was a call I didn't expect but I was more than happy to help. I'd only met Roger a few times but liked him. A very talented man—an important man, in the culture.

I concentrated on the South. It wasn't that tough; I knew a KKK informant who'd had run-ins with the guy. Petry changed his surname in the Fifties—to Jones—but his cronies still called him "Wriggle."

DENZEL WASHINGTON My son just saw *Hollow* for the first time—don't know what took him so long—and loved it. Scared the sweetbreads out of him. We started talking about scary movies. *Get Out* and *Blair Witch*, all that. I told him he needed to see [Polanski's] *Repulsion*. . . . Then I said—'cause I'd just got off the phone with Jordan [Peele]—I said, "You know, Jordan wants to make a film about your godfather Roar." My son said, "Everybody wants to make a freakin' movie about Roar." He's right about *that*. I said to Jordan, "Why don't you do the Bird Rabineau story? She's more interesting!" Naw, I'm not being serious, 'cause Roar's life was interesting as fuck.

Jordan was telling me how these big, traumatic things always tended to happen to Roar right around the time of his movie premieres. It's true. Roar had that boyfriend with the funny name—Boodles—who died on the day *Hollow* opened. And when *Arrival* was having its premiere at the old Carthay Circle Theater in L.A., he's standing on the red carpet when he learns that his biological father is *alive*—for the time being, anyway. The man who raped his mama and got her pregnant is alive, on death row, in Bibb County! That's just a few miles from where we shot *Grace War*. Put *that* in a movie, and the critics'll hammer you to a cross. But they'll find a way to do that anyhow.

BOOK FOUR
Imaginary Prisons
1985–2000

CHAPTER THIRTEEN

Hallelujah Boogie

SIMON CALLOW At heart, he was a "completist." No stone left unturned. He was that way in art and in life. But searching for his father was something I don't believe he'd have done—I think he'd have left it floating out there if Bird hadn't given him that clue. Because narratively, it was far more appealing if the man was impossible to find. Roar *found* his mother; why gild the lily? Sometimes we're not meant to have all the pieces of the puzzle. If it's too tidy, it becomes man-made, novelistic. But that's what Roger got: the curse of resolution.

RICHIE "SNOOP" RASKIN After a few weeks, I got lucky. Not through an informant but a warden at GDCP [Georgia Diagnostic and Classification Prison]—"Wild Bill" Calhoun. GDCP's in Bibb, where the death house is. When I told "Wild Bill" I was looking for an old *peculiar*[156] named Wriggle, he just laughed. "The Wriggleman right here, Snoop Dog."

Here's a piece of trivia that might interest you. At one point, Woody Harrelson's father shared a cell with Wriggle.[157] Harrelson escaped under Calhoun's watch, and Jones nearly went with him. They transferred Harrelson to the Supermax in Colorado after that.

WOODY HARRELSON I met Roar in the Nineties—auditioned for him— and we talked about all that. The parallels were a little eerie. I was born on the

---

156 Klansman.—*ed.*

157 In 1979, Charles Harrelson, the father of actor Woody Harrelson, was convicted of assassinating federal judge, John H. Wood Jr. Harrelson died in prison of a heart attack in 2007.

same day as my dad; Roar and his father were born on the same day too. In Japan, they say it means you're not even his son—you're *him*. I don't know what the shrinks would say about that. Another thing was that my dad was acquitted in the murder of a man named Alan Berg, back in '68. And Roar's dad was indicted as one of the Klansmen who killed Alan Berg—but a *different* Alan Berg.

Another little piece of strangeness.

SAMUEL L. JACKSON (*actor*) When I came in to read for *Hallelujah Boogie*, I found out that we shared some common ground. I grew up in Chattanooga, and Roar was born in Nashville, which I already knew; everybody knew about him and Bird by then. He asked about my folks and I told him about my father, who I'd only met one time in my life. That seemed to get his . . . attention. I brought up his sister because Laughlin used to run with Stokely and I *knew* Stokely. Knew a bunch of the Panthers. And I'd met Laughlin in Atlanta.

When I mentioned Atlanta, Roar said, "That's where my dad is."

He said his father was on death row, and that got *my* attention. It was spontaneous—because at that time, no one outside the inner circle knew.

He said, "Keep that under your hat."

I told him, "Friend, not one of my hats had anything crawl out of it yet."

* * * * * * * * *

JONES v. THE STATE.
20791.
(215 Ga. 376)
(360 SE2d 197)
(1972)

GREGORY, Justice.
Murder, etc. Bibb Superior Court. Before Judge Remaine.

This is a death penalty case. Appellant Colson "Wriggle" Jones was indicted in Bibb County for the rape and murder of a young girl and elderly woman. He was tried, convicted, and sentenced to death. The case was affirmed on direct appeal. His sentence was subsequently vacated by the United States Court of Appeals, Eleventh Circuit, on the basis of virtually identical deficiencies in the sentencing instructions given at his trial.

Jones was returned to Bibb County for retrial as to sentence. His motion for change of venue was granted, and a resentencing trial was held in Morgan County in December 1970. Jones was again sentenced to death and now appeals. See OCGA 11-10-55 (f).

In June of 1966, the Georgia Pardons and Parole Board released Wriggle Jones from prison after he had served only seven years on a ten-year sentence for a variety of charges, including burglary, arson, receiving stolen property and attempted prison break. He was released despite the report from the prison psychologist that said Jones's "test scores reveal the possibility of sociopathic disorders. This individual may be dangerous to himself or others."

On August 7, 1972, Jones was arrested in Ideal, Georgia, for failing to pay for gasoline. Shortly afterward, Appling County Sheriff B. J. Roundtree charged Jones with the murder of Mrs. Becky Hildstrom, seventy-six years of age, and her great-granddaughter, Aurora Hildstrom, 12, who had been robbed, raped, and shot in Mrs. Hildstrom's home, ten miles south of Montezuma on Jan. 26.

Mrs. Hildstrom and her great-granddaughter, ankles and wrists tied with wire hangers, were strangled while being raped. Jones later told a cellmate that Aurora Hildstrom watched the assault on her great-grandmother before being killed herself. The victims had panties stuffed far enough down their throats that this detail was not discovered until autopsy.

* * * * * * * * * *

DAVID STEINBERG His father had been on death row for seventeen years, and it didn't look like they were going to kill him anytime soon. Roar gave himself a reprieve. He'd say, "The minute I hear Truman's doing a book about *Wrigley*"—he never called him Wriggle—"I'll rush down to meet him." The joke being, the writing of *In Cold Blood* hastened the execution of the killers.

LAUGHLIN ORR I guess you could say my brother and I were estranged at the time. We never *officially* stopped talking but it was all surface stuff, you know, how-are-you-I'm-fine-how-are-you—or estate-related issues. I wanted to get to know Bird, but he just wouldn't let me in. She did her best to broker a détente but . . . *nunca mas.* She was wonderful. A very Christian lady, a peacemaker. Years later, we did get close. I adored her.

So, the phone rings in the middle of the night—I'm in St. Bart's. I pick up and that *voice* says, "Hey, Big Sis. Can ya talk?" He hadn't called me that— Big Sis—in forever. I sat bolt upright like I'd had a thousand cups of coffee. He told me he found the man who raped Bird—his technical father—and I was the first person he was telling. We talked until dawn. About everything: Seraphim, Kerouac, the crazy parties Mom and Dad used to throw . . . our generally fucked-up, generally blesséd lives. So dreamy, so *intimate,* like we were on MDMA. He even brought up his friend Jan Morris, how he was seriously thinking of starting hormone treatments because he was tired of having a body that didn't make sense to him. Well, *that* was a surprise. And I loved that he told me! He said that he and Suze—and Scatter!—played dress-up when they were kids. How could I not have known that? "I looked better in Mom's gowns than Suze did"—he was just so funny and sweet. He said he made Suze call him Coco—as in Chanel. I cried a lot on that call and a lot when we hung up.

Best phone call of my life.

BEVERLY D'ANGELO When he told me about his father, I started to hyperventilate. I said, "Are you gonna see him?" He shrugged. You know, like, what's the rush?

DICK GREGORY He wasn't ready. Who would have been? You *can't* get ready for shit like that. He'd joke about it. You know, slip back into stand-up and fantasize about having a meeting with his old man.

"They put us in a room, and I get macho. I tell the guards to unshackle him—motherfucker's seventy years old! How much damage could he *do?* They leave us alone, to get acquainted. And we're smilin' at each other— we're cryin'—it's *complicated*—and he mentions the first time he met Mom. Starts talkin' about how pretty she was, like a hot, tiny, anorexic Aunt Jemima . . . then, *wham*—I'm on the floor. Klansman's cold-cocked me! And when I come to, my Savile Row slacks are bunched up around my ankles and he's drilling the Supremacist shit out of me! But once the *shock* wears off . . . I start to enjoy it! I get *into* it. I'm yellin', *Fuck it, Papa! Fuck your bastard nigger son's man-pussy!* The Imperial Wizard's ridin' me all kinds of *hard*, callin' me all kinds of *Birdies*, and starts reciting poetry—'cause he's a fan of Langston Hughes! Tells me that back in the day, he raped Langston too! That dick's so deep in my ass, I can feel it in my throat. '"Hold fast to your dreams, son! For if dreams die, life is a broken-winged bird that cannot fly!"'[158] Then we both come."

The riffs were his way of coping. What's the name of that play? *Don't Bother Me, I Can't Cope!* [*laughs, chokes, spits out his food, keeps laughing*]

JACK RAPKE (*agent*) I ran into him at the Ivy and asked what he wanted to do next.

He said, "A black comedy."

"Like *Strangelove*?"

"Like *Car Wash*."

DAVID "DOC" O'CONNOR (*agent*) He talked a lot about a script he wrote back in the Sixties, a contemporary version of a story from *1,001 Nights*. He changed the name from "The Hunchback's Tale" to *Gift from God*. It became one of his most beloved films.

SUE MENGERS Roar said different things to different people. With directors, he'd talk about the next movie he had in mind; with writers, about the novel he was planning; with musicians, he'd say, "I'm going to do an opera." With Francis [Bacon] or his dealer, it was about a new suite of paintings or sculptures. He dreamt aloud and in living color.

JOSEPH HELLER (*novelist*) He kept journals but always wanted to write fiction. Jesus, his life *was* fiction. Around the time he learned who his father was, he became captivated by a book called *Child's Play: Memoirs of a Boy Soldier*, written by a young man named Ishmael Beah. Beah was just a kid when the rebels conscripted him to fight in the Ugandan civil war; by the time he was eleven, he'd slaughtered men, women, and children. UNICEF

---

158 From "Dreams," by Langston Hughes, 1922.—*ed.*

rescued and rehabilitated him. At twenty, he wrote a *New York Times* best-seller and did a very successful book tour in America.

Roger's protagonist was Zachariah Boswell—which was perfect, because Roar was both hero and hero's chronicler—a Black teenager living in Los Angeles, adopted by white parents when he was four years old. Zachariah's gifted, he's in all the school plays and aspires to be a movie star. When his adoptive mother gets sick, they have to sell the house to pay her medical bills. But when Zachariah sees Ishmael Beah on *Oprah* promoting his book, he gets "a very Big Idea"—to travel the country *impersonating* Beah on the lecture circuit, giving talks for money he'd send home for his mother's care. It had all the themes that obsessed Roar, and the poetically contrived parallels too: a genius Black boy adopted by white parents; the confidence game all artists are engaged in; the fungibility of life and Art, of reality and dreams. Roar wanted to find the America of himself. He loved *On the Road*, but that was then, this was now. He was long past the adolescent raptures of Kerouac. His sights were much higher: to reach the unreachable dreams of *Quixote*, to out-giant *Gargantua and Pantagruel*. The beacon of *Candide* was in there too. His estimation of contemporary American literature was dismal. He'd say, "Joey? I'm going to Vol*taire* the *New Yorker* crowd a brand new arsehole."

I was a little envious because the theme was so rich. He joked that he might change the kid's name from Zachariah to Yossarian.

AMANDA GORMAN It was so meta! Zachariah's a natural mimic and spends days listening to the *Child's Play* audiobook, mastering Ishmael Beah's mellifluous accent. What's amazing about the novel is its sheer poetry. I was twelve years old when I read it. Didn't *understand* a lot of it but so much of *The Jungle Book* inspired me, not just as a writer but as a Black woman. Zachariah quotes Vachel Lindsay, who I'd never even *heard* of and I couldn't believe what I was reading: "Torch-eyed and horrible, foam-flanked and terrible. BOOM, steal the pygmies, BOOM, kill the Arabs, BOOM, kill the white men, HOO HOO HOO! Lissen to the yell of Leopold's ghost, burning in Hell for his hand-maimed host!" Oh, I know there are lots of people who still have trouble with that man Lindsay, they say he's just a race-carpetbagger, a privileged white man who didn't know a thing about the Black experience—but Langston Hughes loved him. Lindsay was a *jazzman*. And the Beats loved him too. He was really interesting—went on these epic walking journeys, selling poems for food and lodging. Deliberately drank a draught of lye and killed himself . . . kind of a holy fool. Lindsay said his poems were meant to be "read aloud or chanted" and I took that to heart.

That's just *one* of the ways Roger Orr made me who I am.

JONATHAN MILLER (*theater director*) The title—*The Jungle Book*—I thought quite brilliant. He'd always been abundantly fond of Kipling, particularly *Kim*, with its admixture of spiritualism and adventure.

COLSON WHITEHEAD (*novelist*) That book is the Wizard behind the curtain of everything I've ever done. But a *real* wizard, not a balderdash one. It's Mark Twain on a magic carpet.

DICK CAVETT In *Six Degrees of Separation*, a young Black hustler convinces everyone he's Sidney Poitier's son. John [Guare] told me *The Jungle Book* gave him the idea.

JOHN GUARE Dick said that? Well, he misspoke. Look, I thought—and still do—Roger's *Jungle Book* was Voltaire, Twain, and Bellow all wrapped in the same gift box. An absolutely extraordinary, singular achievement.

But that peskily persistent rumor about it being the inspiration for *Six Degrees* just isn't true. I got the idea—rather famously—from friends of mine who got hustled in the same way the Kittredge couple did in my play. I'm embarrassed to say that The *Catcher in the Rye* was another influence. Roger laughed when I told him that. He said, "Killers love *Catcher in the Rye*. Of course, playwrights are killers too. The good ones, anyway."

WES CRAVEN (*director*) He was working on two scripts at one time: revising *Gift from God* for the millionth time—and something called *Hallelujah Boogie*. But *The Jungle Book* consumed him. In the novel, his hero Zachariah jumps from place to place, from library to book club, giving charming, lucrative talks about what it was like to be drafted as a child soldier in Africa and forced to commit atrocities. But the grifter's more often the victim in Roger's picaresque, and he felt the book needed the verisimilitude, *l'esprit des lieux* that inspires the divine; Roar decided to "light out for the territories" on adventures of his own that mirrored Zachariah's, at least geographically. Thank God D. A. [Pennebaker] tagged along.

He already knew Pennebaker through Stephen Sondheim because D. A. filmed the cast recording of *Company* in 1970. Roar called D. A. and told him what he was up to. "Hey, come film it. We'll only be reconnoitering for two weeks. 'Tis the storm season—we might even bump into an F5 by the time we hit Tornado Alley." The image of churches and farm animals being sucked into the vortex of God was all D. A. needed. He met up with everyone in Texas two days later.

ALEX GIBNEY (*documentarian*) [D. A. Pennebaker's] *Holy Highway* follows Orr and his posse as they set out to Duluth from Laredo. It's shambolic, it's infuriating, it's absolutely *glorious*. It's always described as being unfinished but is one of those rare works of art whose "unfinishedness" actually completes it. Part *The Epic That Never Was*, part *Lost In La Mancha*, one keeps waiting for Werner Herzog—or Alejandro Jodorowsky!—to make an appearance. But of course, *Highway* is quite different, in that it isn't about the making of a movie but rather the chronicle of a great director's research for a novel he was about to write.

Which turned out to be one of the towering novels of our time.

REV. THOMAS REVEILLE I hope you don't find it too vainglorious but I'll confess I'm the one who suggested they begin their itinerary in Laredo. You see, I knew men who preached in Encinal. The I-35—the mighty interstate—goes straight up from Laredo to the Great Lakes. The Holy Rollers down there call that concrete river "the Holy Highway" and like to say it's named for Isaiah 35:8. The verse goes, "And a highway shall be there, and it shall be called the Holy Way; the unclean shall not pass over it, and fools shall not err therein." Roger seemed quite taken by all that.

NICK BROOMFIELD (*filmmaker*) I'd made a film about a brothel in Pahrump[159] and Roar rang me up. He was gaga for it. He said he was going on the road to research a book and invited me to "audit" the I-35 trip. I thought that meant he wanted me to shoot it, but *noooo*, he said, "D. A.'s doing that." Which enraged me. I nearly hung up the phone—but then I

---

159 *Chicken Ranch* (1986).

thought it might be nice *not* to have a camera because Roar was such great fun. And I needed a break. Why not? And as far as Pennebaker went, it'd be easier to take the piss.

You can see Roar ballooning up in the documentary. His gut—his bloody *face*—get bigger day by day. We were hardly out of Texas when he said, "I've gained fifteen pounds in seventy-two hours." He wasn't exaggerating. We found a dodgy doctor along the way, an alkie who said Roar was retaining water. They always say that, don't they, the medical men. Bloody cunts. It *can't* be something serious—you're either depressed or allergic or retaining water. Apparently he'd gained quite a bit of weight in the months before the trip, and everyone was glad—*at first*—because he'd always kept himself too thin. His motto was, "No one likes a tree trunk. It's the joyful twigs who get sveltefucked." His happy little neologism. By the time we got to Oklahoma, Roar was having vicious migraines. We had a powwow and decided: time to go home. We thought he'd give us a fight but he was relieved—further evidence things had gone absolutely pants. The man was a doctor himself and must have known how dire his situation was. None of us asked him to rule out what the *possibilities* might be; we were too flaming terrified to know.

Then the chief of police, a big fan of Roar's by the way, dropped by to politely inform that our motel had thoughtlessly placed itself in the path of an F fucking 4. We got a full lights-and-siren two-car escort to the YMCA and hunkered in the basement, where Roar immediately puked up every meal since San Anton'. The walls started shaking, and it sounded like a jet plane was on top of us. I lost my bottle! D. A.'s camera jammed, and the sequence never made it to the film. I had a moment of schadenfreude, you know, "That'd have never happened on my watch!"

D. A. just about hanged himself. Was depressed about it for months.

RACHEL TORST (*intern*) I touched his head to see if he had a fever and a clump of hair fell out. I think I gasped because everyone turned to look. I was so frightened. I thought: He's going to die.

STACY PENNEBAKER (*daughter of D. A. Pennebaker*) Suddenly, he had this bright red rash. And his face just—swelled up like some kind of rotten melon. But the weirdest thing was, a big bump appeared on the back of his neck, right in the middle.

It looked like a *hump*. Fucking Charles Laughton! He called himself "notre dame de Notre Dame"!

NICK BROOMFIELD His doctor in L.A. said, "Get him to a hospital!" but Roar was adamant about hightailing it to L.A. He didn't want to be treated in Tulsa and I'm sure he was right about that. "What gets treated in Tulsa, stays in Tulsa." As they say! The tornados were gone, and we chartered a plane to get us out of there the next morning.

As we took off, he was in good spirits. He started singing and we all joined in: "I'm *NOT* doin' fine, Oklahoma! Oklahoma *NOT* O.K.!"

STACY PENNEBAKER He started having trouble seeing—I don't know *what* state we were flying over at the time. *Oh fuck. Oh no. He's going to die— he's totally going to die on the fucking plane.* It was like *Dark Victory.*

LAUGHLIN ORR The problem was, he was making too much cortisol. The doctors thought it was Cushing's disease, but they found a tumor on his pituitary gland. That was the culprit. He went into surgery right away.

ALI BERK I was shooting *Was It Something I Said*, Nancy Meyers's first film as a director. I was *so* flipped out and Nancy was great. They shot around me on Friday, and I flew home to be with him for the long weekend. They had to go through his *nostrils*—they did a craniotomy or craniostomy, whatever. It's fucking *brain surgery*. So much can go wrong! It was much harder for me than it was for Uncle Roary.

When I saw him in the ICU, his mouth lagged to the side like he'd had a stroke. I sat there and held his hand, tears welling. Then he opened his eyes and said, "I'm just practicing my Randle McMurphy lobotomy look." He set me up! I wanted to shoot him.

But I was *so happy*. Because I knew he would be himself again.

LAUGHLIN ORR A week later, he came home to Bel Air. He was getting stronger but still doing the full-retard *Cuckoo's Nest* routine. He'd get that post-stroke *look* and say to whoever came in the room, "Are you my mother?" Me, Bird, the caregivers . . . "Are you my mother?"

But it was a hoot. He made everyone laugh—always.

BIRD RABINEAU I prayed every day, and every day my prayers were answered. *God is good. God is great. Praise Jesus.*

LAUGHLIN ORR We had an amazing chef and nutritionist. I hired a trainer to get him back in shape. He had his own RN too, Kava Santana. Kava was a friend of Debbie Rowe, the nurse who worked in Arnie Klein's office. The one who had kids with Michael Jackson.

When I found out Kava was pregnant, I wasn't too kind. You hear stories about gold-digging caregivers, and I wasn't very gracious. She turned out to be a great gal—and I got a wonderful nephew out of it. But at the time, something her friend Debbie said was rattling around in my brain. She was talking about how she got pregnant with Michael Jackson's kids and said it was the same way her mares were impregnated for breeding. "Just like I stick sperm up my horse. I was Michael's Thoroughbred."

It kinda turned my stomach.

MELLIE KOCH I was selfish. All I wanted was for *Hallelujah Boogie* to get made! The script was perfect. He called me up one night and said, "Mell? Let's make a movie." He put *The Jungle Book* and the never-ending *Gift from God* on hold. He was ready to roll. But *Gift from God* wouldn't die. It was the vampire that kept breathing, even with a stake through its incessantly revised heart.

DAVID "DOC" O'CONNOR *Hallelujah Boogie* started out as an ensemble piece, a broad comedy. It didn't exactly end up that way. The premise was genius: a Black hair-care billionaire's favorite son joins a Moonie-like cult and the mogul hires a ragtag group of African Americans to infiltrate it, then kidnap and deprogram him—*The Suicide Squad* meets *Barbershop*. There's a lady prison guard who did time for helping a convict escape, a Black professor whose racist school keeps denying him tenure, a flamboyant gay pimp, and a heartbroken preacher who felt God had abandoned him.

The billionaire makes them offers they can't refuse.

JORDAN PEELE When *Boogie* came out, the Moonies were still in the news—white kids were being deprogrammed like crazy. Roar told Dick

Gregory, "Black people *never* go for that shit." So, he thought it'd be funny to do a movie about a Black kid who did. He's rebelling against his rich, controlling dad—and joins a cult that worships whiteness! He's the only Black person and *no one* acknowledges the color of his skin. In three months, he's walking, talking, and acting white. Dave Chappelle based Chuck Taylor on the kid—the white anchor from "News 3."

It was *Get Out*, minus the horror. Or some of it!

ART LINSON (producer) He said he wanted to do *Car Wash* but I didn't *want* him to do fucking *Car Wash*. He was bullshitting, really, because Roger Orr couldn't have done *Car Wash* if he tried. *Boogie* was much closer to Sturges. . . . What he did seems impossible: to skewer whites *and* blacks, yet make you forget about color; by the end of the movie, you just can't see it. Like all his movies, it's about human nature, the fallibility and hypocrisies and fragility of *people*. I think of it as an R-rated ballet. I watched it again the other day and, man, does it hold up. It cast a pretty large shadow. Just the other day, Richard Linklater told me *Dazed and Confused* was a total rip-off of *Boogie*, style-wise. I hear stuff like that from directors all the time. Roger told me *he* ripped off Jacques Tati. Steal from the best, right?

AVA DUVERNAY (filmmaker) I was fifteen when I saw *Hallelujah Boogie* with my father in Alabama. It blew me away. I laughed so hard I peed my pants! That's for real. But halfway through, it took this . . . whole other *direction*. It was still funny—it was *always* funny—but got serious at the same time. I said, "What's goin' on?" *Whatever* was going on had my undivided attention. I'd never seen anything like it. That opened the world for me. Because up till then I thought, it's either got to be one thing—or another. Can't be both. I never saw something with so many flavors. And I had a mad crush on Tyler Perry, who played the billionaire's son.

I didn't know who Roger Orr was. On the way home, my daddy told me that the director was a Black man who thought he was white.

Just like in the movie!

TYLER PERRY I was seventeen and answered an open call for *Hallelujah Boogie* in New Orleans. He put me at ease. I was up for the kid in the cult and hadn't acted before. I learned so much from the man; he became the father I never had. I never thought that was possible because for me, fathers were the ones you never *could* have. They were the carrot on a stick—"the men who got away." [*sings*] *"The road gets rougher, it's lonelier and tougher. . ."* I shared everything, all my deep, dark secrets, and he kindly returned the favor. When I told him about being molested, he topped that in two seconds without breaking a sweat. Whatever I said seemed silly and inconsequential, but I was *heard*. I was really heard. And that lifted a great burden off my shoulders. It was obvious his sexuality was fluid but he never came *close* to being inappropriate. He didn't have a bone like that in his body.

When I did *Madea*, he loved it! Roar said, "That's what I'm going to look like when I get old, Ty—but with real tits. And a tight ol' Black pussy."

WHOOPI GOLDBERG (*actress*) It was a good time for me. I'd done my Broadway show and followed that with *The Color Purple*. After *Color*, I wanted to do comedy and jumped my ass into *Jumpin' Jack Flash*, which didn't thrill me. I knew Roar's work—my God, I was in awe. Those songs! The *comedy* tapes he did when he was fuckin' *six years old*. Ha! And he was an amazing actor. In a lotta ways, a few notches above Mike [Nichols], which technically isn't even possible. Look, Roger Orr's on his own planet—don't take any of this personally, Mike! The *movies* . . . I mean, if he'd only made *Grace War*, it'd have been more than enough. And don't get me started about Bird Rabineau. She's his *mother*? Say, *what*? Like, how cosmically insane and fabtabulous is *that*? So, when my manager sent over *Boogie*, I said fuck yeah without reading the script. Steven [Spielberg] had a little introduction supper for me and Roar, and it was *done*. The next dinner was at Roar's beach house with Spike [Lee], Sam [Jackson], Wesley [Snipes], and Kevin [Costner]. Sat right between Harry Belafonte and Sidney Poitier, and across from Bird Rabineau.

I pretty much died that night and went to Heaven.

And Tyler was there too but didn't say word one. He was terrified! Looked like he was twelve years old, which wasn't too far from the truth.

SPIKE LEE I was getting my Master's at Tisch [School of Fine Arts] and said something flip about *Yes I Can* in a student paper interview. How the hell did he even see that? It was like he had *gnomes* going through newspapers, name-checking and shit. I'd just shown *We Cut Heads* at Lincoln Center, and that big head of mine probably needed a buzz cut. He wrote me a beautiful note. You know, the man's a genius and I was out of line. Young and arrogant and all that. I thought he was going to call me out but all he said was how much he loved *We Cut Heads* and if there was anything he could do to help, I should pick up the phone and call him. He left his number at the bottom of the page.

So, when I was having trouble getting the money together for *She's Gotta Have It*, I called. The person on the other end said, "Hotel Pierre"—ha! I loved that. And he was true to his word. Sent over a check for $25,000 that day. The whole movie cost a hundred-and-seventy-five. He was the first investor, and that did a lot for my confidence.

Got his money back too.

SCATTER HOLBROOK We all went to Cannes [1988] when *Hallelujah Boogie* closed the festival—me and Suze and Ali and Laughlin and Bird. Roar almost boycotted because he was miffed at not being in competition. He thought that was an insult because most of the time, it's the big Hollywood movies that open and close the festival. Maybe I'm wrong, but I don't think they put art films in those slots. *Boogie* was both: a "people's choice" *and* art. So, I guess they didn't know what to do with it.

A typical dilemma for my brother-in-law.

ART LINSON All the stars were there—Belafonte, who had a tiny role, and Poitier, Sam, Kevin, and Whoopi. Even Tyler, who didn't have a dollar. We flew him over. *Hallelujah* stole the show but the true queen of the festival was Bird Rabineau. She was royalty in France.

Clint Eastwood had *Bird* in competition, and Clint was more than a little enamored with *our* Bird, who of course knew Charlie Parker. Sung with him, shot up with him. Did all kinds of things with him.... Clint was in awe. Get in line, Clint. It's legendary now but after Forest [Whitaker] won the Palme d'Or [for *Bird*], Stavros Niarchos threw a party on his boat. Did all kinds of things with him.... Clint stood in front of a black velvet drape—it was one of those megayachts, before megayachts were a thing—and none of us, not even Roar, knew what was about to happen. Clint said, "Ladies and Gentlemen . . . Bird Rabineau and Dizzy Gillespie." When the curtain rose, they did "Lover Boy," and everyone lost their minds.

* * * * * * * * *

HALLELUJAH BOOGIE (1988)
Two Thumbs Heavenward!
by Roger Ebert[160]

The movie that burned the arthouse down at Cannes, melting even the chilliest of *Cahiers du Cinéma* hearts, also happens to be the funniest one of the year. Roger Orr, its light-fingered director, stole from the breakneck, cinematic pace of events in his own life as well. The Renaissance man who learned in middle age that his biological mother is the famous black jazz singer Bird Rabineau has a glorious sense of the divinely random—and the rightness that a string of felicitous wrong turns may bring. His approach to the kaleidoscopic conga line of *Hallelujah Boogie* has all the derring-do, romance, and panache of a zoot-suited jewel thief in a sparkling heist comedy. Orr never takes himself too seriously, allowing the audience to relax, sit back, and enjoy the ride—before being walloped at the end by bittersweet observations on race, loyalty, love and pain and the whole damn thing.

In its own way, it's an instruction manual for living. And boy, can we use that now.

* * * * * * * * * *

TOP-GROSSING FILMS (DOMESTIC) FOR 1988					
1	*Hallelujah Boogie*	Jul 4, 1988	Paramount Pictures	Comedy	$172,438,218	36,902,376
2	*Coming to America*	Jun 29, 1988	Paramount Pictures	Comedy	$128,152,301	31,180,608
3	*Good Morning Vietnam*	Dec 23, 1987	Walt Disney	Comedy	$121,650,966	29,598,775
4	*Big*	Jun 3, 1988	20th Century Fox	Comedy	$112,555,170	27,385,686
5	*Crocodile Dundee*	May 25, 1988	Paramount Pictures	Adventure	$109,306,210	26,595,184

(Continued on next page)

---

160 "Hollywood Unshuffled," *Chicago Sun-Times*, 1988.

6	3 Men and a Baby	Nov 25, 1987	Walt Disney	Comedy	$80,091,739	19,487,041
7	Cocktail	Jul 29, 1988	Walt Disney	Drama	$78,222,753	19,032,300
8	Moonstruck	Dec 16, 1987	MGM	Romantic Comedy	$77,051,120	18,747,231
9	Die Hard	Jul 15, 1988	20th Century Fox	Action	$74,138,586	18,038,585

* * * * * * * * * *

JOHN LAHR They got that huge response when they sang "Tenderness" on *60 Minutes* but Roar turned down all the concertizing offers; Bird wasn't in the best of shape and he thought touring would be too much of a "sideshow vibe." But by the time *Hallelujah Boogie* came out, she was much stronger. She had that spark again. Watching his mother perform with Dizzy at Cannes, seeing the joy it brought her, tipped him over. Roar suggested she might be ready to take her act on the road. Bird said she would, under two conditions: that he join her onstage—and Bobby Short accompany them.

A few months later, they did a peerless three-week gig at the Carlyle.

HILTON KRAMER (*art critic*) Bird was nervous before the Carlyle show. To soothe her nerves, Roger took her shopping for extravagant bangles, ribbons, and bows . . . lunches with Sondheim and Lenny [Bernstein] at Elaine's and the Russian Tea Room—both were places she'd never been. He even brought her to an exhibition at Gagosian. There were Basquiats in one room, Iwana Kants in the other. Of course, Larry [Gagosian] knew all about the reclusive "Iwana Kant," but no one else did. There *were* starting to be rumors Kant didn't exist; that she was an elaborate stratagem, concocted by Roger Orr. I'm not sure how that gossip started, but things did get a little sloppy when he left the Marlborough. He *may* have told Donald Judd about the Iwana ruse—and remember, [Judd] was repped by Bruno Bischofberger, who was a terrific tittle-tattle. By the way, Bruce, I've just seen a marvelous film about this sort of thing, which they call "catfishing." If you haven't seen it, you *must* . . . Still, the rumors were outlandish enough to be dismissed out of hand. During an interview, someone had the impudence to ask Roger about the Kant connection, and his response was just brilliant. "That's terribly sexist!"—he took great umbrage—"They'd never say that about a *male* artist who valued his privacy. I just say, enjoy the work she's created. And if she wants to be Garbo, more power to her. How refreshing that an artist of such immense talent is completely uninterested in self-promotion." What a clever boy.

Anyway, that day at the Gagosian, his mother breezed through the Basquiats. Roger said she clicked her tongue and scratched her chin. "I'd like to see what this boy does when he grows up." Isn't that marvelous? Then, she strolled into the Kant exhibition and spent half-an-hour staring at the paintings and sculptures. Didn't say a word. Finally, on the street, she turned to look toward the gallery and said, "That lady has a strong heart."

To my knowledge, I don't think he ever told her.

BOBBY ZAREM (*publicist*) It was just impossible to see them at the Carlyle. Tickets were being scalped for *thousands* of dollars. But every night, Roar gave precious ducats away: to cops and street bums, to starving students at Juilliard, to moms and their handicapped kids, some of whom were in wheelchairs. A *very* famous star who shall remain nameless asked to be moved because he didn't want to be sitting next to a poor girl with cerebral palsy. He said her breathing was too noisy. When Roar had the man escorted out, half the audience stood up and applauded!

"Suzy" was there, but apparently she owed the rude celebrity a favor and kept the incident out of her column.[161]

GEORGE PLIMPTON *Everyone* was there, and I'm not even exaggerating: Sinatra and Sammy . . . Andy, of course, with Brigid [Berlin] and Bob [Colacello] and Fred Hughes, Viva and Taylor Mead. Just two weeks later, Andy was dead. I mean, he gets shot in the stomach and survives but has to wait twenty more years for the kindly doctors and nurses to finish the job. Nathan Lane came to every show . . . and Bliss Broyard, Anatole's daughter. (Her dad was a no-show.) The list is longer than the *On the Road* scroll, I'm just telling you whoever pops into my head. . . . Dylan swept in one night under cover of darkness after the show started. They conjured a table for him out of thin air, like the waiters did for Ray Liotta in *Goodfellas*. He was with

---

161 The offender was later identified as Larry Hagman, of the hit television show *Dallas.*—*ed.*

three lovely ladies: Karen Dalton, Lainie Kazan, and what *appeared* to be a black hooker. Mel Brooks and Zero Mostel sat together. . . . Larry Rivers . . . and Carl Andre, celebrating his recent acquittal on a second-degree murder charge; his wife, if you'll recall, jumped or got pushed from their fortieth-floor apartment during an argument—my own jury's still out on that one! Berry Gordy and Diana Ross . . . Max Julien and Gordon Parks. . . Nicky Haslam and Jane White—that's Walter F. White's daughter. He was an important civil rights activist, a black man who was white as Roar and Anatole. *The Times* used to call him "a negro by choice." That's just awful. Carole King and Natalie Cole . . . and Woody [Allen], who'd just started playing at the hotel with his jazz band. Doris Troy, the amazing R&B singer who the Beatles signed on Apple . . . Streisand and Sondheim and Lenny [Bernstein], *naturally*. Bette Midler. John Guare and Joseph Heller. And Gore [Vidal], *naturally* . . . Patti Smith came with Mapplethorpe, who died the next year. Iggy, with Lou Reed . . . Germaine Greer, Philip Glass, Fran Lebowitz . . . Sontag and Ned [Rorem] shared a table with Andrew Sarris and Germaine Greer . . . Allan Arbus, Diane's widower. Let me think. Let me think who else was—ah! the amazing Tobias Schneebaum, a *wonderful* writer—a gay anthropologist who lived in the East Village. Literally dropped himself down into a Peruvian jungle *nude* and had "affairs" with all the primitives. Allen Ginsberg brought Burroughs—and Gregory Corso, who got thrown out—*naturally*—for heckling Princess Firyal, who sat at a table with armed bodyguards just *itching* to kill him! Peter Beard brought Jackie O., who'd just published one of his beautiful Africa books. Even Donald Judd and his kids showed up.

It made Capote's Black and White Ball look like one of those Dummy books. You know, "Glamour for Dummies."

BOB COLACELLO Basquiat was in Maui, in rehab. He was so upset about not seeing the Carlyle show that he almost went AWOL. He called to tell us he was getting on the next plane but Andy talked him out of it because he didn't think that was a very good idea. Andy calmed him down by saying that Roger promised that he and Bird would do their whole act in his suite at the Pierre when Jean-Michel got back from Hawaii. And that was the truth.

GORE VIDAL Kissinger sat up front on the night I came. He and Bobby [Short] were having a thing—or should I say, Hank was having Bobby's thing, which, rumor had it, was about as short as the day is long. When I asked if that Teutonic kike was a top or bottom, Bobby winked and said, "I don't Kissinger and tell." His nickname for Hank was "Oh Henry!" because they were madcap coprophiliacs—isn't that nutty?

BETTE MIDLER (*singer*) Roar opened with "Heaven Can't Wait" and "Catapult." Then he introduced *Mom*—she walked out from the wings and we all got goosebumps. Bird did "Storming Heaven" and "Soar Eyes" and it took your breath away. One of the amazing things I remember is them sitting on stools singing a soft, balladic "Piece of My Heart"—nothing like Janis's version. That's kind of a dumb thing to say, 'cause how could it have been? People shouted requests if they were drunk enough. Someone asked her to sing "God Bless the Child" but she politely demurred. "That's Billie's song, that's for Billie to sing. And she sings it every day. If you ever need a boost, look up to the heavens, close your eyes and open your ears. You'll hear her."

BOBBY SHORT (*pianist, cabaret singer*) Every night after the show a whole group of us ferried over to Ceeley's, the speakeasy. It was the after-party of the century—the first, to my knowledge, ever to get covered by both *Jet* and *Vogue*. You had about fifty limos caravanning to Harlem under the watch of a dozen unmarked police cars. But no one had to worry: Bird was like a queen. With *her* in the neighborhood, Harlem was safer than Englewood Cliffs.

She usually sat with Bumpy Johnson's widow. One night, Sammy and George Hamilton joined them and George started talking about how glamorous the evening had been, which led him to reminisce about the Elmo [El Morocco club]. George said that's where he had his twelfth birthday, thrown by the woman he was going to bed with at the time—his stepmother! I thought he was joking but he wasn't. Bird threw her head back and laughed. She got a kick out of George.

Then Sammy recalled the night the Elmo treated him very badly. He made a little joke and said, "They didn't *cotton* to Blacks."

Bird said, "To Jews neither."

Sammy said, "We've come a long way."

Bird just stared back and said, "Have we, baby? Have we?"

MICHAEL FEINSTEIN (*singer, pianist*) No one took too much notice of Kava Santana. Everyone was too busy twisting their necks around to see whatever famous person they could see. During the weeks of the Carlyle concerts, the chiropractors must have done bang-up business.

Kava didn't do much to accentuate her natural prettiness. And the couple was very low-key; I didn't even know she and Roger were together until the third or fourth night at Ceeley's. Kava was a great listener. She was the only person I ever knew who'd been in the paper for beating the hell out of a cougar that attacked her while she was bicycling in the Malibu Hills. I asked how they met and that's when I learned she'd been Roger's nurse; I didn't know about the tumor he had. No one really did, and that's another way Kava made you feel special—that she trusted you enough to take you into her confidence.

I thought they were a mismatch, you know, that it wouldn't last. A lot of people thought that. But the more time you spent around them, the more sense it made.

KAVA SANTANA (*wife of Roger Orr*) Ceeley's was so much fun. I'd never been to anyplace like it, though not too many have. Roar'd be darting around, so I spent most of the time with Valerie, Joe Heller's wife. They'd just gotten married. Joe'd been real sick with Guillain-Barré, he was paralyzed for a while. Valerie was his night nurse at the hospital. And she *loved* that I met Roger the same way. She said, "You're a *gold* digger, I'm an *old* digger"—because I think Joe was around sixty-five when they met. I told her about my other nurse friend, Debbie [Rowe], who had a crush on her doctor's patient, Michael Jackson. She high-fived me and said, "Tell Debbie good luck with *that*. But isn't Michael Jackson a boy scout? I mean, don't he scout boys?" Val was a hoot.

She liked to wear a T-shirt that said RNs HAVE MORE FUN. On the back it said, WE'RE GOOD IN BEDPAN.

BEVERLY D'ANGELO You could tell Kava your deepest, darkest secret and she'd smile and say, "That's so great!" A quality I always found comforting and unsettling at the same time. Roger thought she was an enlightened being. He called her "my pocket Avalokiteśvara"—the Buddha of compassion. I think. Or maybe that's a bodhisattva, not a Buddha.

Whatever.

And Kava *loved* to fuck.

PICO IYER (*author*) Roger told Kava about his "mind-body" problem. I believe he told her shortly after they met. Kava said, "That is so great."

Part of him was embarrassed, not for the reasons one might expect, but because he knew deep down that identifying oneself as either man or woman was fundamentally flawed. The true Self didn't have such preoccupations; those were the preoccupations of Mind.

I remember him telling me that Kava said, "You can be both. You're *one*, and you're working on becoming the *other*. Once you've been both, you can work on being neither."

Which I thought quite beautiful, really. And wise.

ANGELA BOWIE (*actress*) Roar and Kava did their share of sack-hopping. They went through the bloody phone book; that's why David and I left it a one-nighter. AIDS was taking so many friends . . .

I know they were with Michael Stipe for a while. Michael was brilliant, *so* beautiful, and a big fan of Roar's. They were all in bed one morning and Roar said Michael reminded him of a family friend who got horribly burned in Vietnam. How he became a doctor, just so he could save him. And how he failed.

Michael was deeply moved.

That day in the studio, he was recording "The One I Love." The chorus was a last-minute addition. "This one goes out to the one I love. This one goes out to the one I left behind"—then you hear *Fire! Fire!* That was his enraptured throwaway, his *incantation* to the story that touched him so.

MAUREEN ORTH (*journalist*)[162] The famous director and his companion, Kava Santana, knew Cunanan by one of his aliases, Andrew DeSilva. He was a valet at the Beverly Hills Hotel—a gilded hunting ground, if one's game was the rich and famous—and was certain to bring Orr his car when the couple appeared after lunch at the Polo Lounge.

"DeSilva" was charming and erudite, with an impressive knowledge of Orr's artistic oeuvre and personal life. As he branched out from seducing the wealthy businessmen that he courted in La Jolla and Palm Springs, deep-dive

---

162 From *Vulgar Favors: The Hunt for Andrew Cunanan, the Man Who Killed Gianni Versace*, pp. 83–86 (Bantam, 2010).

"homework" on celebrity targets became the killer's hallmark. Roar told him to come to the house when his workday was over; he stayed for two weeks. The ménage à trois ended as quickly as it began, when Cunanan said he needed to tend to a "sick friend" up north. He'd read in the paper that Gianni Versace was in San Francisco, fitting costumes for a production of Philip Glass's opera *In the Penal Colony.* An opportunity to meet his longtime obsession wasn't something Cunanan could pass up.

Orr later quipped, "Traded up by rough trade. Story of my life."

LAUGHLIN ORR Folks were starting to die. *Friends.* Perry [Ellis] and Halston. Nureyev and Peter Allen weren't far behind. Keith Haring and Steve Rubell . . . but it wasn't just AIDS. I was coming up on sixty, and Roar was almost fifty. Not all that old but that's kinda when random shit starts to hit the mortality fan. I lost Abbie [Hoffman] in '89—*such* a drag. I knew him from way back, from the Diggers, and he lit up my life. David [Dellinger] said . . . a *bunch* of people said it wasn't suicide but I never believed Abbie was killed by the CIA. There were people who thought *everyone* was killed by the motherfuckin' CIA. I think Abbie just got tired and took himself out. He was about the same age as Roger and bipolar too. And it really fucked with me because he swallowed a bucket of pills, and I couldn't get the image out of my head of him lying on the floor of his room like my brother at the Pierre. Then Huey [Newton] went—ugh. That hit harder than I thought it would. I went to Oakland for the funeral, and it was Old Home Week. Just, thousands of people in the streets.

Bird had her losses too: Sarah Vaughan, Art [Blakey], Dexter Gordon. Sarah was the big one. She and "Sassy"—that's what Bird called her—were the same age. But she seemed to take it in stride. She'd say, "They're in the arms of the Lord now." I'm agnostic but it was a comfort for me to hear that. Roger's go-to grief song was "Motherless Child." He hummed it every time another one bit the dust. Bird told him he didn't have the right to sing that anymore, 'cause he'd found his Mama. So, when he read the obituaries in the paper, he sang "Get Happy" instead.

But Roger knew *so* many people. Cassavetes went, then Mapplethorpe, who he'd gotten tight with through Patti . . . then Bruce [Chatwin]. The rumor was, Bruce got AIDS from one of Mapplethorpe's lovers. When Christine Jorgensen died, Roger wrote that amazing piece about her for *New York* magazine, "Christine on a Cross." Jan Morris sent him a lovely note about it and they became close again. Another person who passed that year was an African American sculptor, Richmond Barthé. In the Seventies, Roger's gallery in London forwarded a fan letter from Barthé to Iwana Kant. My brother wasn't in love with Barthé's work, but the note was so openhearted and intelligent that "Iwana" wrote back. Roger sent money to him in the last few years of his life; Barthé died alone in a little apartment in Pasadena. They never met, but Roar got *very* depressed when the gallery called to say the actor James Garner had been trying to get in touch with "Ms. Kant" to inform her that Richmond had passed—and to thank her for her help through the years. It turned out that Jim had been giving the man money too but I don't know the original connection. There wasn't a deep relationship there, but it didn't matter. It was cumulative. It all had meaning to my brother.

BEVERLY D'ANGELO 1990 was horrible, just horrible. It started with Bernstein dying. He *loved* Lenny. He always said, "That's the career I want to have"—and of course Lenny always said he wanted Roar's career, and meant it. Then Bliss Broyard called to say her father passed. Bliss said that her mom finally told her that Anatole was Black and when Roar heard that— Kava told me this—he dropped the phone and *bellowed.* More than anyone, Roger understood the crushing weight of identity and deception. He adored Anatole and couldn't stop blaming himself for not reaching out to mend things between them. But he *did* reach out, I was there! I have no idea why he forgot about that. Anatole stonewalled him.

Roar told Bliss that he and her dad were "brothers from another Other"— the same line he and Phil Dick used with each other. Phil was dead coming up on eight years, but Anatole's death somehow exhumed him. Which led to Aurelia and Seraphim, and so many others . . . It was just like the story "I Hope I Shall Arrive Soon." The Great Computer was stirring things up, whiplashing Roar from one loss to another.

SUZE BERKOWITZ Roger rang me up to say he'd been having a recurring dream that Ali would forget him when he died. He was crying during the call—he barely got the words out. I said, "Darling! Darling! She won't, she can't! Because you are *unforgettable*—don't you know that? You're the most unforgettable person I've ever known."

But there was no talking sense to him. He was in a panic.

LAUGHLIN ORR Then Sammy died. Oh Lord. He went with him for his chemo and radiation. My brother kept his spirits up, you know, silly things, like changing the lyrics of "The Candy Man" to "The Cancer Man." Which I *myself* didn't find too funny. But apparently Sammy laughed so hard he started to choke. Roger had to run for the nurses.

ALTOVISE DAVIS Toward the end, Sam got very down. He knew he didn't have much time. Roar told him, "You will live on. Because I'm going to have one eye removed and learn to tap dance." Roar said that after the funeral, he was going to start proceedings to have Sam's name legally changed to "Mr. Bojangles"—because he knew how much Sam hated that song!

I'm just glad Roar was there at the end. So much gratitude for that.

ROGER ORR[163] That time when Sammy hired a helicopter to drop in on me in Maui, I told him that the movie he was shooting [*Tora! Tora! Tora!*] would corner the Jewish demographic—"your *people*"—with a single, simple change.

The next day, I sent a thousand business cards with embossed gold lettering and kept a few for myself.

As they lowered him into Maw Earth, just a short walk from Spence and Bogie, I dropped one in, with a handwritten correction:

Sammy Davowitz Jr.

Las Vegas

Forest Lawn, Glendale

Torah! Torah! Torah!

. . .

LAUGHLIN ORR But nothing—*nothing*—prepared us for losing Jonny. It was something we never *considered*. It never crossed out minds—why would it? He was Baby Brother.

He was going to live for fucking ever.

---

163 From *Long Day's Journal*, Vol. 2, pp. 318–323 (Harcourt Brace, 2002).

CHAPTER FOURTEEN

It Was a Very Good Year

ROGER ORR[164] I was asked to be a pallbearer and was grateful because I'd heard through the years that some family members still held a grudge over the tempest of *Yes I Can*; not that Sammy had been "suckered"—he was his own man—but because it hurt his career. Meaning, as one of his relatives put it, that he got hit in the pocketbook.

On my side of the casket was Bill Cosby, Bob Wagner, Reverend Jackson, and Fred MacMurray; on the other, Frank, Dean, Michael Jackson, and Billy Crystal, with Slip 'n' Slide[165] appropriately bringing up the rear.

If you wanted someone watching your back, Slip 'n' Slide was your man. He'd watch it, eat it, fuck it—then wash it and watch it dry.

An hour after I got home, Kava walked into the den. More of a lurch—or a launch—than a walk. She looked like she'd just been tapped with one of the Commodore's cattle prods. Then she had a strange seizure, a *caesura* made from words: *Your sister's on the phone.* I have no idea how I managed to translate the sentence because I'm convinced it would have been unintelligible to anyone else's ears.

The first thing I thought was, *Bird's gone!*

Then, no—it's *Suze.* My Suze is dead . . .

—Ali! I've lost Ali . . .

Then Scatter, then Beverly, then . . . *everyone* was dead—a fire, a wreck, a shooting. The unspeakable iterations happened in milliseconds. When she

---

164 *Roarshock* by Roger Orr, pp. 65–71 (Liveright, 2003).
165 Orr's nickname for Little Richard.—*ed.*

said it was Jonny, I remained calm, because I didn't believe it. And still don't, to this day.

LAUGHLIN ORR We went straight to Coos Bay. I'd been to Harvest Sun a few times but Roger never had and raked himself over the coals for that. He was shocked at how spectacular it was.

KAVA SANTANA It was a *lot* different than Sammy's funeral. Ha! Right? Jerry Garcia was there, for one. People were on acid. Everyone was dancing, laughing, crying. Roar called it tie-dye grief. But it was *so beautiful*. Actually, it was a lot like being on MDMA—just . . . like stretching your arms out in the rain, in a downpour of feelings. And there *was* rain. It wouldn't let up. It was like being washed in tears.

LAUGHLIN ORR A monk at the burial said, "Does the moon reflected in the water—or images in a mirror—have origination and extinction?"
 I whispered to Roger, "I love that."
 He whispered back, "Yeah, it's great. Fuck 'em if they can't take a koan."

ALI BERK One of the farmhands—or commune girls or whatever—sang Leonard Cohen's "Hallelujah," and this was *way* before singing that song became a party trick. She was about fifteen, flaxen-haired, totally Pre-Raphaelite. It killed. There were, like, these *hurricanes* of sobs that practically knocked you to the ground.

AMARANTH "CHICKWEED" ORR (*Jonny's wife*) They were just— Roar and Laughlin were just so glamorous. That's the only word I can use to describe it. They were beautiful too, I mean, physically beautiful. Of course, everyone was sad we'd lost Jonny, but they brought this *energy* that really lifted me up. A life force that filled the void left by his passing. It sounds funny that we'd never met—I'd spoken to Laughlin once or twice on the phone— Jonny and I had only been together about a year, and there hadn't been the opportunity. He didn't really like to leave Harvest Sun. Had some little issues about that. We got married a few months before he died but Jonny didn't want to tell them. I was cool. I didn't really want to overthink it. It might have had something to do with Roar still being mad at Jonny and his sister for not telling them about the adoption. Jonny filled me in on all that. Families are weird; I know mine is. But they did seem surprised when I told them I was his wife. Not in a good way or bad way. Just surprised. It was awkward for about a second.

But he *always* talked about them—especially about Roar—talked about them like they were these . . . mythic, luminous creatures. And when I finally met them, I thought, you know, "It's true." I was asking all kinds of questions about what he was like when he was little. And they kept saying "Stage Door" did this, "Stage Door" did that. He never said that was their nickname for him. Laughlin said their dad used to call him that because Jonny was always waiting by the door for his big brother to get home. I thought that was the sweetest, most adorable thing! I never really heard that expression, "Stage Door Johnny." Someone who hangs around the theater because he's in love with a chorus girl. And waits for her to come out.

SCATTER HOLBROOK Our plane was delayed and by the time we got there, they were about to bury him. I'm sure they'd have waited for us, but they didn't have to. A doctor friend of Jonny's did a prayer to the "six directions." I didn't know there were six, I thought there were four. Apparently not. The doctor was the head of a psych hospital in Corvallis. He was a famous "journeyer"—a guide for people tripping on mushrooms, acid, whatever. Eye of newt and toe of frog. An absolute sweetheart who reminded me of Linus in the *Peanuts* cartoons. Very compassionate, very present and soft-spoken, with a constant smile on his face. Like he'd just heard the punchline to the Cosmic Joke and wondered if you'd heard it too.

SUZE BERKOWITZ Jonny's death was so absurd. A horse fell on him. End of story. That only happens in rodeos, right? Like, *maybe*.

AMARANTH "CHICKWEED" ORR It was super muddy and Hendrix lost his footing. When I told Roar that Jonny loved that horse to death, he said, "Hendrix returned the favor." But it's true. Jonny loved that horse like it was his child.

What's funny is, Jonny's dashas were in Saturn and Jupiter when he died. His Purva-phalguni . . . *all* aspects were auspicious. What the universe sees as auspicious often has a different interpretation on this plane. I can hear Jonny laughing about it. I mean, of all the ways to go out—Hendrix? I hear him laugh and say, "Really?" The way he used to. And I look back at him and say, "Yeah, really." The way *I* used to.

BEVERLY D'ANGELO I was in Ireland with Neil [Jordan], shooting *The Miracle*. I didn't find out until a week after. It was beyond castastrophe.

Jonny was just forty-four.

AMARANTH "CHICKWEED" ORR Grace Slick and Marty Balin sang Jonny's all-time favorite song, "Miracles." They sang it a capella. I was crying and crying because I hadn't told anyone I was pregnant. That was the *real* miracle.

STEWART BRAND I hadn't seen Roger in a long while. Not great circumstances, but as they say, God has other plans. He told me that he and Jonny didn't talk that much; they sent each other funny postcards instead. They used aliases. Jonny signed off with "gosh oh!" instead of *gassho*[166] and Roger would write at the bottom "All my love: Uh-oh-7." He brought a few cards from Jonny with him and passed them on for my reading pleasure. One said, "A doctor told a patient to stop masturbating. The patient said, 'Why?' The doc said, 'Because I have to examine you now.'" Another said, "The czar and the czarina were being murdered in the basement. And the rest of us were next."

Then he showed me the last one Jonny wrote from a few weeks back. On the front of the card was a horse. On the other side, Jonny wrote, "The MANE event." Roger said it was the only one Jonny never signed.

I got a chill when I saw it. Got one just now.

AMARANTH "CHICKWEED" ORR Roar showed that postcard to me. That's a *lungta*—Tibetan for wind horse. We have them all over the house. Lithographs and little sculptures. Jonny kind of collected them.

After the ceremony, Roar wanted to meet Hendrix so we went over. He did a *gassho* in front of the barn before going inside. Then he just stood there,

---

166 "Gassho," or Añjali Mudrā, is the classic gesture in which palms are pressed together in front of the chest, signifying prayer, greeting, or reverence.—*ed.*

staring at the stall Hendrix lived in. It was about twenty feet away—it's a pretty big barn. There were other horses too but he seemed to know right away which one was Hendrix; he looked over at me to make sure and I nodded. He slowly walked to the stall then stood stock-still. Staring and smiling, kind of in wonder. Like a child. Hendrix moved closer—which I thought was *very* interesting because usually when people come that he doesn't know, he kind of retreats. Roar stroked him and looked into his eyes. He whispered something in Hendrix's ear.

When we left the barn, he *gassho'*d again then backed out through the door.

Once we were outside, he smiled and said, "Never turn one's back on one's teacher."

KAVA SANTANA The dumb thing was, I really liked Chickweed. The unforgiveable thing. She was a little "different," but so was Jonny, from everything I heard. Unfortunately, I never had the pleasure of meeting him.

It's crazy but something came over me, some *woman* thing, and I said, "Are you pregnant?" She beamed and said, "Fuck! How did you *know*?" I said, "Because I am too, baby." There was a lot of pent-up anxiety between us—we'd both been keeping big secrets—and the two of us started howling. Sheer spontaneous release and delight. Sisterhood and all that bullshit. The music was pretty loud by then—the wake was in full swing—and folks were getting high. So our wolfing it up didn't seem out of place. We decided to have a double ceremony and make the announcement.

BEVERLY D'ANGELO I was happy for him about the baby, but it was kind of a mixed bag. Roar and I hadn't been a "couple" for a long time—had we ever?—but it brought back memories of that shitty, shitty time: Roger trying to off himself at the Pierre—and me, alone, bleeding out in a backstage bathroom at the Opry. It was just, ugh. But I love love *loved* him and hoped his being-a-daddy karma finally worked itself out. I wanted that for him, I truly did. And had a feeling in my heart that this time everything would be okay.

LAUGHLIN ORR It was that classic thing—with every death comes new life. Roger and Jonny were having babies! Everyone's hearts were breaking and bursting at the same time. Totally like a scene from a movie; there *is* a scene like that in *Romantic Comedy*.

So, the funeral, as untraditional as it was, became a bacchanal.

SAM KASHNER[167] One of the many "day players" I spoke to was Mimsy Hargitay, who sang "Hallelujah" at Jonny's memorial. Mimsy ran away from a troubled home in Lansing, Michigan, when she was fifteen. After a month of hitchhiking, she fatefully landed at Harvest Sun. Now forty-three, she's a married schoolteacher living in Vancouver.

The sacred gloom turned festive after a surprise bulletin: Roger's girlfriend, Kava Santana, and Jonny's widow, Amaranth "Chickweed" Orr, suddenly announced to the throng that they were pregnant. But it was a *second* surprise that took Mimsy's breath away.

"The thing I'll always remember is Roger leading Hendrix into the field with a long rein. That was the horse that killed his brother in a freak accident. Fell on him during a storm. I'd ridden and groomed him and Hendrix was the gentlest, chillest creature on Earth. You could put a baby on his back and set off explosives and he wouldn't have moved a muscle. It took a minute—not everyone saw them at first—but the music finally stopped and there was . . . complete silence. Roger walked that horse right into the middle of three hundred people like it was some kind of sun god. Then a little three-year-old boy screamed "Jonny!"—he knew Hendrix was Jonny's horse and that's what he meant, that it was Jonny's horse. He was super happy, bouncing up and down, yelling "Jonny! Jonny!" And it was spooky at first, 'cause children *see* things we can't, but broke through all the tension. Cheers went up—the trees seemed to explode when the birds flew out of them!—and everyone started laughing and crying and dancing. The little boy was right: it *was* Jonny, Jonny was totally *there*. Jonny never left!

I still dream about it. When I die, I'll be back in that field again, I *know* I will. I really do believe that. I'll be there with Jonny and all those wonderful people who taught me, protected me, who *cared* for me when I left home. The people who loved me—and taught me how to love in return."

167 From the preface of *Roger Orr, His Lives and Time: An Orral History* by Sam Kashner and Ash Carter, pp. ix–xv (Macmillan, 2017).

SCATTER HOLBROOK The wake lasted five or six days. Toward the end, Roger got a desperate flurry of messages on his answering service—agents, lawyers, the whole shebang. Then all of us started getting messages because a rumor was going around that *Roger* was the one who died!

The Morris office faxed the sadistic cover of *The Enquirer*, who always had it in for Roar, even more than the *Post*:

ROGER ORR NAGGED TO DEATH!!!

It was so macabre and ridiculous that we laughed out loud.

We found out later that Roger's obituary almost ran in the *Times*—they have archives of obits written "pre-need." Roar made calls to a handful of people, to inform he was alive and well. Folks who mattered, like Dick [Gregory] and Beverly . . . Bev was in Ireland and hadn't heard a thing about his demise. But while he had her on the phone, he told her that Kava was pregnant.

JERRY SEINFELD (*comedian*) He released a statement through William Morris, one of the great ones of all time. "Reports of my death are barely exaggerated." He acknowledged that "certain respectable journalists" had mixed him up with his brother but magnanimously forgave them. "Even a professional can write something on the hoof."

How great is that?

* * * * * * * *

LAZARUS LAUGHS [*Vanity Fair*, 1990]
by Dominick Dunne
Photos by Annie Leibovitz

There's that famous photo Jerry Schatzberg took of Roger Orr, John Lennon, and Marvin Gaye, dining together at Elaine's in 1975. Orr had already been shot, just a few years after his friend Andy Warhol; Lennon and Gaye would suffer the same fate, with fatal results. In September, when word spread like inkpot wildfire that Orr had been killed in a fall from his favorite horse—his younger, adoptive brother was the actual victim—the image of that haunting black-and-white

mise-en-scène was dredged up by tabloids and respectable newspapers alike, nationally and around the globe. After the smog of rumor
cleared, the scent of subtext remained:

Just how many more lives does this sorcerer have?

In middle age, he learned his biological mother was the legendary jazz singer Bird Rabineau. Now, at fifty, the prodigy who
changed the face of comedy before he had acne, the acclaimed actor
(*Philip Phaethon, Who Loves Ya, Baby*), the pioneering dermatologist and honored songwriter ("Try a Little Tenderness," "Piece of
My Heart"), the director of eight defiantly uncategorizable films in a
panoply of genres (*They Sleep by Night, Yes I Can, Hollow, Romantic
Comedy, Arrival, Grace War, Hallelujah Boogie*)—many of them divi-
sive, many of them critics' darlings—the magus is showing no signs
of hanging up his magic wand.

We first met in 1950, at Parnassus, the fabulous Greco-Roman
Pacific Heights mansion that Roar's adoptive mother, the elegantly
indomitable socialite Bunny Orr, bought on the casual suggestion of
her close friend Doris Duke. . . .

* * * * * * * *

SUZE BERKOWITZ Roger and Bird grew particularly close after Jonny's
funeral, and I'll tell you why. Because I had a long talk with him about this,
one of our all-nighters. We put on the hair dryer big-time.

The shock of their impossible reunion overshadowed everything else.
And *yes*, it was the bright, shiny thing, but you can't sustain the euphoria.
I think both sensed that something was missing. They started to bicker.
Neither of them were the easiest people to get along with, but Bird could
be *very* tough. Prideful, hardheaded, unsentimental. I wasn't around all that
much, but when I was, I didn't like what I was seeing. I thought, What's
wrong with this picture? You know, either this nasty pimple's gonna pop or
it's gonna get seriously infected . . . They were living on the *surface* of things,
like walking headlines—when they were in the same room, it was two
billboards shouting, "FAMOUS BIOLOGICAL SON!" "LEGENDARY
BIOLOGICAL MOTHER!" I'm exaggerating. A little. But *beneath* the billboards, there was fear. A walking on eggshells. Which was understandable,

I guess, but you just can't sustain it. Maybe they thought there was danger in digging too deep. Because this precious *miracle* had happened—they'd found each other—they couldn't live with it becoming *unprecious*. You know, watching it die, which is where it seemed to be heading. When the magic dies, the honeymoon's over, bubbeluh.

Something had to change.

Roger hadn't said a word to her about finding his father. He'd really been struggling with the idea of going to see him at the prison in Georgia. Over whether he should do that or not. Struggling over telling *Bird* about it. . . . *Another* thing they never talked about was the death of Bird's daughter, Neva. Even though it was public knowledge, they wouldn't touch *that* topic with a ten-foot pole. And Bird *knew* about the very big deal of her son losing Seraphim. She knew about our baby Aurelia too, because Laughlin told her—I think she even knew about losing the baby he was going to have with Beverly. But Bird's default was to rubber-stamp everything with "They're with the Lord now. Praise God." That kind of crap. Which *isn't* crap but for Bird it became a gloss. Got on my fuckin' last nerve.

Jonny's death was the galvanizing event.

Before that, Roger wanted to share things with his mom but didn't, because that wasn't their "way." He'd tell me, *It's not our way.* You know, "We don't do that." The bullshit was getting calcified. But after Jonny died, he got courageous. Started talking about his childhood—the childhood Bird missed. How he used to play dress-up with Seraphim, the true love of his life, and that when she died, he wanted to die too. Just vomited everything out and bared his soul: laying in that warehouse in Oakland beside the raped girl as she drew her last breath. How he abandoned us and was thousands of miles away when Aurelia died in her crib. . . . He stopped short of telling her about wanting to become a woman, so it wasn't a full disclosure of his heart—but was sure as hell close enough.

When he was done, Roger said that Bird got real quiet.

The radio had been on, softly—Bird always had it tuned to one of the jazz stations. On comes Chet Baker, singing "But Not For Me."

And that's when she told him about Neva.

LAUGHLIN ORR Something changed between them after our brother died. They stopped scrapping—I was shocked to see how harsh they'd become with one another—and would sit holding hands, listening to music. Overnight, it felt like they'd been together all along, that he'd never been taken from her. It was so beautiful to watch that.

SCATTER HOLBROOK Suze told me that after the Big Conversation, he finally told Bird that he found the man who raped her. The man who was his father. That he was in prison, in Georgia, on death row. When she didn't say anything back, Roger told her he'd been thinking about going to see him but decided against it.

He was ready for her wrath; he thought Bird would feel betrayed. When she *still* didn't say anything, it only made things worse.

At last, Bird said, "Is he a child of God?"

Roger was stymied.

She asked again. "Is he a child of God?"

Roger said, "Yes."

And Bird said, "Why would you shun a child of God? Why would you be afraid of a child of God?"

Because he *was* afraid.

But the truth is, he desperately wanted to see his father, for all *kinds* of messy reasons. And when she gave him permission, their bond got stronger. It was unbreakable now.

BRUCE WAGNER We had planned to meet in New York to talk about my book, *The Empty Chair*—that was right before the suicide attempt. *Not* the best omen . . . I tucked the whole experience into the Amazing Anecdote file, and we hadn't spoken since; I didn't want to be the one to make an overture. You know, "Hey! How you doin'? We were going to talk about me adapting my book but then you tried to kill yourself. Remember?"

DEBORAH DROOZ, ESQ. (*attorney*) There was a moment where he flirted with making a film of a novel called *The Empty Chair*. He decided to adapt it for the theater instead and direct the play in London. He hired the novelist to do a stage version; the book lent itself to that because it was essentially two long monologues. One belongs to a bisexual man who marries a woman who's a fervent Buddhist. Their nine-year-old son ends up hanging himself, to achieve enlightenment—a misguided effort to please his mother.

The second monologue is given by an older, very wealthy bohemian gal who falls in love with a gangster when he murders the pimp who stabbed her. The gangster, a spiritual seeker, takes her along to India when she's just seventeen. Both characters, "Queenie" and "Charley," take a gimlet-eyed look back on their lives.

DAVID THOMSON (*film critic*) [168] *The Empty Chair* had a lot of the themes that captivated Orr: India and spiritualism, the death of a child, unimaginable violence, unimaginable wealth. But most of all, it was about unmoored people—literal and metaphorical wanderers. Both protagonists, Queenie and Charley, are eternally on the road, running from freedom as they run toward it.

Orr joked that an alternate title would have been *Slouching Toward Nirvana*.

WALLACE SHAWN (*actor, playwright*) The conflicted gay man in the novel was Roger; the rich hippie was Laughlin. His attraction to the material was that simple. I really should say, his *initial* attraction. Because those two things wouldn't have been enough. They were a place to *start*.

BRUCE WAGNER I finished a draft of the play in less than three weeks. It was a cut-and-paste job. The novel's a two-hander; two long monologues. By the time I was done I thought, "This should never have been a novel. It's meant to be a play." I sent it to Roar and started biting my nails. It took longer for him to get back to me than it took to write it.

One morning at ten a.m., the phone rings.

"Is this Bud Wiggins?"

Bud Wiggins is an alter ego who's masochistically starred in a few of my books—a hapless, delusional loser always suffering some humiliation or another. When I heard "Bud Wiggins," I thought, *Uh oh. This ain't gonna be good.* Not just because he'd identified me as "Wiggins" but because Roar *never* called me in the morning—it was always late at night. The *middle* of

---

168 *A Light In the Dark: A History of Movie Directors* by David Thomson, p. 361 (Cavalcade, 2007).

the night. I was thinking, *Okay, you're in the half-hour morning death slot where agents and producers call to kill your babies. Deal with it.*

I said, "Please hold for Mr. Wiggins, he's still wiping."

He laughed and said, "Ah! Then I'll patiently await a long cable from the Coast . . . But *do* tell him Uh-oh-7 is on the line." The friendliness of his voice made it even more certain he was going to cut my head off. "Tell Mr. Wiggins that Uh-oh wishes to inform that Ms. Vanessa Redgrave and Mr. Wallace Shawn have agreed to do his glorious adaption of *The Empty Chair*. Rehearsals begin at the Royal National in 45 days."

KAVA SANTANA We didn't name the baby for months. We went back and forth. Roger was big on "Lungta" for a while, then lobbied for "Seraph" and even "Buñuel"! I said, "That is *not* going to happen." He was really surprised when it was a boy. I said to him—when we were back in the hospital room and he was holding the baby—"You were shocked to see that little cupid dick, huh." He smiled and said, "It's not so little! More like a cupid's *arrow*. . . . But yeah, I was surprised." A long pause, then: "Surprised that it lived."

It wasn't until he said it that I realized how crazed he'd been, how worried he was about me losing the baby—or that it'd be stillborn. God bless him, he never showed me that. Never let me see it. He was cool as cool could be, even in the delivery room.

AMARANTH "CHICKWEED" ORR I loved that they named him "Hendrix." When Kava told me, I just thought it was so amazing. I mean, who would have even *thought* of that but Roger and Kava?

It really fed my heart.

I named *ours* "Moon"—Jonny told me to, in a beautiful dream.

Jonny and Frank Zappa were old friends. I'd met Moon, Frank's daughter—she visited Harvest Sun—but never met Frank. They were both going to come for the funeral but Frank was real sick. He held on a few years more. I *loved* the name Moon—I don't know if I would have added "Unit"!—but Moon was so beautiful. So witchy . . . and a few months before he died, Jonny bought some property up by Saunders Lake for a "companion" commune that he wanted to call Harvest Moon—another reason the name was so perfect.

The foundation I started, Hold Your Horses, is there now. An equine therapy camp for inner city kids.

KAVA SANTANA Chickweed and I are always telling Roger how Moon and Hendrix are gonna get married one day. My husband's all for it. He said the first cousin thing happens all the time in the *Arabian Tales.* "We'll call 'em the Thousand and One Night Kids. They'll be sultans. Sultans of swing." I said, "Maybe. But for now, they're sultans *on* swings."

He never laughs at shit I say but he really laughed at that one!

PANKAJ MISHRA (*author, critic*) *The Empty Chair* was Roar's way of taking a break. Because he had to be working. Here was a chance to direct a play, something he'd always wanted to do, without creating something from whole cloth. Thematically, it was really a kind of rehearsal for his film *Gift from God.* And he loved London. He had so many friends there. Lotta history in London.

REGINA TAYLOR (*actress, playwright*) Bird was in pretty good shape. Bird was in *great* shape. Roar threw a big party for her at the house in Bel Air for her sixty-fifth. Everybody came. You'd scan the room and just about fall down. Denzel'd be talking to Harrison over here and the Bishop [Desmond Tutu] would be talking to Streisand and Q [Quincy Jones] over there. Bob Thiele and Artie Shaw . . . and Joni Mitchell and Peter Coyote, getting into an argument about Buddhism. Arguments about Buddhism! But that was Joni. She's a brawler. And all the actresses were there, you know, angling to play Bird in some unknown future epic. Trying to catch Roar's eye.

Q brought his daughter Rashida and her friend Joan [Wicks]. Years later, Joan had a baby and that baby grew up to be Amanda Gorman. The world appears to be *very* small. Gets smaller by the day!

THE RZA (*musician, producer*) Quincy went a long-ass way back with both of 'em. He did the soundtrack for *Yes I Can*—and helped Bird get on her feet after she sang at the Oscars. Produced *Flygirl* as well. I think that's her best album, or close to it. So, the two of them owed Q a debt. Not that anyone's arm needed to be twisted to work with Quincy. But that was the birthday party where she agreed to do the album that became *Solitary Bird.*

NENA VON SCHLEBRÜGGE Bird was very religious, very spiritual. About a hundred years ago, Alice Coltrane turned her on to John of the

Cross. Bird always kept a dog-eared copy of *Dark Night of the Soul* nearby. Her favorite part was when he writes about the five conditions of a solitary bird—"it flies to the highest point; it does not suffer for company, not even of its own; it aims its beak to the skies; it does not have a definite color; it sings very softly." She tried to emulate that and came awful close.

God *loves* "awful close."

BOB THIELE Roar never stopped writing songs. He wrote "You Are Here" for the album Bird did with Q—wrote it in an airport then jumped on a plane and finished "Would I Lie to You" before they hit Heathrow. That became a huge hit for Charles & Eddie in 1992.

Let me tell you where that came from.

"Would I lie to you" was a pet phrase he and Laughlin liked to use. He was mad at her for so long about "lying" to him about the adoption. Eventually, they cleaned all that up and got real tight again. But whenever he was skeptical about some outrageous piece of gossip that Laughlin told him, she'd say, "Brother! Would I lie to you?" The first time she said it, he laughed his ass off. Then *he* started using it. They did their little act right up until he died.

SAM KASHNER Roar was already incredibly famous, but in the Nineties he was everywhere. The Beastie Boys tagged him in "Carumba": "Cat just came through the bedroom door/Got more lives than Roger Orr." He was about to get a star on the Hollywood Walk of Fame. The Kennedy Center was preparing to honor him . . . and Bird wasn't far behind. Patrick Demarchelier shot her for the cover of *Vogue*; she was Oprah's new best friend; and Spielberg was desperate to do a movie about her. She didn't want to tour, but the Morris Agency represented her for select things, like being flown on a private plane to sing at some Saudi prince's birthday party. One time she gigged at a ball in Venice that Paul Allen threw. Got a million dollars for that. Roger thought that sort of thing was beneath her. Bird would shush him and say, "It's the folks who know how to *die* that know how to *live*. You oughta know that by now, boy." When she called him boy instead of son, look out. She was just about the only one who could shut him down. It was important to Bird that she made her own money. She didn't want anyone's charity, *especially* his. It took him a while, but he finally understood.

JONATHAN MILLER When he came to London for *The Empty Chair*, he reconnected with Bacon—and of course, Simon [Callow], Edna O'Brien, and Harold [Pinter] and Antonia [Fraser]. Ultra Violet tore herself away from her studio in Nice to come see him. . . . Frank Bowling and David Hockney, Ethel Adnan—the old crowd of ne'er-do-wells and rabble-rouser *manqués*. The very amicable David Bailey and Pat Litchfield, that sort. He reacquainted himself with trans street life, which had evolved into something simultaneously stylish and dodgy. Raffish King's Cross dinners with Kenneth Branagh, with whom he'd had an unexpected, whirlwind affair after Ken auditioned for *Arrival*.

Roger paraphrased his sister by calling it "Old Homo Week."

LADY COLIN CAMPBELL (socialite) Roar, Kava, and Hendrix stayed in two huge, connected suites at the old favorite, Claridge's. His brother's widow—she of subsequent *ill-repute*, with that utterly *ridiculous* name—let's call her "Stinkweed"—well, she showed up with her baby but I never saw that much of them. Thank God for small favors. And large ones too.

Oh, there was new blood too. The Tears for Fears fellow who Patti Smith sent Roar's tape—and wound up cadging it for "Mad World." . . . Roar became quite fond of Damien [Hirst] and Tracey Emin. He met them through Charles Saatchi, "Iwana Kant"'s gallerist at the time. Damien was showing his first shark in a YBA show at Saatchi's. They got *Roaring* drunk [*laughs*] and began a party game of renaming the piece: "Jekyll and Formaldehyde," "Noah's Shark," that sort of childish bollocks. Roar loved Tracey—she reminded him of Sandra Bernhard in *King of Comedy*. (She was a big fan of Iwana Kant, by the way.) Roar and Hockney went to her brilliant show at the White Cube. She'd been raped and suffered multiple abortions, which was all Roar needed to hear: he was all in. So darkly funny too. And Damien never knew his dad— as you know, "the Artful Roger" adored his tribe of cast-offs.

Though probably the most important reunion was with Jan Morris.

JAN MORRIS[169] Roger was never a cynic, but learning the truth about his real mum had rather suffused him with the ineffable—that word sounds like the way a drunk would pronounce "inevitable," doesn't it? And we *were*

---

169 From *Allegorizings* by Jan Morris, p. 118 (Liveright, 2021).

drunk, but drank ourselves sober. The night we dined at Sweetings, he said he'd found his biological father as well and was going to meet him. "Jan," he said. "I'm running out of regrets"—his way of sneaking up on telling me he was ready to start HRT.[170] I gave him the name of the best surgeon in London, Dr. Reggie Switch, of all names. He made a little joke, a play on that hoary old one, about at last setting off on his journey to the Switch Alps.

"And when that's done, I'll have just one regret left—but there's no doctor alive who can help me."

I said, "Oh? And what's that?"

"I shall always regret that I didn't write 'Nice 'n' Easy.'" I laughed, of course—I hadn't been expecting that. "The best lyric ever written bar none," he said. "'We're on the road to romance, that's safe to say. *But let's make all the stops along the way.*'"

"You're lucky," I said. "You've made more stops than most."

He smiled and put his hand on mine. He said, "It's nice to know there's not too many left."

I wouldn't say it was ominous yet a great sadness overtook me.

ULTRA VIOLET (*a.k.a. Isabelle Collin Dufresne, author, Warhol Superstar*) There was a reason Kava and Chickweed weren't out and about—they were having a mad affair and kept close quarters. Roger absolutely knew. . . . And was relieved because he had some guilt over his own extramarital carryings-on. Hadn't slowed a whit in that department, an adventurer to the end. If the mouse must play while the cat's away, he'd rather Kava ring up room service than go out to eat.

FRANCIS BACON I'd been doing a portrait of a trans gal and Roger was quite keen to meet her. Inge came to my studio—"Iwana" had been using one of the rooms to paint in when not in rehearsal for *The Empty Chair*—and rather too quickly, Roger asked her to undress. He wanted to see her cunt. Inge was a good sport, especially when he told her he planned on having the same procedure. The interview left him positively giddy and emboldened. It was the nudge he needed.

But on the way back to Claridge's he came across a morose crowd. On

---

170 Hormone replacement therapy.—*ed.*

further investigation, a pedestrian had been struck by a hit-and-dash; the ambulance hadn't yet come. The poor woman's purse spilled its jejune secrets into the street and her shabby heels knocked kilty in the roadway. There was no question she was dead. When Roger came closer, he saw the bald head—the wig got knocked off too and lay next to its owner like a bereft pet. He thought it a terrible premonition, a sign from the heavens telling him not to go through with the surgery. I told him that was nonsense, but he couldn't be swayed. Roger could be quite punchy.

I said, "Don't do it, if your mind's made up. But promise you'll see a gentleman I've found indispensable in the resolution of such esoteric matters."

I was speaking of the extraordinary palmist Mir Bashir, of course.

WALLACE SHAWN Roar swore by the palm reader Francis Bacon recommended. He wanted *me* to make an appointment but I was *afraid*. I didn't want anyone looking at my palm—then dropping it, you know, in horror at what they'd seen. I had enough problems.

Roar told Bashir about coming across a body in the street. He didn't tell him about his *plans*—you know, to have gender surgery. And the palm reader said those sort of encounters—random encounters with death—were *good* omens because they were reminders of the fleetingness of life, and its dual nature: the body he came across was male *and* female because it represented what was coming for us *all*. Death was gender-blind. . . . So, in *that* way, Roar took it as a humbling, cosmic assent to go forward with the surgery. Life is short, so you may as well die with your heels on. Or off, like that sad person in the street! The palm reader was saying none of it mattered! At least, that's how Roar took it.

Then Bashir said something I found quite extraordinary—because Roar still hadn't said anything about his specific *fascination* with that dead body. Bashir went on to say that Roar would die in a dress! He said, "But you will not die in the street. You will be at home, surrounded by loved ones—wearing a dress."

Which is certainly a strange thing to be told by *anyone*. I mean, if Coco Chanel herself told me that, I wouldn't necessarily be *comforted*. I wouldn't jump up and down and say, "Merci, Madame Chanel!" But Roar thought it was quite lovely. I mean, I hate to say it, but when he told me what the palm reader said, it was hard to keep a straight face.

BRUCE WAGNER In my novel, Queenie and Charley's stories are separate. And I kept the same form when adapting it for the stage—a greenhorn move. I showed up for rehearsal and was handed a new script: Roger cut and pasted the two halves, interweaving them like a dark, luminous braid. As I began to read, I felt like the dunce in a master class. I literally hung my head in shame at the rightness, the *obviousness* of what he did. "Don't beat yourself up, kid," he said. "Let me do that!"

Anyway, the work became richer by the tenth power. He designed the set himself, a lazy Susan, soundlessly, breathtakingly, spellbindingly swiveling in front of the ravenous audience.

VANESSA REDGRAVE (*actress*) I'd done five films back-to-back—*five*— but the last thing I did onstage was the Shaw play [*Heartbreak House*]. I was dying to play Queenie. Such a wild, damaged spirit. And dying to work with Roar.

WALLACE SHAWN I had incredible respect for Vanessa. As a human being. I'd actually gone to the courthouse when Vanessa sued the San Francisco Symphony for firing her because of her support for the Black Panthers. I went with Janet Malcolm. Roar's sister, Laughlin, testified—with Lenny Bernstein—on Vanessa's behalf. She was *very* courageous. And just this . . . *incredible* actress. I'd be on the other side of the revolving stage waiting for my turn and be completely rapt by her performance, completely caught up in listening to "Queenie"'s monologue. When the stage began to move, I really had to make an effort to snap out of it.

* * * * * * * *

from Arms and the Man[171]
"The Empty Chair"
by Michael Billington

. . . Orr's direction is a marvel of restraint, a Rolls-Royce engine driving its audience through a landscape of smoke and mirrors that never

---

171 *The Guardian,* Theater Arts, 1992.

quite obscures the facade of a transcendent castle on the hill—the makeshift castle of ruined banquets and empty chairs that is the poignant birthright of human yearning. It is nothing short of a major triumph.

In this life, like a Kali or Durga, Mr. Orr has held a multitude of weapons in his many arms—weapons of love, of hate, of hilarity—but perhaps never held them closer (to the audience as well) as in his first directed theater piece. Perhaps because of his lauded gift of song, the move from celluloid to stage is effortless, and effortlessly musical.

Adapted from Bruce Wagner's chatty, discursive, eponymous novel, he has pulled together the essentials in a way that eclipses the original work. Vanessa Redgrave and Wallace Shawn, by turns, have never been more idiosyncratic, ragged and debased, more holy and comedic.

* * * * * * * *

MELLIE KOCH *Gift from God* is a modern version of a somewhat underrepresented story in the *Arabian Nights*. A sultan's in love with a beautiful young girl. Her rich and powerful father protects her as long as he can from the royal suitor's overtures; he's about to give in to the pressure when a handsome young man appears in a dream and tells him to be patient. "For, I'm destined to marry your daughter." The girl continues to rebuff the sultan's advances, and he spitefully forces her to marry a hunchback. On the eve of the wedding day, some mischievous genies abduct the hunchback while he's in the loo—and conjure the boy from her father's dream. The two fall instantly in love and make a baby. The genies, still out for a laugh, spirit the lover thousands of miles away, where he awakens in the middle of a curious crowd. He thinks he's lost his mind but eventually gathers his wits and becomes apprentice to a baker. When the girl tells her father what happened, they go into hiding to avoid the wrath of the sultan. She gives birth to her dream groom's son. Years go by, and the little boy's constantly fighting because the kids call him a bastard. So, the three of them—father, daughter, and grandson—go searching for her true husband.

STEVEN PRESSFIELD (*writer*)[172] What the *scenarist* Orr loved was a detail that is only revealed at the very end of "The Hunchback's Tale."

Ten years before, when the girl told her father that it wasn't the hunchback with whom she'd conceived a child—but rather, the young man who visited his dream—he immediately sealed the room where they made love, meticulously leaving things as they were. In that sense, it became a Dickensian ghost house (Miss Havisham with a happy ending), awaiting the metaphorical kiss of a revenant prince to awaken it. The bedsheets were left *just so*, stained with the crumbs of postcoital dessert the lovers had been enjoying before the djinns impishly intervened.

When at last they find the baker's apprentice, he's drugged and locked in a box for the thousand-mile journey of return: a metaphor for every writer's journey *to lock in Story and bring it home.* Upon arrival, the woozy young man is placed in bed—beside his waiting bride—*just so.*

When he awakens, he looks around in confusion, scratches his chin and says, "I had the strangest dream: that after we made love, some genies stole me away for ten long years. . ."

PICO IYER *Gift from God* had some favorite themes Roger visited again and again: the plasticity of time and memory, the sheer happenstance of fate. And of course, the strands of Advaita,[173] which became so dear to his heart . . . Thomas Merton wrote in one of his journals that he had to relinquish spirituality in order to give himself to God. Roger did that by making movies. Each one—as worldly as the act of creating a film may be—was a stripping-away of Self, a stepping stone on the path to God.

He described his cinematic detours from the Path in a most delightfully tantric way: "A Funny Thing Happened on the Way to the Formless."

DAVID THOMSON [*Gift from God* is] a weighty film—far more poignant and ecstatically mournful than it is sentimental—yet as light as the puff pastry that its protagonist, the long-lost baker-hero, becomes famous for. It's deftly comedic, with incomparable performances by Gwyneth Paltrow and

---

172 From *The War of Art: Winning the Inner Creative Battle* by Steven Pressfield, 85–88 (Orion, 2003).

173 The Hindu philosophy of nondualism.—*ed.*

River Phoenix. The inherent drama of homecoming creates a tension whose resolution is nothing short of magnificent. It's the closest anyone will ever get to Lubitsch's *The Shop Around the Corner*. In some ways, I think it's superior.

GWYNETH PALTROW I'd only done *Hook*, with Steven [Spielberg], and a few TV movies. Then I did *Flesh and Bone*, which was a pretty big deal for me. But *Gift from God* was the real beginning of my career—and in a lot of ways, my life. Roger showed David Fincher the dailies and because of that, he hired me for *Se7en*. *Everything* about that time was special. River and I were madly in love. Oh, River! He died three months after we wrapped.

That film prepared me for life . . . and death.

I can never be grateful enough to Roar.

MELLIE KOCH He wrote the sultan part for Richard Harris. And because it was contemporary, Roger made him a Mike Milken–like billionaire. A junk bond guy. Richard was positively Shakespearean.

BRIAN COX (*actor*) I've talked about this in many interviews so I'm afraid it's not breaking news: Logan Roy is based on Harris's performance. One thousand percent.

BRIAN GRAZER (*producer*) Roar knew Helen Mirren from *Philip Phaethon* and she signed on to play Gwyneth's mom. Michael [Douglas] wanted the part of Gwyneth's father so badly that he did an audition tape. And was wonderful. But for *my* money, Ben Kingsley stole the show as the hunchbacked Wall Street trader. Each time Ben won an award, they came up with three more that you never knew even existed.

BEN KINGSLEY (*actor*) Roar gave me a clue. He said, "Play him like Feste in *Twelfth Night*—but Feste with a large and serious hard-on."

I took that ball and ran like hell with it!

LAUGHLIN ORR It was a big year. Hendrix turned a happy and healthy four years old. *Gift from God* swept the Oscars—we thought *Gump* and *Shawshank* were going to win everything. A month later, Roger got his star on Hollywood Boulevard. *The Empty Chair* finally came to Broadway and

won two Tonys—Roger for directing, Vanessa for lead actress. It won Best
Play from the New York Drama Critics' Circle too. *Solitary Bird* got an arm-
ful of Grammys, and Bird did that two-hour special with Oprah. "Childless
Mother" was on its way to becoming a standard; Bird stole the title from a
joke Roar used to make—his spin on "Motherless Child"—and he never let
her hear the end of it. It pulled ahead of "Tears in Heaven" in the horse race
for Saddest Motherfucking Song Ever.[174] When she and Tony Bennett came
out to present the award for Best Jazz Instrumental they got the longest ovation in Grammy history. Tony, being the class act he is, stepped back and let it
all go to Bird. Which is kinda where the applause was heading anyway.

RICHIE "SNOOP" RASKIN I kept in touch with "Wild Bill" Calhoun, over
at GDCP. Roger still had me on retainer so I thought of it as a professional
obligation. But I enjoyed the warden. We became friendly and Bill liked to
talk. *Talk* and talk and talk. He could drink too and at the end of each day—I
don't think he had a wife he loved coming home to much—he'd pour himself
a brandy and get on the horn. I tried to avoid it but if I happened to be near
a phone, I'd pick up. "Is this Cool Hand Snoop?" That's what he liked to call
me. I called him Hot Head Bill right back. So, there we were: Cool Hand and
Hot Head, having a colloquy over the wire. Talkin' shit, talkin' women, talkin'
country music. He loved Porter Wagoner. Loved *any* country song ending in
a murder, especially if the killer wound up in jail. Porter has a song, "The Cold
Hard Facts of Life," about a man who stabs his wife and her lover to death.
Sings the whole sad tale from his cell. Loved Kenny Rogers, too—"Ruby,
Don't Take Your Love To Town"—the part where the quadriplegic says he'd
get a gun and put his whore wife in the ground if he wasn't paralyzed. Hell, I
didn't even remember that. He probably liked those songs because they were
about men who had the courage to do what he couldn't. I wondered if his
wife was cuckolding him. I started thinking about that woman. You know,
wondering if she was some kinda bombshell.

Wild Bill smoked his cigar, probably with his feet up on the desk, and
told me what went on that day in the "Georgia Department of Erections

---

174 In 1991, Eric Clapton's four-year-old son fell from the fifty-fourth-floor New York apartment of a friend. "Tears In Heaven," written in memoriam, won three Grammy Awards,
including Song of the Year.—*ed.*

Facility." Laugh while doing it too. He talked about a female guard, a nympho who fucked all the trustees. Bill said he let the guards watch. Said it was a pretty good show and the guards were appreciative. "But I don't allow 'em to pull their peckers." Jesus. He told me about some skinny punk that looked at him the wrong way when he passed through the Yard so he threw him in a cell with a three-hundred-pound psycho. The kid got raped six times from Sunday before gettin' "chicken choked." Bill thought that was a hoot.

One day, I pick up—I'm in L.A., it's about four in the afternoon, so it's seven in Georgia—and he says, "Cool Hand? You better tell your little buddy to get his rich and famous fag ass out here *pronto.*" I'm thinking *Oh shit, they're fixin' to execute the motherfucker.* I doubt if "fixin'" was the actual word, but you *do* tend to start thinking the way Bill talks.

"What's up?"

"The Wriggleman just had himself a big ol' scary heart attack."

CHAPTER FIFTEEN

Daddy Dearest

DAVID STEINBERG We tried to learn his father's status—*Is he alive or is he fucking dead?*—but had to rely on whatever Raskin was able to get from the warden. Which didn't work out so well because "Wild Bill" had reasons of his own for *encouraging* Roar to come down; he thought he could talk him into making a movie of his life. The man was delusional. I can't believe these guys' names. "Wild Bill" and "Snoop" Raskin. So friggin' cheesy. Anyway, Roar had been having long conversations with Woody [Harrelson]. He told him everything and they wound up flying to Georgia together.

WOODY HARRELSON As it turned out, Roar's father and my dad were cellmates at one point. That blew us away. "There are more things in heaven and earth, Horatio, than are dreamt of in your philosophy."

Amen, brother. Amen.

His alias when we checked into the motel was Horatio Hornblower.

KAVA SANTANA Roger had already started hormone therapy—Dr. Switch hooked him up with a surgeon in L.A. So, here you have this incredibly famous person, this genius who wants to become a *woman*, who didn't find out he was adopted until his forties . . . and is suddenly told that his biological mom is *equally* famous, you know, and *Black*, this legendary Black jazz singer . . . and now he/she's on their way to meet Biological Dad—the Klansman who raped his mother, on death row for a bunch of *murders*.

Come *on*, right?

If it was a movie you were pitching, they'd show you the door.

LAUGHLIN ORR He'd just finished taping *Celebrity Jeopardy!* The stars played for their favorite charities and the show matched whatever they won. Roar was playing for Hold Your Horses, the foundation Chickweed started with the money Jonny left her. Buzz Aldrin and Eartha Kitt were the other panelists. Eartha loved Hold Your Horses because she started a nonprofit for underprivileged kids way back in the Sixties. She was an early LGBTQ activist too. A pretty amazing woman. The *strange* thing is, Eartha and Bird had only met in passing. Which didn't make sense to me because they were around the same age and shared so many people in common. Roar asked Bird about it, you know, "How come you never knew each other?" She was blasé. "I can't be knowin' everybody, baby." Kind of blew him off.

He had a theory about that.

See, Eartha was a child of rape, just like Bird. Her mother was raped by the son of the owner of the plantation where they lived. Her mom's new boyfriend was disgusted by Eartha's pale skin so she passed Eartha off to be raised by her auntie. . . . Roar called it the Shame Mirror—Bird and Eartha kept their distance because looking at each other was like looking in a mirror. I couldn't understand that. But when Roger explained it, it made sense. The very thing that you imagine would bring two people together turns out to be the thing that keeps them apart.

WOODY HARRELSON On the plane to Atlanta, we talked about all kinds of things. I'm not sure how Eartha Kitt came up but he said she was born of a rape, like his mom. He said Bird and Eartha never got close because "birds of a certain feather don't flock together."

"And what does *that* mean?"

He paused—he liked to be dramatic, to draw things out.

"Bird had PBS. And Eartha probably had it too." I thought he was talking about public television. "Painted Bird Syndrome, brother."

He told me about *The Painted Bird*,[175] a great novel I hadn't heard of. In the book, a man paints a bird in all kinds of different colors. When he releases it, the flock think she's a threat and savagely peck her out of the sky. I didn't quite get the full metaphor but I knew what he was saying. Being the child of

---

175 By Jerzy Kosinski (Huffington Mifflin, 1965).

a rape, you wear a kind of scarlet letter. It marks you for life as an outsider and condemns you to be a "solitary bird."

VIOLA DAVIS When he told Bird about his "mirror" theory, she laughed. But she liked the part about the painted bird. She said, "That's just the Joseph story. His father, Jacob, gave him a coat of many colors and Joseph's brothers were jealous. The brothers threw Joseph into a pit then sold him to Ishmaelite traders for twenty pieces of silver. They soaked his tattered coat in goat blood then brought it to Jacob and said that his favorite son had been killed by wild pigs."

She ended the little debate by singing the Dolly song, *But I was rich as I could be. In my coat of many colors that Mama made for me.*

Bird was always singing that song.

WOODY HARRELSON When we got to GDCP it was pouring rain. I had memories of my own about that place; it was the first jail I visited my father in. By the time we went to see "Wriggles" [*sic*], Dad had long been incarcerated in Colorado, but it was still hard. Actors learn about a thing called sense memory—the way your body feels during emotional or traumatic events. A lot of those old Georgia feelings washed over me. Like I time-traveled and was about to see my father again, for the first time. My body couldn't tell the difference.

In a lot of ways, Roar and I were having the exact same experience.

* * * * * * * * *

ROGER ORR[176]

The warden looked like the wiry, sadistic Hume Cronyn in Jules Dassin's *Brute Force* but a little more jovial and a lot less wiry; about two hundred pounds less. He knew Woody from years ago, when he'd come to see his father. Before he was famous. Woody said the warden had always been a real shit and made the visits intolerable.

---

176 *Roarshock* by Roger Orr, pp. 190–198 (Liveright, 2003).

He said they almost came to blows once. But today, Woody yessir'd and no sir'd and stared at the ground like a half-wit choirboy.

Our host reintroduced himself, mostly to me, as "Wild Bill—but my friends call me Bill. Hell, my enemies call me that and I seem to have much more of *those*. I'm an Aries so that's to be expected. The only one who *don't* call me Bill is the mother-in-law. To this day, that cunt thinks my name is Sir." He apologized for the weather and said the airports were a mess. "You boys fly charter?" I delivered the painful news that we hadn't and he didn't take it too personally. A *Natural Born Killers* poster in his office awaited Woody's signature.

Woody hunched over the desk with a pen while the panjandrum droned, "I just *love* Oliver Stone, I'll see anything that man does. Wonderful director, best we have. The wife won't go—too violent. Did you get along, Woody? Did you get along with Ollie?"

"Like pigs in shit."

The warden slapped his knee and said, "Ha! Easy to get along with?"

"Easy as 1-2-3."

"Well, goddammit, how did I know that?"

Suddenly I forgot who I was, where I was, and why I'd come.

As we walked to the infirmary, Woody saw that I was unsteady on my feet. He put a hand under my armpit to prop me up while the warden prattled on about Woody's dad.

"How's he holding up? Tough man, Charles. We had our disagreements but there was always a mutual respect"—Woody looked at me sideways because I'd heard all the stories—"Now *that's* a movie Oliver Stone should make. What do you think, Woody? What do you think of a movie about your dad and me?"

"Most definitely, Warden. I think he'd be *very* interested."

Woody had an *I'm going to grind this good ol' boy* glint in his eye.

"Do you?" said the Warden, in astonishment. "Well . . . I was hoping you'd say that because I've typed up a few pages—I'm no writer—but I could show 'em to you and you could let me know if there's something there. Or pass it on to Mr. Stone if you don't have the time . . . they're nothin' too special but I do think I maybe might've caught me some lightning in a bottle. It's either lightning or static electricity—Oliver'd be the one to tell me which.'"

Another sidewise glance from Woody.

"Ollie's always looking for new material." He winked and said, "And as you know, Warden, I have an 'in.'"

"Well, that's—that's just *fantastic*. You made my day, son!"

"You can give me those pages today or you can fax 'em."

The Warden cogitated as we stood in the hall outside the hospital wing. "Well . . . lemme sit on 'em a day or two. I'd like to look them over again. I don't want to embarrass myself *too* much. . . it's been a while. See, I didn't know you were coming with your friend until a few days ago, so I couldn't adequately prepare."

"You've got to give it your best shot."

"Well, this all strikes me as just some kind of fate!"

By the looks of me, Woody knew I needed a few moments to gather myself, and stalled for time by devilishly asking Wild Bill if he ever saw a movie by the name of *Grace War*.

"Nope, never did. And I sure as hell should have, 'cause they shot it over at Bibb where the old jail used to be. The wife saw it. She's got a heart that'll bleed on your carpet. And you won't need luminol to see it. When it comes to the interracial theme, her pussy wets up every time. I only told her that once, 'cause I'm getting too old to dodge a frying pan."

Woody respectfully hung back as the warden walked me to a small grey room where Colson "Wriggle" Jones was the only patient.

There was an EKG and a bag of fluids but neither were hooked up.

The warden turned to me with a smile and said, "The Wriggleman's good people," before making a swift exit.

An ancient, emaciated, urine-smelling creature in a blood-flecked, threadbare hospital gown stared back at me. For years, I conjured a mountain man, a young, hooded hellion crushing down and into Mother as she watched the strange fruit of galaxies wheel through the heavens—a ferocious, acne-pitted ruined child of God creating ruinous new worlds in her unconsenting womb: the world of Me. He was eighty years old now; I was fifty-five. The title of the Philip K. Dick story I based a movie on, "I Hope I Shall Arrive Soon"—about a man whose arrival home is an illusion—lit up the room in neon.

A scabby, whitewashed arm floated up, and we shook hands.

"Pleased to meet you," he said. He coughed then laughed. "You may not be pleased to meet *me*. But I do thank you for coming."

I balked at using the whimsically sinister name I'd first heard from my mother's mouth. "What should I call you?"

"Oh, all kinds of names," he said. He was trying to charm me with what strength he had. "If you got one I never heard before, I'll let you know. But I think I've heard 'em all."

"How about Colson."

"That'll do fine. I never liked Wriggle. But names just stick. Always been that way, always will be. They get stuck."

"I know. They call me 'Roar,' and I can't get away from it."

He laughed then coughed again.

"You've got a soft hand for a lion."

* * * * * * * * *

WOODY HARRELSON We went back to the hotel and played chess. He always kicked my ass, and that night was no different. It was obvious his head was somewhere else. Why wouldn't it be? He was in shock. His sister called and they chatted. Then I had to go. I was shooting *The People vs. Larry Flynt*. Roar's old friend Miloš was directing. I told Miloš I had personal business—I didn't want to break a confidence—and needed a day off. He didn't want to let me go. He wasn't a prick about it but we were on a very tight schedule. I called Roar and said, "Miloš is giving me some trouble here. If he knows what it's about, he'll shoot around me." Roar didn't want to call Miloš himself but gave me the okay. And when I told him, Miloš doubled over and coughed—I thought it was a cough but he'd burst into tears. That set *me* off and we bawled like there was no tomorrow. It was a beautiful moment.

Roar walked me to the cab. He looked up at the sky and said, "She did it. She outwitted the stars." I knew who he was talking about: Bird. And knew where that was from—it's the name of a chapter in one of our favorite books, *Autobiography of a Yogi*. Yogananda's talking about the "astrological inscription" of the stars, and how our lives—and deaths—are already mapped out. "One by one, we can escape from creation's prison of duality."

The great escape. . . .

He started to sing, real soft. "You are here to watch over some heart that is broken, by a word someone left unspoken . . ." I asked what that was from. He said it's the song his mama heard on the radio while she was being attacked. Tommy Dorsey. [*smiles*] Yogananda says you can *outwit* what's been planned for you. You can alter your destiny and set yourself free.

If you're lucky.

LAUGHLIN ORR I'll *never* call that man his father. His first name and last name have never crossed my lips. I don't care what Bird's Jesus says. My Jesus says something else.

SUZE BERKOWITZ After he met Colson Jones, he flew right home to see Bird. She was waiting up for him in the dark, in her favorite living room chair. He told me that he felt like a kid who broke curfew. "A shotgun in her lap would have completed the picture." He started to wonder if he'd done wrong by going to Georgia. She'd actually encouraged him to see the man—but that was a while ago and Rodge started to get paranoid. He was thinking, Oh shit, that was some kind of loyalty test. A test he'd righteously failed.

He told her about Woody coming along "to hold my hand" because Woody's dad was in the penitentiary too. Also for murder. He did a little routine for her, imitating the warden talking about Oliver Stone. He finally gets to the part where he meets his father.

"I thought he'd be a minotaur but he was just a sickly, broken-down jailbird."

Now, his mother usually had a lot to say but she didn't say a *word*. And that fucked with his head. They sat in the dead quiet. Then Bird says, "Pray for him."

Roger took a deep breath to tamp down his righteousness. "He did that unforgivable thing to you. He took the lives of an old woman and a twelve-year-old girl—not before he tortured them first. Who knows how many people he's killed? I don't want to pray for him."

"I didn't say you had to want to. And I didn't say you had to like it. I'm just saying you need to do it." Another five minutes go by. Five minutes! Then she says, "And pray for your brother's father too. Pray for Woody's dad."

"I'll try, Mother. I'll try."

"Well," says Bird, "that's a start. A *good* start. And that word you mentioned, son?" She always called him 'son' when she was about to impart some of that ol' biblical wisdom. "That word 'unforgivable'? You need to get some of that correction fluid you like to use so much and just . . . *brush it across*. Go ahead and brush it right through. White it out. 'Cause that word may belong in the dictionary, but it don't belong in God's Book. How many people have I killed with a look? How many times have you tortured yourself worse than any professional could? Never forget, baby: 'jailbird' and 'bird' are two sides of the same motherfuckin' coin. When you spend your money, the merchant don't look at neither side. *He just takes the coin.* God has a different kind of coin in His realm. It's made of something stronger than steel. Stronger than diamonds. It's minted with love and compassion and forgiveness.

"And God don't look at the sides neither."

KAVA SANTANA Roar had a ranch in Texas. Ten thousand acres, just south of Amarillo—on the edge of the parcel that originally belonged to his mother's family, the Desmoines. Bunny's family. I *hate* saying "adoptive mother" and "birth mother." Roger had two moms, people! Is that *okay*? It's so dumb to fall into a language trap, and I've never been one to get off on being technically correct. Anyway, we had this big, beautiful ranch and he went down there to process. Not just the meeting with that horrible, ugly man—though in *that* case, I make an exception and *do* say "biological father"—but to think about where he was going. What to do next. The hormone treatments made him extra-emotional, extra-vulnerable. I told him it would take time. That for a minute anyway, he was a man without a country. Know what he said? "No, a man without a cunt. But not for long."

BRYAN BURROUGH (*journalist*)[177] The Four Deuces was acquired in the 1890s by the Desmoine family. Orr's adoptive mother, Bunny Orr, was the sole inheritor upon her father's death in 1940. When Bunny and her husband Mug "the Commodore" Orr passed away in 1962, the Orr children inherited the ranch. Jonny sold his portion in the mid-Seventies; he was never a big fan of Texas.

In its heyday, the Four Deuces spanned a million acres. The ranch got its

---

177 From *The Big Rich: The Rise and Fall of the Greatest Texas Oil Fortunes* by Bryan Burrough, pp. 417–421 (Penguin Books, 2004).

name because the seed land was won by Pharaoh Desmoine in a card game. His grandson Langdon took it over in 1916. It was hard going but he had financial assistance from his lover, Electra Waggoner, owner of the famous Waggoner Ranch. She was married, with two sons—one died of syphilis and the other of cirrhosis. (Her husband never knew that Langdon was the father of their boys.) The "Electra Field"—its secret name—was drilled on The Four Deuces in the early Twenties; overnight, Langdon Desmoine became the wealthiest man in America. He was profligate and wanton and his Olympian new power acted as an aphrodisiac to his violent nature. The Ku Klux Klan became the target of his savagery. While unspoken, it was generally known that the Desmoines were Jews but the issue was moot until he struck oil. As threats against him and his family grew, he formed a private army and many Klansmen vanished without a trace, including Hiram Wesley Evans—a Dallas dentist by day and Imperial Wizard by night. It was said that Langdon tracked down a man who threatened his twelve-year-old daughter Bunny and butchered him with a jackknife.

When Electra Waggoner caught him in bed with a ranch hand, she shot both men dead before turning the gun on herself.

LAUGHLIN ORR Mama used to tell us that story about Grandpa killing that man with a pocket knife. She said it was a wizard and that upset me because I thought you weren't supposed to kill wizards. But Roger and I sat there spellbound. The details changed, depending on her mood. One day, it was a switchblade; another, an acetylene torch; another day, he strangled him with hands bigger than three men's put together.

Orr family bedtime stories.

SCATTER HOLBROOK Kava and Chickweed's kids—Hendrix and Moon—were the same age and their moms spent a lot of time together. *Quality* time, if you know what I mean. Chickweed basically moved in. Roger's libido was challenged from all the hormones, *un gran problema* because for Kava, sex was kind of a big deal. And Chickweed was no slouch in that *departmento*.

He walked around having a colloquy with his dick. He'd peer down and say, "Don't give me that *look*, bubba. Number your days." I'd tell him, hey, it ain't goin' nowhere. They're just going to butterfly the fucker and shove it up your new asshole. Roger said, "He's had his head up a thousand assholes—it's poetic justice that mine will be the last he'll ever see!"

DR. EUNICE LAVAR Roger made trips to see Douglas Ousterhout in San Francisco. Doug was an old friend of mine, a craniofacial guy who pioneered surgical feminization for trans women. He owned a vineyard too and helped Roger learn the wine business when he did the ROAR label in the Aughts. By coincidence, Doug and his wife lived in the house in Atherton that Roger used for *Hollow*.

While he was away, Kava and Chickweed got deeper into their thing, and it's my understanding that Roger encouraged it.

ARSENIO HALL (*talk show host, personality*) Roger was in his *Being There* phase. You know, "I like to watch." He'd call while his wife and his brother's widow were having a scene. It was crazy! We'd be talking and he'd shout over to them, "Guess who *I'm* on the phone with? Arsenio!" I'd hear the girls go "Woof! Woof! Woof!" then get right back into it. It was *crazy*. I'd say, "I'm on my way down, dog!" And I was serious too.

KAVA SANTANA It's still hard to talk about all that. About *any* of it. Laughlin called and said something was wrong at Hold Your Horses. The Foundatiion. The first thing I thought was there'd been some kind of accident, you know, one of the kids got hurt. Fell from a horse or whatever. I said, What happened? She said there was money missing. A *lot* of money. And that Chickweed had something to do with it. My back went up. I said, Laughlin, how do you even know this? That's when she told me the family accountants were still involved, which surprised me, because I thought Jonny cut his ties, you know, that the Foundation was independent and had its own overseers. Evidently though, because Roger and Laughlin were still on the board, their people did an audit. At Laughlin's bidding, not Roger's. I said, How much? How much is missing? It was a crazy number—like $9,000,000. Laughlin said the Foundation was about to go belly-up. I wasn't too kind. We had a rift for a while. I was stone in love with Chickweed and saw her as oppressed. I thought she was being spied on and it was all bullshit; for a while, I thought *Laughlin* took the money and was using Chickweed to cover her tracks.

My heart wasn't thinking straight.

ERIC LERNER (*author, screenwriter*) Laughlin told Roger about the swindle but he stayed out of the fray. The situation reminded me of when Leonard's [Cohen] former manager, a woman he'd been intimate with, stole money from him and went to jail. Leonard was laissez-faire. Like Roger, he had years of Buddhism behind him and was practicing what had been preached. Of course, none of the Orrs would have to go on the road like Leonard did, to recoup their losses. They *owned* the roads.

RICHIE "SNOOP" RASKIN I was aware that Kava and Chickweed were having an affair and that Laughlin was worried about Chickweed having access to family finances. I did a little digging at her behest. Turned out Chickweed was madly in love with a gambler and all-around scumbag named Roy Mars. She'd been funneling this guy millions over the years. Just like Sharon Stone in *Casino*—you know, where she's totally addicted to that piece of shit "Lester Diamond." James Woods was fantastic in the role, played it to a tee. I've known too many Lester Diamonds. Of course, the next thing I wondered was if Moon was Jonny's daughter—or Scumbag Mars's.

KAVA SANTANA After she was sentenced, I got a court order for a paternity test. Snoop Raskin found Roy Mars at the Mustang Ranch[178] and had a doctor do the DNA test right there. Roger actually got very pissed off, which I welcomed, because up till then he'd been so *Buddhist* about everything, and that was infuriating. He'd say, "And what if Moon *isn't* Jonny's daughter? What are you going to do, Kava? Tell her to go fuck herself?"

As it turned out, she was. She was Jonny's. And I was so happy and relieved that Jonny was *represented*. I think Roger was glad too but he wouldn't even give me that. I guess it stirred up stuff about the past. You know, a child who becomes a pawn in a game that it never signed up for.

SUZE BERKOWITZ Chickweed went to jail for three years. Moon formally moved in with Kava and Roger, but she'd practically been living with them anyway. Kava talked about adopting her but Roger thought that was a can of worms.

The one time Kava went to see her in prison, she saw Roy Mars in the

---

178 In 1971, Mustang Ranch became Nevada's first licensed brothel.—*ed.*

parking lot, waiting to go in. He was on the phone, sitting in an expensive car—bought with the money Chickweed stole from the foundation.

SAM WASSON His time at the ranch in Texas was productive. He finally wrote his script about Hemingway [*Gigi*] but vowed not to shoot it until he finished his novel. He went on a final road trip to gather material for *The Jungle Book* but this time without the Pennebaker circus. Just him and an assistant. It was also a way of being out in the world with his new, softer looks, even though the physical changes were still pretty subtle. He wanted not just to see but to be seen. A dry run for a new incarnatiion.

Roar made another promise to himself: to visit his father again. He'd done as Bird asked, praying for Colson Jones each day, and something inside him was shifting. He took it a step further and met the families of the women Jones was convicted of murdering.

DAVID THOMSON[179] The next time he saw Colson Jones, the warden was mercifully absent. "Wild Bill" had gon' fishin'—he was on vacation in Hollywood, to get closer to the action. The warden managed to wangle a meeting with Oliver Stone by saying that Woody referred him. He's what they used to call a real character.

A. KITMAN HO (*producer*) Woody was mortified when Oliver called to say he had Wild Bill in his office. But Oliver was gracious about it. He started to laugh when Woody told him that the warden was insane—Oliver's face looks like a crazy pumpkin when he laughs and he had to cover the phone so his guest wouldn't hear Woody's rant. After he hung up, he politely told the warden he'd be happy to read a script but wasn't putting anything into development at this time. I think Oliver got a kick out of him.

Wild Bill walked out of there like he was on cloud nine.

KRISTINE MCKENNA (*journalist, critic*) Before he left Hollywood, "Wild Bill" Calhoun and his wife were on a bus tour of stars homes. A writer for the *LA Weekly* was also on the tour, incognito, doing one of those

---

179 *A Light In the Dark: A History of Movie Directors* by David Thomson, p. 313 (Cavalcade, 2007).

tried-and-true *Day of the Locust* features about heartland folks dropping down from the sky into Babylon. The warden strikes up a conversation and the *Weekly* gal's curiosity is piqued. He tells *all*. When she hears about Woody and Roger going to Georgia—to see Roger Orr's biological father on death row!—she just about has a heart attack. The first thing she does when she jumps off that bus is authenticate the warden. Because the story's so crazy that she needed to make sure he wasn't a nut; if he *was* nuts, it'd be a great *Weekly* story anyway. It's a win-win. But everything checks out. She pitches it to her editor and two weeks later it's in thousands of newsracks alongside the *Free Press* and the porn rag *LA Xpress*. Scoop of the century.

CHARLES CHAMPLIN The *L.A. Times* picks it up and a day later, the Gray Lady lifts her skirts. Wild Bill denied *everything*, but a spokesperson for the prison was forced to walk that back. They said the warden had been explicit in telling the *Weekly* writer that "any comments made would be strictly off the record, and that she agreed."

A lie, of course. But it was marvelous farce.

QUENTIN TARANTINO Supposedly, the media response to Death Row Dad was *way* crazier than when the news broke about Bird being his mom. The tour bus scene in *Once Upon A Time In Hollywood* with Squeaky talking to "the warden" as they roll by Lucille Ball's mansion was a direct lift from that story. John Carroll Lynch was an *awesome* Wild Bill!

DAVID UNGER Roger was on the road for his last *Jungle Book* research trip. He started in Key West and was going to hit all those plantations you can pass through on the way to Manhattan. Ali was about to fly out to join him for that leg of the trip but when Roger heard the news on the radio, he flew straight home. I think he was more disgruntled then pissed off; it was the second time the whole "parent" narrative got away from him. He'd been through all that with Bird, so it was déjà vu.

The Morris office forwarded a message that Arsenio Hall wanted him on his show, obviously to talk about the new development.

LAUGHLIN ORR As usual, a voice in his head said, "What would Bird do?" It was Sunday when he called and she was on her way to church. "Mama?

Arsenio wants me to come on television and talk about Colson Jones." Long pause, as usual. She said, "Do you like Arsenio?" He said, yeah, I like Arsenio. "Do you trust him?" Yeah, I trust him. "Well, that train's left the station. But if you hurry, you and Arsenio can hop on and elbow the conductor out of the way. And that's a little better than a derailment."

RAYMOND C. SAINT JOHN (*author*)[180] When he invited Roar on the show, Arsenio was hurting; when they put Letterman on opposite him, Arsenio's ratings got MC *hammered.* Then the Louis Farrakhan thing happened and his shit was doomed.[181]

HENRY LOUIS GATES JR. Roar wasn't a fan of Farrakhan, not by a long shot. Louis had a Jekyll-and-Hyde thing with the Jews. Roar considered himself a Jew—and not just because his adoptive parents were Jewish. Jews were the eternal outsiders. But for Louis, they were either the most brilliant and accomplished people on the planet—or "evil bloodsuckers." There was no in-between. It was a kind of pathology.

Though he did soften toward Louis when they finally met. Roar was pretty quick to suss the root of a person, the root of their heart. We had dinner at the Farrahkan's, in Chicago. Louis confided that his own father was a Jew and *that* was a mindblower. We had a good time, laughed a lot. Louis put on some of Bird's records, and they talked about their mutual experience on Arsenio's show. [*Orr had yet to tape the episode about Colson Jones*] Louis admired Roar's talent and was impressed by his resilience. I remember him saying, "Brother? You've lived more lives than even me."

DICK GREGORY Arsenio was a friend. When Arsenio's mom got sick, Roger and Bird filled in and cohosted the show. Arsenio had been good to Sammy too and helped a long way toward his public rehabilitation after all the *Yes I Can* bullshit. Roger knew Arsenio was on his last legs and thought, "I'm gonna help the brother." Anyway, he knew he'd get a full hour, like

---

180 From *Things We Talk About When We Talk About Talk Shows* by Raymond C. Saint John and Morbley Everson (Paley Center, 2011).

181 In 1995, Hall was denounced for devoting most of the show's hour to the controversial Nation of Islam leader—the death knell that ended the show on May 27 of that year.—*ed.*

Farrakhan. And that was important. Letterman wanted him too—everyone did—but *nobody* was going to offer him a full hour. Nobody but Arsenio Hall. He didn't want to be sitting on a couch with Joey Heatherton and the wild animal guy. I take that back. Joey, he wouldn't have minded. He had a *thang* for Joey—didn't we all. Stabbed her boyfriend and was *still* lookin' good at fifty years old. Girl had heart. Don't get me started.

JIMMY KIMMEL (*talk show host*) I watch that on YouTube all the time. I was just talking about it on the Stern show. The audience gave Roar a standing ovation. He was beloved. It was the highest-rated Arsenio show ever—but too late to turn the tide. A month later, he was gone.

* * * * * * * * *

The Arsenio Hall Show
[transcript, April 14, 1995]

ARSENIO HALL: Your life has been like a movie.

ROGER ORR: One the critics would no doubt tear apart. The *quibble* being, "This would never happen," "That could never happen." They'd throw popcorn at the screen.

ARSENIO: Hey, if that's *all* they throwin', you're *good* . . .

ORR: As long as it's buttered.

ARSENIO: But Roger, have you ever thought of making a movie about it? About your life? I mean, you must have. Who else could do it better?

ORR: Every screenwriter can write a bang-up first act, Arsenio. The second act's more challenging. You tend to lose focus. It gets muddled—life's like that, too, but a *movie* needs to be compelling. The third act is what makes or breaks a picture. I think I have a pretty good first act. And the makings of a good act 2. Right now, I'm just interested in watching act 3 unfold. It's a helluva lot easier to watch than it is to write!

ARSENIO: Siskel and Ebert were here last week and they love your ass.

ORR: Roger's been very kind; Siskel not so much.

ARSENIO: We'll get the three of you together for another show. . . . But I want to talk about something heavy now. Because it is—it's very heavy.

ORR: [*trying to make light*] "He ain't heavy, he's my father."

ARSENIO: I disagree. What was it like, knowing you were going to actually meet this—this monster. A racist, a violent man, now in prison for—

ORR: The rape and murder of a woman and her great-granddaughter. [*audience gasps*]

ARSENIO: He was never convicted for the rape of your mother.

ORR: Never even accused. It's fifty years or so past the statute of limitations, and there's no DNA. DNA's the only thing that can negate the statute of limitations.

ARSENIO: Is she, is Bird—are *you*—and I don't mean this to be disrespectful—are both of you certain Colson Jones was the one?

ROGER: That question was on my mind. But Jones admitted it—not the first time we met, but the second. He confessed, which I admired. It would have been so easy, with no physical evidence, for him to say, "I'm no angel, but I didn't do that to your mother." Because in prison, rapists are considered to be just a hair above child molesters. He told me certain things that my mother later ratified. No, it couldn't have been anyone but him. The minute I saw him, I knew he was the one.

ARSENIO: Which brings me to my next question. What was it *like* when you put your eyes on the man? You're in a room with a monster . . .

ORR: . . . and saw that he *wasn't* a monster. He was just a man. Just a man. Whether we've acted out or not, we've all done monstrous things in our heads and heart. I don't want to sound too preachy, because for years I had fantasies about killing him. And when I first saw him in the prison infirmary, the thought did cross my mind. An old, sick, defenseless man . . . It would have been so easy. A picture flashed in front of me: being led away in handcuffs. The trial, the sentencing. I even thought, "They'll give me probation. It was impulsive, a crime of passion. The jury and public opinion will be on my side." I was weighing it all out. Something I'm not particularly proud of, but it is what it is.

ARSENIO: There's the end of your second act right there. Your arrest!

ORR: I'd rather not begin my third act in a cell, for the same crime my father committed. I'm a big fan of irony but that's a bit much. [*quiet audience laughter*] The truth is, I didn't want—I don't want to live that way—to suffer the sins of the father. We share DNA, there's no way around that. But I needed to do a magic trick, if I wanted to come out the other end. I needed to outwit the stars. My mother helped me with that. Bird helped me to forgive.

ARSENIO: I want to talk about Bird—there's so *much* I want to ask you, man!—but I love that phrase "outwit the stars." That's fly! I want to hear more about that. [*to camera*] We'll be right back.

* * * * * * * * *

BENNY LERONDE (*editor,* Jet *magazine*) Richard Pryor was at a benefit. He was already debilitated by MS—having trouble walking—and just *rolled* onto the red carpet in that pink polka dot scooter of his. Some blond fool puts a microphone in his face and asks when he's gonna do a picture with Roar. Richard's high! Richard says, "Paramount's gonna do a movie about Bird and Roar's daddy—might be a part in there for me—but they want to make it a *romance.* 'Let's turn that rape into a meet cute'!' And that pissed my friend Roar *off.* He said, 'What the fuck you talkin' about? That man was KKK! Mama was black and underage!'" The poor interview lady hadn't been that shade of pale since the doctor slapped her backside. Then Richard turns on his *white* voice. Every time Chappelle does it, I think of Richard . . . and Tyler, in *Hallelujah Boogie.* Richard transforms himself into a white studio boss. "'Calm down, Roger. Just *calm. The fuck. Down.* This requires *cool heads.* Let me give you the—what do you people call it? We call it the 'skinny' but I think *y'all* call it the 4-1-1. Now, what *you* see as an angry, black, purple-headed *pole,* our *distributors* see . . . as a *tent*-pole! The *good* news, Roger, is that our projections are telling us *this rape has legs!*'"

TOM WOLFE The first time Roar encountered Colson Jones, the man was on his putative deathbed. But when Roar saw him next, eight months later, Jones was fit as a fiddle and hitched to a pen pal—one of those morbidly obese

Miss Lonelyhearts who get their feeble jollies romancing caged heartthrobs. I mean, Jones was *marriage material!* Letitia Galvy was Black, about twice his size. Conjugal visits weren't going to happen—*no jodas*—a true blessing for Convict Jones because if she lay on top him, the State would have made whoopee over the early execution. Which was probably a better way to go than getting bitch-slapped by the sloppy needle of an abecedarian executioner.

WALTON FORD (*painter*) He met the whole Galvy family. Letitia's grandmother loved Bird Rabineau, and Letitia's mom dutifully saw every movie Roger Ebert told her to—Roar was an Ebert favorite.

TA-NEHISI COATES After taping Arsenio's show, Roar went back to finish the East Coast leg of *The Jungle Book* safari. He told his publisher he'd already written 150,000 words and was halfway through. Halfway! That gave them pause. They hadn't seen *any* pages yet. They'd bought it off the pitch that he was giving *Candide* a makeover; it excited them that Voltaire's book was one of the shorter ones you could find on the shelf. (Though most Americans never heard of it.) While long books were in vogue—*Infinite Jest*, to be published the following year, clocked in at over a thousand pages—they *definitely* didn't want to go that way with what they considered a one-trick prose pony by a preeminent filmmaker and songwriter. *Not* a novelist.

ALI BERK[182] I joined him in Key West. We drove up the coast—plantation after plantation, filled with tourists. This country is *so* fucking strange. We went to Savannah with a cute, campy guide who showed us that house from *Midnight In the Garden of Good and Evil*. Uncle Roary was really interested because it once belonged to his friend Johnny Mercer, who wrote "Moon River." A murder took place there and the guide walked us to a cemetery with a famous sculpture of two hands reaching out from the grave. The next day, a *different* campy guide introduced us to an old, wrinkled Gullah who I think was "part of the show"—more theater for tourists, but Roar said it was perfect for *The Jungle Book*. The old Gullah man sat us down in another graveyard—that part of the world is filled with cemeteries, pro-life billboards, Masonic temples, and Piggly Wiggly's—and said, "Now, we all learned when

---

182 *Travels with My Uncle: A Remembrance* by Ali Berk, pp. 137–145 (Pantheon, 2019).

we were kids if you ever see a man of the Root, you don't be curious. You don't ask questions. You don't look him in the eye. And if his hat blows off in that warm Charl'ton wind, well you don't pick it up. Because if you pickin' up his hat, you pickin' up his craft. See, a root doctor ain't nothing but a herbalist gone bad. I don't go into most graveyards. Here in this one, graves are all east to west. That way the sun rise up on you. But if you die under *mysterious reasons*, they bury ya north to south, that way the spirit never settles so it can go after the unknown people who kilt it. Grandmamma always said to me, 'You gonna be buried north to south.' A root doctor tol' her that."

Then Roary peeled off to Georgia. He was going to meet the relatives of some of his father's victims, and I begged to go with, but he said he didn't want me to meet anyone who had anything to do with that man. He didn't want me "picking up his craft."

DR. JOAN WICKS (*teacher*) He visited Jubilee and Tamara Hildstrom, in Durbanville. Jubilee was the daughter of the old woman Colson Jones killed, and Tamara was Jubilee's daughter—the mother of Aurora, the little girl who was attacked when she dropped by her great-grandma's house after school. Good, God-fearing people.

SAM WASSON He told me that the Hildstroms were wary of meeting him. Tamara was the most vocal, but her mother, Jubilee, convinced her. Jubilee had only spoken to Roger on the phone but "looked into his heart through the wire." It didn't hurt that Roar was a movie star who'd been in one of her favorites, *Who Loves Ya, Maybe*. So, Tamara finally gave in.

Tamara was about Roar's age now. And when she saw him, she loved him right away, loved that he cried on a dime—all those hormones!—but he'd have done that anyway. He was softer-looking now too, and blended in with the Hildstrom womenfolk, a real Southern matriarchy. He spent three days and nights as a guest in their home. When it was time to leave, they just didn't want him to go.

CICELY TYSON Bird wanted to meet the Hildstroms, and I was asked to go along. That was a great privilege. A beautiful and important thing in my life. Bird and Roger weren't like family, they *were* family. We shared so many precious experiences together. They came to Miles's [Davis] funeral and helped prop me up because I was in ruins. And I met so many people through them. It was because of Roger that I wound up being godmother to both Denzel's and Tyler's [Perry] kids.

Lord, that trip to Durbanville! It was truly something. Jubilee Hildstrom was just . . . *lit up* with Christ. She'd forgiven Colson Jones for what he did— but not Tamara. Tamara didn't want to hear the word "forgiveness" spoken. Now, I was *very* interested in Tamara because I had the notion of playing her in a film. That was something Roger would have nothing to do with—I never would have asked—but he gave his blessing. Tamara prayed every day that Colson Jones would suffer, suffer in Hell. Her sheer *murderousness* was impressive. Bird would say, "It's not an eye for an eye—it's an 'I' for a 'Thou.'" What she meant was, that's the price of vengeance. You lose your humanity . . . but when it came to Tamara's wrath, Roger whispered to me, "The world needs its tigers." He respected her. Tamara and Jubilee were two sides of the same coin, as Bird would say.

She kept her daughter Aurora's room like a museum. There was a fresh little outfit laid out on the bed for school.

STEPHEN SONDHEIM[183] . . . he wrote a song about that mordant household bedroom pietà and called it "Costume Drama." The melody and words meandered but all the signature lovelinesses were there. It was someplace between an aria and a recitative.

It'd have fit nicely in *Passion*.

CICELY TYSON The Hildstroms learned about Colson Jones's jailhouse marriage from watching the news. Tamara just about lost her mind over the unfairness of that, of allowing the man who took her baby and her grandma away from her to have a wedding. The press made a big joke of it. Whenever Tamara went to the supermarket, she'd see a row of tabloids at the checkout stand with the bride splashed across the cover. Letitia Galvy was a big girl but by the time those magazines got through with their tricks that sweet-faced child looked the size of a minivan. One of the covers said, "YES I CAN—YES 'I DO'!!!"—they dragged Roger in, oh yes they did. All this racist stuff. They

---

183 From *Look, If You Don't Like the Hat, Return It* by Stephen Sondheim, p. 145 (Random House, 2018).

called her a death row *Cinder*-ella who left a slipper behind that the prison guards thought belonged to Bigfoot. I don't know how they got away with it but they did. That truly was a different time. In some or many ways.

Roger told Tamara ain't no use in raging against what we can't control. He showed her how to meditate, and she'd calm down for five minutes then go crazy again. What can you say to a woman who's shouting, "Aurora's supposed to turn thirty-seven next week! *She's* supposed to have got married! I'd've had me grandbabies!" She called Letitia "a stinky, big fat retarded n-word"—but she didn't say "n," she used the word itself—I don't like to use the word—before realizing she was talking to a crowd of Black folk. When she caught herself, she got down on her knees and said how sorry she was. Roger lifted her up, sat her on the sofa, and got on *his* knees. Got down on his knees and kissed her hands. Bird stayed in her chair because she wasn't feeling that well, but I kneeled right down beside him.

To see a mother like that, to watch a soul burn, it humbles you. The n-word don't mean a thing when you see that kind of pain.

ALI BERK[184] The Galvys didn't live too far from the Hildstroms. About ten miles. Uncle Roary said Letitia was polite and a little withdrawn, but you knew right away that she was "off." They call it neurodiverse now. But *somethin'* was going on. . . . Her mother was a big fan of Bird's, and Roary said she collected her records. "All of 'em. And I mean, every single one." By then, Bird and Cicely had gone back to L.A.; they didn't have any interest in meeting the bride. *I* did—but couldn't because I was in New York doing *Picasso at the Lapin Agile.* I think Roary would have let me, all "craft" aside.

Letitia's mother said they played "Try a Little Tenderness" on a cassette recorder for the jailhouse wedding. How crazy and fucked up is that? The bride and groom were separated by a thick wall of glass. When Uncle Roary asked what she felt about her daughter marrying a man who was so much older—he left Jones's evil deeds out of it—her Mom said, "If she's happy, I'm happy. My baby's had so much unhappiness in her short life."

Letitia showed my uncle her room. It was in total disarray. There were posters of Elvis and Michael Jackson on the walls . . . and Jason Priestley and the boy from *Wonder Years.* But one corner of the room was super orderly,

---

184 *Travels With My Uncle: A Remembrance,* pp. 214–23.

with neatly stacked files: her prisoner correspondence. Roary said there were thousands of letters. Letitia said it took a week of working day and night to let all the incarcerated men know that she was going to be wed. She said, "I wore my pencils down to the nub." She'd only heard back from a few of them, but letters were starting to trickle in. She said they were happy for her but hoped it didn't mean she would stop writing—an idea that never occurred to her.

Then Roary couldn't hold it in anymore.

"Do you know what Colson is in jail for?"

He'd broken the promise he made to himself not to go there—what was the point?—but didn't have much to lose. She'd likely report back to Colson about the visit; he was willing to take the chance that his father would be pissed, and refuse to see him again. My uncle wasn't sure anymore why he kept going down to that jail and would have welcomed a ban because he couldn't seem to ban himself.

"Yes," she said. "He killed that poor woman and her daughter."

"Not her daughter. Her great-granddaughter. She was twelve years old. Did you know that he raped them? He raped them before and after he killed them. He raped the old woman's dead body and forced the little girl to watch. He stuffed panties down their throats."

With tears in her eyes, Letitia said, "Isn't that terrible?"

Uncle Roary wanted to stop but couldn't.

"He raped my mother too. He was your age when he did that." She was blubbering now. "Did you know that he was in the Ku Klux Klan, Letitia?"

"Oh yes, he told me that!" She brushed tears away with the heels of both hands. "He tells me everything—I'm his wife. That's what wives are for, to listen to their husbands. I wish we could have a child, but the warden won't let us. I'd like to have a son who looks like Michael Jackson and Jason Priestly and grows up to love Colson as much as you do. A son who'd come all the way to visit him in prison, like you do. Because he loves him so much."

JANET MALCOLM (*journalist*)[185] That conversation with Letitia Galvy, a.k.a. Mrs. Colson Jones, opened the door.

Orr resolved to confront his father the next time they met.

He was becoming irritated with him anyway. Jones sent letters nagging

---

185 From *Auteur-da-fé: The Strange Case of Roger Orr and Colson Jones*, pp. 188–191 (Princeton Press, 2003).

him to "put a hundred or two" in his canteen account. (Orr also learned that Jones convinced Letitia that once they got married she'd be legally compelled to turn over her monthly disability checks.) The asks got bigger, with an element of absurdism. He wanted Orr to bring in a private doctor to oversee his medical care. "You never know," he wrote, "when a man'll go full Richard Speck. Might want me some shiny new titties."[186] He began pressing Orr to hire an attorney "like Woody did for his dad" to get him back to the general population—and help lobby for conjugal visits, which were denied men on death row. "The mountain came to Mohhamed [*sic*] but it's high time for Mohhamed to come all over that big black mountain." Notes like that made Orr cringe. Jones threw in that he'd been working on something "with the secret help of Wild Bill," a screenplay that was "*Shawshank* meets *Gess* [*sic*] *Who's Coming to Dinner* all rolled together. I'll bet you win another Oscar and get me a pass to come out to L.A. for the big show."

His act was getting old.

* * * * * * * * *

ROGER ORR[187]

"I saw that movie you made, *Grace War*. The warden arranged for me to have a machine in the cell that could play it. I found it *very* interesting you had a character who was on death row. The Denzel character. Fine actor. Niggers make good actors, 'cause they're acting all their lives. Acting white. . . . Now, you didn't know about me at the time yet there you were, writing about this man—a colored man—on death row. You were writing about you, and you were writing about me, without even knowing it. Isn't that strange?"

"Yes. It's strange."

"Wild Bill said you even filmed it close by. Was that a coincidence? Or was that the hand of God?"

"What would you know about the hand of God?"

---

186 In 1988, the notorious serial killer Richard Speck was approved to have state-funded breast implants.—*ed.*

187 From *Roar of the Greasepaint: Roger Orr on Broadway* (2003).

"It's always guided me."

"How so?"

"God's hand moved me around the checkerboard. Moved me here, moved me there. Moved me to Leipers Fork where I met your mother . . . moved her to *me*. 'Cause everybody gets moved by God's hand, no way around it. Once you were created, you got moved around too. Then one day that hand moved you here, to GDCP. To see *me*. What I liked most in that movie was a story the monk told Denzel about the fellow who went crazy. The fellow who started cutting off people's fingers. That's a buddha story from a thousand years ago but reads like it was yesterday. Fellow was the teacher's pet but the teacher done him wrong and he went off his head. A sensitive fellow—like you. Starts ambushing people in the valley and slicing their fingers off. Made a necklace out of 'em, a real badass. His mama was gonna try talking sense into him, but he was finnin' to cut *her* finger off! *Badass*. The king was about to send an army to kill him; I don't think they'd have come out smelling like no roses. It'd take more than an army to kill that badass. That's when the cavalry shows up: the big kahuna himself, Mr. Siddhartha Buddha. And you know what? ('Course you do.) Mr. Big Fat Buddha turns out to be more of a badass than the fellow with the finger necklace! A real gangster. Hand of God, hand of Buddha, it's all the same. . . . The fat man saves the day. Stops him dead in his tracks, and that crazy bandit ceases his nefarious ways and becomes a saint—a protector of children. In your movie, when Denzel reads that story, it changes him. I think that's a little too neat, a little too easy, but I relate to it."

"You raped my mother when she was still a child."

"Bird was already fourteen."

"Don't use her name. Don't put her name in your mouth."

"If you say so."

"You were fifty years old when you strangled a little girl. You raped and strangled her, and when she was dead, you raped her again. Does that make you a protector of children?"

Jones smiled, as if he knew that was coming. "I was wondering when you'd get a spine. Good for you. You've been so . . . *soft*. That's the nigger in you. The slave. The faggot slave nigger from your mama's side. You *are* a fag, aren't you? I knew that from the moment we shook hands. Soft, like a lady's . . . tiny little fag-whore wrist. I'll bet you've had that whole arm up a booty, all the way to the elbow. Greased, locked and loaded. But I don't judge you, son. It's no shame to me that my son's queer and most definitely a nigger. Rich one, too! It's just nice to see you grow a dick. If it weren't for this mesh between us, we'd have us a little swordfight! I'd fuck that nigger bitchcunt you got, fuck it silly. But I'm glad you grew a pair of balls today. That's nice to see. Just remember—that thing that hangs between your legs belongs to *Colson Jones*. That's *mine*, you got that from *me*, and don't you forget it. That's Wriggleman cock. Wave it proud."

* * * * * * * * * *

EDDIE IZZARD He had that final, onerous confrontation with his dad—just what the doctor ordered!—and never returned to the state of Georgia. No, sorry—not true. The two of them did have one last encounter. . . . The point is, he finally freed himself from Colson Jones's web. But not *completely*. He continued with the hormones and little cosmetic procedures but wouldn't be able to commit to GRS [gender reassignment surgery] until "Wriggleman"'s dark shadow left the earth. The energy acquired from wrapping up those protracted *Jungle Book* road trips, combined with the decapitation of his father, allowed him to finish his novel in a six-month burst.

He turned it in to his publisher and waited for the response.

MELLIE KOCH We began to cast *Gigi*, his script about Hemingway's transgender son Gregory. Gregory had been more or less erased from the biographies—from the Hemingway *myth*—and Roar was going to restore his rightful place in the legacy. His life had so many uncanny parallels to Roar's: he was a prodigy, a drug addict, a wonderful writer who became a medical doctor. He'd been in all the same fancy nuthouses Roar had. As a boy, he dressed up in his mother's clothes and, toward the end of his life was in the middle of sex surgery. . . . Gregory's relationship with Papa—a violent, homophobic, domineering hunter—was a kind of mirror to Roar's relationship with his own father.

He'd been planning this film for decades, long before the business with

Colson Jones. The script was prescient, not just personally but culturally. In the end, if Roar had never met his biological father at all, it still would have gotten made. And been a great film. But I do believe those prison meetings in Georgia took it to a whole other level. They were the crucible—like Superman crushing coal in his hand, Roar made a diamond masterwork that will outlive us all.

CHAPTER SIXTEEN

Painted Red

DR. EUNICE LAVAR Let me give you a little background music on *Gigi*. Roger traveled in many circles, as we all know. But somehow he never really knew about Gregory Hemingway; virtually no one did, not even Papa's most avid readers. He *may* have known that Hemingway's youngest, gifted son was a twenty-four-karat mess. Gore and Tennessee *may* have told him that Gregory—also known as "Gloria" or "Giggy"— was a weekend cross-dresser. But that was morning coffee for Gore, and Roger didn't pay much attention. Gore's first cup of trash talk before the nine a.m. cabana boy blow job.

Long story short, I'm medicine in Montana. Town of Jordan. This is, what, '82, '83? I call up Roger and say, "Well, *here's* something that may interest you. There's a new sheriff in town: Dr. Gregory Hemingway just hung up his general practitioner shingle. After a busy workday, the physician enjoys ambling over to Esmeralda's to get drunk, said ambling done more often than not in a dress and strapless heels. Usually wears a little calico number, poorly cut, though it does show his curves."

Roger flew out forthwith!

JANIE LACOSTE (*bartender, Esmeralda's*) Gloria and Roar—I called 'em "Roaria"—were thick as thieves. No other way to describe those two. From the minute they clapped eyes on each other it was let the good times roll. They'd get drunk as skunks and buy out the ladies' section at Shabby Chic Mercantile. All the hosiery and frilly things and whatnot. Cheap costume jewelry that fell apart before they got back to the bar. In the morning, there'd be beads all over the sidewalk. I should tell you though that sometimes they came in wearing *suits*. That's when I called 'em the Brooks Brothers. Roar

337

would say, "How dare you call the McGuire Sisters that!" You never could tell what they were up to, and that was part of the fun.

If we weren't too busy, I kicked back and listened. Lord, it was a hoot. Couldn't understand half what they were saying—like a pair of secret-coding Navajo drag queens. The town folk here are very tolerant. You know, "Long as he's good at doctoring, we don't care much what the man does after office hours." 'Course, it helped that he was a Hemingway. And a *helluva* doc. Saved a few lives, I know that for a fact. But Roaria? They didn't just finish each other's sentences, they finished each other's freaking *thoughts*. And vulgar to beat the band! Roar would say—'cause Gloria'd had the surgery—"Show me that dirty old scalpeled cunt!" *Gregloria* shouted back, "It's cleaner than that shithole you *wish* was a cunt." You never heard such things coming out of a mouth. I banned 'em to the back room, but people followed them in because they were so entertaining. They were *too* entertaining.

I was glad Roar came on the scene though, because Dr. H was getting too hot to handle. I wouldn't serve him unless he turned in his car keys. Roar mellowed him out. Maybe "mellow" isn't the right word, but Gloria sure liked the companionship. They both did.

PAUL HENDRICKSON (*author, professor*)[188] I think Roar met his match. Gregory's father was more famous than Bird; he wrote like an angel[189]; was definitely a bigger drug addict; and had the audacity to go through with the gender surgery that Roar endlessly postponed out of fear. Belying his nickname, Roger still thought of himself as the Cowardly Lion in that regard. Gregory told him, "Stop being Jake Barnes and grow a pair like Lady Brett! It takes balls to have an orchiectomy, sweetie."

ALAN CUMMING When he was four years old, Gregory put on his mother's stockings—like Roar did with Bunny's. When he got older, he stole Martha Gellhorn's panties, which *Martha* thought was hysterical but made Papa absolutely furious. Later, he got arrested for boosting lingerie; then

---

188 From the author's new preface to *Hemingway's Boat: Everything He Loved in Life, and Lost, 1934–1961,* Paul Hendrickson, pp. iii–vii (Bodley Head, 2018).

189 Gregory was critically lauded for his book, *Papa: A Personal Memoir* (Scribner's 1976)—*ed.*

busted in the wrong bathroom of a movie theater for cross-dressing. Hey, not everyone can be Babe Paley.

His father set the mood for all that. He made his wives shave their heads and dress like boys. A real ass-fucker, Papa. Which in the end—no pun intended—is the mark of a real man.

GWYNETH PALTROW Roar told me once that he needed to get to San Francisco for more hormone injections. Gregory said, "I'll save you the plane fare." He had a stash of estrogen and gave him a shot in the butt, right at the bar at Esmeralda's. They used to joke about how they'd end up like the suicidal, drug-addicted gynecologists in *Dead Ringers*. You know, roaming around an apartment with their implants and surgical vajayjays, getting high and losing their minds.

PHILIP SEYMOUR HOFFMAN (*actor*) He reached out to me about playing Gregory in a film. I don't think he'd finished the script yet. He'd been working on it forever. Roar was just so. . . intrigued that Papa's macho-ism—anagram for masochism!—well, sort of—had this power to erase the proclivities of his favorite son—"mesmeric" was the word Roar used—that Papa's toxic masculinity could mesmerically erase the possibilities, the *reality* of Gregory's transsexualism. That intrigued him to no end. Intrigued me too! Because I'd *heard* the rumors about him having the surgery, and it was just too unbelievable to accept. Mass Mesmerism! Like those stories you read about people being abducted by UFOs. Ho-ho bullshit.

Gregory said he wanted to change sexes because it was the one and only place that embargoed his father—the undiscovered country that wouldn't stamp Papa's passport because of his lack of nerve. He seriously felt that gender change was the Big Safari Papa *really* wanted to go on, but was afraid to. . . . Roar thought that was a lie but liked the poetry of it—"'Isn't it pretty to think so,'" he said, like Jake Barnes would—but thought it too pat, too convenient. *I* liked it, personally, and used it for the movie. I think Papa dominated Giggy in a lot of the ways Colson Jones dominated Roar.

There's that beautiful scene in *Gigi* where Gregory sits down to write his memoir. Which he won the Pulitzer for, by the way. He's working at a stand-up desk like his father used to. On the typed page, there's a close-up of the title he's come up with: "Rising Son: My Life With Papa." He draws a line through "Rising Son" and replaces it with "Also Rises." Scratches out "Also Rises" and draws a line through "My Life." Then draws *another* line through "With"—until only "Papa" remains. Because that's what defined him. That was his higher power: his father. Makes me cry just thinking of it.

JULIANNE MOORE I remember watching Phil shoot that "scratching out" scene and how emotional he was. I used to love watching him, watching Phil's choices. I'd show up even when I wasn't working and always learn something. Everyone in Hemingway's life—like, *every single person*—wrote a memoir. It's like a Monty Python sketch! In another scene, Roar has Mary, Papa's widow, sitting down to write *hers*. She's in bed with a legal pad. The title she's written is "My Life With Papa." She crosses out "My" and replaces it with "A." So now it's "A Life With Papa." Then she crosses out "With" and crosses out "Papa," until just "A Life" is left. Then she scratches through all of it and tears up the pages. Because in the end, no one felt they'd had a life. Or a right to one, anyway.

MARIEL HEMINGWAY (*actress, daughter of Gregory's brother Jack*) Uncle Gregory respected Roar as an artist. He envied him—but that never got in the way of celebrating his new friend. Gregory was incredibly generous and unselfish with the people he loved and admired . . . Can you imagine what it would be like wanting to be a writer, knowing you had this amazing, natural gift to give to the world—and your father is Ernest Hemingway?

When Gregory was a boy, he won an award at school for a short story he plagiarized from Turgenev. It was quite the scandal when everyone found out. My grandfather never forgave him, but Roger told Gregory it was the greatest thing *ever*, there was a trickster genius to it as good as any story Turgenev could have written. . . . Adulation from Roar meant everything. Because of that, their relationship was a profound healing. And it was healing for Roar too, because in so many ways Gregory was a role model. I know that sounds a little crazy but it's true. He was the father my uncle never had—and the mother too!

PETER BOGDANOVICH Once he met Gregory, everything fell into place. Roar never mentioned the screenplay he'd spent years laboring over, because he knew he needed to scrap it and start fresh. Somewhat ironically, Gregory was the cure for writer's impotence. He said, "It became so clear to me that

Gregory was the big fish, not Papa; *Gregory* was the magnificent, impossible catch, and Papa was just a reef shark, nibbling away . . . So there I was, the old man wrestling with those two cunts. 'The Old Man and the C-Words.'"

When he finally informed him of his plan, Gregory was enthralled. Roar would to restore him as the hero of his own life—and the hero of his narcissistic father's life as well.

MARY V. DEARBORN (*biographer*)[190] One of Gregory's childhood names was Giggy, altered by his father, whose letters sometimes began and ended, "Dear Gigi . . . Love, Papa."

When Roger Orr told him that he was going to call the movie *Gigi*, Gregory had an alternate suggestion: *Moby Dickless*.

BEVERLY D'ANGELO The hormones gave Roger breasts—quite comely. The shots added weight to his hips, and his skin was smoother; the hair on his chest and back was gone. He loved showing me his body. Sometimes that led to a show and tell . . .

It was exciting. It was always exciting. We never lost that.

SCATTER HOLBROOK Did Roar and Giggy have an affair? Yes, because it was irresistible—I should say inevitable. They climbed the mountain because it was *there*. The mutual amorality was towering, but their libidos were a bit challenged, for a number of reasons. Gregory had to shoot something into his cock to get hard and they laughed about that. Roger said, "We switch off playing Auden and Robert Graves but the Golden Bough broke and the cradle's off its rocker." His biggest laugh was Gregory saying, "You've got the body of Shelley Winters with the tits of Shelley Duvall."

MELLIE KOCH Phil Hoffman had that special fierce vulnerability and emotional genius required for the role. Roar loved him in *Happiness*, but Phil wasn't yet the huge star *Gigi* would make him.

Makeup was key. The script was organized by flashbacks and Phil was Gregory's age—early thirties—at the time of Papa's suicide in '61. But the

---

190 *Ernest Hemingway: A Biography* by Mary V. Dearborn, pp. 414–423 (reprint edition, Vintage, 2001).

story was essentially told from the present, bringing Gregory to the end of the century when he was seventy years old. Roar was in touch with Dick Smith, who'd worked with us on *Hollow* and went on to do both *Godfathers* and everything else under the sun. The movie Roar was really thinking of was *Little Big Man*; if Dick could make Dustin [Hoffman] into a 120-year-old man, he could sure as hell make Phil look like a battle-worn, transsexual, drug-addicted retiree. Dick had just done *House on Haunted Hill* and decided he was going to concentrate on teaching but Roger talked him out of retirement. *Gigi* was his final screen credit.

DAVID UNGER Brando almost played Hemingway but bailed at the last minute. *Not* fun. Anthony Hopkins was Roar's next choice, so we got him on the phone. Which wasn't easy because Tony was somewhere in Wales and it took a little showbiz witchcraft to track him down. We had an ace up our sleeve because of Julianne Moore. She'd committed to be our Martha [Gellhorn] and Tony had just signed to do *Hannibal* the next year—with Julie. They were getting an ungodly amount of money for that. Before even reading the script, Tony called to talk to her about *Gigi*. Julie's heart is *always* going to be in the small, radical film—which *Gigi* was—especially if the director's a genius. When he asked about Phil Hoffman, she said, "We have *two* geniuses working on this film: Roar . . . and Phil. A third would be the charm." When Tony was still a bit hesitant, she said, "One for love, Hoppy, one for money."

His casting was controversial, because Hemingway was a sacrosanct American character. You know, What gives a "British" person the right? A tempest in a teapot, but the ruckus made Tony even more committed to doing the role. And he was perfect. He said it was as challenging—and satisfying—as playing Lear. Tony was exactly Hemingway's age when he died and gained sixty pounds for the role. Ridley wasn't too happy about that, but he managed to take the weight off before *Hannibal*.

Tony and Phil were extraordinary together. No one'd seen anything like it since Taylor and Burton in *Who's Afraid of Virginia Woolf*! I mean, one of the tortured love stories of our time.

MICHAEL CHAPMAN (*cinematographer*) *Gigi* was going to shoot in the summer of 1999 and wrap before Thanksgiving. We got permission from the Cuban government to film at the Finca Vigía in Havana and that was a very big deal. Roar gave the Cubans a dummy script because there was no way they would have allowed us to set foot in that house if they knew what we were up to. He gave the same script to the executor of the Hemingway estate because the family would have flipped out as well. Gregory was under strict orders from Roger to keep his mouth shut if any of the Hemingways started probing about the project; it wasn't a secret because the trades announced that Roar was finally doing his "Papa film." As far as I know, Gregory kept his word.

A lot of the shoot took place on a replica of Hemingway's boat, the *Pilar*. That went a little rougher than we'd have liked. We had to stop for a few days when Tony took a fishing hook to the cheek. Roger wrote a new scene where the same thing happens to Papa, for continuity.

MARGARET DRABBLE (*novelist*) Meanwhile, he was waiting for Knopf's response to *The Jungle Book* and began to smell something rotten. He was getting rather churlish about it. His editor was the legendary Robert Gottlieb, who'd worked with his old friends Joe Heller and Antonia Fraser. Bob was also Toni Morrison's editor—*and* Anthony Hopkins's! (Tony was working on a memoir.) The long delay became a source of embarrassment; Roger called it "indecent." He rang up his agent Andrew Wylie twice a day, but Bob wasn't returning Andrew's calls, either. And *no one* doesn't return Andrew's calls.

I had the chance to ask Bob about it years later. He said, "*I* was the one who was embarrassed. Because I just hated the book. Hated it."

ANDREW WYLIE (*literary agent*) It was puzzling. Because the novel was extraordinary. In my career, the only book I can compare it to—that feeling of something revolutionary—was Knausgård's *My Struggle*. Of course, they couldn't have been more different, but the feeling was the same.

STANLEY CROUCH (*critic, novelist*) The truth is, Roger was uncertain of what he'd made. Apart from his agent, only three people saw the manuscript before he gave it to Knopf—to my knowledge. He never sent it to *me*. [*laughs*] I was told that Roger was nervous about how I might judge it because I hadn't *loved* Toni Morrison's book [*Beloved*]. Which to my mind was silly and somewhat uncharacteristic of him to pigeonhole himself like that, and wrongly so. Because *The Jungle Book* is far superior to *Beloved*.

One of the few that read the manuscript was Ralph Ellison, who Roger met through Anatole Broyard in the early Seventies. Ralph came to one of shows they did at the Carlyle, and even went to the after-party in Harlem, at Ceeley's. I never got invited to *that*. [*laughs*] When Roger started to work in earnest on *The Jungle Book* in 1989, he sent pages to Ralph, whom he credited with giving him the courage to continue. Ralph was nearly eighty and would be dead in five years. After reading the novel's first ten chapters, he summoned Roar to his home in Washington Heights. You didn't just go to Ralph's place, you were *summoned*. [*laughs*] He confessed to Roger that he'd been struggling with a second book—it'd been almost forty years since *Invisible Man*. Now, everybody knew Ralph Ellison was the patron saint of writers' block. He told Roger, "*The Jungle Book* is the one I *wished* I could write but am simply unable to do so." It was kind and generous, and correct in its assessment—it *is* a book he wasn't able to write. No one else could, either! I mean, cut off Voltaire and Rabelais's head, sew Jimmy Baldwin and Saul Bellow's on there and it still won't get writ. That was a one-man band, playing for one night only. God was the audience.

And God saw what Roar made, and behold, it was good.

KAVA SANTANA We were doing some spring cleaning, and I came across a little box, one of those cheap lacquered ones you get in Chinatown. I opened it, and there were dead flowers. I showed it to Roger and he got this big grin on his face. "Ralph Ellison gave those to me." He said they were blue cornflowers. After Roger died, I was reading a biography of Ellison—I don't know why, just a way of randomly connecting with people who knew my husband. I still do stuff like that. You know, read stuff, or google people, google their names and Roger's just to see what comes up. I start reading this passage that said when Ellison was just a boy, he was visiting his father at the hospital before he died. And as he leaves, his dad gives him a blue cornflower for his lapel.

Oh, that killed me!

HILTON ALS (theater critic) Another engaged reader of the prepub *Jungle Book* was Claude Brown. They met through Tom Wolfe—strange bedfellows all. But the most unlikely coconspirator was Harold Bloom. Now in his early sixties, Bloom had long been the éminence grise of American lit criticism. It was somehow fitting that two of Roger's biggest champions were an iconic

Black novelist—a shoeshine boy who went to Tuskegee—and a notorious Jewish polymath who was a professor at both Harvard *and* Yale. I'm talking simultaneously.

* * * * * * * * *

HAROLD BLOOM[191]

Dear Mr. Orr,

It is with some irony I admit to being a member of the cabal that believes no unsolicited greeting should go unpunished. If I hear nothing back, my estimation of you may grow; though if it grew any more, I fear it would swallow the sun.

Ralph Ellison was a dear friend and couldn't contain his heart nor loyalty to the *daemon* when he stumbled across the Real Thing. For that reason, he had the temerity, over the years, to share pages of your magisterial *Jungle Book*. He ordered me to keep that under my hat, which I have until now, to its broken brim. I promised him I would take said confidence to the grave but didn't say *whose*.

So, the jungly torch song has been passed.

I presumptively send encouragement to carry on with your sacred, Blakean, Talmudic picaresque. If it remains incomplete, it shall have eternal life in the Heavenly Canon. Until then, or never, I remain

Your heedless, heartfelt, humbled reader,

Harold Bloom

* * * * * * * * *

SAM WASSON In his more paranoid moments, he thought Bloom was "a grouper-mouthed satyr" putting the make on him; and that Ellison had been

---

191 From the Harold Bloom/Charles Eliot Norton Archive at Harvard.

senile all along, projecting his own grandiose fantasies of the novel he could never finish onto *The Jungle Book*. But it didn't really matter because in better moments—there were a lot of them—Bloom's avalanche of recondite mash notes, telegrams and late-night phone calls were the wind he needed in his sails. It gave Roar the energy to go back and alter things in the book that were bothering him.

For example, the first draft had Zachariah raising money to pay for his adoptive mother's medical treatments. He changed all that. She doesn't get cancer. Instead, she decides to retire as a schoolteacher and become a hospice worker, a spiritual vocation that ties her to the child she and her husband lost—the death that inspired them to adopt Zachariah in the first place. In a comic twist of fate, the hospice "school" won't accept the woman because she doesn't have a healthcare background. (Roar's acid commentary on the "business" of compassion.) She becomes deeply depressed and takes to her bed. It's Zachariah's "Big Idea" to make money impersonating the famous Ishmael Beah then give a large donation to the hospice school, thus forcing them to accept her as a trainee.

* * * * * * * * *

ROBERT GOTTLIEB[192]

Roger,

First, my apologies for the delay. There really is no excuse; I've had my secretary scour the office for one but alas it can't be found.

Secondly, I read *TJB* ms with great, enraged interest.[193] There is much gold here. Let's find time to explore. Champagne, helmets, pickaxes, and shiny (if used) Wellies await.

Bob

---

192 Estate of Roger Orr—*ed.*

193 When Andrew Wylie asked Gottlieb what he meant by "enraged interest," the publisher said it was a typo: he'd meant to say "engaged." This explanation further "engaged" Orr.—*ed.*

* * * * * * * * *

SUSAN KAMIL (*editor*) It was the forced whimsicality of Bob's note—the glib disrespect and implicit rejection—that made Roger apoplectic. His worst fears were realized: a lukewarm (translation: terrible) response from one of the premier book editors of the age. But Roger's shame and anxiety emboldened him. He had Andrew Wylie tell Bob to pull the book unless Knopf agreed to get it into galleys by Christmas, a month after *Gigi* wrapped.

Bob blinked.

It was a business decision. If he let the novel go and the sales did even reasonably well at another house—if the book were a succès d'estime, at the very least—it'd be a black eye for Knopf. If Knopf took on *The Jungle Book* and it flopped, it would be an acceptable loss; they couldn't be blamed for endorsing the literary misfire of a protean national treasure.

He told Andrew he'd commit to twenty thousand copies for a release in the summer of 2000 and it was done.

KAVA SANTANA Roar threw himself into *Gigi*, a good thing because the whole Gottlieb standoff was tearing him apart . . . The studio lawyers told him there would likely be defamation issues with the script, even though Roger bought Gregory's life rights for an exorbitant sum—not issues with Gregory, but everyone else. None of the stuff with Papa was a problem because he was dead. But the *living* were a different story. Roar had to shell out his own money for an additional insurance policy.

Gregory came to the set for the first few weeks and was happy as a dog with two tails. I was designated his chaperone and all-around "minder." He was a pleasure to be around. Very respectful, very grateful, just a delight. And he was sober—if he wasn't, you would never have known. Tony and Julianne adored him. He thought Julie just *became* Martha Gellhorn. (Of course she did.) They'd be in her trailer during lunch, giggling their asses off, comparing nail polish and trying on different outfits. He got along great with Phil but never could look him in the eye. It was a little strange. Phil said he tried to make a bridge, but "the pontoons were leaking." Not so sure what that meant! Then something happened when Phil shot the karaoke scene.

JULIANNE MOORE Phil was in full makeup. Total Kabuki. Roger was *obsessed* with Kabuki. Actually, it was a mix of Kabuki Theater and Peking Opera . . . Phil looked every ruined inch of the seventy-year-old "Gigi"— while the *real* Gigi watched aghast from behind the director's chair.

Playback starts and Phil begins singing. That *other* Phil song, "Against All Odds." He's got this . . . black bra underneath a torn, cheap dress—[*sings*] "Take a look at me now!"—and these scuffed, electric blue platform heels that Roar said he saw on a woman in London who'd been hit by a car and was laying in the street—[*sings*] "and you coming back to me is against all odds, it's the chance I have to take." It's funny at the start—weird and goofy and clownish and maca-bre—but so outrageous you have to laugh. Then *verrrrry* slowly, it becomes one of the most tragic, nuanced performances, *I* think, in movie history. I look over, barely moving my head, and Gregory's face is this . . . mask of utter horror, and—I don't know how else to describe it. Human, too human . . . but not human at all. Like Phil was singing to the ghosts of his parents—Papa and Pauline—and you could not look away. Did you know what Papa said to Gregory? What he always told him? That he'd killed his mother because of his "corrupted" ways? That's what he would say, that Gregory dressing up in women's clothes was directly responsible for her death. So monstrous, that man! And there he is—there *they* are—singing, *Take a good look at me now*—"I'll still be standing here"—look! Look what you made me into, this . . . *ogre*. This *deformity* who will always be waiting, waiting for you—waiting for you *to love me*. [sings] "And you coming back to me is against all odds—it's the chance I gotta take". . . because Gregory always said that as much as he hated his father, he loved him. To death . . .

I just shiver thinking about it.

And knowing what Philip was waiting for—what was waiting for *him*—that Philip was going to die—makes everything so much worse.

DAVID UNGER The karaoke scene marked the end of his movie visitation rights. Gregory started openly drinking and became disruptive. Roar was sweet—he invented a story that the actors were so in awe of him, and so wanted to please him, that their performances were suffering and it was bet-ter he went back to New York. It really depressed Phil when Gregory left. As an actor, it was such a gift to have him on set, "on tap," to observe and connect with. Like a constant workshop. But I think everyone understood there was a cruelty in having him there too. You know, it's all fun and games until some-one loses an eye. Or a wig. [*laughs*] I'm sorry, that was mean.

ALI BERK I played Valerie Danby-Smith, the wife in Gregory's longest marriage. It was a really good part. I'd just worked with Miloš on *Man In the Moon* and was so happy to go from Uncle Miloš to Uncle Roary. I subscribed to the whole Coppola thing—movies as a family enterprise. A family love fest. It was so amazing to work with Tony and Julie . . . and Phil, of course. I'd just gotten engaged to my agent [David Unger] and Roar was the only person I told outside of Mom and Dad. We were keeping it quiet for all kinds of reasons. David was the sweetest, most debonair, the *smartest* man I'd ever met—aside from Roar!—and wanted to protect what was still so new. He didn't want anyone overthinking it when he suggested me for a part. So that's how we were going to deal with it until we got married. You know, everyone always wants to give you shit for falling in love with your agent. Carrie Fisher married her agent and told me, "Get ready for the worst jokes of all time." Boy, was she right. People would literally say, "You don't have to love him all the way, he'll be happy with ten percent." I heard that a hundred times and they'd say it like it was the wittiest thing anyone ever heard. Anyway, Roar knew David's father, Anthony, because he produced *Philip Phaethon*. Roar loved David.

And then I did a very bad thing.

A *horrible* thing.

I'm only going to tell you because David said I could.

I had an absolutely huge crush on Philip. He was single. And a few months after all this, he met his beautiful soulmate, the amazing costume designer Mimi O'Donnell. . . . About a week into *Gigi*, I wake up one morning and think, *Oh shit! I'm pregnant.* I get one of the P.A.s to sneak out and get me a test. And it's positive. Right? Now, Philip and I have been flirting for *days*, and my hormones kick into a whole new level. I'm fantasizing about him nonstop. I'm on the phone with David in L.A.—fantasizing about Philip! A *nightmare*. But it's a runaway train. And one day it just . . . happens. We were alone in his trailer and finished shooting for the day. I can't believe I'm telling you this! I mean, I knew I was going to, but . . . and it only happened *once*, Bruce—that's the absolute truth! I felt so awful *afterward* that I ended up telling Philip *everything*. That not only am I engaged but I'm pregnant! He was so compassionate. Such a gentleman. He didn't get fully dressed but was covering himself up . . . like a modesty blanket. He said it's not the end of the world, that he was sorry, and it was a one-time deal. You know, like, *We're good. Trust me, we're good.* He totally meant it. "Think of it as your bachelorette party." He was reminding me that people are complicated and on the scale of things it was a pretty cool thing. I mean, of course he was trying to minimize. . . but there's always a part of a girl that gets worried and thinks *What if he has feelings for me?* Whether or not he did—I still like to think he did!—Philip was letting me know that it wouldn't become a problem. Because if he *did* have feelings, it might *become* a problem, for one of us or for *both*. You know how *that* can go. I think he said something like, "You acted like a guy, big deal. I don't mean that to be sexist because guys act like girls too." That's when we noticed what he'd been holding over his middle part for the *whole conversation*—one of Gregory's dresses! We became completely hysterical. Before I left, he said, "What happens on set stays on set." I went back to my own trailer and called Beverly first, then Mom. The first thing both did when I told them was laugh!

Oh my God, I *hated* telling you this, Bruce! And I hate you for making me! (*nervous laughter*)

MIMI O'DONNELL (*widow of Philip Seymour Hoffman*) I love Ali. She told me that story years later. I don't know if I would have thought it was so funny if Phil and I had already met! But the *way* she told it was outta control. She said she was worried Phil's sperm would bully its way in and "all that'd be left of David was his ten percent."

She's just one of the funniest people I know.

ALI BERK I waited a few years after we were married to tell him. I seriously thought, "If David wants a divorce, we'll have had a few good years. And I got our beautiful twins out of it." I was so scared and nervous that my hair started falling out. I totally got rosacea. I probably should have kept my mouth shut but I had to tell him—mostly because other people knew. Even if it was only Mom and Bev, I *hated* David not knowing. Sigh . . . I yam who I yam. He listened to the spiel, very agent-like. You know, assessing damage, how to spin what he was hearing, spin it for *himself.* That sort of thing.

It was an awkward few weeks.

Then one night he said, "I've been thinking . . . let's consider Phil your hall pass. But I haven't used *mine* yet." "Deal." I didn't ask who he had in mind. I didn't want to know! I have a feeling he's used a *few* hall passes since. He says he hasn't, but—you know agents.

KAVA SANTANA Hendrix was nine years old, and Roar wanted him to play Gregory in some of the flashbacks. Hendy looked a lot like Greg when he was a boy. He was a natural. Moon was with us—her first time on a movie set. They were the cutest. They took lessons with the teacher between scenes.

I had a shit-ton of anxiety because Chickweed was being released from prison at Christmastime. Ho ho ho. She blew through so much money before the arrest that we had to sell the commune land to cover her debt. She even found a way to eat into Moon's trust—such a betrayal. She stole from me directly as well. A brooch that belonged to Bunny went missing from the ranch house, and Snoop Raskin learned that Roy Mars pawned it for $10,000. It was probably worth fifty times that. Somehow Mars never got busted. What's that saying—God favors drunks, children, and scumbag repeat offenders. Snoop said it was because he was an FBI informant in the middle of testifying against AB guys in a murder. Aryan Brotherhood. They didn't want the case to fall apart.

SUZE BERKOWITZ Kava talked to lawyers about adopting Moon, but they said it would be tough, even with Chickweed being an ex-convict and all. Kava was super depressed. She couldn't sleep or hold down food. A zombie barf machine. She had major guilt about having let that wolf get so deep into the chicken house. She felt responsible for the shit that went down. And hated herself for loving that wolf, for loving to be fucked by that wolf. She whined about it to Roger, and he'd say, "Welcome to the dark side of the hood, Red Riding."

JULIANNE MOORE They shot the bullfight in Nogales; it stood in for Pamplona. There's a scene where everyone's drunk and Papa campaigns for Gigi to be the *sobrasiente*. That's a great honor—Gregory explained it to me. *Sobrasientes* are aficionados, volunteers who kill the bull if the matador gets wounded. I don't really know how it works, but it's a pretty big deal to be a *sobrasiente*, a big honor, and not just anyone off the street can do it. There's this training required—Gigi's clueless—so they have to bypass all that and sneak him in. The matador allows it because he loves Papa so much. And Gigi winds up having an appendicitis attack, right in the ring! So, he's useless when the matador gets gored, a fiasco that nearly ends with Gigi *and* the matador dying. Gigi's girlfriend misses the fight but hears that he's in the hospital and assumes he was wounded during an act of bravery. No one tells her about the appendicitis.

She goes to the hospital and weeps by her lover's bed. She can barely speak English and asks to see where he got "bored." It's a total comic scene, but Roar repeats it later in the movie, in a dream sequence, after Giggy has the surgery to remove his penis.

* * * * * * * * *

from the *Gigi* screenplay
[dream sequence]

>   GERTA
> Today I could not come—then I hear *mi*
> *sobrasiente* he was bored. I am so sorry
> your stomach is bored!

>   GIGGY
> It's not so bad.

>   GERTA
> *Mi héroe*! But there is pains for you?

>   GIGGY
> No pains, no gains. It's just a scratch.

>   GERTA
> May I see the scares? Where the bull was
> attacked?

Giggy lowers the sheet and untapes the bandage to reveal the stitches from his phallectomy; the penis is gone. Gerta recoils in horror.

>   GERTA
> But where is your *pene*!

>   GIGGY
> Chola? You've just asked the 64,000-peseta
> question.

* * * * * * * * *

ELVIS MITCHELL (*film critic*) The most outrageously beautiful scene, and most controversial, is the death of Papa. All through the movie—the flashbacks when Gregory was a young boy, the arrests for cross-dressing, the scenes where he sits in bars as "Gloria" (he calls that particular incarnation "Gloria in excelsis deo")—all through the movie there's a theme of bright red lipstick, bright red nail polish. Bright, blood red. Even in the *sobrasiente* scene, when they ritualistically dress him for his entrance to the ring, they have Gigi in those shocking red panties. It's explained that *sobrasientes* need to wear special sterile "panties" to minimize the chance of infection if the fabric should enter a wound. Roar told David Cronenberg that their redness was an homage to the stylized red surgical gowns the twin brothers wore in *Dead Ringers*.

Now, in real life, Gregory wasn't there when his father killed himself. But Roar *puts* him there and that's poetic justice. Roar made the moment into a Grand Guignol, a danse macabre. From his room, Gigi hears the clap of the gunshot and comes bolting down the stairs to see Papa with the rifle between his legs . . .

* * * * * * * * *

from *Gigi* screenplay
[stage directions]

Papa's back is propped against the wall, gun resting between his knees. His skull is blown off at the nose; all that's left is a shiny red shelf. Giggy yelps then slips, falling on his hands and knees, FACEDOWN in the gore. He slowly gets into a sitting position and rests against the banister, stunned.

PUSH IN on Giggy's lips and fingertips, painted a perfect lipstick red by his father's blood.

Mary appears and screams at the top of her lungs at the tableau. The screaming doesn't stop.

* * * * * * * * * *

MERV GRIFFIN (*talk show host, entrepreneur*) I'm a San Mateo boy, and Bunny heard me sing on a radio show called *Sketchbook*. Gee, that was 1944. I wasn't even twenty years old. She rang up the station manager and said, "Hey, I'd like that kid to sing at a party I'm having Saturday night." I show up at Parnassus—I think I've got the wrong address, it looked like an embassy!— and there I am, singing for Doris Duke and Charlie Chaplin. I thought, Who sold me a ticket to Paradise? I was a hundred pounds overweight and Bunny helped me lose all that. I called it "the Starstruck Diet" because I didn't want to be a fatso in front of all those legends.

I had a different path than Bird Rabineau, which might just be the understatement of all time. I ran with Freddy Martin and Doris Day; Bird ran with Artie Shaw and Billie Holiday. I worshipped the ground she sang on. Starting in the Sixties, Bird was a fixture on my television show over the years. Through thick and thin—there was a lot of thin—she always knew I saved a seat for her. She was and still *is* the grandest of ladies. So, when she got in touch about her idea for "a little daytime show with my friend Cicely," I was tickled pink. She wanted to call it *Ladies Talk the Blues*, which I thought witty and lovely but the network felt would be confusing. We went with the reliably dull *The Bird & Cicely Show* instead. An hour of chitchat, cooking and musical guests. Cicely couldn't be on all the time because she was busy with her movie career, so Bird's old friend Nathan Lane filled in. He was a wonderful sidekick. In one *week*, she had Whitney, Janet Jackson, Queen Latifah, Whoopi, Jada Pinkett, and Lauryn Hill. Dick Gregory and Tyler Perry dropped by . . . Denzel, Quincy, Richard [Pryor].

Bird had a ball, but you could see it was taking its toll. She was in good shape for seventy-six, but it was a lot for an old broad.

MELLIE KOCH We were in Idaho, with just a few days left of shooting on *Gigi*. I saw the first AD say something to Roger, who goes ashen. Bird had collapsed on the set of that show she did with Cicely. She was at Hollywood Presbyterian, but they wouldn't tell us anything on the phone.

Roar chartered a plane.

KAVA SANTANA That was a tough flight. One of the things that goes through your head, the most obvious, is that she died and they didn't want to tell him over the phone. Like, you know, their policy. We get to the hospital and the press is already there, all kinds of trucks and news vans. The paparazzi see us and go insane. We're all having a *bad*, bad feeling.

A guard brings us straight to the ICU. We step off the elevator and hear laughter—Bird's! It was just like the scene we shot a few days before, when Gregory gets word on his Tanganyikan game reserve that Papa died in a plane crash in Entebbe. He gets to the hospital and immediately hears uproarious laughter down the hall. Papa's bullshitting with his cronies in the ICU—when he sees Gregory, he gleefully holds up a newspaper headline, HEMINGWAY, WIFE, KILLED IN AIR CRASH.

In Bird's case, it was cholecystitis—gallstones.

The first thing she said was, "I cheated life again." She didn't say death, she said life.

ALI BERK The trip back to Ketchum was a lot different than the trip to Hollywood Pres. There was jubilation. It was a mile-high party.

Before we left L.A., Joe Heller called to say that Roary was getting a Kennedy Center Honor next year. My uncle wanted to know who else was on the list—I think it was Placido Domingo, Baryshnikov, and Liz Taylor, can't remember the rest. That's when Quincy jumped on; he and Joe were together! Just hangin'. The interesting part was, they wanted to give it to Roary *and* Bird. Something like that had never happened, you know, giving the Kennedy to a parent and child. They'd given it to couples—Paul Newman and Joanne Woodward, Hume Cronyn and Jessica Tandy—but never to a mother and son. Q said the list had like a dozen people on it because it was a year away "and there's always a die-off. Some of these folks are mutherfuckin' *old*." Haha! Quincy's hilarious, but he was being serious. And what most people don't know is that the honorees are chosen only by *past* honorees. Which was a lucky thing for Roary, because he knew a lot of those people personally: Lenny, Jerome Robbins, Harold Prince . . . Sinatra, Sondheim, Edward Albee. Not that my uncle needed luck—his achievements spoke for themselves. And not that he gave a shit either. He never really cared too much about awards.

But anytime they wanted to honor his mom, he was thrilled.

SUZE BERKOWITZ After wrapping a film, coming to see us became the ritual. Bird loved Hawaii, and, besides, it was Thanksgiving. The big news was that Ali and David were getting married next summer on the mainland but wanted to have a "secret ceremony" in Maui, over Christmas. Just for family. So, everyone came for a month. Kava was getting crazy, because Chickweed was almost out of jail. She knew she would have to let Moon go and felt like she was handing a lamb to the slaughter. Not too far from the truth.

Beverly showed up and we had some serious all-girl slumber parties. Bev thought *she* had scandalous stories—she did!—but Bird put her to shame. Some of the things that woman told us . . . I mean, they'd arrest you for just listening.

SCATTER HOLBROOK I had some heart-to-hearts with Roger. He was in a strange, sour mood, a very dark place. He gets that way when he finishes a project. I think that's common with most artists. But it was a double whammy because he'd finished *two* projects: a book and a film. I don't think the hormones had anything to do with any of it. I really don't.

He said *The Jungle Book* had "a rogues' gallery" of supporters, but the publisher wasn't behind it. Which was equivalent to a studio dumping a film. He was depressed but seemed resigned to the hand he'd been dealt. He quoted Hemingway: "You know what makes a good loser? Practice." And regarding *Gigi*, he confided that it wasn't finished, at least not to his satisfaction. He was unhappy with the ending; according to Roger, it didn't *have* an ending. All it had was "a rip-off of *Godfather 2*"—with Gigi in full drag, sitting on a bench like Pacino as the leaves skitter, reflecting on the weirdness of his life. I don't think it was literally that but whatever it was, from the way he talked, the movie was in deep shit. He'd wake up in the morning and be up to his eyeballs.

BEVERLY D'ANGELO He wished Gregory would die. I know how awful that sounds. But he was a slave to Story, a slave to Myth—a mercenary artist—and knew Gregory's death would push the narrative into a transcendent place. He *identified* with that perverse desire because part of Roar wanted to die too.

He talked a lot about *In Cold Blood*. That was how he tiptoed around his feelings. About how Truman *needed* the killers to die in order to finish his book. . . . and Truman's anguish because he didn't know how long it would take for them to be executed. He'd say, "Tru could wait them out—but I've got a release date." He flirted with pulling the film and finishing it "postmortem." "I don't care if he goes tomorrow or twenty years from now." Morally, he knew that was completely bankrupt, it was bad faith on *so* many levels.... He paced and literally wrung his hands. He felt debauched, satanic, ashamed—the implosive self-hatred and paralysis of the impotent. His body was the perfect metaphor. He wasn't one thing and he wasn't the other; he couldn't decide *what* to be. He was just a sexless vulture now, admitting he'd failed on an epic level because not even Gregory's death guaranteed a film he'd be proud of.

The deaths of Perry Smith and Dick Hickock became an "answered prayer" that haunted Truman. But the man I loved was *never* haunted by answered prayers—only unanswered ones.

His art and his life depended on that.

ANDREW JARECKI (*filmmaker*) At his lowest moment, he said of *Gigi*, "I wanted to make *Parsifal* but made a TV movie instead."

ALI BERK That first week of December in Maui was the calm before the storm. It was like the water receded way out, beaching the fishes and uncovering all the rocks and shells you never see.

That's what happens before a tsunami hits.

SUZE BERKOWITZ First, Valerie called to say that Joe [Heller] died. He had a heart attack at home in East Hampton. Roger and Kava wanted to fly out to New York, at least for a few days, but Val forbid it. I don't think their hearts were really into it; something was telling them to stay close to the hearth. Valerie did them a great kindness.

KAVA SANTANA To makes things worse, a few weeks before Joe died, Roger took the plunge and finally told Andrew Wylie to send along a copy of *The Jungle Book*. Valerie said it was on Joe's nightstand and he'd "been so enjoying it." Roger thought that was a terrible omen. Yet another!

SCATTER HOLBROOK The next thing that happened—there were lots of next things!—it was a *month* of next things—"Thing Next" was the car crash. Richie Raskin called to say that Roy Mars picked Chickweed up at Florence McClure, the old Southern Nevada Women's Correctional Facility. She'd been transferred there a year into her sentence, don't ask. Ask Richie Raskin. And by the way, Florence McClure has a death row for the *ladies*, if you can believe it. I know I couldn't. Mars picks her up and takes her to see Rodney Dangerfield's show at the Sands. Because hey, who *wouldn't* want to see Rodney after a stretch in the clink? Pia Zadora was opening for Rodney—that sticks in my head because at the time Pia was married to a guy I used to know, a film director and one-hit former wunderkind named Jonathan Kaufer. After the show, on their way to L.A., Roy and Chickweed got T-boned by a drunk; for once, those two had nothing to do with their misfortune. They were on the 95, north of Needles, the same place Sam Kinison was killed by a DUI. Kinison was with his old lady, too, but she lived; the kid who slammed into Sam got a year's probation, and the guy who took out Roy and Chickweed got the same—though he should have been given a medal. The funny thing is, Jonathan Kaufer fell asleep at the wheel on his way back to L.A. from Vegas. I think he was visiting the little girl he had with Pia. Got ejected from the vehicle and died. They say it was instant but they always used to say that. Everything's on video now, so you can usually tell. Just click on YouTube and when you see a car on fire in an intersection, listen for the screams.

I stopped driving to Vegas a long time ago. Well, duh.

ALI BERK When we heard the news, one of the nannies grabbed Hendrix and Moon and hustled them off to the guesthouse. There was a family huddle. What to be done? Do we tell Moon? We *had* to, but . . . how? *When?* She hadn't seen her mom in years, because Chickweed didn't want to be "humiliated" by Moon visiting her in jail. Said she didn't want to "scar" the kid, which none of us really understood. Like she already wasn't scarred enough by having a psycho for a mom? How do you not see your baby girl. . . . It was just indicative of the weird sea change Chickweed underwent. Some of it no doubt was the Rasputin-like influence of Roy Mars. He didn't like kids at *all, especially* Moon. Apparently, he had this plan that he and Chickweed would travel the world. How does the song go? "Two grifters off to see the world, there's such a lot of world to see . . ." [*laughs*] I just realized that's from *Moon* River, oh my God! Anyway, dragging a kid along didn't fit the *plan*. And Chickweed swallowed it whole, like some cultist. That's *exactly* what it reminds me of now. That woman—Lori Vallow? The one who looks like Chelsea Handler? Her husband was a "prophet," said her children were dark spirits, and the cops found them buried in the backyard. That's just what would have happened to Moon—she'd be buried somewhere on the commune. Only it was way too big a place to dig up.

SCATTER HOLBROOK Kava wanted to fly back with Moon and make the funeral arrangements but Roar said, "Go! Just don't drag Moon into your necrophiliac soap opera. She can do her grieving from *here*." He was pissed, because he sensed that Kava was still perversely attached to her old lover. He kind of showed his jealousy hand, and that was rare.

SUZE BERKOWITZ Ali wanted to cancel the wedding but Roar wouldn't hear of it. It wasn't his decision to make, but Ali was usually pretty swayed by her uncle's wishes. . . . David was very much the agent-gentleman and hung back. Bird said, "Life goes on. You've got new life inside you—that's a thing to celebrate." She was definitely starting to show. Roar came up with another nice save: to announce to Moon on the wedding day that he and Kava had legally adopted her. It wouldn't be technically true but the lawyers already assured them it was imminent. Judges *love* fast-tracking that shit. The kiddie court loves a happy ending.

DAVID UNGER We got married on Christmas Day. It was lovely. I think by then Moon had been told her mom was in a bad car accident that wasn't her fault—I'm not sure who gave her the news. Probably Kava because she felt it was her responsibility. She was nine years old, and didn't really process what happened. She still ran around with Hendrix, laughing and being a kid. I can't remember her crying, but she may have done that in the privacy of her room. Kava was worried about her not having a bigger reaction. She got on the phone with Roar's shrink, who said that was totally normal, to just give it time and let the girl do her thing.

Then, on New Year's Eve—my birthday!—Roger gets a call that his father died, of a heart attack. At that point, everyone . . . I mean, after the initial shock of hearing it, we all just—*laughed*. I know that sounds weird, but everything was so surreal. It was cathartic to laugh. And I think actually the healthiest response, because what else could you do?

KAVA SANTANA Roger had a primal impulse to honor the man who brought him into the world. A very Buddhist thing to do, because that would *not* have been my response. I remember he went to the terrace overlooking the ocean and lit about a hundred candles for Colson Jones. He was going to be buried in the prison cemetery on New Year's Day, and Roar called the warden to say he was coming.

We were done with our Maui "chores" and he thought it was a kickass way to begin 2000.

BEVERLY D'ANGELO I think going back to Georgia was the closure he needed. In a way, it was a trade-off for Gregory *not* dying. Sorry to keep hitting that. It makes Roar sound evil. In any event, it stopped him from torturing himself over *Gigi*. He'd convinced himself it was a catastrophe and any break from obsessing was welcome.

WOODY HARRELSON He told me "Wild Bill" gave him a tour before he went out to the graveyard, alone. Showed him the electric chair—the old, nonworking one that's on display somewhere else in the building. The warden said they used to give folks $15 to flip the switch and there'd be a line of volunteers a block long. The chosen switch-flipper watched while a handful of runners-up threw saltwater on the prisoner, so he'd have more of a charge.

CICELY TYSON Usually when he went to see his father, he'd go visit the Hildstroms—Tamara and Jubilee. But he kept to himself this trip. Those graves don't have names on them, only numbers. A grave is cold but a grave without a name? That's a freezing thing.

HIRAM WHIDDLE (*groundskeeper*) There weren't no ceremony. We don't have those here, Warden won't allow it. The state tried to make him but Warden wouldn't have it. State don't rule this place. Nobody does. It's a sacred ground but the lives it cost for these folk to end up here are sacred too. The people here can have their ceremonies elsewhere. We just don't do it. We put a black ribbon round the cross, that's enough. Keep it there till it falls away. Got one that stayed three years. Unusual.

The wife was there—"Mrs. Colson Jones" I guess is what you'd call her. That's an unholy union. That's against God. That big black, crying thing looked like a mountain with the shakes. She weren't no trouble though. She was all the way on the other side of the cemetery when the movie director was here. He might have seen her but kept his distance. Didn't look her way at all. I think she must have been confused. She was none too bright. I told her where Jones is, I said, *Over there*, where that *man* just come from. But she just stayed there crying at the wrong grave.

JULIANNE MOORE His father gave him a great parting gift. Roar felt something lift off of him. Standing at that unmarked grave, he realized for the first time it was Colson Jones who'd been holding him back. He needed that man to die in order to make good on an old unresolved New Year's resolution: To become a woman, once and for all.

LADDIE CAVANAUGH SOTTER (*biographer*)[194] He decided to take the train to New York but wouldn't be traveling that far just yet. First, he went to Florida. Phil Hoffman alerted him that Gregory had been arrested in Miami for indecent exposure and resisting arrest and was being held in a Women's Detention Center in Dade County.

"Gloria" died before Roar got there to bail her out.

She was sixty-nine years old.

In the booking photo, she grins at the camera with loony, defiant cheerfulness. Beneath an open blouse is a deflated breast—the implant removed months prior, due to infection. A medical exam logged a prolapsed vagina and scores of tracks from years of injecting opiates. *The Sun* printed a full, leaked transcript of the pathologist's dictation. This being Florida, the doctor, appraising the body before beginning the autopsy, remarked, "Hooey! This gal's been through a helluva bullfight."

The director returned to New York to ensure Gregory's place in the pantheon of immortals. The *sobrasiente* makes a pact to kill the bull if the matador is gored and Orr would do just that. He shot several new scenes that defiantly altered the destiny of the Old Man's big catch, whose transfigured body, lashed beside the broken-masted skiff, would remain forever whole, impervious to the elements, time, sharks—and Papa.

---

194 *Also Rises: The Victory of Gregory Hemingway* by Laddie Cavanaugh Sotter, pp. 419–426 (Leviathan, 2004).

* * * * * * * * * *

from the *Gigi* screenplay

INT. HOSPITAL. MORGUE—DAY

Giggy (69) lies on a metal gurney as a pathologist dictates into a small tape recorder.

>   PATHOLOGIST
>   "The ears, nose and mouth have no
>   abnormalities. The earlobes are pierced
>   one time each. There is slight female
>   breast development, with the left breast
>   larger than the right. The external
>   genitalia are phenotypically female with
>   labia, urethra, and vagina . . ."

Another doctor ENTERS.

>   DOCTOR
>   That the Hemingway gal?

>   PATHOLOGIST
>   Yup. Meet Ernestine.

>   DOCTOR
>   (scrutinizes the chest)
>   Lose an implant?

>   PATHOLOGIST
>   Had it removed a few years ago, I'm told.

>   DOCTOR
>   That's coyote ugly. Better be sure it's
>   not Ernestine Borgnine.

>   PATHOLOGIST
>   Have some respect, she was a doctor.

                    DOCTOR
Dr. Frankenstein maybe. And "she" my ass.

                  PATHOLOGIST
Mind if I get back to this? I want to
try and get out of here eventually.

                    DOCTOR
Knock yourself out.

The doctor EXITS and the pathologist continues
dictation.

                  PATHOLOGIST
" . . . the extremities are symmetric;
joints are not deformed. All digits are
present. The fingernails are long and
painted blood red. The toenails are
thick and painted blood red . . ."

BLACKOUT.

BOOK FIVE

Bye Bye Blackbird
2000–2018

CHAPTER SEVENTEEN

Smuggler's Cove

SAM WASSON With all that death behind him, he was on fire. He wrote new scenes for *Gigi*, but the studio balked. They thought the movie worked the way it was, one of the worst business decisions ever, because it ended up grossing more than its awards competitor, *American Beauty*—and was a *real* art film, not a fake one. Roar spent $500,000 of his own money and never did another movie for Fox again.

JAMES WOLCOTT (*critic*) Knowing what we know now about Gregory "Gloria" Hemingway's lurid death, the final psychedelic scene of his bloated, transfigured body lashed to the boat, like a predator-repellant—Papa dead on deck as if having slipped on his own Big Bwana peel, exhausted and luminous from the epic struggle of reeling in his mascara'd, errant, errand-boy son—the film would have capsized in the hands of a less *haute* auteur. It's the overblown, porn-comedic iceberg to sink all titanic directorial egos. But Orr is no hack: he's proven himself as the celestial marlin-fucker of all time, and the devil and angels get their due. Hopkins's Papa Lecter is reduced to tenderized animus in the end, and Philip Seymour Hoffman, with his bright red she-man's mani-pedi, becomes Saint Gregory, patron saint of torn breasts, cheap dresses, failed gender surgeries, and sacred hearts. It's the Roadrunner meets God. And, I believe, the most astonishing denouement in the history of world cinema.

MICHAEL CHAPMAN Rhythm & Hues was the groundbreaking company that did the last shot, and it was expensive. R & H had just bought VIFX, a special effects arm of 20th Century Fox. [195] They famously did the work on *Life of Pi* [2012], all that beautiful stuff with the ocean and the tiger. The first time we saw the footage we were blown away. The camera pushes in on Gigi's face as it bobs in the water, half-submerged. He's this grinning leviathan, a godlike version of that final mugshot taken in Florida—emerald and sapphire eyes, flying fish and barracuda leaping, encrusted by starfish necklaces, and topped by a tangled seaweed crown—a Cycladic marble figurine gone awry. It reminded me of the fetus in *2001*, but that's something I never told Roar. He'd have taken it the wrong way.

JANET MASLIN (*film critic*) The camera begins its long, slow push-in on Gigi as the haunting end-crawl captions begin—accompanied by Howard Shore's "Sirens," a weird symphonic echo, per Roger's request, of the majestic, bathetic theme from *The Best Years of Our Lives*. One by one, the roll call of dynastic suicides appears onscreen: Papa's father, 1928 . . . Papa's mom, '35 . . . Papa himself, 1961 . . . Papa's sister, '66 . . . Papa's brother in '82. . . the sister and brother's nanny, '91 . . . Papa's niece—the actress Margaux—in '96 . . . Papa's grand- and great-grandchildren, '93–2000 . . . and all the various sparring partners, bullfighters, household pets, biographers, and fishermen buddies who took their own lives. Then, comes a long pause before the last triumphant chyron:

Gigi Hemingway died of natural causes in 2000.

As "Against All Odds" thunderously kicks in—*Take a look at me now*—we're on an extreme close-up of his lips, bright red with algae—Papa's *and* Neptune's blood.

In real life, Gregory Hemingway sometimes called himself the "capo di tutti Capezios." But Orr made him into the Matador of Matadors.

The King and Queen of Hearts.

PAUL SCHRADER (*filmmaker*) All of Orr's films are "man in a room" narratives. He's like Dreyer that way. Pauline [Kael] said, "Orr's a funky Ozu" but I think he's closer to Béla Tarr. The paradigmatic man in a room story is, of course, Renoir's *Homme Dans Un Chambre*. It's sublime. There's a tie

---

195 In 2020, the company was dissolved, having suffered a financial downturn during the pandemic.—*ed.*

for second: Bresson's *Curé Dans Un Chambre* and Bergman's *Man I Ett Rum*. Tarkovsky's человек в комнате[196] is extraordinary. You've never seen a man *or* a room like that. The theoretical aesthetic culminated in the Beckettian distillation of 2015's *Room*.[197] Curiously, Brian Wilson's "In My Room" is the first boy in a room modality. In the Fifties, the template leaked into television with the seminal *Make Room for Danny . . .* Orr told me he wanted to call one of his films *Man the Torpedoes and the Room!* but the studio wouldn't allow it. I talk about all this in *Paul Schrader: Man In A Room*.[198]

DAVID STEINBERG He finished the reshoots and additional scenes with Philip Hoffman and Anthony Hopkins in April and cut them together in May. The film was coming out in June, the same month as his novel, by design. Once he locked *Gigi*, he got swallowed up again by that emotional sinkhole, *The Jungle Book*. He was scared. I'd never seen him that neurotic—and that's saying something. Roar had been through a lot of film premieres but never had a book come out, let alone one of such ambition. His anxiety was contagious; I knew better, but started to think he'd punched above his weight. Team Roar was just trying to stay on top of it and keep him away from the speed and narcotics. Carrie Fisher took him to a shitload of AA meetings.

GEORGE PLIMPTON Right before your book is released, the publisher or agent usually give a heads-up about where it's going to be reviewed. "Updike's doing it for *The New Yorker*." "Garner's got it for the cover of the Sunday *Book Review*." But a dome of silence dropped down. I tried everyone I knew—no luck. Very strange and foreboding. Then, on the day *Gigi* opened, Michi [Kakutani] reviewed it in the daily [*New York Times*]. She could be very tough—fair, yet tough—but this was a hit-piece, beyond-the-pale horrific. Toward the end, she did her usual token-respectful, damn-with-faint-praise soft-shoe, but it was too late.

Make no mistake: this was a burial.

* * * * * * * * *

---

196 "Man in a Room"—*ed.*
197 Directed by Lenny Abrahamson.
198 Directed by Alex Ross Perry (2022).

MICHIKO KAKUTANI

[*The New York Times*, June 1, 2000]
The Jungle Book
by Roger Orr

. . . one catches glimmers of the author's capacious heart and vir-
tuosic spirit but Orr cannot see the jungle for the trees. The cries
and whispers of the ghosts of Kipling and Conrad, of Jessie Redmon
Faucet's *Plum Bun* and Nella Larson's *Quicksand*, of five-and-dime
Candide and Yabba Dabba Rabelais, of botched Baldwin and bowd-
lerized *Beloved* (with a soupçon of *Nat Turner*) cannot make this
"loose baggy monster" into anything more than it is: not the fire next
time but the heartburn of America's oldest Renaissance Wonderboy
rifling through the Great Books shelf for another notch in his belt.
One can't help but feel jilted by a novel that more faithfully might
have been called *The Bride of Faulknerstein*.

* * * * * * * * * *

DR. JOAN WICKS After the Michi takedown, it was a damn pile-on.
Just so awful and unfair. One of the reviews—was it *Harper's*? or maybe
Commentary—literally had the headline "Uncle Tom-Tom," because of "the
contrived percussiveness of its prose." Racist smokescreen *bullshit*! And no
one even called them out. Can you imagine something like that happening
now? Oh, they ran riot. I still have the reviews: "The Color Purple Prose,"
"Way Too Visible Man"—one was called "Ain't Too Swift" [*laughs*] . . . it was
a friggin' *contest*. But really, it was just that old American pastime called character assassination. Roar'd been on top too long and excelled in so many different areas; his life was a great kaleidoscope of the sociocultural wars, and
always so *prescient*, that I think there was this consensus to bring him down.
And it didn't help that he was a wealthy person of color—a very *wealthy*
person of color—what they liked to call, for whatever godforsaken reason,
an "arriviste." All those literary snobs ganged up and gathered the wagons.
Movies and songs were one thing but how dare he write serious fiction! You
know, *stay in your lane, boy.*

I hate to say it but it reminded me of Clarence's Thomas's remark about a high-tech lynching.

STANLEY CROUCH The [*Gigi*] reviews were actually quite decent. They ranged from polite to three stars but no one wanted to eke out that fourth asterisk. They didn't know what to make of it; they still don't. Oh, there were some doozies like the Rex Reed though no one took that crunchy little faggot seriously.

And then came Queen Pauline [Kael].

If folks thought her *Last Tango* review was radically seminal, she took the *Gigi* panegyric to a whole other level. She compared *Tango* to *Le Sacre du printemps*—but tuned up *Gigi* to van Gogh's *The Potato Eaters*, Courbet's *L'Origine du monde*, Phil Spector's Wall of Sound, Lunchables Fun Snacks, and Mike Nesmith's mom's invention of Liquid Paper®. That essay single-handedly froze all film and art criticism for the next five years. She died two weeks after it ran, as if the writing of it was a self-immolation—her body just couldn't sustain the generated heat.

CHARLES B. WESSLER (*producer*) What Roar *hated* were the notes and emails from friends downplaying the debacle of critical response to *The Jungle Book*—or not mentioning it at all, like that was doing him a favor. It was lose-lose. For a while, his phone had the recording, "You've reached the Schadenfreude's. Please leave a smirk at the tone." Even worse was people saying, "Win some, lose some." Because he knew in his heart what he'd made: a masterwork. Finally, he took a step back.

The Buddhism kicked in.

KAVA SANTANA I remember Valerie Heller sending Roger a supportive reminder that *Catch-22* was rejected a thousand times before being published . . . and that the geniuses at Knopf turned down *On the Road*, *The Diary of Anne Frank*, and the first American edition of *Animal Farm*. The trouble was, all of those books were anointed when at last they saw the light of day; *The Jungle Book* was a dumpster fire.

ALI BERK The twins were born in June, and that was a good distraction because he'd been so low about how his book had been treated. We named them Ava and Emma. People kept asking, "For Ava Gardner?" "Emma from Jane Austen?" And I'd say *no*, it's just fucking Ava and Emma. (Of course, I wasn't that rude.) They're identical, and Uncle Roary loved that. He was kind of obsessed with twins. He'd hold one in each arm—they were so tiny!—and sing that old blues song "Double Trouble."

GEORGE PLIMPTON Then came the wrath of God: a full month after the book's release, the Toni Morrison *alleluia* hit the cover of the *New York Times Book Review* like a rogue wave—the first major review she'd written since winning the Nobel in '93. Her name was in huge letters, stamped like an invincible endorsement over Sendak's wittily shocking, definitive portrait of the artist as a queer, biracial, adrogynous, avenging Renaissance Angel, that now-famous rotogravure of Roger, part-Rembrandt, part-Arbus . . . with the shadowy nimbus of a whited-out wimple!

Perfectly scandalous, scandalously perfect, and true.

A lot of critics went into hiding that day.

* * * * * * * * *

TONI MORRISON
[*The New York Times*, July 4, 2000]
The Jungle Book
by Roger Orr
"Underground Grailroad"

We know—we all do—the myth of Roger Orr, a Roar by any other name that would smell as acrid as it does sweet: born of a rape, this Manchild of the Compromised Land grew up in outlandish white privilege and black oblivion. Yet his DNA tugged like a shackled helix on the wrists, and the voice could not be stilled: anthems shot from the pelvises of forgotten women ("Try a Little Tenderness" and "Piece of My Heart") whilst the avant-gardist loaded and fired from his thoroughly modern canon a fusillade of films both popular and seditious, exploring not just skin but gender. Nearly martyred by a bullet to the belly—not because of his subversive "genocidal" adaptation of Sammy Davis Jr.'s *Yes I Can* (forgive them, for they know not what they do!)—he affirmed his canny instincts to yet again be in the right place at the right time: the carny shooting gallery of Assassination America.

And we know—we know *now*, we really do—that he's written a novel that will flourish long after race is buried, along with the strange rinds and wondrous fruits of an earth where hatred too shared so many gardens.

The Jungle Book is a chronicle as funny as it is jingle-jangle tragic; and so craftily named it could only have been written by a man who did not know who he was—or is—nor has the audacity to claim the scales fell from his eyes after the mythopoeic, tabloid-leaked Revelations brought his scrambled persona into filmy focus. It may have been impossible to write this novel from an aspect of certitude and clarity. For, this Big Black Book of Life came from the heart and its genetics, from the voodoo ether—the ether-Orr—from the balls and breasts of the mythic thing he has become, and is becoming still. As he said in an interview, like a poster art slogan that befitted one of his earlier horror films, "It came from the sphinxter."

Like the author, its narrator Zachariah Boswell is raised by white parents, though not in the bastion of Pacific Heights social aristocracy but rather the gear-slipping middle-class white hood of hardscrabble Riverside, California. When his adoptive mother becomes housebound with severe depression, Zach gets a Big Idea: he shall become her Great Black Hope and savior. He sets out to right the wrongs in that All-American quarterback way: running the long con of impersonating a child soldier mercenary, the real-life Ishmael Beah, who—again, easy and American as apple pie—has already made his fortune by writing a bestselling memoir of his experience as a child soldier in Sierre Leone. Zachariah goes on the road, a soldier of fortune in his own right, stealing the identity of Mr. Beah as he performs for bleeding, gullible hearts at well-attended, well-paid lectures in libraries and book clubs across the land, meeting killers and lovers along the way—Aunt Bees and Uncle Toms; blackened whites and whitened blacks—uncovering the soft-hard underbelly of the soul of a nation. His journey is much like Candide's, and Orr is at his best when mixing and stirring the surreality of these United

States. But the eternal, nocturnal return goes "South to a Very Old Place"—of mashed-up cabbages and trainyard kings with their kind coronets of stately durags, of junkies and schizophrenic Gullah wannabes, of hollowed-eyed children of the black bottom cornrows, of hallucinatory savagery and tender Africanist mercies. Zachariah bleeds and bloodhounds for what he calls the Big Idea, much larger than a grifter's cheat: it's the *grail* that he's after, the giant-killer, and though it takes his entire short life to find it, the idea finally comes to him in the very jail cell (the animated cel) that our holy fool—our divine poseur—will wrongfully die in. The Big Idea finally breaks him out and breaks the Reader too. Dying in confinement, eyes open in beatified Awareness, is a rightful death.

The biggest idea of them all.

* * * * * * * * *

ANGELA JANKLOW (*publisher*) Everything followed from Morrison's review: the cover of *Time*; those big "Roar" portraits flyposted all over the city and hung in the windows of bookstores, with Roger right beside George Sand, Kafka and Virginia Woolf; *The Paris Review* interview with his old friend George Plimpton. The Pulitzer. The Anisfield-Wolf. The PEN/Faulkner. Oprah's Book Club. It was off the hook. But *he* didn't feel that way. Off the hook, I mean. [*laughs*]

JONY IVE (*designer*) Steve [Jobs] was a fan and got in touch with him personally. He wanted Roar for the "Think Different" campaign. It was a heady crew: Einstein, Dylan, Gandhi, Martin Luther King, Picasso. But there were "populists" too, like Robin Williams and Jim Henson. Roar said the only way he'd do it was if the campaign were changed to "Think Same." He didn't want to be the poster boy for *different* anymore. Steve had a sense of humor about it. He said, "Oh, come on. You wore a fur coat for Blackglama in the Nineties. Was that 'Think Same'?" Which was true—Roar did the *What becomes a legend most?* campaign, right after Jessica Tandy and just before Jessye Norman. Roar's comeback was, "The aim of art is the creation of a strange object covered with fur, that breaks your heart." He was paraphrasing Donald Barthelme.

Then he said, "Plus, they gave me the coat, Steve."

JULIAN BARNES (*author*) Well, yes, Flaubert—of course. Emma with her arsenic, a toxic *adultère*. *Reading* Flaubert, *reading* Orr: the Great Stuffed Pair. Always Flaubert, and yet. Flaubert! *Flaubert.* From the desk of.

FREDERICK SEIDEL (*poet*)

I'm rich
I'm rich
I live in the LRB:
Push PH to floor me.
Got stanzas of Bugatti's
Stravaganzas of Ducati's
and slum with Schlumberger's.
Egg me on—
I'll shit Fabergé's
fab as Shelley Fabares'.
I'm rich
I'm rich

Dead rich.

PATRICIA LOCKWOOD (*author, poet, critic*)[199] Oops! (*Love* me a jump through some oops.) Roger Orr couldsta-shouldsta called his gangsta Voltairean *echt*-opus "Candida"—'cause (and that's *probable* 'cause to you, buckaroo) *The Jungle Book* is yeasty, Yeatsy, and Richard Yatesy too. Reading this book made me scream like a whiteface Candace Owens OnlyFans strap-on trans swimmer planecrashed *Yellowjackets* Kardashian kunt.

As the Rutles once said, "All you need is Ove."

ANDREW WYLIE [Robert Gottlieb] was humbled. He knew he had misjudged the work. I really don't think it was the Morrison piece that changed his mind; I believe he took time off and reread the novel in Connecticut. As a grand mea culpa, he sent Roar a piece of sculpture, a very costly stone-carved figure of a woman bowing down in humility to unseen gods. The sublime

---

199 From *The London Review of Books*, 2022.

irony is that when Bob called Larry Gagosian for suggestions, Larry devilishly said, "I have the perfect thing." It was, of course, an Iwana Cant.

LAUGHLIN ORR After the Kennedy Center Honors—Spielberg introduced him—and the Academy Awards the next year—Julianne, Tony, and Phil were shut out, but *Gigi* won Best Screenplay and Best Special Effects—after all that, he was just so tired. We thought, "Something's wrong." His endocrinologist ran tests and couldn't find anything, which made sense. He was clinically depressed. As it turned out.

KITASHA STEIN-STEIN (*artist, activist*) Everyone wanted them[200] to make a movie of *The Jungle Book*, but they couldn't have cared less. It was a *book*, not a book-to-film. They wanted someone else to sink or swim while they sat back and watched the fun. So, Robert Zemeckis filmed the adaptation, which was perfect. Ha! "Back to the Colonial Future." The whitest man on Earth doing a half-animated live-action version of one of the masterpieces of Two-Spirit World literature. It was like Ron Howard trying to paint a Basquiat.

GRIFFIN DUNNE (*actor, director*) Zemeckis! He could've given it to anyone but he gives it to *Zemeckis*. I like Bob, he's enormously talented, but wasn't exactly the dream director for *The Jungle Book.* . . . I think it was one of Roar's "subversions." He just wasn't proprietary; he had *zero* maternal instincts when it came to protecting his babies. He'd cross those shaved legs and say, "Go ahead! Piss on it." That was his way of showing the world that nothing lasts. You know—all is vanity. "You think your little creations are so perfect and precious and everlasting? *Fuck you.*"

Once they were out of the nest, he washed his wings of them.

SPIKE LEE People said, "Spike, you need to make *The Jungle Book*!" That

---

200 While there continues to be controversy around the topic, Stein-Stein chose to use the pronoun "they" when referring to Orr. Ali Berk said, "Uncle Roary found it all so silly—the pronoun game. Though he did say he was happy to be called *anything*." For this interview, Stein-Stein went on record: "I use 'they' to honor their posthumous wishes. I'm against deadpronouning, *especially* when a Pangender, Neutrois, Librafluid spirit is actually, literally dead."—*ed.*

would have been like signing my death warrant. . . . John Singleton wanted to do it, in the worst way. He and Roger might even have talked about that. But . . . Zemeckis! And I got it, I really did. I finally *understood* Roar's radical prankster shit, almost like for the first time. And appreciated it, appreciated the recklessness of it. That book is perfect. That book is inviolable. That book is the Black *Quixote*, ain't nobody can *touch* it, ain't nobody could make a *movie* of it, not even Roar! So, he did the next best thing and gave it to the highest bidder. He said to me, "They want a slave auction? Well, here you go. Send the motherfuckin' check." And it was a *big* motherfuckin' check.

ALI BERK He was really depressed. I'd seen him like that before, but this time Roary he didn't hide it like he used to. He was past all that. He just laid there and watched TV, twenty-four-seven. Ballooned up on Cheetos and watched true-crime shows. Kids getting raped and buried alive, women being stabbed a thousand times. . . . The worst that humanity had to offer. I never brought the twins when I visited because I didn't want them to be around that kind of energy. I felt bad about it, you know, selfish, because he always brightened when he saw them. But it wasn't their role in life to be his emotional support animals.

Once when I came over, he was watching Bird on *American Idol*. They were doing a week of songs honoring her and Uncle Roary. She was kind of a coach for everyone that night. During commercials, he'd flip back to the murder channel—from the sacred to the profane. I couldn't deal.

BEVERLY D'ANGELO He gained a hundred pounds. There was a lot of talk about suicide, a lot of *joking* about it, but I never really felt that was something he'd try again. There were too many children in his life that he loved—Moon and the twins, *Hendrix*—and leaving them behind was a dealbreaker. He said so himself. But I still thought, *Ooh, Bev, you don't want to be wrong about this.*

Whenever he started listening to "Shallow Brown," we knew he was in trouble. That was his go-to into-the-void soundtrack. It was on a loop in his house, for weeks. You could hear it in every room.

GABRIELA LENA FRANK (*composer*) "Shallow Brown" was a sailor song, a mordant sea shanty written by a weird Australian named Percy Grainger. It's sometimes called "Challo" Brown, *challo* being slang for mixed-breed; yet another sign that the song had somehow been directly written about *him*. It was all mixed up with Gregory Hemingway too, who still floated on the Sea of Roger's horizon like an existential leviathan.

STEPHEN SONDHEIM Grainger was a soul brother—a beautiful boy who looked much like Roger did when he was young. They shared the same pro-clivities—Percy was a sadomasochist who collected albums filled with rope cuttings and bloodstained fabric. He liked to whip and be whipped. His rela-tionship with his mother was a bit close for comfort; when a friend accused her of having sexual relations with her son, she jumped from the eighteenth floor of a building in midtown. That'll show 'em! She signed the suicide note, "Your Insane Mama" . . . Oh, they had lots in common! Loved the same art-ists too. Ol' Percy was buddies with Vaughan Williams *and* Duke Ellington.

NED ROREM I met Grainger at his home in White Plains. He wasn't at all well, but I was enthralled. He was obsessed with music-making machines, had invented all kinds. I mean, mechanical devices that went *far* beyond the theremin. Very much a prophet. He died when Roar was twenty-one. They'd have gotten along famously.

MISTY COPELAND (*ballet dancer*) Grainger set poems and stories to music. The strange thing is, he'd done that with Kipling's *Jungle Book*—when Roger found out, something in him snapped and he *became* Percy Grainger. We thought it was a pose and let him have his way. He loved playing make-believe. He tried on lots of new costumes before embarking on a big project.

TOM STOPPARD For the longest time, Roger spoke of doing a one-man show. All the doors were open, of course, but he decided to go with the Public Theater because Joe [Papp] gave him carte blanche to do whatever he wanted without the usual rehearsal time. That was important to Roger because there was this strange urgency; he didn't want to spend months or even weeks in preview. He didn't want to spend a day! It was against Joe's bet-ter judgment but when George Wolfe and Roger Orr walk in, it's hard to say no. So instead of what was expected, what he'd *implied*—a tragicomic rococo memory palace, a poetic, moving remembrance of things past, present, and future—he trod the boards in one of those ghastly Mark Twain impression thingies. An "impersonation," and a saucy one at that: ladies and gentlemen, Roger Orr *is* Percy Grainger! It was madcap. And not just because no one knew who Percy Grainger was . . . He minced and he bellowed; simulated masturbation; and played the most peculiar musical instruments, doubtless jerry-rigged hours before. There was even a scene with his mother—*Percy's* mother—defenestrating herself. (Offstage, thank God.) Hitch [Christopher Hitchens] was my date and we both agreed it was the strangest evening either of us had ever spent at the theater. It all ended rather dramatically: the men with the butterfly nets hauled him away. *Not* part of the performance. An ambulance had been rung up during intermission and they took him straight off the stage before he was about to harm himself—or any of us whom were still left watching!

DICK GREGORY Oh, I *heard* about that! [*laughs uproariously*] The night they drove ol' Dixie down! [*more laughter*] Oh shit, oh shit. I almost made it to that show. Wished I *had*. It only played one night—one *hour*—maybe *half* an hour—and I just couldn't get it *togethuh*. The gal I was with was too fine. [*laughs*] But seriously, they had no right to let him go onstage in the condition he was in, so shame on them. But that's the Roar Effect. The man's seductive even when he's *psychoactive*. Hahaha! I think he pulled his dick out onstage and jacked it. Mother of God. Mother of God. When Roar *jacked*, they *straitjacketed*. Hahaha! They put that unruly member on a seventy-two-hour hold. All those psych nurses he knew at Payne Whitney were happy to see him again! *Welcome home, baby*. Laughlin flew out and she and the wife—Kava—took him back to California, where he was hospitalized *again*.

Two days later came 9/11. That's what I nicknamed him when I visited him out in Cali: "9/11." 'Cause that's *exactly* what happened to the motherfucker: God and Al Qaeda flew a plane into *both* his heads—'cause my boy had more than one. He put that on his door when he got out of lockdown, taped a sign up that said Room 9-11. Started calling Ava and Emma the *Twins Tower* but Ali wouldn't put up with that shit *at all*. She said, "One more time and you'll never see them again." That shut him up good.

LAUGHLIN ORR We put him in Thalians, at Cedars. Carrie Fisher told me it'd be the last breakdown Roger would ever have—"the Mother of nervous breakthroughs, the one that puts the pieces back together for life"—and she was right. That woman knows from whence she speaks. It was so extraordinary to watch, and what the show at the Public *should* have been: the man of a thousand faces became Peter Gramm, negotiating the deal to adopt him in Nashville; became Doris Duke and Sunny Radcliffe, Mom's two best friends; became both Seraphims—our baby sister *and* that poor girl who died in his arms in the warehouse in Oakland. Became *all* of the Beats: and the two Gregorys—Corso and Hemingway—morphing into each other like a vision through a rainy-day windowpane . . . it went on and on, like that movie *Dead of Night*—did you ever see it, Bruce? At the end, the freaked-out hero finds himself sprinting through the sets of the film you've been watching, literally running through all the previous scenes as if in a funhouse hall of mirrors, breaking the fourth, fifth, and sixth walls. Breaking the cosmic egg! And *oh, oh, oh.* [*briefly overcome*] Roger's "Jonny" was so heartbreaking . . .

He changed mannerisms and sexes, even the way he wore his clothes. He became Mug, getting fucked by god knows who or what, *merged* with Mug then merged with *me*—me!—dissolved into Scatter and Suze, then Ali and the twins, cross-fading into the strange, beautiful parade we call our lives . . .

Hendrix the son, Hendrix the horse!

. . . *Moon* and *Chickweed* and even that sonofabitch Roy Mars—

It was something he needed to do *not to die.* A last supper for all the ones he'd loved and lost: Boodles—and those beautiful dead babies, Beverly's and Suze's—Neva, Bird's little girl—Lenny and Anatole and Phil Dick and the late great Sammy D—oh! Kava and I would sit with him and feel like we'd taken some heroic dose of psilocybin.

Things took a dark turn when Roger inhabited Colson Jones. [*pauses to gather herself*] I've had my share of journeying and sometimes you become all Mothers, the mothers and fathers who've lost their children—the Great Mother, keening over the deaths of all the tiny precious beings who ever died in their cribs—or the sons and brothers and fathers who perished on battlefields, modern or medieval—you sit with it—sit with *them*—with their bodies—before the new leaves can grow. That horrible time when there's only death, without birth . . . and toward the end of his run, Roger became the martyred victims of Colson Jones: the ones who died slowly or suddenly, the ones whose names will never be known, the ones who fell prey to him and his kind—I watched my brother become the men that were executed at the Georgia prison, become that poor put-upon simpleton Letitia Galvy, become the old Hildstrom woman and her great-granddaughter—*become the panties stuffed deep down their throats!*

The panties "Gigi" coveted all his life . . .

And at long last, become Mother Courage: Bird.

The doctor was great, he really was. He was into TM—not a stranger to the spiritual. They had long talks about India, of gurus and such, but he finally said, "Laughlin, we need to try ECT because he can't sustain this. There's a danger of him never coming back." The shock treatment broke the fever of madness. Roger looked like some newborn. A clear, clean, *placental* wetness covering his skin like a sheen.

You could only do justice to everything I've just told you if you animated it, you know, like that movie Richard Linklater did. Not *A Scanner Darkly*, but—what's it called—*Waking Life*.

It would have to be beautiful like *Waking Life*.

BEVERLY D'ANGELO I'm trying to figure out how Roar and Carrie [Fisher] met. Carrie knew *everyone* but I think it was through Paul [Simon] because Roger went on that boat trip on the Nile—when Paul and Carrie got married. So, they knew each other from at least the early Eighties. . . . Whenever either of them went into psychiatric lockdown, they'd send each other flowers with a little card that read, "Wish you were here." Over the years, that changed to "Wish you were queer," "Fishing for tears," "Dish Norman Lear." Carrie still has all the cards he sent. They're framed on a wall of the Coldwater house. They'd crash psych wards, ERs and ICUs—a game to see who could travel the farthest and fastest to get there. They called it "the surprise snakepit talk show celebrity walk-on." Sometimes they brought friends. Roar got on a plane once with Hedy Lamarr and dropped in on Carrie at the NPI. When Carrie was in halfway houses, he'd show up with Bird, Billy Wilder, or Bernardo [Bertolucci]. . . . They were always trying to top each other. She'd bring Joni Mitchell and Jennifer Jones to Payne Whitney or wherever. And Debbie [Reynolds], of course. She brought the ashes of ZaSu Pitts. No idea how she wound up with *those*.

When Roar was in Thalians that last time, Carrie brought someone she intuitively thought was a romantic match. Which neither had ever done before because they just hadn't *thought* of it. Carrie's friend was from the

South, not even five-feet tall—a cross between an elf and a nightstand, as she put it. (She liked to say he was one of the Munchkins from *Under the Rainbow*, the movie she did with Chevy.)

Roar was coming out of the toilet in one of those flimsy, hideous hospital gowns when the two walked in. Carrie said, "Put your ass away, I want you to meet your new husband." Roger said, "I do! I do!" then Carrie's friend said, "I do declare."

Et voila: Roger and Leslie Jordan's meet-cute.

APRIL D. (*friend of Carrie's*) Leslie's told this story so often that I don't think he'll mind. One night, he found himself sitting next to Carrie at the Wednesday AA meeting in Brentwood. They called it the Big Top because it was the largest Alcoholics Anonymous meeting in the world—a thousand recovering drunks under one roof. Carrie always sat with her sponsor, Clancy Imislund, who was kind of a legend and the head of the Midnight Mission. And the putative ringmaster of Big Top. Leslie, being newly sober and extremely gay (and extremely *short*), couldn't believe he was sharing an armrest with one of his all-time idols. He was so nervous that he blabs his whole life story. About how his mother's a very proper Southern Baptist woman and how embarrassed she was about a photo of her son in drag that appeared in her favorite, *The National Enquirer*. Outside after the meeting, Carrie rushes up and hands Leslie her cell phone. "Someone wants to talk to you." And it's Debbie Reynolds. *Of course* it is. Debbie winds up calling Leslie's mom in Chattanooga and chilling her out over the tabloid *scandale*. *Classic* Carrie.

LILY TOMLIN (*actress, comedian*) When Jordy [Leslie Jordan] and Roar laid eyes on each other it was a "coming home." Which makes no outward sense but is a testimony to Carrie's witchy ways. How would she have known? What's funny is they'd actually met a few years before at the premiere for *Get Bruce!* Jordy and I were there to support Bruce [Vilanch], and Nathan Lane introduced us. *Jordy* claims that Roar ignored him. But the thing of it is, Bird was there too—Bird Rabineau!—and everyone was in falling-down awe of them *both*. Bird and Roger. We all went blotto. Whoopi and Robin were . . . *aflutter*. Roar can be shy; he tunes out when he's overwhelmed. And I totally get that. *Jordy* said that Roar "just looked through the big ol' empty space above my *haid*." Guess it took a hospital room, a broken brain, and a bare ass for Roar to pull focus. [*laughs*]

JOANNE CARSON (*talk show host, socialite*) No one could believe they had a sexual relationship—who cared? It was no one's business. I'd lived through my share of odd couples with Truman. . . . it was just so interesting to be with them. To watch and to listen. I didn't have to say a word! Leslie was four-foot-something, even shorter than Tru. Shorter than *Paul Williams*. They made each other laugh. Leslie's so debonair and gemütlich, but with a dark side—maybe not on par with Roger but *oh* he could go dark, and Roger loved that about him. They had little nicknames for each other. He called Leslie "Life" just so people would ask why. "Because Life's *too short*." So corny but the two of them just went berserk. They had "royal" farting contests and Leslie'd say, "Oh dear. I do believe Her Majesty has sharted." Roger would cackle and call him "Bad Air" Jordan. . . . The *great* thing was, Leslie was sober. Great not only for Leslie but for Roger. He'd only been sober a few years before they met but had a very strong program. I think that rubbed off on Roger. Definitely.

LAUGHLIN ORR [Leslie] always reminded me of someone in the back of my head but I could never put a finger on it. Then one day it came to me: the photographer Steve Schapiro. I knew Steve from the freedom marches. He took all those amazing, famous pictures of Martin Luther King and everyone else . . . pictures of *everybody*, including Bird and Billie when they were on tour. Portraits of Andy—and those haunting images of Edie and Samuel Beckett. Steve did all the photos for that gorgeous edition of Jimmy's *The Fire Next Time*. I said to Roger about Leslie, "The face! The height! They're the same people!" He looked at me like I was crazy. For some reason, he just couldn't see it. Love is blind.

ALI BERK Leslie had identical twin sisters who he doted over. He adored Ava and Emma—they were crazy about him too—but they didn't have to be twins for Les to love 'em like he did. He was just so wonderful with children. It's a cliché to say that was because he was a kid himself, but it was true. *Big* people loved him too 'cause he was wise as fuck. A smart, sophisticated Southern gentleman who was "nuttier than a porta potty at a peanut festival," as he used to say. Ava and Emma loved the nutty parts.

LESLIE JORDAN (*actor*) Well, I told everyone not to tell him this because I didn't want his head to swell up any larger than a head has a right to, but I was just *obsessed* with the man. Always had been, for years and years and years. There was Roar—and there was Carrie. My two lodestars. I met him at a premiere once and just shut down. I thought, *I need to make myself even smaller than I am.* Which is a pretty neat trick. They should do a movie about that night and call it *The Incredible Shrinking Violet.* I was just so in awe. And I couldn't believe that Nathan knew him—*and* Bird Rabineau. It was all beyond my ken. I couldn't wrap my tiny hands, tiny brain, and tiny eyeballs around it. I was about a thousand miles past "I am not worthy." He's a genius, and how often do you meet one of *those*? The faucets still turn on when I think of him, of his life, his career. That man got me through some dark times—long before I met him—but I still hear that from folks every day. That's what a genius of the heart *does*, that's why God put 'im here. I mean, "Try a Little Tenderness"? Come *on.* "Piece of My Heart"? Now, now. Come now. I'd sit there at Film Forum watching his movies in chronological order and just *collapse.* I even saw the all-drag queen revival of *Unselected Poems*, his play about Sylvia Plath and Anne Sexton! Saw it three times! On Oscar night, I'd be glued to the set. And that *novel*? *The Jungle Book*? Sorry, the faucets are starting to drip, someone hand me a hankie. The star turn of *Philip Phaedon*? No no *no. Arrival*? Brother, please. And did you know there's a crazy midnight show—I think it's still running—where people dress up like the characters in *Who Loves Ya, Maybe*? All right, I'm gonna stop now. You know, Carrie once told me she was an enthusiastic agnostic who'd be thrilled to be proven wrong. Well [*tears up*] . . . when I met Roger Orr, I looked up at the sky and said, "He's the proof." Praise Jesus.

I'm just so blessed to have found him. I pinch myself every day. Pinch *him* too—but mostly to see if he's real. I don't want him flickering out on me. Don't you dare.

SHEILA WELLER (*biographer*)[201] They didn't have a physical relationship anymore, and Kava was happy for Roar to have found a sane, devoted companion. He grounded Roar. There was something so pure, respectful, and courtly about their relationship. Their love and admiration never wavered. "Not even," said Leslie, "in death."

---

201 *Roar! The Many Lives and Loves of Roger Orr*, pp. 313–21 (Simon & Schuster, 2019).

LESLIE JORDAN The biggest thing we shared was depression. I found an answer—Paxil—but I don't think Pfizer's come up with a pill that'll "fix" Roger Orr. Maybe he's not meant to be fixed. Not everyone is. I don't think God *wants* everything fixed, because She's happy with what She made— "come as you are"—though now that I think of it, God probably uses a pronoun for Herself that we all haven't heard of. One that we can't pronounce. Maybe Her pronoun is the sound we make when we take our last breath. . . . On the Orr Scale of Depression, mine was prolly about a three-point-two. *His* was stuck around nine. I mean, the man invented the scale, so it's only right that he's higher up. My dark moods wore petticoats; Roar's were draped in a black Balenciaga haute couture cape. Vintage. Oh, we had lots in common. We were both superfans of crystal meth. I mean, Roar's appetites were a tad more Promethean than mine, which makes sense because his divine hunger was his superpower.

Goodness gracious, we were Southern Baptist, so there wasn't much drinking in my family. I had a good friend who was "ewhiskeypalian" and did *we* have fun. It didn't help that Daddy died in a plane crash when I was eleven. . . . One of the stranger things I recall is running away to Atlanta when I wasn't quite of *age*. Ran away to be a drag queen. Doesn't every boy? This was 1972. One day at the house in Malibu I was telling him about my father and how I missed him and Roar finally told me about *his*, which was something he hadn't done, at least not with me. And I don't mean the Commodore, I mean that other nasty fellow. We never talked about it, not directly. But this time, he bared his soul. Told me all the truly terrible things that man did—of course, I already knew the *details* because the whole damn soap opera played out on a national scale. Hearing it from the horse's mouth was quite a different experience. . . . I felt like I was on *60 Minutes*! When he mentioned the Hildstroms, that poor woman and her granddaughter [*sic*], it *clicked*: it's a one-in-a-million deal, but I *knew* that family. A Hildstrom cousin was queer, and we used to hang out and drink, *all the time*. He didn't show up one night and the bartender said, "Some of his people done got 'emselves murdered."

KAVA SANTANA I was so happy he found Leslie because Roar had so many destructive lovers in the past. Boodles and what have you. Whenever he went "night-crawling," I'd stay home waiting for the other shoe to drop. The other knife, the other gun. All I had to do was think of his friends and favorites—Joe Orton, Pasolini, and that German director, von Fassenbender [*sic*]. They died in the street. . . . I thought of our little tryst with Andrew Cunanan. I wanted him to put those days behind him, behind *us*, and he did.

Leslie was gentle, compassionate and caring. He took care of me too, he really did. He became an instant member of the family.

SUZE BERKOWITZ When Roar got out of Thalians, he bought the place way up in Malibu, in Paradise Cove. It was fucking spectacular. The Cove was still kind of a secret place. It *was* paradise, especially for Hendrix and Moon, who spent weekends there. That land belonged to the Chumash and was once called Smuggler's Cove. How magical is that? The Rindge family owned it and then the Morrises. The little café's still there—Bob Morris still owns it but spends most of his time in the south of France—but the billionaires have taken over. Laurene Jobs, Larry Ellison. The Snapchat guy and his gorgeous wife. Blah. But oh God, we had so much fun in that house.

It's Leslie's now.

LESLIE JORDAN Sandy Gallin had a place out there. Ours was nothing to sneeze at, more Big Sur than it was a classic Bu beach house. Sandy's was on the *grandiloquent* side, but ours was a mishmash of towering wood and huge glass windows, and all that *macramé* Roar was indulgent enough to let me strew around the joint. I'm a fool for macramé. Roar always called it "the teardown." We'd be in New York or the ranch in New Mexico or in Tennessee visiting Mom and the twins. When he had enough, he'd say, "Life?"—though sometimes he called me *Lifer*—"Life? The teardown awaits!" His sense of design was impeccable but he let me do my thing. Tony Duquette used to drop by and give me ideas.

We had lots of parties at the Cove, but it was funner to go to Sandy's because you always have a better time if you're not the host. Sandy was Dolly Parton's manager. Streisand's too—and Michael Jackson's. Debbie [Rowe] and Michael would show up with their toddlers because Kava and Deb were old friends from nursing days. I'd just look around at the caliber of guests and have me two heart attacks an hour. Thank God there was lots of amyl nitrate around! I'd always be early—Roar always came *late*—and there'd be Howard Rosenman and Barry Diller, David [Geffen] and Calvin [Klein] and Joel [Schumacher]. And Steve Martin—be still my heart!—he was in one of Howard's films [*Father of the Bride*]—Steve would show up with Michael Kors. I think Steve might have been . . . *experimenting*. Ahem ahem. Now, I'm just a poor queer boy from Chattanooga, but dontcha know, I started feelin' *very* gay mafia. We called ourselves "button men" as a joke but "bottom men" was prolly more accurate. Whoever started gaining weight was "Luca Brasi" until they took it off; bottoms were called "Fredos"; a Fredo who had the misfortune of leaving blood on the sheets was called a horsehead or a Khartoum. Oh—know what's funny? Someone once asked Roger if there was such a thing as a *Jewish* mafia in Hollywood, and he said, "If I tell you, I'll have to bill you."

LAUGHLIN ORR Kava was still living in the Bel Air house and looking after Bird. Hendrix and Moon divided their time between Bel Air and the "teardown." Kava really stepped up as a mom—and as a mom to Bird, who didn't need mothering but was touched by Kava's daughterly love. You could see it in her eyes. She got this *look* when Kava fussed over her, the same look she had when Moon and Hendy or the twins came into a room. Of content-ment, and quiet joy. Of family. . . . I think she was seeing Neva again, seeing her in all things. Neva would have been fifty years old if she'd lived. Bird was in pretty good shape but was getting close to eighty, and it was lovely to see this final chapter.

ZVI HOWARD ROSENMAN (*producer*) I'd known Roar a long time and always wanted to work with him. Every time we tried, he'd say, "Close but no shofar." We did have some interesting things in common though. He was a dermatologist and I'd been a pretty serious med school student in the Sixties—inspired by Dr. Kildare, who I had a massive crush on. But when I met Lenny [Bernstein], he said, "Stay where you are, boychik, and you won't wind up in a white coat, you'll be *chased* by men in white coats." So, I became a Broadway baby and kept tabs on the sky for the meteor that was Roger Orr. I was always saying to Lenny and Stephen [Sondheim], "Who do I have to get fucked by to work with Mr. Roar?" Lenny said, "Bend over." Then Stephen said, "Bend over." [*laughs*] . . . When he got out of Thalians, he needed that downtime at the beach. He wasn't *ready* to make a film. But he was a workaholic and hated being idle. Look, Roger Orr being idle was like the rest of us in the middle of a raging manic episode.

His agency was starting to test the waters but word got back that the studios were leery of getting involved because of his nineteenth nervous breakdown—not nineteenth, Juneteenth! Hahaha. They said he wasn't insurable, that old bugaboo. Who *hasn't* had a breakdown in L.A.? Tom Hanks? Maybe. The artists who *haven't* had breakdowns are the ones they should fucking blackball. Plus, there'd been a string of shitty articles about him in the press. They were trying to make him into Brian Wilson—you know, out there somewhere taking shits in a groovy golden sandbox. *New York* magazine did that famous *schmegegge* cover portrait of Roar made up to look like "Gloria" Hemingway in the mugshot before she died. At the bottom, it said, "Who Framed Roger Orr?"—always the *zetz*—a dumb, cryptic, totally exploitative lead that implied paranoia, gender dysphoria and whatever general has-been bullshit madness the casual reader wanted to fill in. It was *zilten kempe*—even *worse*, because the allusion was to Zemeckis, who begat that awful, anodyne adaptation of *The Jungle Book*. *And* directed the Roger Rabbit movie. *Roger down the rabbit hole.* That was it, in a nutshell.

Then, HBO called. I helped, as a friend not a manager. Cable was so new.

TOM HANKS (*actor*) HBO said to Roar, "What about Suzan-Lori Parks?" I remember because I was doing *Band of Brothers* and would have lunch on the set with Colin [Callender]. Suzan-Lori had a big hit with *Topdog/Underdog* at the Public and just debuted *Negritude Cuckoo's Clock, Parts 1 Through 4*— which won her a second Pulitzer, the Lucille Lortel, the Drama Desk, the Drama Critics Circle, the Outer Critics Circle, the Inner Critics Circle, the Circle of Critics' Desks, the Critics Intersecting Dramaturge Circles, two Tonys, three Jennifers, a Josh, a Jane, and a Jim. *NCC 1-4* was an adaption of *One Flew Over the Cuckoo's Nest* that Kesey gave his blessing to at the end of 2001, a few days before he died. Suzan-Lori called it a "plantation play" and it was a seven-hour astonishment, performed over three nights; *perfect* for the renegade, wild-ass ambitions of cable at that time. But Colin said that Roar wasn't in love with it. And besides, he didn't want to "go black." Roar said as much to me at a party at Sandy Gallin's . . . [*mimicking Orr doing Black minstrel*] "Tommy? Once you's goes black, sometimes you jus' *loves* to go back— to da *white* shit!" I think he proposed a few other things to Colin as a kind of test. There was an Alan Ayckbourn play, a Eudora Welty short story called "A Curtain of Green" . . . the most outrageously *white* things he could come up with. None of it mattered. Colin was so anxious, rightfully so, to have Roger in the fold, he'd have let him shoot *The Protocols of the Elders of Zion*.

ZVI HOWARD ROSENMAN So we made the deal with HBO. I sent him a shofar when it closed. I don't know if he ever blew it. If you've never blown a shofar, it isn't pretty. There's a Joan Rivers joke in there somewhere.

BERNIE WEINRAUB (*journalist*) He could have done anything he wanted but wound up doing *The Sunshine Boys*—yup—and making some "alterations" with Neil Simon's consent. Neil wasn't stodgy about his plays and took pleasure that Roger was going to shake things up; I don't think Neil realized just how *much*. The comedians were played quite younger, by Ben Stiller and Leslie Jordan—HBO wanted Will Ferrell and Steve Carrell—and *anyone* but Leslie. Roar wouldn't budge. And Leslie won the Emmy, not Ben. In Roger's version, *both* comics suffer from dementia. Their once-famous act becomes surreal, dominating the last act of what became a two-part, four-hour teleplay. Roger pulled from everywhere, even material he wrote for the amazingly precocious LPs that his sister put out in the Fifties. So, half the play is more or less traditional, and the other half goes completely off the rails. It was a rehearsal for his *Little Shop on the Corner* "subversion"—and the germination of his great play, *The Cancel Ward*, which was Orton writ large.

SHONDA RHIMES (*writer, showrunner*) It won Primetime Emmys for Outstanding Made for TV movie, Outstanding Directing, Outstanding Writing—ultimately, Neil Simon forced HBO to call it *Roger Orr's The Sunshine Boys*. Which pleased Roar to no end! Leslie and Ben both got SAG awards; it won the Humanitas *and* the Peabody. Coincidentally, there was a revival of the original *Sunshine Boys* on Broadway, with people expecting to see the HBO version—which Neil started calling *The Nightmare Boys*. In a friendly way. I mean, he'd given his permission, right? And certainly wasn't returning the cash HBO forked over for the rights.

DAVID UNGER CBS did *Hallelujah Boogie* as a sitcom, and that was a big payday. He hated it. It was canceled after two seasons.

RICHIE "SNOOP" RASKIN Roger got ripped off in a Ponzi, so the *Boogie*

TV money helped. Helped psychologically—'cause, don't get me wrong, it's not like Roger went broke, not even close. He was too big to fail, the resources were too vast. And the man was smart; he never kept his eggs in one basket. There were a lot of eggs! What happened was, the notorious Ken Starr took him for thirteen mil. Remember him? One of Starr's clients was Uma Thurman, whose dad, Bob Thurman, was an old friend of Roger's. Bob gave Starr a hearty endorsement and couldn't forgive himself for that; this was before, of course, Uma said goodbye to three mil herself. When Neil Simon was looking for someone to handle his money, Roger said, "Ken Starr's your man." Starr was the *real* "nightmare boy"! It was the domino effect; a lot of Hollywood folk wound up taking a bath. That's a showbiz rite of passage, but it hurt. It was like the ghosts of Chickweed and Roy Mars making a visitation to keep Roar humble. Starr got seven-and-half-years in the pen.

DICK GREGORY Oh baby, I been there. Screwed, blued, and tattooed. I've been there and *back*. Getting' buncoed is a bitch. Don't matter what kind of fuck-you money you got, you still feel like a punk. But I don't think it rattled Sad Man too much. I told him, "Don't worry. Mr. Starr'll probably get raped in the joint." Roger just smiled and said, "My dream since I was little." [*laughs*]

BEVERLY D'ANGELO He drifted away from the Sandy Gallin crowd. He'd wear a dress to Sandy's but said he was starting to feel like "a rich old fag hag." The parties he and Leslie threw were more like salons. One time, Garry Shandling showed up with Thich Nhất Hạnh, who everyone called "Tie." I mean, Thich Nhất Hạnh was *not* someone you'd find yukking it up with Dolly Parton, Tommy Tune, and Marty Erlichman.[202] But I didn't think he was someone who'd be yucking it up with Garry Shandling, either. The people who made Tie laugh the most were Elmore Leonard and Ed Ruscha. Go figure. It was always this bizarre assemblage of genius-level people. A lot of doctors too—neurologists, trans surgeons, and a plethora of dermatologists. Arnie Klein was still very much in the mix, though he probably belonged more at Sandy's. This was before poor Arnie hung himself; he'd been treating

---

202 Barbra Streisand's longtime manager.—*ed.*

Bobbi Brown[203] for migraines and accidentally killed her with a botox over-dose. Which was weird because when he did my lips, he was fuckin' *stingy*. Bruce and Kris Jenner lived nearby, and Carrie was a frequent guest. She'd bring Maureen O'Hara or Helmut Newton or Montgomery Clift—sometimes Meryl—or Gavin [de Becker], a childhood friend, also a buddy of Roar.

Charlie Kaufman hung out. He was a superfan. Roar was this . . . father figure. He was so in awe, that for the first hour he couldn't even speak. Charlie was riding high off *Adaptation* and just finishing the script of *Eternal Sunshine of the Spotless Mind*. He was kind of obsessed with Roar's idea of "subversions" and they talked about collaborating on a film. I don't think Roger was serious but he did like Charlie's screenplays. Charlie talked about *Synecdoche*, a movie he wouldn't make for another five years. Roger said, "*Please* do not call it that, Charles, I beg of you. Do not call it *Synecdoche*!" It was the first thing he'd say to Charlie when he dropped by—and the last thing when Charlie left. "You must never call *anything* 'Synecdoche.'"

DREW BARRYMORE (*actress*) Frank Gehry designed this *amazing* funicular that went down to the beach. One night, Frank, Charlie Kaufman, Roger and Leslie, and Bruce Jenner—he wasn't Cait yet, so I'm not deadnaming!—were crammed in as it descended to the tiki torches on the sand. Everyone started singing this ditty Roger and Leslie wrote called "Synecdoche Blues," sung to the tune of [Queen's] "Bohemian Rhapsody." They'd spent all afternoon *rehearsing*. A surprise to Charlie, of course.

> He's just a poor boy
> from a poor family,
> spare him his life from this monstrosity
> You're a cocky phony cunt
> and it's a SYN
> you DOUCHE
> to name a thing that way!
> The Sinning-douche from Synecdoche

---

203 Bobbi Kristina Brown was the daughter of singers Whitney Houston and Bobby Brown.—*ed.*

Needs a title-ectomy
Sinning-douche, Scary-douche,
Do the Fag-django!
And die, you pompous little shit!

Charlie laughed it off—but never made another film after *Synecdoche*. The song was a curse! The film made him a laughingstock all over the world and because of that weird, pretentious, unpronouncable title, his work is now forgotten. So sad.

SAM RAIMI (*director*) Joel and Ethan spent a lot of time at the "teardown" and sometimes I went along. They loved movies about Hollywood—just huge fans of *8½* and *The Bad and the Beautiful*—though at the time, they'd only done *Barton Fink*. Which was *great* but they wanted to do something less niche. Something epic and contemporary. Preston Sturges's classic, *Sullivan's Travels*, checked all the boxes. I think it must have been on their minds because the title of their last—*O, Brother, Where Art Thou?*—is actually an allusion to *Sullivan's Travels*. "O Brother Where Art Thou?" is the name of a fictitious book about the Great Depression that its protagonist, a burned-out comedy director, flirts with adapting, as part of his quest for gravitas and sociological relevance. Going for the laughs isn't cutting it anymore.

Roar loved *O, Brother*—all that Klan stuff especially, which is ironic!— and loved the music T-Bone put together. He was fairly bedeviled by "I Am A Man of Constant Sorrow," the dark-waters incantatory feel of that tune; it reminded him of a sea shanty he was obsessed with. Roar was also a tremendous fan of Sturges. What director isn't? Over dinner one night, Joel said, "We're doing *Sullivan's Travels* and want you to play the director." His eyes lit up because he hadn't acted in a long time and missed being in front of the camera. Anyway, it was such a genius idea: Roger Orr as a rich, famous, existentially conflicted film director! That was him to a *T*. His career in movies and music caromed between the esoteric and the spiritual yet always kept an eye on the "star maker machinery behind the popular song." Part of their proposal was that he score the soundtrack as well. It was perfect because Ethan always wanted to do *Pennies From Heaven*—and Roar long aspired to make his own version of a favorite BBC show, *The*

Singing Detective. Both shows brilliantly intermingled drama with song and dance.

It was a match made in heaven.

LESLIE JORDAN It was a good thing, a *very* good thing, and not just because he was in the capable hands of the fabulous furry Coen Brothers. It was good because it got him out of the friggin' house. I was doin' all kinds of television but he was just sittin' around the Teardown packin' away the pounds. Started looking like a big old orange Cheeto.

I called him Grey Garden. 'Course, I was Little Edie, and he was Big Edie, 'cause he was a fat fuck.

IAN NATHAN (*film writer*) [204] With a nod to Voltaire, the Coen Brothers finished production on [the retitled] *Candide Camera* in the fall of 2004. Just as Orr went younger for *The Sunshine Boys*, the Coen's went older: Meryl Streep was forty-five and Orr was sixty-five. (In *Sullivan's Travels*, Joel McCrea was in his mid-thirties and Veronica Lake had just turned nineteen.) It worked, and gloriously so. As expected, their version was far more violent and idiosyncratic than Sturges's yet also went deeper; but the persistent theme of the cynical yet innocent vagabond on the road to redemption was a mighty river that flowed through much of the Coens' oeuvre—and Orr's as well, reaching its zenith in his prose masterwork *The Jungle Book*.

While the Coen Brothers' natural, interpretive predilections push many scenes to the border of feeling staged and shabbily colloquial, even treading on the outré, Orr invariably comes to the rescue with his signature, deftly improvisational touch. Effortlessly embodying the cranky, luminously convivial itinerant holy man, a leitmotif in his own life and work, he brings welcome warmth and humor to what is often the somewhat brittle, androidal comedy stylings of the Brothers Coen.

THOMAS SOWELL (*social theorist*) Roger's contributions to the script were substantial. Joel and Ethan offered a screen credit but he declined.

If the man ever thought of making a film of his own life, it was no longer

---

204 *On the Road With the Coen Brothers: From* Blood Simple *to* The Man Who Wasn't There, by Ian Nathan, pp. 219–23 (Camera Obscura/Pantheon 2002).

necessary. *Candide Camera*'s most astonishing hat trick was near the end, when the film director is jailed on a trumped-up charge of murder. Deeply depressed, he joins the rest of prisoners on "movie night." In the famous scene in *Sullivan's Travels*, a Chaplin film provides the epiphany that laughter is the best medicine. But Joel had a better idea—they swapped out Chaplin for *Hallelujah Boogie*, effectively eliminating any artifice when it came to who and what *Candide* was really about. It was as daring of the Brothers as what Roar did at the end of *Gigi*; a sink-or-swim moment that can ruin everything that came before it. But it swam. How it swam!

ROGER DEAKINS (*cinematographer*) In another moment of life imitating art imitating life, we shot the *Candide Camera* penitentiary sequence in Georgia. Not at the prison that housed Colson Jones—and not at the little jail where Roar shot *Grace War*—but in Macon, still a little too close to his father's grave for comfort. I wondered if he was going to make a pilgrimage to see that sonofabitch but he never did.

MERYL STREEP [One of] the most extraordinary experiences of my life. I was reluctant, initially, because the character reminded me too much of the one I played in *Ironweed* [1987]. But the Coens gently disabused me of that notion. . . . Working with Roar was sheer joy. We talked about our kids and just . . . ruminated on the dream of our lives. My husband visited when we were shooting in Michigan. Don's a sculptor, and they got into long, passionate conversations about art. We knew he was great friends with Francis Bacon, and Don soaked it up. My God, the life Roger Orr had! The *lives . . .*

I can't remember how it happened but they were talking about Iwana Cant, an artist Don just *loves*; he keeps a little figurine of hers in his studio for inspiration. I walked into Roar's trailer and heard Don say, "Do you know her? Have you met her?" Something like that. I wasn't sure who he was talking about at first. And that's when Roar told us. It started very kind of, you know, *roundabout*. He's a marvelous storyteller. He talked about how he'd been showing his sculptures to Francis—he was making them in Francis's studio, where he was staying—and how encouraging Francis had been. How Francis brought the pieces to his own gallery without saying whose they were. And they *immediately* said they wanted to represent whoever made them. Roger and Francis got drunk because they had to come up with a cover story—and "Iwana Cant" was born. Then the whole thing just skyrocketed, snowballed, the critics and collectors went cuckoo-for-cocoa-puffs over Ms. Cant. Over time, became one of the art world's best-kept secrets. And I could see this little bitty shadow of *regret* that he had taken us into his confidence, you know, one of those *oh-SHIT-that-was-dumb-why-the-fuck-did-I-tell-them* moments. Well, of course we thought he was joking because he wasn't above that sort of thing. Roar liked to prank. But something shifted and we knew he was being truthful. And it was just so *poignant* . . . and *devastating* in some weird way, you know, for someone to have that *in* them, to have so *much* in them, so much more than most of us are lucky enough to be burdened with. He made us promise never to tell anyone. We had to lift our arms in a pledge: that we must *never*, at any cost, mention it to anyone we knew. . . . and *especially* not Larry [Gagosian]! I think he was embarrassed that hubris drove him to his confession. I don't believe it's true—that it was hubris—because Roar was one of the least self-aggrandizing people I'd ever met. But gosh, he may even have said *Kava* didn't know—or Leslie! We were just floored. Honored. Humbled. And on and on and on and on. In that way, it was a big weight of responsibility . . . We were positively giddy. Giddy and scared!

Then, comes a rap at the door.

A P.A., telling us we needed to be on set.

And that was that . . .

Don and I didn't talk about it until I got back to L.A. There was kind of a superstitious feeling about saying anything *about* it, even when it was just the two of us, in the privacy of our own home! Like an Ear in the Sky would hear us break our covenant. I remember we were in bed and just looked at each other, shook our heads and laughed. We knew what each other was thinking but *still* didn't mention it. There was nothing to say.

CARTER BURWELL (*film composer*) I knew Roger was writing songs but Joel and Ethan weren't sure what they'd use. They showed me the film to see if I'd be interested in scoring, as kind of a backup. That's pretty common; you try to cover yourself as best you can. I asked if Roger had finished anything and they played a rough track of him singing, accompanying himself on— God, a cello? Anyway, it was that haunting, marvelous song, "Directions." I said, "There's your theme, guys. You don't need my services." In the end, I did do some orchestral and choral transcriptions—from songs and melodies Roger had written.

LAUGHLIN ORR I was working on my memoir[205] and showed him a draft. My brother's main comment was that I needed to stop ending each chapter with a bang and a cliffhanger. I guess it was my insecurity as a writer. My editor kept pushing me toward the Big Climaxes but Roger helped me see how clichéd that was. He said, "*Trust the reader*. You don't need to work that hard. Your writing's wonderful; the reader's already on your side. Stop playing to the cheap seats and make it more like *life*. In life, when a chapter ends, most of the time we don't even know it."

SUZE BERKOWITZ It wasn't a bestseller but it's a beautiful book. And *so* beautifully written. The critics said the best thing about Laughlin's memoir was its pace—that it meandered like the stream of life and avoided splashy resolutions.

SAM WASSON He loved quoting Virginia Woolf from *A Room of One's Own*: "Literature is strewn with the wreckage of those who have minded beyond reason the game of fool's gold that closes one chapter with the shattering of a vase then begins another with the sweeping up of broken glass."

LAUGHLIN ORR The day my book was published was the day we found out Hendrix was in jail; Bird lay dying; Roar'd had his sex surgery done in secret; and our beloved Scatter would soon to be scattered to the winds—*oh shit*. I just remembered an important appointment. That fucking idiot new assistant didn't put it in the calendar.

Can we pick this up tomorrow, Bruce?

---

205 *The Last Laughlin: A Memoir*, Laughlin Orr, p. 218 (Blue Rider, 2006).

CHAPTER EIGHTEEN

Changes

* * * * * * * * * *

Bird Rabineau, Jazz Singer, Dies at 80; Grandson Sought
by RADIE SCOTT WILLS
August 6, 2006

Grammy-winning jazz and gospel singer Bird Rabineau, whose tragic yet triumphant life was the stuff of American Myth—she called it a "revival act"—died on Friday in the Bel Air home she shared with her son, the protean film director Roger Orr, and his wife, grandson, and adopted niece.

Hendrix Orr, 16, was captured several blocks away and brought into custody. He was booked on a charge of manslaughter.

Rabineau was taken to Cedars-Sinai Medical Center. A witness reportedly told police that the singer had been shoved during an altercation with her grandson, who fled the scene. He was apprehended in the backyard of movie director Arthur Penn.

Ali Berk, a family friend, called the police when she found the unresponsive Ms. Rabineau at the scene. It is not believed she was a witness to what occurred. The person who told police about the events is a minor, whose identity has not yet been released.

Hendrix Orr is being held at Edgemont Hospital, a psychiatric facility, and is on suicide watch.

* * * * * * * * * *

ALI BERK . . . all this glass on the floor when I came in. A big vase had been broken. I had this random thought, "Why isn't anyone sweeping up the glass?" Like, what happened to the housekeeper? It was so obvious something wasn't right. And thank God I didn't have the twins with me. I can't remember why I was there, other than, you know, that I used to stop by when I was in L.A. Usually unannounced. So, I'm standing there kind of scratching my head and I hear someone crying. It sounded like a cat. I turn the corner and see Moon, cradling Bird's head in her arms but it was so surreal that I couldn't process what I was seeing. She just looked at me and said, "He didn't mean to! It was a mistake. It was a mistake!" Very deadpan, very soft, you know, in shock. I got out my BlackBerry to call 911 and that's when I heard sirens. Hendrix called them before he left.

Which turned out to be a good thing that he did. A mitigating thing, in terms of his sentencing.

JUDD APATOW (*writer, producer*) He was always troubled. Gifted but troubled—the rotten apple of Roar's eye. But all Roar could see was this beautiful boy, his only son. He even sardonically called him that to his face: "Only Son." I should say *half*-sardonically. Hendrix would walk into the room and Roar would say, "Only son!"—the only begotten son of God—because the thing he saw was the kid's aborted genius. Hendrix was like a clone that went bad. Always climbing out of shit. Or stepping into it. There were a lot of parallels to Gregory and Papa. Roar even joked about that. Hemingway used to say that his son was the better writer, the better shot, a "natural" who didn't have to work at it. I think in his heart, with a father's blind love, Roar did believe that his son was a genius, which he *was*: a genius of promise and mayhem.

A genius of rage.

BECCA SMYTHE-HENRIQUEZ (*therapist, Crossroads School*) Hendrix had a crush on Hilary Hahn when he was ten—he was very musical—and asked his mother for a violin. He'd go to Kava with that kind of request, never to Roger. He always had a plan: to paint something, write something, learn to play a musical instrument, then surprise his dad. He felt he needed to *perform*. The sun rose and set on his father, on pleasing his Dad. Kava said he was always bringing Roger trophies, "Like a dog brings its owner a dying animal in its teeth."

PATTON OSWALT (*comedian*) "Only Son" *did* learn to play the violin—in that strange, primordial, Frankenstein way he had of learning things . . . kinda by swallowing them whole. He took lots of different lessons but quickly lost interest in his teachers. Roger respected that he "didn't want to be tamed." Or couldn't be, anyway.

LESLIE JORDAN We got along pretty well but I'd be lying if I said I wasn't a skosh scared of Mr. Hendrix. Maybe wary is the better word. I hate that phrase "bad energy," just hate it, but here it is comin' out of my mouth. Hendrix just attracted it. I mean, every *day* I expected the phone to ring with some awful news. He'd robbed a *bank* or mowed down some pedestrians with a stolen *car*—I thought all these terrible things! "Boy's gonna set a house afire." But an act of violence on Bird? Wasn't in my repertoire. That was a left-field deal.

ESA-PEKKA SALONEN (*conductor*) Roar wanted to do a new version of *The Beggar's Opera*; Jim Maraniss[206] and I had many dinners at the house. I got to know his son pretty well, or as well as one could know him. He was a bit of a locked box. I remember that Hendrix was consumed by Bruch's *Scottish Fantasy*. He listened to it constantly—when he came to dinner, his earphones were plugged into a Walkman and he sat in the chair doing what the rabbis did; he davened. Roar said Hendrix seemed to have found his very own "Shallow Brown," the Grainger piece that became a Eucharist for Roar. He inherited from his dad that single-minded, almost autistic devotion to what I call vibrational heart songs or romantic dirges. Threnodies . . . it's why his father was such a great composer. He could tap into that vibrational consciousness. The *Scottish Fantasy*'s in E-flat Minor, a place where Hendrix and Roger seemed to live. . . . The boy never learned the whole thing, just the part that called to him—the *Adagio Cantabile* based on the Irish song "Through the woods, Laddie." I have a cassette of him playing that'll give you gooseflesh; you can hear Roar weeping in the background. And it's absolutely, divinely haunting in its way, especially because it was so painstakingly, lovingly transcribed. The *effort* it must have taken breaks your heart and humbles you. In its gangling, cloddish transcendence, that two-minute unaccompanied tape captures the

---

206 James Maraniss won a Pulitzer Prize in 2000 for an opera based on the early seventeenth-century drama *La Vida es sueño* by Pedro Calderon de la Barca.—*ed.*

tragedy of the boy, the magnificent miscarriage of what is—and isn't meant to be. The yearning and shame, the spring-coiled violence.

It can't have been easy to be Roger Orr's son. But I suppose it isn't easy being anybody's son.

LAUGHLIN ORR From the moment Kava and Chickweed announced their pregnancies at Jonny's funeral, they joked with Roger about their babies getting married one day. And when Hendrix and Moon were seven or eight, it became obvious to everyone that they *would*. Like, it wasn't a joke anymore. They were inseparable. It was eerie because they reminded me of Roger and Seraphim at that age. Moon was such a strange child—a moonchild for real. One night at the Cove house, we couldn't find her. I went into her room at midnight and she was *gone*. Hendrix was sleeping; we woke him up, but he didn't have a clue where she was and I believed him. She was eleven but a very *young* eleven. She was either very young or very old—but it was the very young Moon I lost sleep over. I know that sounds like it should be the other way around. The *waxing crescent* worried me. . . . Chickweed and I would say to each other, "Is she full or she is waxing?" Sounds dirty! But that was our little code. *Full* meant she was playing at being a woman; *waxing* meant she was reveling in being a child. We had a small search party out—the house had so many rooms—then went outside to look. After a few minutes, Chick and I see a tiny figure in a white dress, dancing on one of the low terraces. The *real* moon was full that night and threw a spotlight on her as if to say, *She's mine. All mine* . . . the waves were just roaring—behind, below, and everywhere else. The Santa Anas blew the world around like draughts from a sorcerer's cauldron.

We got closer and I saw the red, red stain on that white, white dress. Her first period came. One of the wickedest, loveliest things I ever saw in my life. She kept dancing as the waves crashed—then reached out her arms to us in an invitation to the dance. Have you ever seen a painting by Winslow Homer called *A Summer Night*? Google it, Bruce, it's worth it. You should put it somewhere in the book! The Homer hung in Parnassus for years. We sold it at auction, something I will always regret . . .

The three of us looked just like it: a coven of witches dancing on an overlook, splashed by moon and blood, painted by God, the Devil, and the black emerald sea.

BILLIE LOURD (*actress*)[207] We all went to Crossroads together—Jory, Hannah and Frances,[208] me and Austen (the boy I'd marry and have kids with), and Hendrix and Moon. We were *totally* obsessed with Moon and Hendrix, *everyone* was. Hendrix was beyond handsome and Moon was beautiful too, in a quiet, mysterious way. They were my crush and it was intense. Like that crush you get on kids at school when they're from other countries. Everything fascinates you about them: their *accent*, their *clothes*, the way they wear their hair. Their *smell*. . . . Hendrix was sweet but kinda scary because you couldn't read him, you were never sure what he'd do. He might do *anything*. That was the vibe. My mom was the only one he was intimidated by because he probably thought she was smarter and crazier than he was, I mean, of *course*. Sometimes they visited [the house on] Coldwater and if he was acting out or saying stupid shit, Mom would shout, "*Stop being an asshole*," and he would totally stop! He didn't have a comeback. Or she'd sneak up on him and say is this growly whisper, "What is it that we're pretending not to know?" He'd get spooked because he thought she could read his mind.

No one could scare my mother.

Hendrix and Moon were sleeping together *way* before anyone was doing that. I mean, millennials can be kind of prudish but Hendrix and Moon had a free love vibe. With a touch of Manson. That's why I never let them come over when I was babysitting the twins. No way!

MARE STRATTON (*Crossroads teacher*) Moon was a talented girl but whenever she tried to shine, Hendrix would shoot her a glance and that would be that. She had this *voice*, husky, but just dripped in honey. Her singing voice was so different from her speaking voice. Like two different people.

She auditioned one year for *A Little Night Music*. She was singing "Send In the Clowns"—it was wonderful—and at "Don't bother, they're here," Hendrix appeared at the back of the auditorium, right on cue. There was that glance, that *look*, and I knew she wouldn't be our Desirée. We begged but she just wouldn't do it.

FRANCES BEAN COBAIN (*artist*) She didn't have an identity apart from

---

207 Lourd is the daughter of Bryan Lourd and Carrie Fisher.—*ed.*
208 Frances Bean Cobain, the daughter of Courtney Love and Kurt Cobain.—*ed.*

him. At that age, we were all trying to find ourselves. Distancing ourselves from our parents, trying on all kinds of silly costumes. We changed the color of our hair, gave ourselves secret ballpoint pen tattoos, even changed our names . . . but *those* two were in a world of their own. We called them Moondrix, but that didn't really stick because Moon didn't merge, she got *absorbed* and disappeared. A lunar eclipse! As dominating as he was, Hendrix was lost without her. Which was kind of a beautiful thing. He was tough and weird and showoffy but couldn't live without her. He constantly watched her, gauging her reactions. You could see him making little changes to whatever he said, like they were communicating telepathically and she was giving comments through brainwaves. I guess that's textbook codependent? They had a *big* sex thing, super incestuous, by definition—the same last names! But no one really teased them about that. We were afraid to. [*laughs*]

LAUGHLIN ORR He was violent like Roger, who by the way did a *lot* of acting out when he was Hendrix's age. My brother saw himself in his son, big-time. The worst part was when Hendrix tore into his dad in this grossly homophobic way. He was *so* sadistic about Roger's feminization—and his plan to fully transition. It was intolerable. Horrible.

That shit came to a head when Roger made the announcement he was changing his name to Rory. Rory Rabineau, to honor his mother. "Roger" felt stupid to him now—he never liked it anyway—and loved that Ali called him Roary, though he didn't retain the "a" she put in when she wrote him notes and letters . . . My God, Hendrix would pinch Roger's *tits*, I mean, *hard*, and that was just awful to be around. "Nice tits, *Rory!*" Yuck. Just *yuck*. And it really scared me, because it was like all those stories you read about pit bulls suddenly leaping up to rip out their owner's throats. That's why, after the Bird thing happened, I thought: *well, of course it did*. Roger winced in pain when he got pinched, and shoved Hendrix away—he was *fifteen* for chrissake, *not* a kid. But lots of fifteen-year-olds get put away for murder. I said, "Roger, we need to get this kid *help*, he cannot be around you, he's going to *hurt* you." He'd get very Zen about it. You know, "He's working through stuff. It'll pass. He's angry about my big, noisy life and he's still trying to find his own." But trouble was definitely brewing.

Never name your kid after the animal that kills your brother.

BEVERLY D'ANGELO Hendrix had only seen one of his dad's films, the zombie flick, *They Sleep by Night.* The one starring the amazing Beverly D'Angelo. [*grins*] I always thought that was telling. Because he was old enough to be a little more curious, a little more thoughtful. I'd say, "You should see his other movies, it's disrespectful." He'd just smile.

It was fucked up.

We were all in a restaurant once, and "Try a Little Tenderness" came on. Not the Otis or the Frank or the Sammy but the Erma Franklin, which was interesting because it was kind of obscure and you never heard it much on the radio. We were listening and enjoying. Then Hendrix came back from the restroom and started yelling at the waitstaff, "Turn it off! Turn it off!" So embarrassing and disruptive. Roger acted like he didn't give a shit, which wasn't true. But Moon loved all the movies and the songs. She knew Bird's whole catalogue—her "Come to Me" was poignantly epic. She sang it for her grandma but only when Hendrix wasn't around.

NILE NIAMI (*producer, real estate developer*) When they found him, he was hiding in Arthur Penn's backyard—Arthur bought the house from Judd Marmor's estate when Judd died. I lived three doors down but we had huge hedges and a monster gate. You'd think Hendrix would have done something crazy like carjack someone and die in a freeway chase on TV. I guess he wanted to get caught. Which was probably a good thing. I'd like to *think* it's a good thing.

Arthur found him crouching in some bushes and sort of talked him down, because Hendrix wasn't fully coherent. I guess if you've worked with Faye Dunaway,[209] you can handle anything. He was eighty-five years old but nothing fazed him; his son had his share of trouble back in the day too, and that's probably why he was so chill. Anyway, he recognized Hendrix—and thank God it had a happy ending. You know, thank God Arthur wasn't the next bitch-slapped float in the Hendrix Orr elder abuse parade. Roar went over to the house the next day and thanked him. He admired Arthur as a director but I can't say they were close. Roar and his mom took walks around the neighborhood, and they'd run into Arthur and his caregiver.

BEVERLY D'ANGELO I think it was harder for Kava than it was for Roar,

---

209 Penn directed *Bonnie and Clyde* (1967)—*ed.*

I really believe that. Because she was somehow outside the dynamic—that weird psychosomatic throuple of Bird, Roar, and Hendrix. She always felt like a trespasser. I came and stayed with her a while because she couldn't sleep. If you can't sleep, that leads to *very* bad things. Been there, done that. If you don't sleep, you either die or lose your mind. Hopefully not in that order.

* * * * * * * * *

DETECTIVES' PRECINCT INTERROGATIONS

HENDRIX ORR: Moon and I saw *Talladega Nights.*

DETECTIVE: What time do you think you got home?

HENDRIX: We went to an afternoon show.

DETECTIVE: So, roughly.

HENDRIX: Six. Six-thirty.

DETECTIVE: Okay. And where was your grandma when you got home?

HENDRIX: In her room, I guess. She spends a lot of time in her room!

DETECTIVE: What did you do when you and Moon got home?

HENDRIX: Moon made some sandwiches and we danced around.

DETECTIVE: Danced around?

HENDRIX: Playing music in the living room.

DETECTIVE: Had you been smoking grass?

HENDRIX: Naw.

DETECTIVE: Or taking anything else?

HENDRIX: Naw.

DETECTIVE: No pills? No drinking? Your eyes look red.

HENDRIX: They're always that way.

DETECTIVE: Okay. And your grandmother . . .

HENDRIX: She came down because the music was too loud.

DETECTIVE: She was upset about the noise?

HENDRIX: She never really got upset about anything.

DETECTIVE: Did she tell you to turn it down?

HENDRIX: Yeah.

DETECTIVE: And did you?

HENDRIX: Not really. [*laughs*]

DETECTIVE: What did you end up doing?

HENDRIX: Roughhousing I guess.

DETECTIVE: Roughhousing?

HENDRIX: That's what she called it. It was kind of a joke.

DETECTIVE: Can you explain?

HENDRIX: Sometimes I roughhouse with Dad and Grammy.

DETECTIVE: You roughhouse with an eighty-year-old woman and a sixty-five-year-old man?

HENDRIX: It's pretend. Can I ask you a question, sir?

DETECTIVE: Fire away.

HENDRIX: Is my dad here?

DETECTIVE: I believe he may be at the hospital.

HENDRIX: Then Grammy's okay?

DETECTIVE: I don't have that information just now.

HENDRIX: Would it be possible if—if . . . I'd like to see Moon. Is she here?

* * * * * * * * *

DETECTIVE: Did you see what happened?

MOON ORR: Yes.

DETECTIVE: Tell me in your own words.

MOON: Bird came down . . .

DETECTIVE: From upstairs?

MOON: . . . and Hendy started doing the Baby Jesus scene from Talladega.

DETECTIVE: What's that? I haven't seen the movie yet. My kids love Will Farrell.

MOON: "Ricky Bobby"—Will Farrell—is saying grace. Hendrix thought it was funny because Grammy's so religious. Ricky Bobby says, "Dear Tiny Jesus and your golden fleece diapers with your tiny fat little balled-up fist . . ." I can't remember the rest.

DETECTIVE: I'll have to go see it. So, he did that little scene for Bird?

MOON: Uh huh.

DETECTIVE: And was Grammy—was Bird angry or upset? Because he was making fun of Jesus or whatever?

MOON ORR: Not really. She just wanted the music turned down.

DETECTIVE: And did you turn it down?

MOON ORR: Uh huh. But Hendy turned it up again and started dancing with her but she shook him off because she said she was tired. I tried to stop him but he was spinning her around and she fell.

DETECTIVE: Okay. How long did he spin her around for?

MOON ORR: Like two or three minutes?

DETECTIVE: Then what happened?

MOON ORR: She fell. [pause] Can I ask you a question?

DETECTIVE: Sure.

MOON ORR: Can I see Hendrix if he's here?

* * * * * * * * *

BIRD RABINEAU[210] Tell Baby [Hendrix] it's all right. Gonna be all right. Tell Baby, Grammy in the arms of the Lord and be jus' fine. She's already wearing the garments He provided. Tell Baby not to feel bad 'bout what he done. Gotta whole life to fill up with roughhousin' [unintelligible] that'll bring Baby close to the Lord. Tell Baby he forgiven, Baby was *born* forgiven. Tell Baby he was dancing with Grammy then the Lord cut in. Lord got [the] next dance. Grammy likes a strong lead. Tell Baby he don't need to pray 'cause God prays *for* him. That's how much He loves him.

LESLIE JORDAN Roar felt tremendous guilt. Because Kava was always pushing the boy into therapy but Roar was *très* laissez-faire. He worshipped his son but when he looked in his eyes, saw the warped genetics of Colson Jones. He joked about it. He'd sing that song but changed the title to "Me and Mr. Jones." [*sings*] "We got a thing goin' on . . . I know it's wrong but DNA's much too strong to let it go now." When Bird died, he fell apart. I'd sit up with him all night and say, "You can't control the world, honeybear. The world is not a film you're directing, the world is not a book you are writing. The world isn't a song you wrote, either—it's the *Song of Songs*. It's a spiritual, written by 'Anonymous.'"

I stood in the doorway of Bird's room at Cedars. He wanted me to come closer but it was just too intimate. She was fading and I didn't want to intrude. He had this little tape recorder running the whole time—that was Roar. The

210 Orr taped his mother's remarks in the last hours of her life (transcript provided by the Estate of Roger Orr).—*ed.*

compulsive documenter, the Impassioned Observer. In her last moments on Earth, she talked about running through the neighborhood with her friend Callico in Leipers Fork. "She used to call me Kiki. Oh, we used to kiss like *movie stars*." Movie stars—I loved that. Then Bird blinked and said, "Henry?" That's what she called Chet Baker. She thought Roger was Chet. Right before she died, she pointed to something in the window. He put the cassette on for me later and her voice was so soft, he had to play it four or five times before I could understand. She looked toward the window and sang "Summertime" . . . the most beautiful thing I ever heard. [*sings*] ". . . then you'll spread your wings and take to the sky."

We wrapped our arms around each other and *wailed*. Cried the eyes out of our hearts for, gee, must've been ten whole minutes. And I think that was the first time he'd cried, *really* cried. Might've been the last too, 'cause by the time he finished, there weren't no tears left. And I'll testify to that in court.

PHILIP GLASS Bird and Roger visited Alice [Coltrane] at Shanti Anantam, her ashram in Agoura Hills. That was in 2002, 2003. She had about fifty acres up there in the Santa Monica Mountains. Her guru, Swami Satchidananda, suggested Alice change her name to Swami Turiyasangitananda, which means "the highest song of God." Bird's birthname was Mika—"God's gift"— so, they were a pair to draw to. By that time, Alice's music was completely devoted to the spiritual. Bird used to say, "Alice and me, we got to the same place. Jesus is Buddha, and Buddha is Christ."

I don't know if it's apocryphal but apparently Bird took one look at the stunning landscape and said, "Hey, guess what? They're gonna bury me here." That was the very first thing she said to Alice when she got out of the car.

HELEN MIRREN Alice and Roar had long chats about their mutual travels in India. They'd both spent time, independently, in Dalhousie and Rishikesh . . . both had major revelations in that country, experiencing what Hindus call *tapas*—Sanskrit for "heat and ardor." Rather Merchant-Ivory, isn't it? Much better than "Heat and Dust," I think.

TOM MORELLO (*musician, activist*)[211] I had the privilege of knowing

---

211 Morello, a founder of the rock group Rage Against the Machine, was born of an Irish American mother and a Kenyan father.—*ed.*

both of them. The funny thing was, people always said Roar and I were loo-kalikes. A *lot* of people said that. I knew Alice too . . . When Bird passed, Roar and I spoke on the phone. I was surprised when he said his mama was going to be buried up there at the ashram. I said, "She didn't want to be with Neva?" Her little girl who died. Roar said, "I guess she felt Billie had that covered." Because Billie Holiday was buried right next to Neva. "Mom probably said to herself, 'You hold down the East Coast, Lady; I'll hold down the West.'"

RICHIE "SNOOP" RASKIN Hendrix was convicted on a charge of invol-untary manslaughter but the judge suspended the sentence. He was sent to a camp in New Mexico, not far from the family ranch. The agreement with the court was that he'd stay for twenty-four months.

ALI BERK Uncle Roary wanted their son at the funeral but Kava wouldn't have it. It was sad but I understood. No one needed that. This was Bird's day, and Hendrix would have been a distraction.

LAUGHLIN ORR[212] Roar and Alice wrote a piece for the memorial, "When Push Comes to Love." The innuendo being that Bird had been pushed to her death. Alice played the harp, and Roger played the organ. Alice was a devotee of organs because there didn't need to be a pause for breath—she called it "the sublime third leg of the inhalation-exhalation stool." A bit over my non-musical head but I got what she was saying. Sort of.

  Just before they started, Roger introduced "Push" with an alternate title: "Kirtans for You, Ma."

ALI BERK The funeral was tough, because Dad couldn't travel. He'd just been diagnosed with the tumor and didn't want Uncle Roary to know. "He's got too much on his plate. It'll keep." Mom didn't want to leave Maui because he was starting to have seizures—so I was the designated mourner. I *hated* lying to Laughlin and my uncle, but didn't think I had a choice. Though I probably should've listened to my husband: "Just tell them." It was all so fucked.

---

212 The following was ultimately excised from the published memoir (from the Estate of
    Laughlin Orr).—*ed.*

My father talked to Roary on the phone a few days before and said they couldn't come, some random bullshit about having a pneumothorax. I had to look up what that even meant. Then Mom called Roary back from a separate room and said it was "a little worse than a collapsed lung"—that's *all* she said—and how upset they were about not being able to come for the memorial. That she didn't feel comfortable leaving him by himself, bla. I was listening and the hardest part was you could tell that Roary was starting to probe—he's not an idiot—and Mom kept saying, "Oh, the doctor says he's going to be fine! We'll see you in L.A. next month."

LESLIE JORDAN The funeral was small, because Roar thought Bird's life had been enough of a spectacle. It was mostly music, and I'll take that anytime over the spoken word, *especially* over the godforsaken eulogies people work like hell to come up with. Charlie Haden played. There must've been, gee, only twenty, twenty-five folks. Laughlin and Ali and the twins. Moon—sans Hendrix. Quincy and Etta . . . Dick Gregory. Cicely, of course. It was a gorgeous day. Hot, but cool in the shade. Like Bird!

And she was really *there*. It's such a cliché but everyone kept whispering to each other, "Can you feel her?" We said it all day long.

MICHELLE COLTRANE (*singer*) Our mother died just a few months after Bird. We buried her next to Papa, in Suffolk County. A town called Babylon. But I'm glad Bird stayed behind, sprinkling that place with her fairy dust. [*smiles*] The ashram burned in the Woolsey fire[213]—the Buddha gave his fire sermon, for real! The Buddha said, "All is burning: eyes, forms, gazes, minds, ideas all burning." Mama taught us a lot of Buddhist scripture. Mama used to say, *ashes to ashram, dust to dust.* . . . But you can't burn a Phoenix. A phoenix will always rise. And that's Bird Rabineau.

LESLIE JORDAN Suze finally told Roar what was going on with Scatter, and he flew to Maui right away. I was in the middle of a TV series and couldn't go. I do think it was better he went alone. They had all that history. It wasn't my place.

---

213 In 2018.

KAVA SANTANA They were a sight to see! Scatter had six months to live—his tumor was incredibly aggressive—and made all these jokes about beginning to look like a Francis Bacon painting. Because one side of his face was scary-distended and streaky. You'd be talking to him and he'd have these petit mal seizures, nothing dramatic, just off he'd go in a fugue state. When he came out of it about a minute later, he'd say, super deadpan, "Now, where were we?" Oh my God. [*laughs*] Roar had an army of assistants combing through his archives to find the T-shirt he made for Anne Sexton when they got "married"—GO FUGUE YOURSELF—but they never could find it. Roar was still wiry—his weight was back down to fighting form—but he was really looking womanly, with perfect little breasts and lovely skin. His skin was better than *mine*, I was friggin' *jealous*. And he was starting to experiment with wigs.

The two of them were like the vaudeville act from Hell.

DR. EUNICE LAVAR He called me about the case, and it was fun—it brought us back to our medical school days. We talked about leukocyte counts and neutrophil granulocyte levels, just like we used to. Scatter had an epileptic lesion in the left temporal and parietal lobes, what we call grade IV. He didn't want to have radiation therapy, and I thought that was smart. It wouldn't have been the cure killing the patient because technically, the patient was already dead. That's how far along the disease process was.

ROBERT THURMAN The part of Roger that was a physician was fascinated. The part that was an *artist* was fascinated. The Buddhist part that had done Maraṇasati in Rishikesh—charnel ground meditation—was both resigned and utterly intrigued. At death, the body bloats and turns colors; then it stinks; then becomes unrecognizable; then, skeletal. The bones detach and become strewn and bleached before breaking into bits that no longer look like bones. The last phase is when bones become dust. He knew where Scatter was going, that would follow soon enough, and began to consider his [reassignment surgery] a whimsical detour in the general defilement. That's not my word, it's *his*: "whimsical." He regarded the surgery as folly, but a divine one! He thought, if none of this *matters*, why not go ahead with it anyway? "The whole cooked hog," is how he put it. . . . If conditioned existence—all physical and mental events—is impermanent, what difference would it make? He used to tell me, "A young man can be hung upside down, tortured, and take two weeks to die; an old man dies in his sleep on a private plane en route to a grand ceremony where he's being given the highest award in the land. In the end, no difference." When I asked which of those two fates he'd prefer, he said, "Baby? I intend to be in Philadelphia."

Roar felt the same way about the art he created. He knew that eventually, it would bloat, stink, bleach, detach—then disappear. The facts of it never trampled or negated his joy, his vigor, and love for life.

SUZE BERKOWITZ[214] It was a little confusing. He *was* a woman now, with a woman's parts—and occasionally I'd use the wrong pronoun, not that he gave a shit. If I dare apologize, he'd say, "Oh no! Et tu, Suze-tus? Gawd!" He felt there was nuance to what he was doing, there was abstraction, and to be too linear—taxonomic was the word he used—was dumb farce that turned you into "the world." Turning into the world was the worst insult she could hurl at you—there, I said it! The S-word! [*laughs*] In other words, she didn't care *what* you called her but if you broke into a sweat about it, you were an asshole who didn't appreciate or understand the magnitude of what he/she/they was doing, of what he/she/they had done. But I was trying to be respectful, not just to Roger but to a whole *community*. I'd spent my life honoring and supporting movements, and I wasn't about to make an exception for my cranky genius ex-husband. Put that in your surgical cunt and smoke it!

---

214 From this point on, I chose to retain the pronouns employed by our narrators, even if they were "mix and match." (The same as I've handled proper nouns—"Rory," "Roar," "Roary," "Roger," et alia.) Political correctness aside, the homogenization of nomenclature bears a freight of presumption too heavy for this editor's shoulders to bear. Orr's surgical reversion in the last year of his life further complicates matters, both clouding and clarifying the narrators' individual preferences. A good example of the latter are the comments of Suze Berkowitz, recorded after Orr's death; while many of Ali Berk's interviews (and Ms. Berkowitz's as well) were conducted before the event. To the immense irritation of my proofreader, and perhaps the at-home reader as well, there will be instances when Orr is referred to as both "he" and "she" in a single paragraph. Again, I've chosen to retain the poignant dissonance of usage, as it reflects fluidity not only of gender but of cognition. And since I have the reader's attention—arguably—I'll end this footnote by acknowledging the messiness of sometimes capitalizing Black, and sometimes not, depending not only upon the personality of the historian but upon the era from which he/she/they speak. —*ed.*

ALI BERK The most amazing thing were these behind-closed-doors explorations they did of their bodies. *Oh. My. God.* Dad was *obsessed* with Roary's
vagina. I was too! But he never showed it to *me*. I don't know why; he certainly wasn't shy. In fact, my uncle—aunt?—was the *worst* showboater. It was
kind of sweet that he wouldn't though. Sweet to see she had *some* boundaries.
. . . David was invited to what they called their "atrocity exhibitions" but my
husband wanted no part of it. Dad couldn't get enough! He was just in awe
of the technical aspects of it. We'd hear them guffawing and Mom would say,
"Roary must be dilating her vadge again." [*laughs uproariously*] Dad would
tell Roary how pretty she was, he'd say shit like, "I'd fuck your brains out if
this tumor would let me. But it's very possessive." Roary would say, "I'd fuck
your brains out but the tumor got there first!" Mom and I would be on the
other side of the door collapsing in hysteria then segue into horrific yowls
and lamentations. We sounded like cats, you know, *caterwauling*, knowing
what was coming for Dad. . . . We'd sprint to the beach, run into the waves and
scream at the top of our lungs. We didn't want anyone hearing that.

A few times, I'd walk in on them with Dad's favorite popcorn. (He liked
it burnt.) I always put it in a sterling silver bucket belonging to Bunny that
Laughlin gave to us for our wedding. I'd kinda linger and if they didn't throw
me out, I'd sit on an ottoman with my legs tucked under my butt and try to
make myself scarce. This was about a month before Dad passed away. He
really wanted to know why Uncle Roary—*Aunt* Roary—Dad wanted to
know why he went through with it. With the surgery. It was cool listening
because I had a lot of the same questions. He'd say, "Why now? When you're
old? Look at me: I don't have much time. Look at *you*: do you think you have
twenty years? Do you think you even have *ten*? So, tell me true, light of my
life: why'd you do it?" Roar got that wiseman smile and became super serious. He said, "I woke up one day and didn't have a choice anymore, Scat. It's
probably more accurate to say I'd been heading somewhere all my life—in a
certain direction, anyway—then suddenly, I *arrived*. A voice inside and out
said, 'Now.' So, it was a *need*, but also—mostly—a tingle in the heart. A tingle
in the head and the soul—and the heart—the exact same tingle I get before
starting a new film. Or a new song. A new *anything*. The agony, the *mess* goes
on for a long time, and then you get a *tingle*. You sit down at the piano to
write. Or show up on set at 6:30 a.m. . . . after years of thinking about your
film, after months of preproduction, there you are setting up that first shot.

Then *wham* you're on the red carpet—the premiere. Or listening to your song on the radio of the car next to you at the stoplight. You *are* a song; the whole world is. You're a movie and a song. You're in bookstores and theaters, in wide release. And that's about as good as it gets."

Oh my God, I was in tears!

Then she sang this amazing song for us that Roary said she wrote years before—about the rage at being born in a man's body. A ballad. I don't know if rage is the right word because there were so many things she said he *loved* about being a man. But that's how it came across, a "goodbye-to-you" song. (I think it was originally called "Good Riddance.") At the end, he sang, "The truth of the matter is, replacing you is so easy," and it was so emotional, so raw, because obviously it *wasn't* easy—it was this crazy, heroic struggle that consumed her for so many years . . .

Whenever I see Judy Garland on YouTube, I remember the time he sang that song for me and my dad, and cry like hell. Funny, huh.

LESLIE JORDAN When he was visiting Scatter in Maui, Roar and I talked every night on the phone for hours. I suppose I should say here, Bruce, that I *refused* to call 'im Rory—never called him anything but *Roar* post-surgery. I just *love* Roar. I love "Roger" too but *Roar* says it all. "Roar" is the thing he *is*: nonsectarian, non-gender, non-genre, non-*pronoun*. . . . You know, I always called him "genrequeer"! And guess what, when I'm pissed, *that's* when I use "she" or "her." Or *Rory*! I used "him" after they carved the hole . . . called it my Hymn to the Vanished Him—I know, I know, I'll be canceled when people read this but who gives a shit. I know I don't.

One thing I do remember and think about quite often is Roar saying how lovely it was to watch the twins clamber around on his dying friend. They'd curl up and sleep in that hospital bed, and Ali encouraged it. How wonderful is that? Because usually you'd have a parent shouting, "Don't do that!" You know, *let your mothertruckin' Grandpa die in peace.* And there's all those sick-room smells they think kids should be insulated from . . . the death taboo is something you've got to be carefully taught, as the song goes. But I just think it was so wonderful and natural, very much in keeping with that unique and beautiful person Suze and Scatter brought into this world: Ali Louise Berk. Why *not* have Emma and Ava as tiny little flower girls helping him into the other world? Roar said Scatter smiled nonstop when they got in that bed. I have pictures Roar took that would break your heart. If a heart has to break—and it does!—well, wow, bring it. That's the way I want to go, in bed with friends and family, with babies crawling up my oxygen-deprived snout. None of this standoffish shit, *please*. Not for me.

LAUGHLIN ORR That terrible Lifetime movie came out about Bird—and Hendrix. Because that's *mostly* what it was about. Not so much about her life, but *lots* about the lurid mini-drama of her end. We had the lawyers on it and forced them to change a bunch of stuff, but there was nothing we could really do. I was in Maui when the show came on and didn't think Roger even knew. Some of his fool friends must have reminded him and he insisted on watching. I said, "We are not going to watch that piece of shit!" But he insisted, so all of us gathered in the screening room. Ava and Emma were there, and Ali and a neighbor or two—she had some pretty great, supportive friends—and Scatter's Fijian caregiver, Kamini. Scat was sort of out of it; it was all about the morphine and the buttered popcorn now. So, *on* comes *Flight Lessons*, and I'm *dreading* it. The credits begin: "starring Liam Hemsworth"—as Hendrix!—"Elizabeth Debicki"—as Moon!—Gail Fisher from *Mannix*—as Mama Bird! But the funniest part was the actor who played my brother—Bernie Mac! I mean, how Black is Bernie? Blacker than *shit*.

We start to watch and there's this *dead silence*. You can hear the urine draining into Scatter's catheter bag . . . and it's a complete smash. *Just* what we needed—the best thing that could have happened to that deranged, motley, grief-stricken crew. Whenever Bernie came on, I thought Roger was going to have a heart attack he was laughing so hard. A night to fucking remember. In *spades*!

Sorry! Don't cancel me, Bruce!

ALI BERK Daddy died the next morning, and the joke was, *Flight Lessons* finished him off. Personally, I think it was the popcorn. [*laughs, then goes quiet. Struggles*] Okay, I think I'm done for now.

SUZE BERKOWITZ We were all there when my darling husband left the building. In that breathtaking room overlooking the ocean. The smell of his favorite incense, the crashing of waves. The crashing of tears . . . I held it in pretty well, but the rest of the group was, like, a fountain of ugly cry. I laid beside him like the twins used to. He only wanted to hear the country music we had on a mixtape that Ali and Moon made. Roar called it "the undiscovered country music from which no cowpoke returns." I wondered why Scat didn't want to hear his favorites—Frank doing Cole Porter. But Roar said country was just a two-step away from the American Songbook. He said, "Don't Get Around Much Anymore" and "Nice 'n' Easy" were *great* country songs. I just prayed "He Stopped Loving Her Today" didn't come on.

When Scat took his last breath, it was to "Whiskey River."

God Bless Willie.

God Bless us, every one!

ROGER ORR[215] It was another deathbed scene; I was getting rather good at them. I'd done a fair amount of hospice work while researching *The Jungle Book* because Zachariah's adoptive mother aspired to that line of work. But nothing prepares you for the hallucinations and the grace. My old friend Scatter spoke insistently of balsa wood—balsa wood!—and I followed along blindly like a good soldier of transfiguration.

He kept saying, *Remember? Remember?*

Which of course I didn't.

Months later, I finally understood . . .

At seven years old, we visited the shop of a master craftsman who made miniature replicas of boats for the Commodore: clipper ships, pirate galleons, barques and brigs, four-masted schooners and ancient Greek war galleys. The smell of the workshop with its wood shavings, its solder gun burnt offerings and glue, suddenly made a visitation, toppling me to my knees like Scatter's last breath: He was making a boat to take him across the Charon. Soon I would soon join him; Charon share alike, as the saying goes.

SUZE BERKOWITZ Rory brought a painting with him when he first got to the island and hung it on the wall of Scatter's room. I didn't really take it in—there was too much going on. But I knew it was a Bacon; I'm not a total philistine. Anyway, she brought it with her from L.A. because we'd be on the phone, and I'd be trying to prepare her for what she was going to see. You know, that my husband's face had changed. I told her that Scatter was calling

---

215 From *Either/Orr: The Rest of Roger Orr*, p. 213 (Juvenal, 2021).

himself "a thriftshop Francis Bacon"—so she thought it only fitting to hang the real thing on the wall, as a goof. Which Scatter *thoroughly* appreciated. They shared that dark, impish sense of humor.

I was sitting in Scat's room after he was gone. I wanted to get that hospital bed *outta* there. That room has the best view in the house; before he got sick, it was my meditation and yoga spot. I sat on a mat with my back to the ocean—another kind of meditation—with my eyes half-open. Suddenly, I focus on the painting above the bed. I stand and come close, you know, scrutinizing. I googled it—it's one of the last things Bacon did before he died.[216] He left it to Rory in his will because over the years they'd talked a lot about the Hemingway movie he wanted to make. Roar had been planning that for decades. Bulls were a very big thing for Francis, the way minotaurs were for Picasso. But he gave Roar the painting because he loved her.

I called and said, "You forgot your painting." He said, "No, no, Scatter wanted it, so I gave it to him." I knew that wasn't true because Scat never accepted *anything*—money or gifts—from the Orrs. Ever. He'd get cantankerous about it when they offered. We did okay, but money was tight the last few years, and the medical bills didn't help. I told Rory I couldn't accept it and she said, "Look, Suze. You're going to have to *live*. The twins need to go to *Harvard*. And you're going to need to get a house in L.A. so you can be close to your daughter and grandkids." The minute he said it, I knew he was right. *I will be leaving this house.* It hadn't occurred to me until then! "Give the little painting to Sotheby's forthwith and don't be a cow."

I did some research and when I saw what "the little painting" was worth, I—

. . .

LESLEE DART (*publicist*) Rory decided to have a coming-out—to announce the reassignment surgery in a big way. It was a matter of time, because the paparazzi were snap-snap-snapping; she looked a lot different, and dressed like a woman now. It was the perfect moment to tell the world, because since Bird's death, Rory had been almost completely out of the public eye. She'd been off the radar, caring for a sick friend in Hawaii . . .

---

216 *Study of a Bull* (1991), completed a year before the artist's death.

Rory called David Letterman and told him what was up. She said an appearance on his show would go a long way toward normalizing gender surgery and of course she was right: that's why the Wachowskis and Caitlyn and Elliot Page all went into such astonishing detail about their surgeries. Rory was the pioneer who made it de rigueur—it was everybody's business now. Goop has a whole imprint specializing in SRS before-and-after "picture books" and you'll find down-market knockoffs at Walmart and Costco. *Metoidioplasties and Vaginoplasties For Dummies* at the Barnes & Noble.

Dave was thrilled and honored.

But something happened that pushed things back a few months.

DIANE WARREN (*songwriter*) Beyoncé was always trying to collab with Roar—why did I just say that? I hate that word, I've lost my mind—Beyoncé wanted to *work* with him on a song, a script. . . . Just a huge fan of Roar and a huge fan of Bird. Aren't we all? They knew each other but it'd been a few of years. Roar and I had a couple of dinners with Beyoncé and Jay—I wouldn't do something with her until 2012[217]—and he could really make them laugh. That night, "Rory" went on about them producing his remake of *Imitation of Life*—with Beyoncé as an R&B singer hiding the fact that her mom is white! It was crazy, but Jay indulged him because he knew that with every ten wack ideas, one or two would be pure gold. And maybe his idea for *Imitation* wasn't so wack after all . . .

He sent them a tape of "Good Riddance" and Beyoncé loved it. It wasn't like he was saying, "This is for *you*." I think he just loved the song and wanted them to hear it—I can relate!—but Beyoncé, being *Beyoncé*, started fucking with it because she couldn't get it out of her head. She knew its background, that it was so personal, you know, his *anthem* and his pain. So, she was walking on eggshells a little because she knew one day she'd need to pick up the phone and say, "Hey I really wanna do this but I changed your fuckin' anthem!" Oops. It was a ballad, a *slow* ballad, and Beyoncé and Jay juiced it. "Riddance" was in E and they transposed it to Bb, adding the 808 and that acoustic guitar—played, I may add, by the uncredited lady herself: Rory Rabineau!

---

217 Warren wrote "I Was Here," a track on Beyoncé's album 4 (2011)—*ed.*

MARK RONSON (*producer, songwriter*) The original "Irreplaceable"—he called it "Good Riddance"—was torchy. It would have been perfect for Amy [Winehouse]. But Roar loved the mordant swagger of Beyoncé's take. The truth is, he was tired of it. Tired of hearing himself sing it to a "looking glass." He gave it to Beyoncé not just because he thought she was great but because he wanted to pass it on, in whatever incarnation. At one point, he said, "I should have given it to Britney first. Or Ludacris. Or both." I'm sure he was joking but with Roar you never knew.

TEDDY GEIGER (*singer-songwriter, producer*) It was a triumphant good-bye to the toxic male self—the part whispering, "You're just a freak who'll never make it as a woman." That's what the boxes of clothes in it were all about. You know, "Take your suits and ties and baseball caps"—take all your *male costumes* with you—"and don't come back." Beyoncé changed the lyric from "Standing in front of the looking glass" to "Standing in the front yard"—little things like that. But the best trivia thing is "To the left, to the left." Roar wrote in one of his books[218] that he heard the surgeon say *to the left, to the left* during the orchiectomy. How genius is that. He wasn't sure if he heard it or dreamed it.

* * * * * * * * * *

from the Late Show With David Letterman (2006)

DAVID LETTERMAN: Ladies and gentlemen, you've heard the phrase "national treasure"—cabdrivers call me that all the time—I just say, "Oh, *stop*"—"No, not here! I'm going to 72nd and Park!"—but my next guest is the very real deal. A Grammy-Award–winning songwriter and Academy Award–winning director and actor, his novel *The Jungle Book* has been called one of the best books of this or any other century. He's here tonight to talk about many things, including a wonderful new song he wrote with Beyoncé called "Irreplaceable." Please welcome an old friend of the show—and *new* friend as well. The amazing—and lovely—Rory Rabineau.

---

218 *Long Day's Journal into Night, Vol. 3,* pp. 419–441 (Harcourt Brace, 2008).

Orr enters in a one-piece gown. The audience is startled, then delighted; his softer, womanly looks don't jibe with the "Roger" of public memory. A two-minute standing ovation ensues, the longest in the show's history.

RORY [*to audience*]: "Thank you sir, may I have another?" [*They stand again. Shouts, applause. Rory waves at them to sit*]

LETTERMAN: Is that from *Animal House*? Or *Oliver Twist*?

RORY: I'm afraid it's *Animal House*. [*laughter*]

LETTERMAN: Is that right? I thought it was Dickens.

RORY: Well, you're not far off. That dear boy Oliver said something close: "Please sir, I want some more."

LETTERMAN: [*a scampish grin*] Oh, he did, did he now?

RORY: Oliver was an absolute degenerate. [*laughter*]

LETTERMAN: [*amused*] A *degenerate*?

RORY: Legendarily so. That's the "twist." [*laughter*]

LETTERMAN: You think he's a wonderful little boy but he's just no good.

RORY: Every story needs a twist, and Dickens knew that better than us all.

LETTERMAN: As far as twists go, I'd say you're right up there with Mr. Dickens. [*laughter, sustained applause*]

RORY: Well played, Dave.

LETTERMAN: I'm so happy to see you.

RORY: Happy to be here. As we say in a certain circle, happy to be *anywhere*.

LETTERMAN: Now, I'd like to get serious for a moment.

RORY: Oh don't do that. [*laughter*] Must we?

LETTERMAN: I promise to keep the serious part brief, but I wanted you to bring everyone up to speed. I'm sure the studio audience and the folks at home are curious. A lot has happened, or *seems* to have happened, since the last time you were on the show. For one, your name has changed.

RORY: Is that all? [*laughter*] But yes, it has.

LETTERMAN: The last time you were here I introduced you as Roger Orr. You are now formally—and legally I imagine, as well—"Rory Rabineau." Can ya tell us a little about that?

RORY: Happy to. I thought I needed a new name to go along with my new look. [*gentle laughter*] But to be *serious*, Dave, we do change all the time. Our head hits the pillow at night and we're often quite different people than whoever we were when we woke up that morning.

LETTERMAN: Now, you make a *very* good point. What you're saying is that it's simplistic to—

RORY: That's right. It's the nature of time and human experience to *change*. We change opinions, change moods, hairstyles . . . we change *husbands and wives.*

LETTERMAN: Speak for yourself. [*laughter*]

RORY: The change I underwent is something perhaps more drastic—but only on the surface. Because on the inside, you see, I haven't changed at all.

LETTERMAN: This is something—the "change," which involved surgery— something I imagine you thought about for a while.

RORY: Oh yes, yes. From before I was verbal. Which is far more common than one thinks or would believe. It's rather typical.

LETTERMAN: And brave. [*applause*]

RORY: Well, thanks for the applause but I think of myself as a coward. A cowardly lion, who had a heart but was searching for . . . a vagina. [*uproarious laughter, applause*]

LETTERMAN: O-*kay*! Ha! My goodness. Speaking of lions, you've long been known to the world as "Roar." Do you mind if people still call you that?

RORY: Could care less. Call me anything—just don't forget to call. [*laughter*]

LETTERMAN: So, "Rory" makes sense, and it's a lovely name. But you've taken the surname of your mother, the great Bird Rabineau.

RORY: May she rest in peace. [*prolonged applause. To audience:*] Thank you. I'm sure she heard that. But yes, I thought it a fitting way to honor her. No disrespect to my adoptive family, who generously graced me with their name. It was just time . . . for something new.

LETTERMAN: When it comes to "something new," you don't mess around, do you? You're wearing a dress—a lovely one, I might add. Can you talk about that?

RORY: It's vintage Diane von Furstenberg. Which, aside from fitting well, is fitting. Because I'm nothing if not vintage.

LETTERMAN: [*laughs*] Can you tell us more?

RORY: Behind every great dress is a great woman. [*applause*] Long story short: I had gender surgery.

LETTERMAN: Now, for the folks who don't know exactly what that is—

RORY: The long and now *very* short of it is, they remove the *offending organ*—the one that gets men into so much trouble—and give it a makeover.

LETTERMAN: A makeover . . .

RORY: It's actually quite brilliant what the doctors do. Without getting too graphic—I know this is a family show—the penis and scrotum are reconfigured to create a vagina.

LETTERMAN: That's, uhm, fascinating. It really is.

RORY: They create a vaginal canal and labia.

LETTERMAN: And this . . . "vagina"—

ROAR: Oh, take the quotation marks away from the word, Dave. You can do it!

LETTERMAN: [*laughs*] There were no quotation marks!

RORY: Free the vagina! Free the vagina! [*shouts, applause*]

LETTERMAN: [*awkward, curious*] Do you have any plans to use this new addition?

RORY: I thought you'd never ask. [*laughter*] Let me put it in actor's terms: there've been a few promising auditions but she hasn't yet been offered a role. But of one thing you can be sure: the old girl *will* get her Oscar.

* * * * * * * * * *

KAVA SANTANA That ugly side of America came out, which used to be cyclical but seems to be the only side America has now. Roar's iconic status didn't make him immune. After the Letterman show, we got calls every few weeks from the FBI—"credible threats." Don't make a public appearance here, better not do a book-signing there. He always ignored them. I was happy to have Gavin de Becker's protectors go along. I'd call Gavin in the middle of the night at his place in Fiji and say, "I just can't *do* this anymore," and he'd talk me down.

SAM KASHNER He had the idea to put all the hate mail into an omnium gatherum called *The Golden Anthology of American Humor*. But no one would publish it because of the title—they said it was "misleading." Of course, the title had little to do with their reticence, which was a foreshadowing of our brave new world's cancel mania. He finally published it himself. He wanted Shel Silverstein to do the illustrations but when he reached out, learned

Shel's condition was "quite grave."[219] He approached Art Spiegelman, who declined.

Roar wound up doing the whimsical drawings himself, a perfect counterpoint to the book's heinous contents.

* * * * * * * * * *

"The Golden Anthology of American Humor"[220]

† † †

Dear ½-NIGGERCUNT &fullblood JEW,
you are corgially invited to a lynch party, we shove a fat black COCK
with RAZERS up that fake white girl pussy watch you bleed at the
end of a rop. your fag children will be there to cellibrait
    corijially yours,
    a FRIEND

† † †

Dear Mr. Orr,
I was a fan of your songs and movies ("who loves you maybe") but
alack, am a fan no more. You are a complete and utter disgrace! I had
to tell my teenager you were a sick man and we burned the DVDs
and records in the barbacue. I hope you need all the help you get.

† † †

Roger/Rory/Thing,
Yr slave mother is turning over in her grave. Even a dead junkie whore
that yr autistic son murdered on yr orders deserves more repect.

---

219 Orr's euphemism, as he was informed by the family that Silverstein had passed away the
    day before.—*ed.*
220 *The Golden Book of American Humor*, edited and with an introduction by Roxane Gay,
    afterword by Louis C.K. (Ask the Dust Jacket Press, 2009).

God hates you and made you into Frankenmonster for His sport and our fun. The community is praying you suffer as you die while G-d laughs. But I liked your dress on lettrman. It will look good being lifted by Satan prier to butt-intercourse in hell.

Have a nice day

* * * * * * * * * *

JANE HARPER (*cultural critic*)[221] The "wokening" industry swallowed Orr's latest incarnation—the new, improved Rory Rabineau—as a perfect antidote to the perceived poison of his uninsurable "mental instability." Which, at least for the last few years, consigned him to the directorial B-list, if that. Suddenly, he was out of movie jail and looking good: as Orr himself put it, "Papa's got a brand new Birkin bag." The studios pounced on the opportunity to welcome a proven moneymaker back into the billfold. In a cynically revisionist consensus, Orr's past erratic behavior was attributed to seismic activity along the fault lines of repressed gender identity issues— neatly resolved by the cathartic earthquake of affirmation surgery. The brilliant, heroic (and convenient) narrative, ripped from the *Tootsie* playbook, was simply untrue. But sometimes myth becomes reality. Corporate reality, anyway.

And Hollywood didn't disappoint with cash and prizes.

It pimped up to the plate by offering Orr a jewel in the Marvel crown— *Spider-Man: Web Dawn.*

LESLIE JORDAN The *Spider-Man* budget was north of $200 million, so he did feel a certain amount of pressure. On the first day of filming, he left for work in a very demure pantsuit. It was touching because he was trying to be a good little presentable girl; all the studio bigwigs were waiting for him on set. I told him, "Oh honey. You look just like Hillary Clinton." He said, "Don't you worry, Life. I'll come home stained like Monica."

EMMA STONE (*actress*) I was *so* nervous—he was *such* a hero of mine. When we heard she was directing, Andrew and I just said *What*? I mean, we

---

221 From Salon.com, "Bottom Surgery and Tinseltown's Bottom Line," vol. 33, 2003.

were in shock. *Rory Rabineau?* We thought it was a prank. But that was Laura [Ziskin]; it was her idea to reach out to Rory. Her instincts were always so amazing. Laura was *fierce.*

LUPE SANTIAGA (*script supervisor*) Alvin Sargent[222] wrote the script, but Tom Stoppard did an uncredited pass. Rory called in friends to help with additional dialogue—like Haruki Murakami and Susan Sontag. It was over-kill but somehow it worked. Rory made a joke of it. She'd whisper to me between takes, "Get Gabo [Gabriel García Márquez]! Get Nabokov! Get Turgenev! *Get Christie Love!*"

J. K. SIMMONS (*actor*) On the first day of principal photography, he gath-ered the actors around—everyone was in that first scene—and got us in a prayer huddle. I should probably say "she," so let me correct myself. And the adrenaline's pumping, just a fantastic feeling. She says this and that, how happy she is to begin this journey with us, the standard pep-talky thing. I'm looking her over out of the side of my eye—I'm focused on that frig-gin *pantsuit.* I just thought, "This is the greatest thing *ever.*" A few minutes in, she says, *very* seriously, "Now, the studio doesn't know this but there's something I'd like to try. And contractually, I have creative control. I have final cut." Which I didn't know and kind of took the top of my head off. Like, how did *that* happen? 'Cause *no one* gets final cut on movies like this. I wanted to find out who his agent was! [*laughs*] She goes on to say, "I've thought about this a *lot* and I think it's going to . . . *revolutionize* the fran-chise. We are going to make *history.* Gwen?"—he used character names, and Gwen was Emma—"Peter?—that's Andrew—"Peter and Gwen are going to *switch roles.* Andrew, I've had Chanel and Maison Margiela (Did I pro-nounce that right?) make you some lovely, amazing gowns. And Emma . . . when you're not in your Spidey costume, you'll be wearing three-piece her-ringbone Brioni suits."

Well, I watched poor Emma and Andrew—especially Andrew!—with these *frozen* smiles. The blood drained from their faces, but they didn't say a word because they're respectful kids, plus they were in awe of

---

222 The legendary screenwriter was the husband of *Spider-Man: Web Dawn* producer Laura Ziskin.—*ed.*

him—her—like everyone else. No one really knew if she was being serious . . . because he's *Roger friggin' Orr!*—she's Rory friggin' Rabineau!—and *usually* a friggin' genius knows better than *you* do. And at the moment, it's very intimate: you're huddled with the gal who has your fate in her hands for the next five months. She's Mommy, Daddy, and God—in Roar's case, *literally* all three!—wrapped in one package. You don't want to piss her off. You don't want to say, you know, "Are you sure about this?" But then she says, "Emma? Wait till you see the prosthetic penis. It's ten inches and shoots long, sticky webs!"

They completely lose it—we all did. Absolute hysterics. A *great* icebreaker because everyone's freaked out on Day One.

Long, sticky webs! [*laughs*]

SEEGER ST. JACQUES (*writer*)[223] The shoot went well but after they wrapped, the "Spideycurse" kicked in. The production designer went to work on *Django Unchained;* he stroked out and died on the set. Laura Ziskin passed away a few days later of breast cancer. Roar's composer, Jim Horner, was flying his plane back to L.A. from Camarillo and crashed—all this before *Web Dawn* even came out. The *eerie* thing is that Horner hit one of the buildings in Alice Coltrane's ashram, right by the lake where Bird's ashes were scattered. Horner and three meditators were killed.

But in the end, all was well. *Spider-Man: Web Dawn* made $4 billion for Sony. The series was a hundred percent resuscitated. Rory Rabineau dubbed herself "the new old Queen"—and Hollywood bent the knee.

OWEN GLEIBERMAN (*film critic*) The man who'd survived so many literal and figurative crashes had one last astonishing joyride in him. There were more honors and a few more songs . . . he'd write his prophetic play, *The Cancel Ward*—and finally make his "subversion," the Lubitschian *Act of Kindness.*

And his final film, the towering, magnificent adaptation of George Saunders's *Lincoln in the Bardo*, would be the apotheosis of lifelong themes that outshone John Huston's ultimate, *The Dead*.

---

223 From *The Advocate,* "Tangled Webs," vol. 7, 2009.

LESLIE JORDAN He used to say, "Life?"—he called me that till there was life no more—"I'm like a piñata—stuffed with shit and surprises, and most of 'em *cheap*. But oh God, what fun it's been to watch all the blindfolded kiddies have a good whack.

"And when they *hit*—oh, Life! It hurt so good."

CHAPTER NINETEEN

The Costume Party

NORMA STEVENS (*biographer*)[224] After Roger was shot, Warhol wanted Dick [Richard Avedon] to take his picture but for whatever reason it never happened. Well, in 2012, Roger asked his old friend William Eggleston to do a portrait of his new, post-reassignment body. He knew Eggleston from the Factory days when Bill was having a fling with Viva. Viva had "encounters" with Roger *and* Boodles, but her relationship with Bill lasted decades.... Bill and Roger had tremendous respect for one another's work. It was Roger's idea to wear a black leather jacket—an homage to Warhol and the portrait Avedon did of Andy's gunshot wounds—but Bill made the brilliant suggestion to add those glorious yellow Wolford tights.

GRAYDON CARTER (*editor*) When I saw Bill's portrait, I thought there were so many echoes and reverberations: the immediate reference to *Gigi*—that notorious mugshot of Gregory Hemingway grinning at the world like a hellish pinup. And apart from the naughty bits (or lack thereof), you could even see his scars from being shot.... We got pulled from all the news racks but sold over a million copies, still the magazine's biggest seller. Not even Caitlyn's cover [2015] bested it.

It was the perfect note for me to leave on. I was beginning to feel I'd stayed too long at the *VF* party—old girls, they do get weary. To paraphrase Roar.

TAMARA SZYMAŃSKI (*photo editor*) The cover was fairly explicit but the close-up of Roar's vaginoplasty never made it into the magazine. I pushed,

---

224 Coauthor, with Steven M. L. Aronson, of *Avedon: Something Personal* (Random House, 2017).

but Graydon, I think rightfully now, pushed back. He said something funny like, "Sorry, Tam, I just sold that image to JAMA [*The Journal of the American Medical Association*] for their centerfold." But the photo did wind up in Eggleston's wonderful shows at the Getty and the National Portrait Gallery in London. Down the hall from the Bacons.

DAVID STEINBERG Roar called the Eggleston portrait "Monster Mash." Which he amended to "'Bangers and Mash'—but hold the banger."

CAITLYN JENNER I was relieved that he did it *first*. So, you know, I didn't have to boldly go where no man had gone before! Because that wasn't what I wanted—and wasn't really Annie [Leibovitz]'s style. When Annie and I got together, we talked about the Eggleston cover, how could we not? We both said "been there, done that." What would the next step be? We wanted something elegant . . . because it was time. We stood on the shoulders of a giant and that gave us a wonderful view. Roar was always the pioneer, the trailblazer, as was Mr. Eggleston. Annie's a giant too, don't get me wrong. She's almost as tall as I am! [*laughs*] But the world didn't need lightning to strike again in the same place. It was *still* a lightning bolt—why not wrap it up it in an ivory bustier? I didn't want to "roar," baby. I wanted to purr.

KATE McKINNON (*comedian***)** The public's fixation with Cait finally took the focus off Rory. It knocked her off the pedestal, and she was grateful for that. As Ms. Rabineau liked to say, "There's a new *she*-riff in Transtown."

ALI BERK Mom'll wind up back in Maui one day. I think we all will. But the twins needed their "gramjam" stateside! That's what they called her: Gramjam. David and I had a house in Mandeville, and Mom bought a place in the Palisades with the money she got from that painting Roary gave her. And believe me, there was plenty left over. The lady was *not* hurting. My uncle sold the house in Bel Air; he and Leslie stayed in the Cove whenever they were in L.A. Moon and Hendrix wanted to "housesit," but Kava wouldn't allow it. No way was she gonna let them be squatters. She didn't trust them— not Hendrix, anyway. Besides, she thought it was high time those two managed on their own. Kava had a big place in Ojai too, but hired guards to ward off potential Teardown trespassers. Meaning Hendy and Moon, I guess.

But the twins and I went camping at the Cove, whether Roary and Les were in town or not. It was such a magical place. I was holding on to those girls by my teeth—watching them, listening to them talk, loving them. Ava and Emma were at that heartbreaking age, "the edge of thirteen," when a Mom starts practicing to herself those deep, wrenching, empty nest goodbyes. I'd be meditating and catch myself having elaborate fantasies: weddings, babies, the whole megillah. I even saw myself in bed dying, with grandkids crawling on me like Ava and Emma did with Daddy. I know it's morbid, but there's something beautiful about it too. Circle of life, right?

LAUGHLIN ORR I started spending more time with my little bro. We had get-togethers at the Teardown—we never called them parties, they were always "get-togethers." Caitlyn hung out a lot with Roar, because she was seeing his doctor, Doug Ousterhout, for her feminization. Roar was Cait's guru! I guess that's common knowledge but no one knew it *then*. Everything with Cait was hush-hush. Donald Judd's kids would drop in, and Bill Eggleston's too—Andra and Bill Junior. Billie [Lourd] came with her mom. Joan [Wicks] and her beautiful daughter Amanda [Gorman]. Amanda was just a few years older than the twins. There'd always be the spiritual contingent: Stephen Levine, his son Noah, and a roving monk or two. And the star posse—Gwyneth and Emma Stone, Robert Downey Jr. and Joaquin [Phoenix]. And sometimes—*sometimes*—Hendrix and Moon. Under close supervision! I think they were living somewhere in Venice. Hopefully not on the Boardwalk.

GWYNETH PALTROW "Moondrix"—that's what the twins called them!—were sweet but kept to themselves. Sometimes I didn't even know they were there. They usually wouldn't sit at the big table for meals, with everyone else. That was by choice because we all encouraged them to. They'd sort of stand and giggle on the sidelines. Stoners! But potheads who didn't *eat*. They were insanely gorgeous. They'd ride the funicular to the beach and take marathon walks. One time when they didn't return, Roar said, "I think they walked back to Venice."

LESLIE JORDAN They'd both just turned twenty-one. For a while, they stayed in Topanga at a place Eileen Myles owned—this was right before

Transparent changed her life but she'd already won every grant known to God and man and acquired lots of property along the way. She was the richest poorest poet in history. Hendrix was working at Moonjuice, if you can believe that. Have you been? Do you know the place I'm talking about, Bruce? You'd think Hendy had *enough* moon juice but the boy needed more! Well, I was young once too. He made these marvelous smoothies whenever he came to the Cove. Wouldn't take money from his dad, and Roger respected that. Kava didn't know it'd been *offered* and I'm glad she didn't 'cause all hell would've broke loose. I know he did occasionally slip Moon an envelope of cash. She'd take it and *erupt* in giggles. Strange, eccentric girl. I don't know if she told Hendy about the money, prob'ly not, because he'd have gotten mad. And you didn't want to make Hendy mad. I think she was saving it for a rainy day. And that day did come. Always does, doesn't it.

NOAH LEVINE (*Buddhist teacher, writer*) I got in trouble when I was young. Felonies, dope, juvie hall. Suicide attempts. I was in total rebellion against my father's world. What's that quote of Oscar Levant's? "I'm a study of a man in chaos in search of frenzy." That's me when I was young. The dissonance was that I grew up in a house with traditions—mindfulness, breathwork, Ānāpānasati—and the company of serious scholars and teachers like Bob Thurman and Jack Kornfield. I didn't know it but all those things were the wind and water that shaped the stone. But I guess you could say the *formal* beginning of my journey was seeing *Grace War* when I was nineteen years old. I really responded to Denzel's journey to become a monk. It brought me back to my years of incarceration because he does it all from his jail cell—the prayers, prostrations and studies—which led me to eventually become involved with the Prison Dharma Network. I practice and teach in the Theravada and Mahayana traditions.

Roar wanted me to invite his son to a vipassana retreat I was doing at Esalen. I liked Hendrix and saw a lot of myself in him. The violence, the rebellion, the low self-esteem. My dad was—is—kind of a rock star in the Buddhist community so I understood the shadow Hendrix grew up in. I had a much smaller shadow, comparatively, but I got it.

He showed up with Moon, took a few classes then disappeared. I understood that too.

LESLIE JORDAN He started gaining weight, kind of his thing, especially when he started a new project ... They ballyhooed *Act of Kindness* as a "subversion"—and I hate that, 'cause *all* of Roger's work was a subversion! But he'd get depressed when he got fat, it was a vicious circle. He walked around naked, and I thought that comical. He'd pass a mirror, give a sidelong glance, and say, "Well, *that's* a helluva gunt." He loved using that terrible, horrible word!

BEVERLY D'ANGELO He brought out the best in the paparazzi, per usual. His girth was memorialized in telephoto lenses, exploding from dresses and pantsuits. The *Enquirer* splashed "MAN OVERBOARD!!!" and the *Star* bannered THE INCREDIBLE UNSHRINKING WOMAN. Even Carrie couldn't resist pasting the cover of *The Sun* on her fridge—Roar meditating under the headline OBESE WAN KENOBI.

JOHN WATERS Come Halloween, *porcine* drag queens took to the streets with a fury, in custom button-popping, break-at-the-seams Rory Rabineau finery. There were only two choices for a plus-size miscreant: Oprah—or Rory. Rory Rabineau dethroned Divine, at last. Threw him under the bus like a bear swatting a salmon.

DR. WITT DJELLIN (*personal physician*) Weight gain is more common in transmasculines than transfeminines but I really don't think that had much to do with it. Roger had a history of BED [binge eating disorder] long before his surgery. Add to that, he was depressed—and when you're depressed, you eat. Some of us *overeat*. The root of his latest despondency, of course, was that Roger wanted an excuse to detransition. He felt he'd made a terrible mistake and had been secretly entertaining the thought for months. It embarrassed the hell out of him, deepening the depression. I told him to sit with it a while because what he was going through wasn't uncommon. It happens. People make choices, then people make new choices—that's what makes them people. In the moment, though, detransitioning seemed an unavoidable, *very* scary option. He knew he'd be rebranded as a general lunatic, while at the same time getting bullied and body-punched by the trans community. He said, "For chrissake, Witt, I just won the fucking Pioneer Award!"—he called it the "GLAAD bag award," you know, "the one they give old bags." At least he still had a sense of humor. But I could see that his mind was made up; he just didn't have it in him for another donnybrook. Roger was tired of fighting the world and wanted a medical alibi that would explain to his angry "wominions" why he was "rowing back to the Isle of Man, like a sad dog with its vaginoplasty between its legs." He wanted to know if it was feasible to announce that his body had "rejected" the surgery. I said, "No, it *isn't*—and it's none of anyone's fucking business. My body, my choice. Remember that?"

I finally did say, "Grow a pair!" and that really made him laugh.

GEORGE C. WOLFE (*director*) I got late-night phone calls. And it *was* a sticky wicket. I told him, yes, folks in the community are going to be angry, but he didn't *owe* anyone. "You don't owe anyone but yourself." I understood why he was upset. He didn't want to repudiate what he still felt was a brave and revolutionary act—for *others*. He didn't want to set back "the cause." He said, "I'm too old to play Judas." I told him, "Baby, you're too old to play Jesus too. You've betrayed the public your entire life. That's what Genius *is*, when it's done right: the constant betrayal of a public that expects one thing but always gets something else."

In the end, God bless him, he was beholden to no one.

· · ·

ALI BERK I hadn't worked in a while and was thrilled that he asked me to be in *Act of Kindness*. It was the most perfect script I'd ever read.

DAVID UNGER He'd been talking about directing *Kindness* for years. I thought it was one of those things that would never get made—a hole-in-the-bucket-list dream project. Because every major artist has one or two that got away. But the Spider-Man movie made so much money, they would have let him do a frame-by-frame remake of *Heaven's Gate*.

BRUNO DELBONNEL (*cinematographer*) He wanted to shoot *Act of Kindness* in black and white. An homage to the gentle, luminous Americana of Lubitsch, Cukor, and Capra—and what he called the sprawling, transcendent "hope opera" of William Wyler's *The Best Years of Our Lives*.

PAM KOFFLER (*producer*) He showed up the first day in a man's suit. He'd had implants, right? Something small, maybe 125, 150 cc's—what are they called, "gummy bears"?—but you couldn't see them. I think he taped them down. There was only one day when he wore a dress: the day we wrapped the shooting script and began the "ghost pages."

JENNIFER LAWRENCE We knew he was going to do five additional days of shooting but he never gave us pages. He'd just sort of wink and say, "You'll see." We trusted him implicitly. Oh my God! With our lives.

BRADLEY COOPER (*actor*) As meticulous and reassuring as Roar was, you never lost that sense of danger. Real danger. There was always a kind of tension on the set, which I think can be a good thing as long as it's the right director. Part of that was respect: you knew you were working with a genius. You're trying to do your best work and at the same time trying not to disappoint him. But *some* of that anxiety had to do with the "subversions"—he'd been talking about them for years, in interviews. So, all of us—myself, Jennifer, Scarlett—had the sick-stomach feeling *somethin's comin'*. That he was going to light a match and burn the house down. With us in it! [*laughs*] And because we *loved* what we'd already shot, and knew we had something beyond special, our egos were a little involved. We got *worried*. "Oh no! He's going to ruin our precious film! No Academy Award for *moi*." I'm kidding about that, because we'd all done pretty well and weren't really in the awards headspace anymore. But we *did* fall into that middle-class trap. Weirdly, that was one of the allures of working with him—that the man was capable of burning it all down in a minute and dancing on the ashes. We knew *he* could walk on hot coals, but weren't so sure we could do the same. Ever seen marshmallows at a campfire? [*laughs*]

SCARLETT JOHANSSON Jen and I used to joke about the infamous "five additional days." We tried to find out what the fuck was in those "ghost" pages—BOO!—but *no one* knew what Roar was up to. We didn't ask the script supervisor because we were afraid she'd tattle. Jen would say to me, "What if he actually *doesn't* shoot any more scenes . . . What if the only thing he actually *shoots* is—*us*! With a gun! I mean, just *mows us all down*." [*laughs uproariously*] We saw ourselves crouching in the honey wagon and dialing

911, you know, *Help! Help! Active shooter! Might be wearing a dress!* But the paranoia seeped in and I started to get . . . *concerned.* [*giggles*] I told my agent, "Jen and I think he's going to kill us." Bryan [Lourd] just laughed, but with this *different* laugh, different than usual. When I told Jen about it, she said, "Oh my God, he *knows.* Bryan knows we're gonna die!"

KELLY SÚILLEABHÁIN (*First AD*) The actors got their sides "on the day." They were elated with the ghost pages but didn't really have time to process what was happening. Even though they knew it was a "subversion," I still think they believed it was an elaborate prank Roar was pulling on the studio. They were sworn to secrecy. It felt like a game you'd play on a sleepover when you were a kid. And you're slaphappy, struggling not to wake the parents.

SAM WASSON A wonderful movie had been made that was wedded to a coda that retained the *feeling* of the characters and the film itself but broke rank in this hallucinatory way. *Act of Kindness* was emotionally and aesthetically in the style of Fifties Cinemascope-melodramorama—but the "ghost pages" were a cross between the kinetic surrealism of Fellini's *Toby Dammit*[225] and the deadpan dadaism of *The Discreet Charm of the Bourgeoisie.* And he shot them in living color!

LINDA LICHTER (*attorney*) The studio had their hands full with *Guardians of the Galaxy* and *Captain America,* and Roger managed to fly under the radar. He padded the script with scenes that he knew weren't going to be shot and used the money for those extra, unauthorized five days. MGM argued that the budget for the "after-shoot" had never been approved and took him to court with the intent of nullifying his right of final cut "due to subterfuge and bad faith." But we brought a gun to that fight. When I pointed out that he wrapped under budget, the studio lost. In an "act of vengeance," they opened *Kindness* in twenty theaters instead of twelve hundred. It wound up making about nine million in the States and three times that in Europe—less than the contractual cost of P&A [prints and advertising].

Without the "subversion," the film was in a league with *It's A Wonderful*

---

225 Fellini's contribution to the omnibus film *Spirits of the Dead* (1968)—*ed.*

Life and *It Happened One Night*; instead, it was a shotgun wedding between Capra and Lars von Trier.

PETER BRADSHAW (*film critic*) It absolutely dominated Cannes. Julianne Moore won Best Actress for her bravura performance in David Cronenberg's *Maps to the Stars* but *Act of Kindness* swept everything else: Best Film, Best Director, Best Screenplay—and Bradley Cooper for Best Actor. Orr was tremendously impressed with Xavier Dolan, the twenty-five-year-old Cannes prodigy and auteur poster boy. Dolan's film *Mommy* had already won the Jury Prize but when Jane Campion [Jury President] gave Orr the trophy for Best Film, he leapt into the audience and thrust the Palme d'Or into the stunned Dolan's hands. A rudely magnanimous, poignantly memorable moment.[226]

KATHY GRIFFIN (*comedian*) Some article quoted Roar kvelling that "Xavier Dolan is the son I never had." That was dumb but sometimes words just come out of your mouth. What can you do. The terrible thing is, Hendrix somehow saw it. He sent a "Cannes-gratulations!" gift to the Cove house, a pair of scuzzy gold pumps, obviously bought at a thrift store—with *shit* on the heels. The note said, *"To the father I never had!* Because I never wanted a FAGGOT NIGGER WITH A MUTANT CUNT." So ugly. So, so ugly. . . . It was the last Roar heard from him. If he'd known that, if he *believed* he'd never see that boy again, I don't think he could have lived. As fucked up and complicated as things were, that's the truth. I know it sounds dramatic. But there are things we'll never know nor should be privileged to know about that relationship.

LESLIE JORDAN We were at the Cove watching the Kardashians on TV. Caitlyn was on the couch with us—how's *that* for keeping up with the Kardashians! And of course we knew everything going on with Cait, though it was another year before she came out publicly. She was wearing a slinky little number because she felt comfortable around us, but Roger had on baggy old clothes. He was still quite heavy—his Kirstie *Alley Fat Actress* phase. And

---

226 *Mommy's* soundtrack showcased both "Try a Little Tenderness" and "Irreplaceable"; Orr personally negotiated a reduction in licensing fees, whose cost would have been prohibitive for the young director.—*ed.*

vaping, which bothered me *no end*. Everyone kept saying how safe it was to vape but how *could* it be? Every time I looked over, he was blowin' out smoke like a foghorn. I thought: *uh oh*. Heart attack time.

Caitlyn was aware of Roger wanting to reverse the surgery. It wasn't something that was going to sway her own plans, but she was *very* interested. She was curious. The last thing Roger wanted to do was plant seeds of doubt in Cait—not that he *could* have—he just didn't want to influence anybody. He was always careful to say he had no regrets, you know, that he was grateful to have had the surgery. Is that a paradox? He was a mincing paradox! You *could* say he doth protest too much but I think it was true. And there wasn't a time frame for the detransition deal, so none of us knew if he'd actually go through with it. Part of me didn't *want* him to, because the *first* surgery weren't no walk in the park. There were some complications. And they'd have to make him a brand-new whatsit—I mean, what could possibly go wrong? [*laughs*] What the surgeons taketh away, they giveth back. Or try like hell to, anyway.

Roar was so upset he'd made such a mess of things. And everything gets much worse when you're depressed. Everything becomes symbolic of . . . overall failure. Doesn't matter *what* you've accomplished in life, you hate the world, and as far as you're concerned the world hates you right back. He usually got that way after a big wingding like the Oscars or Grammys or Cannes—the carriage turns into a pumpkin and there he is back home, stewing in his own thoughts like a big trans dog sniffing its caca. Not a good look. The whole Hendrix blowout added a new layer. I knew he was preoccupied—just tormented something terrible—by Only Son.

So there we were with Couch Caitlyn, watching TV Caitlyn. And Roger blurts something out—I didn't know if he was talking to us or the tube—he liked talking to the tube—then topples off the couch and upchucks. A blood-curdling yelp came out of me, Caitlyn told me that later, she said it sounded like a wolf with its paw caught in a steel trap. Now, I don't remember that at all. I was just so certain he was going to die. We're way out in the Cove and it felt like three days before the paramedics got there. I think it was closer to twenty minutes. And I was alone with Roger because Caitlyn ran out to PCH to flag 'em down. In her dress! Six-foot-three, in heels. If the sight of that gal didn't get emergency service's attention, *nuthin'* would. I held his head in my lap and said all the dumb things folks say in a situation like that. "You're gonna be okay." . . . "*Hang on.*" I was so mad about the damn vaping. Then you switch over to "I love you" and "Don't die on me, honey, you *cannot*. I will not allow it." You're thinking: game over. You kinda go from rescue to recovery.

KAVA SANTANA Leslie called but he didn't *sound* like Leslie. I was in Ojai, about to get a massage. He said, in this very kind of *stentorian* voice, "We're at Saint John's, you better come down right away." Your head goes to funny places when you hear something like that. Like, Did I forget I was supposed to be there? Was that in my iPhone calendar? I immediately thought *car wreck*. "Les, what happened?" He said Roger probably had a heart attack and when I asked if he was alive, he said, *I don't know, Kava! They won't let me in!* and hung up.

LAUGHLIN ORR I was in San Francisco and chartered a plane. I just didn't want to be with a hundred strangers. I really thought, *The moment has come.* I already saw myself at the hospital, touching the body. I was pretty calm. A voice in my head kept saying "The road narrows." I'd been in this situation with my brother before but there were always people I could reach out to— Jonny, Scatter, Sammy, Phil Hoffman . . . all gone. I was convinced Roger was gone now too.

In that moment, I was sure of it.

DAVID UNGER He was still in the ER when we got there. I went outside for a cigarette—I was still smoking then—and the trucks started rolling in and setting up: TMZ, Eyewitness News, Action News . . . all the vulture culture soldiers. I spent much of my life in Europe and remember thinking, "Get me out of here." Not get me out of Hollywood. Get me out of America.

ALI BERK The doctor said Uncle Roary had what they call the "widow-maker." The artery was completely blocked and he was lucky not to have died right there on the floor of the Teardown.

LESLIE JORDAN Well, he stopped calling me Life. My new name—wait for it!—was Widow-Maker. I said, "*No*, that'd be *you*." But I didn't give a hoot. If he'd called me shit for brains, I'd have been happy. I'd have been overjoyed. He was still weak but sang "I'm Still Here" from the hospital bed—that boy did a mean Elaine Stritch. I just cried and cried and cried. I'm a helluvan audience.

I started calling him Black Widow-Maker but changed it to "Blackish Widow." He got a kick out of that.

DAVID UNGER When I saw him in the ICU, he said, "Am I gonna need a new ticker? They better not give me Altman's." He joked about having a "one-stop" heart transplant/gender reversal, you know, at the same time. "They can throw in a butt lift while they're at it." Phil Hoffman died a few months before, and Roger said, "See if you can pull some strings and get Phil's heart. We'll soak it, detox it, then sew the fucker right in. Might improve my acting skills."

KAVA SANTANA He lost fifty pounds on what he called the "Live and Let Diet." We got him a trainer. He was on the treadmill a lot, which I thought was counterintuitive but turned out to be the best thing for his recovery. The doctors didn't want him to think about the FTM [female to male] until he was fully back on his feet. They took him off hormones, something Roar wanted to do anyway. The cardiac shit was hereditary; Colson Jones died of the same thing. Talk about the *real* "widow-maker." How's that for poetic justice?

DOUGLAS OUSTERHOUT (*surgeon*) Late-life gender confirmation surgeries are becoming more common. People of "a certain age," a certain generation, finally say, "Why not?" Some are widows or widowers whose partners may not have been in alignment with their desires—or may never have even known. Suddenly, they're free. They simply don't want to die in a body that all their lives was foreign to them. Usually, age isn't an issue in terms of the procedure. A gal in England did it for her eighty-first birthday. She was a pilot in the Royal Air Force—rather like Jan Morris, who was in the Royal Lancers. Though I can't recall anyone who had the surgery as late as Roger did, then decided to detransition. He's the anomaly. As always.

LESLIE JORDAN He began having second thoughts about the reversal. He was having third, fourth and *fifth* thoughts. You can say what you like, but Her Majesty was a royal pantsful. He *mulled* . . . other ideas were germinating. He reached out to his Buddhist friends.

ZACKARY DRUCKER (*artist, producer*) There's a prurient interest in the sex lives of trans folk. You know, "Does that hole they dug work?" A natural curiosity but most of it's a by-product of porn culture—in that way, I'm not sure the *Vanity Fair* cover helped or hurt. I understood what Roar was doing. What he *thought* he was doing, the outcome he wanted, which was to demystify. I just don't think that's always a good thing. Sometimes it's corrupting to take away mystery. It degrades. That's what porn does; numbs, degrades, erases. But people are insatiable, they want to *see*. Anything. You know, CLICK to see pregnant woman having baby carved from stomach with car key by wannabe mom. CLICK to see baby elephant screaming while Mom gets hacked and detusked by poachers. CLICK to see boy run over by steamroller in slow-motion—and it's *not* the dark web, it's ABC News. They always have a "content warning": *some viewers may find the following video offensive . . .* "Hey, not me! Not me! Bring it!"

It's all entertainment now.

TEDDY SWIMS (*singer-songwriter*) I talked to Leslie about it once. You know, how's the sex? A veiled way of asking about Roar's shiny new equipment. *Is it functional? Or is it a shitshow?* He got that twinkle in his eye and said, "My lips are sealed. His lips, too—but I ain't sayin' which." I had the feeling their relationship wasn't all that sexual to begin with, but I could be wrong. I regretted asking because, *yo*, it wasn't any of my business. I apologized. Said the devil made me do it—I used to say that to my granddaddy, a Pentecostal preacher. Leslie just laughed and said, "You'd look good in a devil blue dress, Teddy boy. But the beard has got to go."

LESLIE JORDAN He walked around in that old terrycloth robe muttering, "I'm done, I'm done"—it was very *Scrooge*. But Roger was *never* done. He'd always talked about doing "my Joe Orton play." He'd tell me dribs and drabs but the general theme has now become the norm: death by internet, victim culture. That's what he was going to call it—"Victims"—but changed it to "The Cancel Ward." I probably looked a bit nonplussed by the new title. When he thought I wasn't getting it, he said, "*Solzhenitsyn*, you illiterate redneck."

Cleared it right up. [*laughs*]

BEN BRANTLEY (*theater critic*) It was by far the most outrageous, most comical, most taboo thing he'd ever done. (That's saying a lot.) If the subversion at the end of *Act of Kindness* was the cherry bomb on top, *The Cancel Ward* was pure napalm in two acts. In the play, if you'll recall, someone's directing a film about a little girl who drowns. A mob shows up—mothers and fathers of drowned children—to shut the film down. They argue that the girl should *actually* drown; any artifice would be sacrilege. And because the "real" drowned girl that the movie director based his character on had thrown herself in the river because she'd been bullied for her gayness, the PODC (Parents of Drowned Children) insist he cast a gay or trans actor to be sacrificed.

You could see all of Roar's heroes in there: Buñuel, Kovacs, and Orton of course. But the immanent ingredient, the spark that made the fires burn and cauldrons bubble was sheer Orrian witchcraft.

STEPHEN KOPEL, CSA (*casting*) In the end, we hired twenty actors: personal hygiene-challenged, differently abled, corpulent-proud, neurodiverse BIPOCs without housing. We even had a schizophrenic with scleroderma and a Cavusgender boyflux "multiple"—one of their personalities was a horrible racist who identified as woke. Most had never acted before. Before each audition, Roar met them in private and broke down what the play was about—at least, what he was aiming for—because he didn't want them to feel they were being judged. The cast greatly appreciated it because they knew who it was coming from: a biracial transfeminine self-identifying Jew—who'd survived an *assassination attempt*, for God's sake.

On his birthday, they sang "Tenderness" from the stage. I sat a few rows behind him and thought he was laughing. But after a while there was something too rhythmic about it. You know, his shoulders going up and down, up and down. I took a peek—he was bawling his eyes out.

SIOBHAN BYRNE (*dramaturge*) The day we auditioned animals for the scene where everyone boards a plane with their emotional support pets was total anarchy. Wranglers brought peacocks and potbelly pigs, snakes, ponies, marmosets, and miniature horses. The actors and stagehands watched from the seats and had a ball. It was touching to see Simone Chevrolet "listening" to a companion as he signed into her cupped hand what was happening onstage. Simone fell on the floor laughing but kept her arm stretched up so she could keep getting the play-by-play.

MARGOT LION (*producer*) In "The Cancel Ward," the estate of Eugene O'Neill tries to censure the five-hundred-pound, blind, deaf, and incontinent trans Aborigine from playing Mary Tyrone in *Long Day's Journey*—but the court rules against them. Of course, Roar couldn't use any of the real words from the O'Neill play, but what he wrote sounded *exactly* like O'Neill. In life imitating art, the O'Neill estate sued Roar for "appropriation" but wound up with egg on its face when our attorneys pointed out that none of the original dialogue from *Long Day's Journey* had been used; hence, it fell under the rubric of parody and satire. It was an embarrassment to the family, and Roar said he felt bad for them. "But not *that* bad."

The showstopper was that now-famous scene where Simone sweeps in from the wings with her ASL [American Sign Language] interpreter—regal, luminous, incontinent—her nightgown was rigged to sporadically drop perfect strawy clumps of dung onto the stage—and "signs" a pretaped morphine-drenched monologue, blasted from speakers by an AI voice generator! There were standing ovations every night. And her Tony *acceptance* speech! She signed into the interpreter's hand while he translated, nervously, ecstatically, in his own very human voice: "If I could *roar*, I would. But my heart is roaring. Thank you, Mr. Orr, for this long day's journey . . . to *tonight*."

How blessed we were to find such a profoundly disgusting, disabled actress.

· · ·

HANSON G. D. WEIL (*biographer*)[227] He seemed finished with movies. He didn't watch them anymore, either, except old ones on TCM. Leslie Jordan said his partner had that "view from the bridge"—an indifferent yet joyful feeling that all his debts had been paid. He felt liberated.

But everything changed when George Saunders sent him an early manuscript of his novel *Lincoln in the Bardo*. Years ago, Saunders sent Orr a fan note about *The Jungle Book* and "to my utter dismay and jubilation, he wrote back." They maintained a correspondence through the years that Saunders characterized as "a very Lawrence Durrell/Henry Miller colloquy whose missives

227 *Roger Orr: Extended Engagement*, Hanson G. D. Weil, pp. 163–168 (Samuel French, 2019).

typically ended with my washing of his epistolary feet—silent, humble, grateful. Though not as humble or silent as he might have wished."[228]

TIG NOTARO (*comedian*) He wanted to go to the [Hotel] Roosevelt to see a drag queen do "An Evening with Rory Rabineau." Addie Wool, an amazing, talented kid that Leslie knew from *Will & Grace*, was getting a lot of press for his Rory impersonation.

Roar had fond memories of the Roosevelt. When he saw Jim Bailey do Judy Garland there, in '68—at the Cinegrill—the *real* Judy wound up crashing the show! Climbed right onstage and sang "Bye Bye Blackbird" with Jim . . . so, it was kind of, "I wanna see how this Addie Wool kid measures up." And I think Roger was *mentally prepared* to do the same knockout thing, the whole bring-the-house-down surprise. That just may have been the plan, 'cause there's no business like show business. (No business I know, anyway.) The thing was, no one recognized him, because he'd lost so much weight! *And* was wearing men's clothing. *And* we were with André Leon Talley . . . so everyone was looking at *André*. It was hard not to.

Addie did all the songs—"Tenderness," "Dreamcoat," "Irreplaceable," "Pray Tell," "Piece of My Heart"—and obscure ones too, like "There Can Be No Mountains." And at the end, this crazy, beautiful thing happened: *another* drag queen comes out onstage, fuck, she must have been eighty years old. Everyone gasped because it was like Bird had risen from the grave. They did this banter together and Roar started whispering to himself, "Mom said that . . . yes . . . yes! . . . she said *that* too. . . ." She was *totally* channeling his mother. Then Addie and the old woman did a "Come To Me" duet—every few seconds people just *sobbed*—then jumped to their feet in a thunder of applause and tears. I looked over and Roar was *quaking*, which made me cry even harder. Kill me, I'm dead.

And Leslie? Forget about it. He was a fuckin' puddle.

---

228 In his Man Booker Prize acceptance speech for *Lincoln in the Bardo*, Saunders said, "I want to thank my wife Paula for her lustrous, unconditional love and support. Paula, I could not do what I do without you. And, begging her pardon, I'd like to thank my *other* wife, Rory Rabineau—also known as Roger Orr—no name can define or contain such a force of nature—whose novel, *The Jungle Book*, allowed me to begin dreaming of my own picaresque. Perhaps the trembling instilled by the epic sweep and geography of that monumental work—its ambition, gloriously fulfilled—led me to set my own 'road' novel in the humble confines of a graveyard, where all roads lead."

CHRISTINE VACHON (*producer*) He optioned *Lincoln in the Bardo* and began working on the script. George wasn't quite finished with his novel and the only proviso was that he didn't want the book and film to come out at the same time. This wasn't something George *ever* considered as a movie. It's kind of an experimental work, a not-so-crazy quilt of "talking corpse head" monologues taking place in the bardo—what Buddhists call the state of transition between death and rebirth, a dream-purgatory—and George's characters aren't fully aware of their condition. They don't know that they're dead. And everyone's buried in the same cemetery as President Lincoln's recently deceased twelve-year-old son. So, no one's thinking, "This would make a great movie!" But *Lincoln in the Bardo* was compelling to Roger because its themes were personally irresistible: child death, transition, confusion, transcendence. Most importantly, it allowed him to describe the metaphorical death of his own son, Hendrix. Which was still an open wound. So, it was *Roger in the Bardo*. And became a self-eulogy, a panoramic tone poem, a tip of the hat to what he called "a dream coat . . . for Technicolored girls and boys who've considered suicide when the rainbow wasn't enough."

PAK LOPEZ (*personal assistant*) There was a year between the opening of "The Cancel Ward" and the first day of principal photography of *Lincoln in the Bardo*. Roger scheduled his back-to-male surgery during the hiatus—about a month after the play premiered to nearly universal acclaim.

He'd gotten heavy again, but the doctors were confident everything would go well.

KATT WILLIAMS (*comedian*) I loved that man. He'd been through some serious shit in his life but always came out swingin'. Came out smilin' too. The reviews were in for "Cancel Ward" and it was all good. Hell, it was *more* than good—no swingin', only smilin' this time. But he was gonna have the surgery now and wanted to rest up before the docs built him a new dick. He slimmed down but the paps took some *baaaad* pics—you know the one, where he trips and falls on the way to the public shitter? Shows his flabby cottage cheese ass and *bystanders* have to help him up? Oh, the humanity! That's happened to me more than once. Anyway, rumors swirled like they do and he winds up on DeathList2016.com . . . they do an annual pool of who's gonna croak by New Year's Eve—and Roar's Number 38! Right under Stan

Lee and right above Boutros-Boutros Butthead—and *those* two fuckers were ninety-four years old! I admit Roar wasn't the picture of health, but the man grew tails faster than a fuckin' starfish. I mean, come on. When Roar made the list, Stan Lee sent flowers and a *Deadpool* poster. Wrote on the bottom, "Better late than never—but better never than late."

That was pretty cool.

NORMAN SNIDER (*screenwriter*) David [Cronenberg] told me that he phoned Roger when he heard about him detransitioning. David was . . . *interested.* He compared Roger to the protagonist of a script he wrote years before called *Painkillers*, about a performance artist who does surgery on himself and begins growing "illegal" internal organs. Apparently, Roger loved that— the idea of himself as a performance artist of the body. I wish he'd lived long enough to see the film.[229]

ALI BERK My uncle postponed the surgery. He knew there wasn't much time; in just a few months, he'd be in preproduction on *Lincoln in the Bardo*. He wanted to visit Ram Dass—they were really close. Mom said that when Roary was in India, he spent time with Ram Dass's teacher, Neem Karoli Baba. It's funny, because Roary and Ram Dass didn't meet each other until way after. I guess that was their karma.

Ram Dass lived in Maui, near our old house. Roary wanted to sit with him because he was floundering. He didn't want a woman's body anymore—but didn't want a man's, either! He just felt so neurotic, so defeated. When he called Ram Dass to make a plan, someone picked up and put him on speaker. Ram Dass's stroke made it hard to understand what he was saying; the sound of a didgeridoo in the background made it even harder. Roary had called during a "healing session" and the didgeridoo was part of that. It was being played by Ram Dass's personal physician, "Handsome" Joel Friedman. Joel's an interesting guy, kind of a cross between an old Jewish hippie and a Florida Republican—though maybe those two things are the same! He was actually my father's doctor. So kind and caring in Dad's last days. . . . Anyway, Ram Dass knew all about my uncle's "conundrum," as he called it. I guess they'd

---

229 *Painkillers*, retitled *Crimes of the Future*, won Cronenberg the Palme d'Or for Best Director in 2022.—*ed.*

been talking. He strongly suggested Roary attend a workshop in Northern California before coming out to see him. He didn't go into much detail. All Ram Dass would say was that the workshop's theme was "pertinent."

Roary said the didgeridoo seemed to agree!

THUBTEN CHODRON (*author, abbess*) The talks were given by the *tulku* Chökyi Nyima Rinpoche and centered around the Vimalakirti Sutra, the Dharmakaya, and the Dakini—and Mandarava, a female guru-deity in Tantric Buddhism or Vajrayana. [The Rinpoche] spoke of *ma ning*, a Tibetan term meaning neither man nor woman, with no opposite.... The Vimalakirti Sutra tells the story of Śāriputra, a male disciple of the Buddha, who mocks a goddess for her inferior woman's form; as a rejoinder to his provocation, she switches their bodies. Point taken, point made: all is illusion.

If you're going to have your knuckles rapped, it may as well be by a goddess. That's what *I* say. [*laughs*]

FRITJOF CAPRA (*physicist*) Lots of old friends were there, heavyweights in the Buddhist community. The usual suspects. Stephen Levine and Jack Kornfield. Stephen's son Noah drove up. And Joan—Joan Halifax. I'm trying to . . . let's see, oh, Bob Thurman, Sharon Salzberg. And a woman named Janet Gyatso, a scholar at the Harvard Divinity School who wrote quite intelligently about the "third gender." Alice Walker came. And that wonderful writer George Saunders dropped in for lunch because he was in California on a book tour. So, the literary crowd was quite well-represented . . . now, was Michael Stipe—? No. [*pauses to reflect*] Was it Michael or was it Moby? The brain fog's rolling in thick today . . . uneasy is the head that wears the crown of predementia! [*laughs*] Oh—*ah*. Yes. Herbie Hancock played music, with Krishna Das. But the social aspect fell away once the workshop formally began.

SAFFRON DEMILLE (*yoga teacher*) It was *so good*. I didn't go to all the lectures and classes but loved learning about dakinis. They're kind of like the feminine part of men. But it was great to hear how *women* need dakinis too—they can be super helpful because women can get just as stuck in Self as the males. Joan Halifax was so funny, she'd say, "It doesn't matter what you weigh, you'll always look great in a dakini." And did you know *men* can become dakinis? That's so wise and ahead of its time. It's really woke. I think Buddhism is by far the most inclusive of the religions. Though it's not really a religion, it's more a "school." A school of thought and heart.

JANET GYATSO (*author, scholar*) Roger was warm, clever, charming—he called the *tantra* [esoteric teachings] "the tantrums." At that time, though, he was quite beleaguered. He was in what we call a liminal state. Tremendous suffering. He *was* transitioning, true, yet not back to a male body. He misread his doubts and impulses because he had nowhere to put them. The Rinpoche helped him find a safe place.

MAXINE HONG KINGSTON (*novelist*) It isn't that Roger no longer considered himself to be predominantly female. No, no, *no*. The trouble was, he didn't want to be predominantly *anything*. You must understand that about him, really, you must, or you do him a great disservice. You do yourself one. The concept of identity—one must be this, one must be that—was death to him. Worse than death, because it was so obviously a human construct. All his life he strived not to be human. He'd say, "No good comes from that. No art comes from that." The sacredness of our humanity shines through the impersonal art we make; art reflects it back like broken glass. Human beings do not *make* art, art pours *through* them. At this stage of his life, he was moving very close to the "third gender" that Janet Gyatso talks about in her marvelously titled book.[230] He was saying goodbye to the body. He'd loved it, hated it, sanctified it, mutilated it. He was moving toward the Land of No Regrets.

And as he liked to say, "The journey's a real bitch."

SAFFRON DEMILLE After the final dharma talk, Chökyi Nyima met with Roar in a cabin by the creek. The Rinpoche was brilliant. He giggled a lot and wore Nikes under his robes—and really knew his celebrities. A little too well! I wouldn't have been surprised if one of his guilty pleasures was watching shows like *Two and a Half Men* or *Dancing with the Stars.* . . .

I was taking a walk when I saw Roger leave the cabin. It looked like the weight of the world had been lifted off. I waved and he waved back

---

230 *Apparitions of the Self: The Secret Autobiographies of a Tibetan Visionary,* Janet Gyatso (Princeton University Press, 1999).

with a smile that just lit up the daylight. I didn't want to ask him what the Rinpoche said. I found out, though, when I read the journal published after his death.

* * * * * * * * * *

ROGER ORR[231]

I had so many talks with so many people during those two beguiling weeks at Spirit Rock that I was thoroughly disenchanted—not with them but with myself. When I wasn't seized by fear and poisonous self-loathing, moments of clarity, brief yet luminous, carried me through. Yet as the days passed, stuck in my bipolar ways, I wanted out. As Tony Newley put it, "Stop the world—I want to get off." Because I wasn't getting off on the world, not anymore, and the feeling was mutual. I *did* want to "stop the world," in the Castanedaean sense, but it was impossible to step outside the incessant, useless demands of Self. "There is no more time for what we used to do," said don Juan Matus. "Now you must employ all the *not-doing* I have taught you and *stop the world*."[232] What to do? Or not-do—that was the question. A life of too-much-doing had dramatically lowered any chance of escape.

The Rinpoche and I sat quietly. He smiled like a celestial psychoanalyst as I shrugged my shoulders, an action he playfully mimicked. My anxiety doubled down. The babbling brook outside the window began to sound like an unruly mob.

"You know what is dementia?" he said.

"Do you think I have it?"

"Not yet! Not yet!" he said, cracking up. His accent was thick and I listened with every fiber of my being so that I could understand. "I read a man like you in a magazine. Had surgery and became woman. Went 'under the knife.' I don't know *where* I read, but this

---

231 *False Posthumous: The Rest of Roger Orr*, pp. 198–203 (Cavalcade, 2022).

232 *Journey to Ixtlan: The Lessons of Don Juan* by Carlos Castaneda, p. 243 (Simon & Schuster, 1972).

was no joke. This real! She very happy with new body. Very content. What she always *wanted*. Time goes by and becomes—she *acquires* Alzheimer's. Aha! The wrinkle in the story! Something she did not expect. They place her in home—the children place her—in 'memory home.' I like it called memory home. But I think 'dream home' better . . . the challenge the caretakers, the *challenge* caregivers have each morning . . . is she is *different*. Different! She forgets. One morning she is female, next morning male. Yes, yes! *She is returning to essential form.* Caregivers very good, very nice, very understanding. Caregivers did not judge. 'Dreamgivers' better than 'caregivers,' no? But *caregiver* better than care*taker* . . . 'caretaker' much better than 'dreamtaker'! . . . Body is hotel. You already know this! You are very, very smart. Smart man, smart woman. You know many things, much more than most! Body is hotel. Body is *Four Seasons*. Body is *Three* Seasons—third gender." The Rinpoche whispered, "Ask for late checkout! Late checkout, sleep in."

He walked me to the door, where we embraced.

"Don't check out too soon."

"I won't."

"Put 'do not disturb' on door. Sleep in. Keep maid out."

"I will."

"Good! Make movies, write songs! Don't be a desperate housewife."

* * * * * * * * *

LAUGHLIN ORR My brother asked me along and that was sweet. I hadn't seen Richard [Ram Dass] in thirty years. I drove down from Big Sur—I was at Esalen—and we flew out from Santa Monica on a private plane.

If there's an example of proof being in the practice, it's Ram Dass. If I had a stroke like that, I'd be trying to hire one of those killer nurses I'm always watching documentaries about on TV, to put me down. He was so joyous— all love, all the time. Roger'd been to some Buddhist workshop Richard recommended; when he imitated one of the monks, Richard laughed so hard I thought he was going to have another brain bleed. The big surprise was my brother announcing he wasn't going to have the surgery after all, but was going to make everyone *think* he did. I thought he was joking. Richard had another conniption fit. May as well die laughing, right?

He said, "Yes! It's like a koan."

And Roger said, "Fuck 'em if they can't take a koan"—the same thing he said to me at Jonny's funeral. One of his hit parade remarks.

DR. EUNICE LAVAR The team of course knew Roger had decided against reversing his bottom surgery. All he wanted was to have the breast implants removed and they were probably glad to avoid the opportunity for complications. In FTM, they do a vaginectomy, then lengthen the urethra so the person can stand while urinating. They do a flap, using skin from the thigh— then a urethroplasty and a phalloplasty. A royal pain in the Mr. Winky. It's like trying to put the stolen family jewels back in the shattered display cases of a museum.

LESLIE JORDAN He hid out in the Cove for the recuperation charade— the implants were taken out but that was it. Only a few of us knew. The rest of the world thought he had hisself reversed. My husband was just so hard-headed. Plain ornery. He seemed *aroused* by all that bile and rage directed against him for his "betrayal" . . . like his new mission in life was a vendetta on the community he once loved, for having judged him. He wanted to do *damage*. Strutted around in the raw like a rooster, jubilantly quoting the last line of *The Stranger*: "For me to feel less alone, I imagined a large crowd of spectators on the day of my execution, greeting me with shouts and imprecations." Notched another subversion on his gun!

Oh, he was an impossible spitfire. But he was *my* impossible spitfire.

LAUGHLIN ORR There was something sad about it. About the lie, the bombastic subterfuge. It reminded me of when Mom went to La Piedra after the miscarriage, pretending to still be pregnant. I've heard all the theories— you know, my brother as coyote trickster. I never really bought it. I think he was just all-around ashamed, plain and simple. But it came out as a fuck you to the world.

SUZE BERKOWITZ I *love* Laughlin. She's an amazing woman, an amazing person. But there was so much about her brother that she got wrong, so much she didn't understand. As out there as she was in life, as loyal and committed to causes way past most people's comfort zones, Laughlin had a core that was . . . I want to say middle-class but it's the wrong adjective. "Traditional" isn't right, either. I guess what I'm trying to say is there was a fundamental *igno-rance* when it came to who Roger was. And not just as an artist. There was an ignorance about who he was—and who he *wasn't*.

LESLIE JORDAN Caitlyn got that big award and asked him to come as her "honored guest." And *that* was an offer he couldn't refuse. He loved the theat-ricality of it—Caitlin had a real flair that way. He said to me, "Widow-maker? Put on your dancin' shoes! It's *showdown* time." 'Cause Roger hadn't been seen in public since the, ahem, detransitioning. Now, Caitlyn knew *everything* and certainly wasn't planning to out him. You know, "Hey, everyone! Our boy here's still got his magic poontang! *Gotcha*." The great thing about Cait is, she *never* judges. She understood and respected *whatever* he chose to do, she's a really enlightened person that way. He was a big important person in her life and she'd been through so much herself. We're talking about an *Olympic decathlete* here. One tough lady. She wasn't one to fold her cards and sure as hell wasn't going to fold anyone else's.

She introduced him from the stage—no one knew what was coming— as the person who gave her the courage to do what she'd done. Then Roger appears in a suit and a banker's haircut, another goad, because he never looked like that in his *life*. When the audience finally realized it wasn't a joke they gasped and went *totally schizophrenic*. Sounded like a bad loop group. Oh, it was rock 'n' roll, honey, it was rage 'n' rapture . . .

Dylan went electric that night all over again.

Someone even shouted "Traitor!"

Her Majesty was happy as a tick on a plus-sized hiker.

SARAH PAULSON (*actress*) Caitlyn's famous "stand up" speech was . . . I don't mean to compare it to "I have a dream"—she would hate me doing that!—but listening to her, I got the same kind of chills when I was eleven years old and heard Martin Luther King.

* * * * * * * * *

CAITLYN JENNER
[GLAAD Media Awards, 2016]

Roar bows his head as he stands next to her, weathering the catcalls and epithets. She extends her arms, gently signaling the audience to stop.

. . . Try a little tenderness. Try a little tenderness. [*slowly, the crowd begins to settle*] Many people in this room know what it's like to suffer. To suffer privately in one's room. To suffer publicly—in a room just like this. Many of you know what it's like to suffer privately and to suffer publicly for simple reasons. Many of you know what it's like to suffer privately and publicly for complicated ones. Roger Orr *and* Rory Rabineau have suffered. It's simple and it's complicated but I think that's a fair definition of what it is to be human: we are simple and we are complicated and we suffer. (We are also happy, joyous, and free.) We are not one thing nor are we another. [*looks at Roar and smiles*] We are not so black and white. [*back to audience*] "Young girls they do get weary." Young boys, too. And young girls who want to be boys and young boys who want to be girls . . . they do get weary. [*some laughter, applause*] Rory Rabineau and Roger Orr have made movies about their suffering. Rory Rabineau and Roger Orr have written songs of their suffering. Written books about their suffering. *The Jungle Book*— my God. Just, "My God." [*pause*] There can be no one in this room who has not been touched and thrilled and *altered* by the works of art he/she/they has created. [*pause*] And I want to ask the people in this room tonight who wish to condemn a genius of the heart and spirit who for so many years has spoken *for* you, *to* you, for *us* . . . I'd like you to remain seated. I want to ask the people in this room tonight who wish to condemn the person standing beside me, who is all of us, who is all of *you*, in your splendor and your suffering, in your best and worst moments . . . I want to ask you to be seated. I want to ask the people in this room tonight who wish to *judge* the collection of persons known to us by the single name of "Roar" . . . please remain seated. If there is anyone in this room that grew up with rocks being thrown at them, literal *and* metaphorical, anyone who is still dodging those rocks, if there is anyone who has picked up those stones out of anger and is ready to use them as weapons *tonight . . . please remain seated.* I am asking those who feel comfortable denouncing Roar in their throats and hearts to remain seated. My grandpa used to say, "Why stand when you can sit?" Grandma would scowl and say, "Because when you stand, fool, you're a little closer to God." For non-believers, please remain seated. *You will not be judged.* But if you've ever listened to Roar's music, if you've ever watched the movies and ever read the books, if you've ever laughed and cried and thought, "My God, that's me, that's me, that's me"—stand up! [*after a pause, a rustle of chairs as some begin to rise*] Go ahead. Go ahead. Take your time. We got all night. Come on. I know you can do it. [*more rustling of chairs*] That's right . . . that's right. That's lovely. Join me. Join us . . . . [*her voice crescendoing now, to be heard over the dragging of chairs*] If you were ever afraid to tell your family the secrets you held—if some of you are *still* afraid—if you ever caught Mama or Daddy or Sister or Brother humming or singing along to one of Roar's songs during their *own* private sufferings—*dancing* to them—crying to them or laughing and crying to one of the movies—or smiling as they read one of *her* novels or *his* diaries—if you saw that their hearts seemed to grow larger—and their heads closer to God . . . please stand up.

Stand up! Stand up! [*all are standing now*] Stand up, stand up, stand up, stand up, stand up, stand up!

* * * * * * * * *

ELLIOT PAGE (*actor*) Every single person was on their feet. She'd admonished them in the most beautiful way. It was a master class in humility. In Christianity, in compassion.

I never cried so hard in my life.

NATHAN LANE Roar openly wept, which absolutely took him by surprise. Because he walked on that stage feeling hatred and contempt—a defense mechanism, but it was real.

The first thing he said was, "Roger and Rory thank you from the broken bottoms of their gratefully ungendered, unbroken hearts."

Classic Roar: funny and tender and *authentic*. It broke the ice.

KAVA SANTANA A month later, Obama gave him the Medal of Freedom. Cicely and Tom [Hanks] got one too. We all flew to Washington together. My husband wasn't feeling great, and the honorees and presenters made pilgrimages to the room to pay their respects. Bruce Springsteen and Diana Ross! It was ridiculous. Michael Jordan, Lorne Michaels . . . I thought the Obamas themselves would show up because Michelle was a such a fan of Bird's. Roger greeted everyone with "Welcome to the Three Seasons Hotel, desperate housewives!" He was drinking again, nothing out of control, and a little wine really seemed to help. He'd imitate the guru he met up north: "No late checkout—get *early* checkout. Late checkout for pussies. Housekeeper need to clean!" No one knew what he was talking about.

. . .

DR. WITT DJELLIN Roger had to take a physical before we went into production on *Lincoln in the Bardo*. That didn't work out so well. The EKG results weren't good. He had some fairly serious arrhythmias—what they call a prolonged QT interval—that deservedly made the insurance company nervous. It was suggested we find a director who could step in if something happened.

ANTHONY UNGER Roger left his ego at the door. He needed to make this movie and was going to do whatever was necessary.

MORGAN MASON (*screenwriter, blockchain investor*) *Lincoln in the Bardo*—the novel—came out on Valentine's Day, to just *astonishing* acclaim. When Roar read the reviews, he made the same joke Saunders did in his Man Booker speech: "It's all downhill from here." Which happens to be the same thing my father said when he finished *Odd Man Out*.[233]

PAMELA KOFFLER Roar suggested an alternate director: Xavier Dolan, the enfant terrible of Cannes. The insurance folks did their research and said, "Zut alors!" Was *not* going to happen. They even said no to Todd Haynes. . . . We were getting nervous because Roar asked the Wachowskis, who would have been amazing, but their parents weren't doing well and they didn't feel

---

233 Mason's father, James Mason, starred in Carol Reed's acclaimed film (1947).

comfortable making a four-month commitment. So, he gave Gus Van Sant a call. They'd known each other a long time and Roar loved his sensibilities. Gus happens to be a very good painter too; Roar gave him an Iwana Cant sculpture when we wrapped.

CHRISTINE VACHON We started production in the summer of 2017. He was almost seventy-seven years old and pretty much right away had shortness of breath. He'd go into his trailer on breaks and breathe oxygen but eventually it was out in the open and he was on the tanks all the time. We put him in a wheelchair because walkers weren't doing it for him anymore. That's where he directed from—like John Huston did, for *The Dead*.

ANJELICA HUSTON (*actor*) It was painful seeing that. It was déjà vu. I'd look over and see my father in that wheelchair in front of the monitors. And the film was all about ghosts—people trapped in the bardo, the space between life and death. I had nightmares Dad was still trapped.

ZAZIE BEETZ (*actor*) I'd worked with wonderful directors but no one on that scale. How often do you get the chance? When I auditioned, he knew a *lot* about me. I don't know, people probably do their googling homework but Roar made you think he was genuinely interested—which he was! He had a quality that seems in short supply these days, a way of making you feel you were the most important person in the room. For example, he knew I'd been named after a novel by Raymond Queneau. He's the only person I ever met who'd actually *heard* of Queneau! . . . It was crazy but it was love at first sight. I don't know about *his* sight, but it was love at mine.

BOB SAGET (*comedian*) One of the amazing things about Roar was that he didn't look at your career, he looked at *you*. Not *through* you but *into* you. He saw things that others didn't or couldn't. And he loved comedians—he was one himself—because of the sorrow that was there, deep down. You know the Smokey song? [*sings*] "If you look closer, you're able to see the tracks of my tears." He probably wrote that! Right? I used to sit around with Louie [Anderson], and we were just so grateful to be working on *Bardo*. The script was amazing, and after I was hired, I got curious about the book. It was hard to read, but the script sort of prepared me. It's so interesting what it explores.

That fine line between life and death. I used to wonder with Louie and Gilbert [Gottfried], "What if that happens to us?" Joking but not joking. What if *we're* confused about being dead? Louie'd say, "Not gonna happen, Saget. I'll just tell the reaper, 'Sorry, buddy, life used up all my confusion. Got nuthin' left for ya.'"

KEVIN HART (*comedian, actor*) What Saget said is true. Roar saw me as a soldier in the Civil War. He'd seen all my comedies but *still* saw me as a dead soldier in the Civil War. The far-out thing is that I once had a psychic reading at one of those Hollywood parties where they have all kinds of mentalists, jugglers, psychics—you know, they got petting zoos and mechanical *bull*-shit . . . and this psychic said exactly that: *You were a soldier in the Civil War.* "You were in the Colored Troops"—that's what they called the Black regiments. And this girl was *white.* This girl was whiter than Taylor Swift!

PETE DAVIDSON (*comedian, actor*) He called me himself. I thought I was being pranked. Apatow told me that was Roar's thing—picking up the phone and bypassing the agencies, whatever. Judd said that it meant he was really excited about me being in his movie. Apart from thinking Roger Orr was cooler than shit, I had another kind of personal connection. My sister had a birthday party at some karaoke place in Long Island when I was six years old. Dad sang "Try a Little Tenderness," and it was a big hit. That was a year before he died and my mom played it at his funeral. It's funny I'm talking to you now because I just removed the ROAR tattoo from my forehead that I put over the KIM that I removed after I removed the APATOW. The skin on the forehead is thin so you can still kind of see them. Which is cool, because now they're like all in the bardo of my forehead.

I was only on *Bardo* for a week. He never really gave notes as a director. He trusted actors. Old school. He *did* come up to me once between takes with this aggressively serious look. I thought, *Oh shit*, I must have really fucked up. He leaned over and whispered, "I want you to be in my next picture." That's what he called it: a *picture.* Loved that. He said, "I want you to play *Don Knotts.* We're going to see a side of Mr. Limpet no one's seen before."

I think he was serious.

SANDRA OH (*actor*) I couldn't believe who was there my first day on set. Look! It's Idris and Meryl! And Julianne Moore . . . look over *there*: it's Denzel and Tom Hanks! And Elliot Page! I said, *Wha?* It was like a crazy *Vanity Fair* Hollywood issue cover that I didn't belong in. I turned the corner and bumped into these guys I think are crew, I mean, literally *ran into them.* Adam Driver and Harry Styles! Oh my God, I needed a friggin' diaper. Adam said something nice about *Grey's Anatomy*, something *really* nice, and I was shocked. He didn't know my name but knew I was a *Grey's Anatomy* person . . . which was *more* than enough. Fuck! This was Adam Driver! And Harry Styles! Who'd just been so amazing in *Dunkirk*. . . . *Killing Eve* wasn't until the next year so people kinda sorta knew who I was though not really. But *Lincoln in the Bardo* made me feel like, "Girl? You have *arrived*."

KEVIN SPACEY (*actor*) I knew Roar from the Old Vic days. He was a friend of Jonathan Miller—and Jack [Lemmon]—and used to come to rehearsals of *Long Day's Journey*. I think that's what gave him the idea to call his diaries "Long Day's Journals." He'd sit in back, making notes in the dark. He usually went out to dinner with Jonathan after. I never had the stones to invite myself along. I cannot put into words the respect I had for that man. The awe.

When his movie started shooting, I was entering a bardo of my own, though it felt a lot closer to death. The "transition" was quick; "the quick and the dead." The allegations came out a few months before and by the time I shot *Bardo*, I'd already been fired from *House of Cards*—and replaced by Chris [Christopher Plummer] on *All the Money In the World*. I had a small part in *Bardo*—most of us did, it was a true ensemble piece—but was proud of the work I did. And my God, that movie . . . a masterwork on the scale of *Long Day's Journey*. I wasn't in the final cut and never faulted him for that. People say that he hired me just to make a political statement—the studio fought him, you know—and that he never planned on leaving me in the film. I don't believe it. This is a man who'd just done a Pulitzer-winning play called *The Cancel Ward*; a man who'd been vilified for being white and vilified for being Black; a man whom a not inconsiderable segment of LGBTQ had turned their backs on. So, no, it's not that simple. Was there tremendous power exerted to have me removed from *Bardo*? No question. But Roger Orr *always* spoke truth to power, so I think hiring me was more than a "gesture." In the end, nothing mattered but the film itself, as it should. My presence would have overshadowed the beautiful thing he had made—*Lincoln in the*

Bardo would have suffered both critically *and* in the public's eye. I don't say that out of arrogance because one likes to believe "the thing speaks for itself" and that one doesn't have such power.

Sadly, that's no longer true.

PHILIP KENNICOTT (*film critic*) *Lincoln in the Bardo* was the most harrowing film I'd seen since Christi Puiu's *The Death of Mr. Lazarescu.* I sat in the dark for twenty minutes when it ended. I didn't know what to do with my hands, my legs, my heart. A large part of me still doesn't.

LESLIE JORDAN He edited the film from the studio he built at the Cove. He looked terrible. His breathing was a little better but his skin was mottled. I thought, oh God, his liver's failing, but the docs said it wasn't that. His liver was fine—everything *else* was failing. At the end of the day, I bundled him up and we rode the funicular. Down and up, up and down . . . we never did get out of that little gondola and walk on the beach. Just stayed all snug, blasting Rachmaninoff from the speakers—"Vocalise"—and rap music too. He loved rap, loved the wordplay. He thought the best of it was just as sophisticated as anything Cole Porter wrote. I couldn't see it, let alone *listen* to it, but when he broke some of the lyrics down, I understood what he meant.

KAVA SANTANA They were giving him the Mark Twain in April [2018] . . . this avalanche of accolades was beginning, and it was pretty apparent that the general feeling was, "Get him while the body's still warm." The National Book Foundation's Lifetime Medal for Distinguished Contribution to American Letters; the AFI Lifetime Achievement; the DGA Lifetime Achievement; the BET Lifetime Achievement; the Grammy Lifetime Achievement . . . It made me a little uncomfortable, mostly because he often wanted to go in person and that was challenging, healthwise. Of *course* he deserved all of it, and more! But at one point, I remember my husband saying, "Can't wait for the Golden Noose—the Deathtime Achievement. Last rope on the block."

LESLIE JORDAN He always called me Life so I started calling him Lifetime Achievement. He shortened that to "Lifetime Channel." I'd already banned "Widow-Maker" from the house. I just didn't want to hear it.

He was too sick to go to Washington for the Mark Twain Prize. He said, "I'm afraid the Twains shall never meet." They gave it to their backup, Dave Chappelle, and Roger was so happy about that.

After the second heart attack, we set up a wing at the Cove with full-time nurses. So many friends were doctors; the Teardown was lousy with medicos! Lots of Buddhists too. We had the East and the West covered.

One night he said, "Life? There's something you should know: I've started seeing someone—I'm in love and can't live without her. She wants me to die in her arms."

He was talking about morphine, bless his heart.

ALI BERK Laughlin came and stayed a few days. The woman was eighty-five years old and still a gypsy. She and Suze were in better shape than I was. They both wore Fitbits and *squealed* when the alarm went off telling them they got their ten thousand steps.

LAUGHLIN ORR I knew he didn't have long. I know none of us do, in the scheme of things . . . but it's just so hard to talk about, Bruce! Don't make me. . . . He—he was my baby brother. I loved him so!

CARRIE FISHER (*writer, actress*) Leslie keeps getting asked, "What were his last words?" A dumb question, because unless you've been thinking about it your entire fucking life, your last words *will not* be memorable! Not many of us are Oscar Levant, or even Goethe. We tend not to look toward the window and shout "*More light,*" even in German. We tend not to be Emily Dickinson, who kind of said the opposite—"I must go in, the fog is rising." Isn't that *fantastic*? My favorite part is "I must go in." Mustn't we all? Not too many of us are Steve Jobs, either, who said *Oh wow, oh wow, oh wow.* Which is still the *best.* For my money—and Steve's too. These days, *everyone* says "Oh wow" when they're dying. It's *trending.* It wasn't till a few years later that Leslie finally spilled the beans—on Mayim Bialik's podcast. Of course! Where else *would* you? If you can't reveal, for the first time, your husband's last words to a gal who's a neuroscientist *and* the star of *The Big Bang Theory*, who *can* you tell? According to Les, Roar said, "Tell Eartha I'll yell when I see her." Which is a lot different than saying "Oh wow." Or maybe not. Well, of course, Mayim wanted to know what that meant—wouldn't you? I mean, even if you *weren't* a neuroscientist, you'd really want to know, right? So, Leslie told the story of Eartha Kitt screaming at the top of her lungs as she left the world. It's a true story, she *screamed*. Her daughter was there when it happened, I googled it— talk about raging against the dying of the light. . . . I googled *my* last words but couldn't find them. All I could find were my *first* words, which apparently were, "Oh wow." Search engines are clearly overrated. They should call them Search Party engines. Anyway, Leslie told the TV star/neuroscientist the story about Eartha dying, and then he said, "Roger was too weak to do any screaming—sadly, because it had always been the plan."

Don't you *love* that? That screaming as he died was *the plan*?

Screaming should *always* be the plan.

SUZE BERKOWITZ Ali and I went for a walk on the beach. Ava and Emma stayed at the house with Roger. They'd just turned eighteen and brought him a gift. That was a ritual they had—giving gifts to people on their birthday. It was this gorgeous photo album. Those *pictures*! Where did they *find* them? There were just so many amazing images—of Scatter and Roger and me, at Parnassus. We must have been six years old . . . pictures of the *wedding*, the crazy Chicago wedding. [*cries*] O! I'm sorry. I'm sorry, I didn't mean— I didn't think I'd get so emotional. There he was on Jack Paar, singing that song—there he was holding Hendrix in the delivery room—there he was with Bird—and Sammy . . . directing *Spider-Man* in some kind of ludicrous ball gown [*laugh-cries*]—oh! One of the nurses took a picture with Ava's iPhone of Roger right before he died, all stoned and smiling, the girls in bed with him like they were with Scatter. Oh! Oh! Oh—

ALI BERK As we headed back to the house, the twins were racing toward us with contorted faces. And we knew he was gone.

Mom *very slowly* walked toward the room. I was right behind her. Kava stood in the doorway, looking in. She turned to us and smiled. She motioned us to come closer and we stood at the door too. Leslie was on the edge of the bed, staring at Roary. He looked up and whispered, "He did it. Honeychile done *did* it and did it *right*. Honeychile did *everything* right." His face was wet, with that beautiful leprechaun grin. We all hugged. Then he went back to Roary and said, "Bravo. Brava. I'm so proud of you. You called me Life but you were my life." Then he beamed at us—the twins were crying in the doorway now—and said, "Look at Her Majesty. Isn't she just the most beautiful thing?"

KAVA SANTANA Suze and I were on both sides of the bed, stroking his forehead. She said, "Sleep now. Let those thousand lives sleep." Then she looked at Roar and her eyes got wide. She said, "What is he *wearing*?" You know, with a smirk of shocked delight. Because the sheet had drifted down.

LESLIE JORDAN Sometimes when he was feeling better—and the morphine kicked in!—he changed out of his pajamas. He'd say, "Lifer? Let's slip into something more comfortable."

That was my cue to open the closet where all the dresses were.

He'd point and say, "That one! No, *that* one. No—*this* one." The Royal Curator. But on the last day, he said, "Get the flat box on the floor, behind all the shoes." I opened it; there was a little frock but nothing special. The nurses helped me put it on him, which seemed to give them great, chortling pleasure. It was a tiny thing and fit him like a dream because he'd lost so much weight.

ALI BERK When Mom asked what Uncle Roary was wearing, I took a good look . . . *Bird* liked to slouch around the house that dress! But Mom swore it was the "shaggy" one, you know, the "Try a Little Tenderness" nightie that she wore on the eve of their wedding. Mom said it had "magical properties" but disappeared years ago. "Walked off by itself."

It was always a mystery what happened to it.

LESLIE JORDAN That dress! That dress . . . we *all* wear that dress. For a while, we thought, Oh, he was trying to go back in time. That time of *relative* innocence when they were young marrieds in Chicago and loved each other so much. Before all the fame and the deaths and psych ward *tsuris*. The time when the only one he'd lost was Seraphim . . . But I think that's wrong because he was *not* a nostalgic person. And he loved Suze, he truly did, but it wasn't romantic, all that ended years and years before. She was a sister to him and it wasn't—there was no *longing* there, no loose ends that needed to be tied. I spoke to Suze about this before she died and she agreed. We *did* think it funny he had the dress in his possession though. And funny how Bird took to it like a kitten to warm milk.

It was Suze's. It was Bird's. And it was Roar's too: tailored by the Almighty. I hear the Buddha was a pretty good dressmaker himself.

My mama told me that Bible story all the time and she just *loved* the wonderful Dolly song, "Coat of Many Colors."

> Although we had no money I was rich as could be
> In my coat of many colors my mama made for me.

LAST LOOKS

ALI BERK When I read about what happened to Peter Beard, I started having these recurring dreams.

Peter and Roary knew each other from the Warhol days. They were born around the same time and both their families were rich. Not long after my uncle died, Peter did an interview for a magazine, one of those deals where they want to know your favorite airport, your favorite exotic hotel, that sort of silly thing. When they asked about his favorite artist, he said, "Roger Cant and Iwana Orr." Obviously, he knew they were the same person. So it made me think he and Peter had been in touch. Because of course the secret about Iwana finally did go public but a year *after* Peter died. We haven't finished going through all of Roary's personal correspondence. I guess I'll find out.

The way Peter died was so awful. He had dementia and wandered off into the woods around his house. They didn't find his body for three weeks. That's when I started having recurring dreams about Roary. I was in a dark forest—like a fairy tale—and heard him crying, "Ali! Ali! Find me! Save me!" I'd wake up drenched. I'm just so glad Roary died at home with his family and not in some crazy place in Africa or India. Or the godforsaken woods of Montauk.

ANTHONY HADEN-GUEST (*writer, critic*) The *name* of the place they found poor Peter is called Camp Hero—how Joseph Campbell of it all. In my head, Roar and Pete are holding hands, two blessedly subversive geniuses eloping on a moonlit night. Peter in a chic safari suit and Roger in a shaggy dress.

As Sondheim would say, into the woods.

ALI BERK . . . then Uncle Roary became Hendrix, *Hendrix* was the one crying in the forest—the difference was, Hendy never called out. He'd be very close then very far away. That happened for about a week—the dreams of Hendrix—then stopped. I haven't dreamt about either of them since.

SARAH JESSICA PARKER (*actress*) It would have been so horrible if he died in the first year of the pandemic. If he was in the hospital, no one would have been able to see him. He'd have died alone. I mean, except for the nurses and doctors with their faces hidden by masks.

DR. WITT DJELLIN Who said that, an actress? Well, that explains it, because it's claptrap. If he *had* been "in the hospital"—which, trust me, I would never have allowed—but if he *had*, for chrissake it'd have been the Head of State suite at the Mug and Bunny Orr Building at Cedars! His sister *Laughlin* died there, at the height of COVID bullshit medical paranoia and skullduggery—do you think *she* was alone? Well, think again. Can anyone *imagine* I would have let that happen? I wasn't just his doctor, I was his

> *friend in the backseat said 'moon,' is that short for moonshot hahahah and the driver said shoot your best shot jonas. backseat jonas said haha what's your last name and when I told him, he said 'moon ore'—is that like moondust hahaha that's a trip. the driver said she's a hippie, asshole, so be polite. he sweetly said oh sorry then asked was your mom a hippie? I said kinda, her name was chickweed so I guess that made her a hippie. oh did that chick smoke weed? the driver told backseat jonas shut up he thought it was bothering me but it wasn't. I started singing halsey and when I finished he said I should try out for american idol then asked if I was going up to coos bay to see my mom and I told him she was dead. nobody said anything for a while, I watched the hills go by and the ocean on the other side. jonas said do you have a boyfriend I said sort of and giggled. what's his name, 'satellite'? hahaha the driver said shut up but jonas asked me if he's a satellite, does he revolve around you or do you revolve around him. the driver said to backseat jonas that it didn't look like he, jonas, was*

revolving around anyone at the current moment and I could tell the driver was interested, he looked at me sideways sexy like kayce would in yellowstone all scruffy cowboy-cute and handsome. the driver wanted to know what I was going to do in coos bay and I said I used to live there and he said so you're going home. sort of I said again. the backseat boy said you mean like you lived in a commune and I said yeah, I don't remember much about it I haven't been there in a long time but that's where I was born. then I don't know why but I told them my parents owned the commune. the driver said 'I thought no one owns a commune like that's the whole point.' I got embarrassed and said my parents only owned the land and he said well I guess they own the commune then, cause whoever owns the land owns everything on it and it was just like what kayce would say. they were going all the way to reno and when I asked why, the driver said I shot a man there but forgot to watch him die hahahahaha. And that's when we

LESLIE JORDAN scattered Roar's ashes all over the world. I'm gonna have some in my pocket when they bury me in Chattanooga. I used to tell him that was my plan and he'd smile and say, "The eternal return," because we Tennessee boys always go back. I'm still thinking about what I'd put on the stone. Roger always liked YOU ARE HERE—a gentle reminder to whoever's looking at the grave that all things must pass. He called cemeteries the grass menagerie, did I already tell you that? I *might* just do a little plagiarizing though: Jan Morris and her wife had one all ready-set to go, but apparently never used it: "Here are two friends, at the end of one life." And I really do love it because it has a few different meanings that are subject to interpretation. If Roger had a grave, it'd be perfect: two friends, the man and woman sides, together at last. Leaving the costume party for those stars that Bird loved to sing about. *Free at last, free at last, thank God almighty, we are free at last.* And did I tell you, Bruce, that *hendrix called and called before I left but would never say where he was. everyone kept telling me to say where he was, they didn't believe it when I said I didn't know, they thought oh how could she not. I wouldn't have told them anyway because they might've got him locked him up or done whatever. when I said why do you want to know is it because the lawyers finally want to give him the money they looked at me with suspicion or thought I was being nasty. leslie was selling the house in the cove but said I could stay there during construction there was a lot needed to be done before it was sold because the house was in disrepair. that's what leslie kept saying, he liked the word disrepair which struck me as quite southern. anyway I don't think he wanted me to stay but was too gentlemanly to throw me out. when roger died I met with the lawyers there was a trust he left but they never told me how much. my friend sabrina called it a handcuff trust. her boyfriend called it a distrust how witty of him. the lawyers said there would be a tranche, I said what IS that and they said an allowance though I couldn't expect it for a few months. but the only tranche I ever got was so-called emergency money for covid and I spent it all. they said I needed permission if I wanted to make a big purchase like a car or a house were they joking sabrina said I was the new britney every time I saw her she said free moon! free moon! i got tired of it. aunt ali said I would be getting money from laughlin, she died too but nothing came of that, either. it was like a joke, I hate to argue with brandi carlile but the joke was on me not them. hendy and I had a little shitty apartment in venice people were always robbing and one sunday the edison people called and said they were going to shut the electricity off if I didn't pay. I said but it's sunday how can you do that on a sunday and they said they had the legal right because I owed five hundred dollars and they'd just shut everything off if I didn't pay NOW and that I must go to a certain ralphs on olympic and buy a certain giftcard and call back when I had the certain type of card. I had to because I needed to keep my phone charged in case hendy called, he'd been gone for three weeks I didn't know where but i always charged my phone at night when I slept. I called edison back when I had the certain giftcard and they said now I should go to a bitcoin machine I didn't know what that was they asked what part of town I lived and said there was a machine at the 711 on pico. they said to call when I got there then stand at the machine while they gave instructions to punch in the numbers on the giftcard so I did. the next day they called to say there was an error I needed to put more in if I didn't want power shut off and should just go to the bank and withdraw money because the bitcoin machine would take cash. they said to call from the machine when I had the cash and gave more instructions what to punch in and the machine took the hundred-dollar bills one by one by one. it kept happening over the next few days they were very apologetic they put on the bitcoin or edison manager and he said he never saw a situation like this before but the balance kept being higher then they thought and I gave them six thousand dollars because I was scared hendy would call I would miss the call because my phone was uncharged. when I told sabrina what was going on her boyfriend shouted from the background it's a scam it's a scam how could that idiot not know it was a scam and sabrina started laughing I was so embarrassed I hung up packed my worldly goods and went back to the bank and got the fifteen hundred that was left and hitched up PCH. I don't see ali anymore and the twins are in school back east but I didn't want to call and ask for help. I was too embarrassed the bitcoin*

MOLLY HASKELL (*film critic*) shown on TCM sans the seven-minute coda that made movie history. Because without the "subversion," *Act of Kindness* was a throwback American classic—perfect fare for the Turner channel. The family sued, arguing that the film must be presented in its original and intended form. The DGA supported such a view, claiming that "final cut" extended to network television. The outcome was promising: a similar case in France had been settled in favor of the plaintiffs—*The Asphalt Jungle* had been colorized for TV and the courts ruled [that John Huston's] heirs indeed retained *droit moraux*—"moral rights."

The estate of Roger Orr lost.

That's when Orr's goddaughter, the fizzy, resourceful Ali Berk—she describes herself as

"mule stubborn"—enlisted Martin Scorsese's
help. The director, an old friend of the

embarrassed about what happened that i'd been made a fool of i was already
past the age of thirty but why did they put me in that position why had no one
come through for me i didn't even have money for a lawyer not that i would have
pursued like sabrina said i should. i don't think the orrs were like the edison
people i know roar wasn't like that nor ali or laughlin nor leslie but why would
it be taking so long. i did get the allowance but had to call the lawyers even for
that because it always came late i had sex with kayce but left in the middle of
the night because i wasn't in love. i missed hendy so much i looked at my phone
a thousand times a day. i thought he would know to call me once i got to harvest
sun he would feel it something in him would sense it i kept thinking he'd prob-
ably be there when i arrived i knew harvest sun wasn't there anymore but maybe
the new owners kept the bookstore or barns and would give me a job tho the best
thing would be if it was still a commune i didn't want to get my hopes up. i kept
thinking of kevin costner as my TV dad because roar had a picture of jonny that
looked just like him when i thought of hendrix he looked like all the yellowstone
kayces i met on the road, even like the handsome son of the last ride i got to
crescent bay from a driver dad who reminded me of kevin costner he was with
his family and drove an old yellow cadillac he called the 'golden brougham.'
everyone wore masks and he said if i rode with them i needed one too but i said
i didn't have one he had about a hundred of em and gave one to me the family
brought me all the way to crescent city they would have taken me further but i
said just leave me here i'm good.

i walked down to the ocean so wild and different from the cove or venice or
any place i'd seen i slept on a blanket some party people left behind and was warm
because of my trusty north face i sang 'without me' again a duet with the ocean so
loud even the stars could hear if i ever get that money this will be the perfect place
for a house i wanted to stay another night but there was poor reception i needed to
charge my phone so he could reach me it would be like a horror movie if hendrix
went to voicemail

and i remembered dancing at the beach when i was little holding hands
with ali and laughlin we held hands and danced in the moonlight they said we
were witches but not bad witches good witches i wanted to sleep in the funicular

and they wrapped me in blankets under the stars the same stars above me now in crescent bay as i stared at the sky from my golden brougham in the funicular on the night of the witches when my period came my skin tingled with ocean salt the stars twinkled the black world was mine mine mine warm winds dried my tears streamed down mama used to call them angelsaltwater when she came in my room and i cried myself to sleep she'd say stop those tears nancy drew turn off those saltwater tears missy drew give those sweet angels a big timeout and i was so happy I was s